HORROR HISTORIA

RED

HORROR HISTORIA brings together the most influential monsters and
original gothic stories in one blood-curdling collection.

Collect each volume and complete the ultimate nightmare pantheon.

Horror Historia Black
Nightmares and boogeymen of the phantasmagoria.

Horror Historia Brown
Werewolves, hellhounds, and other supernatural beasts.

Horror Historia Green
Carnivorous and lethal vegetation.

Horror Historia Indigo
Practitioners of sorcery and witchcraft.

Horror Historia Pink
Murderers, ghouls, and other monsters of the flesh.

Horror Historia Red
Bloodsuckers and vampire variants.

Horror Historia Violet
Magical beings of folklore and mythology.

Horror Historia White
Ghosts, phantoms, and visitants.

Horror Historia Yellow
Mummies and nightmares of the Nile.

RED

31 Essential Vampire Tales

curated and edited by
C.S.R. Calloway

HORROR HISTORIA RED

Published by CSRC Storytelling
Los Angeles, California

ISBNs:
Hardcover: 978-1-955382-19-9
Paperback: 978-1-955382-21-2
Ebook: 978-1-955382-24-3

Cover designed by Mena Bo

CONTENTS

I

INTRODUCTION TO THE VOLUME

"Wright told me what he remembered about vampires—that they're immortal unless someone stabs them in the heart with a wooden stake, and yet even without being stabbed they're dead, or undead. Whatever that means. They drink blood, they have no reflection in mirrors, they can become bats or wolves, they turn other people into vampires either by drinking their blood or by making the convert drink the vampire's blood. This last detail seemed to depend on which story you were reading or which movie you were watching. That was the other thing about vampires. They were fictional beings. Folklore. There were no vampires."

— OCTAVIA E. BUTLER, *FLEDGLING*

A ngelus. Blade. Bill Compton. Edward Cullen. Lestat de Lioncourt. These names and others make it clear that vampires have long been a part of the cultural conversation. They're romantic leads, effete villains, brutal superheroes, yet they share the same blood. Vampires are the personification of defilement, ranging from contagion to violation. They take what they need, usually blood, and leave their victims with something unwanted: sickness, death, or even immortality. Many ancient civilizations feature vampires or vampiric-like creatures—revenants, living corpses who sustain their parasitic afterlife by feeding on the essence of living beings. The Egyptians had warrior goddess Sekhmet, who enjoyed the taste of blood and used plagues as her messengers. The Greeks had shapeshifter Empusa, who drank the blood of the men she seduced, and the monster Lamia, who drank the blood of children as vengeance for having her own offspring taken by the goddess Hera. Through countless stories, these beings and similar creatures adapted to the needs of the various societies, not pop culture, but culturally significant nonetheless.

In 1746, French Benedictine monk Antoine Augustin Calmet's treatise, *Dissertations sur les apparitions des anges, des démons et des esprits, et sur les revenants et vampires de Hongrie, de Bohême, de Moravie et de Silésie* (*Dissertations on the Apparitions of Angels, of Demons, and Spirits and on Revenants or Vampires of Hungary, Bohemia, Moravia and Silesia*; expanded five years later under the slightly-shorter title *Treatise on the Apparitions of Spirits and on Vampires or Revenants of Hungary, Moravia, Etc.*) brought vampires from lore into literature, laying out a set of beliefs about their capabilities, where they come from, and how to destroy them.

Immediately upon moving from folk tradition to fiction, vampires were eroticized in ways that proved creepy, if not scary. The narrator of Heinrich August Ossenfelder's "Der Vampir" promises that "as softly thou art sleeping / to thee shall I come creeping / and thy life's blood drain away." A quarter of a century later, Gottfried August Bürger published Gothic ballad "Lenore" (1774) which, while not outright about a vampire, detailed a macabre account of the arisen dead and influenced many of the poetry and stories to come. Johann Wolfgang von Goethe, another German author released "The Bride of Corinth" (1797; published as "Die Braut von Korinth"), the only non-prose piece included within this collection. That same year, the vampire finally made its English language debut in a section of *Thalaba the Destroyer*, an epic poem written by Robert Southey.

> In hollow tones she cried to Thalaba;
> "And must I nightly leave my grave
> To tell thee, still in vain,
> God hath abandoned thee?'

John Stagg's considerably shorter "The Vampyre" (1810) followed, as did Lord Byron's "The Giaour" (1813) and Samuel Taylor Coleridge's "Christabel" (1816). Other notable poems centering vampires released throughout the era covered in this collection: "Lamia" (1819) by John Keats, "The Vampire Bride" (1833) by Henry Thomas Liddell, "Strigoiul" (1845) by Vasile Alecsandri, "The Vampyre" (1845) by James Clerk Maxwell ("Beware of that deceitfull spright, / the ghaist that suckle the blude."), "Les Metamorphoses du Vampire" and "Le Vampire" (both 1857) by Charles Baudelaire, "The Vampyre" by Owen Meredith (1882), "The Vampyre" (1883) by Eric Stenbock, "The Vampire" (1896) by Madison Julius Cawein, "Luke Havergal" (1896) by Edward Arlington Robinson, "The Vampire" (1897) by Rudyard Kipling, "The Vampire" (1914) by Conrad Aiken ("And beautiful to kiss; / her mouth is sinister and red / as blood in moonlight is."), and "Oil and Blood" (1933) by William Butler Yeats.

The unattributed poem "The Vampyre of the Fens" is referenced as far back as 1855 by Edmund Ollier in an issue of Charles Dickens's weekly magazine *Household Words*, but there is no proof such a poem has ever truly existed outside of a potential conflation with a few stanzas from the epic poem *Beowulf* about the undefined monster Grendel.[1]

> That did not the monster think to delay,
> But quickly he seized for the first time
> A sleeping warrior, him tore unresisting,
> Bit his bone-frame, drank blood from his veins,

---

[1] *Beowulf*, 739-45; 1912 translation by James M. Garnett. Grendel is only referred to as a "*pyrs*" in the text, which is Old English for "demon.

> In great bites him swallowed: soon then he had,
> Deprived of life, him all devoured,
> Feet even and hands."

Germany remained at the forefront of new frontiers for the vampire in print. Ignatz Ferdinand Arnold wrote the first vampire novel, three-parter *Der Vampir* (1801). No surviving copies are known to exist. In Switzerland, during 1816's "Year Without a Summer," Lord Byron famously challenged his summer guests to write ghost stories. Though Byron himself was unable to complete his followup to "The Giaour," his friend John William Polidori reworked the vampire threads into the progenitorial short story "The Vampyre" (1819; introducing the idea of an aristocratic vampire)—even quoting Byron's earlier poem—and Mary Shelley produced the seminal novel *Frankenstein* (1818) from this same contest. Eventually Byron's partial story was published against his will as "A Fragment" (1816). He expressed his vexation to publisher John Murray in a letter: "and there you tacked it, without a word of explanation, and be damned to you."

A century and a half before Shakespearean actor and opera singer William Marshall chilled hearts as Mamuwalde in two *Blacula* films, readers were introduced to the Black vampire of Haiti in Uriah Derick D'Arcy's "The Black Vampyre; A Legend of St. Domingo."[2] This was a direct response to Polidori's story, even quoting "The Giaour" and making explicit references to Polidori's text. The genre would gain another Black vampire nearly a century later with Harriet Brandt, the "tragic mulatta" lead of Florence Marryat's *The Blood of the Vampire* (1897). Another direct offshoot of Polidori's tale was the novel, *Lord Ruthven, ou les Vampires* (1820) by Cyprien Bérard. Dramatist Charles Nodier adapted Bérard's novel as *Le Vampire* later that year. The success of Nodier's adaptation meant caused the work to be adapted itself, as an English play (*The Vampire, or The Bride of the Isles* by James Planché), a German play (*Der Vampir oder die Totenbrait* by Heinrich Ludwig Ritter) and two separate German operas (both first performed in 1928 and both titled *Der Vampyr*, with composer Heinrich Marschner and librettist Wilhelm August Wohlbrück's adaptation premiering that March in Leipzig, while composer Peter Josef von Lindpainter and librettist Cäsar Max Hegel's variation premiered that September in Stuttgart).

Nodier embraced the successes brought to him by the bloodsucking undead with the surreal *Smarra, or the Night of the Demons* (1821; as *Smarra ou les Demons de la Nuit*). German author Heinrich Zschokke released "Der tote Gast" ("The Dead Guest") the same year, while two years later Germany cranked out yet another classic with Ernst Raupach's "Wake Not the Dead"

---

[2] D'Arcy is assuredly a pseudonym, and "The Black Vampyre" has since been attributed to two different white American writers of the era: Robert C. Sands and pastor Richard Varick Dey. This makes the story one of many firsts, including the first to feature a Black vampire story and the first to be written by an American.

(1823; as "Laßt die Todten ruhen"). Etienne-Léon Lamothe-Langon's *The Vampire or The Hungarian Virgin* (1825; as *La Vampire, ou La Vierge de Hongrie*) introduces Alinska, who drinks blood from the lungs through the mouth of her victims as an instrument of God's wrath. Ten years later Russian writer Nikolai Vasilyevich Gogol wrote of a blood-drinking witch and the man charged to watch her corpse in "The Viy."

Der Vampyre und seine Braut (*The Vampire and his Bride*) was released by Carl Spindler in 1826, *Der Vampyr, oder: Die Todtenbraut* (*The Dead Bride*) by Theodor Hildebrand in 1828, and the year in between saw the first widespread literary vampire hoax with *La Guzla*, which author Prosper Mérimée presented as translations of twenty-nine folk ballads from Bosnia, Croatia, Dalmatia, and Herzegovina.[3] Mérimée's book includes several original narratives, with none as striking as the chapter "Sur le vampirisme" ("On Vampirism"), which features a narrator who tries—and fails—to convince a young girl that her sickness is likely psychological, while she assures her family that she's been vampirized by a recently deceased neighbor.

Returning to Russia, Aleksey Konstantinovich Tolstoy released *The Vampire* (1841; as *Oupyr*) and its poor critical reception prevented him from releasing his additional vampire stories during his lifetime with the sole exception of "Amena" (1849). Although written two years before *The Vampire*, "The Family" (originally written in French as *La Famille du Vourdalak. Fragment inedit des Memoires d'un inconnu*) wasn't published until 1884, nearly a decade after Tolstoy's death.

The next influential vampire story came from—where else?—Germany, with Karl von Wachsmann's *The Mysterious Stranger* (1844; as *Der Fremde*). Not much is known of von Wachsmann, but many of the things unique to von Wachsmann's story at the time—among other details, the vampire Azzo von Klatka lives in the Carpathian mountains in a castle in dreadful need of upkeep—resurfaced half a decade later in what is widely considered to be the best known vampire story. Much more developed before then.

The next significant piece of vampiric fiction came with the penny dreadful *Varney the Vampire; or, the Feast of Blood* (1846-7; serialized) by James Malcolm Rymer and(/or) Thomas Peckett Prest.[4] In this story for the first time, the vampire has fangs which leave puncture wounds on the necks of its victims, has super strength and powers of hypnotism, and treats his condition like an affliction—despite it being his unchangeable nature—long before Anne Rice delved beneath the monster in her thirteen book series *The*

---

[3] There have been a few other high profile literary hoaxes since, which I have chosen not to amplify further by detailing here.

[4] *The Feast of Blood* was published by Edward Lloyd, who did not allow authors' names on their work, meaning that the true authorship has not been confirmed. For the purposes of this collection, only an excerpt of *The Feast of Blood* was included. The full story is 667,000 words long—over three times the length of this book.

Vampire Chronicles (1976–2018). Augustus Hare's *The Vampire Of Croglin Grange* (1900) retells a "true" legend but parallels beats from *The Feast of Blood* to the point that a few scholars and many readers have suggested that Hare plagiarized the older story. Two years after Varney terrorized England, novelists Alexandre Dumas and Paul Bocage included "The Pale Lady" (1849; as "Les monts Carpathes") in their collection *Les mille et un fantômes* (*One Thousand and One Ghosts*),[5] while Pierre-Alexis Ponson du Terrail's hallucinatory take on the Gothic genre, *The Late Baroness* (1853; as *La Baronne Trépassée*), features a vampire that looks strangely like the protagonist's late wife. (*The Late Baroness* was not the first story to portend the onslaught of reincarnated love horror-romances. The vampire in *Thalaba* disguises itself as the titular character's deceased love.) That same year also brought the first "psychic" vampire—a being that drains energy, emotions, or other intangible essences—in *Yieger's Cabinet: Spiritual Vampirism, the History of Etherial Softdown, and Her Friends of the "New Light"* by Charles Wilkins Webber.

William H. G. Kingston broke from Slavic vampire traditions with "The Vampire; or, Pedro Pacheco and the Bruxa: A Legend of Portugal" (1863), focusing on the *bruxa*, a Portuguese monster that amalgamated the common characteristics of vampires and witches. Notably, *bruxas* were living dead bloodsuckers, human in likeness and thought during the day, morphing at night into giant winged and suitably nocturnal creatures (the book specifies owls and bats, though other inexplicit horrors are indicated). Richard F. Burton's *Vikram and the Vampire* (1870) followed, an adaptation of *Kathasaritsagara* which reimagined the *baital* as a bat-like vampire.[6] Vampires played significant supporting roles in other novels like Professor P. Jones's *The Pobratim: A Slav Novel* (1895) and anchored stories in varied collections like William Gilbert's *The Wizard of the Mountain* (1867; "The Last Lords of Gardonal"), G. J. Whyte-Melville's *"Bones and I"; or, The Skeleton at Home* (1868; "A Vampire,"), and Julian Osgood Field's *Aut Diabolus Aut Nihil, and Other Tales* (1893; "A Kiss of Judas").[7]

A trilogy of inventive French vampire novels came next—1860's *Knightshade*, 1865's *The Vampire Countess* and 1874's *The Vampire City* (*Chevalier Ténèbre*, *La Vampire*, and *The Vampire City*; respectively). In this series, Paul Féval, père ignored the increasing homogeny of literary vampires —though he embraced the concept of vampires being sexual beings—and played fast and loose with his own conventions. For instance, *Knightshade*

---

[5] Dumas also wrote *Le Vampire* (1851), a stage play where Polidori's Lord Ruthven combats a necromancer named Ziska.

[6] The *Kathasaritsagara* is an 11th-century collection of Indian legends. Burton loosely adapted a portion of this collection, entitled *Baital Pachisi*, into his own.

[7] Interestingly, though "*pobratim*" translates to "blood brothers," the vampire in this epic is neither of those titular characters.

defines the difference between a vampire and an oupire (one feeds on blood, the other on flesh, essentially treating vampires and the ghouls of Arabic folklore as parallel creatures), while the vampire countess Addhema retains her youth by wearing scalps she tears from living young women. Notably, *The Vampire City* introduces a female vampire hunter (a fictionalized version of Gothic fiction writer Ann Radcliffe), a pillar of good to stand against the undead evil, predating *Buffy the Vampire Slayer* by over one hundred years.

J. Sheridan Le Fanu released the haunting and unmistakably queer— another first—*Carmilla* in 1872. The story may be read as an homage or adaptation of Coleridge's "Christabel," but Le Fanu's bloodsucker became the paradigm for female vampires. Julian Hawthorne contributed Ethelind Fionguala to the array with "Ken's Mystery" (1883), and Sabine Baring-Gould created one of the most unique female vampires with "Margery of Quether" (1884), a literally bloodless tale. Like Webber's Etherial Softdown before her, Margery eschews exsanquination in favor of a different sort of imbibition. The narrator is explicit in this:

> I would not have you suppose that Margery was sucking my blood. Nothing of the sort; that is, not grossly in the manner of a leech. But she really did, in some marvelous manner, to me quite inexplicable, extract life and health, the blood from my veins and the marrow from my bones, and assimilate them herself.

Psychic vampires of varying forms also show up in Eric Stenbock's "The True Story of a Vampire" (1894) and Arabella Kenealy's "A Beautiful Vampire" (1896). Kenealy's narrative is significant in another way, by facing her vampire against a "psychic" detective in her series *Some Experiences of Lord Syfret*. Writers Alice and Claude Askew would pit their own occult detective against a more traditional vampire in 1914's "Aylmer Vance and the Vampire."

Vampire stories were quite varied at this stage, with "Manor" (1885), by Karl Heinrich Ulrichs, weaving a gay love story in the vein of Le Fanu, though its protagonists are devoted long before one becomes a vampire. "A Mystery of the Campagna" (1886) by Baroness Anne Crawford Von Rabe, "The Last of the Vampires" (1893) by Phil Robinson, and "The Tomb of Sarah" (1900) by F. G. Loring are each epistolary works, with Robinson's tale also doing something very unique with his vampire variant. Places and things become important factors to the action in both "The Old Portrait" (1890) by Hume Nisbet and "The Stone Chamber" (1898) by H. B. Marriott Watson.

In 1897, the quintessential vampire novel arrived with *Dracula*.[8] Written by Bram Stoker as a novel first and then a play, the tale and its many

---

[8] The novel's impact is represented here by "Dracula's Guest," which, according to Stoker's widow, was intended as an early chapter in the novel, excised, and later included *Dracula's Guest and Other Weird Stories* (1914).

adaptations have become inseparable from general vampire lore, meaning even the elements not original to Stoker were canonized due to the widespread reach of the story. Count Dracula, it should be noted, was the first vampire who showed no reflection in mirrors. Other traits associated with vampires by this point—aversion to crucifixes and garlic, transforming into bats, etc.—became fixtures of the genre. Additional full-length novels followed, with notable releases from Herbert Moore Pim (*A Vampire of Souls*; 1904) and M. Y. Halidom (*The Woman in Black*; 1906). Short stories published during this initial post-*Dracula* period include J. E. Muddock's "The Woman with the 'Oily Eyes'" (1899), "The Vampire" (1901) by Hugh McCrae (writing as W. W. Lamble), "Count Magnus" (1904) by M. R. James, "For the Blood is the Life" (1905) by F. Marion Crawford, "A Vampire" (1907) by Italian author Luigi Capuana, and two classics by E. F. Benson: "The Room in the Tower" (1912) and "Mrs. Amworth" (1920).

Two additional writers utilized psychic vampires in 1902. Published without attribution in *Tales by Three Brothers* and widely credited to the eldest Robinson brother, Phil, "Medusa" features Edith Tierce, whose reign of psychic terror was quickly eclipsed by Mary Wilkins Freeman's "Luella Miller." The horrifying Reginald Clarke joined them with *The House of the Vampire* (1907), a full-length novel by George Sylvester Viereck that saw its vampire malignantly purloining artistry and skill from unsuspecting victims. Additional variations are found in Vincent O'Sullivan's "Will" (1899), Emilia Pardo Bazán's "Vampiro" (1901), E. F. Benson's "And No Bird Sings" (1926), and D.H. Lawrence's "The Lovely Lady" (1928). Algernon Blackwood conducts this particular offshoot of vampirism to a thrilling eventuality—and a fantastic illustration of the unstoppable force paradox—in "The Transfer" (1911), coming just one year after his significantly more conventional vampire tale "The Singular Death of Morton."

Deviation offered a fresh takes on a vampire mythos that was nearing standardization. Sabine Baring-Gould introduced the notion of vampiric *body parts* with "A Dead Finger" (1904), echoed in concept by Morley Roberts's "The Blood Fetish" (1908; in which a cast of white characters are terrorized by a disembodied Black hand). In "The Feather Pillow" (1907; as "El almohadón de plumas"), author Horacio Quiroga does not reveal the unique source of horror until the last possible moment, and in her slow-burning "Bewitched" (1926), Edith Wharton refuses to reveal anything at all. "The Sumach" (1919) finds Ulric Daubeny putting a botanical spin on bloodsucking.[9]

The film *Nosferatu – Eine Symphonie des Grauens* (*Nosferatu: A Symphony of Horror*) was released in Germany in 1922 as loose, unauthorized adaptation of Stoker's novel. The central vampire's name is Count Orlok, he definitely looks like something monstrous, and instead of being merely weakened by

[9] For more lethal plants and fatal flora, *HORROR HISTORIA GREEN* is a necessary companion to this volume.

the sun, daylight is fatal. After a lengthy and uncompromising legal dispute between the makers of *Nosferatu* and Stoker's widow Florence Balcombe, and after several successful stage adaptations approved and licensed by Balcombe, Dracula finally crossed over into film, with the 1931 Bela Lugosi-starrer from Universal Studios. Lugosi was handsome and elegant and susceptible to romance; unlike the hairy, malodorous Count found in the novel or the clawed, cadaverous Count from the unauthorized film; marrying the image of the male vampire with the eroticism typically reserved for the female vamps going as far back as "Lenore" and "The Bride of Corinth."

By this time pulp magazines filled with action-packed horror stories from authors like Hugh B. Cave, Carl Jacobi, Earl Peirce, Jr., Victor Roman, Clark Ashton Smith, and Manly Wade Wellman. Three of the finer melodramas are included here: Grace Jones Morgan's deceptively-titled "The Wolf-Woman" (1927), Everil Worrell's "The Canal" (1927), and Henry Kuttner's "I, the Vampire" (1937; anthologized here as "Red Thirst").

The vampire was not done; there are many more tales from this foundational era that are less known and less noteworthy—fairly or not—that are worth seeking out, from oft-anthologized stories like Nisbet's "The Vampire Maid" (1890) to lost-in-translation gems such as Marie Nizet's *Le Capitaine Vampire* (1879). To this very day, the vampire continues to grow in popularity and iconography across all media. At this present moment, popular books, filmed projects, video games, and other forms of entertainment add to, interpolate, and subvert familiar themes and archetypes—an adaptable predator maintaining rule over its ever-changing territory. It becomes clearer everyday that these creatures, the life-consuming dead, have embraced a new immortality.

C.S.R. CALLOWAY

NOTES ON THE COLLECTION

Gothic grotesqueries, penny dreadfuls, pulp magazines, and other darkly inventive publications have produced a dread allure across the world, infiltrating culture and influencing language, becoming the source for multiple adaptations across all forms of media. HORROR HISTORIA brings together the most influential monsters and original gothic stories in distinctive blood-curdling collections, existing not as an exhaustive tome or panoptic omnibus, but as one hell of a starter kit for the archetypes, conventions and motifs necessary to build the ultimate nightmare pantheon.

To make HORROR HISTORIA texts more accessible to the contemporary reader, minor changes have been made with spelling, punctuation, capitalization, italicization, hyphenation, and spacing. British spellings ("colour" instead of "color") have been altered throughout. Obvious typographical errors in the original texts have been corrected. Many of these stories contain depictions common during their day among writers from systemically majoritized backgrounds and cultures, though any outright slurs have been altered or removed. Neither the publisher nor the editor endorses any characterizations, depictions, or language which would be considered ableist, racist, xenophobic, or otherwise offensive.

Each book in the HORROR HISTORIA collection is dedicated to **Gerardo Maravilla**.

1

NOTES ON THE COLLECTION

THE BRIDE OF CORINTH

Johann Wolfgang von Goethe

first published as "Die Braut von Korinth" in *Die Horen* (1797)

I.

A youth to Corinth, whilst the city slumbered,
  Came from Athens: though a stranger there,
Soon among its townsmen to be numbered,
  For a bride awaits him, young and fair.
    From their childhood's years
    They were plighted feres,
So contracted by their parents' care.

II.

But may not his welcome there he hindered?
  Dearly must he buy it, would he speed.
He is still a heathen with his kindred,
  She and hers washed in the Christian creed.
    When new faiths are born,
    Love and troth are torn
Rudely from the heart, howe'er it bleed.

III.

All the house is hushed;—to rest retreated
  Father, daughters—not the mother quite;
She the guest with cordial welcome greeted,
  Led him to a room with tapers bright;
    Wine and food she brought,
    Ere of them he thought,
Then departed with a fair goodnight.

IV.

But he felt no hunger, and unheeded
  Left the wine, and eager for the rest

Which his limbs, forspent with travel, needed,
  On the couch he laid him, still undressed.
    There he sleeps—when lo!
    Onwards gliding slow,
  At the door appears a wondrous guest.

V.

By the waning lamp's uncertain gleaming
  There he sees a youthful maiden stand,
Robed in white, of still and gentle seeming,
  On her brow a black and golden band.
    When she meets his eyes,
    With a quick surprise
  Starting, she uplifts a pallid hand.

VI.

"Is a stranger here, and nothing told me?
  Am I then forgotten even in name?
Ah! 'tis thus within my cell they hold me,
  And I now am covered o'er with shame!
    Pillow still thy head
    There upon thy bed,
  I will leave thee quickly as I came."

VII.

"Maiden—darling! Stay, O stay!" and, leaping
  From the couch before her stands the boy:
"Ceres—Bacchus, here their gifts are heaping.
  And thou bringest Amor's gentle joy!
    Why with terror pale?
    Sweet one, let us hail
  These bright gods their festive gifts employ."

VIII.

"Oh, no—no! Young stranger, come not nigh me
  Joy is not for me, nor festive cheer.
Ah! such bliss may ne'er be tasted by me,
  Since my mother, in fantastic fear,
    By long sickness bowed,
    To heaven's service vowed
  Me, and all the hopes that warmed me here.

IX.

"They have left our hearth, and left it lonely,—
  The old gods, that bright and jocund train.

One, unseen, in heaven, is worshipped only.
  And upon the cross a Savior slain;
    Sacrifice is here,
    Not of lamb nor steer,
  But of human woe and human pain."

       X.

And he asks, and all her words doth ponder,—
  "Can it be that in this silent spot,
I behold thee, thou surpassing wonder!
  My sweet bride, so strangely to me brought?
    Be mine only now—
    See, our parents' vow
  Heaven's good blessing hath for us besought."

       XI.

"No! thou gentle heart," she cried in anguish;
  "'Tis not mine, but 'tis my sister's place;
When in lonely cell I weep and languish,
  Think, oh, think of me in her embrace!
    I think but of thee—
    Pining drearily,
  Soon beneath the earth to hide my face!"

       XII.

"Nay! I swear by yonder flame which burneth,
  Fanned by Hymen, lost thou shalt not be;
Droop not thus, for my sweet bride returneth
  To my father's mansion back with me!
    Dearest, tarry here!
    Taste the bridal cheer,
  For our spousal spread so wondrously!"

       XIII.

Then with word and sigh their troth they plighted,
  Golden was the chain she bade him wear,
But the cup he offered her she slighted,
  Silver, wrought with cunning past compare.
    "That is not for me;
    All I ask of thee
  Is one little ringlet of thy hair!"

       XIV.

Dully boomed the midnight hour unhallowed,
  And then first her eyes began to shine;

Eagerly with pallid lips she swallowed
  Hasty draughts of purple-tinctured wine;
    But the wheaten bread,
    As in shuddering dread,
  Put she always by with loathing sign.

XV.

And she gave the youth the cup: he drained it,
  With impetuous haste he drained it dry;
Love was in his fevered heart, and pained it,
  Till it ached for joy she must deny.
    But the maiden's fears
    Stayed him, till in tears
  On the bed he sank, with sobbing cry.

XVI.

And she leans above him—"Dear one, still thee!
  Ah, how sad am I to see thee so!
But, alas! these limbs of mine would chill thee:
  Love! they mantle not with passion's glow;
    Thou wouldst be afraid,
    Didst thou find the maid
  Thou hast chosen, cold as ice or snow."

XVII.

Round her waist his eager arms he bended,
  With the strength that youth and love inspire;
"Wert thou even from the grave ascended,
  I could warm thee well with my desire!"
    Panting kiss on kiss!
    Overflow of bliss!
  "Burn'st thou not, and feelest me on fire?"

XVIII.

Closer yet they cling, and intermingling.
  Tears and broken sobs proclaim the rest;
His hot breath through all her frame is tingling,
  There they lie, caressing and caressed.
    His impassioned mood
    Warms her torpid blood,
  Yet there beats no heart within her breast!

XIX.

Meanwhile goes the mother, softly creeping
  Through the house, on needful cares intent,

Hears a murmur, and, while all are sleeping,
  Wonders at the sounds, and what they meant.
    Who was whispering so?—
    Voices soft and low,
  In mysterious converse strangely blent.

XX.

Straightway by the door herself she stations,
  There to be assured what was amiss;
And she hears love's fiery protestations,
  Words of ardor and endearing bliss:
    "Hark, the cock! 'Tis light!
    But tomorrow night
  Thou wilt come again?" and kiss on kiss.

XXI.

Quick the latch she raises, and, with features
  Anger-flushed, into the chamber hies.
"Are there in my house such shameless creatures,
  Minions to the stranger's will?" she cries.
    By the dying light.
    Who is't meets her sight?
  God! 'tis her own daughter she espies!

XXII.

And the youth in terror sought to cover,
  With her own light veil, the maiden's head,
Clasped her close; but, gliding from her lover.
  Back the vestment from her brow she spread,
    And her form upright,
    As with ghostly might,
  Long and slowly rises from the bed.

XXIII.

"Mother! mother! wherefore thus deprive me
  Of such joy as I this night have known?
Wherefore from these warm embraces drive me?
  Was I wakened up to meet thy frown?
    Did it not suffice
    That in virgin guise,
  To an early grave you forced me down?

XXIV.

"Fearful is the weird that forced me hither,
  From the dark-heaped chamber where I lay;

Powerless are your drowsy anthems, neither
   Can your priests prevail, howe'er they pray.
     Salt nor lymph can cool,
     Where the pulse is full;
   Love must still burn on, though wrapped in clay.

XXV.

"To this youth my early troth was plighted,
   Whilst yet Venus ruled within the land;
Mother! and that vow ye falsely slighted,
   At your new and gloomy faith's command.
     But no god will hear,
     If a mother swear
   Pure from love to keep her daughter's hand.

XXVI.

"Nightly from my narrow chamber driven,
   Come I to fulfill my destined part.
Him to seek to whom my troth was given,
   And to draw the life-blood from his heart.
     He hath served my will;
     More I yet must kill,
   For another prey I now depart.

XXVII.

"Fair young man! thy thread of life is broken.
   Human skill can bring no aid to thee.
There thou hast my chain—a ghastly token—
   And this lock of thine I take with me.
     Soon must thou decay,
     Soon thou wilt be gray,
   Dark although tonight thy tresses be!

XXVIII.

"Mother! hear, oh, hear my last entreaty!
   Let the funeral-pile arise once more;
Open up my wretched tomb for pity,
   And in flames our souls to peace restore.
     When the ashes glow,
     When the fire-sparks flow,
   To the ancient gods aloft we soar."

THE VAMPYRE

John William Polidori

first published in the *New Monthly Magazine* (April 1819)

INTRODUCTION

The superstition upon which this tale is founded is very general in the East. Among the Arabians it appears to be common: it did not, however, extend itself to the Greeks until after the establishment of Christianity; and it has only assumed its present form since the division of the Latin and Greek churches; at which time, the idea becoming prevalent, that a Latin body could not corrupt if buried in their territory, it gradually increased, and formed the subject of many wonderful stories, still extant, of the dead rising from their graves, and feeding upon the blood of the young and beautiful. In the West it spread, with some slight variation, all over Hungary, Poland, Austria, and Lorraine, where the belief existed, that vampyres nightly imbibed a certain portion of the blood of their victims, who became emaciated, lost their strength, and speedily died of consumptions; whilst these human blood-suckers fattened—and their veins became distended to such a state of repletion, as to cause the blood to flow from all the passages of their bodies, and even from the very pores of their skins.

In the London Journal, of March, 1732, is a curious, and, of course, credible account of a particular case of vampyrism, which is stated to have occurred at Madreyga, in Hungary. It appears, that upon an examination of the commander-in-chief and magistrates of the place, they positively and unanimously affirmed, that, about five years before, a certain Heyduke, named Arnold Paul, had been heard to say, that, at Cassovia, on the frontiers of the Turkish Servia, he had been tormented by a vampyre, but had found a way to rid himself of the evil, by eating some of the earth out of the vampyre's grave, and rubbing himself with his blood. This precaution, however, did not prevent him from becoming a vampyre himself; for, about twenty or thirty days after his death and burial, many persons complained of having been tormented by him, and a deposition was made, that four persons had been deprived of life by his attacks. To prevent further mischief, the inhabitants having consulted their Hadagni,[10] took up the body, and found it (as is supposed to be usual in cases of vampyrism) fresh, and entirely free from corruption, and emitting at the mouth, nose, and ears, pure and florid blood. Proof having been thus obtained, they resorted to the accustomed remedy. A stake was driven entirely through the heart and body of Arnold Paul, at which he is reported to have cried out as dreadfully as if he had been alive. This done, they cut off his head, burned his body, and threw the ashes into his grave. The same measures were adopted with the corses of those persons who had previously died from vampyrism, lest they should, in their turn, become agents upon others who survived them.

This monstrous rodomontade is here related, because it seems better adapted to illustrate the subject of the present observations than any other instance which could be adduced. In many parts of Greece it is considered as a sort of punishment after death, for some heinous crime committed whilst in existence, that the deceased is not only doomed to vampyrise, but compelled to confine his infernal visitations solely to those beings he loved most while upon earth—those to whom he was bound by ties of kindred and affection.— A supposition alluded to in the "Giaour."

> But first on earth, as Vampyre sent,
> Thy corse shall from its tomb be rent;
> Then ghastly haunt the native place,
> And suck the blood of all thy race;
> There from thy daughter, sister, wife,
> At midnight drain the stream of life;
> Yet loathe the banquet which perforce
> Must feed thy livid living corse,
> Thy victims, ere they yet expire,
> Shall know the demon for their sire;
> As cursing thee, thou cursing them,
> Thy flowers are withered on the stem.
> But one that for thy crime must fall,
> The youngest, best beloved of all,
> Shall bless thee with a father's name—
> That word shall wrap thy heart in flame!
> Yet thou must end thy task and mark
> Her cheek's last tinge—her eye's last spark,
> And the last glassy glance must view
> Which freezes o'er its lifeless blue;
> Then with unhallowed hand shall tear
> The tresses of her yellow hair,
> Of which, in life a lock when shorn
> Affection's fondest pledge was worn—

---

[10] Chief bailiff.

But now is borne away by thee
Memorial of thine agony!
Yet with thine own best blood shall drip;
Thy gnashing tooth, and haggard lip;
Then stalking to thy sullen grave,
Go—and with Gouls and Afrits rave,
Till these in horror shrink away
From spectre more accursed than they.

Mr. Southey has also introduced in his wild but beautiful poem of *Thalaba*, the vampyre corse of the Arabian maid Oneiza, who is represented as having returned from the grave for the purpose of tormenting him she best loved whilst in existence. But this cannot be supposed to have resulted from the sinfulness of her life, she being portrayed throughout the whole of the tale as a complete type of purity and innocence. The veracious Tournefort gives a long account in his travels of several astonishing cases of vampyrism, to which he pretends to have been an eyewitness; and Calmet, in his great work upon this subject, besides a variety of anecdotes, and traditionary narratives illustrative of its effects, has put forth some learned dissertations, tending to prove it to be a classical, as well as barbarian error.

Many curious and interesting notices on this singularly horrible superstition might be added; though the present may suffice for the limits of a note, necessarily devoted to explanation, and which may now be concluded by merely remarking, that though the term Vampyre is the one in most general acceptation, there are several others synonymous with it, made use of in various parts of the world: as Vroucolocha, Vardoulacha, Ghoul, Broucoloka, etc.

THE VAMPYRE

I t happened that in the midst of the dissipations attendant upon a London winter, there appeared at the various parties of the leaders of the ton a nobleman, more remarkable for his singularities, than his rank. He gazed upon the mirth around him, as if he could not participate therein. Apparently, the light laughter of the fair only attracted his attention, that he might by a look quell it, and throw fear into those breasts where thoughtlessness reigned. Those who felt this sensation of awe, could not explain whence it arose: some attributed it to the dead grey eye, which, fixing upon the object's face, did not seem to penetrate, and at one glance to pierce through to the inward workings of the heart; but fell upon the cheek with a leaden ray that weighed upon the skin it could not pass. His peculiarities caused him to be invited to every house; all wished to see him, and those who had been accustomed to violent excitement, and now felt the weight of ennui, were pleased at having something in their presence capable of engaging their attention. In spite of the deadly hue of his face, which never gained a warmer tint, either from the blush of modesty, or from the strong emotion of passion, though its form and outline were beautiful, many of the female hunters after notoriety attempted to win his attentions, and gain, at least, some marks of what they might term affection: Lady Mercer, who had been the mockery of every monster shewn in drawing-rooms since her marriage, threw herself in his way, and did all but put on the dress of a mountebank, to attract his notice:—though in vain:—when she stood before him, though his eyes were apparently fixed upon her's, still it seemed as if they were unperceived;—even her unappalled impudence was baffled, and she left the field. But though the common adultress could not influence even the guidance of his eyes, it was not that the female sex was indifferent to him: yet such was the apparent caution with which he spoke to the virtuous wife and innocent daughter, that few knew he ever addressed himself to females. He had, however, the reputation of a winning tongue; and whether it was that it even overcame the dread of his singular character, or that they were moved by his apparent hatred of vice, he was as often among those females who form the boast of their sex from their domestic virtues, as among those who sully it by their vices.

About the same time, there came to London a young gentleman of the name of Aubrey: he was an orphan left with an only sister in the possession of great wealth, by parents who died while he was yet in childhood. Left also to himself by guardians, who thought it their duty merely to take care of his fortune, while they relinquished the more important charge of his mind to the care of mercenary subalterns, he cultivated more his imagination than his judgment. He had, hence, that high romantic feeling of honor and candor, which daily ruins so many milliners' apprentices. He believed all to sympathize with virtue, and thought that vice was thrown in by Providence merely for the picturesque effect of the scene, as we see in romances: he thought that the misery of a cottage merely consisted in the vesting of clothes, which were as warm, but which were better adapted to the painter's eye by their irregular folds and various colored patches. He thought, in fine, that the dreams of poets were the realities of life. He was handsome, frank, and rich: for these reasons, upon his entering into the gay circles, many mothers surrounded him, striving which should describe with least truth their languishing or romping favorites: the daughters at the same time, by their brightening countenances when he approached, and by their sparkling eyes, when he opened his lips, soon led him into false notions of his talents and his merit. Attached as he was to the romance of his solitary hours, he was startled at finding, that, except in the tallow and wax candles that flickered, not from the presence of a ghost, but from want of snuffing, there was no foundation in real life for any of that congeries of pleasing pictures and descriptions contained in those volumes, from which he had formed his study. Finding, however, some compensation in his gratified vanity, he was about to relinquish his dreams, when the extraordinary being we have above described, crossed him in his career.

He watched him; and the very impossibility of forming an idea of the character of a man entirely absorbed in himself, who gave few other signs of his observation of external objects, than the tacit assent to their existence, implied by the avoidance of their contact: allowing his imagination to picture every thing that flattered its propensity to extravagant ideas, he soon formed this object into the hero of a romance, and determined to observe the offspring of his fancy, rather than the person before him. He became acquainted with him, paid him attentions, and so far advanced upon his notice, that his presence was always recognized. He gradually learnt that Lord Ruthven's affairs were embarrassed, and soon found, from the notes of preparation in —— Street, that he was about to travel. Desirous of gaining some information respecting this singular character, who, till now, had only whetted his curiosity, he hinted to his guardians, that it was time for him to perform the tour, which for many generations has been thought necessary to enable the young to take some rapid steps in the career of vice towards putting themselves upon an equality with the aged, and not allowing them to appear as if fallen from the skies, whenever scandalous intrigues are mentioned as the subjects of pleasantry or of praise, according to the degree of skill shewn in carrying them on. They consented: and Aubrey immediately mentioning his intentions to Lord Ruthven, was surprised to receive from him a proposal to join him. Flattered by such a mark of esteem from him, who, apparently, had nothing in common with other men, he gladly accepted it, and in a few days they had passed the circling waters.

Hitherto, Aubrey had had no opportunity of studying Lord Ruthven's character, and now he found, that, though many more of his actions were exposed to his view, the results offered different conclusions from the apparent motives to his conduct. His companion was profuse in his liberality; —the idle, the vagabond, and the beggar, received from his hand more than enough to relieve their immediate wants. But Aubrey could not avoid remarking, that it was not upon the virtuous, reduced to indigence by the misfortunes attendant even upon virtue, that he bestowed his alms;—these were sent from the door with hardly suppressed sneers; but when the profligate came to ask something, not to relieve his wants, but to allow him to wallow in his lust, or to sink him still deeper in his iniquity, he was sent away with rich charity. This was, however, attributed by him to the greater importunity of the vicious, which generally prevails over the retiring bashfulness of the virtuous indigent. There was one circumstance about the charity of his Lordship, which was still more impressed upon his mind: all those upon whom it was bestowed, inevitably found that there was a curse upon it, for they were all either led to the scaffold, or sunk to the lowest and the most abject misery. At Brussels and other towns through which they passed, Aubrey was surprised at the apparent eagerness with which his companion sought for the centers of all fashionable vice; there he entered into all the spirit of the faro table: he betted, and always gambled with success, except where the known sharper was his antagonist, and then he lost even more than he gained; but it was always with the same unchanging face, with which he generally watched the society around: it was not, however, so when he encountered the rash youthful novice, or the luckless father of a numerous family; then his very wish seemed fortune's law—this apparent abstractedness of mind was laid aside, and his eyes sparkled with more fire than that of the cat whilst dallying with the half-dead mouse. In every town, he left the formerly affluent youth, torn from the circle he adorned, cursing, in the solitude of a dungeon, the fate that had drawn him within the reach of this fiend; whilst many a father sat frantic, amidst the speaking looks of mute hungry children, without a single farthing of his late immense wealth, wherewith to buy even sufficient to satisfy their present craving. Yet he took no money from the gambling table; but immediately lost, to the ruiner of many, the last gilder he had just snatched from the convulsive grasp of the innocent: this might but be the result of a certain degree of knowledge, which was not, however, capable of combating the cunning of the more experienced. Aubrey often wished to represent this to his friend, and beg him to resign that charity and pleasure which proved the ruin of all, and did not tend to his own profit;—but he delayed it—for each day he hoped his friend would give him some opportunity of speaking frankly and openly to him; however, this never occurred. Lord Ruthven in his carriage, and amidst the various wild and rich scenes of nature, was always the same: his eye spoke less than his lip; and though Aubrey was near the object of his curiosity, he obtained no greater gratification from it than the constant excitement of vainly wishing to break that mystery, which to his exalted imagination began to assume the appearance of something supernatural.

They soon arrived at Rome, and Aubrey for a time lost sight of his companion; he left him in daily attendance upon the morning circle of an Italian countess, whilst he went in search of the memorials of another almost deserted city. Whilst he was thus engaged, letters arrived from England, which he opened with eager impatience; the first was from his sister, breathing nothing but affection; the others were from his guardians, the latter astonished him; if it had before entered into his imagination that there was an evil power resident in his companion, these seemed to give him sufficient reason for the belief. His guardians insisted upon his immediately leaving his friend, and urged, that his character was dreadfully vicious, for that the possession of irresistible powers of seduction, rendered his licentious habits more dangerous to society. It had been discovered, that his contempt for the adultress had not originated in hatred of her character; but that he had required, to enhance his gratification, that his victim, the partner of his guilt, should be hurled from the pinnacle of unsullied virtue, down to the lowest abyss of infamy and degradation: in fine, that all those females whom he had sought, apparently on account of their virtue, had, since his departure, thrown even the mask aside, and had not scrupled to expose the whole deformity of their vices to the public gaze.

Aubrey determined upon leaving one, whose character had not yet shown a single bright point on which to rest the eye. He resolved to invent some plausible pretext for abandoning him altogether, purposing, in the mean while, to watch him more closely, and to let no slight circumstances pass by unnoticed. He entered into the same circle, and soon perceived, that his Lordship was endeavoring to work upon the inexperience of the daughter of the lady whose house he chiefly frequented. In Italy, it is seldom that an unmarried female is met with in society; he was therefore obliged to carry on his plans in secret; but Aubrey's eye followed him in all his windings, and soon discovered that an assignation had been appointed, which would most likely end in the ruin of an innocent, though thoughtless girl. Losing no time, he entered the apartment of Lord Ruthven, and abruptly asked him his intentions with respect to the lady, informing him at the same time that he was aware of his being about to meet her that very night. Lord Ruthven answered, that his intentions were such as he supposed all would have upon such an occasion; and upon being pressed whether he intended to marry her, merely laughed. Aubrey retired; and, immediately writing a note, to say, that from that moment he must decline accompanying his Lordship in the remainder of their proposed tour, he ordered his servant to seek other apartments, and calling upon the mother of the lady, informed her of all he knew, not only with regard to her daughter, but also concerning the character of his Lordship. The assignation was prevented. Lord Ruthven next day merely sent his servant to notify his complete assent to a separation; but did not hint any suspicion of his plans having been foiled by Aubrey's interposition.

Having left Rome, Aubrey directed his steps towards Greece, and crossing the Peninsula, soon found himself at Athens. He then fixed his residence in the house of a Greek; and soon occupied himself in tracing the faded records of ancient glory upon monuments that apparently, ashamed of chronicling the deeds of freemen only before slaves, had hidden themselves beneath the sheltering soil or many colored lichen. Under the same roof as himself, existed a being, so beautiful and delicate, that she might have formed the model for a painter wishing to portray on canvass the promised hope of the faithful in Mahomet's paradise, save that her eyes spoke too much mind for any one to think she could belong to those who had no souls. As she danced upon the plain, or tripped along the mountain's side, one would have thought the gazelle a poor type of her beauties; for who would have exchanged her eye, apparently the eye of animated nature, for that sleepy luxurious look of the animal suited but to the taste of an epicure. The light step of Ianthe often accompanied Aubrey in his search after antiquities, and often would the unconscious girl, engaged in the pursuit of a Kashmere butterfly, show the whole beauty of her form, floating as it were upon the wind, to the eager gaze of him, who forgot the letters he had just deciphered upon an almost effaced tablet, in the contemplation of her sylph-like figure. Often would her tresses falling, as she flitted around, exhibit in the sun's ray such delicately brilliant and swiftly fading hues, it might well excuse the forgetfulness of the antiquary, who let escape from his mind the very object he had before thought of vital importance to the proper interpretation of a passage in Pausanias. But why attempt to describe charms which all feel, but none can appreciate?—It was innocence, youth, and beauty, unaffected by crowded drawing-rooms and stifling balls. Whilst he drew those remains of which he wished to preserve a memorial for his future hours, she would stand by, and watch the magic effects of his pencil, in tracing the scenes of her native place; she would then describe to him the circling dance upon the open plain, would paint, to him in all the glowing colors of youthful memory, the marriage pomp she remembered viewing in her infancy; and then, turning to subjects that had evidently made a greater impression upon her mind, would tell him all the supernatural tales of her nurse. Her earnestness and apparent belief of what she narrated, excited the interest even of Aubrey; and often as she told him the tale of the living vampyre, who had passed years amidst his friends, and dearest ties, forced every year, by feeding upon the life of a lovely female to prolong his existence for the ensuing months, his blood would run cold, whilst he attempted to laugh her out of such idle and horrible fantasies; but Ianthe cited to him the names of old men, who had at last detected one living among themselves, after several of their near relatives and children had been found marked with the stamp of the fiend's appetite; and when she found him so incredulous, she begged of him to believe her, for it had been, remarked, that those who had dared to question their existence, always had some proof given, which obliged them, with grief and heartbreaking, to confess it was true. She detailed to him the traditional appearance of these monsters, and his horror was increased, by hearing a pretty accurate description of Lord Ruthven; he, however, still persisted in persuading her, that there could be no truth in her fears, though at the same time he wondered at the many coincidences which had all tended to excite a belief in the supernatural power of Lord Ruthven.

Aubrey began to attach himself more and more to Ianthe; her innocence, so contrasted with all the affected virtues of the women among whom he had sought for his vision of romance, won his heart; and while he ridiculed the idea of a young man of English habits, marrying an uneducated Greek girl, still he found himself more and more attached to the almost fairy form before him. He would tear himself at times from her, and, forming a plan for some antiquarian research, he would depart, determined not to return until his object was attained; but he always found it impossible to fix his attention upon the ruins around him, whilst in his mind he retained an image that seemed alone the rightful possessor of his thoughts. Ianthe was unconscious of his love, and was ever the same frank infantile being he had first known. She always seemed to part from him with reluctance; but it was because she had no longer any one with whom she could visit her favorite haunts, whilst her guardian was occupied in sketching or uncovering some fragment which had yet escaped the destructive hand of time. She had appealed to her parents on the subject of Vampyres, and they both, with several present, affirmed their existence, pale with horror at the very name. Soon after, Aubrey determined to proceed upon one of his excursions, which was to detain him for a few hours; when they heard the name of the place, they all at once begged of him not to return at night, as he must necessarily pass through a wood, where no Greek would ever remain, after the day had closed, upon any consideration. They described it as the resort of the vampyres in their nocturnal orgies, and denounced the most heavy evils as impending upon him who dared to cross their path. Aubrey made light of their representations, and tried to laugh them out of the idea; but when he saw them shudder at his daring thus to mock a superior, infernal power, the very name of which apparently made their blood freeze, he was silent.

Next morning Aubrey set off upon his excursion unattended; he was surprised to observe the melancholy face of his host, and was concerned to find that his words, mocking the belief of those horrible fiends, had inspired them with such terror. When he was about to depart, Ianthe came to the side of his horse, and earnestly begged of him to return, ere night allowed the power of these beings to be put in action;—he promised. He was, however, so occupied in his research, that he did not perceive that day-light would soon end, and that in the horizon there was one of those specks which, in the warmer climates, so rapidly gather into a tremendous mass, and pour all their rage upon the devoted country.—He at last, however, mounted his horse, determined to make up by speed for his delay: but it was too late. Twilight, in these southern climates, is almost unknown; immediately the sun sets, night begins: and ere he had advanced far, the power of the storm was above—its echoing thunders had scarcely an interval of rest—its thick heavy rain forced its way through the canopying foliage, whilst the blue forked lightning seemed to fall and radiate at his very feet. Suddenly his horse took fright, and he was carried with dreadful rapidity through the entangled forest. The animal at last, through fatigue, stopped, and he found, by the glare of lightning, that he was in the neighborhood of a hovel that hardly lifted itself up from the masses of dead leaves and brushwood which surrounded it. Dismounting, he approached, hoping to find someone to guide him to the town, or at least trusting to obtain shelter from the pelting of the storm. As he approached, the thunders, for a moment silent, allowed him to hear the dreadful shrieks of a woman mingling with the stifled, exultant mockery of a laugh, continued in one almost unbroken sound;—he was startled: but, roused by the thunder which again rolled over his head, he, with a sudden effort, forced open the door of the hut. He found himself in utter darkness: the sound, however, guided him. He was apparently unperceived; for, though he called, still the sounds continued, and no notice was taken of him. He found himself in contact with someone, whom he immediately seized; when a voice cried, "Again baffled!" to which a loud laugh succeeded; and he felt himself grappled by one whose strength seemed superhuman: determined to sell his life as dearly as he could, he struggled; but it was in vain: he was lifted from his feet and hurled with enormous force against the ground:—his enemy threw himself upon him, and kneeling upon his breast, had placed his hands upon his throat—when the glare of many torches penetrating through the hole that gave light in the day, disturbed him;—he instantly rose, and, leaving his prey, rushed through the door, and in a moment the crashing of the branches, as he broke through the wood, was no longer heard. The storm was now still; and Aubrey, incapable of moving, was soon heard by those without. They entered; the light of their torches fell upon the mud walls, and the thatch loaded on every individual straw with heavy flakes of soot. At the desire of Aubrey they searched for her who had attracted him by her cries; he was again left in darkness; but what was his horror, when the light of the torches once more burst upon him, to perceive the airy form of his fair conductress brought in a lifeless corse. He shut his eyes, hoping that it was but a vision arising from his disturbed imagination; but he again saw the same form, when he unclosed them, stretched by his side. There was no color upon her cheek, not even upon her lip; yet there was a stillness about her face that seemed almost as attaching as the life that once dwelt there:—upon her neck and breast was blood, and upon her throat were the marks of teeth having opened the vein:—to this the men pointed, crying, simultaneously struck with horror, "A Vampyre! a Vampyre!" A litter was quickly formed, and Aubrey was laid by the side of her who had lately been to him the object of so many bright and fairy visions, now fallen with the flower of life that had died within her. He knew not what his thoughts were—his mind was benumbed and seemed to shun reflection, and take refuge in vacancy—he held almost unconsciously in his hand a naked dagger of a particular construction, which had been found in the hut. They were soon met by different parties who had been engaged in the search of her whom a mother had missed. Their lamentable cries, as they approached the city, forewarned the parents of some dreadful catastrophe.—To describe their grief would be impossible; but when they ascertained the cause of their child's death, they looked at Aubrey, and pointed to the corse. They were inconsolable; both died broken-hearted.

Aubrey being put to bed was seized with a most violent fever, and was often delirious; in these intervals he would call upon Lord Ruthven and upon Ianthe—by some unaccountable combination he seemed to beg of his former companion to spare the being he loved. At other times he would imprecate maledictions upon his head, and curse him as her destroyer. Lord Ruthven, chanced at this time to arrive at Athens, and, from whatever motive, upon hearing of the state of Aubrey, immediately placed himself in the same house, and became his constant attendant. When the latter recovered from his delirium, he was horrified and startled at the sight of him whose image he had now combined with that of a Vampyre; but Lord Ruthven, by his kind words, implying almost repentance for the fault that had caused their separation, and still more by the attention, anxiety, and care which he showed, soon reconciled him to his presence. His lordship seemed quite changed; he no longer appeared that apathetic being who had so astonished Aubrey; but as soon as his convalescence began to be rapid, he again gradually retired into the same state of mind, and Aubrey perceived no difference from the former man, except that at times he was surprised to meet his gaze fixed intently upon him, with a smile of malicious exultation playing upon his lips: he knew not why, but this smile haunted him. During the last stage of the invalid's recovery, Lord Ruthven was apparently engaged in watching the tideless waves raised by the cooling breeze, or in marking the progress of those orbs, circling, like our world, the moveless sun;—indeed, he appeared to wish to avoid the eyes of all.

Aubrey's mind, by this shock, was much weakened, and that elasticity of spirit which had once so distinguished him now seemed to have fled forever. He was now as much a lover of solitude and silence as Lord Ruthven; but much as he wished for solitude, his mind could not find it in the neighborhood of Athens; if he sought it amidst the ruins he had formerly frequented, Ianthe's form stood by his side—if he sought it in the woods, her light step would appear wandering amidst the underwood, in quest of the modest violet; then suddenly turning round, would show, to his wild imagination, her pale face and wounded throat, with a meek smile upon her lips. He determined to fly scenes, every feature of which created such bitter associations in his mind. He proposed to Lord Ruthven, to whom he held himself bound by the tender care he had taken of him during his illness, that they should visit those parts of Greece neither had yet seen. They travelled in every direction, and sought every spot to which a recollection could be attached: but though they thus hastened from place to place, yet they seemed not to heed what they gazed upon. They heard much of robbers, but they gradually began to slight these reports, which they imagined were only the invention of individuals, whose interest it was to excite the generosity of those whom they defended from pretended dangers. In consequence of thus neglecting the advice of the inhabitants, on one occasion they travelled with only a few guards, more to serve as guides than as a defense. Upon entering, however, a narrow defile, at the bottom of which was the bed of a torrent, with large masses of rock brought down from the neighboring precipices, they had reason to repent their negligence; for scarcely were the whole of the party engaged in the narrow pass, when they were startled by the whistling of bullets close to their heads, and by the echoed report of several guns. In an instant their guards had left them, and, placing themselves behind rocks, had begun to fire in the direction whence the report came. Lord Ruthven and Aubrey, imitating their example, retired for a moment behind the sheltering turn of the defile: but ashamed of being thus detained by a foe, who with insulting shouts bade them advance, and being exposed to unresisting slaughter, if any of the robbers should climb above and take them in the rear, they determined at once to rush forward in search of the enemy. Hardly had they lost the shelter of the rock, when Lord Ruthven received a shot in the shoulder, which brought him to the ground. Aubrey hastened to his assistance; and, no longer heeding the contest or his own peril, was soon surprised by seeing the robbers' faces around him—his guards having, upon Lord Ruthven's being wounded, immediately thrown up their arms and surrendered.

By promises of great reward, Aubrey soon induced them to convey his wounded friend to a neighboring cabin; and having agreed upon a ransom, he was no more disturbed by their presence—they being content merely to guard the entrance till their comrade should return with the promised sum, for which he had an order. Lord Ruthven's strength rapidly decreased; in two days mortification ensued, and death seemed advancing with hasty steps. His conduct and appearance had not changed; he seemed as unconscious of pain as he had been of the objects about him: but towards the close of the last evening, his mind became apparently uneasy, and his eye often fixed upon Aubrey, who was induced to offer his assistance with more than usual earnestness—"Assist me! you may save me—you may do more than that—I mean not my life, I heed the death of my existence as little as that of the passing day; but you may save my honor, your friend's honor."—"How? tell me how? I would do any thing," replied Aubrey.—"I need but little—my life ebbs apace—I cannot explain the whole—but if you would conceal all you know of me, my honor were free from stain in the world's mouth—and if my death were unknown for some time in England—I—I—but life."—"It shall not be known."—"Swear!" cried the dying man, raising himself with exultant violence, "Swear by all your soul reveres, by all your nature fears, swear that, for a year and a day you will not impart your knowledge of my crimes or death to any living being in any way, whatever may happen, or whatever you may see. "—His eyes seemed bursting from their sockets: "I swear!" said Aubrey; he sunk laughing upon his pillow, and breathed no more.

Aubrey retired to rest, but did not sleep; the many circumstances attending his acquaintance with this man rose upon his mind, and he knew not why; when he remembered his oath a cold shivering came over him, as if from the presentiment of something horrible awaiting him. Rising early in the morning, he was about to enter the hovel in which he had left the corpse, when a robber met him, and informed him that it was no longer there, having been conveyed by himself and comrades, upon his retiring, to the pinnacle of a neighboring mount, according to a promise they had given his lordship, that it should be exposed to the first cold ray of the moon that rose after his death. Aubrey astonished, and taking several of the men, determined to go and bury it upon the spot where it lay. But, when he had mounted to the summit he found no trace of either the corpse or the clothes, though the robbers swore they pointed out the identical rock on which they had laid the body. For a time his mind was bewildered in conjectures, but he at last returned, convinced that they had buried the corpse for the sake of the clothes.

Weary of a country in which he had met with such terrible misfortunes, and in which all apparently conspired to heighten that superstitious melancholy that had seized upon his mind, he resolved to leave it, and soon arrived at Smyrna. While waiting for a vessel to convey him to Otranto, or to Naples, he occupied himself in arranging those effects he had with him belonging to Lord Ruthven. Amongst other things there was a case containing several weapons of offense, more or less adapted to ensure the death of the victim. There were several daggers and yataghans. Whilst turning them over, and examining their curious forms, what was his surprise at finding a sheath apparently ornamented in the same style as the dagger discovered in the fatal hut—he shuddered—hastening to gain further proof, he found the weapon, and his horror may be imagined when he discovered that it fitted, though peculiarly shaped, the sheath he held in his hand. His eyes seemed to need no further certainty—they seemed gazing to be bound to the dagger; yet still he wished to disbelieve; but the particular form, the same varying tints upon the haft and sheath were alike in splendor on both, and left no room for doubt; there were also drops of blood on each.

He left Smyrna, and on his way home, at Rome, his first inquiries were concerning the lady he had attempted to snatch from Lord Ruthven's seductive arts. Her parents were in distress, their fortune ruined, and she had not been heard of since the departure of his lordship. Aubrey's mind became almost broken under so many repeated horrors; he was afraid that this lady had fallen a victim to the destroyer of Ianthe. He became morose and silent; and his only occupation consisted in urging the speed of the postilions, as if he were going to save the life of someone he held dear. He arrived at Calais; a breeze, which seemed obedient to his will, soon wafted him to the English shores; and he hastened to the mansion of his fathers, and there, for a moment, appeared to lose, in the embraces and caresses of his sister, all memory of the past. If she before, by her infantine caresses, had gained his affection, now that the woman began to appear, she was still more attaching as a companion.

Miss Aubrey had not that winning grace which gains the gaze and applause of the drawing-room assemblies. There was none of that light brilliancy which only exists in the heated atmosphere of a crowded apartment. Her blue eye was never lit up by the levity of the mind beneath. There was a melancholy charm about it which did not seem to arise from misfortune, but from some feeling within, that appeared to indicate a soul conscious of a brighter realm. Her step was not that light footing, which strays where'er a butterfly or a color may attract—it was sedate and pensive. When alone, her face was never brightened by the smile of joy; but when her brother breathed to her his affection, and would in her presence forget those griefs she knew destroyed his rest, who would have exchanged her smile for that of the voluptuary? It seemed as if those eyes,—that face were then playing in the light of their own native sphere. She was yet only eighteen, and had not been presented to the world, it having been thought by her guardians more fit that her presentation should be delayed until her brother's return from the continent, when he might be her protector. It was now, therefore, resolved that the next drawing-room, which was fast approaching, should be the epoch of her entry into the "busy scene." Aubrey would rather have remained in the mansion of his fathers, and fed upon the melancholy which overpowered him. He could not feel interest about the frivolities of fashionable strangers, when his mind had been so torn by the events he had witnessed; but he determined to sacrifice his own comfort to the protection of his sister. They soon arrived in town, and prepared for the next day, which had been announced as a drawing-room.

The crowd was excessive—a drawing-room had not been held for a long time, and all who were anxious to bask in the smile of royalty, hastened thither. Aubrey was there with his sister. While he was standing in a corner by himself, heedless of all around him, engaged in the remembrance that the first time he had seen Lord Ruthven was in that very place—he felt himself suddenly seized by the arm, and a voice he recognized too well, sounded in his ear—"Remember your oath." He had hardly courage to turn, fearful of seeing a spectre that would blast him, when he perceived, at a little distance, the same figure which had attracted his notice on this spot upon his first entry into society. He gazed till his limbs almost refusing to bear their weight, he was obliged to take the arm of a friend, and forcing a passage through the crowd, he threw himself into his carriage, and was driven home. He paced the room with hurried steps, and fixed his hands upon his head, as if he were afraid his thoughts were bursting from his brain. Lord Ruthven again before him—circumstances started up in dreadful array—the dagger—his oath.— He roused himself, he could not believe it possible—the dead rise again!— He thought his imagination had conjured up the image his mind was resting upon. It was impossible that it could be real—he determined, therefore, to go again into society; for though he attempted to ask concerning Lord Ruthven, the name hung upon his lips, and he could not succeed in gaining information. He went a few nights after with his sister to the assembly of a near relation. Leaving her under the protection of a matron, he retired into a recess, and there gave himself up to his own devouring thoughts. Perceiving, at last, that many were leaving, he roused himself, and entering another room, found his sister surrounded by several, apparently in earnest conversation; he attempted to pass and get near her, when one, whom he requested to move, turned round, and revealed to him those features he most abhorred. He sprang forward, seized his sister's arm, and, with hurried step, forced her towards the street: at the door he found himself impeded by the crowd of servants who were waiting for their lords; and while he was engaged in passing them, he again heard that voice whisper close to him—"Remember your oath!"—He did not dare to turn, but, hurrying his sister, soon reached home.

Aubrey became almost distracted. If before his mind had been absorbed by one subject, how much more completely was it engrossed, now that the certainty of the monster's living again pressed upon his thoughts. His sister's attentions were now unheeded, and it was in vain that she intreated him to explain to her what had caused his abrupt conduct. He only uttered a few words, and those terrified her. The more he thought, the more he was bewildered. His oath startled him;—was he then to allow this monster to roam, bearing ruin upon his breath, amidst all he held dear, and not avert its progress? His very sister might have been touched by him. But even if he were to break his oath, and disclose his suspicions, who would believe him? He thought of employing his own hand to free the world from such a wretch; but death, he remembered, had been already mocked. For days he remained in this state; shut up in his room, he saw no one, and ate only when his sister came, who, with eyes streaming with tears, besought him, for her sake, to support nature. At last, no longer capable of bearing stillness and solitude, he left his house, roamed from street to street, anxious to fly that image which haunted him. His dress became neglected, and he wandered, as often exposed to the noon-day sun as to the midnight damps. He was no longer to be recognized; at first he returned with the evening to the house; but at last he laid him down to rest wherever fatigue overtook him. His sister, anxious for his safety, employed people to follow him; but they were soon distanced by him who fled from a pursuer swifter than any—from thought. His conduct, however, suddenly changed. Struck with the idea that he left by his absence the whole of his friends, with a fiend amongst them, of whose presence they were unconscious, he determined to enter again into society, and watch him closely, anxious to forewarn, in spite of his oath, all whom Lord Ruthven approached with intimacy. But when he entered into a room, his haggard and suspicious looks were so striking, his inward shudderings so visible, that his sister was at last obliged to beg of him to abstain from seeking, for her sake, a society which affected him so strongly. When, however, remonstrance proved unavailing, the guardians thought proper to interpose, and, fearing that his mind was becoming alienated, they thought it high time to resume again that trust which had been before imposed upon them by Aubrey's parents.

Desirous of saving him from the injuries and sufferings he had daily encountered in his wanderings, and of preventing him from exposing to the general eye those marks of what they considered folly, they engaged a physician to reside in the house, and take constant care of him. He hardly appeared to notice it, so completely was his mind absorbed by one terrible subject. His incoherence became at last so great, that he was confined to his chamber. There he would often lie for days, incapable of being roused. He had become emaciated, his eyes had attained a glassy luster;—the only sign of affection and recollection remaining displayed itself upon the entry of his sister; then he would sometimes start, and, seizing her hands, with looks that severely afflicted her, he would desire her not to touch him. "Oh, do not touch him—if your love for me is aught, do not go near him!" When, however, she inquired to whom he referred, his only answer was, "True! true!"

and again he sank into a state, whence not even she could rouse him. This lasted many months: gradually, however, as the year was passing, his incoherences became less frequent, and his mind threw off a portion of its gloom, whilst his guardians observed, that several times in the day he would count upon his fingers a definite number, and then smile.

The time had nearly elapsed, when, upon the last day of the year, one of his guardians entering his room, began to converse with his physician upon the melancholy circumstance of Aubrey's being in so awful a situation, when his sister was going next day to be married. Instantly Aubrey's attention was attracted; he asked anxiously to whom. Glad of this mark of returning intellect, of which they feared he had been deprived, they mentioned the name of the Earl of Marsden. Thinking this was a young Earl whom he had met with in society, Aubrey seemed pleased, and astonished them still more by his expressing his intention to be present at the nuptials, and desiring to see his sister. They answered not, but in a few minutes his sister was with him. He was apparently again capable of being affected by the influence of her lovely smile; for he pressed her to his breast, and kissed her cheek, wet with tears, flowing at the thought of her brother's being once more alive to the feelings of affection. He began to speak with all his wonted warmth, and to congratulate her upon her marriage with a person so distinguished for rank and every accomplishment; when he suddenly perceived a locket upon her breast; opening it, what was his surprise at beholding the features of the monster who had so long influenced his life. He seized the portrait in a paroxysm of rage, and trampled it under foot. Upon her asking him why he thus destroyed the resemblance of her future husband, he looked as if he did not understand her—then seizing her hands, and gazing on her with a frantic expression of countenance, he bade her swear that she would never wed this monster, for he—But he could not advance—it seemed as if that voice again bade him remember his oath—he turned suddenly round, thinking Lord Ruthven was near him but saw no one. In the meantime the guardians and physician, who had heard the whole, and thought this was but a return of his disorder, entered, and forcing him from Miss Aubrey, desired her to leave him. He fell upon his knees to them, he implored, he begged of them to delay but for one day. They, attributing this to the insanity they imagined had taken possession of his mind, endeavored to pacify him, and retired.

Lord Ruthven had called the morning after the drawing-room, and had been refused with every one else. When he heard of Aubrey's ill health, he readily understood himself to be the cause of it; but when he learned that he was deemed insane, his exultation and pleasure could hardly be concealed from those among whom he had gained this information. He hastened to the house of his former companion, and, by constant attendance, and the pretense of great affection for the brother and interest in his fate, he gradually won the ear of Miss Aubrey. Who could resist his power? His tongue had dangers and toils to recount—could speak of himself as of an individual having no sympathy with any being on the crowded earth, save with her to whom he addressed himself;—could tell how, since he knew her, his existence, had begun to seem worthy of preservation, if it were merely that he might listen to her soothing accents;—in fine, he knew so well how to use the serpent's art, or such was the will of fate, that he gained her affections. The title of the elder branch falling at length to him, he obtained an important embassy, which served as an excuse for hastening the marriage, (in spite of her brother's deranged state,) which was to take place the very day before his departure for the continent.

Aubrey, when he was left by the physician and his guardians, attempted to bribe the servants, but in vain. He asked for pen and paper; it was given him; he wrote a letter to his sister, conjuring her, as she valued her own happiness, her own honor, and the honor of those now in the grave, who once held her in their arms as their hope and the hope of their house, to delay but for a few hours that marriage, on which he denounced the most heavy curses. The servants promised they would deliver it; but giving it to the physician, he thought it better not to harass any more the mind of Miss Aubrey by, what he considered, the ravings of a maniac. Night passed on without rest to the busy inmates of the house; and Aubrey heard, with a horror that may more easily be conceived than described, the notes of busy preparation. Morning came, and the sound of carriages broke upon his ear. Aubrey grew almost frantic. The curiosity of the servants at last overcame their vigilance, they gradually stole away, leaving him in the custody of an helpless old woman. He seized the opportunity, with one bound was out of the room, and in a moment found himself in the apartment where all were nearly assembled. Lord Ruthven was the first to perceive him: he immediately approached, and, taking his arm by force, hurried him from the room, speechless with rage. When on the staircase, Lord Ruthven whispered in his ear—"Remember your oath, and know, if not my bride to day, your sister is dishonored. Women are frail!" So saying, he pushed him towards his attendants, who, roused by the old woman, had come in search of him. Aubrey could no longer support himself; his rage not finding vent, had broken a blood-vessel, and he was conveyed to bed. This was not mentioned to his sister, who was not present when he entered, as the physician was afraid of agitating her. The marriage was solemnized, and the bride and bridegroom left London.

Aubrey's weakness increased; the effusion of blood produced symptoms of the near approach of death. He desired his sister's guardians might be called, and when the midnight hour had struck, he related composedly what the reader has perused—he died immediately after.

The guardians hastened to protect Miss Aubrey; but when they arrived, it was too late. Lord Ruthven had disappeared, and Aubrey's sister had glutted the thirst of a VAMPYRE!

THE BLACK VAMPYRE;
A LEGEND OF ST. DOMINGO

Uriah Derick D'Arcy

(1819)

So have I heard on Afric's burning shore,
Another lion give a grievous roar,
And the first lion thought the last a boar.

WILLIAM BARNES RHODES
BOMBASTES FURIOSO

INTRODUCTION

I f any person should have patience to read the following narrative, and can discover the Author's drift, it is more than he can do himself. If it be thought exquisite nonsense, it is more than the writer dares hope: and if it be pronounced simple, stupid, and unadulterated absurdity, his own private opinion will perfectly coincide with that of the public. He began to write without any fable, and before he had found any had spun out the thread of his ideas.

This tangled skein of absurdities is now exposed to criticism, from the laudable motive of showing, of how much nonsense an individual may be delivered, in the short space of two afternoons; without any excuse but idleness, or any object but amusement.

The prominent descriptions, which it is here attempted to ridicule, are fresh in the memory of all who have read the "White Vampyre;" and to those who have not, the Superstition must be so familiar, that it is unnecessary to make useless extracts.

That the Author may not, however, be misunderstood, it may be necessary to state, that in the speech of the Vampyre, he had no design of descending to that meanest of all intellectual exercises, a travesty on authors who are justly admired: but meant, if any thing, simply to show how passages, which were fine in their original use, when garbled by the ignorant and tasteless, become a melancholy rhapsody of nonsense.

"But first on earth, as Vampyre sent,
Thy corse shall from its tomb be rent;
Then ghastly haunt thy native place,
And suck the blood of all thy race;
There from thy *daughter, sister, wife,*
At midnight drain the stream of life;
Yet loathe the banquet, which perforce
Must feed thy livid living corse.
Thy victims, ere they yet expire,
Shall know the demon for their sire;
The Black Vampyre
As cursing thee, thou cursing them,
Thy flowers are withered on the stem.
But one that for *thy crime* must fall,
The youngest, best beloved of all,
Shall bless thee with a *father's* name—
That word shall wrap thy heart in flame!
Yet thou must end thy task and mark
Her cheek's last tinge—her eye's last spark,
And the last glassy glance must view
Which freezes o'er its lifeless blue;
Then with unhallowed hand shall tear
The tresses of her yellow hair,
Of which, in life a lock when shorn
Affection's fondest pledge was worn—
But now is borne away by thee
Memorial of thine agony!
Yet with thine own best blood shall drip
Thy gnashing tooth, and haggard lip;
Then stalking to thy sullen grave,
Go—and with Ghouls and Afrits rave,
Till these in horror shrink away
From spectre more accursed than they."

BYRON.

THE BLACK VAMPYRE

Mr. Anthony Gibbons was a gentleman of African extraction. His ancestors emigrated from the eastern coast of Guinea, in a French ship, and were sold in St. Domingo remarkably cheap; as they were reduced to mere skeletons by the yaws[11] on the passage; and all died shortly after their arrival, except one small negro, of a very slender constitution, and fit for no work whatever. The gentleman who purchased *him*, charitably knocked out his brains; and the body was thrown into the ocean. The tide returning in the night, it was washed upon the sands; and the moon then shining bright, the gentleman was taking a walk to enjoy the coolness of the evening; judge of his surprise, when the little corpse got up, and complaining of a pain in its bowels, begged for some bread and butter!

The Planter supposing his business to have been but half done, kicked him back in the water. The element seemed very familiar to him; and he swam back with much grace and agility; parting the sparkling waves with his jet black members, polished like ebony, but reflecting no single beam of light. His complexion was a dead black;—his eyes a pure white;—the iris was flame color;—and the pupils of a clear, moonshiny luster;—but so peculiarly constructed, that, though prominent, they seemed to look into his own head. His hair was neither curled nor straight; but feathery, like the plumage of a crow. Having paddled again on shore, he came crawling crab fashion, to the feet of Mr. Personne. The latter gentleman, in considerable alarm, (not knowing whether it was Satan, Obi, or some other worthy, with whom he had to deal,) mustered up sufficient resolution, to tie a large stone round the boy's middle: then, with a main exertion of strength, he hurled him into the sparkling ocean. He fell where the reflection of the moon was brightest, and sunk like lead; but immediately rose again like cork, perpendicularly, with the stone under his arm; while the radiant luster of the planet retreated from his dark figure, exhibiting in its most striking contrast its utter blackness!

In this predicament, he came buoyant to land; surrounded, as he seemed, by a sphere of magic luster. He now walked up to the Frenchman, with his arms akimbo, and looking remarkably fierce. Mr. Personne's particular hairs stood up on end,

_____ Tunc perculit horror
Membra ducis, riguere comæ, gressumque coercens Languor in extrema tenuit vestigia ripa.

LVC.

but being ashamed that a little negro of ten years old, should put him in bodily fear, he knocked him down. The Guinea-man rose again, without bending a joint; as fast as Mr. Personne could upset him, he recovered his altitude; just like one of those small toys, fabricated from pith, tipt with lead, called witches and hobgoblins by the rising generation!

The Planter, in utter amazement and despair, took hold of the child by both his extremities; and pressing him to the earth, set down upon him! Then,

[11] A contagious skin disease of lesions.

halloing for is attendants, he ordered a tremendous fire to be kindled on the sand!! This was accordingly done. The Gaul[12] congratulated himself on his perseverance and sagacity; and as he had never heard of ignaqueous animals, was confident that though the water fiend was so expert in his own element, he could not stand the fiery ordeal. The boy, meanwhile, lay perfectly passive, as if he had been a mere log; but presently, when the pile was all in a light blaze, with a sudden expansion, like that of a compressed Indian Rubber, he popped Mr. Personne up into the air many yards, and he alighted head-foremost into the fire, where he had intended to have dedicated the sable brat, with his nine lives, to Moloch!!!

Whatever the negro was, it is notorious that Mr. Personne was no salamander. He was rescued from the pyre, which, like Hercules, he had, (though unwittingly,) erected for himself; looking like a squizzed cat, and having apparently no life left in his body. The attention of the domestics was drawn entirely to their master; who soon betrayed signs of animation, though he exhibited a most awful spectacle: being one continual sore and blister. "His whole body was one wound," as Virgil or some other poet has hyperbolically expressed himself.

Mr. Personne, when he perfectly recovered his senses, found himself in his own bed, wrapt in greasy sheets, and smarting as if in a Cayenne bath. He called for a glass of brandy,—his dear wife Euphemia,—and his infant son, who had not yet been christened. His lady, with streaming eyes, presented herself before him; and, after tenderly inquiring into the state of his health, told him, (with a voice interrupted with sobs and hiccups,) that when she went in the morning to see her baby, whom she had left in the cradle, there was nothing to *be* seen, but the *skin*, *hair*, and *nails!!!* She declared that there never was such another object; except, indeed, the exsiccation in Scudder's Museum!

On the receipt of this horrid intelligence, Mr. Personne was seized with a violent spasmodic affection; and shortly after expired, muttering something about *sacré*, and the Guinea-negro!

The amiable, but unfortunate Euphemia, was thrown into several hysterical convulsions; as well she might be, poor woman! when her husband had been made a holocaust, and served up like a broiled and peppered chicken, to feed the grim maw of death; and her interesting infant, the first pledge of her pure and perfect love, had been precociously sucked, like an unripe orange, and nothing left but its beautiful and tender skin. The disconsolate widow caused her husband to be embalmed; and he was buried amid the lamentations and tears of all the funeral; much regretted by all who had the honor of his acquaintance, particularly by his negroes; who could not soon forget him; as he had left too many sincere marks of his regard upon their backs, to be ever obliterated from their recollections.

---

12 Frenchman.

Time, as all the Greek tragedians, Solomon, and others have remarked, is a benevolent deity. Mrs. Personne's grief yielded to the soothing hand of the consoling power; and her bloom and spirits returned with more luster and elasticity than they had before exhibited: as the rose, that had drooped in the fury of the passing storm, erects its blushing honors, and shows more beautiful and vivid tints, when the squall is over!

Many years after these occurrences took place, while Euphemia was in second mourning for her third husband, she was indulging in the luxury of solitary grief; and reading *Burton's Anatomy of Melancholy*, and *The Melancholy Poems of Dr. Farmer*, in an orangerie. The refreshing breezes from the ocean, which now tempered the sultry heats of the declining day,—the soft perfume of the opening blossoms;—and the mellow tints of the evening sky, shedding that holy light, so dear to sensitive hearts, diffused a calm over her soul, wrapt in the contemplation of departed days. While lost in this pensive reverie, she perceived two strangers approaching her, in the extremity of the long vista of the grove. One of them was a colored gentleman, of remarkable height, and deep jetty blackness; a perfect model of the Congo Apollo. He was dressed in the rich garb of a Moorish Prince; and led by the hand a pale European boy, in an Asiatic dress; whose languid countenance, slender form and tristful gait, were strongly contrasted with the portly appearance and majestic step of his conductor!

They both saluted the lovely widow, and after an interchange of compliments, accepted her polite invitation to set down, and take tea with her in the bower. She learned from the elder stranger, that he had brought out a cargo of slaves, whom his subjects had lately taken prisoners in war; and whom he had resolved to dispose of himself; as he was desirous of seeing the world. His Page, he said, was an orphan, left by a slave merchant in Africa.

The manners and conversation of the Prince had an irresistible charm. The regal port was manifest in his gigantic and well proportioned frame; and majesty was conspicuous on his brow, without its diadem. The turban and crescent had never graced a nobler front; but the winning condescension of his tones and language, while they could not banish the feeling of the presence of royalty, removed every restraint incident to that consciousness. He criticized the works, which Euphemia had been perusing, with masterly precision; and displayed more knowledge than even the accomplished ideologist of Lady Morgan; with infinitely more discretion and good sense.

It is remarked by the Abbe Reynal, that there is a peculiar elegance and beauty in the complexion of the Africans, (when the eyes and nose are accustomed to their hue and odor.) This truth was realized by Euphemia, as she gazed on the open visage of her illustrious guest. She thought surely that in him Nature might stand up and say "This was a man!" And certainly it is only the weakness and imperfection of our human senses, which, penetrating no further than the surface, is forever deceived by superficial shadows. The empyrean is always blue, whatever vapors may float in our contracted atmosphere. And if we gaze on the rows of skulls, which festoon and garnish

Surgeon's Hall, we can apply no standard, to determine their relative beauty. They are all equally ugly; and the block of Helen might be mistaken for that of Medusa. Shakespeare, true to nature, has also remarked, "Black men are pearls in beauteous ladies' eyes."

The beauty then, the royalty, gentility, and various accomplishments of the Bambuck monarch, made captive the too sensible heart of the French widow. She forgot her ogles, graces, and even her loquacity; rooted to her seat, and fixed in immoveable contemplation of the African's face. What peculiar feature or lineament attracted her attention, she knew not: his eyes, though bright, did not sparkle; and the iris, though of a more vivid red than the roseate line in the rainbow, emitted no scintillations. In fact, *his whole countenance seemed to look, and to perambulate her own.*

The conversation gradually assumed a more impassioned and amorous complexion; and the little page, (who, though meagre and emaciated, evidently showed that he was no gump for his years,) taking certain broad hints, cast a mournful and intelligent look on the widow, said he would fetch a short walk in the plantation, and left the orangerie.

The Prince then spreading his glittering sash upon the grass, went down on his knees upon it; and broke out into the most ardent exclamations, of love and admiration; and professions of constant attachment. He said that the flat-nosed beauties of Zara; the scarred, squab figures of the golden coast; the well proportioned Zilias, Calypsos, and Zamas on the banks of the Niger; and even the great Hottentot Venus herself, had never for a moment made the least impression on his heart! His passion was a mystery to himself; its origin secret as the sources of the Nile; but full and impetuous as its ample channel, when replenished from the celestial fountains of Abyssinia; while if Mrs. Dubois would shine upon its waves, its enlivened currents would fertilize his vast dominions, in the luxuriant realms of central Africa; making them to fructify yet more abundantly, with burning gold, and radiant diamonds!!!

What female heart could resist such pleadings, and the compliment implied in such a preference? When Zembo (the page) returned, the parties had agreed to be privately united on the same evening. The ceremony was accordingly performed, on the spot, by the family chaplain of Mrs. Dubois: not without many remonstrances on his part, as to the impropriety of marrying a negro. The Prince did not see to resent the affront; which, by the by, he had no right to do; as the priest got nothing for the job. Zembo, too, was extremely restless; till Mrs. Dubois gave him some sweetmeats, which seemed to quiet his conscience; after which he took some stiff punch, and fell asleep!

About midnight, the Prince came to him; and, shaking him by the ears, bad him rise and follow him. His bride was hanging on his arm, in an enchanting dishabille; and did not seem to be in perfect possession of her right senses. Zembo mournfully followed the new married pair.

They went silently out of the back door, with cautious steps, and proceeded through the orangerie. No breath of wind was stirring. The moon was on the zenith, surrounded by a pale halo of ghostly luster. When they had crossed the plantation, they came to a place of sepulture; where the dark cypresses, and lugubrious mahogany, admitted but sparse and glimmering streaks of funereal light; which, falling on the rank foliage, the white monuments and broken ground beneath, presented a thousand dusky shapes, flitting in the dim uncertainty dear to superstition.

Vague terrors seized on the mind of the bride; and she began very naturally to inquire, what was the use of getting out of a comfortable bed, and trailing through the heavy dew, in her undress, to such an unusual spot for midnight recreation.

They now stood near the spot, where her three husbands, several children, and the *skin*, *hair* and *nails* of her first baby, were deposited in a row. At the foot of a tamarind, lay her third son; whose christian name was Spooner, and who died, according to the tombstone, in a fit of intoxication, aged seven years and six months. On him she had bestowed a greater share of tenderness, than any of her other offspring; and his loss had caused her most affliction. The African, making observations on the grave, began to strip himself very expeditiously, assisted by Zembo; who seemed to recover from his blues; and by his activity and eagerness, manifested his expectation of soon seeing some fine sport.

Presently the two genii, or gentlemen, or whatever they were, turned towards the East, and performed certain antic prostrations; throwing handfuls of earth three times over their heads. Then returning to the tomb, they tore up the sods with ravenous fury; and soon drew out the last-mentioned son of the Lady, and threw him on the grass, beside the grave. Zembo fell as fiercely upon the corpse, as a hungry dog upon his dinner; but was arrested by the African, who lent him a severe box on the ear, which sent him blubbering to a corner of the cemetery.

What added both to the mother's horrors and admiration, was, that the body of her child was perfectly fresh, and the olfactory nerves experienced no unsavory sensation from its proximity; while its cheeks were diffused with so deep a tinge of scarlet, that they shone like ruddy fireballs in the darkness of the spot. Her husband drew a golden goblet from beneath a large stone; then, bending over the corse, he scooped out the heart, with his long and polished nails; and, having pressed the blood into the chalice, mingled with it some dark particles, gathered from the newly turned up earth. From the pure and scanty lymph, which gushed near by and flickered like a streak of quicksilvery-light in the moonbeam, he added a third ingredient of the potion. Then seizing his passive and trembling spouse by the throat, and presenting the unnatural mixture to her lips; he cried in a hollow voice, whose very inflection thrilled through each fibre of its victim,—"Swear, or if that is against your principles, affirm, by this dirty blood,—and bloody dirt;—by this watery blood,—and bloody water;—by this watery dirt, and dirty water;—

that you will never disclose in any manner, aught of what you have seen and shall see this night. Call them all to witness your wish, that in the moment when you even conceive the thought of perjury, your bowels may burst out, and your bones rot! Swear and drink!"

The affrighted woman murmured, (as articulately as the iron gripe of the monster would suffer her,) that she was not thirsty; and had not breath enough to aspirate such a terrible conjuration. "No trifling," roared the fiend, "you have not a moment to deliberate." But his bellowing and threats were vain; and he found to his mortification that he had gotten the wrong sow by the ear, or rather by the throat. She stuttered out, in the most pitiful accents, which would have softened any heart (but a Vampyre has none,) that though she was by no means partial to the delectable confectionary of the pharmacopeia, calomel and jalap, ipecacuanha, rhubarb, and tartar-emetic, she would rather take them all, collectively and individually, than the unchristian decoction he held against her teeth.

Foaming with madness, till the white slaver flowed down his sable limbs, the African hurled Mrs. Personne, Dubois, etc. etc. on the grave of her first husband, and stamping violently on the earth, it seemed to heave as with the throes of an earthquake. Immediately the tumuli yawned. The ponderous stones and slabs were shaken from their ancient sockets; and the ghastly dead, in uncouth attitudes, crawled from their nooks; with their hair curling in tortuous and serpent twinings; and their eyeballs of fire bursting from their heads; while, as they extended their withered arms, and tapering fingers, furnished with blood-hound claws, their gory shrouds fell in wild drapery around them, transiently revealing their forms, bloated as if to bursting, and often incarnadined with clotted blood, yet warm and dripping!!!

The Lady, (as those who have been in similar predicaments may suppose,) soon lost her recollection; not, however, before she had seen Zembo busily employed in tearing up the grave of her first husband; she saw herself surrounded by the specters, and lost all consciousness.

When reason and sense returned, she found herself in the same place; and it was also the midnight hour. She was laying by the grave of Mr. Personne, and her breast was stained with blood. A wide wound appeared to have been inflicted there, but was now cicatrized. Imagine if you can, her surprise; when, by a certain carnivorous craving in her maw, and by putting this and that together, she found she was a—Vampyre!!! and gathered from her indistinct reminiscences, of the preceding night, that she had been then sucked; and that it was now her turn to eject the peaceful tenants of the grave!

With this delightful prospect of immortality before her, she began to examine the graves, for subject to a satisfy her furious appetite. When she had selected one to her mind, a new marvel arrested her attention. Her first husband got up out his coffin, and with all the grace so natural to his countrymen, made her a low bow in the last fashion, and opened his arms to receive her!

What were the emotions of this fond couple, when, after a lingering separation for sixteen years, they again embraced each other, with the ardor of an affection equal to their earliest transports, and which their long divorce served only to increase; tenderly inquiring into the state of each other's health; and the accidents which had befallen them during their disjunction. They forgot even their hunger and thirst; and sitting down on a tombstone, made a thousand inquiries; which, however, they related to family concerns, might not be as interesting to the reader as they were to the parties concerned.

Mr. Personne, however, looked rather glum, when he learned that his Lady had been thrice married, since his decease. But she assured him, that she would never more tolerate the addresses of another suitor: and as for the two husbands, they were rotten enough by this time; as she was confident they had not attended the Vampyre Ball, on the preceding night. As for her sable spouse, she trusted that he would never again appear to interrupt their happiness. But while she was expressing this hope, the gentleman in question, (like his relation below, according to the old proverb,) came upon the ground, with Zembo. Mr. Personne, having neither sword nor pistols at hand, armed himself with a gigantic thigh-bone; and warned the Black Prince to stand upon his guard as he meant to punish him severely.

But Zembo, rushing between the parties, raised his hands in a supplicating posture; while the generous monarch, making a Salaam to his antagonist, begged him, keep himself quiet, and look behind him. They both turned round on this intimation, when, to the utter confusion of the Lady, her second and third husbands, Messieurs Marquand and Dubois, arose from the graves, where they had been lovingly deposited by the side of each other. They both advanced to salute their wife; but Mr. Personne, brandishing his thigh-bone, warned them to stand off, as he had the first title to the Lady. Much confusion would have ensued, had not the African Prince interfered. He told the gentlemen that so delicate a point could only be settled in an *honorable* way; and proposed that Mr. Marquand and Mr. Dubois should first settle their difference in a personal encounter; after which Mr. Personne might give the survivor *gentlemanly satisfaction*. To this all parties assented.

As they were already stripped, the combatants shook hands, to show their mutual goodwill; and proceeded to action, without further ceremony. Mr. Dubois soon brought claret from Mr. Marquand; who, in returning the compliment, fibbed Mr. Dubois so severely in the bowels, that he lost his wind; and gasping for breath, smote the air on all sides, without any of his blows telling. He came to the ground, and his bones rattled as he fell. But soon recovering his breath, he made a desperate attack on Mr. Marquand'S sconce; and favored him with so terrible a facer under the gills, that he fell incontinently like a bull smitten in his front; but entangling his own heels with those of Mr. Dubois, they both came simultaneously to the ground; striking their heads against different tombstones; and knocking out their own brains.

They rose again, refreshed like the giant of old, by their grappling with the earth, and all the better for the loss of their wits, which, indeed, was a mere trifle. But the African, who had no time to see more sport, fixed them to the sod by his superior strength; and Zembo dexterously pinned them fast, by driving stakes through their hearts, with a large sledge hammer, (which he carried about his person for such emergencies.) During the operation, their roaring surpassed that which is performed by the Lioness, when bereft of her whelps; but as soon as they were fairly nailed to the counter, they lay motionless and breathless—a horrible pair of spectacles of sin and misery!

The African assured the Lady, that she need never fear their second resurrection; and Mr. Personne politely offered to settle their controversy, in any mode most agreeable to the Prince:—either to box with him on the spot, or appoint a meeting in future, with pistols, rifles, small or broad sword; or else they might toss up, who should set fire to a barrel of gunpowder. The Prince said that quarreling was all nonsense, and offered his hand; but Mr. Personne refused, saying, "Don't be too familiar, Blackey;" and renewing his threats of cracking him over the noddle with the thigh-bone.

The generous monarch pocketed the affront. "You have been," he said, "sufficiently rewarded, for the cruelties you practiced upon my person, several years ago. I forgive you, my dear sir, what you performed, and intended to perform on me. Here is your son, who has grown considerably, as you may observe; and I assure you that his education has not been neglected. To his exertions last night you are indebted for your revivification. And as, you may remember, you were embalmed, you have kept quite sweet and fresh ever since your interment. Amiable and virtuous Vampyres! may you long enjoy that tranquillity and contentment, which your merit and accomplishments so eminently deserve! A vessel lies in the port, ready to sail for Europe in an hour. The Island is no longer a place for you. Here is money to pay your passages, and all I have to say, is, that the sooner you're off the better.— Farewell!" So saying he departed, without waiting for the acknowledgments of the party.

Mr. Personne and his Lady, whom we shall again call by her first marriage name, did not exactly comprehend what their dingy benefactor meant, by bidding them take French leave of the Island, like pickpockets and outlaws; but, as they were yet wondering at their own existence, like Adam and Eve, the first day of their creation, and as they had reason to believe the Prince a potent magician, who could rouse the dead from their searments, and turn the planets from their courses;—for these reasons, they concluded to follow his bidding, without any impertinent scruples. But as the keen edge of their hunger had been whetted by delay, they would fain have taken supper, and digested a little something wherewithal to strengthen them, before they set out.

Zembo, who had filled his own breadbasket very lately, and was in no such urgent necessity, protested with all the vehemence which filial reverence would permit, against the unseasonable gratification of their unnatural craving; and recited with just emphasis and good discretion, an extract from Counsellor Phillips's harangue, about "the cannibal appetite of his rejected altar;" which his parents did not understand, and of course thought very sublime! But even this master-piece of mystical eloquence would have been delivered in vain; had not the boy given other reasons of such cogency, that they licked their lips—cast a longing, lingering look at the grave-yard,—and followed him without more opposition.

They prosecuted their nocturnal march, through closely woven and solemn groves; until they descended into a profound valley, where the light of the pale planet of magic adoration, streamed and quivered on serried files of bright armory. The leader of the band seemed to have expected their arrival; and mutual tokens of recognition passed between him and Zembo. The whole company then set forward their array in silence;—

> No cymbal clash'd, no clarion rang,
> Still were the pipe and drum;
> Save heavy tread, and armor's clang,
> The sullen march was dumb.

By continual descent, they seemed to have penetrated the bowels of a cavern, whose ramifications ran under the sea; as they heard a murmuring roar, as of the ocean, above their heads. The party, by the instructions of Zembo, dispersed themselves in different directions; until they had enclosed the interior of the rock where its largest chamber was, to speak catachrestically, so artfully concealed by nature, that no one, not instructed by an adept in its subterranean topography, could ever have detected the secret of its existence. It had been, in former days, a place of deposit and asylum for the Buccaniers; and its situation had been since known only to the Professors of the Obeah art, who held here their midnight orgies.

Mr. and Mrs. Personne, guided by their son, were placed in a situation, where, through the crevices of the inner partition of the rock, they could observe what was passing in the interior.

It seemed, at first view, a vast hall of Arabian romance; supported by immense shafts, and studded with precious stones; so various and beautiful were the hues, which the different spars assumed, in the light of an hundred torches, blazing in every quarter, and illuminating the farthest recesses of the cave. The walls were decorated with other appendages, which added to the mystery, if not to the embellishment of the scene; being irregularly stained with blood; decorated with rude tapestry of many colored plumage;—and stuccoed with the beaks of parrots;—the teeth of dogs, and alligators;—bones of cats;—broken glass and eggshells; plastered with a composition of rum and grave-dirt, the implements of Negro witchcraft!

At one extremity of the extensive apartment, on a kind of natural throne, sat several Blackamoors in sumptuous Moorish apparel; whom, by their swollen forms, and remarkable eyes, Mrs. Personne knew to be Ghouls; and among whom she recognized her late husband. The whole range of this vast amphitheater, sweeping from before the throne, was occupied by slaves, rudely attired, and imperfectly armed with clubs and missiles; a decent platoon of black-guards were posted before the Vampyre monarchs; and, in the centre, a band of musicians performed an exquisite symphony. The soft strains of the Merriwang;—the lively notes of the Dundo;—and the martial accompaniment of the Goombay, made, with their united noises, a discordant harmony, whose powers the lyre of Orpheus could not equal; and which would certainly be enough to frighten all the hosts of Pandemonium.

The oratorio being finished, the African Prince arose, and making an obeisance to the company,—cleared his throat, and began to address them as follows:—"Gentlemen and Vampyres!"—but the Vampyres expressing their resentment against this breach of etiquette, he corrected himself:—"Vampyres and Gentlemen!"—but the Negroes were no more willing to come last, than the Vampyres, and a loud growl accompanied by a slight hiss, again interrupted the orator. He was not, however, disconcerted, but like Mr. Burke, thundered out an iteration of the offensive sentence.

"Yes," said he, "I repeat it, Vampyres and Gentlemen? Shall not the immortal precede the mortal?—Shall not those whose diet surpasses the nectar and ambrosia of celestials, precede the ephemeral race, who fatten on the unclean juice of brutes,—the rank essence of esculent, edible, productions,—or the nauseous liquor of the distillery? *(applause—hear! hear! and see-boy! from the Vampyres—groans from the negroes!)* Gentlemen of color! I appeal to yourselves; shall not the descendants of the Gods be named before the offspring of the earth-born image, whom Titan impregnated with celestial fire?—For Prometheus was the first Vampyre. You must all know, as you have undoubtedly read Æschylus, that the vulture, who preyed on his liver, was neither fish, flesh, nor fowl. He is called a dog, which makes him a quadruped;—he is represented as ερπωυ, creeping, which proves him an insect; and is said to have wings, which shows that he was a bird. Now, from this amphibious monster have descended the Crows,—the Jackalls,—and the Bloodhounds;—the pirate Bat of Madagascar,—and the man-killing Ivunches of Chili;—the Sharks;—the Crocodiles;—the Krakens;—the Horse-leeches;—the Cape-cod Sea Serpents;—the Mermaids;—the Incubi; —and the Succubi!!! *(loud cheering from the Vampyres.)* From Titan himself, descended the Cyclopes, and all other ancient and modern Anthropophagi; and, in lineal descent, the Moco tribe of our own Eboes, to whom I have the honor of being related. Those of you, too, are his posterity, who, after your deaths, return to your native land—the true Elysium; where the balmy bowl of the coco, the soft bloom of the anana, and the coal-black beauties of the clime of love, shall forever reward your fortitude, and steep in forgetfulness the memory of your wrongs. *(hear! hear! from the negroes.)* But none of these genera or species of our order, must longer engage your dignified and charitable attention. I come to ourselves, full-blooded—unadulterated—immortal bloodsuckers!—To ourselves—whether Ghouls,—or Afrits,—or Vampyres;—Vroucolochas,—Vardoulachos,—or Broucolokas—To ourselves—the terror of the living and of the dead, and the participants of the nature of both;—To ourselves—the emblems at once of corruption and of vitality;—blotted from the records of existence, and replenished to repletion with circulating life;—abandoned by the quick, and unrecognized by the dead:—'at once relics and relicts;—rocked on the bases of our own eternities;—the chronicles of what was—the solemn and sublime mementoes of what must be.' *(unqualified approbation from both sides of the house.)*

"The estate of Vampyrism is a fee-tail, and may be docked in two different ways. The first mode is the sanguinary practice of perforating the subject with a stake; and this is final. The other is produced by the gentler operation of the narcotic potion you behold in this phial; by whose lenient and opiate influence, the individual is restored to the plight, in which he was previous to his death, or his becoming a Vampyre, and belongs to the Obeah mysteries.

"But to come to the object of our present meeting. Sublime and soul-elevating theme!—The emancipation of the Negroes!—The consecration of the soil of St. Domingo to the manes of murdered patriots in all ages!—No matter whether the bill of sale was scrawled in French or in English;—No matter whether we were taken prisoners, in a battle between the Leophares and the Jaloffs, or in a skirmish between the Samboes and the Sawpits;—No matter whether we were bought for calico and cotton, or for gunpowder or for shot;—No matter whether we were transported in chains or in ropes—in a brig, or a schooner, or a seventy-four—the first moment we come ashore on St. Domingo, our souls shall swell like a sponge in the liquid element;—our bodies shall burst from their fetters, glorious as a curculio from its shell;—our minds shall soar like the car of the aeronaut, when its ligaments are cut; in a word, O my brethren, we shall be free!—Our fetters discandied, and our chains dissolved, we shall stand liberated,—redeemed,—emancipated,—and disenthralled by the irresistible genius of UNIVERSAL EMANCIPATION!!!" *(Unparalleled bursts of unprecedented applause!!!)*

Such was the report of this oration, taken down in short hand by Zembo; of whose extraordinary sagacity so many proofs have been exhibited; and who was never unprovided with materials for any emergency. The fiery oratory of the Prince communicated such inspiration to the auditors, that the whole mass of their thick blood leaped up with the quickening pulse of anticipated freedom; they danced and sung, with violent gesticulations, like perfect Corybantes; but unfortunately, their phyrricks were interrupted by the glittering bayonets of the soldiery; who poured in upon them from every quarter, and hemmed them in, with a bristling *chevaux-de-frise* of steel. The Vampyres, surprised but undaunted, unsheathed their sabers, and drew up in a gallant style, as if determined to die game; being, indeed, assured, that like so many Phoenixes, they would rise from their own ashes, as often as they might be cut down.

A desperate conflict ensued, during which Mrs. Personne observed the phial, mentioned by the Prince, lying on the ground; and very thoughtfully put it in her reticule. The slaves, seeing how the business was likely to terminate, prudently sneaked off, while the attention of the military was occupied by the Vampyres. The former were violently exasperated to find all their labor so unprofitable; since while they themselves were wounded by every blow of their opponents, the latter, like so many ninepins, were set up, as fast as they were bowled down; bending to the storm, like masts on a tempestuous ocean, and rising again upon the billow in perpendicular triumph.

But, being instructed by Zembo, the soldiers pinioned them as fast as they fell; and prevented their rising, by sitting in great numbers on their bodies; though the task was somewhat like that of detaining quicksilver beneath the fingers. The Prince, however, still fought desperately. Brandishing a huge scimitar in either hand, he swayed his arms like the sails of a windmill; while limbs, heads, and bodies flew about him, curvetting and dancing in the air; as when the ingenious Mr. Maffey pulls to pieces a coach, or an old woman, children, chickens, friars, and petticoats dance about in wild confusion, till the artist's hand again brings order out of chaos:—Or, as when the renowned knight of the Bed-Chamber, whose name eternal vases shall record, saw the ungenerous caricature on the wall, wielding a ponderous jug, he smote the innocent tables, chairs, and bed-posts, and strode victorious over the gory field: So fought the Prince; till being neatly pricked in the spine, unexpectedly, he soused (as Johannes Porco Latinus remarks) "*in principia fundimentalia*," and was immediately set upon by a host. So when a Gaetulian lion is pierced by the light bamboo, overpowered by the hunters, he struggles in his thrall like an Enceladus under Aetna, and dies at last with heart-wrung tears of anguish, and reverberating roars of hatred!!!

Stakes were immediately procured, and the whole infernal fraternity securely disposed of: as their compeers, described by Homer,

> *With burning chains fixed to the brazen floors*
> *And lock'd by hell's inexorable doors.*

With their bellowings, the vast chambers of the subterranean rung like the caverns of Delphos, when the inflammable air was fired by the crafty priests. The Inhabitants of the Island started up from their slumbers in shuddering terror, and believed that an earthquake was rumbling beneath their feet.

Mr. and Mrs. Personne and Zembo lost no time in trying the effects of the African's stolen prescription. Being thrown into a tranquil slumber they were conveyed to their plantation; and awoke the next morning, perfectly well, excepting slight colds in the head. Mr. Personne, having been in status quo, for sixteen years, was now much younger than his lady; a circumstance, for which she was not at all sorry; and which he himself declared by no means displeased him. The remainder of their life was serene as a tropic night;—illumined by the mild effulgence of domestic love;—fanned by the soft aspirations of peaceful bosoms;—and enlivened by the fire-fly scintillations of rapture!!!

Zembo, to whose taste and ingenuity they were indebted for their happiness, and who was baptized with the Christian name of Barabbas, after an uncle of his mother's, recorded what the reader has perused. One only circumstance, like one of those claps of thunder, frequently heard in the unclouded sky, passed over the tranquillity of their bosoms. Mrs. Personne's fourth husband's child was a mulatto, and of Vampyrish propensities; of which his mother and Mr. Personne were never able entirely to cure him, having used up all the African's preparation.

The intelligent reader, (if any such there be,) will remember that this narrative commenced with the name of Mr. Anthony Gibbons, of whom nothing has since been said; and whose adventures (to use a Forum trope) "must remain buried in the bowels of futurity," until a more convenient opportunity. He is a lineal descendant from the last-mentioned mulatto; and the manuscript, which is now given to the public, was transmitted to him from his ancestors. He is a resident in Essex county, New Jersey; and candor requires us to state, that he is no relation to his celebrated namesake at Elizabeth-Town; as it is notorious to all who have had the pleasure of witnessing the size of the latter gentleman's waist, that he has too much bowels for so diabolical a profession; and it is to be hoped in charity, that though he is such a delicate morsel, when he is laid in the sepulcher of his fathers, he may not prove a titbit, to *glut the thirst of a VAMPYRE!!!*

MORAL

I n this happy land of liberty and equality, we are free from all traditional superstitions, whether political, religious, or otherwise. Fiction has no materials for machinery;—Romance no horrors for a tale of mystery. Yet in a figurative sense, and in the moral world, our climate is perhaps more prolific than any other, in enchanters,—Vampyres,—and the whole infernal brood of sorcery and witchcraft.

The accomplished dandy, who in maintaining his horses,—his tailor, etc. —absorbs in the forced and unnatural excitement of his senseless orgies, the life-blood of that wealth which his prudent Sire had accumulated by a long devotion to the counter,—What is he but a Vampyre?

The fraudulent trafficker in stock and merchandize, who, having sucked the whole substance of an hundred honest men, is consigned for a few weeks to the sepulcher of the jail; and then, by the potent magic of an insolvent law, stalks forth, triumphant with bloated villany, more elated in his shameless resurrection to renew his career of iniquity and of disgrace,—what is he but a Vampyre?

The corrupted and senseless Clerk, who being placed near the vitals of a moneyed institution, himself exhausted to feed the appetite of sharpers, drains, in his turn, the coffers he was appointed to guard,—is *he* not, I appeal to the Stockholders,—is *he* not a Vampyre?

Brokers, Country Bank Directors, and their disciples—all whose hunger and thirst for money, unsatisfied with the tardy progression of honest industry, by creating fictitious and delusive credit, has preyed on the heart and liver of public confidence, and poisoned the currents of public morals, are they not all Vampyres?

The whole tribe of Plagiarists, under every denomination;—The Critic, who, by eviscerating authors, and stuffing his own meagre show of learning with the pilfered entrails, ekes out his periodical fulmination against public taste;—the Forum Orator, who, without compunction, barbarously exonerates Burke, and Curran, and Phillips,—the Second-handed Lawyer,—Scholar,—Theologue,—who quote from quotations, and steal stolen property:—the Divine, who preaches Tillotson and Toplady;—what are they all but Vampyres?

The Empiric, who fills his own stomach, while he empties his shop into the bowels of the hypochondriac;—the Bibliopolist, "who guts the fobs" of the whole reading community, by ascribing to Lord Byron works which that author never saw; the philanthropic Contractor for the Army, who charges more for lime and horse-beef, than his quantum-meruit for the best provisions; who sets up his carriage and his palace, by blistering the mouths and destroying the intestines of thousands,—what are these but Vampyres?

The Professors and Disciples of Surgeon's Hall, who, when a fine fat corse is rolled out of the resurrectionist's budget, set up a howl of horrible transport, like he anthropophagous Caribs in Robinson Crusoe;—glut their gloating eyes with the pinguidity and unctuousness of the subject; and whet their blades like Shylock, impatient to attack the ilia,—what are they but Vampyres?

And I, who, as Johnson said of an hypochondriac Lady, "have spun this discourse out of my own bowels," and made as free with those of others—I am a VAMPYRE!

VAMPYRISM; A POEM

I.

In this blest land, where valor burst
The links which bound his children erst,
And rent the vail whose darkness hid

Legitimacy's monstrous creed;—
Where all that since the world began
Had sway'd the sacred rights of man,
With ancient dreams had past away,
And bare in all its weakness lay;—
Here reason, in triumphal hour,
Asserted too her conquering power:
From mountain, valley, plain and flood,
She exorcised the shadowy brood.

II.

When freshening gales had swept the mists,
That wildly wreath'd the mountain crests,
No cloudy spectre o'er the storm
Reveal'd the terrors of his form;—
When evening breezes curl'd the wave
No wraiths disturb'd the wandering brave,—
When lost in darkness, down the side
Of craggy mount their path they tried,
And stunn'd by torrents deafening roar,
Downward were hurl'd, to rise no more;
Men said their balance they had lost,
But never laid it to a ghost.

III.

No more, around the guarded gold,
Their wake were pirates seen to hold;—
No elves the midnight circle tript;
No fairies lunar vigils kept;
Genii nor devils rose—except,
Indeed, that once in godly Salem
Blue laws and preachings seem'd to fail 'em;
Bed bugs and rats their slumbers broke,
On Beelzebub they laid the joke;
Took brandy to expel the fiend,
Which answered quite another end!
Old ladies then to swim were taught,
In amorous league with Satan caught;—
And some were hang'd:—but now no more
'Tis fit to rake up that old sore.

IV.

Of late the pole its fiends has sent,
The 'tarnal Yankees to torment;
By water witchcraft long distrest,

In vain with all their might they *guest;*
Till when their *gumption* seem'd to fail
One captain got him by the tail;
But metamorphos'd, (such their story,)
The wizard gave the man the go-by
Turn'd out a tunny fish to be,
The "shallowest monster" of the sea.

V.

And now they swear with might and main,
That Monsieur Tonson's come again:
And Marshal Prince, his wife and daughters,
Off Nahant, saw him walk the waters.
The coachman there and Mrs. Prince
Got at the odd fish several squints;
But Mr. Prince, for weak his eye was,
Look'd at him through a mast-head spy-glass;
And took, lest men his word should doubt,
An ugly likeness of his snout,
With all the bumps the monster bore—
He says, thirteen—his wife, two more.

VI.

In Morristown we've heard a ghost
Wrought wonders to the people's cost.
'Tis not long since, on New Year's night,
The devil gave three bad boys a fright;
Who o'er their whiskey took to cursing,
Spoke disrespectfully of his person,
His government began to libel,
And on the back-log put the bible.—
But these things are of little moment,
Unworthy of a further comment.

VII.

Yet *superstition!* though thy throne
Be rear'd in wilds and woods alone,
Where the rude wanderer of the glen
Invokes the souls of martial men;—
Adores the torrent thundering loud;
Calls on the spirits of the cloud;—
And o'er the black and bursting heaven,
Sees Ariouski's chariot driven;—
Yet, queen of terror's sheetedband!
Fiends worse than thine affright our land,

While, stalking from their ghastly homes,
The Vampyre host infuriate roams!

VIII.

Behold that exquisitE divine,
Fit to hang up for fashion's sign.
In classic mould his wig is shear'd—
So Saunders says—by all rever'd—
(Yet much, with deference, due I doubt
If Saunders' science could make out
Apollo's nob, if slic'd off well,
From John G. Bogert's bust to tell—
Both are stuck up in the Academy—
Yet for this query think not bad o' me.
But to the Dandy—'neath his chin
Hog's bristles fiercely fence him in;
One corset back his shoulders throws;
His bowels other bones enclose;
His *ample* chest is bullet proof,
With cotton cram'd and such like stuff;
And for his clothes—but here's enough.
For ere the printer's tardy imp,
Shall bid in type this doggrel limp,
The swifter ninth part of a man
Shall change the passing mode again;
And waists now short shall then be long.
All that's now right shall then be wrong!

IX.

How came that puppy by his gig?
What taught him how to look so big?
For this behind the measur'd board
His father scrap'd the growing hoard—
Like him the pyramids who rear'd,
To leave behind no name rever'd
For, on the bowels of the heap,
His revels shall this Vampyre keep;
Till vigils late—and generous wine,
And—things that suit no lay of mine;
Have left him soon to die and rot,
Be laugh'd at, pitied, and forgot!
His species and his line to trace,
And count the honors of his race,
Let Mr. Wynkoop soar as high,
As Scythia's Cynocephali,

And Mr. Langstaff dive as low
As he, and he alone, can go;"
Let this quote Greek—that crack stale jokes,
The theme is worthy of such folks.

X

Lo! thro' the bustling world of trade,
What monsters march in long parade;
Gorg'd with the substance of a host,
Swelling they strut with empty boast;
The bubble burst, and credit fled,
The money'd quack proclaims them dead;—
Bailiffs in haste the corpse escort;—
The turnkey says his service short;—
Awhile in jail their bones repose,
Till lo! the dungeon doors unclose!
Insolvent laws, with potent spell,
Have wrought the wondrous miracle;
Their words of might the dead restore;
And even more bloated than before,
From that deep sepulcher, to prey
On all the gudgeons in his way,
Of shameless resurrection vain,
The Vampyre *bankrupt* stalks again!

XI.

Temples of Mammon! O beware
What priests the golden chalice bear!
And let not hands profane approach
The tempting, costly shrines to touch!
Have we not seen what secret stealth
Has suck'd the vitals of your wealth,
When the weak dupe, quite drain'd himself,
Grew hungry for the luscious pelf;
Nor did his secret orgies end,
Till fail'd a whole year's dividend.
And now once more in open air,
Have we not seen the Vampyre *pair*,
Stalk forth, from jails and juries free,
In all the pride of infamy?

XII.

O Hermes of these latter times,
I hail thee in unworthy rhymes!

Great alchemist, whose art alone
Has found the philosophic stone!
Thou arch magician! to whose hand
Alone is given the hazel wand,
That finds the veins of glittering ores,
Great Dousterswivel of conjurors!
What though thine art itself despair,
And all the pageant fade in air?
While harmless mobs thy doors assail,
And blustering butchers curse and rail,
Above thine own Flaminian roll'd,
Shall thy triumphal chariot hold
Its course majestical along,
Before the whole admiring throng!

XIII.

O Jacob! Jacob! thou art keen,
As thy great namesake;—him, I mean.
Who manag'd for himself to keep
The best of crafty Laban's sheep.
Immortal Vampyre of our age!
O might this unassuming page
Be read by all, whose fobs must bleed,
Thy ravenous appetite to feed,
Behind thy coach and four might I
Roll in an humbler tilbury;
Beneath thy wings might D'Arcy's name
Soar to the solar blaze of fame!

XIV.

Plumb from the giddy height I fall,
Amid whole herds of Vampyres small,
Critics, who worn out common place
With Author's pilfer'd entrails grace
The Forum spouter—barbarous Turk!
Who rips up Curran, Phillips, Burke,
And thunders forth bombastic centos,
Of wasted time the sad mementoes;
All those who *quote* at second hand,
And what they quote don't understand;
The Parson who in sleepy tone
Evangelizes Tillotson;
All Plagiarists,—concise to be,—
Are Ghouls of high or low degree.

XV.

    The Quack with brick dust who provides,
    Wherewith to line his own insides;
    Who fills up all his hungry chinks,
    While to a ghost his patient shrinks;
    Thomas who vends as Byron's own
    The works of doggrelists unknown;
    Honest Contractors, who are able
    To cheat both government and rabble;
    Who, worthy of the scourge and gallows,
    Set up their equipage and palace;
    While blister'd mouths deep curses pour
    And tortur'd soldiers writhe and roar,
    Who eat the beef of horses dead,
    And craunch corroding lime for bread—
    These, as the sufferers all agree,
    Are of the Ghoul fraternity.

XVI.

    There are whose tongues around them throw
    The gall with which their hearts o'erflow,
    Like those from old Medusa's head,
    Where'er its venom'd drops are shed,
    Earth's verdure fades;—rank poison springs;
    Snakes hiss, and dragons spread their wings
    Pale Dian's hopeless votary old
    Crabb'd, ancient dames, and bachelors cold,
    Nay e'en the blooming maid—will hie
    To the foul feast of calumny;
    On wisdom, worth, and reverend age,
    Beauty and wit, they glut their rage;
    And fondly hope, that as they tear
    The limbs of murder'd character,
    Their own fair fame shall prouder swell,
    Fatten'd upon the feast of hell!

XVII.

    There is a spot, unknown to fame,
    Where Vampyres haunt their hold of shame
    When Envy left her noxious cave,
    Along Passaic's winding wave,
    (Though Ovid has this fact forgot,)
    She linger'd by one cherish'd spot;
    She left her benediction here,
    The ground became forever sere;

Infected by her scatter'd slime
And tainted to all after time;
Whoever tastes its baleful food,
A Vampyre longs to feed on blood—
The blood of honor, virtue free,
Fame, confidence and chastity!

XVIII.

But wouldst thou, in thy purpose bold,
The demon orgies foul behold—
Mark where the Sons of Surgeon's Hall,
Upon their foul purveyor call;
And lo, the plunderer of the tomb
Brings up his budget in the room;
Rolls out, their ardent gaze before,
A huge, fat negress on the floor;
Then with a savage howl they roar!
Like cannibals, prepar'd to roast
Their pris'ners on some barbarous coast;
Like Shakespeare's Jew, the joyous band
Whet their keen blades with eager band;
While all the putrid limbs excite
Their foul and Vampyre appetite.—

XIX.

And what am I, whose spider skill
Has thus contrived this sheet to fill;
From my own bowels spun the lay,
Until I find no more to say?
Before to all I bid adieu,
Confess,—*I am a Vampyre too!*

WAKE NOT THE DEAD

Ernst Raupach

first published as *Laßt die Todten ruhen* in *Minerva* (1823)

this translation was first published in *Popular Tales and Romances of the Northern Nations, Vol. 1* (1823)

Wake not the Dead:—they bring but gloomy night
And cheerless desolation into day;
For in the grave who mouldering lay,
No more can feel the influence of light,
Or yield them to the sun's prolific might;
Let them repose within their house of clay—
Corruption, vainly wilt thou e'er essay
To quicken:—it sends forth a pest'lent blight;
And neither fiery sun, nor bathing dew,
Nor breath of spring the dead can e'er renew.
That which from life is pluck'd, becomes the foe
Of life, and whoso wakes it waketh woe.
Seek not the dead to waken from that sleep
In which from mortal eye they lie enshrouded deep.

"Wilt thou forever sleep? wilt thou never more awake, my beloved? but henceforth repose forever from thy short pilgrimage on earth? O yet once again return! and bring back with thee the vivifying dawn of hope to one whose existence hath, since thy departure, been obscured by the dunnest shades. What! Dumb? Forever dumb? Thy friend lamenteth, and thou heedest him not? He sheds bitter, scalding tears, and thou reposest unregarding his affliction? He is in despair, and thou no longer openest thy arms to him as an asylum from his grief? Say then, doth the paly shroud become thee better than the bridal veil? Is the chamber of the grave a warmer bed than the couch of love? Is the spectre death more welcome to thy arms than thy enamored consort? O return, my beloved, return once again to this anxious, disconsolate bosom." Such were the lamentations which Walter poured forth for his Brunhilda, the partner of his youthful, passionate love: thus did he bewail over her grave at the midnight hour, what time the spirit that presides in the troublous atmosphere, sends his legions of monsters through mid-air; so that their shadows, as they flit beneath the moon and across the earth, dart as wild, agitating thoughts that chase each other o'er the sinner's bosom:—thus did he lament under the tall linden trees by her grave, while his head reclined on the cold stone.

Walter was a powerful lord in Burgundy, who, in his earliest youth, had been smitten with the charms of the fair Brunhilda, a beauty far surpassing in loveliness all her rivals; for her tresses, dark as the raven face of night, streaming over her shoulders, set off to the utmost advantage the beaming luster of her slender form, and the rich dye of a cheek whose tint was deep and brilliant as that of the western heaven: her eyes did not resemble those burning orbs whose pale glow gem the vault of night, and whose immeasurable distance fills the soul with deep thoughts of eternity, but rather as the sober beams which cheer this nether world, and which, while they enlighten, kindle the sons of earth to joy and love. Brunhilda became the wife of Walter, and both equally enamored and devoted, they abandoned themselves to the enjoyment of a passion that rendered them reckless of aught besides, while it lulled them in a fascinating dream. Their sole apprehension was less aught should awaken them from a delirium which they prayed might continue forever. Yet how vain is the wish that would arrest the decrees of destiny! as well might it seek to divert the circling planets from their eternal course. Short was the duration of this frenzied passion; not that it gradually decayed and subsided into apathy, but death snatched away his blooming victim, and left Walter to a widowed couch. Impetuous, however, as was his first burst of grief, he was not inconsolable, for ere long another bride became the partner of the youth.

Swanhilda also was beautiful; although nature had formed her charms on a very different model from those of Brunhilda. Her golden locks waved bright as the beams of morn: only when excited by some emotion of her soul did a rosy hue tinge the lily paleness of her cheek: her limbs were proportioned in the nicest symmetry, yet did they not possess that luxuriant fullness of animal life: her eye beamed eloquently, but it was with the milder radiance of a star tranquillizing to tenderness rather than exciting to warmth. Thus formed, it was not possible that she should steep him in his former delirium, although she rendered happy his waking hours: tranquil and serious, yet cheerful, studying in all things her husband's pleasure, she restored order and comfort in his family, where her presence shed a general influence all around. Her mild benevolence tended to restrain the fiery, impetuous disposition of Walter: while at the same time her prudence recalled him in some degree from his vain, turbulent wishes, and his aspirings after unattainable enjoyments, to the duties and pleasures of actual life. Swanhilda bore her husband two children, a son and a daughter; the latter was mild and patient as her mother, well contented with her solitary sports, and even in these recreations displayed the serious turn of her character. The boy possessed his father's fiery, restless disposition, tempered, however, with the solidity of his mother. Attached by his offspring more tenderly towards their mother, Walter now lived for several years very happily: his thoughts would frequently, indeed, recur to Brunhilda, but without their former violence, merely as we dwell upon the memory of a friend of our earlier days, borne from us on the rapid current of time to a region where we know that he is happy.

But clouds dissolve into air, flowers fade, the sand of the hour-glass runs imperceptibly away, and even so, do human feelings dissolve, fade, and pass away, and with them too, human happiness. Walter's inconstant breast again sighed for the ecstatic dreams of those days which he had spent with his equally romantic, enamored Brunhilda: again did she present herself to his ardent fancy in all the glow of her bridal charms, and he began to draw a parallel between the past and the present; nor did imagination, as it is wont, fail to array the former in her brightest hues, while it proportionably obscured the latter; so that he pictured to himself, the one much more rich in enjoyment, and the other, much less so than they really were. This change in her husband did not escape Swanhilda; whereupon, redoubling her attentions towards him, and her cares towards their children, she expected, by this means, to reunite the knot that was slackened; yet the more she endeavored to regain his affections, the colder did he grow,—the more intolerable did her caresses seem, and the more continually did the image of Brunhilda haunt his thoughts. The children, whose endearments were now become indispensable to him, alone stood between the parents as genii eager to effect a reconciliation; and, beloved by them both, formed a uniting link between them. Yet, as evil can be plucked from the heart of man, only ere its root has yet struck deep, its fangs being afterwards too firm to be eradicated; so was Walter's diseased fancy too far affected to have its disorder stopped, for, in a short time it completely tyrannized over him. Frequently of a night, instead of retiring to his consort's chamber, he repaired to Brunhilda's grave, where he murmured forth his discontent, saying: 'Wilt thou sleep forever?'"

One night as he was thus reclining on the turf, indulging in his wonted sorrow, a sorcerer from the neighboring mountains, entered into this field of death for the purpose of gathering, for his mystic spells, such herbs as grow only from the earth wherein the dead repose, and which, as if the last production of mortality, are gifted with a powerful and supernatural influence. The sorcerer perceived the mourner, and approached the spot where he was lying.

"Wherefore, fond wretch, dost thou grieve thus, for what is now a hideous mass of mortality—mere bones, and nerves, and veins? Nations have fallen unlamented; even worlds themselves, long ere this globe of ours was created, have moldered into nothing; nor hath any one wept over them: why then should thou indulge this vain affliction for a child of the dust—a being as frail as thyself, and like thee the creature but of a moment?"

Walter raised himself up:—"Let yon worlds that shine in the firmament," replied he, "lament for each other as they perish. It is true, that I who am myself clay, lament for my fellow-clay: yet is this clay impregnated with a fire, —with an essence, that none of the elements of creation possess—with love: and this divine passion, I felt for her who now sleepeth beneath this sod."

"Will thy complaints awaken her: or could they do so, would she not soon upbraid thee for having disturbed that repose in which she now is hushed?"

"Avaunt, cold-hearted being: thou knowest not what is love. Oh! that my tears could wash away the earthy covering that conceals her from these eyes; —that my groan of anguish could rouse her from her slumber of death!—No, she would not again seek her earthy couch."

"Insensate that thou art, and couldst thou endure to gaze without shuddering on one disgorged from the jaws of the grave? Art thou too thyself the same from whom she parted; or hath time passed o'er thy brow and left no traces there? Would not thy love rather be converted into hate and disgust?"

"Say rather that the stars would leave yon firmament, that the sun will henceforth refuse to shed his beams through the heavens. O that she stood once more before me;—that once again she reposed on this bosom!—how quickly should we then forget that death or time had ever stepped between us."

"Delusion! mere delusion of the brain, from heated blood, like to that which arises from the fumes of wine. It is not my wish to tempt thee;—to restore to thee thy dead; else wouldst thou soon feel that I have spoken sooth."

"How! restore her to me," exclaimed Walter casting himself at the sorcerer's feet. "Oh! if thou art indeed able to effect that, grant it to my earnest supplication; if one throb of human feeling vibrates in thy bosom, let my tears prevail with thee: restore me my beloved; so shalt thou hereafter bless the deed, and see that it was a good work."

"A good work! a blessed deed!"—returned the sorcerer with a smile of scorn; "for me there exists nor good, nor evil; since my will is always the same. Ye alone know evil, who will that which ye would not. It is indeed in my power to restore her to thee: yet, bethink thee well, whether it will prove thy weal. Consider too, how deep the abyss between life and death; across this, my power can build a bridge, but it can never fill up the frightful chasm."

Walter would have spoken, and have sought to prevail on this powerful being by fresh entreaties, but the latter prevented him, saying: "Peace! bethink thee well! and return hither to me tomorrow at midnight. Yet once more do I warn thee, 'wake not the dead.'"

Having uttered these words, the mysterious being disappeared. Intoxicated with fresh hope, Walter found no sleep on his couch; for fancy, prodigal of her richest stores, expanded before him the glittering web of futurity; and his eye, moistened with the dew of rapture, glanced from one vision of happiness to another. During the next day he wandered through the woods, lest wonted objects by recalling the memory of later and less happier times, might disturb the blissful idea, that he should again behold her—again fold her in his arms, gaze on her beaming brow by day, repose on her bosom at night: and, as this sole idea filled his imagination, how was it possible that the least doubt should arise; or that the warning of the mysterious old man should recur to his thoughts.

No sooner did the midnight hour approach, than he hastened towards the grave-field where the sorcerer was already standing by that of Brunhilda. "Hast thou maturely considered?" enquired he.

"Oh! restore to me the object of my ardent passion," exclaimed Walter with impetuous eagerness. "Delay not thy generous action, lest I die even this night, consumed with disappointed desire; and behold her face no more."

"Well then, answered the old man," return hither again tomorrow at the same hour. But once more do I give thee this friendly warning, 'wake not the dead.'"

In all the despair of impatience, Walter would have prostrated himself at his feet, and supplicated him to fulfill at once a desire now increased to agony; but the sorcerer had already disappeared. Pouring forth his lamentations more wildly and impetuously than ever, he lay upon the grave of his adored one, until the grey dawn streaked the east. During the day, which seemed to him longer than any he had ever experienced, he wandered to and fro, restless and impatient, seemingly without any object, and deeply buried in his own reflections, inquest as the murderer who meditates his first deed of blood: and the stars of evening found him once more at the appointed spot. At midnight the sorcerer was there also.

"Hast thou yet maturely deliberated?" enquired he, "as on the preceding night?"

"On what should I deliberate?" returned Walter impatiently. "I need not to deliberate: what I demand of thee, is that which thou hast promised me—that which will prove my bliss. Or dost thou but mock me? if so, hence from my sight, lest I be tempted to lay my hand on thee."

"Once more do I warn thee," answered the old man with undisturbed composure, 'wake not the dead'—let her rest."

"Aye, but not in the cold grave: she shall rather rest on this bosom which burns with eagerness to clasp her."

"Reflect, thou may'st not quit her until death, even though aversion and horror should seize thy heart. There would then remain only one horrible means."

"Dotard!" cried Walter," interrupting him, "how may I hate that which I love with such intensity of passion? how should I abhor that for which my every drop of blood is boiling?"

"Then be it even as thou wishest," answered the sorcerer; "step back."

The old man now drew a circle round the grave, all the while muttering words of enchantment. Immediately the storm began to howl among the tops of the trees; owls flapped their wings, and uttered their low voice of omen;

the stars hid their mild, beaming aspect, that they might not behold so unholy and impious a spectacle; the stone then rolled from the grave with a hollow sound, leaving a free passage for the inhabitant of that dreadful tenement. The sorcerer scattered into the yawning earth, roots and herbs of most magic power, and of most penetrating odor, so that the worms crawling forth from the earth congregated together, and raised themselves in a fiery column over the grave: while rushing wind burst from the earth, scattering the mould before it, until at length the coffin lay uncovered. The moon-beams fell on it, and the lid burst open with a tremendous sound. Upon this the sorcerer poured upon it some blood from out of a human skull, exclaiming at the same time:—"Drink, sleeper, of this warm stream, that thy heart may again beat within thy bosom." And, after a short pause, shedding on her some other mystic liquid, he cried aloud with the voice of one inspired: "Yes, thy heart beats once more with the flood of life: thine eye is again opened to sight. Arise, therefore, from thy tomb."

As an island suddenly springs forth from the dark waves of the ocean, raised upwards from the deep by the force of subterraneous fires, so did Brunhilda start from her earthy couch, borne forward by some invisible power. Taking her by the hand, the sorcerer lead her towards Walter, who stood at some little distance, rooted to the ground with amazement.

"Receive again," said he, "the object of thy passionate sighs: mayest thou never more require my aid; should that however happen, so wilt thou find me, during the full of the moon, upon the mountains in that spot and where the three roads meet."

Instantly did Walter recognize in the form that stood before him, her whom he so ardently loved; and a sudden glow shot through his frame at finding her thus restored to him: yet the night-frost had chilled his limbs and palsied his tongue. For a while he gazed upon her without either motion or speech, and during this pause, all was again become hushed and serene; and the stars shone brightly in the clear heavens.

"Walter!" exclaimed the figure; and at once the well-known sound, thrilling to his heart, broke the spell by which he was bound.

"Is it reality? is it truth?" cried he, "or a cheating delusion?"

"No, it is no imposture: I am really living:—conduct me quickly to thy castle in the mountains."

Walter looked around: the old man had disappeared, but he perceived close by his side, a coal-black steed of fiery eye, ready equipped to conduct him thence; and on his back lay all proper attire for Brunhilda, who lost no time in arraying herself. This being done, she cried: "Haste, let us away ere the dawn breaks, for my eye is yet too weak to endure the light of day." Fully recovered from his stupor, Walter leaped into his saddle, and catching up, with a mingled feeling of delight and awe, the beloved being thus mysteriously restored from the power of the grave, he spurred on across the wild, towards the mountains, as furiously as if pursued by the shadows of the dead, hastening to recover from him their sister.

The castle to which Walter conducted his Brunhilda, was situated on a rock between other rocks rising up above it. Here they arrived, unseen by any, save one aged domestic, on whom Walter imposed secrecy by the severest threats.

"Here will we tarry," said Brunhilda, "until I can endure the light, and until thou canst look upon me without trembling: as if struck with a cold chill." They accordingly continued to make that place their abode: yet no one knew that Brunhilda existed, save only that aged attendant, who provided their meals. During seven entire days, they had no light except that of tapers; during the next seven, the light was admitted through the lofty casements only while the rising or setting-sun faintly illumined the mountain-tops, the valleys being still enveloped in shade.

Seldom did Walter quit Brunhilda's side: a nameless spell seemed to attach him to her; even the shudder which he felt in her presence, and which would not permit him to touch her, was not unmixed with pleasure, like that thrilling, awful emotion felt when strains of sacred music float under the vault of some temple; he rather sought, therefore, than avoided this feeling. Often too as he had indulged in calling to mind the beauties of Brunhilda, she had never appeared so fair, so fascinating, so admirable when depicted by his imagination, as when now beheld in reality. Never till now had her voice sounded with such tones of sweetness; never before did her language possess such eloquence as it now did, when she conversed with him on the subject of the past. And this was the magic fairyland towards which her words constantly conducted him. Ever did she dwell upon the days of their first love, those hours of delight which they had participated together when the one derived all enjoyment from the other: and so rapturous, so enchanting, so full of life did she recall to his imagination that blissful season, that he even doubted whether he had ever experienced with her so much felicity, or had been so truly happy. And, while she thus vividly portrayed their hours of past delight, she delineated in still more glowing, more enchanting colors, those hours of approaching bliss which now awaited them, richer in enjoyment than any preceding ones. In this manner did she charm her attentive auditor with enrapturing hopes for the future, and lull him in dreams of more than mortal ecstasy; so that while he listened to her siren strain, he entirely forgot how little blissful was the latter period of their union, when he had often sighed at her imperiousness, and at her harshness both to himself and all his household. Yet even had he recalled this to mind would it have disturbed him in his present delirious trance? Had she not now left behind in the grave all the frailty of mortality? Was she not cheerful as the morning hour in spring —affectionate and mild as the last beams of an autumnal sun? Was not her whole being refined and purified by that long sleep in which neither passion nor sin had approached her even in dreams? How different now was the subject of her discourse! Only when speaking of her affection for him, did she betray any thing of earthly feeling: at other times, she uniformly dwelt upon themes relating to the invisible and future world; when in descanting and declaring the mysteries of eternity, a stream of prophetic eloquence would burst from her lips.

In this manner had twice seven days elapsed, and, for the first time, Walter beheld the being now dearer to him than ever, in the full light of day. Every trace of the grave had disappeared from her countenance: a roseate tinge like the ruddy streaks of dawn again beamed on her pallid cheek; the faint, mouldering taint of the grave was changed into a delightful violet scent; the only sign of earth that never disappeared. He no longer felt either apprehension or awe, as he gazed upon her in the sunny light of day: it was not until now, that he seemed to have recovered her completely; and, glowing with all his former passion towards her, he would have pressed her to his bosom, but she gently repulsed him, saying: "Not yet: spare your caresses until the moon has again filled her horn."

Spite of his impatience, Walter was obliged to await the lapse of another period of seven days; but, on the night when the moon was arrived at the full, he hastened to Brunhilda, whom he found more lovely than she had ever appeared before. Fearing no obstacles to his transports, he embraced her with all the fervor of a deeply-enamored and successful lover. Brunhilda, however, still refused to yield to his passion. "What!" exclaimed she, "is it fitting that I who have been purified by death from the frailty of mortality, should become thy concubine, while a mere daughter of the earth bears the title of thy wife: never shall it be. No, it must be within the walls of thy palace, within that chamber where I once reigned as queen, that thou obtainest the end of thy wishes,—and of mine also," added she, imprinting a glowing kiss on his lips, and immediately disappeared.

Heated with passion, and determined to sacrifice every thing to the accomplishment of his desires, Walter hastily quitted the apartment, and shortly after the castle itself. He travelled over mountain and cross heath, with the rapidity of a storm, so that the turf was flung up by his horse's hoofs; nor once stopped until he arrived home.

Here, however, neither the affectionate caresses of Swanhilda, or those of his children could touch his heart, or induce him to restrain his furious desires. Alas! is the impetuous torrent to be checked in its devastating course by the beauteous flowers over which it rushes, when they exclaim: "Destroyer, commiserate our helpless innocence and beauty, nor lay us waste?"—the stream sweeps over them unregarding, and a single moment annihilates the pride of a whole summer.

Shortly afterwards, did Walter begin to hint to Swanhilda, that they were ill-suited to each other;—that he was anxious to taste that wild, tumultuous life, so well according with the spirit of his sex, while she, on the contrary, was satisfied with the monotonous circle of household enjoyments:—that he was eager for whatever promised novelty, while she felt most attached to what was familiarized to her by habit; and lastly, that her cold disposition, bordering upon indifference, but ill assorted with his ardent temperament: it was therefore more prudent that they should seek apart from each other, that happiness which they could not find together. A sigh, and a brief acquiescence in his wishes was all the reply that Swanhilda made: and, on the following morning upon his presenting her with a paper of separation, informing her that she was at liberty to return home to her father, she received it most submissively: yet, ere she departed, she gave him the following warning: "Too well do I conjecture to whom I am indebted for this our separation. Often have I seen thee at Brunhilda's grave, and beheld thee there even on that night when the face of the heavens was suddenly enveloped in a veil of clouds. Hast thou rashly dared to tear aside the awful veil that separates the mortality that dreams, from that which dreameth not, O! then woe to thee, thou wretched man, for thou hast attached to thyself that which will prove thy destruction." She ceased: nor did Walter attempt any reply, for the similar admonition uttered by the sorcerer flashed upon his mind, all obscured as it was by passion, just as the lightning glares momentarily through the gloom of night without dispersing the obscurity.

Swanhilda then departed, in order to pronounce to her children, a bitter farewell, for they, according to the custom of his nation, belonged to the father; and, having bathed them in her tears, and consecrated them with the holy water of maternal love, she quitted her husband's residence, and departed to the home of her fathers.

Thus was the kind and benevolent Swanhilda, driven an exile from those halls, where she had presided with such grace;—from halls which were now newly decorated to receive another mistress. The day at length arrived, on which Walter, for the second time, conducted Brunhilda home, as a newly-made bride. And he caused it to be reported among his domestics, that his new consort had gained his affections by her extraordinary likeness to Brunhilda, their former mistress. How ineffably happy did he deem himself, as he conducted his beloved once more into the chamber which had often witnessed their former joys, and which was now newly gilded and adorned in a most costly style: among the other decorations were figures of angels scattering roses, which served to support the purple draperies, whose ample folds o'ershadowed the nuptial couch. With what impatience did he await the hour that was to put him in possession of those beauties, for which he had already paid so high a price, but, whose enjoyment was to cost him most dearly yet! Unfortunate Walter! reveling in bliss, thou beholdest not the abyss that yawns beneath thy feet, intoxicated with the luscious perfume of the flower thou hast plucked, thou little deemest how deadly is the venom with which it is fraught, although, for a short season, its potent fragrance bestows new energy on all thy feelings.

Happy however, as Walter now was, his household were far from being equally so. The strange resemblance between their new lady and the deceased Brunhilda, filled them with a secret dismay,—an undefinable horror; for there was not a single difference of feature, of tone of voice, or of gesture. To add too to these mysterious circumstances, her female attendants discovered a particular mark on her back, exactly like one which Brunhilda had. A report was now soon circulated, that their lady was no other than Brunhilda herself, who had been recalled to life by the power of necromancy. How truly horrible was the idea of living under the same roof with one who had been an inhabitant of the tomb, and of being obliged to attend upon her, and acknowledge her as mistress! There was also in Brunhilda, much to increase this aversion, and favor their superstition: no ornaments of gold ever decked her person; all that others were wont to wear of this metal, she had formed of silver: no richly colored, and sparkling jewels glittered upon her; pearls alone, lent their pale luster to adorn her bosom. Most carefully did she always avoid the cheerful light of the sun, and was wont to spend the brightest days in the most retired and gloomy apartments: only during the twilight of the commencing, or declining day did she ever walk abroad, but her favorite hour was, when the phantom light of the moon bestowed on all objects a shadowy appearance, and a sombre hue; always too at the crowing of the cock, an involuntary shudder was observed to seize her limbs. Imperious as before her death, she quickly imposed her iron yoke on every one around her, while she seemed even far more terrible than ever, since a dread of some supernatural power attached to her, appalled all who approached her. A malignant withering glance seemed to shoot from her eye on the unhappy object of her wrath, as if it would annihilate its victim. In short, those halls which, in the time of Swanhilda were the residence of cheerfulness and mirth, now resembled an extensive desert tomb. With fear imprinted on their pale countenances, the domestics glided through the apartments of the castle; and, in this abode of terror, the crowing of the cock caused the living to tremble, as if they were the spirits of the departed; for the sound always reminded them of their mysterious mistress. There was no one but who shuddered at meeting her in a lonely place, in the dusk of evening, or by the light of the moon, a circumstance that was deemed to be ominous of some evil: so great was the apprehension of her female attendants, that they pined in continual disquietude, and, by degrees, all quitted her. In the course of time even others of the domestics fled, for an insupportable horror had seized them.

The art of the sorcerer had indeed bestowed upon Brunhilda an artificial life, and due nourishment had continued to support the restored body; yet, this body was not able of itself to keep up the genial glow of vitality, and to nourish the flame whence springs all the affections and passions, whether of love or hate; for death had forever destroyed and withered it: all that Brunhilda now possessed was a chilled existence, colder than that of the snake. It was nevertheless necessary that she should love, and return with equal ardor the warm caresses of her spell-enthralled husband, to whose passion alone she was indebted for her renewed existence. It was necessary that a magic draught should animate the dull current in her veins, and awaken her to the glow of life and the flame of love—a potion of abomination—one not even to be named without a curse—human blood, imbibed whilst yet warm, from the veins of youth. This was the hellish drink for which she thirsted: possessing no sympathy with the purer feelings of humanity; deriving no enjoyment from aught that interests in life, and occupies its varied hours; her existence was a mere blank, unless when in the arms of her paramour husband, and therefore was it that she craved incessantly after the horrible draught. It was even with the utmost effort that she could forbear sucking even the blood of Walter himself, as he reclined beside her. Whenever she beheld some innocent child, whose lovely face denoted the exuberance of infantine health and vigor, she would entice it by soothing words and fond caresses into her most secret apartment, where, lulling it to sleep in her arms, she would suck from its bosom the warm, purple tide of life. Nor were youths of either sex safe from her horrid attack: having first breathed upon her unhappy victim, who never failed immediately to sink into a lengthened sleep, she would then in a similar manner drain his veins of the vital juice. Thus children, youths, and maidens quickly faded away, as flowers gnawn by the cankering worm: the fullness of their limbs disappeared; a sallow hue succeeded to the rosy freshness of their cheeks, the liquid luster of the eye was deadened, even as the sparkling stream when arrested by the touch of frost; and their locks became thin and grey, as if already ravaged by the storm of life. Parents beheld with horror this desolating pestilence devouring their offspring; nor could simple or charm, potion or amulet avail aught against it. The grave swallowed up one after the other; or did the miserable victim survive, he became cadaverous and wrinkled even in the very morn of existence. Parents observed with horror, this devastating pestilence snatch away their offspring—a pestilence which, nor herb however potent, nor charm, nor holy taper, nor exorcism could avert. They either beheld their children sink one after the other into the grave, or their youthful forms withered by the unholy, vampire embrace of Brunhilda assume the decrepitude of sudden age.

At length strange surmises and reports began to prevail; it was whispered that Brunhilda herself was the cause of all these horrors; although no one could pretend to tell in what manner she destroyed her victims, since no marks of violence were discernible. Yet when young children confessed that she had frequently lulled them asleep in her arms, and elder ones said that a sudden slumber had come upon them whenever she began to converse with them, suspicion became converted into certainty, and those whose offspring had hitherto escaped unharmed, quitted their hearths and home—all their little possessions—the dwellings of their fathers and the inheritance of their children, in order to rescue from so horrible a fate those who were dearer to their simple affections than aught else the world could give.

Thus did the castle daily assume a more desolate appearance; daily did its environs become more deserted: none but a few aged decrepit old women and grey-headed menials were to be seen remaining of the once numerous retinue. Such will, in the latter days of the earth, be the last generation of mortals, when child-bearing shall have ceased, when youth shall no more be seen, nor any arise to replace those who shall await their fate in silence.

Walter alone noticed not, or heeded not, the desolation around him; he apprehended not death, lapped as he was in a glowing elysium of love. Far more happy than formerly did he now seem in the possession of Brunhilda. All those caprices and frowns which had been wont to overcloud their former union had now entirely disappeared. She even seemed to dote on him with a warmth of passion that she had never exhibited even during the happy season of bridal love; for the flame of that youthful blood, of which she drained the veins of others, rioted in her own. At night, as soon as he closed his eyes, she would breathe on him till he sank into delicious dreams, from which he awoke only to experience more rapturous enjoyments. By day she would continually discourse with him on the bliss experienced by happy spirits beyond the grave, assuring them that, as his affection had recalled her from the tomb, they were now irrevocably united. Thus fascinated by a continual spell, it was not possible that he should perceive what was taking place around him. Brunhilda, however, foresaw with savage grief that the source of her youthful ardor was daily decreasing, for, in a short time, there remained nothing gifted with youth, save Walter and his children, and these latter she resolved should be her next victims.

On her first return to the castle, she had felt an aversion towards the offspring of another, and therefore abandoned them entirely to the attendants appointed by Swanhilda. Now, however, she began to pay considerable attention to them, and caused them to be frequently admitted into her presence. The aged nurses were filled with dread at perceiving these marks of regard from her towards their young charges, yet dared they not to oppose the will of their terrible and imperious mistress. Soon did Brunhilda gain the affection of the children, who were too unsuspecting of all guile to apprehend any danger from her; on the contrary, her caresses won them completely to her. Instead of ever checking their mirthful gambols, she would rather instruct them in new sports; often too did she recite to them tales of such strange and wild interest as to exceed all the stories of their nurses. Were they wearied either with play or with listening to her narratives, she would take them on her knees and lull them to slumber. Then did visions of the most surpassing magnificence attend their dreams: they would fancy themselves in some garden, where flowers of every hue rose in rows one above the other, from the humble violet to the tall sun-flower, forming a party-colored broidery of every hue, sloping upwards towards the golden clouds, where little angels, whose wings sparkled with azure and gold, descended to bring them delicious cates, or splendid jewels; or sung to them soothing melodious hymns. So delightful did these dreams in short time become to the children, that they longed for nothing so eagerly as to slumber on Brunhilda's lap, for never did they else enjoy such visions of heavenly forms. Thus were they most anxious for that which was to prove their destruction:—yet do we not all aspire after that which conducts us to the grave—after the enjoyment of life? These innocents stretched out their arms to approaching death, because it assumed the mask of pleasure; for, while they were lapped in these ecstatic slumbers, Brunhilda sucked the life-stream from their bosoms. On waking, indeed, they felt themselves faint and exhausted, yet did no pain, nor any mark betray the cause. Shortly, however, did their strength entirely fail, even as the summer brook is gradually dried up: their sports became less and less noisy; their loud, frolicsome laughter was converted into a faint smile; the full tones of their voices died away into a mere whisper. Their attendants were filled with horror and despair; too well did they conjecture the dreadful truth, yet dared not to impart their suspicions to Walter, who was so devotedly attached to his horrible partner. Death had already smote his prey: the children were but the mere shadows of their former selves, and even this shadow quickly disappeared.

The anguished father deeply bemoaned their loss, for, notwithstanding his apparent neglect, he was strongly attached to them, nor until he had experienced their loss, was he aware that his love was so great. His affliction could not fail to excite the displeasure of Brunhilda: "Why dost thou lament so fondly," said she, "for these little ones? What satisfaction could such unformed beings yield to thee, unless thou wert still attached to their mother? Thy heart then is still hers? Or dost thou now regret her and them, because thou art satiated with my fondness, and weary of my endearments? Had these young ones grown up, would they not have attached thee, thy spirit and thy affections more closely to this earth of clay—to this dust, and have alienated thee from that sphere to which I, who have already passed the grave, endeavor to raise thee? Say is thy spirit so lumpish, or thy love so weak, or thy faith so hollow, that the hope of being mine forever is unable to touch thee?" Thus did Brunhilda express her indignation at her consort's grief, and forbade him her presence. The fear of offending her beyond forgiveness, and his anxiety to appease her soon dried up his tears; and he again abandoned himself to his fatal passion, until approaching destruction, at length awakened him from his delusion.

Neither maiden, nor youth, was any longer to be seen, either within the dreary walls of the castle, or the adjoining territory:—all had disappeared; for those whom the grave had not swallowed up, had fled from the region of death. Who, therefore, now remained to quench the horrible thirst of the female vampire, save Walter himself? and his death she dared to contemplate unmoved; for that divine sentiment that unites two beings in one joy and one sorrow was unknown to her bosom. Was he in his tomb, so was she free to search out other victims, and glut herself with destruction, until she herself should, at the last day, be consumed with the earth itself; such is the fatal law, to which the dead are subject, when awoke by the arts of necromancy from the sleep of the grave.

She now began to fix her blood-thirsty lips on Walter's breast, when cast into a profound sleep by the odor of her violet breath, he reclined beside her quite unconscious of his impending fate: yet soon did his vital powers begin to decay; and many a grey hair peeped through his raven locks. With his strength, his passion also declined; and he now frequently left her in order to pass the whole day in the sports of the chase, hoping thereby, to regain his wonted vigor. As he was reposing one day in a wood beneath the shade of an oak, he perceived, on the summit of a tree, a bird of strange appearance, and quite unknown to him; but, before he could take aim at it with his bow, it flew away into the clouds; at the same time, letting fall a rose-colored root which dropped at Walter's feet, who immediately took it up, and, although he was well acquainted with almost every plant, he could not remember to have seen any at all resembling this. Its delightfully odoriferous scent induced him to try its flavor, but ten times more bitter than wormwood, it was even as gall in his mouth; upon which, impatient of the disappointment, he flung it away with violence. Had he, however, been aware of its miraculous quality, and that it acted as a counter-charm against the opiate perfume of Brunhilda's breath, he would have blessed it spite of its bitterness: thus do mortals often blindly cast away in displeasure, the unsavory remedy that would otherwise work their weal.

When Walter returned home in the evening, and laid him down to repose as usual by Brunhilda's side, the magic power of her breath produced no effect upon him; and, for the first time during many months did he close his eyes in a natural slumber. Yet hardly had he fallen asleep, ere a pungent, smarting pain disturbed him from his dreams; and, opening his eyes, he discerned, by the gloomy rays of a lamp, that glimmered in the apartment, what for some moments transfixed him quite aghast, for it was Brunhilda, drawing with her lips, the warm blood from his bosom. The wild cry of horror which at length escaped him, terrified Brunhilda, whose mouth was besmeared with the warm blood. "Monster!" exclaimed he, springing from the couch, "is it thus that you love me?

"Aye, even as the dead love," replied she, with a malignant coldness.

"Creature of blood!" continued Walter, "the delusion which has so long blinded me is at an end: thou art the fiend who hast destroyed my children— who hast murdered the offspring of my vassals." Raising herself upwards, and, at the same time, casting on him a glance that froze him to the spot with dread, she replied: "It is not I who have murdered them:—I was obliged to pamper myself with warm youthful blood, in order that I might satisfy thy furious desires—thou art the murderer!"—These dreadful words summoned, before Walter's terrified conscience, the threatening shades of all those who had thus perished; while despair choked his voice. "Why," continued she, in a tone that increased his horror, "why dost thou make mouths at me like a puppet? Thou who hadst the courage to love the dead—to take into thy bed, one who had been sleeping in the grave, the bed-fellow of the worm—who hast clasped in thy lustful arms, the corruption of the tomb—dost thou, unhallowed as thou art, now raise this hideous cry for the sacrifice of a few lives?—They are but leaves swept from their branches by a storm.—Come, chase these idiot fancies, and taste the bliss thou hast so dearly purchased." So saying, she extended her arms towards him; but this motion served only to increase his terror, and exclaiming: "Accursed Being,"—he rushed out of the apartment.

All the horrors of a guilty, upbraiding conscience became his companions, now that he was awakened from the delirium of his unholy pleasures. Frequently did he curse his own obstinate blindness, for having given no heed to the hints and admonitions of his children's nurses, but treating them as vile calumnies. But his sorrow was now too late, for, although repentance may gain pardon for the sinner, it cannot alter the immutable decrees of fate—it cannot recall the murdered from the tomb. No sooner did the first break of dawn appear, than he sat out for his lonely castle in the mountains, determined no longer to abide under the same roof with so terrific a being; yet vain was his flight, for, on waking the following morning, he perceived himself in Brunhilda's arms, and quite entangled in her long raven tresses, which seemed to involve him, and bind him in the fetters of his fate; the powerful fascination of her breath held him still more captivated, so that, forgetting all that had passed, he returned her caresses, until awakening as if from a dream he recoiled in unmixed horror from her embrace. During the day he wandered through the solitary wilds of the mountains, as a culprit seeking an asylum from his pursuers; and, at night, retired to the shelter of a cave; fearing less to couch himself within such a dreary place, than to expose himself to the horror of again meeting Brunhilda; but, alas! it was in vain that he endeavored to flee her. Again, when he awoke, he found her the partner of his miserable bed. Nay, had he sought the centre of the earth as his hiding place; had he even imbedded himself beneath rocks, or formed his chamber in the recesses of the ocean, still had he found her his constant companion; for, by calling her again into existence, he had rendered himself inseparably hers; so fatal were the links that united them.

Struggling with the madness that was beginning to seize him, and brooding incessantly on the ghastly visions that presented themselves to his horror stricken-mind, he lay motionless in the gloomiest recesses of the woods, even from the rise of sun till the shades of eve. But, no sooner was the light of day extinguished in the west, and the woods buried in impenetrable darkness, than the apprehension of resigning himself to sleep drove him forth among the open mountains. The storm played wildly with the fantastic clouds, and with the rattling leaves, as they were caught up into the air, as if some dread spirit was sporting with these images of transitoriness and decay: it roared among the summits of the oaks as if uttering a voice of fury, while its hollow sound rebounding among the distant hills, seemed as the moans of a departing sinner, or as the faint cry of some wretch expiring under the murderer's hand: the owl too, uttered its ghastly cry as if foreboding the wreck of nature. Walter's hair flew disorderly in the wind, like black snakes wreathing around his temples and shoulders; while each sense was awake to catch fresh horror. In the clouds he seemed to behold the forms of the murdered; in the howling wind to hear their laments and groans; in the chilling blast itself he felt the dire kiss of Brunhilda; in the cry of the screeching bird he heard her voice; in the mouldering leaves he scented the charnel-bed out of which he had awakened her. "Murderer of thy own offspring," exclaimed he in a voice making night, and the conflict of the element still more hideous, "paramour of a blood-thirsty vampire, reveler with the corruption of the tomb!" while in his despair he rent the wild locks from his head. Just then the full moon darted from beneath the bursting clouds; and this sight recalled to his remembrance the advice of the sorcerer, when he trembled at the first apparition of Brunhilda rising from her sleep of death;—namely, to seek him, at the season of the full moon, in the mountains, where three roads met. Scarcely had this gleam of hope broke in on his bewildered mind than he flew to the appointed spot.

On his arrival, Walter found the old man seated there upon a stone, as calmly as though it had been a bright sunny day, and completely regardless of the uproar around. "Art thou come then?" exclaimed he to the breathless wretch, who, flinging himself at his feet, cried in a tone of anguish: "Oh save me—succor me—rescue me from the monster that scattereth death and desolation around her."

"I am acquainted with all," returned the sorcerer; "thou now perceivest how wholesome was the advice—'wake not the dead.'"

"And wherefore a mere mysterious warning? why didst thou not rather disclose to me, at once, all the horrors that awaited my sacrilegious profanation of the grave?"

"Wert thou able to listen to any other voice than that of thy impetuous passions? Did not thy eager impatience shut my mouth at the very moment I would have cautioned thee?"

"True, true:—thy reproof is just: but what does it avail now;—I need the promptest aid."

"Well," replied the old man, "there remains even yet a means of rescuing thyself, but it is fraught with horror, and demands all thy resolution."

"Utter it then, utter it; for what can be more appalling, more hideous than the misery I now endure?"

"Know then," continued the sorcerer, "that only on the night of the new moon, does she sleep the sleep of mortals; and then all the supernatural power which she inherits from the grave totally fails her. 'Tis then that thou must murder her."

"How! murder her!" echoed Walter.

"Aye," returned the old man calmly, "pierce her bosom with a sharpened dagger, which I will furnish thee with; at the same time renounce her memory forever, swearing never to think of her intentionally, and that, if thou dost involuntarily, thou wilt repeat the curse."

"Most horrible! yet what can be more horrible than she herself is?—I'll do it."

"Keep then this resolution until the next new moon."

"What, must I wait until then?" cried Walter, "alas ere then, either her savage thirst for blood will have forced me into the night of the tomb, or horror will have driven me into the night of madness."

"Nay," replied the sorcerer, "that I can prevent;" and, so saying, he conducted him to a cavern further among the mountains. "Abide here twice seven days," said he; "so long can I protect thee against her deadly caresses. Here wilt thou find all due provision for thy wants; but take heed that nothing tempt thee to quit this place. Farewell, when the moon renews itself, then do I repair hither again." So saying, the sorcerer drew a magic circle around the cave, and then immediately disappeared,

Twice seven days did Walter continue in this solitude, where his companions were his own terrifying thoughts, and his bitter repentance. The present was all desolate and dread; the future presented the image of a horrible deed, which he must perforce commit; while the past was empoisoned by the memory of his guilt. Did he think on his former happy union with Brunhilda, her horrible image presented itself to his imagination with her lips defiled with dropping blood: or, did he call to mind the peaceful days he had passed with Swanhilda, he beheld her sorrowful spirit, with the shadows of her murdered children. Such were the horrors that attended him by day: those of night were still more dreadful, for then he beheld Brunhilda herself, who, wandering round the magic circle which she could not pass, called upon his name, till the cavern re-echoed the horrible sound. "Walter, my beloved," cried she, wherefore dost thou avoid me? art thou not mine? forever mine—mine here, and mine hereafter? And dost thou seek to murder me?—ah! commit not a deed which hurls us both to perdition—thyself as well as me." In this manner did the horrible visitant torment him each night, and, even when she departed, robbed him of all repose.

The night of the new moon at length arrived, dark as the deed it was doomed to bring forth. The sorcerer entered the cavern; "Come, said he to Walter, let us depart hence, the hour is now arrived:" and he forthwith conducted him in silence from the grave, to a coal-black steed, the sight of which recalled to Walter's remembrance the fatal night. He then related to the old man Brunhilda's nocturnal visits, and anxiously enquired whether her apprehensions of eternal perdition would be fulfilled or not. "Mortal eye," exclaimed the sorcerer, "may not pierce the dark secrets of another world, or penetrate the deep abyss that separates earth from heaven." Walter hesitated to mount the steed. "Be resolute," exclaimed his companion, "but this once is it granted to thee to make the trial, and, should thou fail now, nought can rescue thee from her power."

"What can be more horrible than she herself?—I am determined:" and he leaped on the horse, the sorcerer mounting also behind him.

Carried with a rapidity equal to that of the storm that sweeps across the plain, they in brief space arrived at Walter's castle. All the doors flew open at the bidding of his companion, and they speedily reached Brunhilda's chamber, and stood beside her couch. Reclining in a tranquil slumber; she reposed in all her native loveliness, every trace of horror had disappeared from her countenance; she looked so pure, meek and innocent that all the sweet hours of their endearments rushed to Walter's memory, like interceding angels pleading in her behalf. His unnerved hand could not take the dagger which the sorcerer presented to him. "The blow must be struck even now:" said the latter, "shouldst thou delay but an hour, she will lie at day-break on thy bosom, sucking the warm life-drops from thy heart."

"Horrible! most horrible!" faltered the trembling Walter, and turning away his face, he thrust the dagger into her bosom, exclaiming: "I curse thee forever!"—and the cold blood gushed upon his hand. Opening her eyes once more, she cast a look of ghastly horror on her husband, and, in a hollow dying accent said:—"Thou too art doomed to perdition."

"Lay now thy hand upon her corse," said the sorcerer, "and swear the oath."—Walter did as commanded, saying:—"Never will I think of her with love, never recall her to mind intentionally, and, should her image recur to my mind involuntarily, so will I exclaim to it: be thou accursed."

"Thou hast now done every thing," returned the sorcerer;—restore her therefore to the earth, from which thou so foolishly recalled her; and be sure to recollect thy oath: for, shouldst thou forget it but once, she would return, and thou wouldst be inevitably lost. Adieu: we see each other no more." Having uttered these words he quitted the apartment, and Walter also fled from this abode of horror, having first given directions that the corse should be speedily interred.

Again did the terrific Brunhilda repose within her grave; but her image continually haunted Walter's imagination, so that his existence was one continued martyrdom, in which he continually struggled, to dismiss from his recollection the hideous phantoms of the past; yet, the stronger his effort to banish them, so much the more frequently and the more vividly did they return; as the night-wanderer, who is enticed by a fire-wisp into quagmire or bog, sinks the deeper into his damp grave the more he struggles to escape. His imagination seemed incapable of admitting any other image than that of Brunhilda: now he fancied he beheld her expiring, the blood streaming from her beautiful bosom: at others he saw the lovely bride of his youth, who reproached him with having disturbed the slumbers of her tomb: and to both he was compelled to utter the dreadful words, "I curse thee forever." The terrible imprecation was constantly passing his lips; yet was he in incessant terror lest he should forget it, or dream of her without being able to repeat it, and then, on awaking, find himself in her arms. Else would he recall her expiring words, and, appalled at their terrific import, imagine that the doom of his perdition was irrecoverably passed. Whence should he fly from himself? or how erase from his brain these images and forms of horror? In the din of combat, in the tumult of war and its incessant pour of victory to defeat; from the cry of anguish to the exultation of victory—in these he hoped to find at least the relief of distraction: but here too he was disappointed. The giant fang of apprehension now seized him who had never before known fear: each drop of blood that sprayed upon him seemed the cold blood that had gushed from Brunhilda's wound; each dying wretch that fell beside him looked like her, when expiring, she exclaimed: "Thou too art doomed to perdition," so that the aspect of death seemed more full of dread to him than aught beside, and this unconquerable terror compelled him to abandon the battle-field. At length, after many a weary and fruitless wandering he returned to his castle. Here all was deserted and silent, as if the sword, or a still more deadly pestilence had laid every thing waste: for the few inhabitants that still remained, and even those servants who had once shewn themselves the most attached, now fled from him, as though he had been branded with the mark of Cain. With horror he perceived that, by uniting himself as he had done with the dead, he had cut himself off from the living, who refused to hold any intercourse with him. Often, when he stood on the battlements of his castle, and looked down upon desolate fields, he compared their present solitude with the lively activity they were wont to exhibit, under the strict but benevolent discipline of Swanhilda. He now felt that she alone could reconcile him to life, but durst he hope that one, whom he had so deeply aggrieved, could pardon him, and receive him again? Impatience at length got the better of fear; he sought Swanhilda, and, with the deepest contrition, acknowledged his complicated guilt; embracing her knees he beseeched her to pardon him, and to return to his desolate castle, in order that it might again become the abode of contentment and peace. The pale form which she beheld at her feet, the shadow of the lately blooming youth, touched Swanhilda. "Thy folly," said she gently, "though it has caused me much sorrow, has never excited my resentment or my anger. But say, where are my children? To this dreadful interrogation the agonized father could for a while frame no reply: at length he was obliged to confess the dreadful truth. "Then we are asundered forever," returned Swanhilda; nor could all his tears or supplications prevail upon her to revoke the sentence she had given.

Stripped of his last earthly hope, bereft of his last consolation, and thereby rendered as poor as mortal can possibly be on this side of the grave, Walter returned homewards; when, as he was riding through the forest in the neighborhood of his castle, absorbed in his gloomy meditations, the sudden sound of a horn roused him from his reverie. Shortly after he saw appear a female figure clad in black, and mounted on a steed of the same color: her attire was like that of a huntress, but, instead of a falcon she bore a raven on her hand; and she was attended by a gay troop of cavaliers and dames. The first salutations being passed, he found that she was proceeding the same road as himself; and, when she found that Walter's castle was close at hand, she requested that he would lodge her for that night, the evening being far advanced. Most willingly did he comply with this request, since the appearance of the beautiful stranger had struck him greatly; so wonderfully did she resemble Swanhilda, except that her locks were brown, and her eye dark and full of fire. With a sumptuous banquet did he entertain his guests, whose mirth and songs enlivened the lately silent halls. Three days did this revelry continue, and so exhilarating did it prove to Walter, that he seemed to have forgotten his sorrows and his fears; nor could he prevail upon himself to dismiss his visitors, dreading lest, on their departure, the castle would seem a hundred times more desolate than before, and his grief be proportionably increased. At his earnest request, the stranger consented to stay seven days, and again another seven days. Without being requested, she took upon herself the superintendence of the household, which she regulated as discreetly and cheerfully as Swanhilda had been wont to do, so that the castle, which had so lately been the abode of melancholy and horror, became the residence of pleasure and festivity, and Walter's grief disappeared altogether in the midst of so much gaiety. Daily did his attachment to the fair unknown increase; he even made her his confidante; and, one evening as they were walking together apart from any of her train, he related to her his melancholy and frightful history. "My dear friend," returned she, as soon as he had finished his tale, "it ill beseems a man of thy discretion to afflict thyself, on account of all this. Thou hast awakened the dead from the sleep of the grave, and afterwards found,—what might have been anticipated, that the dead possess no sympathy with life. What then? thou wilt not commit this error a second time. Thou hast however murdered the being whom thou hadst thus recalled again into existence—but it was only in appearance, for thou couldst not deprive that of life, which properly had none. Thou hast too, lost a wife and two children: but, at your years, such a loss is most easily repaired. There are beauties who will gladly share your couch, and make you again a father. But you dread the reckoning of hereafter:—go, open the graves and ask the sleepers there whether that hereafter disturbs them." In such manner would she frequently exhort and cheer Walter, and, so successful were her efforts, that, in a short time, his melancholy entirely disappeared. He now ventured to declare to the unknown the passion with which she had inspired him, nor did she refuse him her hand. Within seven days afterwards the nuptials were celebrated with the utmost magnificence: with the first dawn of day commenced the labors of those who were busied in preparing the festival; and, if the walls of the castle had often echoed before to the sounds of mirth and revelry, the very foundations now seemed to rock from the wild tumultuous uproar of unrestrained riot. The wine streamed in abundance; the goblets circled incessantly: intemperance reached its utmost bounds, while shouts of laughter, almost resembling madness, burst from the numerous train belonging to the unknown. At length Walter, heated with wine and love, conducted his bride into the nuptial chamber: but, oh horror! scarcely had he clasped her in his arms, ere she transformed herself into a monstrous serpent, which, entwining him in its horrid folds, crushed him to death. Flames crackled on every side of the apartment; in a few minutes after, the whole castle was enveloped in a blaze that consumed it entirely: while, as the walls fell in with a horrid crash, a voice exclaimed aloud—"WAKE NOT THE DEAD."

CLARIMONDE

Théophile Gautier

TRANSLATED BY LAFCADIO HEARN

first published as "La morte amoureuse" in *La Chronique de Paris* (June 1836)

translation first published in *Clarimonde and Other Stories* (1908)

Brother, you ask me if I have ever loved. Yes. My story is a strange and terrible one; and though I am sixty-six years of age, I scarcely dare even now to disturb the ashes of that memory. To you I can refuse nothing; but I should not relate such a tale to any less experienced mind. So strange were the circumstances of my story, that I can scarcely believe myself to have ever actually been a party to them. For more than three years I remained the victim of a most singular and diabolical illusion. Poor country priest though I was, I led every night in a dream—would to God it had been all a dream!—a most worldly life, a damning life, a life of Sardanapalus. One single look too freely cast upon a woman well-nigh caused me to lose my soul; but finally by the grace of God and the assistance of my patron saint, I succeeded in casting out the evil spirit that possessed me. My daily life was long interwoven with a nocturnal life of a totally different character. By day I was a priest of the Lord, occupied with prayer and sacred things; by night, from the instant that I closed my eyes I became a young nobleman, a fine connoisseur in women, dogs, and horses; gambling, drinking, and blaspheming; and when I awoke at early daybreak, it seemed to me, on the other hand, that I had been sleeping, and had only dreamed that I was a priest. Of this somnambulistic life there now remains to me only the recollection of certain scenes and words which I cannot banish from my memory; but although I never actually left the walls of my presbytery, one would think to hear me speak that I were a man who, weary of all worldly pleasures, had become a religious, seeking to end a tempestuous life in the service of God, rather than a humble seminarist who has grown old in this obscure curacy, situated in the depths of the woods and even isolated from the life of the century.

Yes, I have loved as none in the world ever loved—with an insensate and furious passion—so violent that I am astonished it did not cause my heart to burst asunder. Ah, what nights—what nights!

From my earliest childhood I had felt a vocation to the priesthood, so that all my studies were directed with that idea in view. Up to the age of twenty-four my life had been only a prolonged novitiate. Having completed my course of theology I successively received all the minor orders, and my superiors judged me worthy, despite my youth, to pass the last awful degree. My ordination was fixed for Easter week.

I had never gone into the world. My world was confined by the walls of the college and the seminary. I knew in a vague sort of a way that there was something called Woman, but I never permitted my thoughts to dwell on such a subject, and I lived in a state of perfect innocence. Twice a year only I saw my infirm and aged mother, and in those visits were comprised my sole relations with the outer world.

I regretted nothing; I felt not the least hesitation at taking the last irrevocable step; I was filled with joy and impatience. Never did a betrothed lover count the slow hours with more feverish ardor; I slept only to dream that I was saying mass; I believed there could be nothing in the world more delightful than to be a priest; I would have refused to be a king or a poet in preference. My ambition could conceive of no loftier aim.

I tell you this in order to show you that what happened to me could not have happened in the natural order of things, and to enable you to understand that I was the victim of an inexplicable fascination.

At last the great day came. I walked to the church with a step so light that I fancied myself sustained in air, or that I had wings upon my shoulders. I believed myself an angel, and wondered at the sombre and thoughtful faces of my companions, for there were several of us. I had passed all the night in prayer, and was in a condition well-nigh bordering on ecstasy. The bishop, a venerable old man, seemed to me God the Father leaning over His Eternity, and I beheld Heaven through the vault of the temple.

You well know the details of that ceremony—the benediction, the communion under both forms, the anointing of the palms of the hands with the Oil of Catechumens, and then the holy sacrifice offered in concert with the bishop.

Ah, truly spake Job when he declared that the imprudent man is one who hath not made a covenant with his eyes! I accidentally lifted my head, which until then I had kept down, and beheld before me, so close that it seemed that I could have touched her—although she was actually a considerable distance from me and on the further side of the sanctuary railing—a young woman of extraordinary beauty, and attired with royal magnificence. It seemed as though scales had suddenly fallen from my eyes. I felt like a blind man who unexpectedly recovers his sight. The bishop, so radiantly glorious but an instant before, suddenly vanished away, the tapers paled upon their golden candlesticks like stars in the dawn, and a vast darkness seemed to fill the whole church. The charming creature appeared in bright relief against the background of that darkness, like some angelic revelation. She seemed herself radiant, and radiating light rather than receiving it.

I lowered my eyelids, firmly resolved not to again open them, that I might not be influenced by external objects, for distraction had gradually taken possession of me until I hardly knew what I was doing.

In another minute, nevertheless, I reopened my eyes, for through my eyelashes I still beheld her, all sparkling with prismatic colors, and surrounded with such a penumbra as one beholds in gazing at the sun.

Oh, how beautiful she was! The greatest painters, who followed ideal beauty into heaven itself, and thence brought back to earth the true portrait of the Madonna, never in their delineations even approached that wildly beautiful reality which I saw before me. Neither the verses of the poet nor the palette of the artist could convey any conception of her. She was rather tall, with a form and bearing of a goddess. Her hair, of a soft blonde hue, was parted in the midst and flowed back over her temples in two rivers of rippling gold; she seemed a diademed queen. Her forehead, bluish-white in its transparency, extended its calm breadth above the arches of her eyebrows, which by a strange singularity were almost black, and admirably relieved the effect of sea-green eyes of unsustainable vivacity and brilliancy. What eyes! With a single flash they could have decided a man's destiny. They had a life, a limpidity, an ardor, a humid light which I have never seen in human eyes; they shot forth rays like arrows, which I could distinctly *see* enter my heart. I know not if the fire which illumined them came from heaven or from hell, but assuredly it came from one or the other. That woman was either an angel or a demon, perhaps both. Assuredly she never sprang from the flank of Eve, our common mother. Teeth of the most lustrous pearl gleamed in her ruddy smile, and at every inflection of her lips little dimples appeared in the satiny rose of her adorable cheeks. There was a delicacy and pride in the regal outline of her nostrils bespeaking noble blood. Agate gleams played over the smooth lustrous skin of her half-bare shoulders, and strings of great blonde pearls—almost equal to her neck in beauty of color—descended upon her bosom. From time to time she elevated her head with the undulating grace of a startled serpent or peacock, thereby imparting a quivering motion to the high lace ruff which surrounded it like a silver trellis-work.

She wore a robe of orange-red velvet, and from her wide ermine-lined sleeves there peeped forth patrician hands of infinite delicacy, and so ideally transparent that, like the fingers of Aurora, they permitted the light to shine through them.

All these details I can recollect at this moment as plainly as though they were of yesterday, for notwithstanding I was greatly troubled at the time, nothing escaped me; the faintest touch of shading, the little dark speck at the point of the chin, the imperceptible down at the corners of the lips, the velvety floss upon the brow, the quivering shadows of the eyelashes upon the cheeks—I could notice everything with astonishing lucidity of perception.

And gazing I felt opening within me gates that had until then remained closed; vents long obstructed became all clear, permitting glimpses of unfamiliar perspectives within; life suddenly made itself visible to me under a totally novel aspect. I felt as though I had just been born into a new world and a new order of things. A frightful anguish commenced to torture-my heart as with red-hot pincers. Every successive minute seemed to me at once but a second and yet a century. Meanwhile the ceremony was proceeding, and I shortly found myself transported far from that world of which my newly born desires were furiously besieging the entrance. Nevertheless I answered "Yes" when I wished to say "No," though all within me protested against the violence done to my soul by my tongue. Some occult power seemed to force the words from my throat against my will. Thus it is, perhaps, that so many young girls walk to the altar firmly resolved to refuse in a startling manner the husband imposed upon them, and that yet not one ever fulfills her intention. Thus it is, doubtless, that so many poor novices take the veil, though they have resolved to tear it into shreds at the moment when called upon to utter the vows. One dares not thus cause so great a scandal to all present, nor deceive the expectation of so many people. All those eyes, all those wills seem to weigh down upon you like a cope of lead, and, moreover, measures have been so well taken, everything has been so thoroughly arranged beforehand and after a fashion so evidently irrevocable, that the will yields to the weight of circumstances and utterly breaks down.

As the ceremony proceeded the features of the fair unknown changed their expression. Her look had at first been one of caressing tenderness; it changed to an air of disdain and of mortification, as though at not having been able to make itself understood.

With an effort of will sufficient to have uprooted a mountain, I strove to cry out that I would not be a priest, but I could not speak; my tongue seemed nailed to my palate, and I found it impossible to express my will by the least syllable of negation. Though fully awake, I felt like one under the influence of a nightmare, who vainly strives to shriek out the one word upon which life depends.

She seemed conscious of the martyrdom I was undergoing, and, as though to encourage me, she gave me a look replete with divinest promise. Her eyes were a poem; their every glance was a song.

She said to me:

"If thou wilt be mine, I shall make thee happier than God Himself in His paradise. The angels themselves will be jealous of thee. Tear off that funeral shroud in which thou art about to wrap thyself. I am Beauty, I am Youth, I am Life. Come to me! Together we shall be Love. Can Jehovah offer thee aught in exchange? Our lives will flow on like a dream, in one eternal kiss.

"Fling forth the wine of that chalice, and thou art free. I will conduct thee to the Unknown Isles. Thou shalt sleep in my bosom upon a bed of massy gold under a silver pavilion, for I love thee and would take thee away from thy God, before whom so many noble hearts pour forth floods of love which never reach even the steps of His throne!"

These words seemed to float to my ears in a rhythm of infinite sweetness, for her look was actually sonorous, and the utterances of her eyes were reechoed in the depths of my heart as though living lips had breathed them into my life. I felt myself willing to renounce God, and yet my tongue mechanically fulfilled all the formalities of the ceremony. The fair one gave me another look, so beseeching, so despairing that keen blades seemed to pierce my heart, and I felt my bosom transfixed by more swords than those of Our Lady of Sorrows.

All was consummated; I had become a priest.

Never was deeper anguish painted on human face than upon hers. The maiden who beholds her affianced lover suddenly fall dead at her side, the mother bending over the empty cradle of her child, Eve seated at the threshold of the gate of Paradise, the miser who finds a stone substituted for his stolen treasure, the poet who accidentally permits the only manuscript of his finest work to fall into the fire, could not wear a look so despairing, so inconsolable. All the blood had abandoned her charming face, leaving it whiter than marble; her beautiful arms hung lifelessly on either side of her body as though their muscles had suddenly relaxed, and she sought the support of a pillar, for her yielding limbs almost betrayed her. As for myself, I staggered toward the door of the church, livid as death, my forehead bathed with a sweat bloodier than that of Calvary; I felt as though I were being strangled; the vault seemed to have flattened down upon my shoulders, and it seemed to me that my head alone sustained the whole weight of the dome.

As I was about to cross the threshold a hand suddenly caught mine—a woman's hand! I had never till then touched the hand of any woman. It was cold as a serpent's skin, and yet its impress remained upon my wrist, burnt there as though branded by a glowing iron. It was she. "Unhappy man! Unhappy man! What hast thou done?" she exclaimed in a low voice, and immediately disappeared in the crowd.

The aged bishop passed by. He cast a severe and scrutinizing look upon me. My face presented the wildest aspect imaginable: I blushed and turned pale alternately; dazzling lights flashed before my eyes. A companion took pity on me. He seized my arm and led me out. I could not possibly have found my way back to the seminary unassisted. At the corner of a street, while the young priest's attention was momentarily turned in another direction, a Negro page, fantastically garbed, approached me, and without pausing on his way slipped into my hand a little pocket-book with gold-embroidered corners, at the same time giving me a sign to hide it. I concealed it in my sleeve, and there kept it until I found myself alone in my cell. Then I opened the clasp. There were only two leaves within, bearing the words, "Clarimonde, at the Concini Palace." So little acquainted was I at that time with the things of this world that I had never heard of Clarimonde, celebrated as she was, and I had no idea as to where the Concini Palace was situated. I hazarded a thousand conjectures, each more extravagant than the last; but, in truth, I cared little whether she were a great lady or a courtesan, so that I could but see her once more.

My love, although the growth of a single hour, had taken imperishable root. I did not even dream of attempting to tear it up, so fully was I convinced such a thing would be impossible. That woman had completely taken possession of me. One look from her had sufficed to change my very nature. She had breathed her will into my life, and I no longer lived in myself, but in her and for her. I gave myself up to a thousand extravagancies. I kissed the place upon my hand which she had touched, and I repeated her name over and over again for hours in succession. I only needed to close my eyes in order to see her distinctly as though she were actually present; and I reiterated to myself the words she had uttered in my ear at the church porch: "Unhappy man! Unhappy man! What hast thou done?" I comprehended at last the full horror of my situation, and the funereal and awful restraints of the state into which I had just entered became clearly revealed to me. To be a priest!—that is, to be chaste, to never love, to observe no distinction of sex or age, to turn from the sight of all beauty, to put out one's own eyes, to hide forever crouching in the chill shadows of some church or cloister, to visit none but the dying, to watch by unknown corpses, and ever bear about with one the black soutane as a garb of mourning for oneself, so that your very dress might serve as a pall for your coffin.

And I felt life rising within me like a subterranean lake, expanding and overflowing; my blood leaped fiercely through my arteries; my long-restrained youth suddenly burst into active being, like the aloe which blooms but once in a hundred years, and then bursts into blossom with a clap of thunder.

What could I do in order to see Clarimonde once more? I had no pretext to offer for desiring to leave the seminary, not knowing any person in the city. I would not even be able to remain there but a short time, and was only waiting my assignment to the curacy which I must thereafter occupy. I tried to remove the bars of the window; but it was at a fearful height from the ground, and I found that as I had no ladder it would be useless to think of escaping thus. And, furthermore, I could descend thence only by night in any event, and afterward how should I be able to find my way through the inextricable labyrinth of streets? All these difficulties, which to many would have appeared altogether insignificant, were gigantic to me, a poor seminarist who had fallen in love only the day before for the first time, without experience, without money, without attire.

"Ah!" cried I to myself in my blindness, "were I not a priest I could have seen her every day; I might have been her lover, her spouse. Instead of being wrapped in this dismal shroud of mine I would have had garments of silk and velvet, golden chains, a sword, and fair plumes like other handsome young cavaliers. My hair, instead of being dishonored by the tonsure, would flow down upon my neck in waving curls; I would have a fine waxed mustache; I would be a gallant." But one hour passed before an altar, a few hastily articulated words, had forever cut me off from the number of the living, and I had myself sealed down the stone of my own tomb; I had with my own hand bolted the gate of my prison! I went to the window. The sky was beautifully blue; the trees had donned their spring robes; nature seemed to be making parade of an ironical joy. The *Place* was filled with people, some going, others coming; young beaux and young beauties were sauntering in couples toward the groves and gardens; merry youths passed by, cheerily trolling refrains of drinking-songs—it was all a picture of vivacity, life, animation, gaiety, which formed a bitter contrast with my mourning and my solitude. On the steps of the gate sat a young mother playing with her child. She kissed its little rosy mouth still impearled with drops of milk, and performed, in order to amuse it, a thousand divine little puerilities such as only mothers know how to invent. The father standing at a little distance smiled gently upon the charming group, and with folded arms seemed to hug his joy to his heart. I could not endure that spectacle. I closed the window with violence, and flung myself on my bed, my heart filled with frightful hate and jealousy, and gnawed my fingers and my bedcovers like a tiger that has passed ten days without food.

I know not how long I remained in this condition, but at last, while writhing on the bed in a fit of spasmodic fury, I suddenly perceived the Abbé Sérapion, who was standing erect in the center of the room, watching me attentively. Filled with shame of myself, I let my head fall upon my breast and covered my face with my hands.

"Romuald, my friend, something very extraordinary is transpiring within you," observed Sérapion, after a few moments' silence; "your conduct is altogether inexplicable. You—always so quiet, so pious, so gentle—you to rage in your cell like a wild beast! Take heed, brother—do not listen to the suggestions of the devil The Evil Spirit, furious that you have consecrated yourself forever to the Lord, is prowling around you like a ravening wolf and making a last effort to obtain possession of you. Instead of allowing yourself to be conquered, my dear Romuald, make to yourself a cuirass of prayers, a buckler of mortifications, and combat the enemy like a valiant man; you will then assuredly overcome him. Virtue must be proved by temptation, and gold comes forth purer from the hands of the assayer. Fear not. Never allow yourself to become discouraged. The most watchful and steadfast souls are at moments liable to such temptation. Pray, fast, meditate, and the Evil Spirit will depart from you."

The words of the Abbé Sérapion restored me to myself, and I became a little more calm. "I came," he continued, "to tell you that you have been appointed to the curacy of C———. The priest who had charge of it has just died, and Monseigneur the Bishop has ordered me to have you installed there at once. Be ready, therefore, to start tomorrow." I responded with an inclination of the head, and the Abbé retired. I opened my missal and commenced reading some prayers, but the letters became confused and blurred under my eyes, the thread of the ideas entangled itself hopelessly in my brain, and the volume at last fell from my hands without my being aware of it.

To leave tomorrow without having been able to see her again, to add yet another barrier to the many already interposed between us, to lose forever all hope of being able to meet her, except, indeed, through a miracle! Even to write to her, alas! would be impossible, for by whom could I dispatch my letter? With my sacred character of priest, to whom could I dare unbosom myself, in whom could I confide? I became a prey to the bitterest anxiety.

Then suddenly recurred to me the words of the Abbé Sérapion regarding the artifices of the devil; and the strange character of the adventure, the supernatural beauty of Clarimonde, the phosphoric light of her eyes, the burning imprint of her hand, the agony into which she had thrown me, the sudden change wrought within me when all my piety vanished in a single instant—these and other things clearly testified to the work of the Evil One, and perhaps that satiny hand was but the glove which concealed his claws. Filled with terror at these fancies, I again picked up the missal which had slipped from my knees and fallen upon the floor, and once more gave myself up to prayer.

Next morning Sérapion came to take me away. Two mules freighted with our miserable valises awaited us at the gate. He mounted one, and I the other as well as I knew how.

As we passed along the streets of the city, I gazed attentively at all the windows and balconies in the hope of seeing Clarimonde, but it was yet early in the morning, and the city had hardly opened its eyes. Mine sought to penetrate the blinds and window-curtains of all the palaces before which we were passing. Sérapion doubtless attributed this curiosity to my admiration of the architecture, for he slackened the pace of his animal in order to give me time to look around me. At last we passed the city gates and commenced to mount the hill beyond. When we arrived at its summit I turned to take a last look at the place where Clarimonde dwelt. The shadow of a great cloud hung over all the city; the contrasting colors of its blue and red roofs were lost in the uniform half-tint, through which here and there floated upward, like white flakes of foam, the smoke of freshly kindled fires. By a singular optical effect one edifice, which surpassed in height all the neighboring buildings that were still dimly veiled by the vapors, towered up, fair and lustrous with the gilding of a solitary beam of sunlight—although actually more than a league away it seemed quite near. The smallest details of its architecture were plainly distinguishable—the turrets, the platforms, the window-casements, and even the swallow-tailed weather-vanes.

"What is that palace I see over there, all lighted up by the sun?" I asked Sérapion. He shaded his eyes with his hand, and having looked in the direction indicated, replied: "It is the ancient palace which the Prince Concini has given to the courtesan Clarimonde. Awful things are done there!"

At that instant, I know not yet whether it was a reality or an illusion, I fancied I saw gliding along the terrace a shapely white figure, which gleamed for a moment in passing and as quickly vanished. It was Clarimonde.

Oh, did she know that at that very hour, all feverish and restless—from the height of the rugged road which separated me from her, and which, alas! I could never more descend—I was directing my eyes upon the palace where she dwelt, and which a mocking beam of sunlight seemed to bring nigh to me, as though inviting me to enter therein as its lord? Undoubtedly she must have known it, for her soul was too sympathetically united with mine not to have felt its least emotional thrill, and that subtle sympathy it must have been which prompted her to climb—although clad only in her nightdress—to the summit of the terrace, amid the icy dews of the morning.

The shadow gained the palace, and the scene became to the eye only a motionless ocean of roofs and gables, amid which one mountainous undulation was distinctly visible. Sérapion urged his mule forward, my own at once followed at the same gait, and a sharp angle in the road at last hid the city of S——— forever from my eyes, as I was destined never to return thither. At the close of a weary three-days' journey through dismal country fields, we caught sight of the cock upon the steeple of the church which I was to take charge of, peeping above the trees, and after having followed some winding roads fringed with thatched cottages and little gardens, we found ourselves in front of the façade, which certainly possessed few features of magnificence. A porch ornamented with some moldings, and two or three pillars rudely hewn from sandstone; a tiled roof with counterforts of the same sandstone as the pillars—that was all. To the left lay the cemetery, overgrown with high weeds, and having a great iron cross rising up in its centre; to the right stood the presbytery under the shadow of the church. It was a house of the most extreme simplicity and frigid cleanliness. We entered the enclosure. A few chickens were picking up some oats scattered upon the ground; accustomed, seemingly, to the black habit of ecclesiastics, they showed no fear of our presence and scarcely troubled themselves to get out of our way. A hoarse, wheezy barking fell upon our ears, and we saw an aged dog running toward us.

It was my predecessor's dog. He had dull bleared eyes, grizzled hair, and every mark of the greatest age to which a dog can possibly attain. I patted him gently, and he proceeded at once to march along beside me with an air of satisfaction unspeakable. A very old woman, who had been the housekeeper of the former curé, also came to meet us, and after having invited me into a little back parlor, asked whether I intended to retain her. I replied that I would take care of her, and the dog, and the chickens, and all the furniture her master had bequeathed her at his death. At this she became fairly transported with joy, and the Abbé Sérapion at once paid her the price which she asked for her little property.

As soon as my installation was over, the Abbé Sérapion returned to the seminary. I was, therefore, left alone, with no one but myself to look to for aid or counsel. The thought of Clarimonde again began to haunt me, and in spite of all my endeavours to banish it, I always found it present in my meditations. One evening, while promenading in my little garden along the walks bordered with box-plants, I fancied that I saw through the elm-trees the figure of a woman, who followed my every movement, and that I beheld two sea-green eyes gleaming through the foliage; but it was only an illusion, and on going round to the other side of the garden, I could find nothing except a footprint on the sanded walk—a footprint so small that it seemed to have been made by the foot of a child. The garden was enclosed by very high walls. I searched every nook and corner of it, but could discover no one there. I have never succeeded in fully accounting for this circumstance, which, after all, was nothing compared with the strange things which happened to me afterward.

For a whole year I lived thus, filling all the duties of my calling with the most scrupulous exactitude, praying and fasting, exhorting and lending ghostly aid to the sick, and bestowing alms even to the extent of frequently depriving myself of the very necessaries of life. But I felt a great aridness within me, and the sources of grace seemed closed against me. I never found that happiness which should spring from the fulfillment of a holy mission; my thoughts were far away, and the words of Clarimonde were ever upon my lips like an involuntary refrain. Oh, brother, meditate well on this! Through having but once lifted my eyes to look upon a woman, through one fault apparently so venial, I have for years remained a victim to the most miserable agonies, and the happiness of my life has been destroyed forever.

I will not longer dwell upon those defeats, or on those inward victories invariably followed by yet more terrible falls, but will at once proceed to the facts of my story. One night my door-bell was long and violently rung. The aged housekeeper arose and opened to the stranger, and the figure of a man, whose complexion was deeply bronzed, and who was richly clad in a foreign costume, with a poniard at his girdle, appeared under the rays of Barbara's lantern. Her first impulse was one of terror, but the stranger reassured her, and stated that he desired to see me at once on matters relating to my holy calling. Barbara invited him upstairs, where I was on the point of retiring. The stranger told me that his mistress, a very noble lady, was lying at the point of death, and desired to see a priest. I replied that I was prepared to follow him, took with me the sacred articles necessary for extreme unction, and descended in all haste. Two horses black as the night itself stood without the gate, pawing the ground with impatience, and veiling their chests with long streams of smoky vapor exhaled from their nostrils. He held the stirrup and aided me to mount upon one; then, merely laying his hand upon the pommel of the saddle, he vaulted on the other, pressed the animal's sides with his knees, and loosened rein. The horse bounded forward with the velocity of an arrow. Mine, of which the stranger held the bridle, also started off at a swift gallop, keeping up with his companion. We devoured the road. The ground flowed backward beneath us in a long streaked line of pale gray, and the black silhouettes of the trees seemed fleeing by us on either side like an army in rout. We passed through a forest so profoundly gloomy that I felt my flesh creep in the chill darkness with superstitious fear. The showers of bright sparks which flew from the stony road under the ironshod feet of our horses remained glowing in our wake like a fiery trail; and had any one at that hour of the night beheld us both—my guide and myself—he must have taken us for two specters riding upon nightmares. Witch-fires ever and anon flitted across the road before us, and the night-birds shrieked fearsomely in the depth of the woods beyond, where we beheld at intervals glow the phosphorescent eyes of wild cats. The manes of the horses became more and more disheveled, the sweat streamed over their flanks, and their breath came through their nostrils hard and fast. But when he found them slacking pace, the guide reanimated them by uttering a strange, guttural, unearthly cry, and the gallop recommenced with fury. At last the whirlwind race ceased; a huge black mass pierced through with many bright points of light suddenly rose before us, the hoofs of our horses echoed louder upon a strong wooden drawbridge, and we rode under a great vaulted archway which darkly yawned between two enormous towers. Some great excitement evidently reigned in the castle. Servants with torches were crossing the courtyard in every direction, and above lights were ascending and descending from landing to landing. I obtained a confused glimpse of vast masses of architecture— columns, arcades, flights of steps, stairways—a royal voluptuousness and elfin magnificence of construction worthy of fairyland. A Negro page—the same who had before brought me the tablet from Clarimonde, and whom I instantly recognized—approached to aid me in dismounting, and the major-domo, attired in black velvet with a gold chain about his neck, advanced to meet me, supporting himself upon an ivory cane. Large tears were falling from his eyes and streaming over his cheeks and white beard. "Too late!" he cried, sorrowfully shaking his venerable head. "Too late, sir priest! But if you have not been able to save the soul, come at least to watch by the poor body."

He took my arm and conducted me to the death-chamber. I wept not less bitterly than he, for I had learned that the dead one was none other than that Clarimonde whom I had so deeply and so wildly loved. A *prie-dieu* stood at the foot of the bed; a bluish flame flickering in a bronze pattern filled all the room with a wan, deceptive light, here and there bringing out in the darkness at intervals some projection of furniture or cornice. In a chiseled urn upon the table there was a faded white rose, whose leaves—excepting one that still held —had all fallen, like odorous tears, to the foot of the vase. A broken black mask, a fan, and disguises of every variety, which were lying on the armchairs, bore witness that death had entered suddenly and unannounced into that sumptuous dwelling. Without daring to cast my eyes upon the bed, I knelt down and commenced to repeat the Psalms for the Dead, with exceeding fervor, thanking God that He had placed the tomb between me and the memory of this woman, so that I might thereafter be able to utter her name in my prayers as a name forever sanctified by death. But my fervor gradually weakened, and I fell insensibly into a reverie. That chamber bore no semblance to a chamber of death. In lieu of the fetid and cadaverous odors which I had been accustomed to breathe during such funereal vigils, a languorous vapor of Oriental perfume—I know not what amorous odor of woman—softly floated through the tepid air. That pale light seemed rather a twilight gloom contrived for voluptuous pleasure, than a substitute for the yellow-flickering watch-tapers which shine by the side of corpses. I thought upon the strange destiny which enabled me to meet Clarimonde again at the very moment when she was lost to me forever, and a sigh of regretful anguish escaped from my breast. Then it seemed to me that someone behind me had also sighed, and I turned round to look. It was only an echo. But in that moment my eyes fell upon the bed of death which they had till then avoided. The red damask curtains, decorated with large flowers worked in embroidery and looped up with gold bullion, permitted me to behold the fair dead, lying at full length, with hands joined upon her bosom. She was covered with a linen wrapping of dazzling whiteness, which formed a strong contrast with the gloomy purple of the hangings, and was of so fine a texture that it concealed nothing of her body's charming form, and allowed the eye to follow those beautiful outlines—undulating like the neck of a swan—which even death had not robbed of their supple grace. She seemed an alabaster statue executed by some skillful sculptor to place upon the tomb of a queen, or rather, perhaps, like a slumbering maiden over whom the silent snow had woven a spotless veil.

I could no longer maintain my constrained attitude of prayer. The air of the alcove intoxicated me, that febrile perfume of half-faded roses penetrated my very brain, and I commenced to pace restlessly up and down the chamber, pausing at each turn before the bier to contemplate the graceful corpse lying beneath the transparency of its shroud. Wild fancies came thronging to my brain. I thought to myself that she might not, perhaps, be really dead; that she might only have feigned death for the purpose of bringing me to her castle, and then declaring her love. At one time I even thought I saw her foot move under the whiteness of the coverings, and slightly disarrange the long straight folds of the winding-sheet.

And then I asked myself: "Is this indeed Clarimonde? What proof have I that it is she? Might not that black page have passed into the service of some other lady? Surely, I must be going mad to torture and afflict myself thus!" But my heart answered with a fierce throbbing: "It is she; it is she indeed!" I approached the bed again, and fixed my eyes with redoubled attention upon the object of my incertitude. Ah, must I confess it? That exquisite perfection of bodily form, although purified and made sacred by the shadow of death, affected me more voluptuously than it should have done; and that repose so closely resembled slumber that one might well have mistaken it for such. I forgot that I had come there to perform a funeral ceremony; I fancied myself a young bridegroom entering the chamber of the bride, who all modestly hides her fair face, and through coyness seeks to keep herself wholly veiled. Heartbroken with grief, yet wild with hope, shuddering at once with fear and pleasure, I bent over her and grasped the corner of the sheet. I lifted it back, holding my breath all the while through fear of waking her. My arteries throbbed with such violence that I felt them hiss through my temples, and the sweat poured from my forehead in streams, as though I had lifted a mighty slab of marble. There, indeed, lay Clarimonde, even as I had seen her at the church on the day of my ordination. She was not less charming than then. With her, death seemed but a last coquetry. The pallor of her cheeks, the less brilliant carnation of her lips, her long eyelashes lowered and relieving their dark fringe against that white skin, lent her an unspeakably seductive aspect of melancholy chastity and mental suffering; her long loose hair, still intertwined with some little blue flowers, made a shining pillow for her head, and veiled the nudity of her shoulders with its thick ringlets; her beautiful hands, purer, more diaphanous, than the Host, were crossed on her bosom in an attitude of pious rest and silent prayer, which served to counteract all that might have proven otherwise too alluring—even after death—in the exquisite roundness and ivory polish of her bare arms from which the pearl bracelets had not yet been removed. I remained long in mute contemplation, and the more I gazed, the less could I persuade myself that life had really abandoned that beautiful body forever. I do not know whether it was an illusion or a reflection of the lamplight, but it seemed to me that the blood was again commencing to circulate under that lifeless pallor, although she remained all motionless. I laid my hand lightly on her arm; it was cold, but not colder than her hand on the day when it touched mine at the portals of the church. I resumed my position, bending my face above her, and bathing her cheek with the warm dew of my tears. Ah, what bitter feelings of despair and helplessness, what agonies unutterable did I endure in that long watch! Vainly did I wish that I could have gathered all my life into one mass that I might give it all to her, and breathe into her chill remains the flame which devoured me. The night advanced, and feeling the moment of eternal separation approach, I could not deny myself the last sad sweet pleasure of imprinting a kiss upon the dead lips of her who had been my only love... Oh, miracle! A faint breath mingled itself with my breath, and the mouth of Clarimonde responded to the passionate pressure of mine. Her eyes unclosed, and lighted up with something of their former brilliancy; she uttered a long sigh, and uncrossing her arms, passed them around my neck with a look of ineffable delight. "Ah, it is thou, Romuald!" she murmured in a voice languishingly sweet as the last vibrations of a harp. "What ailed thee, dearest? I waited so long for thee that I am dead; but we are now betrothed: I can see thee and visit thee. Adieu, Romuald, adieu! I love thee. That is all I wished to tell thee, and I give thee back the life which thy kiss for a moment recalled. We shall soon meet again."

Her head fell back, but her arms yet encircled me, as though to retain me still. A furious whirlwind suddenly burst in the window, and entered the chamber. The last remaining leaf of the white rose for a moment palpitated at the extremity of the stalk like a butterfly's wing, then it detached itself and

flew forth through the open casement, bearing with it the soul of
Clarimonde. The lamp was extinguished, and I fell insensible upon the bosom
of the beautiful dead.

When I came to myself again I was lying on the bed in my little room at
the presbytery, and the old dog of the former curé was licking my hand,
which had been hanging down outside of the covers. Barbara, all trembling
with age and anxiety, was busying herself about the room, opening and
shutting drawers, and emptying powders into glasses. On seeing me open my
eyes, the old woman uttered a cry of joy, the dog yelped and wagged his tail,
but I was still so weak that I could not speak a single word or make the
slightest motion. Afterward I learned that I had lain thus for three days,
giving no evidence of life beyond the faintest respiration. Those three days do
not reckon in my life, nor could I ever imagine whither my spirit had
departed during those three days; I have no recollection of aught relating to
them. Barbara told me that the same coppery-complexioned man who came
to seek me on the night of my departure from the presbytery had brought me
back the next morning in a close litter, and departed immediately afterward.
When I became able to collect my scattered thoughts, I reviewed within my
mind all the circumstances of that fateful night. At first I thought I had been
the victim of some magical illusion, but ere long the recollection of other
circumstances, real and palpable in themselves, came to forbid that
supposition. I could not believe that I had been dreaming, since Barbara as
well as myself had seen the strange man with his two black horses, and
described with exactness every detail of his figure and apparel. Nevertheless it
appeared that none knew of any castle in the neighborhood answering to the
description of that in which I had again found Clarimonde.

One morning I found the Abbé Sérapion in my room. Barbara had
advised him that I was ill, and he had come with all speed to see me.
Although this haste on his part testified to an affectionate interest in me, yet
his visit did not cause me the pleasure which it should have done. The Abbé
Sérapion had something penetrating and inquisitorial in his gaze which made
me feel very ill at ease. His presence filled me with embarrassment and a
sense of guilt. At the first glance he divined my interior trouble, and I hated
him for his clairvoyance.

While he inquired after my health in hypocritically honeyed accents, he
constantly kept his two great yellow lion-eyes fixed upon me, and plunged his
look into my soul like a sounding-lead. Then he asked me how I directed my
parish, if I was happy in it, how I passed the leisure hours allowed me in the
intervals of pastoral duty, whether I had become acquainted with many of the
inhabitants of the place, what was my favorite reading, and a thousand other
such questions. I answered these inquiries as briefly as possible, and he,
without ever waiting for my answers, passed rapidly from one subject of
query to another. That conversation had evidently no connection with what
he actually wished to say. At last, without any premonition, but as though
repeating a piece of news which he had recalled on the instant, and feared

might otherwise be forgotten subsequently, he suddenly said, in a clear vibrant voice, which rang in my ears like the trumpets of the Last Judgment:

"The great courtesan Clarimonde died a few days ago, at the close of an orgy which lasted eight days and eight nights. It was something infernally splendid. The abominations of the banquets of Belshazzar and Cleopatra were reenacted there. Good God, what age are we living in? The guests were served by swarthy slaves who spoke an unknown tongue, and who seemed to me to be veritable demons. The livery of the very least among them would have served for the gala-dress of an emperor. There have always been very strange stories told of this Clarimonde, and all her lovers came to a violent or miserable end. They used to say that she was a ghoul, a female vampire; but I believe she was none other than Beelzebub himself."

He ceased to speak, and commenced to regard me more attentively than ever, as though to observe the effect of his words on me. I could not refrain from starting when I heard him utter the name of Clarimonde, and this news of her death, in addition to the pain it caused me by reason of its coincidence with the nocturnal scenes I had witnessed, filled me with an agony and terror which my face betrayed, despite my utmost endeavors to appear composed. Sérapion fixed an anxious and severe look upon me, and then observed: "My son, I must warn you that you are standing with foot raised upon the brink of an abyss; take heed lest you fall therein. Satan's claws are long, and tombs are not always true to their trust. The tombstone of Clarimonde should be sealed down with a triple seal, for, if report be true, it is not the first time she has died. May God watch over you, Romuald!"

And with these words the Abbé walked slowly to the door. I did not see him again at that time, for he left for S―――― almost immediately.

I became completely restored to health and resumed my accustomed duties. The memory of Clarimonde and the words of the old Abbé were constantly in my mind; nevertheless no extraordinary event had occurred to verify the funereal predictions of Sérapion, and I had commenced to believe that his fears and my own terrors were over-exaggerated, when one night I had a strange dream. I had hardly fallen asleep when I heard my bed-curtains drawn apart, as their rings slid back upon the curtain rod with a sharp sound. I rose up quickly upon my elbow, and beheld the shadow of a woman standing erect before me. I recognized Clarimonde immediately. She bore in her hand a little lamp, shaped like those which are placed in tombs, and its light lent her fingers a rosy transparency, which extended itself by lessening degrees even to the opaque and milky whiteness of her bare arm. Her only garment was the linen winding-sheet which had shrouded her when lying upon the bed of death. She sought to gather its folds over her bosom as though ashamed of being so scantily clad, but her little hand was not equal to the task. She was so white that the color of the drapery blended with that of her flesh under the pallid rays of the lamp. Enveloped with this subtle tissue which betrayed all the contour of her body, she seemed rather the marble statue of some fair antique bather than a woman endowed with life. But dead or living, statue or woman, shadow or body, her beauty was still the same, only that the green light of her eyes was less brilliant, and her mouth, once so warmly crimson, was only tinted with a faint tender rosiness, like that of her cheeks. The little blue flowers which I had noticed entwined in her hair were withered and dry, and had lost nearly all their leaves, but this did not prevent her from being charming—so charming that, notwithstanding the strange character of the adventure, and the unexplainable manner in which she had entered my room, I felt not even for a moment the least fear.

She placed the lamp on the table and seated herself at the foot of my bed; then bending toward me, she said, in that voice at once silvery clear and yet velvety in its sweet softness, such as I never heard from any lips save hers:

"I have kept thee long in waiting, dear Romuald, and it must have seemed to thee that I had forgotten thee. But I come from afar off, very far off, and from a land whence no other has ever yet returned. There is neither sun nor moon in that land whence I come: all is but space and shadow; there is neither road nor pathway: no earth for the foot, no air for the wing; and nevertheless behold me here, for Love is stronger than Death and must conquer him in the end. Oh what sad faces and fearful things I have seen on my way hither! What difficulty my soul, returned to earth through the power of will alone, has had in finding its body and reinstating itself therein! What terrible efforts I had to make ere I could lift the ponderous slab with which they had covered me! See, the palms of my poor hands are all bruised! Kiss them, sweet love, that they may be healed!" She laid the cold palms of her hands upon ray mouth, one after the other. I kissed them, indeed, many times, and she the while watched me with a smile of ineffable affection.

I confess to my shame that I had entirely forgotten the advice of the Abbé Sérapion and the sacred office wherewith I had been invested. I had fallen without resistance, and at the first assault. I had not even made the least effort to repel the tempter. The fresh coolness of Clarimonde's skin penetrated my own, and I felt voluptuous tremors pass over my whole body. Poor child! in spite of all I saw afterward, I can hardly yet believe she was a demon; at least she had no appearance of being such, and never did Satan so skillfully conceal his claws and horns. She had drawn her feet up beneath her, and squatted down on the edge of the couch in an attitude full of negligent coquetry. From time to time she passed her little hand through my hair and twisted it into curls, as though trying how a new style of wearing it would become my face. I abandoned myself to her hands with the most guilty pleasure, while she accompanied her gentle play with the prettiest prattle. The most remarkable fact was that I felt no astonishment whatever at so extraordinary ah adventure, and as in dreams one finds no difficulty in accepting the most fantastic events as simple facts, so all these circumstances seemed to me perfectly natural in themselves.

"I loved thee long ere I saw thee, dear Romuald, and sought thee everywhere. Thou wast my dream, and I first saw thee in the church at the fatal moment. I said at once, "It is he!" I gave thee a look into which I threw all the love I ever had, all the love I now have, all the love I shall ever have for thee—a look that would have damned a cardinal or brought a king to his knees at my feet in view of all his court. Thou remainedst unmoved, preferring thy God to me!

"Ah, how jealous I am of that God whom thou didst love and still lovest more than me!

"Woe is me, unhappy one that I am! I can never have thy heart all to myself, I whom thou didst recall to life with a kiss—dead Clarimonde, who for thy sake bursts asunder the gates of the tomb, and comes to consecrate to thee a life which she has resumed only to make thee happy!"

All her words were accompanied with the most impassioned caresses, which bewildered my sense and my reason to such an extent, that I did not fear to utter a frightful blasphemy for the sake of consoling her, and to declare that I loved her as much as God.

Her eyes rekindled and shone like chrysoprases. "In truth?—in very truth? —as much as God!" she cried, flinging her beautiful arms around me. "Since it is so, thou wilt come with me; thou wilt follow me whithersoever I desire. Thou wilt cast away thy ugly black habit. Thou shalt be the proudest and most envied of cavaliers; thou shalt be my lover! To be the acknowledged lover of Clarimonde, who has refused even a Pope! That will be something to feel proud of. Ah, the fair, unspeakably happy existence, the beautiful golden life we shall live together! And when shall we depart, my fair sir?"

"Tomorrow! Tomorrow!" I cried in my delirium.

"Tomorrow, then, so let it be!" she answered. "In the meanwhile I shall have opportunity to change my toilet, for this is a little too light and in nowise suited for a voyage. I must also forthwith notify all my friends who believe me dead, and mourn for me as deeply as they are capable of doing. The money, the dresses, the carriages—all will be ready. I shall call for thee at this same hour. Adieu, dear heart!" And she lightly touched my forehead with her lips. The lamp went out, the curtains closed again, and all became dark; a leaden, dreamless sleep fell on me and held me unconscious until the morning following.

I awoke later than usual, and the recollection of this singular adventure troubled me during the whole day. I finally persuaded myself that it was a mere vapor of my heated imagination. Nevertheless its sensations had been so vivid that it was difficult to persuade myself that they were not real, and it was not without some presentiment of what was going to happen that I got into bed at last, after having prayed God to drive far from me all thoughts of evil, and to protect the chastity of my slumber.

I soon fell into a deep sleep, and my dream was continued. The curtains again parted, and I beheld Clarimonde, not as on the former occasion, pale in her pale winding-sheet, with the violets of death upon her cheeks, but gay, sprightly, jaunty, in a superb traveling-dress of green velvet, trimmed with gold lace, and looped up on either side to allow a glimpse of satin petticoat. Her blond hair escaped in thick ringlets from beneath a broad black felt hat, decorated with white feathers whimsically twisted into various shapes. In one hand she held a little riding-whip terminated by a golden whistle. She tapped me lightly with it, and exclaimed: "Well, my fine sleeper, is this the way you make your preparations? I thought I would find you up and dressed. Arise quickly, we have no time to lose."

I leaped out of bed at once.

"Come, dress yourself, and let us go," she continued, pointing to a little package she had brought with her. "The horses are becoming impatient of delay and champing their bits at the door. We ought to have been by this time at least ten leagues distant from here."

I dressed myself hurriedly, and she handed me the articles of apparel herself one by one, bursting into laughter from time to time at my awkwardness, as she explained to me the use of a garment when I had made a mistake. She hurriedly arranged my hair, and this done, held up before me a little pocket-mirror of Venetian crystal, rimmed with silver filigree-work, and playfully asked: "How dost find thyself now? Wilt engage me for thy valet de chambre?"

I was no longer the same person, and I could not even recognise myself. I resembled my former self no more than a finished statue resembles a block of stone. My old face seemed but a coarse daub of the one reflected in the mirror. I was handsome, and my vanity was sensibly tickled by the metamorphosis.

That elegant apparel, that richly embroidered vest had made of me a totally different personage, and I marvelled at the power of transformation owned by a few yards of cloth cut after a certain pattern. The spirit of my costume penetrated my very skin and within ten minutes more I had become something of a coxcomb.

In order to feel more at ease in my new attire, I took several turns up and down the room. Clarimonde watched me with an air of maternal pleasure, and appeared well satisfied with her work. "Come, enough of this child's play! Let us start, Romuald, dear. We have far to go, and we may not get there in time." She took my hand and led me forth. All the doors opened before her at a touch, and we passed by the dog without awaking him.

At the gate we found Margheritone waiting, the same swarthy groom who had once before been my escort. He held the bridles of three horses, all black like those which bore us to the castle—one for me, one for him, one for Clarimonde. Those horses must have been Spanish genets born of mares fecundated by a zephyr, for they were fleet as the wind itself, and the moon, which had just risen at our departure to light us on the way, rolled over the sky like a wheel detached from her own chariot. We beheld her on the right leaping from tree to tree, and putting herself out of breath in the effort to keep up with us. Soon we came upon a level plain where, hard by a clump of trees, a carriage with four vigorous horses awaited us. We entered it, and the postillions urged their animals into a mad gallop. I had one arm around Clarimonde's waist, and one of her hands clasped in mine; her head leaned upon my shoulder, and I felt her bosom, half bare, lightly pressing against my arm. I had never known such intense happiness. In that hour I had forgotten everything, and I no more remembered having ever been a priest than I remembered what I had been doing in my mother's womb, so great was the fascination which the evil spirit exerted upon me. From that night my nature seemed in some sort to have become halved, and there were two men within me, neither of whom knew the other. At one moment I believed myself a priest who dreamed nightly that he was a gentleman, at another that I was a gentleman who dreamed he was a priest. I could no longer distinguish the dream from the reality, nor could I discover where the reality began or where ended the dream. The exquisite young lord and libertine railed at the priest, the priest loathed the dissolute habits of the young lord. Two spirals entangled and confounded the one with the other, yet never touching, would afford a fair representation of this bicephalic life which I lived. Despite the strange character of my condition, I do not believe that I ever inclined, even for a moment, to madness. I always retained with extreme vividness all the perceptions of my two lives. Only there was one absurd fact which I could not explain to myself—namely, that the consciousness of the same individuality existed in two men so opposite in character. It was an anomaly for which I could not account—whether I believed myself to be the curé of the little village of C———, or *Il Signor Romualdo*, the titled lover of Clarimonde.

Be that as it may, I lived, at least I believed that I lived, in Venice. I have never been able to discover rightly how much of illusion and how much of reality there was in this fantastic adventure. We dwelt in a great palace on the Canaleio, filled with frescoes and statues, and containing two Titians in the noblest style of the great master, which were hung in Clarimonde's chamber. It was a palace well worthy of a king. We had each our gondola, our *barcarolli* in family livery, our music hall, and our special poet. Clarimonde always lived upon a magnificent scale; there was something of Cleopatra in her nature. As for me, I had the retinue of a prince's son, and I was regarded with as much reverential respect as though I had been of the family of one of the twelve Apostles or the four Evangelists of the Most Serene Republic. I would not have turned aside to allow even the Doge to pass, and I do not believe that since Satan fell from heaven, any creature was ever prouder or more insolent than I. I went to the Ridotto, and played with a luck which seemed absolutely infernal. I received the best of all society—the sons of ruined families, women of the theatre, shrewd knaves, parasites, hectoring swashbucklers. But notwithstanding the dissipation of such a life, I always remained faithful to Clarimonde. I loved her wildly. She would have excited satiety itself, and chained inconstancy. To have Clarimonde was to have twenty mistresses; ay, to possess all women: so mobile, so varied of aspect, so fresh in new charms was she all in herself—a very chameleon of a woman, in sooth. She made you commit with her the infidelity you would have committed with another, by donning to perfection the character, the attraction, the style of beauty of the woman who appeared to please you. She returned my love a hundred-fold, and it was in vain that the young patricians and even the Ancients of the Council of Ten made her the most magnificent proposals. A Foscari even went so far as to offer to espouse her. She rejected all his overtures. Of gold she had enough. She wished no longer for anything but love—a love youthful, pure, evoked by herself, and which should be a first and last passion. I would have been perfectly happy but for a cursed nightmare which recurred every night, and in which I believed myself to be a poor village curé, practising mortification and penance for my excesses during the day. Reassured by my constant association with her, I never thought further of the strange manner in which I had become acquainted with Clarimonde. But the words of the Abbé Sérapion concerning her recurred often to my memory, and never ceased to cause me uneasiness.

For some time the health of Clarimonde had not been so good as usual; her complexion grew paler day by day. The physicians who were summoned could not comprehend the nature of her malady and knew not how to treat it. They all prescribed some insignificant remedies, and never called a second time. Her paleness, nevertheless, visibly increased, and she became colder and colder, until she seemed almost as white and dead as upon that memorable night in the unknown castle. I grieved with anguish unspeakable to behold her thus slowly perishing; and she, touched by my agony, smiled upon me sweetly and sadly with the fateful smile of those who feel that they must die.

One morning I was seated at her bedside, and breakfasting from a little table placed close at hand, so that I might not be obliged to leave her for a single instant. In the act of cutting some fruit I accidentally inflicted rather a deep gash on my finger. The blood immediately gushed forth in a little purple jet, and a few drops spurted upon Clarimonde. Her eyes flashed, her face suddenly assumed an expression of savage and ferocious joy such as I had never before observed in her. She leaped out of her bed with animal agility—the agility, as it were, of an ape or a cat—and sprang upon my wound, which she commenced to suck with an air of unutterable pleasure. She swallowed the blood in little mouthfuls, slowly and carefully, like a connoisseur tasting a wine from Xeres or Syracuse. Gradually her eyelids half closed, and the pupils of her green eyes became oblong instead of round. From time to time she paused in order to kiss my hand, then she would recommence to press her lips to the lips of the wound in order to coax forth a few more ruddy drops. When she found that the blood would no longer come, she arose with eyes liquid and brilliant, rosier than a May dawn; her face full and fresh, her hand warm and moist—in fine, more beautiful than ever, and in the most perfect health.

"I shall not die! I shall not die!" she cried, clinging to my neck, half mad with joy. "I can love thee yet for a long time. My life is thine, and all that is of me comes from thee. A few drops of thy rich and noble blood, more precious and more potent than all the elixirs of the earth, have given me back life."

This scene long haunted my memory, and inspired me with strange doubts in regard to Clarimonde; and the same evening, when slumber had transported me to my presbytery, I beheld the Abbé Sérapion, graver and more anxious of aspect than ever. He gazed attentively at me, and sorrowfully exclaimed: "Not content with losing your soul, you now desire also to lose your body. Wretched young man, into how terrible a plight have you fallen!" The tone in which he uttered these words powerfully affected me, but in spite of its vividness even that impression was soon dissipated, and a thousand other cares erased it from my mind. At last one evening, while looking into a mirror whose traitorous position she had not taken into account, I saw Clarimonde in the act of emptying a powder into the cup of spiced wine which she had long been in the habit of preparing after our repasts. I took the cup, feigned to carry it to my lips, and then placed it on the nearest article of furniture as though intending to finish it at my leisure. Taking advantage of a moment when the fair one's back was turned, I threw the contents under the table, after which I retired to my chamber and went to bed, fully resolved not to sleep, but to watch and discover what should come of all this mystery. I did not have to wait long, Clarimonde entered in her nightdress, and having removed her apparel, crept into bed and lay down beside me. When she felt assured that I was asleep, she bared my arm, and drawing a gold pin from her hair, commenced to murmur in a low voice:

"One drop, only one drop! One ruby at the end of my needle... Since thou lovest me yet, I must not die!... Ah, poor love! His beautiful blood, so brightly purple, I must drink it. Sleep, my only treasure! Sleep, my god, my child! I will do thee no harm; I will only take of thy life what I must to keep my own from being forever extinguished. But that I love thee so much, I could well resolve to have other lovers whose veins I could drain; but since I have known thee all other men have become hateful to me... Ah, the beautiful arm! How round it is! How white it is! How shall I ever dare to prick this pretty blue vein!" And while thus murmuring to herself she wept, and I felt her tears raining on my arm as she clasped it with her hands. At last she took the resolve, slightly punctured me with her pin, and commenced to suck up the blood which oozed from the place. Although she swallowed only a few drops, the fear of weakening me soon seized her, and she carefully tied a little band around my arm, afterward rubbing the wound with an unguent which immediately cicatrized it. Further doubts were impossible. The Abbé Sérapion was right. Notwithstanding this positive knowledge, however, I could not cease to love Clarimonde, and I would gladly of my own accord have given her all the blood she required to sustain her factitious life. Moreover, I felt but little fear of her. The woman seemed to plead with me for the vampire, and what I had already heard and seen sufficed to reassure me completely. In those days I had plenteous veins, which would not have been so easily exhausted as at present; and I would not have thought of bargaining for my blood, drop by drop. I would rather have opened myself the veins of my arm and said to her: "Drink, and may my love infiltrate itself throughout thy body together with my blood!" I carefully avoided ever making the least reference to the narcotic drink she had prepared for me, or to the incident of the pin, and we lived in the most perfect harmony.

Yet my priestly scruples commenced to torment me more than ever, and I was at a loss to imagine what new penance I could invent in order to mortify and subdue my flesh. Although these visions were involuntary, and though I did not actually participate in anything relating to them, I could not dare to touch the body of Christ with hands so impure and a mind defiled by such debauches whether real or imaginary. In the effort to avoid falling under the influence of these wearisome hallucinations, I strove to prevent myself from being overcome by sleep. I held my eyelids open with my fingers, and stood for hours together leaning upright against the wall, fighting sleep with all my might; but the dust of drowsiness invariably gathered upon my eyes at last, and finding all resistance useless, I would have to let my arms fall in the extremity of despairing weariness, and the current of slumber would again bear me away to the perfidious shores. Sérapion addressed me with the most vehement exhortations, severely reproaching me for my softness and want of fervor. Finally, one day when I was more wretched than usual, he said to me: "There is but one way by which you can obtain relief from this continual torment, and though it is an extreme measure it must be made use of; violent diseases require violent remedies. I know where Clarimonde is buried. It is necessary that we shall disinter her remains, and that you shall behold in how pitiable a state the object of your love is. Then you will no longer be tempted to lose your soul for the sake of an unclean corpse devoured by worms, and ready to crumble into dust. That will assuredly restore you to yourself." For my part, I was so tired of this double life that I at once consented, desiring to ascertain beyond a doubt whether a priest or a gentleman had been the victim of delusion. I had become fully resolved either to kill one of the two men within me for the benefit of the other, or else to kill both, for so terrible an existence could not last long and be endured. The Abbé Sérapion provided himself with a mattock, a lever, and a lantern, and at midnight we wended our way to the cemetery of ———, the location and place of which were perfectly familiar to him. After having directed the rays of the dark lantern upon the inscriptions of several tombs, we came at last upon a great slab, half concealed by huge weeds and devoured by mosses and parasitic plants, whereupon we deciphered the opening lines of the epitaph:

Here lies Clarimonde
Who was famed in her life-time
As the fairest of women.

"It is here without a doubt," muttered Sérapion, and placing his lantern on the ground, he forced the point of the lever under the edge of the stone and commenced to raise it. The stone yielded, and he proceeded to work with the mattock. Darker and more silent than the night itself, I stood by and watched him do it, while he, bending over his dismal toil, streamed with sweat, panted, and his hard-coming breath seemed to have the harsh tone of a death rattle. It was a weird scene, and had any persons from without beheld us, they would assuredly have taken us rather for profane wretches and shroud-stealers than for priests of God. There was something grim and fierce in Sérapion's zeal which lent him the air of a demon rather than of an apostle or an angel, and his great aquiline face, with all its stern features, brought out in strong relief by the lantern-light, had something fearsome in it which enhanced the unpleasant fancy. I felt an icy sweat come out upon my forehead in huge beads, and my hair stood up with a hideous fear. Within the depths of my own heart I felt that the act of the austere Sérapion was an abominable sacrilege; and I could have prayed that a triangle of fire would issue from the entrails of the dark clouds, heavily rolling above us, to reduce him to cinders. The owls which had been nestling in the cypress-trees, startled by the gleam of the lantern, flew against it from time to time, striking their dusty wings against its panes, and uttering plaintive cries of lamentation; wild foxes yelped in the far darkness, and a thousand sinister noises detached themselves from the silence. At last Sérapion's mattock struck the coffin itself, making its planks re-echo with a deep sonorous sound, with that terrible sound nothingness utters when stricken. He wrenched apart and tore up the lid, and I beheld Clarimonde, pallid as a figure of marble, with hands joined; her white winding-sheet made but one fold from her head to her feet. A little crimson drop sparkled like a speck of dew at one corner of her colorless mouth. Sérapion, at this spectacle, burst into fury: "Ah, thou art here, demon! Impure courtesan! Drinker of blood and gold!" And he flung holy water upon the corpse and the coffin, over which he traced the sign of the cross with his sprinkler. Poor Clarimonde had no sooner been touched by the blessed spray than her beautiful body crumbled into dust, and became only a shapeless and frightful mass of cinders and half-calcined bones.

"Behold your mistress, my Lord Romuald!" cried the inexorable priest, as he pointed to these sad remains. "Will you be easily tempted after this to promenade on the Lido or at Fusina with your beauty?" I covered my face with my hands, a vast ruin had taken place within me. I returned to my presbytery, and the noble Lord Romuald, the lover of Clarimonde, separated himself from the poor priest with whom he had kept such strange company so long. But once only, the following night, I saw Clarimonde. She said to me, as she had said the first time at the portals of the church: "Unhappy man! Unhappy man! What hast thou done? Wherefore have hearkened to that imbecile priest? Wert thou not happy? And what harm had I ever done thee that thou shouldst violate my poor tomb, and lay bare the miseries of my nothingness? All communication between our souls and our bodies is henceforth forever broken. Adieu! Thou wilt yet regret me!" She vanished in air as smoke, and I never saw her more.

Alas! she spoke truly indeed. I have regretted her more than once, and I regret her still. My soul's peace has been very dearly bought. The love of God was not too much to replace such a love as hers. And this, brother, is the story of my youth. Never gaze upon a woman, and walk abroad only with eyes ever fixed upon the ground; for however chaste and watchful one may be, the error of a single moment is enough to make one lose eternity.

THE FEAST OF BLOOD
(EXCERPT)

Anonymous

(COMMONLY ATTRIBUTED TO JAMES MALCOLM RYMER AND/OR THOMAS PECKETT PREST)

(1845)

"How graves give up their dead,
And how the night air hideous grows
With shrieks!"

The solemn tones of an old cathedral clock have announced midnight —the air is thick and heavy—a strange, death like stillness pervades all nature. Like the ominous calm which precedes some more than usually terrific outbreak of the elements, they seem to have paused even in their ordinary fluctuations, to gather a terrific strength for the great effort. A faint peal of thunder now comes from far off. Like a signal gun for the battle of the winds to begin, it appeared to awaken them from their lethargy, and one awful, warring hurricane swept over a whole city, producing more devastation in the four or five minutes it lasted, than would a half century of ordinary phenomena.

It was as if some giant had blown upon some toy town, and scattered many of the buildings before the hot blast of his terrific breath; for as suddenly as that blast of wind had come did it cease, and all was as still and calm as before.

Sleepers awakened, and thought that what they had heard must be the confused chimera of a dream. They trembled and turned to sleep again.

All is still—still as the very grave. Not a sound breaks the magic of repose. What is that—a strange pattering noise, as of a million fairy feet? It is hail—yes, a hail-storm has burst over the city. Leaves are dashed from the trees, mingled with small boughs; windows that lie most opposed to the direct fury of the pelting particles of ice are broken, and the rapt repose that before was so remarkable in its intensity, is exchanged for a noise which, in its accumulation, drowns every cry of surprise or consternation which here and there arose from persons who found their houses invaded by the storm.

Now and then, too, there would come a sudden gust of wind that in its strength, as it blew laterally, would, for a moment, hold millions of the hailstones suspended in mid air, but it was only to dash them with redoubled force in some new direction, where more mischief was to be done.

Oh, how the storm raged! Hail—rain—wind. It was, in very truth, an awful night.

T here was an antique chamber in an ancient house. Curious and quaint carvings adorn the walls, and the large chimneypiece is a curiosity of itself. The ceiling is low, and a large bay window, from roof to floor, looks to the west. The window is latticed, and filled with curiously painted glass and rich stained pieces, which send in a strange, yet beautiful light, when sun or moon shines into the apartment. There is but one portrait in that room, although the walls seem paneled for the express purpose of containing a series of pictures. That portrait is of a young man, with a pale face, a stately brow, and a strange expression about the eyes, which no one cared to look on twice.

There is a stately bed in that chamber, of carved walnut-wood is it made, rich in design and elaborate in execution; one of those works which owe their existence to the Elizabethan era. It is hung with heavy silken and damask furnishing; nodding feathers are at its corners—covered with dust are they, and they lend a funereal aspect to the room. The floor is of polished oak.

God! how the hail dashes on the old bay window! Like an occasional discharge of mimic musketry, it comes clashing, beating, and cracking upon the small panes; but they resist it—their small size saves them; the wind, the hail, the rain, expend their fury in vain.

The bed in that old chamber is occupied. A creature formed in all fashions of loveliness lies in a half sleep upon that ancient couch—a girl young and beautiful as a spring morning. Her long hair has escaped from its confinement and streams over the blackened coverings of the bedstead; she has been restless in her sleep, for the clothing of the bed is in much confusion. One arm is over her head, the other hangs nearly off the side of the bed near to which she lies. A neck and bosom that would have formed a study for the rarest sculptor that ever Providence gave genius to, were half disclosed. She moaned slightly in her sleep, and once or twice the lips moved as if in prayer—at least one might judge so, for the name of Him who suffered for all came once faintly from them.

She had endured much fatigue, and the storm dose not awaken her; but it can disturb the slumbers it does not possess the power to destroy entirely. The turmoil of the elements wakes the senses, although it cannot entirely break the repose they have lapsed into.

Oh, what a world of witchery was in that mouth, slightly parted, and exhibiting within the pearly teeth that glistened even in the faint light that came from that bay window. How sweetly the long silken eyelashes lay upon the cheek. Now she moves, and one shoulder is entirely visible—whiter, fairer than the spotless clothing of the bed on which she lies, is the smooth skin of that fair creature, just budding into womanhood, and in that transition state which presents to us all the charms of the girl—almost of the child, with the more matured beauty and gentleness of advancing years.

Was that lightning? Yes—an awful, vivid, terrifying flash—then a roaring peal of thunder, as if a thousand mountains were rolling one over the other in the blue vault of Heaven! Who sleeps now in that ancient city? Not one living soul. The dread trumpet of eternity could not more effectually have awakened any one.

The hail continues. The wind continues. The uproar of the elements seems at its height. Now she awakens—that beautiful girl on the antique bed; she opens those eyes of celestial blue, and a faint cry of alarm bursts from her lips. At least it is a cry which, amid the noise and turmoil without, sounds but faint and weak. She sits upon the bed and presses her hands upon her eyes. Heavens! what a wild torrent of wind, and rain, and hail! The thunder likewise seems intent upon awakening sufficient echoes to last until the next flash of forked lightning should again produce the wild concussion of the air. She murmurs a prayer—a prayer for those she loves best; the names of those dear to her gentle heart come from her lips; she weeps and prays; she thinks then of what devastation the storm must surely produce, and to the great God of Heaven she prays for all living things. Another flash—a wild, blue, bewildering flash of lightning streams across that bay window, for an instant bringing out every color in it with terrible distinctness. A shriek bursts from the lips of the young girl, and then, with eyes fixed upon that window, which, in another moment, is all darkness, and with such an expression of terror upon her face as it had never before known, she trembled, and the perspiration of intense fear stood upon her brow.

"What—what was it?" she gasped; "real or delusion? Oh, God, what was it? A figure tall and gaunt, endeavoring from the outside to unclasp the window. I saw it. That flash of lightning revealed it to me. It stood the whole length of the window."

There was a lull of the wind. The hail was not falling so thickly—moreover, it now fell, what there was of it, straight, and yet a strange clattering sound came upon the glass of that long window. It could not be a delusion—she is awake, and she hears it. What can produce it? Another flash of lightning—another shriek—there could be now no delusion.

A tall figure is standing on the ledge immediately outside the long window. It is its finger-nails upon the glass that produces the sound so like the hail, now that the hail has ceased. Intense fear paralyzed the limbs of the beautiful girl. That one shriek is all she can utter—with hand clasped, a face of marble, a heart beating so wildly in her bosom, that each moment it seems as if it would break its confines, eyes distended and fixed upon the window, she waits, froze with horror. The pattering and clattering of the nails continue. No word is spoken, and now she fancies she can trace the darker form of that figure against the window, and she can see the long arms moving to and fro, feeling for some mode of entrance. What strange light is that which now gradually creeps up into the air? red and terrible—brighter and brighter it grows. The lightning has set fire to a mill, and the reflection of the rapidly consuming building falls upon that long window. There can be no mistake. The figure is there, still feeling for an entrance, and clattering against the glass with its long nails, that appear as if the growth of many years had been untouched. She tries to scream again but a choking sensation comes over her, and she cannot. It is too dreadful—she tries to move—each limb seems weighted down by tons of lead—she can but in a hoarse faint whisper cry,—

"Help—help—help—help!"

And that one word she repeats like a person in a dream. The red glare of the fire continues. It throws up the tall gaunt figure in hideous relief against the long window. It shows, too, upon the one portrait that is in the chamber, and the portrait appears to fix its eyes upon the attempting intruder, while the flickering light from the fire makes it look fearfully lifelike. A small pane of glass is broken, and the form from without introduces a long gaunt hand, which seems utterly destitute of flesh. The fastening is removed, and one-half of the window, which opens like folding doors, is swung wide open upon its hinges.

And yet now she could not scream—she could not move. "Help!—help!—help!" was all she could say. But, oh, that look of terror that sat upon her face, it was dreadful—a look to haunt the memory for a life-time—a look to obtrude itself upon the happiest moments, and turn them to bitterness.

The figure turns half round, and the light falls upon its face. It is perfectly white—perfectly bloodless. The eyes look like polished tin; the lips are drawn back, and the principal feature next to those dreadful eyes is the teeth—the fearful looking teeth—projecting like those of some wild animal, hideously, glaringly white, and fang-like. It approaches the bed with a strange, gliding movement. It clashes together the long nails that literally appear to hang from the finger ends. No sound comes from its lips. Is she going mad—that young and beautiful girl exposed to so much terror? she has drawn up all her limbs; she cannot even now say help. The power of articulation is gone, but the power of movement has returned to her; she can draw herself slowly along to the other side of the bed from that towards which the hideous appearance is coming.

But her eyes are fascinated. The glance of a serpent could not have produced a greater effect upon her than did the fixed gaze of those awful, metallic-looking eyes that were bent down on her face. Crouching down so that the gigantic height was lost, and the horrible, protruding white face was the most prominent object, came on the figure. What was it?—what did it want there?—what made it look so hideous—so unlike an inhabitant of the earth, and yet be on it?

Now she has got to the verge of the bed, and the figure pauses. It seemed as if when it paused she lost the power to proceed. The clothing of the bed was now clutched in her hands with unconscious power. She drew her breath short and thick. Her bosom heaves, and her limbs tremble, yet she cannot withdraw her eyes from that marble-looking face. He holds her with his glittering eye.

The storm has ceased—all is still. The winds are hushed; the church clock proclaims the hour of one: a hissing sound comes from the throat of the hideous being, and he raises his long, gaunt arms—the lips move. He advances. The girl places one small foot on to the floor. She is unconsciously dragging the clothing with her. The door of the room is in that direction— can she reach it? Has she power to walk?—can she withdraw her eyes from the face of the intruder, and so break the hideous charm? God of Heaven! is it real, or some dream so like reality as to nearly overturn judgment forever?

The figure has paused again, and half on the bed and half out of it that young girl lies trembling. Her long hair streams across the entire width of the bed. As she has slowly moved along she has left it streaming across the pillows. The pause lasted about a minute—oh, what an age of agony. That minute was, indeed, enough for madness to do its full work in.

With a sudden rush that could not be foreseen—with a strange howling cry that was enough to awaken terror in every breast, the figure seized the long tresses of her hair, and twining them round his bony hands he held her to the bed. Then she screamed—Heaven granted her then power to scream. Shriek followed shriek in rapid succession. The bed-clothes fell in a heap by the side of the bed—she was dragged by her long silken hair completely on to it again. Her beautifully rounded limbs quivered with the agony of her soul. The glassy, horrible eyes of the figure ran over that angelic form with a hideous satisfaction—horrible profanation. He drags her head to the bed's edge. He forces it back by the long hair still entwined in his grasp. With a plunge he seizes her neck in his fang-like teeth—a gush of blood, and a hideous sucking noise follows. The girl has swooned, and the vampire is at his hideous repast!

THE MYSTERIOUS STRANGER

Karl von Wachsmann

published as *Der Fremde* in *Erzählungen und Novellen* (1844)

this translation was first published without accreditation in
Chambers's Repository (February 1854)

Boreas, that fearful north-west wind, which in the spring and autumn stirs up the lowest depths of the wild Adriatic, and is then so dangerous to vessels, was howling through the woods, and tossing the branches of the old knotty oaks in the Carpathian Mountains, when a party of five riders, who surrounded a litter drawn by a pair of mules, turned into a forest-path, which offered some protection from the April weather, and allowed the travelers in some degree to recover their breath. It was already evening, and bitterly cold; the snow fell every now and then in large flakes. A tall old gentleman, of aristocratic appearance, rode at the head of the troop. This was the Knight of Fahnenberg, in Austria. He had inherited from a childless brother a considerable property, situated in the Carpathian Mountains; and he had set out to take possession of it, accompanied by his daughter Franziska, and a niece about twenty years of age, who had been brought up with her. Next to the knight rode a fine young man some twenty and odd years—the Baron Franz von Kronstein; he wore, like the former, the broad-brimmed hat with hanging feathers, the leather collar, the wide riding-boots—in short, the traveling-dress which was in fashion at the commencement of the seventeenth century. The features of the young man had much about them that was open and friendly, as well as some mind; but the expression was more that of dreamy and sensitive softness than of youthful daring, although no one could deny that he possessed much of youthful beauty. As the cavalcade turned into the oak wood the young man rode up to the litter, and chatted with the ladies who were seated therein. One of these—and to her his conversation was principally addressed—was of dazzling beauty. Her hair flowed in natural curls round the fine oval of her face, out of which beamed a pair of star-like eyes, full of genius, lively fancy, and a certain degree of archness. Franziska von Fahnenberg seemed to attend but carelessly to the speeches of her admirer, who made many kind inquiries as to how she felt herself during the journey, which had been attended with many difficulties: she always answered him very shortly; almost contemptuously; and at length remarked, that if it had not been for her father's objections, she would long ago have requested the baron to take her place in their horrid cage of a litter, for, to judge by his remarks, he seemed incommoded by the weather; and she would so much rather be mounted on the spirited horse, and face wind and storm, than be mewed up there, dragged up the hills by those long-eared animals, and mope herself to death with ennui. The young lady's words, and, still more, the half-contemptuous tone in which they were uttered, appeared to make the most painful impression on the young man: he made her no reply at the moment, but the absent air with which he attended to the kindly-intended remarks of the other young lady, showed how much he was disconcerted.

"It appears, dear Franziska," said he at length in a kindly tone, "that the hardships of the road have affected you more than you will acknowledge. Generally so kind to others, you have been very often out of humour during the journey, and particularly with regard to your humble servant and cousin, who would gladly bear a double or treble share of the discomforts, if he could thereby save you from the smallest of them."

Franziska showed by her look that she was about to reply with some bitter jibe, when the voice of the knight was heard calling for his nephew, who galloped off at the sound.

"I should like to scold you well, Franziska," said her companion somewhat sharply, "for always plaguing your poor Cousin Franz in this shameful way; he who loves you so truly, and who, whatever you may say, will one day be your husband."

"My husband!" replied the other angrily. "I must either completely alter my ideas, or he his whole self, before that takes place. No, Bertha! I know that this is my father's darling wish, and I do not deny the good qualities Cousin Franz may have, or really has, since I see you are making a face; but to marry an effeminate man—never!"

"Effeminate! you do him great injustice," replied her friend quickly. "Just because instead of going off to the Turkish war, where little honor was to be gained, he attended to your father's advice, and stayed at home, to bring his neglected estate into order, which he accomplished with care and prudence; and because he does not represent this howling wind as a mild zephyr—for reasons such as these you are pleased to call him effeminate."

"Say what you will, it is so," cried Franziska obstinately. "Bold, aspiring, even despotic, must be the man who is to gain my heart; these soft, patient, and thoughtful natures are utterly distasteful to me. Is Franz capable of deep sympathy, either in joy or sorrow? He is always the same—always quiet, soft and tiresome."

"He has a warm heart, and is not without genius," said Bertha.

"A warm heart! that may be," replied the other; "but I would rather be tyrannized over, and kept under a little by my future husband, than be loved in such a wearisome manner. You say he has genius, too. I will not exactly contradict you, since that would be unpolite, but it is not easily discovered. But even allowing you are right in both statements, still the man who does not bring these qualities into action is a despicable creature. A man may do many foolish things, he may even be a little wicked now and then, provided it is in nothing dishonorable; and one can forgive him, if he is only acting on some fixed theory for some special object. There is, for instance, your own faithful admirer, the Castellan of Glogau, Knight of Woislaw; he loves you most truly, and is now quite in a position to enable you to marry comfortably. The brave man has lost his right hand—reason enough for remaining seated behind the stove, or near the spinning-wheel of his Bertha; but what does he do?—He goes off to the war in Turkey; he fights for a noble thought—"

"And runs the chance of getting his other hand chopped off, and another great scar across his face," put in her friend.

"Leaves his lady-love to weep and pine a little," pursued Franziska, "but returns with fame, marries, and is all the more honored and admired! This is done by a man of forty, a rough warrior, not bred at court, a soldier who has nothing but his cloak and sword. And Franz—rich, noble—but I will not go on. Not a word more on this detested point, if you love me, Bertha."

Franziska leaned back in the corner of the litter with a dissatisfied air, and shut her eyes as though, overcome by fatigue, she wished to sleep.

"This awful wind is so powerful, you say, that we must make a detour to avoid its full force," said the knight to an old man, dressed in a fur-cap and a cloak of rough skin, who seemed to be the guide of the party.

"Those who have never personally felt the Boreas storming over the country between Sessano and Triest, can have no conception of the reality," replied the other. "As soon as it commences, the snow is blown in thick long columns along the ground. That is nothing to what follows. These columns become higher and higher, as the wind rises, and continue to do so until you see nothing but snow above, below, and on every side—unless, indeed, sometimes, when sand and gravel are mixed with the snow, and at length it is impossible to open your eyes at all. Your only plan for safety is to wrap your cloak around you, and lie down flat on the ground. If your home were but a few hundred yards off, you might lose your life in the attempt to reach it."

"Well, then, we owe you thanks, old Kumpan," said the knight, though it was with difficulty he made his words heard above the roaring of the storm; "we owe you thanks for taking us this round, as we shall thus be enabled to reach our destination without danger."

"You may feel sure of that, noble sir," said the old man. "By midnight we shall have arrived, and that without any danger by the way, if—" Suddenly the old man stopped, he drew his horse sharply up, and remained in an attitude of attentive listening.

"It appears to me we must be in the neighborhood of some village," said Franz von Kronstein; "for between the gusts of the storm I hear a dog howling."

"It is no dog, it is no dog!" said the old man uneasily, and urging his horse to a rapid pace. "For miles around there is no human dwelling; and except in the castle of Klatka, which indeed lies in the neighborhood, but has been deserted for more than a century, probably no one has lived here since the creation.—But there again," he continued; "well, if I wasn't sure of it from the first."

"That howling seems to fidget you, old Kumpan," said the knight, listening to a long-drawn fierce sound, which appeared nearer than before, and seemed to be answered from a distance.

"That howling comes from no dogs," replied the old guide uneasily. "Those are reed-wolves; they may be on our track; and it would be as well if the gentlemen looked to their firearms."

"Reed-wolves ? What do you mean?" inquired Franz in surprise.

"At the edge of this wood," said Kumpan, "there lies a lake about a mile long, whose banks are covered with reeds. In these a number of wolves have taken up their quarters, and feed on wild birds, fish and such like. They are shy in the summer-time, and a boy of twelve might scare them; but when the birds migrate, and the fish ate frozen up, they. prowl about at night, and then they are dangerous. They are worst, however, when Boreas rages, for then it is just as if the fiend himself possessed them: they are so mad and fierce that man and beast become alike their victims; and a party of them have been known even to attack the ferocious bears of these mountains, and, what is more, to come off victorious." The howl was now again repeated more distinctly, and from two opposite directions. The riders in alarm felt for their pistols, and the old man grasped the spear which hung at his saddle.

"We must keep dose to the litter; the wolves are very near us," whispered the guide. The riders turned their horses, surrounded the litter, and the knight informed the ladies, in a few quieting words, of the cause of this movement.

"Then we *shall* have an adventure—some little variety!" cried Franziska with sparkling eyes.

"How can you talk so foolishly?" said Bertha in alarm.

"Are we not under manly protection? Is not Cousin Franz on our side?" said the other mockingly.

"See, there is a light gleaming among the twigs; and there is another," cried Bertha. "there must be people close to us."

"No, no," cried the guide quickly. "Shut up the door, ladies. Keep close together, gentlemen. It is the eyes of wolves you see sparkling there." The gentlemen looked towards the thick underwood, in which every now and then little bright spots appeared, such as in summer would have been taken for glow-worms; it was just the same greenish-yellow light, but less unsteady, and there were always two flames together. The horses began to be restive, they kicked and dragged at the rein; but the mules behaved tolerably well.

"I will fire on the beasts, and teach them to keep their distance," said Franz, pointing to the spot where the lights were thickest.

"Hold, hold, Sir Baron!" cried Kumpan quickly, and seizing the young man's arm. "You would bring such a host together by the report, that, encouraged by numbers, they would be sure to make the first assault. However, keep your arms in readiness, and if an old she-wolf springs out— for these always lead the attack—take good aim and kill her, for then there must be no further hesitation." By this time the horses were almost unmanageable, and terror had also infected the mules. Just as Franz was turning towards the litter to say a word to his cousin, an animal, about the size of a large hound, sprang from the thicket and seized the foremost mule.

"Fire, baron! A wolf!" shouted the guide.

The young man fired, and the wolf fell to the ground. A fearful howl rang through the wood.

"Now, forward! Forward without a moment's delay!" cried Kumpan. "We have not above five minutes' time. The beasts will tear their wounded comrade to pieces, and, if they are very hungry, partially devour her. We shall, in the meantime, gain a little start, and it is not more than an hour's ride to the end of the forest. There—do you see—these are the towers of Klatka between the trees—out there where the moon is rising, and from that point the wood becomes less dense."

The travelers endeavored to increase their pace to the utmost, but the litter retarded their progress. Bertha was weeping with fear, and even Franziska's courage had diminished, for she sat very still. Franz endeavored to reassure them. They had not proceeded many moments when the howling recommenced, and approached nearer and nearer.

"There they are again and fiercer and more numerous than before," cried the guide in alarm.

The lights were soon visible again, and certainly in greater numbers. The wood had already become less thick, and the snowstorm having ceased, the moonbeams discovered many a dusky form amongst the trees, keeping together like a pack of hounds, and advancing nearer and nearer till they were within twenty paces, and on the very path of the travelers. From time to time a fierce howl arose from their centre, which was answered by the whole pack, and was at length taken up by single voices in the distance.

The party now found themselves some few hundred yards from the ruined castle of which Kumpan had spoken. It was, or seemed by moonlight to be, of some magnitude. Near the tolerably preserved principal building lay the ruins of a church, which must have once been beautiful, placed on a little hillock, dotted with single oak-trees and bramble-bushes. Both castle and church were still partially roofed in; and a path led from the castle gate to an old oak-tree, where it joined at right angles the one along which the travelers were advancing. The old guide seemed in much perplexity.

"We are in great danger, noble sir," said he. "The wolves will very soon make a general attack. There will then be only one way of escape: leaving the mules to their fate, and taking the young ladies on your horses."

"That would be all very well, if I had not thought of a better plan," replied the knight. "Here is the ruined castle; we can surely reach that, and then, blocking up the gates, we must just await the morning."

"Here? In the ruins of Klatka?—Not for all the wolves in the world!" cried the old man. "Even by daylight no one likes to approach the place, and, now, by night!—The castle, Sir Knight, has a bad name."

"On account of robbers?" asked Franz.

"No; it is haunted," replied the other.

"Stuff and nonsense!" said the baron. "Forward to the ruins; there is not a moment to be lost."

And this was indeed the case. The ferocious beasts were but a few steps behind the travelers. Every now and then they retired, and set up a ferocious howl. The party had just arrived at the old oak before mentioned, and were about to turn into the path to the ruins, when the animals, as though perceiving the risk they ran of losing their prey, came so near that a lance could easily have struck them. The knight and Franz faced sharply about, spurring their horses amidst the advancing crowds, when suddenly, from the shadow of the oak stepped forth a man, who in a few strides placed himself between the travelers and their pursuers. As far as one could see in the dusky light, the stranger was a man of a tall and well-built frame; he wore a sword by his side, and a broad-brimmed hat was on his head. If the party were astonished at his sudden appearance, they were still more so at what followed. As soon as the stranger appeared, the wolves gave over their pursuit, rumbled over each other, and set up a fearful howl. The stranger now raised his hand, appeared to wave it, and the wild animals crawled back into the thickets like a pack of beaten hounds.

Without casting a glance at the travelers, who were too much overcome by astonishment to speak, the stranger went up the path which led to the castle, and soon disappeared beneath the gateway.

"Heaven have mercy on us!" murmured old Kumpan in his beard, as he made the sign of the cross.

"Who was that strange man?" asked the knight with surprise, when he had watched the stranger as long as he was visible, and the party had resumed their way.

The old guide pretended not to understand, and, riding up to the mules, busied himself with arranging the harness, which had become disordered in their haste: more than a quarter of an hour elapsed before he rejoined them.

"Did you know the man who met us near the ruins, and who freed us from our four-footed pursuers in such a miraculous way?" asked Franz of the guide.

"Do I know him? No, noble sir; I never saw him before," replied the guide hesitatingly. "He looked like a soldier, and was armed," said the baron. "Is the castle, then, inhabited?"

"Not for the last hundred years," replied the other. "It was dismantled because the possessor in those days had iniquitous dealings with some Turkish-Sclavonian hordes, who had advanced as far as this; or rather"—he corrected himself hastily—"he is said to have had such, for he might have been as upright and good a man as ever ate cheese fried in butter."

"And who is now the possessor of the ruins and of these woods?" inquired the knight.

"Who but yourself, noble sir?" replied Kumpan. "For more than two hours we have been on your estate, and we shall soon reach the end of the wood."

"We hear and see nothing more of the wolves," said the baron after a pause. "Even their howling has ceased. The adventure with the stranger still remains to me inexplicable, even if one were to suppose him a huntsman—"

"Yes, yes; that is most likely what he is," interrupted the guide hastily, whilst he looked uneasily round him.

"The brave good man, who came so opportunely to our assistance, must have been a huntsman Oh, there are many powerful woodsmen in this neighborhood! Heaven be praised!" he continued, taking a deep breath, "there is the end of the wood, and in a short hour we shall be safely housed."

And so it happened. Before an hour had elapsed, the party passed through a well-built village, the principal spot on the estate, towards the venerable castle, the windows of which were brightly illuminated, and at the door stood the steward and other dependents, who, having received their new lord with every expression of respect, conducted the party to the splendidly furnished apartments.

Nearly four weeks passed before the traveling adventures again came on the tapis. The knight and Franz found such constant employment in looking over all the particulars of the large estate, and endeavoring to introduce various German improvements, that they were very little at home. At first, Franziska was charmed with everything in a neighborhood so entirely new and unknown. It appeared to her so romantic, so very different from her German Fatherland, that she took the greatest interest in everything, and often drew comparisons between the countries, which generally ended unfavorably for Germany. Bertha was of exactly the contrary opinion: she laughed at her cousin, and said that her liking for novelty and strange sights must indeed have come to a pass, when she preferred hovels in which the smoke went out of the doors and windows instead of the chimney, walls covered with soot, and inhabitants not much cleaner, and of unmannerly habits, to the comfortable dwellings and polite people of Germany. However, Franziska persisted in her notions, and replied that everything in Austria was flat, *ennuyant*, and common; and that a wild peasant here, with his rough coat of skin, had ten times more interest for her than a quiet Austrian in his holiday suit, the mere sight of whom was enough to make one yawn.

As soon as the knight had got the first arrangements into some degree of order, the party found themselves more together again. Franz continued to show great attention to his cousin, which, however, she received with little gratitude, for she made him the butt of all her fanciful humors, that soon returned when after a longer sojourn she had become more accustomed to her new life. Many excursions into the neighborhood were undertaken, but there was little variety in the scenery, and these soon ceased to amuse.

The party were one day assembled in the old-fashioned hall, dinner had just been removed, and they were arranging in which direction they should ride. "I have it," cried Franziska suddenly, "I wonder we never thought before of going to view by day the spot where we fell in with our night-adventure with wolves and the Mysterious Stranger."

"You mean a visit to the ruins—what were they called?" said the knight.

"Castle Klatka," cried Franziska gaily. "Oh, we really must ride there! It will be so charming to go over again by daylight, and in safety, the ground where we had such a dreadful fright."

"Bring round the horses," said the knight to a servant "and tell the steward to come to me immediately." The latter, an old man, soon after entered the room.

"We intend taking a ride to Klatka," said the knight: "we had an adventure there on our road.—"

"So old Kumpan told me," interrupted the steward.

"And what do you say about it?" asked the knight.

"I really don't know what to say," replied the old man, shaking his head. "I was a youth of twenty when I first came to this castle, and now my hair is grey; half a century has elapsed during that time. Hundreds of times my duty has called me into the neighborhood of those ruins, but never have I seen the Fiend of Klatka."

"What do you say? Whom do you call by that name?" inquired Franziska, whose love of adventure and romance was strongly awakened.

"Why, people call by that name the ghost or spirit who is supposed to haunt the ruins," replied the steward. "They say he only shows himself on moonlight nights—"

"That is quite natural," interrupted Franz smiling. "Ghosts can never bear the light of day; and if the moon did not shine, how could the ghost be seen? for it is not supposed that any one for a mere freak would visit the ruins by torch-light."

"There are some credulous people who pretend to have seen this ghost," continued the steward. "Huntsmen and wood-cutters say they have met him by the large oak on the cross-path. That, noble sir, is supposed to be the spot he inclines most to haunt, for the tree was planted in remembrance of the man who fell there."

"And who was he?" asked Franziska with increasing curiosity.

"The last owner of the castle, which at that time was a sort of robber's den, and the headquarters of all depredators in the neighborhood," answered the old man. "They say this man was of superhuman strength, and was feared not only on account of his passionate temper, but of his treaties with the Turkish hordes. Any young woman, too, in the neighborhood to whom he took a fancy, was carried off to his tower and never heard of more. When the measure of his iniquity was full, the whole neighborhood rose in a mass, besieged his stronghold, and at length he was slain on the spot where the huge oak-tree now stands."

"I wonder they did not burn the whole castle, so as to erase the very memory of it," said the knight.

"It was a dependency of the church, and that saved it," replied the other. "Your great-grandfather afterwards took possession of it, for it had fine lands attached. As the Knight of Klatka was of good family, a monument was erected to him in the church, which now lies as much in ruin as the castle itself."

"Oh, let us set off at once! Nothing shall prevent my visiting so interesting a spot," said Franziska eagerly. "The imprisoned damsels who never reappeared, the storming of the tower, the death of the knight, the nightly wanderings of his spirit round the old oak, and, lastly, our own adventure, all draw me thither with an indescribable curiosity."

When a servant announced that the horses were at the door, the young girls tripped laughingly down the steps which led to the coach-yard. Franz, the knight, and a servant well acquainted with the country, followed; and in a few minutes the party were on their road to the forest.

The sun was still high in the heavens when they saw the towers of Klatka rising above the trees. Everything in the wood was still, except the cheerful twitterings of the birds as they hopped about amongst the bursting buds and leaves, and announced that spring had arrived.

The party soon found themselves near the old oak at the bottom of the hill on which stood the towers, still imposing in their ruin. Ivy and bramble bushes had wound themselves over the walls, and forced deep roots so firmly between the stones that they in a great measure held these together. On the top of the highest spot, a small bush in its young fresh verdure swayed lightly in the breeze.

The gentlemen assisted their companions to alight, and leaving the horses to the care of the servant, ascended the hill to the castle. After having explored this in every nook and cranny, and spent much time in a vain search for some trace of the extraordinary stranger, whom Franziska declared she was determined to discover, they proceeded to an inspection of the adjoining church. This they found to have better withstood the ravages of time and weather; the nave, indeed, was in complete dilapidation, but the chancel and altar were still under roof, as well as a sort of chapel which appeared to have been a place of honor for the families of the old knights of the castle. Few traces remained, however, of the magnificent painted glass which must once have adorned the windows, and the wind entered at pleasure through the open spaces.

The party were occupied for some time in deciphering the inscriptions on a number of tombstones, and on the walls, principally within the chancel. They were generally memorials of the ancient lords, with figures of men in armor, and women and children of all ages. A flying raven and various other devices were placed at the corners. One gravestone, which stood close to the entrance of the chancel, differed widely from the others: there was no figure sculptured on it, and the inscription, which, on all besides, was a mere mass of flattering eulogies, was here simple and unadorned; it contained only these words: "Ezzelin von Klatka fell like a knight at the storming of the castle"— on such a day and year.

"That must be the monument of the knight whose ghost is said to haunt these ruins," cried Franziska eagerly.

"What a pity he is not represented in the same way as the others—I should so like to have known what he was like!"

"Oh, there is the family vault, with steps leading down to it, and the sun is lighting it up through a crevice, said Franz, stepping from the adjoining vestry.

The whole party followed him down the eight or nine steps which led to a tolerably airy chamber, where were placed a number of coffins of all sizes, some of them crumbling into dust. Here, again, one close to the door was distinguished from the others by the simplicity of its design, the freshness of its appearance, and the brief inscription: "Ezzelinus de Klatka, Eques."

As not the slightest effluvium was perceptible, they lingered some time in the vault; and when they reascended to the church, they had a long talk over the old possessors, of whom the knight now remembered he had heard his parents speak. The sun had disappeared, and the moon was just rising as the explorers turned to leave the ruins. Bertha had made a step into the nave, when she uttered a slight exclamation of fear and surprise. Her eyes fell on a man who wore a hat with drooping feathers, a sword at his side, and a short cloak of somewhat old-fashioned cut over his shoulders. The stranger leaned carelessly on a broken column at the entrance; he did not appear to take any notice of the party; and the moon shone full on his pale face.

The party advanced towards the stranger.

"If I am not mistaken," commenced the knight; "we have met before."

Not a word from the unknown.

"You released us in an almost miraculous manner," said Franziska, "from the power of those dreadful wolves. Am I wrong in supposing it is to you we are indebted for that great service?"

"The beasts are afraid of me," replied the stranger in a deep fierce tone, while he fastened his sunken eyes on the girl, without taking any notice of the others.

"Then you are probably a huntsman," said Franz, "and wage war against the fierce brutes."

"Who is not either the pursuer or the pursued? All persecute or are persecuted, and Fate persecutes all," replied the stranger without looking at him.

"Do you live in these ruins?" asked the knight hesitatingly.

"Yes; but not to the destruction of your game, as you may fear, Knight of Fahnenberg," said the unknown contemptuously. "Be quite assured of your property shall remain untouched—"

"Oh! my father did not mean that," interrupted Franziska, who appeared to take the liveliest interest in the stranger. "Unfortunate events and sad experiences have, no doubt, induced you to take up your abode in these ruins, of which my father would by no means dispossess you."

"Your father is very good, if that is what he meant," said the stranger in his former tone; and it seemed as though his dark features were drawn into a slight smile; "but people of my sort are rather difficult to turn out."

"You must live very uncomfortably here," said Franziska, half vexed, for she thought her polite speech had deserved a better reply.

"My dwelling is not exactly uncomfortable, only somewhat small, still quite suitable for quiet people," said the unknown with a kind of sneer. "I am not, however, always quiet; I sometimes pine to quit the narrow space, and then I dash away through forest and field, over hill and dale; and the time when I must return to my little dwelling always comes too soon for me."

"As you now and then leave your dwelling," said the knight, "I would invite you to visit us, if I knew—"

"That I was in a station to admit of your doing so," interrupted the other; and the knight started slightly, for the stranger had exactly expressed the half-formed thought. "I lament," he continued coldly, "that I am not able to give you particulars on this point—some difficulties stand in the way: be assured, however, that I am a knight, and of at least as ancient a family as yourself."

"Then you must not refuse our request," cried Franziska, highly interested in the strange manners of the unknown. "You must come and visit us."

"I am no boon-companion, and on that account few have invited me of late," replied the other with his peculiar smile; "besides, I generally remain at home during the day; that is my time for rest. I belong, you must know, to that class of persons who turn day into night, and night into day, and who love everything uncommon and peculiar."

"Really? So do I! And for that reason, you must visit us," cried Franziska. "Now," she continued smiling, "I suppose you have just risen, and you are taking your morning airing. Well, since the moon is your sun, pray pay a frequent visit to our castle by the light of its rays. I think we shall agree very well, and that it will be very nice for us to be acquainted."

"You wish it?—You press the invitation?" asked the stranger earnestly and decidedly.

"To be sure, for otherwise you will not come," replied the young lady shortly.

"Well, then, come I will!" said the other, again fixing his gaze on her. "If my company does not please you at any time, you will have yourself to blame for an acquaintance with one who seldom forces himself, but is difficult to shake off."

When the unknown had concluded these words, he made a slight motion with his hand, as though to take leave of them, and passing under the doorway, disappeared among the ruins. The party soon after mounted their horses, and took the road home.

It was the evening of the following day, and all were again seated in the hall of the castle. Bertha had that day received good news. The knight Woislaw had written from Hungary, that the war with the Turks would be brought to a conclusion during the year, and that although he had intended returning to Silesia, hearing of the knight of Fahnenberg having gone to take possession of his new estates, he should follow the family there, not doubting that Bertha had accompanied her friend. He hinted that he stood so high in the opinion of his duke on account of his valuable services, that in future his duties would be even more important and extensive; but before settling down to them, he should come and claim Bertha's promise to become his wife. He had been much enriched by his master, as well as by booty taken from the Turks. Having formerly lost his right hand in the duke's service, he had essayed to fight with his left; but this did not succeed very admirably, and so he had an iron one made by a very clever artist. This hand performed many of the functions of a natural one, but there had been still much wanting; now, however, his master had presented him with one of gold, an extraordinary work of art, produced by a celebrated Italian mechanic. The knight described it as something marvelous, especially as to the superhuman strength with which it enabled him to use the sword and lance. Franziska naturally rejoiced in the happiness of her friend, who had had no news of her betrothed for a long time before. She launched out every now and then, partly to plague Franz, and partly to express her own feelings, in the highest praise and admiration of the bravery and enterprise of the knight, whose adventurous qualities she lauded to the skies. Even the scar on his face, and his want of a right hand, were reckoned as virtues; and Franziska at last saucily declared that a rather ugly man was infinitely more attractive to her than a handsome one, for as a general rule handsome men were conceited and effeminate. Thus, she added, no one could term their acquaintance of the night before handsome, but attractive and interesting he certainly was. Franz and Bertha simultaneously denied this. His gloomy appearance, the deadly hue of his complexion, the tone of his voice, were each in turn depreciated by Bertha, while Franz found fault with the contempt and arrogance obvious in his speech. The knight stood between the two parties. He thought there was something in his bearing that spoke of good family, though much could not be said for his politeness; however, the man might have had trials enough in his life to make him misanthropical. Whilst they were conversing in this way, the door suddenly opened, and the subject of their remarks himself walked in.

"Pardon me, Sir Knight," he said coldly, "that I come, if not uninvited, at least unannounced; there was no one in the ante-chamber to do me that service."

The brilliantly lighted chamber gave a full view of the stranger. He was a man about forty, tall, and extremely thin. His features could not be termed uninteresting—there lay in them something bold and daring; but the expression was on the whole anything but benevolent. There was contempt and sarcasm in the cold grey eyes, whose glance, however, was at times so piercing, that no one could endure it long. His complexion was even more peculiar than the features: it could neither be called pale nor yellow; it was a sort of grey, or, so to speak, dirty white, like that of an Indian who has been suffering long from fever; and was rendered still more remarkable by the intense blackness of his beard and short cropped hair. The dress of the unknown was knightly, but old-fashioned and neglected; there were great spots of rust on the collar and breastplate of his armor; and his dagger and the hilt of his finely-worked sword were marked in some places with mildew. As the party were just going to supper, it was only natural to invite the stranger to partake of it; he complied, however, only in so far that he seated himself at the table, for he ate no morsel. The knight, with surprise, inquired the reason.

"For a long time past, I have accustomed myself never to eat at night," he replied with a strange smile. "My digestion is quite unused to solids, and indeed would scarcely confront them. I live entirely on liquids."

"Oh, then, we can empty a bumper of Rhine-wine together," cried the host.

"Thanks; but I neither drink wine nor any cold beverage," replied the other; and his tone was full of mockery. It appeared as if there was some amusing association connected with the idea.

"Then I will order you a cup of hippocras"—a warm drink composed of herbs—"it shall be ready immediately," said Franziska.

"Many thanks, fair lady; not at present," replied the other. "But if I refuse the beverage you offer me now, you may be assured that as soon as I require it —perhaps very soon—I will request that, or some other of you."

Bertha and Franz thought the man had something inexpressibly repulsive in his whole manner, and they had no inclination to engage him in conversation; but the baron, thinking that perhaps politeness required him to say something, turned towards the guest, and commenced in a friendly tone: "It is now many weeks since we first became acquainted with you; we then had to thank you for a signal service—"

"And I have not yet told you my name, although you would gladly know it," interrupted the other dryly. "I am called Azzo; and as"—this he said again with his ironical smile—"with the permission of the Knight of Fahnenberg, I live at the castle of Klatka, you can in future call me Azzo von Klatka."

"I only wonder you do not feel lonely and uncomfortable amongst those old walls," began Bertha. "I cannot understand—"

"What my business is there? Oh, about that I will willingly give you some information, since you and the young gentleman there takes such a kindly interest in my person," replied the unknown in his tone of sarcasm.

Franz and Bertha both started, for he had revealed their thoughts as though he could read their souls. "You see, lady," he continued, "there are a variety of strange whims in the world. As I have already said, I love what is peculiar and uncommon, at least what would appear so to you. It is wrong in the main to be astonished at anything, for, viewed in one light, all things are alike; even life and death, this side of the grave and the other, have more resemblance than you would imagine. You perhaps consider me rather touched a little in my mind, for taking up my abode with the bat and the owl; but if so, why not consider every hermit and recluse insane? You will tell me that those are holy men. I certainly have no pretension that way; but as they find pleasure in praying and singing psalms, so I amuse myself with hunting. Oh, you can have no idea of the intense pleasure of dashing away in the pale moonlight, on a horse that never tires, over hill and dale, through forest and woodland! I rush among the wolves, which fly at my approach, as you yourself perceived, as though they were puppies fearful of the lash."

"But still it must be lonely, very lonely for you," remarked Bertha.

"So it would by day; but I am then asleep," replied the stranger dryly; "at night I am merry enough."

"You hunt in an extraordinary way," remarked Franz hesitatingly.

"Yes; but, nevertheless, I have no communication with robbers, as you seem to imagine," replied Azzo coldly.

Franz again started—that very thought had just crossed his mind. "Oh, I beg your pardon; I do not know—" he stammered.

"What to make of me," interrupted the other. "You would, therefore, do well to believe just what I tell you, or at least to avoid making conjectures of your own, which will lead to nothing."

"I understand you: I know how to value your ideas, if no one else does," cried Franziska eagerly. "The humdrum, everyday life of the generality of men is repulsive to you; you have tasted the joys and pleasures of life, at least what are so called, and you have found them tame and hollow. How soon one tires of the things one sees all around! Life consists in change. Only in what is new, uncommon, and peculiar, do the flowers of the spirit bloom and give forth scent. Even pain may become a pleasure if it saves one from the shallow monotony of everyday life—a thing I shall hate till the hour of my death."

"Right, fair lady—quite right! Remain in this mind: this was always my opinion, and the one from which I have derived the highest reward," cried Azzo; and his fierce eyes sparkled more intensely than ever. "I am doubly pleased to have found in you a person who shares my ideas. Oh, if you were a man, you would make me a splendid companion; but even a woman may have fine experiences when once these opinions take root in her, and bring forth action!"

As Azzo spoke these words in a cold tone of politeness, he turned from the subject, and for the rest of his visit only gave the knight monosyllabic replies to his inquiries, taking leave before the table was cleared. To an invitation from the knight, backed by a still more pressing one from Franziska to repeat his visit, he replied that he would take advantage of their kindness, and come sometimes.

When the stranger had departed, many were the remarks made on his appearance and general deportment. Franz declared his most decided dislike to him. Whether it was as usual to vex her cousin, or whether Azzo had really made an impression on her, Franziska took his part vehemently. As Franz contradicted her more eagerly than usual, the young lady launched out into still stronger expressions; and there is no knowing what hard words her cousin might have received had not a servant entered the room.

The following morning Franziska lay longer than usual in bed. When her friend went to her room, fearful lest she should be ill, she found her pale and exhausted. Franziska complained she had passed a very bad night; she thought the dispute with Franz about the stranger must have excited her greatly, for she felt quite feverish and exhausted, and a strange dream, too, had worried her, which was evidently a consequence of the evening's conversation. Bertha, as usual, took the young man's part, and added, that a common dispute about a man whom no one knew, and about whom any one might form his own opinion, could not possibly have thrown her into her present state. "At least," she continued, "you can let me hear this wonderful dream."

To her surprise; Franziska for a length of time refused to do so.

"Come, tell me," inquired Bertha, "what can possibly prevent you from relating a dream—a mere dream? I might almost think it credible, if the idea were not too horrid, that poor Franz is not very far wrong when he says that the thin, corpse-like, dried-up, old-fashioned stranger has made a greater impression on you than you will allow."

"Did Franz say so?" asked Franziska. "Then you can tell him he is not mistaken. Yes, the thin, corpse-like, dried-up, whimsical stranger is far more interesting to me than the rosy-checked, well-dressed, polite, and prosy cousin."

"Strange," cried Bertha. "I cannot at all comprehend the almost magic influence which this man, so repulsive, exercises over you."

"Perhaps the very reason I take his part, may be that you are all so prejudiced against him," remarked Franziska pettishly. "Yes, it must be so; for that his appearance should please my eyes, is what no one in his senses could imagine. But," she continued, smiling and holding out her hand to Bertha, "is it not laughable that I should get out of temper even with you about this stranger?—I can more easily understand it with Franz—and that this unknown should spoil my morning, as he has already spoiled my evening and my night's rest?"

"By that dream, you mean?" said Bertha, easily appeased, as she put her arm round her cousin's neck and kissed her. "Now, do tell it to me. You know how I delight in hearing anything of the kind."

"Well, I will, as a sort of compensation for my peevishness towards you," said the other, clasping her friend's hands. "Now, listen! I had walked up and down my room for a long time; I was excited—out of spirits—I do not know exactly what. It was almost midnight ere I lay down, but I could not sleep. I tossed about, and at length it was only from sheer exhaustion that I dropped off. But what a sleep it was! An inward fear ran through me perpetually. I saw a number of pictures before me, as I used to do in childish sicknesses. I do not know whether I was asleep or half awake. Then I dreamed, but as dearly as if I had been wide awake, that a sort of mist filled the room, and out of it stepped the knight Azzo. He gazed at me for a time, and then letting himself slowly down on one knee, imprinted a kiss on my throat. Long did his lips rest there; and I felt a slight pain, which always went on increasing, until I could bear it no more. With all my strength I tried to force the vision from me, but succeeded only after a long struggle. No doubt I uttered a scream, for that awoke me from my trance. when I came a little to my senses, I felt a sort of superstitious fear creeping over me—how great you may imagine when I tell you that, with my eyes open and awake, it appeared to me as if Azzo's figure were still by my bed, and then disappearing gradually into the mist, vanished at the door!"

"You must have dreamed very heavily, my poor friend," began Bertha, but suddenly paused. She gazed with surprise at Franziska's throat. "Why, what is that?" she cried. "Just look: how extraordinary—a red streak on your throat!"

Franziska raised herself, and went to a little glass that stood in the window. She really saw a small red line about an inch long on her neck, which began to smart when she touched it with her finger.

"I must have hurt myself by some means in my sleep," she said after a pause; "and that in some measure will account for my dream."

The friends continued chatting for some time about this singular coincidence—the dream and the stranger; and at length it was all turned into a joke by Bertha.

Several weeks passed. The knight had found the estate and affairs in greater disorder than he at first imagined; and instead of remaining three or four weeks, as was originally intended, their departure was deferred to an indefinite period. This postponement was likewise in some measure occasioned by Franziska's continued indisposition. She who had formerly bloomed like a rose in its young fresh beauty, was becoming daily thinner, more sickly and exhausted, and at the same time so pale, that in the space of a month not a tinge of red was perceptible on the once glowing cheek. The knight's anxiety about her was extreme, and the best advice was procured which the age and country afforded; but all to no purpose. Franziska complained from time to time that the horrible dream with which her illness commenced was repeated, and that always on the day following she felt an increased and indescribable weakness. Bertha naturally set this down to the effect of fever, but the ravages of that fever on the usually dear reason of her friend filled her with alarm.

The knight Azzo repeated his visits every now and then. He always came in the evening, and when the moon shone brightly. His manner was always the same. He spoke in monosyllables, and was coldly polite to the knight; to Franz and Bertha, particularly to the former, contemptuous and haughty; but to Franziska, friendliness itself. Often when, after a short visit, he again left the house, his peculiarities became the subject of conversation. Besides his old way of speaking, in which Bertha said there lay a deep hatred, a cold detestation of all mankind with the exception of Franziska, two other singularities were observable. During none of his visits, which often took place at supper-time, had he been prevailed upon to eat or drink anything, and that without giving any good reason for his abstinence. A remarkable alteration, too, had taken place in his appearance; he seemed an entirely different creature. The skin, before so shriveled and stretched, seemed smooth and soft, while a slight tinge of red appeared in his cheeks, which began to look round and plump. Bertha, who could not at all conceal her ill-will towards him, said often, that much as she hated his face before, when it was more like a death's-head than a human being's, it was now more than ever repulsive; she always felt a shudder run through her veins whenever his sharp piercing eyes rested on her. Perhaps it was owing to Franziska's partiality, or to the knight Azzo's own contemptuous way of replying to Franz, or to his haughty way of treating him in general, that made the young man dislike him more and more. It was quite observable, that whenever Franz made a remark to his cousin in the presence of Azzo, the latter would immediately throw some ill-natured light on it, or distort it to a totally different meaning. This increased from day to day, and at last Franz declared to Bertha, that he would stand such conduct no longer, and that it was only out of consideration for Franziska that he had not already called him to account.

At this time the party at the castle was increased by the arrival of Bertha's long-expected guest. He came just as they were sitting down to supper one evening, and all jumped up to greet their old friend. The knight Woislaw was a true model of the soldier, hardened and strengthened by war with men and elements. His face would not have been termed ugly, if a Turkish saber had not left a mark running from the right eye to the left cheek, and standing out bright red from the sunburned skin. The frame of the Castellan of Glogau might almost be termed colossal. Few would have been able to carry his armor, and still fewer move with his lightness and ease under its weight. He did not think little of this same armor, for it had been a present from the palatine of Hungary on his leaving the camp. The blue wrought-steel was ornamented all over with patterns in gold; and he had put it on to do honor to his bride-elect, together with the wonderful gold hand, the gift of the duke. Woislaw was questioned by the knight and Franz on all the concerns of the campaign; and he entered into the most minute particulars relating to the battles, which, with regard to plunder, had been more successful than ever. He spoke much of the strength of the Turks in a hand-to-hand fight, and remarked that he owed the duke many thanks for his splendid gift, for in consequence of its strength many of the enemy regarded him as something superhuman. The sickliness and deathlike paleness of Franziska was too perceptible not to be immediately noticed by Woislaw; accustomed to see her so fresh and cheerful, he hastened to inquire into the cause of the change. Bertha related all that had happened, and Woislaw listened with the greatest interest. This increased to the utmost at the account of the often-repeated dream, and Franziska had to give him the most minute particulars of it; it appeared as though he had met with a similar case before, or at least had heard of one. When the young lady added, that it was very remarkable that the wound on her throat which she had at first felt had never healed, and still pained her, the knight Woislaw looked at Bertha as much as to say, that this last fact had greatly strengthened his idea as to the cause of Franziska's illness.

It was only natural that the discourse should next turn to the knight Azzo, about whom every one began to talk eagerly. Woislaw inquired as minutely as he had done with regard to Franziska's illness, about what concerned this stranger, from the first evening of their acquaintance down to his last visit, without, however, giving any opinion on the subject. The party were still in earnest conversation, when the door opened, and Azzo entered. Woislaw's eyes remained fixed on him, as he, without taking any particular notice of the new arrival, walked up to the table, and seating himself, directed most of the conversation to Franziska and her father, and now and then made some sarcastic remark when Franz began to speak. The Turkish war again came on the tapis, and though Azzo only put in an occasional remark, Woislaw had much to say on the subject. Thus they had advanced late into the night, and Franz said smiling to Woislaw: "I should not wonder if day had surprised us, whilst listening to your entertaining adventures."

"I admire the young gentleman's taste," said Azzo, with an ironical curl of the lip. "Stories of storm and shipwreck are, indeed, best heard on *terra firma*, and those of battle and death at a hospitable table or in the chimney-corner. One had then the comfortable feeling of keeping a whole skin, and being in no danger, not even of taking cold." With the last words, he gave a hoarse laugh, and turning his back on Franz, rose, bowed to the rest of the company, and left the room. The knight, who always accompanied Azzo to the door, now expressed himself fatigued, and bade his friends good night.

"That Azzo's impertinence is unbearable," cried Bertha when he was gone. "He becomes daily more rough, unpolite, and presuming. If only on account of Franziska's dream, though of course he cannot help that, I detest him. Now, tonight, not one civil word has he spoken to any one but Franziska, except, perhaps, some casual remark to my uncle."

"I cannot deny that you are right, Bertha," said her cousin. "One may forgive much to a man whom fate had probably made somewhat misanthropical; but he should not overstep the bounds of common politeness.

But where on earth is Franz?" added Franziska, as she looked uneasily round. —The young man had quietly left the room whilst Bertha was speaking.

"He cannot have followed the knight Azzo to challenge him?" cried Bertha in alarm.

"It were better he entered a lion's den to pull his mane!" said Woislaw vehemently. "I must follow him instantly," he added, as he rushed from the room.

He hastened over the threshold, out of the castle, and through the court, before he came up to them. Here a narrow bridge with a slight balustrade passed over the moat by which the castle was surrounded. It appeared that Franz had only just addressed Azzo in a few hot words, for as Woislaw, unperceived by either, advanced under the shadow of the wall, Azzo said gloomily: "Leave me, foolish boy—leave me; for by that sun"—and he pointed to the full moon above them—"you will see those rays no more if you linger another moment on my path."

"And I tell you, wretch, that you either give me satisfaction for your repeated insolence, or you die," cried Franz, drawing his sword.

Azzo stretched forth his hand, and grasping the sword in the middle, it snapped like a broken reed. "I warn you for the last time," he said in a voice of thunder, as he threw the pieces into the moat. "Now, away—away, boy, from my path, or, by those below us, you are lost!"

"You or I! you or I!" cried Franz madly, as he made a rush at the sword of his antagonist, and strove to draw it from his side. Azzo replied not; only a bitter laugh half escaped from his lips; then seizing Franz by the chest, he lifted him up like an infant, and was in the act of throwing him over the bridge, when Woislaw stepped to his side. With a grasp of his wonderful hand, into the springs of which he threw all his strength, he seized Azzo's arm, pulled it down, and obliged him to drop his victim. Azzo seemed in the highest degree astonished. Without concerning himself further about Franz, he gazed in amazement on Woislaw.

"Who are thou who darest to rob me of my prey?" he asked hesitatingly. "Is it possible? Can you be—"

"Ask not, thou bloody one! Go, seek thy nourishment! Soon comes thy hour!" replied Woislaw in a calm but firm tone.

"Ha, now I know!" cried Azzo eagerly. "Welcome, blood-brother! I give up to you this worm, and for your sake will not crush him. Farewell; our paths will soon meet again."

"Soon, very soon; farewell!" cried Woislaw, drawing Franz towards him. Azzo rushed away, and disappeared.

Franz had remained for some moments in a state of stupefaction, but suddenly started as from a dream. "I am dishonored, dishonored forever!" he cried, as he pressed his clenched hands to his forehead.

"Calm yourself; you could not have conquered," said Woislaw.

"But I will conquer, or perish!" cried Franz incensed. "I will seek this adventurer in his den, and he or I must fall."

"You could not hurt him," said Woislaw. "You would infallibly be the victim."

"Then show me a way to bring the wretch to judgment," cried Franz, seizing Woislaw's hands, while tears of anger sprang to his eyes. "Disgraced as I am, I cannot live."

"You shall be revenged, and that within twenty-four hours, I hope; but only on two conditions—"

"I agree to them! I will do anything—" began the young man eagerly.

"The first is, that you do nothing, but leave everything in my hands," interrupted Woislaw. "The second, that you will assist me in persuading Franziska to do what I shall represent to her as absolutely necessary. That young lady's life is in more danger from Azzo than your own!"

"How? What?" cried Franz fiercely. "Franziska's life in danger! and from that man? Tell me, Woislaw, who is this fiend?"

"Not a word will I tell either the young lady or you, until the danger is passed," said Woislaw firmly. "The smallest indiscretion would ruin everything. No one can act here but Franziska herself, and if she refuses to do so she is irretrievably lost."

"Speak, and I will help you. I will do all you wish, but I must know—"

"Nothing, absolutely nothing," replied Woislaw. "I must have both you and Franziska yield to me unconditionally. Come now, come to her. You are to be mute on what has passed, and use every effort to induce her to accede to my proposal."

Woislaw spoke firmly, and it was impossible for Franz to make any further objection; in a few moments they both entered the hall, where they found the young girls still anxiously awaiting them.

"Oh, I have been so frightened," said Franziska, even paler than usual, as she held out her hand to Franz. "I trust all has ended peaceably."

"Everything is arranged; a couple of words were sufficient to settle the whole affair," said Woislaw cheerfully.

"But Master Franz was less concerned in it than yourself, fair lady."

"I! How do you mean?" said Franziska in surprise.

"I allude to your illness," replied the other.

"And you spoke of that to Azzo? Does he, then, know a remedy which he could not tell me himself?" she inquired, smiling painfully.

"The knight Azzo must take part in your cure; but speak to you about it he cannot, unless the remedy is to lose all its efficacy," replied Woislaw quietly.

"So it is some secret elixir, as the learned doctors say, who have so long attended me, and through whose means I only grow worse," said Franziska mournfully.

"It is certainly a secret, but is as certainly a cure," replied Woislaw.

"So said all, but none has succeeded," said the young lady peevishly.

"You might at least try it," began Bertha.

"Because your friend proposes it," said the other smiling. "I have no doubt that you, with nothing ailing you, would take all manner of drugs to please your knight; but with me the inducement is wanting, and therefore also the faith."

"I did not speak of any medicine," said Woislaw.

"Oh! a magical remedy! I am to be cured—what was it the quack who was here the other day called it?—' by sympathy.' Yes, that was it."

"I do not object to your calling it so, if you like," said Woislaw smiling; "but you must know, dear lady, that the measures I shall propose must be attended to literally, and according to the strictest directions."

"And you trust this to me?" asked Franziska.

"Certainly," said Woislaw hesitating; "but—"

"Well, why do you not proceed? Can you think that I shall fail in courage?" she asked.

"Courage is certainly necessary for the success of my plan," said Woislaw gravely; "and it is because I give you credit for a large share of that virtue, I venture to propose it at all, although for the real harmlessness of the remedy I will answer with my life, provided you follow my directions exactly."

"Well, tell me the plan, and then I can decide," said the young lady.

"I can only tell you that when we commence our operations," replied Woislaw.

"Do you think I am a child to be sent here, there, and everywhere, without a reason?" asked Franziska, with something of her old pettishness.

"You did me great injustice, dear lady, if you thought for a moment I would propose anything disagreeable to you, unless demanded by the sternest necessity," said Woislaw; "and yet I can only repeat my former words."

"Then I will not do it," cried Franziska. "I have already tried so much, and all ineffectually."

"I give you my honor as a knight, that your cure is certain, but—you must pledge yourself solemnly and unconditionally to do implicitly what I shall direct," said Woislaw earnestly.

"Oh, I implore you to consent, Franziska. Our friend would not propose anything unnecessary," said Bertha, taking both her cousin's hands.

"And let me join my entreaties to Bertha's," said Franz.

"How strange you all are!" exclaimed Franziska, shaking her head; "you make such a secret of that which I must know if I am to accomplish it, and then you declare so positively that I shall recover, when my own feelings tell me it is quite hopeless."

"I repeat, that I will answer for the result," said Woislaw, "on the condition I mentioned before, and that you have courage to carry out what you commence."

"Ha! now I understand; this, after all, is the only thing which appears doubtful to you," cried Franziska. "Well, to show you that our sex are neither wanting in the will nor in the power to accomplish deeds of daring, I give my consent."

With the last words, she offered Woislaw her hand.

"Our compact is thus sealed," she pursued smiling. "Now say, Sir Knight, how am I to commence this mysterious cure?"

"It commenced when you gave your consent," said Woislaw gravely. "Now, I have only to request that you will ask no more questions, but hold yourself in readiness to take a ride with me tomorrow an hour before sunset. I also request that you will not mention to your father a word of what has passed."

"Strange!" said Franziska.

"You have made the compact; you are not wanting in resolution; and I will answer for everything else," said Woislaw encouragingly.

"Well, so let it be. I will follow your directions," said the lady, although she still looked incredulous.

"On our return you shall know everything; before that, it is quite impossible," said Woislaw in conclusion. "Now go, dear lady, and take some rest; you will need strength for tomorrow."

It was on the morning of the following day, the sun had not risen above an hour, and the dew still lay like a veil of pearls on the grass, or dripped from the petals of the flowers, swaying in the early breeze, when the knight Woislaw hastened over the fields towards the forest, and turned into a gloomy path, which by the direction, one could perceive, led towards the towers of Klatka. When he arrived at the old oak-tree we have before had occasion to mention, he sought carefully along the road for traces of human footsteps, but only a deer had passed that way; and seemingly satisfied with his search, he proceeded on his way, though not before he had half drawn his dagger from its sheath, as though to assure himself that it was ready for service in time of need.

Slowly he ascended the path; it was evident he carried something beneath his cloak. Arrived in the court, he left the ruins of the castle to the left, and entered the old chapel. In the chancel, he looked eagerly and earnestly around. A deathlike stillness reigned in the deserted sanctuary, only broken by the whispering of the wind in an old thorn-tree which grew outside. Woislaw had looked round him ere he perceived the door leading down to the vault; he hurried towards it, and descended. The sun's position enabled its rays to penetrate the crevices, and made the subterranean chamber so light, that one could read easily the inscriptions at the head and feet of the coffins. The knight first laid on the ground the packet he had hitherto carried under his cloak, and then going from coffin to coffin, at last remained stationary before the oldest of them. He read the inscription carefully, drew his dagger thoughtfully from its case, and endeavored to raise the lid with its point. This was no difficult matter, for the rusty iron nails kept but a slight hold of the rotten wood. On looking in, only a heap of ashes, some remnants of dress, and a skull were the contents. He quickly closed it again, and went on to the next, passing over those of a woman and two children. Here things had much the same appearance, except that the corpse held together till the lid was raised, and then fell into dust, a few linen rags and bones being alone perceptible In the third, fourth, and nearly the next half-dozen, the bodies were in better preservation: in some, they looked a sort of yellow brown mummy; whilst in others, a skinless skull covered with hair grinned from the coverings of velvet, silk, or mildewed embroideries; all, however, were touched with the loathsome marks of decay. Only one more coffin now remained to be inspected; Woislaw approached it, and read the inscription. It was the same that had before attracted the Knight of Fahnenberg: Ezzelin von Klatka, the last possessor of the tower, was described as lying therein. Woislaw found it more difficult to raise the lid here; and it was only by the exertion of much strength he at length succeeded in extracting the nails. He did all, however, as quietly as if afraid of rousing some sleeper within; he then raised the cover, and cast a glance on the corpse. An involuntary "Ha!" burst from his lips as he stepped back a pace. If he had less expected the sight that met his eyes, he would have been far more overcome. In the coffin lay Azzo as he lived and breathed, and as Woislaw had seen him at the supper-table only the evening before. His appearance, dress and all were the same; besides, he had more the semblance of sleep than of death—no trace of decay was visible —there was even a rosy tint on his cheeks. Only the circumstance that the breast did not heave, distinguished him from one who slept. For a few moments Woislaw did not move; he could only stare into the coffin. With a hastiness in his movements not usual with him, he suddenly seized the lid, which had fallen from his hands, and laying it on the coffin, knocked the nails into their places. As soon as he had completed this work, he fetched the packet he had left at the entrance, and laying it on the top of the coffin, hastily ascended the steps, and quitted the church and the ruins.

The day passed. Before evening, Franziska requested her father to allow her to take a ride with Woislaw, under pretense of showing him the country. He, only too happy to think this a sign of amendment in his daughter, readily gave his consent; so followed by a single servant, they mounted and left the castle. Woislaw was unusually silent and serious. When Franziska began to rally him about his gravity, and the approaching sympathetic care, he replied that what was before her was no laughing matter; and that although the result would be certainly a cure, still it would leave an impression on her whole future life. In such discourse they reached the wood, and at length the oak, where they left their horses. Woislaw gave Franziska his arm, and they ascended the hill slowly and silently. They had just reached one of the half-dilapidated outworks where they could catch a glimpse of the open country, when Woislaw, speaking more to himself than to his companion, said: "In a quarter of an hour, the sun will set, and in another hour the moon will have risen; then all must be accomplished. It will soon be time to commence the work."

"Then, I should think it was time to entrust me with some idea of what it is," said Franziska, looking at him.

"Well, lady," he replied, turning towards her, and his voice was very solemn, "I entreat you, Franziska von Fahnenberg, for your own good, and as you love the father who clings to you with his whole soul, that you will weigh well my words, and that you will not interrupt me with questions which I cannot answer until the work is completed. Your life is in the greatest danger from the illness under which you are laboring; indeed, you are irrecoverably lost if you do not fully carry out what I shall now impart to you. Now, promise me to do implicitly as I shall tell you; I pledge you my knightly word it is nothing against Heaven, or the honor of your house; and, besides, it is the sole means for saving you." With these words, he held out his right hand to his companion, while he raised the other to heaven in confirmation of his oath.

"I promise you," said Franziska, visibly moved by Woislaw's solemn tone, as she laid her little white and wasted hand in his.

"Then, come; it is time," was his reply, as he led her towards the church. The last rays of the sun were just pouring through the broken windows. They entered the chancel, the best preserved part of the whole building; here there were still some old kneeling-stools, placed before the high-altar, although nothing remained of that but the stonework and a few steps; the pictures and decorations had all vanished.

"Say an Ave; you will have need of it," said Woislaw, as he himself fell on his knees.

Franziska knelt beside him, and repeated a short prayer. After a few moments, both rose. "The moment has arrived! The sun sinks, and before the moon rises, all must be over," said Woislaw quickly.

"What am I to do?" asked Franziska cheerfully.

"You see there that open vault!" replied the knight Woislaw, pointing to the door and flight of steps: "You must descend. You must go alone; I may not accompany you. When you have reached the vault you will find, close to the entrance, a coffin, on which is placed a small packet. Open this packet, and you will find three long iron nails and a hammer. Then pause for a moment; but when I begin to repeat the Credo in a loud voice, knock with all your might, first one nail, then a second, and then a third, into the lid of the coffin, right up to their heads."

Franziska stood thunderstruck; her whole body trembled, and she could not utter a word. Woislaw perceived it.

"Take courage, dear lady!" said he. "Think that you are in the hands of Heaven, and that without the will of your Creator, not a hair can fall from your head. Besides, I repeat, there is no danger."

"Well, then, I will do it," cried Franziska, in some measure regaining courage.

"Whatever you may hear, whatever takes place inside the coffin," continued Woislaw, "must have no effect upon you. Drive the nails well in, without flinching: your work must be finished before my prayer comes to an end."

Franziska shuddered, but again recovered herself. "I will do it; Heaven will send me strength," she murmured softly.

"There is one thing more," said Woislaw hesitatingly; "perhaps it is the hardest of all I have proposed, but without it your cure will not be complete. When you have done as I have told you, a sort of"—he hesitated—"a sort of liquid will flow from the coffin; in this dip your finger, and besmear the scratch on your throat."

"Horrible!" cried Franziska. "This liquid is blood. A human being lies in the coffin."

"An *unearthly one* lies therein! That blood is your own, but it flows in other veins," said Woislaw gloomily. "Ask no more; the sand is running out."

Franziska summoned up all her powers of mind and body, went towards the steps which led to the vault, and Woislaw sank on his knees before the altar in quiet prayer. When the lady had descended, she found herself before the coffin on which lay the packet before mentioned. A sort of twilight reigned in the vault, and everything around was so still and peaceful, that she felt more calm, and going up to the coffin, opened the packet. She had hardly seen that a hammer and three long nails were its contents when suddenly Woislaw's voice rang through the church, and broke the stillness of the aisles. Franziska started, but recognized the appointed prayer. She seized one of the nails, and with one stroke of the hammer drove it at least an inch into the cover. All was still; nothing was heard but the echo of the stroke. Taking heart, the maiden grasped the hammer with both hands, and struck the nail twice with all her might, right up to the head into the wood. At this moment commenced a rustling noise; it seemed as though something in the interior began to move and to struggle. Franziska drew back in alarm. She was already on the point of throwing away the hammer, and flying up the steps, when Woislaw raised his voice so powerfully, and it sounded so entreatingly, that in a sort of excitement, such as would induce one to rush into a lion's den, she returned to the coffin, determined to bring things to a conclusion. Hardly knowing what she did, she placed a second nail in the centre of the lid, and after some strokes, this was likewise buried to its head. The struggle now increased fearfully, as if some living creature were striving to burst the coffin. This was so shaken by it, that it cracked and split on all sides. Half distracted, Franziska seized the third nail; she thought no more of her ailments, she only knew herself to be in terrible danger, of what kind she could not guess: in an agony that threatened to rob her of her senses, and in the midst of the turning and cracking of the coffin, in which low groans were flow heard, she struck the third nail in equally tight. At this moment, she began to lose consciousness. She wished to hasten away, but staggered; and mechanically grasping at something to save herself by, she seized the corner of the coffin, and sank fainting beside it on the ground.

A quarter of an hour might have elapsed, when she again opened her eyes. She looked around her. Above was the starry sky, and the moon, which shed her cold light on the ruins and on the tops of the old oak-trees. Franziska was lying outside the church walls, Woislaw on his knees beside her, holding her hand in his.

"Heaven be praised that you live!" he cried, with a sigh of relief. "I was beginning to doubt whether the remedy had not been too severe, and yet it was the only thing to save you."

Franziska recovered her full consciousness very gradually. The past seemed to her like a dreadful dream. Only a few moments before, that fearful scene; and now this quiet all around her. She hardly dared at first to raise her eyes, and shuddered when she found herself only a few paces removed from the spot where she had undergone such terrible agony. She listened half unconsciously, now to the pacifying words Woislaw addressed to her, now to the whistling of the servant, who stood by the horses, and who, to wile away his time, was imitating the evening-song of a belated cow-herd.

"Let us go," whispered Franziska, as she strove to raise herself "But what is this? My shoulder is wet, my throat, my hand—"

"It is probably the evening dew on the grass," said Woislaw gently.

"No; it is blood!" she cried, springing up with horror in her tone. "See, my hand is full of blood!"

"Oh, you are mistaken—surely mistaken," said Woislaw stammering. "Or perhaps the wound on your neck may have opened! Pray, feel whether this is the case." He seized her hand, and directed it to the spot.

"I do not perceive anything; I feel no pain," she said at length, somewhat angrily.

"Then, perhaps, when you fainted, you may have struck a corner of the coffin, or have torn yourself with the point of one of the nails," suggested Woislaw.

"Oh, of what do you remind me!" cried Franziska shuddering. "Let us away—away! I entreat you, come! I will not remain a moment longer near this dreadful, dreadful place."

They descended the path much quicker than they came. Woislaw placed his companion on her horse, and they were soon on their way home.

When they approached the castle, Franziska began to inundate her protector with questions about the preceding adventure; but he declared that her present state of excitement must make him defer all explanations till the morning, when her curiosity should be satisfied. On their arrival, he conducted her at once to her room, and told the knight his daughter was too much fatigued with her ride to appear at the supper-table. On the following morning, Franziska rose earlier than she had done for a long time. She assured her friend it was the first time since her illness commenced that she had been really refreshed by her sleep, and, what was still more remarkable, she had not been troubled by her old terrible dream. Her improved looks were not only remarked Bertha, but by Franz and the knight; and with Woislaw's permission, she related the adventures of the previous evening. No sooner bad she concluded, than Woislaw was completely stormed with questions about such a strange occurrence.

"Have you" said the latter, turning towards his host, "ever heard of Vampires?"

"Often," replied he; "but I have never believed in them."

"Nor did I," said Woislaw; "but I have been assured of their existence by experience."

"Oh, tell us what occurred," cried Bertha eagerly, as a light seemed to dawn on her.

"It was during my first campaign in Hungary," began Woislaw, "when I was rendered helpless for some time by this sword-cut of a janizary across my face, and another on my shoulder. I had been taken into the house of a respectable family in a small town. It consisted of the father and mother, and a daughter about twenty years of age. They obtained their living by selling the very good wine of the country, and the taproom was always full of visitors. Although the family were well to do in the world, there seemed to brood over them a continual melancholy, caused by the constant illness of the only daughter, a very pretty and excellent girl. She had always bloomed like a rose, but for some months she had been getting so thin and wasted, and that without any satisfactory reason: they tried every means to restore her, but in vain. As the army had encamped quite in the neighborhood, of course a number of people of all countries assembled in the tavern. Amongst these there was one man who came every evening, when the moon shone, who struck everybody by the peculiarity of his manners and appearance; he looked dried up and deathlike, and hardly spoke at all; but what he did say was bitter and sarcastic. Most attention was excited towards him by the circumstance, that although he always ordered a cup of the best wine, and now and then raised it to his lips, the cup was always as full after his departure as at first."

"This all agrees wonderfully with the appearance of Azzo," said Bertha, deeply interested.

"The daughter of the house," continued Woislaw, "became daily worse, despite the aid not only of Christian doctors, but of many amongst the heathen prisoners, who were consulted in the hope that they might have some magical remedy to propose. It was singular that the girl always complained of a dream, in which the unknown guest worried and plagued her."

"Just the same as your dream, Franziska," cried Bertha.

"One evening," resumed Woislaw, "an old Sclavonian—who had made many voyages to Turkey and Greece, and had even seen the New World— and I were sitting over our wine, and sat down at the table. The bottle passed quickly between my friend and me, whilst we talked of all manner of things, of our adventures, and of passages in our lives, both horrible and amusing. We went on chatting thus for about an hour, and drank a tolerable quantity of wine. The unknown had remained perfectly silent the whole time, only smiling contemptuously every now and then. He now paid his money, and was going away. All this had quietly worried me—perhaps the wine had got a little into my head—so I said to the stranger: 'Hold, you stony stranger; you have hitherto done nothing but listen, and have not even emptied your cup. Now you shall take your turn in telling us something amusing, and if you do not drink up your wine, it shall produce a quarrel between us.' 'Yes,' said the Sclavonian, 'you must remain; you shall chat and drink, too;' and he grasped —for although no longer young, he was big and very strong—the stranger by the shoulder, to pull him down to his seat again: the latter, however, although as thin as a skeleton, with one movement of his hand flung the Sclavonian to the middle of the room, and half stunned him for a moment. I now approached to hold the stranger back. I caught him by the arm; and although the springs of my iron hand were less powerful than those I have at present, I must have gripped him rather hard in my anger, for after looking grimly at me for a moment, he bent towards me and whispered in my ear: 'Let me go from the gripe of your fist, I see you are my brother, therefore do not hinder me from seeking my bloody nourishment. I am hungry!' Surprised by such words, I let him loose, and almost before I was aware he had left the room. As soon as I had in some degree recovered from my astonishment, I told the Sclavonian what I had heard. He started, evidently alarmed. I asked him to tell me the cause of his fears, and pressed him for an explanation of those extraordinary words. On our way to his lodging, he complied with my request. 'The stranger,' said he, 'is a Vampire!'"

"How?" cried the knight, Franziska, and Bertha simultaneously, in a voice of horror. "So this Azzo was—"

"Nothing less. He also was a Vampire!" replied Woislaw. "But at all events his hellish thirst is quenched forever; he will never return.—But I have not finished. As in my country vampires had never been heard of, I questioned the Sclavonian minutely. He said that in Hungary, Croatia, Dalmatia, and Bosnia, these hellish guests were not uncommon. They were deceased persons, who had either once served as nourishment to vampires, or who had died in deadly sin, or under excommunication; and that whenever the moon shone, they rose from their graves, and sucked the blood of the living."

"Horrible!" cried Franziska. "If you had told me all this beforehand, I should never have accomplished the work."

"So I thought; and yet it must be executed by the sufferers themselves, while someone else performs the devotions," replied Woislaw. "The Sclavonian," he continued after a short pause, "added many other facts with regard to these unearthly visitants. He said that whilst their victim wasted, they themselves improved in appearance, and that a vampire possessed enormous strength—"

"Now I can understand the change your false hand produced on Azzo," interrupted Franz.

"Yes, that was it," replied Woislaw. "Azzo, as well as the other vampire, mistook its great power for that of a natural one, and concluded I was one of his own species.—You may now imagine, dear lady," he continued, turning to Franziska, "how alarmed I was at your appearance when I arrived: all you and Bertha told me increased my anxiety; and when I saw Azzo, I could doubt no longer that he was a vampire. As I learned from your account that a grave with the name Ezzelin von Klatka lay in the neighborhood, I had no doubt that you might be saved if I could only induce you to assist me. It did not appear to me advisable to impart the whole facts of the case, for your bodily powers were so impaired, that an idea of the horrors before you might have quite unfitted you for the exertion; for this reason, I arranged everything in the manner in which it has taken place."

"You did wisely," replied Franziska shuddering. "I can never be grateful enough to you. Had I known what was required of me, I never could have undertaken the deed."

"That was what I feared," said Woislaw; "but fortune has favored us all through."

"And what became of the unfortunate girl in Hungary?" inquired Bertha.

"I know not," replied Woislaw. "That very evening there was an alarm of Turks, and we were ordered off. I never heard anything more of her."

The conversation upon these strange occurrences continued for some time longer. The knight determined to have the vault at Klatka walled up forever. This took place on the following day; the knight alleging as a reason that he did not wish the dead to be disturbed by irreverent hands.

Franziska recovered gradually. Her health had been so severely shaken, that it was long ere her strength was so much restored as to allow of her being considered out of danger. The young lady's character underwent a great change in the interval. Its former strength was, perhaps, in some degree diminished, but in place of that, she had acquired a benevolent softness, which brought out all her best qualities. Franz continued his attentions to his cousin; but, perhaps, owing to a hint from Bertha, he was less assiduous in his exhibition of them. His inclinations did not lead him to the battle, the camp, or the attainment of honors; his great aim was to increase the good condition and happiness of his tenants, and to this he contributed the whole energy of his mind. Franziska could not withstand the unobtrusive signs of the young man's continued attachment; and it was not long ere the credit she was obliged to yield to his noble efforts for the welfare of his fellow-creatures, changed into a liking, which went on increasing, until at length it assumed the character of love. As Woislaw insisted on making Bertha his wife before he returned to Silesia, it was arranged that the marriage should take place at their present abode. How joyful was the surprise of the knight of Fahnenberg, when his daughter and Franz likewise entreated his blessing, and expressed their desire of being united on the same day! That day soon came round, and it saw the bright looks of two happy couples.

KEN'S MYSTERY

Julian Hawthorne

first published in *Harper's New Monthly Magazine*
(November 1883)

One cool October evening—it was the last day of the month, and unusually cool for the time of year—I made up my mind to go and spend an hour or two with my friend Keningale. Keningale was an artist (as well as a musical amateur and poet), and had a very delightful studio built onto his house, in which he was wont to sit of an evening. The studio had a cavernous fire-place, designed in imitation of the old-fashioned fire-places of Elizabethan manor-houses, and in it, when the temperature out-doors warranted, he would build up a cheerful fire of dry logs. It would suit me particularly well, I thought, to go and have a quiet pipe and chat in front of that fire with my friend.

I had not had such a chat for a very long time—not, in fact, since Keningale (or Ken, as his friends called him) had returned from his visit to Europe the year before. He went abroad, as he affirmed at the time, "for purposes of study," whereat we all smiled, for Ken, so far as we knew him, was more likely to do anything else than to study. He was a young fellow of buoyant temperament, lively and social in his habits, of a brilliant and versatile mind, and possessing an income of twelve or fifteen thousand dollars a year; he could sing, play, scribble, and paint very cleverly, and some of his heads and figure—pieces were really well done, considering that he never had any regular training in art; but he was not a worker. Personally he was fine-looking, of good height and figure, active, healthy, and with a remarkably fine brow, and clear, full-gazing eye. Nobody was surprised at his going to Europe, nobody expected him to do anything there except amuse himself, and few anticipated that he would be soon again seen in New York. He was one of the sort that find Europe agree with them. Off he went, therefore; and in the course of a few months the rumor reached us that he was engaged to a handsome and wealthy New York girl whom he had met in London. This was nearly all we did hear of him until, not very long afterward, he turned up again on Fifth Avenue, to every one's astonishment; made no satisfactory answer to those who wanted to know how he happened to tire so soon of the

Old World; while, as to the reported engagement, he cut short all allusion to that in so peremptory a manner as to show that it was not a permissible topic of conversation with him. It was surmised that the lady had jilted him; but, on the other hand, she herself returned home not a great while after, and, though she had plenty of opportunities, she has never married to this day.

Be the rights of that matter what they may, it was soon remarked that Ken was no longer the careless and merry fellow he used to be; on the contrary, he appeared grave, moody, averse from general society, and habitually taciturn and undemonstrative even in the company of his most intimate friends. Evidently something had happened to him, or he had done something. What? Had he committed a murder? or joined the Nihilists? or was his unsuccessful love affair at the bottom of it? Some declared that the cloud was only temporary, and would soon pass away.

Nevertheless, up to the period of which I am writing, it had not passed away, but had rather gathered additional gloom, and threatened to become permanent.

Meanwhile I had met him twice or thrice at the club, at the opera, or in the street, but had as yet had no opportunity of regularly renewing my acquaintance with him. We had been on a footing of more than common intimacy in the old days, and I was not disposed to think that he would refuse to renew the former relations now. But what I had heard and myself seen of his changed condition imparted a stimulating tinge of suspense or curiosity to the pleasure with which I looked forward to the prospects of this evening. His house stood at a distance of two or three miles beyond the general range of habitations in New York at this time, and as I walked briskly along in the clear twilight air I had leisure to go over in my mind all that I had known of Ken and had divined of his character. After all, had there not always been something in his nature—deep down, and held in abeyance by the activity of his animal spirits—but something strange and separate, and capable of developing under suitable conditions into—into what? As I asked myself this question I arrived at his door; and it was with a feeling of relief that I felt the next moment the cordial grasp of his hand, and his voice bidding me welcome in a tone that indicated unaffected gratification at my presence. He drew me at once into the studio, relieved me of my hat and cane, and then put his hand on my shoulder.

"I am glad to see you," he repeated, with singular earnestness—"glad to see you and to feel you; and tonight of all nights in the year."

"Why tonight especially?"

"Oh, never mind. It's just as well, too, you didn't let me know beforehand you were coming; the unreadiness is all, to paraphrase the poet. Now, with you to help me, I can drink a glass of whisky and water and take a bit draw of the pipe. This would have been a grim night for me if I'd been left to myself."

"In such a lap of luxury as this, too!" said I, looking round at the glowing fire-place, the low, luxurious chairs, and all the rich and sumptuous fittings of the room. "I should have thought a condemned murderer might make himself comfortable here."

"Perhaps; but that's not exactly my category at present. But have you forgotten what night this is? This is November-eve, when, as tradition asserts, the dead arise and walk about, and fairies, goblins, and spiritual beings of all kinds have more freedom and power than on any other day of the year. One can see you've never been in Ireland."

"I wasn't aware till now that you had been there, either."

"Yes, I have been in Ireland. Yes—" He paused, sighed, and fell into a reverie, from which, however, he soon roused himself by an effort, and went to a cabinet in a corner of the room for the liquor and tobacco. While he was thus employed I sauntered about the studio, taking note of the various beauties, grotesquenesses, and curiosities that it contained. Many things were there to repay study and arouse admiration; for Ken was a good collector, having excellent taste as well as means to back it. But, upon the whole, nothing interested me more than some studies of a female head, roughly done in oils, and, judging from the sequestered positions in which I found them, not intended by the artist for exhibition or criticism. There were three or four of these studies, all of the same face, but in different poses and costumes. In one the head was enveloped in a dark hood, overshadowing and partly concealing the features; in another she seemed to be peering duskily through a latticed casement, lit by a faint moonlight; a third showed her splendidly attired in evening costume, with jewels in her hair and ears, and sparkling on her snowy bosom. The expressions were as various as the poses; now it was demure penetration, now a subtle inviting glance, now burning passion, and again a look of elfish and elusive mockery. In whatever phase, the countenance possessed a singular and poignant fascination, not of beauty merely, though that was very striking, but of character and quality likewise.

"Did you find this model abroad?" I inquired at length. "She has evidently inspired you, and I don't wonder at it."

Ken, who had been mixing the punch, and had not noticed my movements, now looked up, and said: "I didn't mean those to be seen. They don't satisfy me, and I am going to destroy them; but I couldn't rest till I'd made some attempts to reproduce—What was it you asked? Abroad? Yes—or no. They were all painted here within the last six weeks."

"Whether they satisfy you or not, they are by far the best things of yours I have ever seen."

"Well, let them alone, and tell me what you think of this beverage. To my thinking, it goes to the right spot. It owes its existence to your coming here. I can't drink alone, and those portraits are not company, though, for aught I know, she might have come out of the canvas tonight and sat down in that chair." Then, seeing my inquiring look, he added, with a hasty laugh, "It's November-eve, you know, when anything may happen, provided its strange enough. Well, here's to ourselves."

We each swallowed a deep draught of the smoking and aromatic liquor, and set down our glasses with approval. The punch was excellent. Ken now opened a box of cigars, and we seated ourselves before the fireplace.

"All we need now," I remarked, after a short silence, "is a little music. By-the-by, Ken, have you still got the banjo I gave you before you went abroad?"

He paused so long before replying that I supposed he had not heard my question. "I have got it," he said, at length, "but it will never make any more music."

"Got broken, eh? Can't it be mended? It was a fine instrument."

"It's not broken, but it's past mending. You shall see for yourself."

He arose as he spoke, and going to another part of the studio, opened a black oak coffer, and took out of it a long object wrapped up in a piece of faded yellow silk. He handed it to me, and when I had unwrapped it, there appeared a thing that might once have been a banjo, but had little resemblance to one now. It bore every sign of extreme age. The wood of the handle was honey-combed with the gnawings of worms, and dusty with dry-rot. The parchment head was green with mold, and hung in shriveled tatters. The hoop, which was of solid silver, was so blackened and tarnished that it looked like dilapidated iron. The strings were gone, and most of the tuning-screws had dropped out of their decayed sockets. Altogether it had the appearance of having been made before the Flood, and been forgotten in the forecastle of Noah's Ark ever since.

"It is a curious relic, certainly," I said. "Where did you come across it? I had no idea that the banjo was invented so long ago as this. It certainly can't be less than two hundred years old, and may be much older than that."

Ken smiled gloomily. "You are quite right," he said; "it is at least two hundred years old, and yet it is the very same banjo that you gave me a year ago."

"Hardly," I returned, smiling in my turn, "since that was made to my order with a view to presenting it to you."

"I know that; but the two hundred years have passed since then. Yes; it is absurd and impossible, I know, but nothing is truer. That banjo, which was made last year, existed in the sixteenth century, and has been rotting ever since. Stay. Give it to me a moment, and I'll convince you. You recollect that your name and mine, with the date, were engraved on the silver hoop?"

"Yes; and there was a private mark of my own there, also."

"Very well," said Ken, who had been rubbing a place on the hoop with a corner of the yellow silk wrapper; "look at that."

I took the decrepit instrument from him, and examined the spot which he had rubbed. It was incredible, sure enough; but there wee the names and the date precisely as I had caused them to be engraved; and there, moreover, was my own private mark, which I had idly made with an old etching point not more than eighteen months before. After convincing myself that there was no mistake, I laid the banjo across my knees, and stared at my friend in bewilderment. He sat smoking with a kind of grim composure, his eyes fixed upon the blazing logs.

"I'm mystified, I confess," said I. "Come; what is the joke? What method have you discovered of producing the decay of centuries on this unfortunate banjo in a few months? And why did you do it? I have heard of an elixir to counteract the effects of time, but your recipe seems to work the other way—to make time rush forward at two hundred times his usual rate, in one place, while he jogs on at his usual gait elsewhere. Unfold your mystery, magician. Seriously, Ken, how on earth did the thing happen?"

"I know no more about it than you do," was his reply. "Either you and I and all the rest of the living world are insane, or else there has been wrought a miracle as strange as any in tradition.

"How can I explain it? It is a common saying—a common experience, if you will—that we may, on certain trying or tremendous occasions, live years in one moment. But that's a mental experience, not a physical one, and one that applies, at all events, only to human beings, not to senseless things of wood and metal. You imagine the thing is some trick or jugglery. If it be, I don't know the secret of it. There's no chemical appliance that I ever heard of that will get a piece of solid wood into that condition in a few months, or a few years. And it wasn't done in a few years, or a few months either. A year ago today at this very hour that banjo was as sound as when it left the maker's hands, and twenty-four hours afterward—I'm telling you the simple truth—it was as you see it now." The gravity and earnestness with which Ken made this astounding statement were evidently not assumed. He believed every word that he uttered. I knew not what to think. Of course my friend might be insane, though he betrayed none of the ordinary symptoms of mania; but, however that might be, there was the banjo, a witness whose silent testimony there was no gain-saying. The more I meditated on the matter the more inconceivable did it appear. Two hundred years—twenty-four hours; these were the terms of the proposed equation. Ken and the banjo both affirmed that the equation had been made; all worldly knowledge and experience affirmed it to be impossible. What was the explanation? What is time? What is life? I felt myself beginning to doubt the reality of all things. And so this was the mystery which my friend had been brooding over since his return from abroad. No wonder it had changed him. More to be wondered at was it that it had not changed him more.

"Can you tell me the whole story?" I demanded at length.

Ken quaffed another draught from his glass of whisky and water and rubbed his hand through his thick brown beard. "I have never spoken to any one of it heretofore," he said, "and I had never meant to speak of it. But I'll try and give you some idea of what it was. You know me better than any one else; you'll understand the thing as far as it can ever be understood, and perhaps I may be relieved of some of the oppression it has caused me. For it is rather a ghastly memory to grapple with alone, I can tell you."

Hereupon, without further preface, Ken related the following tale. He was, I may observe in passing, a naturally fine narrator. There were deep, lingering tones in his voice, and he could strikingly enhance the comic or pathetic effect of a sentence by dwelling here and there upon some syllable. His features were equally susceptible of humorous and of solemn expressions, and his eyes were in form and hue wonderfully adapted to showing great varieties of emotion. Their mournful aspect was extremely earnest and affecting; and when Ken was giving utterance to some mysterious passage of the tale they had a doubtful, melancholy, exploring look which appealed irresistibly to the imagination. But the interest of his story was too pressing to allow of noticing these incidental embellishments at the time, though they doubtless had their influence upon me all the same.

"I left New York on an Inman Line steamer, you remember," began Ken, "and landed at Havre. I went the usual round of sight-seeing on the Continent, and got round to London in July, at the height of the season. I had good introductions, and met any number of agreeable and famous people. Among others was a young lady, a countrywoman of my own—you know whom I mean—who interested me very much, and before her family left London she and I were engaged. We parted there for the time, because she had the Continental trip still to make, while I wanted to take the opportunity to visit the north of England and Ireland. I landed at Dublin about the 1st of October, and, zigzagging about the country, I found myself in County Cork about two weeks later.

"There is in that region some of the most lovely scenery that human eyes ever rested on, and it seems to be less known to tourists than many places of infinitely less picturesque value. A lonely region too: during my rambles I met not a single stranger like myself, and few enough natives. It seems incredible that so beautiful a country should be so deserted. After walking a dozen Irish miles you come across a group of two or three one-roomed cottages, and, like as not, one or more of those will have the roof off and the walls in ruins. The few peasants whom one sees, however, are affable and hospitable, especially when they hear you are from that terrestrial heaven whither most of their friends and relatives have gone before them. They seem simple and primitive enough at first sight, and yet they are as strange and incomprehensible a race as any in the world. They are as superstitious, as credulous of marvels, fairies, magicians, and omens, as the men whom St. Patrick preached to, and at the same time they are shrewd, skeptical, sensible, and bottomless liars. Upon the whole, I met with no nation on my travels whose company I enjoyed so much, or who inspired me with so much kindliness, curiosity, and repugnance.

"At length I got to a place on the sea-coast, which I will not further specify than to say that it is not many miles from Ballymacheen, on the south shore. I have seen Venice and Naples, I have driven along the Cornice Road, I have spent a month at our own Mount Desert, and I say that all of them together are not so beautiful as this glowing, deep-hued, soft-gleaming, silvery-lighted, ancient harbor and town, with the tall hills crowding round it and the black cliffs and headlands planting their iron feet in the blue, transparent sea. It is a very old place, and has had a history which it has outlived ages since. It may once have had two or three thousand inhabitants; it has scarce five or six hundred today. Half the houses are in ruins or have disappeared; many of the remainder are standing empty. All the people are poor, most of them abjectly so; they saunter about with bare feet and uncovered heads, the women in quaint black or dark-blue cloaks, the men in such anomalous attire as only an Irishman knows how to get together, the children half naked. The only comfortable-looking people are the monks and the priests, and the soldiers in the fort. For there is a fort there, constructed on the huge ruins of one which may have done duty in the reign of Edward the Black Prince, or earlier, in whose mossy embrasures are mounted a couple of cannon, which occasionally sent a practice-shot or two at the cliff on the other side of the harbor. The garrison consists of a dozen men and three or four officers and non-commissioned officers. I suppose they are relieved occasionally, but those I saw seemed to have become component parts of their surroundings.

"I put up at a wonderful little old inn, the only one in the place, and took my meals in a dining-saloon fifteen feet by nine, with a portrait of George I (a print varnished to preserve it) hanging over the mantel-piece. On the second evening after dinner a young gentleman came in—the dining-saloon being public property of course—and ordered some bread and cheese and a bottle of Dublin stout. We presently fell into talk; he turned out to be an officer from the fort, Lieutenant O'Connor, and a fine young specimen of the Irish soldier he was. After telling me all he knew about the town, the surrounding country, his friends, and himself, he intimated a readiness to sympathize with whatever tale I might choose to pour into his ear; and I had pleasure in trying to rival his own outspokenness. We became excellent friends; we had up a half-pint of Kinahan's whisky, and the lieutenant expressed himself in terms of high praise of my countrymen, my country, and my own particular cigars. When it became time for him to depart I accompanied him—for there was a splendid moon abroad—and bade him farewell at the fort entrance, having promised to come over the next day and make the acquaintance of the other fellows. 'And mind your eye, now, going back, my dear boy,' he called out, as I turned my face homeward. 'Faith, 'tis a spooky place, that graveyard, and you'll as likely meet the black woman there as anywhere else!'

"The graveyard was a forlorn and barren spot on the hill-side, just the hither side of the fort: thirty or forty rough head-stones, few of which retained any semblance of the perpendicular, while many were so shattered and decayed as to seem nothing more than irregular natural projections from the ground. Who the black woman might be I knew not, and did not stay to inquire. I had never been subject to ghostly apprehensions, and as a matter of fact, though the path I had to follow was in places very bad going, not to mention a hap-hazard scramble over a ruined bridge that covered a deep-lying brook. I reached my inn without any adventure whatever.

"The next day I kept my appointment at the fort, and found no reason to regret it; and my friendly sentiments were abundantly reciprocated, thanks more especially, perhaps, to the success of my banjo, which I carried with me, and which was as novel as it was popular with those who listened to it. The chief personages in the social circle besides my friend the lieutenant were Major Molloy, who was in command, a racy and juicy old campaigner, with a face like a sunset, and the surgeon, Dr. Dudeen, a long, dry, humorous genius, with a wealth of anecdotical and traditional lore at his command that I have never seen surpassed. We had a jolly time of it, and it was the precursor of many more like it. The remains of October slipped away rapidly, and I was obliged to remember that I was a traveler in Europe, and not a resident in Ireland. The major, the surgeon, and the lieutenant all protested cordially against my proposed departure, but, as there was no help for it, they arranged a farewell dinner to take place in the fort on All-halloween.

"I wish you could have been at that dinner with me! It was the essence of Irish good-fellowship. Dr. Dudeen was in great force; the major was better than the best of Lever's novels; the lieutenant was overflowing with hearty good-humor, merry chaff, and sentimental rhapsodies about this or the other pretty girl of the neighborhood. For my part I made the banjo ring as it had never rung before, and the others joined in the chorus with a mellow strength of lungs such as you don't often hear outside of Ireland. Among the stories that Dr. Dudeen regaled us with was one about the Kern of Querin and his wife, Ethelind Fionguala—which being interpreted signified 'the white-shouldered.' The lady, it appears, was originally betrothed to one O'Connor (here the lieutenant smacked his lips), but was stolen away on the wedding night by a party of vampires, who, it would seem, where at that period a prominent feature among the troubles of Ireland. But as they were bearing her along—she being unconscious—to that supper where she was not to eat but to be eaten, the young Kern of Querin, who happened to be out duck-shooting, met the party, and emptied his gun at it. The vampires fled, and the Kern carried the fair lady, still in a state of insensibility, to his house. 'And by the same token, Mr. Keningale,' observed the doctor, knocking the ashes out of his pipe, 'ye're after passing that very house on your way here. The one with the dark archway underneath it, and the big mullioned window at the corner. Ye recollect, hanging over the street as I might say—'

"'Go 'long wid the house, Dr. Dudeen, dear,' interrupted the lieutenant; 'sure can't you see we're all dying to know what happened to sweet Miss Fionguala, God be good to her, when I was after getting her safe upstairs—'

"'Faith, then, I can tell ye that myself, Mr. O'Connor,' exclaimed the major, imparting a rotary motion to the remnants of whisky in his tumbler.

"''Tis a question to be solved on general principles, as Colonel O'Halloran said that time he was asked what he'd do if he'd been the Dook

O'Wellington, and the Prussians hadn't come up in the nick o' time at Waterloo. 'Faith,' says the colonel, 'I'll tell ye—'

"Arrah, then, major, why would ye be interruptin' the doctor, and Mr. Keningale there lettin' his glass stay empty till he hears—The Lord save us! the bottle's empty!'

"In the excitement consequent upon this discovery, the thread of the doctor's story was lost; and before it could be recovered the evening had advanced so far that I felt obliged to withdraw. It took some time to make my proposition heard and comprehended; and a still longer time to put it in execution; so that it was fully midnight before I found myself standing in the cool pure air outside the fort, with the farewells of my boon companions ringing in my ears.

"Considering that it had been rather a wet evening indoors, I was in a remarkably good state of preservation, and I therefore ascribed it rather to the roughness of the road than to the smoothness of the liquor, when, after advancing a few rods, I stumbled and fell. As I picked myself up I fancied I had heard a laugh, and supposed that the lieutenant, who had accompanied me to the gate, was making merry over my mishap; but on looking round I saw that the gate was closed and no one was visible. The laugh, moreover, had seemed to be close at hand, and to be even pitched in a key that was rather feminine than masculine. Of course I must have been deceived; nobody was near me: my imagination had played me a trick, or else there was more truth than poetry in the tradition that Halloween is the carnival-time of disembodied spirits. It did not occur to me at the time that a stumble is held by the superstitious Irish to be an evil omen, and had I remembered it it would only have been to laugh at it. At all events, I was physically none the worse for my fall, and I resumed my way immediately.

"But the path was singularly difficult to find, or rather the path I was following did not seem to be the right one. I did not recognize it; I could have sworn (except I knew the contrary) that I had never seen it before. The moon had risen, though her light was as yet obscured by clouds, but neither my immediate surroundings nor the general aspect of the region appeared familiar. Dark, silent hill-sides mounted up on either hand, and the road, for the most part, plunged down-ward, as if to conduct me into the bowels of the earth. The place was alive with strange echoes, so that at times I seemed to be walking through the midst of muttering voices and mysterious whispers, and a wild, faint sound of laughter seemed ever and anon to reverberate among the passes of the hills. Currents of colder air sighing up through narrow defiles and dark crevices touched my face as with airy fingers. A certain feeling of anxiety and insecurity began to take possession of me, though there was no definable cause for it, unless that I might be belated in getting home. With the perverse instinct of those who are lost I hastened my steps, but was impelled now and then to glance back over my shoulder, with a sensation of being pursued. But no living creature was in sight. The moon, however, had now risen higher, and the clouds that were drifting slowly across the sky flung into the naked valley dusky shadows, which occasionally assumed shapes that looked like the vague semblance of gigantic human forms.

"How long I had been hurrying onward I know not, when, with a kind of suddenness, I found myself approaching a graveyard. It was situated on the spur of a hill, and there was no fence around it, nor anything to protect it from the incursions of passers-by. There was something in the general appearance of this spot that made me half fancy I had seen it before; and I should have taken it to be the same that I had often noticed on my way to the fort, but that the latter was only a few hundred yards distant therefrom, whereas I must have traversed several miles at least.

As I drew near, moreover, I observed that the head-stones did not appear so ancient and decayed as those of the other. But what chiefly attracted my attention was the figure that was leaning or half sitting upon one of the largest of the upright slabs near the road. It was a female figure draped in black, and a closer inspection—for I was soon within a few yards of her—showed that she wore the calla, or long hooded cloak, the most common as well as the most ancient garment of Irish women, and doubtless of Spanish origin.

"I was a trifle startled by this apparition, so unexpected as it was, and so strange did it seem that any human creature should be at that hour of the night in so desolate and sinister a place. Involuntarily I paused as I came opposite her, and gazed at her intently. But the moonlight fell behind her, and the deep hood of her cloak so completely shadowed her face that I was unable to discern anything but the sparkle of a pair of eyes, which appeared to be returning my gaze with much vivacity.

"'You seem to be at home here,' I said, at length. 'Can you tell me where I am?'

"Hereupon the mysterious personage broke into a light laugh, which, though in itself musical and agreeable, was of a timbre and intonation that caused my heart to beat rather faster than my late pedestrian exertions warranted; for it was the identical laugh (or so my imagination persuaded me) that had echoed in my ears as I arose from my tumble an hour or two ago. For the rest, it was the laugh of a young woman, and presumably of a pretty one; and yet it had a wild, airy, mocking quality, that seemed hardly human at all, or not, at any rate, characteristic of a being of affections and limitations like unto ours. But this impression of mine was fostered, no doubt, by the unusual and uncanny circumstances of the occasion.

"'Sure, sir,' said she, 'you're at the grave of Ethelind Fionguala.'

"As she spoke she rose to her feet, and pointed to the inscription on the stone. I bent forward, and was able, without much difficulty, to decipher the name, and a date which indicated that the occupant of the grave must have entered the disembodied state between two and three centuries ago.

"And who are you?' was my next question.

"'I'm called Elsie,' she replied. 'But where would your honor be going November-eve?'

"I mentioned my destination, and asked her whether she could direct me thither.

"Indeed, then, 'tis there I'm going myself,' Elsie replied; 'and if your honor 'll follow me, and play me a tune on the pretty instrument, 'tisn't long we'll be on the road.'

"She pointed to the banjo which I carried wrapped up under my arm. How she knew that it was a musical instrument I could not imagine; possibly, I thought, she may have seen me playing on it as I strolled about the environs of the town. Be that as it may, I offered no opposition to the bargain, and further intimated that I would reward her more substantially on our arrival. At that she laughed again, and made a peculiar gesture with her hand above her head. I uncovered my banjo, swept my fingers across the strings, and struck into a fantastic dance-measure, to the music of which we proceeded along the path, Elsie slightly in advance, her feet keeping time to the airy measure. In fact, she trod so lightly, with an elastic, undulating movement, that with a little more it seemed as if she might float onward like a spirit. The extreme whiteness of her feet attracted my eye, and I was surprised to find that instead of being bare, as I had supposed, these were incased in white satin slippers quaintly embroidered with gold thread.

"Elsie,' said I, lengthening my steps so as to come up with her, 'where do you live, and what do you do for a living?'

"Sure, I live by myself,' she answered; 'and if you'd be after knowing how, you must come and see for yourself.'

"Are you in the habit of walking over the hills at night in shoes like that?'

"And why would I not?' she asked, in her turn. 'And where did your honor get the pretty gold ring on your finger?'

"The ring, which was of no great intrinsic value, had struck my eye in an old curiosity-shop in Cork. It was an antique of very old-fashioned design, and might have belonged (as the vender assured me was the case) to one of the early kings or queens of Ireland.

"Do you like it?' said I.

"Will your honor be after making a present of it to Elsie?' she returned, with an insinuating tone and turn of the head.

"Maybe I will, Elsie, on one condition. I am an artist; I make pictures of people. If you will promise to come to my studio and let me paint your portrait, I'll give you the ring, and some money besides.'

"And will you give me the ring now?' said Elsie.

"Yes, if you'll promise.'

"And will you play the music to me?' she continued.

"As much as you like.'

"But maybe I'll not be handsome enough for ye,' said she, with a glance of her eyes beneath the dark hood.

"I'll take the risk of that,' I answered, laughing, 'though, all the same, I don't mind taking a peep beforehand to remember you by.' So saying, I put forth a hand to draw back the concealing hood. But Elsie eluded me, I scarce know how, and laughed a third time, with the same airy, mocking cadence.

"'Give me the ring first, and then you shall see me,' she said, coaxingly.

"'Stretch out your hand, then,' returned I, removing the ring from my finger. 'When we are better acquainted, Elsie, you won't be so suspicious.'

"She held out a slender, delicate hand, on the forefinger of which I slipped the ring. As I did so, the folds of her cloak fell a little apart, affording me a glimpse of a white shoulder and of a dress that seemed in that deceptive semi-darkness to be wrought of rich and costly material; and I caught, too, or so I fancied, the frosty sparkle of precious stones.

"'Arrah, mind where ye tread!' said Elsie, in a sudden, sharp tone.

"I looked round, and became aware for the first time that we were standing near the middle of a ruined bridge which spanned a rapid stream that flowed at a considerable depth below. The parapet of the bridge on one side was broken down, and I must have been, in fact, in imminent danger of stepping over into empty air. I made my way cautiously across the decaying structure; but, when I turned to assist Elsie, she was nowhere to be seen.

"What had become of the girl? I called, but no answer came. I gazed about on every side, but no trace of her was visible. Unless she had plunged into the narrow abyss at my feet, there was no place where she could have concealed herself—none at least that I could discover. She had vanished, nevertheless; and since her disappearance must have been premeditated, I finally came to the conclusion that it was useless to attempt to find her. She would present herself again in her own good time, or not at all. She had given me the slip very cleverly, and I must make the best of it. The adventure was perhaps worth the ring.

"On resuming my way, I was not a little relieved to find that I once more knew where I was. The bridge that I had just crossed was none other than the one I mentioned some time back; I was within a mile of the town, and my way lay clear before me. The moon, moreover, had now quite dispersed the clouds, and shone down with exquisite brilliance. Whatever her other failings, Elsie had been a trustworthy guide; she had brought me out of the depth of elf-land into the material world again. It had been a singular adventure, certainly; and I mused over it with a sense of mysterious pleasure as I sauntered along, humming snatches of airs, and accompanying myself on the strings. Hark! what light step was that behind me? It sounded like Elsie's; but no, Elsie was not there. The same impression or hallucination, however, recurred several times before I reached the outskirts of the town—the tread of an airy foot behind or beside my own. The fancy did not make me nervous; on the contrary, I was pleased with the notion of being thus haunted, and gave myself up to a romantic and genial vein of reverie.

"After passing one or two roofless and moss-grown cottages, I entered the narrow and rambling street which leads through the town. This street a short distance down widens a little, as if to afford the wayfarer space to observe a remarkable old house that stands on the northern side.

"The house was built of stone, and in a noble style of architecture; it reminded me somewhat of certain palaces of the old Italian nobility that I had seen on the Continent, and it may very probably have been built by one of the Italian or Spanish immigrants of the sixteenth or seventeenth century. The molding of the projecting windows and arched doorway was richly carved, and upon the front of the building was an escutcheon wrought in high relief, though I could not make out the purport of the device. The moonlight failing upon this picturesque pile enhanced all its beauties, and at the same time made it seem like a vision that might dissolve away when the light ceased to shine. I must often have seen the house before, and yet I retained no definite recollection of it; I had never until now examined it with my eyes open, so to speak.

"Leaning against the wall on the opposite side of the street, I contemplated it for a long while at my leisure. The window at the corner was really a very fine and massive affair. It projected over the pavement below, throwing a heavy shadow aslant; the frames of the diamond-paned lattices were heavily mullioned. How often in past ages had that lattice been pushed open by some fair hand, revealing to a lover waiting beneath in the moonlight the charming countenance of his high-born mistress! Those were brave days. They had passed away long since. The great house had stood empty for who could tell how many years; only bats and vermin were its inhabitants.

"Where now were those who had built it? and who were they? Probably the very name of them was forgotten.

"As I continued to stare upward, however, a conjecture presented itself to my mind which rapidly ripened into a conviction. Was not this the house that Dr. Dudeen had described that very evening as having been formerly the abode of the Kern of Querin and his mysterious bride? There was the projecting window, the arched doorway. Yes, beyond a doubt this was the very house. I emitted a low exclamation of renewed interest and pleasure, and my speculations took a still more imaginative, but also a more definite turn.

"What had been the fate of that lovely lady after the Kern had brought her home insensible in his arms? Did she recover, and were they married and made happy ever after; or had the sequel been a tragic one? I remembered to have read that the victims of vampires generally became vampires themselves. Then my thoughts went back to that grave on the hill-side. Surely that was unconsecrated ground. Why had they buried her there? Ethelind of the white shoulder! Ah! why had not I lived in those days; or why might not some magic cause them to live again for me? Then would I seek this street at midnight, and standing here beneath her window, I would lightly touch the strings of my bandore until the casement opened cautiously and she looked down. A sweet vision indeed! And what prevented my realizing it? Only a matter of a couple of centuries or so. And was time, then, at which poets and philosophers sneer, so rigid and real a matter that a little faith and imagination might not overcome it? At all events, I had my banjo, the bandore's legitimate and lineal descendant, and the memory of Fionguala should have the love-ditty.

"Hereupon, having retuned the instrument, I launched forth into an old Spanish love-song, which I had met with in some moldy library during my travels, and had set to music of my own. I sang low, for the deserted street re-echoed the lightest sound, and what I sang must reach only my lady's ears. The words were warm with the fire of the ancient Spanish chivalry, and I threw into their expression all the passion of the lovers of romance. Surely Fionguala, the white-shouldered, would hear, and awaken from her sleep of centuries, and come to the latticed casement and look down! Hist! see yonder! What light—what shadow is that that seems to flit from room to room within the abandoned house, and now approaches the mullioned window? Are my eyes dazzled by the play of the moonlight, or does the casement move—does it open? Nay, this is no delusion; there is no error of the senses here. There is simply a woman, young, beautiful, and richly attired, bending forward from the window, and silently beckoning me to approach.

"Too much amazed to be conscious of amazement, I advanced until I stood directly beneath the casement, and the lady's face, as she stooped toward me, was not more than twice a man's height from my own. She smiled and kissed her finger-tips; something white fluttered in her hand, then fell through the air to the ground at my feet. The next moment she had withdrawn, and I heard the lattice close.

"I picked up what she had let fall; it was a delicate lace handkerchief, tied to the handle of an elaborately wrought bronze key. It was evidently the key of the house, and invited me to enter. I loosened it from the handkerchief, which bore a faint, delicious perfume, like the aroma of flowers in an ancient garden, and turned to the arched doorway. I felt no misgiving, and scarcely any sense of strangeness. All was as I had wished it to be, and as it should be; the medieval age was alive once more, and as for myself, I almost felt the velvet cloak hanging from my shoulder and the long rapier dangling at my belt. Standing in front of the door I thrust the key into the lock, turned it, and felt the bolt yield. The next instant the door was opened, apparently from within; I stepped across the threshold, the door closed again, and I was alone in the house, and in darkness.

"Not alone, however! As I extended my hand to grope my way it was met by another hand, soft, slender, and cold, which insinuated itself gently into mine and drew me forward. Forward I went, nothing loath; the darkness was impenetrable, but I could hear the light rustle of a dress close to me, and the same delicious perfume that had emanated from the handkerchief enriched the air that I breathed, while the little hand that clasped and was clasped by my own alternately tightened and half relaxed the hold of its soft cold fingers. In this manner, and treading lightly, we traversed what I presumed to be a long, irregular passageway, and ascended a staircase. Then another corridor, until finally we paused, a door opened, emitting a flood of soft light, into which we entered, still hand in hand. The darkness and the doubt were at an end.

"The room was of imposing dimensions, and was furnished and decorated in a style of antique splendor. The walls were draped with mellow hues of tapestry; clusters of candles burned in polished silver sconces, and were reflected and multiplied in tall mirrors placed in the four corners of the room. The heavy beams of the dark oaken ceiling crossed each other in squares, and were laboriously carved; the curtains and the drapery of the chairs were of heavy-figured damask. At one end of the room was a broad ottoman, and in front of it a table, on which was set forth, in massive silver dishes, a sumptuous repast, with wines in crystal beakers. At the side was a vast and deep fire-place, with space enough on the broad hearth to burn whole trunks of trees. No fire, however, was there, but only a great heap of dead embers; and the room, for all its magnificence, was cold—cold as a tomb, or as my lady's hand—and it sent a subtle chill creeping to my heart.

"But my lady! how fair she was! I gave but a passing glance at the room; my eyes and my thoughts were all for her. She was dressed in white, like a bride; diamonds sparkled in her dark hair and on her snowy bosom; her lovely face and slender lips were pale, and all the paler for the dusky glow of her eyes. She gazed at me with a strange, elusive smile; and yet there was, in her aspect and bearing, something familiar in the midst of strangeness, like the burden of a song heard long ago and recalled among other conditions and surroundings. It seemed to me that something in me recognized her and knew her, had known her always. She was the woman of whom I had dreamed, whom I had beheld in visions, whose voice and face had haunted me from boyhood up. Whether we had ever met before, as human beings meet, I knew not; perhaps I had been blindly seeking her all over the world, and she had been awaiting me in this splendid room, sitting by those dead embers until all the warmth had gone out of her blood, only to be restored by the heat with which my love might supply her.

"'I thought you had forgotten me,' she said, nodding as if in answer to my thought. 'The night was so late—our one night of the year! How my heart rejoiced when I heard your dear voice singing the song I know so well! Kiss me—my lips are cold!'

"Cold indeed they were—cold as the lips of death. But the warmth of my own seemed to revive them. They were now tinged with a faint color, and in her cheeks also appeared a delicate shade of pink. She drew fuller breath, as one who recovers from a long lethargy. Was it my life that was feeding her? I was ready to give her all. She drew me to the table and pointed to the viands and the wine.

"'Eat and drink,' she said. 'You have traveled far, and you need food.'

"'Will you eat and drink with me?' said I, pouring out the wine.

"'You are the only nourishment I want,' was her answer. 'This wine is thin and cold. Give me wine as red as your blood and as warm, and I will drain a goblet to the dregs.'

"At these words, I know not why, a slight shiver passed through me. She seemed to gain vitality and strength at every instant, but the chill of the great room struck into me more and more.

"She broke into a fantastic flow of spirits, clapping her hands, and dancing about me like a child. Who was she? And was I myself, or was she mocking me when she implied that we had belonged to each other of old? At length she stood still before me, crossing her hands over her breast. I saw upon the forefinger of her right hand the gleam of an antique ring.

"'Where did you get that ring?' I demanded.

"She shook her head and laughed. 'Have you been faithful?' she asked. 'It is my ring; it is the ring that unites us; it is the ring you gave me when you loved me first. It is the ring of the Kern—the fairy ring, and I am your Ethelind—Ethelind Fionguala.'

"'So be it,' I said, casting aside all doubt and fear, and yielding myself wholly to the spell of her inscrutable eyes and wooing lips. 'You are mine, and I am yours, and let us be happy while the hours last.'

"'You are mine, and I am yours,' she repeated, nodding her head with an elfish smile. 'Come and sit beside me, and sing that sweet song again that you sang to me so long ago. Ah, now I shall live a hundred years.'

"We seated ourselves on the ottoman, and while she nestled luxuriously among the cushions, I took my banjo and sang to her. The song and the music resounded through the lofty room, and came back in throbbing echoes. And before me as I sang I saw the face and form of Ethelind Fionguala, in her jeweled bridal dress, gazing at me with burning eyes. She was pale no longer, but ruddy and warm, and life was like a flame within her. It was I who had become cold and bloodless, yet with the last life that was in me I would have sung to her of love that can never die. But at length my eyes grew dim, the room seemed to darken, the form of Ethelind alternately brightened and waxed indistinct, like the last flickerings of a fire; I swayed toward her, and felt myself lapsing into unconsciousness, with my head resting on her white shoulder."

Here Keningale paused a few moments in his story, flung a fresh log upon the fire, and then continued:

"I awoke, I know not how long afterward. I was in a vast, empty room in a ruined building. Rotten shreds of drapery depended from the walls, and heavy festoons of spiders' webs gray with dust covered the windows, which were destitute of glass or sash; they had been boarded up with rough planks which had themselves become rotten with age, and admitted through their holes and crevices pallid rays of light and chilly draughts of air. A bat, disturbed by these rays or by my own movement, detached himself from his hold on a remnant of moldy tapestry near me, and after circling dizzily around my head, wheeled the flickering noiselessness of his flight into a darker corner. As I arose unsteadily from the heap of miscellaneous rubbish on which I had been lying, something which had been resting across my

knees fell to the floor with a rattle. I picked it up, and found it to be my banjo
—as you see it now.

"Well, that is all I have to tell. My health was seriously impaired; all the
blood seemed to have been drawn out of my veins; I was pale and haggard,
and the chill—Ah, that chill," murmured Keningale, drawing nearer to the
fire, and spreading out his hands to catch the warmth—"I shall never get over
it; I shall carry it to my grave."

THE FAMILY

Aleksey Konstantinovich Tolstoy

TRANSLATED BY C.S.R. CALLOWAY

first published as **Семья вурдалака** in *The Russian Messenger*
(January 1884)

originally written as *La Famille du Vourdalak. Fragment inedit des Memoires d'un inconnu* (1839)

The year of 1815 brought together in Vienna all who were the most distinguished in terms of European scholarship, brilliant societal minds, and high diplomatic appointments. Even so, the Congress was over.

The royalist emigres were preparing to return conclusively to their castles, the Russian servicemen to see their abandoned homes again and a few unhappy Poles to bring their love of freedom to Cracow and shelter it there under the triple and dubious independence which the prince of Metternich, the prince of Hardenberg and the count of Nesselrode had provided them.

Similar to the end of a lively ball, the once noisy reunion was reduced to a small number of happy-minded people who, fascinated by the charms of Austrian ladies, were slow to pack up and postpone their departure.

This cheerful society, of which I was a part, met twice a week in the castle of the Princess Dowager of Schwarzenberg, a few miles from the town, beyond a small market town called Hitzing. The good manners of the hostess, highlighted by her gracious kindness and the nuances of her wit, made the stay in her residence extremely pleasant.

Our mornings were spent walking; we all had dinner together, either at the castle or in the surrounding area, and in the evenings, sitting by a cozy fireplace, we had fun chatting and telling stories. It was severely forbidden to speak politics. Everyone had had enough, and our stories were borrowed either from the legends of our respective countries or from our own memories.

One evening, when everyone had told something and our minds were in that state of tension that is usually heightened by darkness and silence, the

Marquis d'Urfé, an old emigrant whom we all loved because of his youthful gaiety and the sharp manner by which he spoke of his former good fortunes, took advantage of a moment's silence and spoke:

"Your stories, good fellows," he said to us, "are doubtless very astonishing, but I think they lack an essential point, I mean that of authenticity, because— from what I can tell—none of you has seen with his own eyes the wonderful things he has related, nor can he affirm the truth of them on his word as a nobleman."

We were obliged to agree and the old man continued, stroking the frill on his blouse:

"As for me, good fellows, I know only one adventure of this kind, but it is at the same time so strange, so horrible and so true, that it would be enough by itself to strike terror into the imagination of the most incredulous. I was unfortunately an audience and an actor at the same time, and although I usually do not like to remember it, I will gladly tell you about it this time, if these ladies will allow me."

The agreement was unanimous. A few fearful glances glanced around on the luminous rectangles that the light was beginning to draw on the parquet; but soon the little circle narrowed and everyone fell silent to listen to the story of the marquis. M. d'Urfé took a snuff, inhaled it slowly, and began as follows:

"First of all, ladies, I beg your pardon if, in the course of my storytelling, I happen to talk about my love affairs more often than it would suit a man my age. But I should mention it for the intelligence of my story. Besides, it is forgivable in old age to have moments of oblivion, and it will be your fault, ladies, if, seeing you so beautiful in front of me, I am still tempted to believe myself a young man. I will therefore tell you without further preamble that, in 1759, I was head over heels in love with the pretty Duchess of Gramont. This passion, which I then believed to be deep and lasting, gave me no rest either day or night, and the Duchess, as pretty women often do, was delighted by her coquetry to add to my torment. So much so that, in a moment of vexation, I came to request and obtain a diplomatic mission to the hospodar[13] of Moldavia, who was negotiating matters with the cabinet of Versailles which would be as boring as it would be useless to describe to you. I received the appointment and the day before my departure, I went to see the Duchess. She greeted me with a less mocking air than usual and said in a voice with some emotion:

"'D'Urfé, you do a great folly. But I know you and I know that you will never go back on a resolution made. So, I only ask one thing of you: accept this little cross as a token of my affection and carry it with you until your return. It is a family relic that we hold dear.'

[13] Master of the house.

"With a perhaps inappropriate gallantry for such a moment, I kissed not the relic, but the charming hand which presented it to me, and I put around my neck the cross where it has remained ever since.

"I will not bore you, gracious comrades, with the details of my trip, nor with the observations I made on the Hungarians and the Serbs, these poor and ignorant peoples, but brave and honest and who, enslaved as they were by the Turks, had forgotten neither their dignity, nor their former independence. Suffice it to say that having learned some Polish during a visit I made in Warsaw, I was soon comfortable with Serbian, as both languages—as well as Russian and bohemian—are, as you know, branches of a single language called Slavonic.

"So I knew enough to make myself understood, when one day I arrived in a village whose name would hardly interest you. I found the inhabitants of the house where I went down in a state of anxiety which seemed all the more strange to me since it was a Sunday, a day when the Serbian people used to indulge in different pleasures, such as dancing, archery, wrestling, etc. I attributed the attitude of my hosts to some newly arrived calamity, and was about to retire when a man of about thirty, tall and imposing in face, approached me and took my hand.

"'Come in, come in, stranger,' he said to me, 'don't be put off by our sadness; you will understand it when you know the cause.'

"He then told me that his old father, who was called Gorcha, a man of a restless and obstinate character, got up one day from his bed and unhooked his long Turkish arquebus from the wall.

"'Children,' he had said to his two sons, one Georgi, the other Pierre, 'I am going into the mountains to join the brave men who are hunting this dog Alibek (it was the name of a Turkish robber who had been devastating the country for some time). Wait for me ten days, and if I do not come back on the tenth, say a death mass for me, for I will have been be killed. But,' old Gorcha had added, taking his most serious air, 'if, God forbid, I come back after the ten days have passed, for your salvation do not let me in. I command you in this case to forget that I was your father and pierce me with a stake of aspen, no matter what I say or do, because then I'd be nothing but a damned vourdalak that would suck your blood.'

"It is fitting to tell you, ladies and gentlemen, that the vourdalaks, or vampires of the Slavic peoples, are, in the opinion of the country, nothing more than dead bodies that have risen from their graves to suck the blood of the living. Until then their habits are those of all vampires, but they have another which only makes them more formidable. The vourdalaks, you see, preferably suck the blood of their closest relatives and closest friends who, when dead, become vampires in their turn, so it is claimed to have seen in Bosnia and Hungary entire villages transformed into vourdalaks. Father Augustin Calmet, in his curious studies on the apparitions, cites a few frightening examples. The emperors of Germany repeatedly appointed commissions to investigate cases of vampirism. Reports were drawn up, corpses were exhumed and found to be gorged with blood, and they were burnt in public places after having had their hearts pierced. Magistrates who witnessed these executions claim to have heard the corpses screaming when the executioner drove a stake into their chest. They made a formal statement and corroborated it with their oath and signature.

"From this information, it will be easy for you to understand, my respected listeners, the effect that old Gorcha's words had on his sons. Both of them fell at his feet and begged him to let them go in his place, but in answer he had turned his back on them and walked away humming the chorus of an old ballad. The day I arrived in the village was precisely the day on which the term set by Gorcha was due to expire, and I had no difficulty understanding the concern of his children.

"They were a good, honest family. Georgi, the eldest of the two sons, with strong masculine features, appeared to be a serious and determined man. He was married and the father of two children. His brother Petar, a handsome young man of eighteen, betrayed in his countenance more gentleness than boldness, and seemed the favorite of a younger sister, called Sdenka, who might well pass for the ultimate in Slavic comeliness. Besides this undeniable beauty in all respects, a distant resemblance to the Duchess of Gramont struck me at first. Above all, there was one characteristic feature on the forehead that I've only found in my entire life on these two people. This trait might not appeal at first glance, but you grew overwhelmingly fond of it once you saw it a few times.

"Whether I was very young then, or whether this resemblance, joined to an original and naive mind, was really of an irresistible effect, I did not entertain Sdenka for even two minutes, as I already felt too keen a sympathy for her that threatened to change into a more tender feeling if I prolonged my stay in this village.

"We were all gathered in front of the house around a table lined with cheese and bowls of milk. Sdenka was spinning; her sister-in-law was preparing supper for the children playing in the sand; Petar, with affected carelessness, whistled as he cleaned a yataghan[14]. Georgi, leaning on the table, his head in his hands and his forehead anxious, devoured the main road with his eyes and said nothing.

"As for me, overcome by the prevailing sadness, I gazed wistfully at the evening clouds framing the golden background of the sky and at the silhouette of a convent that a dark pine forest half-concealed.

"This convent, as I learned later, had once enjoyed great fame because of a miraculous image of the Virgin, which, according to legend, had been brought by angels and placed on an oak tree. But, at the beginning of the last century, the Turks had made an invasion in the country; they had slaughtered the monks and desecrated the monastery. All that remained were the walls and a chapel served by a sort of hermit. He led curious visitors through the

14 A long Turkish knife.

ruins and gave shelter to pilgrims who, going on foot from one place of devotion to another, liked to stop at the Convent of the Virgin of the Oak. As I said, I did not learn all this until later, because that evening I had something quite different in mind than the archeology of Serbia. As often happens when you let your imagination run wild, I thought of times past, of the heyday of my childhood, of my beautiful France, which I had left for a distant and wild country.

"I was thinking of the Duchess of Gramont and, why not admit it, I was also thinking of some other contemporaries of your grandmothers, whose images, unbeknownst to me, had crept into my heart following that of the lovely duchess.

"Soon I had forgotten both my hosts and their worry.

"Suddenly Georgi broke the silence.

"'Woman,' he said, 'at what time did the old man leave?'

"'Eight o'clock,' his wife replied. 'I heard the convent bell ringing.'

"'So that's good,' said Georgi, 'it can't be past half past seven.' And he fell silent, fixing his eyes again on the main road which lost itself in the forest.

"I forgot to tell you, ladies and gentlemen, that when the Serbs suspect someone of vampirism, they avoid naming him by name or referring to him directly, because they think that would summon him from the tomb. So for some time now Georgi, speaking of his father, called him only 'the old man.'

"There were a few moments silence, then suddenly one of the children said to Sdenka, pulling her by the apron:

"Auntie, when will Grandpa come home?"

"A slap from Georgi was the answer to this untimely question.

"The child started to cry, but his little brother spoke with a look both astonished and fearful:

"'Why then, father, do you forbid us to speak of Grandpa?

"Another blow shut his mouth. The two children bawled and the adults crossed each other.

"We were there when I heard the convent clock strike eight o'clock slowly. No sooner had the first toll sounded in our ears than we saw a human form separate itself from the wood and head towards us.

"'It's him! God be praised!' cried Sdenka, Petar and her sister-in-law together.

"'God have us in his holy care!' said Georgi solemnly. 'How do you know if the ten days are up or not?'

"Everyone looked at him with dread. The human form was still advancing. He was a tall old man with a silver mustache, a pale, stern face, dragging himself painfully with a stick. As he moved forward, Georgi grew darker. When the new arrival was near us, he stopped and looked over his family with eyes that seemed not to see, they were so dull and sunken in their sockets.

"'Well,' he said in a hollow voice, 'nobody gets up to receive me? What does this silence mean? Can't you see I'm hurt?'

"I then saw that the old man's left side was bloody.

"'Go help your father,' I said to Georgi, 'and you, Sdenka, you should give him some liqueur, for he is on the verge of fainting!'

"'My father,' said Georgi, approaching Gorcha, 'show me your wound. I have enough knowledge and I'll bandage you...

"He made as if to open his coat, but the old man pushed him back roughly and covered his side with both hands.

"'Get away, clumsy,' he said. 'You hurt me!'

"'But it's in the heart that you're wounded!' cried Georgi, quite pale; 'Come on, come on, take off your clothes! You have to, you have to, I tell you!'

"The old man stood up straight and stiff.

"'Beware,' he said in a hollow voice, 'if you touch me, I curse you!'

"Petar got between Georgi and his father.

"'Leave him alone,' he said to his brother. 'You can see what pain he's in!'

"'Don't cross him,' his wife added. 'You know he never tolerated that!'

"At this moment we saw a herd returning from the pasture and moving towards the house in a cloud of dust. Either the dog that accompanied them had not recognized his old master, or he had been impelled by some other motive for as soon as he saw Gorcha, he stopped, his hair standing on end, and began to yowl as if he saw something unnatural.

"'What's wrong with this dog?' asked the old man, looking more and more unhappy. 'What does all this mean? Have I become a stranger in my own home? Have ten days in the mountains changed me so much that even my dogs don't recognize me?'

"'Do you hear him?' Georgi asked his wife.

"'What?'

"'He admits that the ten days have passed!'

"'No, since he's come back on time!'

"'It's okay, it's okay. I know what to do.'

"As the dog continued to howl, Gorcha cried, 'I want him killed! Well, don't you hear me?'

"Georgi did not move; but Petar got up with tears in his eyes and, seizing his father's arquebus, he shot the dog, who rolled in the dust.

"'But he was my favorite dog,' he said in a low voice. 'I don't know why my father wanted him dead!'

"'Because he deserved it,' Gorcha said. 'Come on, it's cold and I want to go inside!'

"While this was going on outside, Sdenka had brewed an herbal tea for the old man of brandy boiled with pears, honey and raisins, but her father pushed her away in disgust. He showed the same aversion to the dish of mutton and rice that Georgi presented him and went to sit in the corner of the fireplace, muttering unintelligible words between his teeth.

"A pine fire sparkled in the hearth, and with its quivering light enlivened the face of the old man so pale and defeated that, without this light, it might have been taken for that of a dead man. Sdenka came and sat down beside him.

"'Father,' she said, 'you don't want to take anything or rest; why don't you tell us about your adventures in the mountains?'

"By saying this, the young girl knew she touched a sensitive chord, because the old man liked to talk about wars and fights. Also, a kind of smile appeared on his bloodless lips, without reaching his eyes, and he replied by passing his hand over her beautiful blond hair:

"'Yes, my daughter, yes, Sdenka, I will tell you what happened to me in the mountains, but it will be another time, because I am tired today. I will tell you, however, that Alibek is no more and that it was at my hand that he perished. If anyone doubts it,' continued the old man, looking over his family, 'here is the proof!'

"He undid a sort of satchel which hung behind his back, and drew from it a discolored, bloody head that competed with his own in pallor! We turned away in horror, but Gorcha, giving it to Petar:

"'Here,' he said, 'tie this above the door for me, so that all passers-by will learn that Alibek is killed and that the roads are cleared of robbers, except perhaps the sultan's janissaries!'

"Petar obeyed with disgust.

"'I understand everything now,' he said, 'that poor dog I had killed only howled because he smelled dead flesh!'

"'Yes, he smelled dead flesh,' replied Georgi, with a somber air, who had gone out without our noticing it, and who was entering at this moment, holding in his hand an object which he placed in a corner. To me, it appeared to be a stake.

"'Georgi,' said his wife in a low voice, 'you don't want to, I hope…'

"'My brother,' added his sister, 'what do you want to do? But no, no, you won't do anything, will you?'

"'Leave me alone,' replied Georgi, 'I know what to do and I won't do anything that's not necessary.'

"In the meantime, when night came, the family went to sleep in a part of the house which was only separated from my room by a very thin partition. I admit that what I had seen that evening had impressed my imagination. My light was out, the moon looked right into a small low window, very close to my bed, and threw pallid gleams on the floor and walls, much as it does now, ladies, in the living room where we are. I wanted to sleep and couldn't. I attributed my sleeplessness to the moonlight; I looked for something that could serve as a curtain, but found nothing. So, hearing confused voices behind the partition, I began to listen.

"'Lie down, woman,' said Georgi, 'and you, Petar, and you, Sdenka. Don't worry about a thing, I'll watch for you.'

"'But, Georgi,' replied his wife, 'it is right for me to watch. You worked last night; you must be tired. Besides, otherwise I must watch over our oldest boy. You know he's been unwell since yesterday!'

"'Be quiet and go to bed,' said Georgi, 'I will watch for both of us!'

"'But, my brother,' Sdenka said then in her softest voice, 'it seems to me that it would be useless to keep watch. Our father is already asleep, and see how calm and peaceful he looks.'

"'Neither of you understand anything,' Georgi said in a tone that left no room for no contradiction. 'I tell you to go to bed and let me watch.'

"There was then a deep silence. Soon I felt my eyelids grow heavy and sleep take hold of my senses.

"I thought I saw my door slowly open and old Gorcha appear on the threshold. But I suspected its shape rather than seeing it, for it was pitch dark in the room he came from. It seemed to me that his dull eyes sought to guess my thoughts and followed the movement of my breathing. Then he put one foot forward, then he put the other forward. Then, with extreme care, he began to stealthily walk towards me. Then he took a leap and landed next to my bed. I had inexpressible anguish, but an invisible force held me still. The old man leaned over me and brought his livid face so close to mine that I thought I could smell his cadaverous breath. So I made a supernatural effort and woke up, bathed in sweat. There was no one in my room, but, glancing towards the window, I distinctly saw old Gorcha who outside had pressed his face against the glass and fixed fearful eyes on me. I had the strength not to scream and the presence of mind to lie down, as if I hadn't seen a thing. However, the old man seemed to have come only to make sure that I was asleep, for he made no attempt to enter, but, after examining me well, he moved away from the window and I heard him walking. In the next room Georgi had fallen asleep and he was snoring enough to make the walls shake. The child coughed then and I could make out Gorcha's voice.

"'Aren't you sleeping, child?' he said.

"'No, Grandpa,' replied the child, 'and I want to talk to you!'

"'Ah, you want to talk to me? And what shall we talk about?'

"'I would like you to tell me how you fought with the Turks, because I too would gladly fight with the Turks!'

"'I thought about it, child, and brought you a little yataghan that I'll give you tomorrow.'

"'Ah, grandpa, rather give it to me now, since you're not sleeping.'

"'But why, child, didn't you talk to me while it was daylight?'

"'Because Daddy wouldn't let me!'

"'He's careful, your father. So, would you like to have your little yataghan?'

"'Oh yes, I would like it, but I can't play with it here, because Daddy might wake up!'

"'But where, then?'

"'If we go out, I promise to be very good and not to make any noise!'

"I thought I heard a snort of laughter from Gorcha and heard the child stand up. I didn't believe in vampires, but the nightmare I had just had got on my nerves and, not wanting to reproach myself afterwards, I stood up and punched the bulkhead. It would have been enough to wake the seven sleepers, but nothing told me it had been overheard by the family. I rushed to the door, determined to save the child, but found it locked from the outside and the bolts did not yield to my efforts. As I tried to push it down, I saw the old man pass by my window with the child in his arms.

"'Get up, get up!' I cried with all my might, and shook the wall with my blows. Only then did Georgi wake up.

"'Where's the old man?' he demanded.

"'Get out quickly,' I shouted at him. 'He just took your child!'"

"Georgi kicked open the door, which like mine had been closed from the outside, and he began to run in the direction of the wood. I finally managed to wake Petar, his sister-in-law and Sdenka. We gathered in front of the house and, after a few minutes of waiting, we saw Georgi return with his son. He had found him passed out on the highway, but soon he had recovered and looked no more ill than before. Pressed with questions, he replied that his grandfather had done him no harm, that they had gone out together to talk more comfortably, but that once outside, he had lost consciousness, without remembering how. As for Gorcha, he had disappeared.

"The rest of the night, as one can imagine, passed without sleep.

"The next day I learned that the Danube, which cut off the main road a quarter of a league from the village, had started to carry icicles, which always happens in these regions in late autumn and early spring. The passage was blocked for a few days, and I could not consider taking my departure. Besides, even if I could, curiosity, combined with a more powerful attraction, would have held me back. The more I saw Sdenka, the more I fell in love with her. I am not one of those people who believe in the sudden and irresistible passions of which the novels offer us examples; but I think there are times when love grows faster than usual. The original beauty of Sdenka, this singular resemblance to the Duchess of Gramont whom I had fled in Paris and whom I found here, in a picturesque costume, speaking a foreign and harmonious language, this characteristic forehead mark for which, in France, I had wanted to be killed twenty times, all this, together with the singularity of my situation and the mysteries which surrounded me, had to contribute to ripening in me a feeling which, in other circumstances, would not have manifested itself, or only in a vague and fleeting way.

"During the course of the day I overheard Sdenka talking to her younger brother.

"'What do you think of all this?' she said. 'Do you also suspect our father?'

"'I dare not suspect it,' Petar replied, 'especially since the child said he didn't harm him. And when it comes to his disappearance, you know he never reported on his absences.'

"'I know it,' sighed Sdenka, 'but then he must be protected, because you know Georgi…'

"'Yes, yes, I know Georgi. Talking to him would be useless, but we'll hide the stake, and he won't look for another, because on this side of the mountains there is not a single aspen!'

"'Yes, let's hide the stake, but let's not tell the children about it, because they could talk about it in front of Georgi!'

"'We will take care not to do so,' said Petar. And they parted.

"Night came without our having learned anything about old Gorcha. I was like the day before lying on my bed and the moon was right in my room. When sleep began to cloud my thoughts, I felt, as if by instinct, the approach of the old man. I opened my eyes and saw his livid face pressed against my window.

"This time I wanted to get up, but it was impossible for me. It seemed to me that all my limbs were paralyzed. After giving me a good look, the old man walked away. I heard him go around the house and knock softly on the window of the bedroom where Georgi and his wife were sleeping. The child rolled over in his bed and moaned in a dream. A few minutes of silence passed, then I heard another knock on the window. Then the child moaned again and woke up ...

"'Is that you, Grandpa?' he said.

"'It's me,' came the hollow-voiced reply, 'and I'm bringing you your little yataghan.'

"'But I don't dare go out; daddy forbade me!'

"'You don't have to go out, just open the window for me and come and kiss me!'

"The child stood up and I heard him open the window. So, recalling all my energy, I jumped out of bed and ran to knock on the partition. In a minute Georgi was up. I heard him swear, his wife let out a loud cry, soon the whole house was gathered around the inanimate child. Gorcha had disappeared like the day before. By dint of care we managed to bring the child back to consciousness, but he was very weak and breathing with difficulty. The poor little one did not know the cause of his fainting. His mother and Sdenka attributed it to the fear of being caught chatting with his grandfather. I didn't say anything. However, the child having calmed down, everyone except Georgi went back to bed.

"Toward dawn I heard him wake up his wife. They spoke to each other in low voices. Sdenka joined them and I heard her sob, as well as her sister-in-law.

"The child was dead.

"I gloss over the family's desperation. No one, however, attributed the cause to old Gorcha. At least, we didn't talk about it openly.

"Georgi was silent, but there was something terrible about his still dark expression now. For two days the old man did not reappear. In the night following the third (the one where the child was buried) I thought I heard footsteps around the house and an old man's voice calling for the younger brother of the deceased. I also thought for a moment that I saw Gorcha's face pressed against my window, but I couldn't tell if that was a reality or a figment of my imagination, for that night the moon was veiled. However, I thought it my duty to tell Georgi about it. He questioned the child, and the child replied that indeed he had heard himself called by his grandfather and had seen him looking through the window. Georgi severely enjoined his remaining son to wake him up if the old man still appeared.

"All these circumstances did not prevent my affection for Sdenka from developing even further.

"I hadn't been able to speak to her without witnesses all day. When night came, the thought of my next departure gripped my heart. Sdenka's room was only separated from mine by a vestibule facing the street on one side and the courtyard on the other.

"My host family was in bed when it occurred to me to take a walk in the countryside to distract myself. Entering the hallway, I saw that Sdenka's door was ajar.

"I stopped involuntarily. A well-known rustle of a dress made my heart beat faster. Then I heard words sung in a low voice. These were the farewells that a Serbian king, going to war, addressed to his beautiful.

> "'Oh, my young poplar,' said the old king, 'I am going to war and you will forget me!
>
> "'The trees that grow at the foot of the mountain are slender and flexible, but your youthful camp is slenderer and more flexible!
>
> "'The rowan fruits that the wind swings are red, but your lips are redder than the rowan fruits!
>
> "'And I am like an old oak tree stripped of leaves, and my beard is whiter than the foam of the Danube!
>
> "'And you will forget me, O my soul, and I will die of anguish, for the enemy will not dare to kill the old king!'
>
> "'And the beauty replied, 'I swear to be faithful to you and not to forget you. And if I break the oath, come to me from the grave and suck the blood of my heart.'
>
> "'And the old king said, 'So be it!' And he left for the war. And soon the beauty forgot him!...'"

"Here Sdenka stopped, as if afraid of ending the ballad. I no longer contained myself. This voice so sweet, so expressive, was the voice of the Duchess of Gramont... Without thinking, I pushed open the door and entered. Sdenka had just taken off a casaquin, a short fitted coat worn by the women of her country. Her shirt, embroidered in gold and red silk, wrapped around her waist with a simple checkered skirt, made up her entire outfit. Her beautiful blonde tresses were loose and her negligee heightened her appeal. Without getting irritated by my sudden entry, she looked confused and blushed slightly.

"'Oh,' she said to me, 'why did you come here? What would people think of me if we were caught?'

"'Sdenka, my soul,' I said to her, 'be quiet, everything around us is asleep. Only the cricket in the grass and the chafer in the air can hear what I have to say to you.

"'Oh, my friend, run away, run away! If my brother catches us, I'm lost!'

"'Sdenka, I will not go until you promise to love me always, as the beauty promised to the king of the ballad. I'm leaving soon, Sdenka, who knows when we'll meet again? Sdenka, I love you more than my soul, more than my salvation… My life and my blood are yours… Will you not give me an hour in return?'

"'A lot can happen in an hour,' Sdenka said thoughtfully; but she left her hand in mine. 'You don't know my brother,' she continued, shivering; 'my intuition says he will come.'

"'Calm down, my Sdenka,' I said to her. 'Your brother is tired of his vigils. He has been lulled to sleep by the wind playing in the trees; very heavy is his rest, very long is the night, and I ask you only for an hour! And then, goodbye…maybe forever!'

"'Oh, no, no, not forever!' said Sdenka hastily; then she recoiled as if frightened by her own voice.

"'Oh, Sdenka!' I cried. 'I only see you, I only hear you, I am no longer in control of myself, I obey a higher force! Forgive me, Sdenka!' And like a madman I hugged her to my heart.

"'Oh, you're not my friend,' she said, freeing herself from my arms, and went to take refuge in the back of her room. I do not know what I replied to her, for I myself was confused by my audacity, not that on such an occasion it did not succeed me sometimes, but because, despite my passion, I could not defend myself from sincere respect for Sdenka's innocence.

"At the beginning I had, it is true, risked some of those phrases of gallantry which did not displease the beauties of our time, but soon I was ashamed of it, and I gave it up, seeing that the simplicity of the young girl prevented her from understanding what you ladies, I can see by your smile, you guessed at half a word.

"I was there in front of her, not knowing what to say to her, when all of a sudden I saw her flinch and gaze in terror on the window. I followed the direction of his eyes and distinctly saw the motionless face of Gorcha watching us from outside.

"At the same moment, I felt a heavy hand rest on my shoulder. I turned around. It was Georgi.

"'What are you doing here?' he demanded of me.

"Baffled by the abruptness of his appearance and the sharpness of his question, I showed him his father who was looking at us through the window and who disappeared as soon as Georgi saw him.

"'I heard the old man and I came to tell your sister,' I lied.

"Georgi looked at me as if he wanted to read the depths of my soul. Then he took me by the arm, led me to my room and left without saying a word.

"The next day the family gathered outside the door of the house around a table laden with dairy products.

"'Where's the kid?' said Georgi.

"'He's in the yard,' his mother replied, 'playing his favorite game on his own and imagining himself fighting the Turks.'

"No sooner had she said these words than to our extreme surprise we saw the tall figure of Gorcha advance from the bottom of the woods, who walked slowly towards our group and sat down at the table as he had done during the day of my arrival.

"'Welcome father, my father,' his daughter-in-law whispered in a barely intelligible voice.

"'Welcome, father,' repeated Sdenka and Petar in low voices.

"'My father,' said Georgi in a casual voice, though his face betrayed his intentions, 'we are waiting for you to say the prayer!'

"The old man turned away, frowning.

"'Prayer right now!' repeated Georgi, 'and make the sign of the cross or by Saint George ...'

"Sdenka and her sister-in-law leaned over the old man and begged him to say the prayer.

"'No, no, no,' said the old man, 'he has no right to order me and if he insists, I curse him!'

"Georgi got up and ran into the house. Soon he returned, fury in his eyes.

"'Where's the stake?' he cried, 'where did you hide the stake?'

"Sdenka and Petar exchanged a look.

"'Corpse!' then said Georgi, addressing the old man. 'What have you done with my eldest? Why did you kill my child? Give me back my son, corpse!'

"And as he spoke like that, he grew paler and paler, and his eyes became more animated.

"The old man gave him a sour look and didn't move.

"'Oh! The stake, the stake!' exclaimed Georgi. 'May he who hid it answer for the misfortunes that await us!'

"At that moment we heard the joyful bursts of laughter from the younger child and we saw him arrive astride a large stake which he was dragging, prancing on it and uttering with his small voice the war cry of the Serbs when they attack. the enemy.

"At this sight, Georgi's gaze blazed. He tore the stake from the child and rushed at his father. The latter gave a howl and began to run in the direction of the wood with a speed so out of keeping with his age that it seemed supernatural.

"Georgi chased him across the fields and soon we lost sight of them.

"The sun had gone down when Georgi came home, deathly pale and his hair standing on end. He sat down by the fire and I thought I heard his teeth chattering. No one dared to question him. About the time when the family used to part, he seemed to recover all his energy and, taking me aside, he said to me in the most natural way:

"'My dear guest, I just saw the river. The ice has melted, the path is clear, nothing stands in the way of your departure. It is useless,' he added, glancing at Sdenka, 'to say your goodbyes to my family. On behalf of them, I wish you all the happiness that one can desire in this world, and I hope that you too will keep us in fond memory. Tomorrow, at daybreak, you will find your horse saddled and your guide ready to follow you. Farewell, and whenever you think of your host, forgive him if your stay here was not as free from tribulation as you would have liked.'

"Georgi's harsh features at that moment had an almost cordial expression. He led me to my room and shook my hand one last time. Then he flinched and his teeth chattered as if he was shivering with cold.

"Left alone, I didn't think of going to bed as you can imagine. Other ideas preoccupied me. I had loved many times in my life. I had had fits of tenderness, spite and jealousy, but never, not even when I left the Duchess of Gramont, had I felt a sadness like the one that was tearing my heart at this moment. Before the sun came out, I put on my traveling clothes and wanted to try one last interview with Sdenka. But Georgi was waiting for me in the hall. Any possibility of seeing her again was abandoned.

"I jumped on my horse and took off at full speed. I promised myself, on my return from Jassy, to return to this village, and this hope, remote though it was, gradually chased my worries away. I was already thinking complacently by the time of the return and my imagination was tracing all the details in advance, when a sudden movement of the horse nearly knocked me off the pommels. The animal came to a stop, stiffened on its front feet, and snorted anxiously to communicate its sensing of danger. I looked closely and saw a wolf digging in the earth a hundred paces ahead of me. At the noise I made he fled, I thrust my spurs into the sides of my mount and managed to push it forward. I then noticed at the spot that the wolf had left a very fresh pit. It also seemed to me to distinguish the tip of a stake a few inches above the ground that the wolf had just stirred. However, I don't say that because I passed this place very quickly."

Here the marquis was silent and took a snuff.

"So is that all?" the company demanded to know.

"Alas no!" replied M. d'Urfé. "What I have to tell you, again, is a much more painful memory to me, and I would give a lot to be delivered from it.

"The business that brought me to Jassy kept me there longer than I expected. I didn't finish for six months. What will I tell you? It is a sad truth to confess, but it is nonetheless a truth that there are few lasting feelings here on earth. The success of my negotiations, the encouragement I received from the cabinet of Versailles, politics in short, this ugly policy which has bored us so much lately, soon weakened the memory of Sdenka in my mind. Then, the wife of the hospodar, a very beautiful person and fluent in our language, from the very first days of my arrival honored me, giving me special preference over the other young foreigners who were staying then in Jassy. Raised, as I was, in the principles of French gallantry, my Gallic blood would have revolted at the idea of paying ingratitude for the benevolence shown to me by beauty. So I courteously responded to advances made to me, and to put myself in a position to assert the interests and rights of France, I began to look at all the rights and all the interests of the sovereign as my own.

"Called back to my country, I took the path that had brought me to Jassy.

"I was no longer thinking of Sdenka or her family, when one evening, riding through the countryside, I heard a bell ringing eight o'clock. This sound did not strike me as unknown and my guide told me it came from a convent not far away. I asked her for the name, and learned that it was the Virgin of the Oak. I quickened my horse's pace and soon we knocked on the convent door. The hermit opened the door for us and led us to the strangers' apartment. I found it so full of pilgrims that I lost the desire to spend the night there and asked if I could find a place to stay in the village.

"'You will find more than one,' replied the hermit, heaving a deep sigh; 'thanks to the disbeliever Gorcha there is no shortage of empty houses!'

"'What does that mean?' I asked. 'Is old Gorcha still alive?'

"'Oh, no, that one is well and beautifully buried with a stake in his heart! But he had sucked the blood of Georgi's son. The child came back one night, crying at the door, saying he was cold and wanted to go home. His foolish mother, although she had buried him herself, didn't have the courage to send him back to the cemetery and opened it for him. So he threw himself on her and sucked her to death. Buried in her turn, she came back to suck the blood of her second son, and then that of her husband, and then that of her brother-in-law. All of them have passed there.

"'And Sdenka?' I said.

"'Oh, that one went mad with pain, the poor thing. It's best not to speak about it!'

"There was some vagueness in his answer, though I lost the courage to inquire any further.

"'Vampirism is contagious,' the hermit continued, crossing himself; 'many families in the village are affected, many families died down to their last member, and if you trust me, you'll pass the night at the convent, because in the village, even if you were not be devoured by the vourdalaks, still, the terror alone is enough to bleach your hair before I'm done ringing matins.

"'I am only a poor religious man,' he continued, 'but the generosity of the travelers has enabled me to provide for their needs. I have exquisite cheeses, raisins that will make your mouth water just looking at them, and a few flasks of Tokay wine which is on par with the one served to His Holiness the Patriarch!'

"At that moment, before my eyes, the hermit seemed to be turning into an innkeeper. I believed that he had told me fairy tales on purpose to give me the opportunity to make myself pleasant in heaven, by imitating the generosity of the travelers *who had enabled the holy man to provide for their needs.*

"And then the word 'fear' has always had on me the effect of a bugle on a steed of war. I would have been ashamed of myself if I hadn't left immediately. My guide, all trembling, asked me permission to stay and I gladly granted it.

"It took me about half an hour to get to the village. I found it deserted. Not a light shone in the windows, not a song was heard. I passed all these houses in silence, most of which were known to me, and finally came to Georgi's. Either sentimental memory or a young man's nerve, it was there that I resolved to spend the night.

"I dismounted and knocked on the porte-cochere. No one answered. I pushed open the door, it opened, creaking on its hinges, and I entered the courtyard.

"I tethered my saddled horse under a shed, where I found a supply of oats sufficient for the night and I proceeded resolutely towards the house.

"No doors were closed, yet all the rooms seemed uninhabited. Sdenka's seemed to have been abandoned only the day before. A few clothes still lay on the bed. Some jewels she had received from me, among which I recognized a small enamel cross that I had bought while passing through Pest, shone on a table in the light of the moon. I couldn't help myself from a pang of heart, although my love had passed. However, I wrapped myself in my coat and lay down on the bed. Soon I fell asleep. I don't remember the details of my dream, but I do know that I saw Sdenka again, beautiful, naive and loving as in the past. Seeing her I reproached myself for my selfishness and inconstancy. How could I, I wondered, abandon this poor child who loved me, how could I forget her? Then the vision of her merged with that of the Duchess of Gramont and I saw in these two images only one and the same person. I threw myself at Sdenka's feet and begged her forgiveness. My whole being, my whole soul mingled in an ineffable feeling of melancholy and happiness.

"I had reached this point in my dream, when I was half awakened by a harmonious sound, like the rustle of a wheat field stirred by the light breeze. I thought I heard the ears of corn clash melodiously and the song of birds mingled with the rolling of a waterfall and the whisper of the trees. Then it seemed to me that all these confused sounds were only the rustle of a woman's dress and I stopped at this idea. I opened my eyes and saw Sdenka by my bed. The moon shone so brightly that I could make out in minute detail the adorable features that had once been so dear to me, but of which only my dream had just made me feel the full value. I found Sdenka more beautiful and more developed. She had the same negligee as the last time, when I had seen her alone; a simple shirt embroidered with gold and silk, and then a skirt tightly drawn above the hips.

"'Sdenka!' I said, getting up from my seat. 'Is that you, Sdenka?'

"'Yes, it's me,' she replied in a soft and sad voice, 'it's your Sdenka that you forgot. Ah, why didn't you come back sooner? It's all over now, you have to go; one more moment and you're lost! Farewell, my friend, farewell forever!'"

"'Sdenka,' I said to her, 'you have had a lot of misfortunes I was told. Come, we will talk together and it will relieve you!'

"'Oh, my friend,' she said, 'don't believe everything that is said about us; but go, go as quickly as possible, for if you stay here your loss is certain.'

"'But, Sdenka, what is this danger that threatens me? Can't you give me an hour, just one hour to speak with you?'

"'Sdenka flinched, and a strange revolution took place in her whole person.

"'Yes,' she said, 'an hour, an hour, isn't it, like when I was singing the old king's ballad and you entered that room? Is that what you mean? Well, okay, I'll give you an hour! But no, no,' she said, pulling herself together, 'go, go away!—Go faster, I tell you, run away! …but run away while you can!

"A savage energy animated her features.

"I didn't bother to understand why she was talking like that, but she was so beautiful that I resolved to stay in spite of herself. Finally yielding to my pleas, she sat down next to me, told me about times gone by and blushed to admit that she had loved me from the day I arrived. However, gradually I noticed a big change in Sdenka. Her former reserve had given way to a strange abandon. There was something bold about her gaze, which had once been so timid. And from the way she behaved with me, I realized with amazement that there was little of that modesty left in her that had once distinguished her.

"'Could it be possible,' I said to myself, 'that Sdenka was not the pure and innocent young girl she seemed to be two years ago? Would she have taken only the appearance for fear of her brother? Would I have been so grossly fooled by her adopted virtue? But then why did she encourage me to leave? Could it be by chance a refined coquetry? And I, who thought I knew her! But whatever! If Sdenka is not a Diana as I thought she would be, I can compare her to another deity, no less lovable and, by God, I prefer the role of Adonis to the role of Actaeon!

"If that classic phrase I addressed to myself seems out of season to you, good fellows, please bear in mind that what I have the honor to tell you was in our year of grace 1758. Mythology was the order of the day then, and I didn't pride myself on going faster than my century. Things have changed a lot since then, and it is not long ago that the Revolution, by overturning memories of paganism, along with the Christian religion, put the goddess Reason in their place. This goddess, ladies, was never my patroness when I found myself in the presence of you, and, at the time of which I speak, I was less willing than ever to offer her sacrifices. I surrendered wholeheartedly to the inclination that drew me towards Sdenka and happily met her aggravations. Some time had already passed in sweet intimacy when, having fun adorning Sdenka with all her jewels, I wanted to put the little enamel cross I had found on the table around her neck. At the movement I made, Sdenka shuddered backwards.

"'Enough childishness, my friend,' she said to me, 'leave these trinkets and let's talk about you and your plans!'

"Sdenka's fluctuation made me think. Examining the cross carefully, I noticed that it no longer had around its neck, as in the past, a crowd of small pictures, reliquaries and sachets filled with incense that the Serbs used to wear from their childhood and that they do not leave until their death.

"'Sdenka,' I said to her, 'where are the images you had around your neck?'

"'I lost them,' she replied impatiently, and immediately changed the conversation.

"Some kind of dark foreboding began to speak in me; I did not immediately realize it. I wanted to leave, but Sdenka held me back.

"'What?' she cried. 'You asked me for an hour, and here you go after a few minutes!'

"'Sdenka,' I said, 'you were right to make me leave; I think I hear some noise and I'm afraid we will be surprised!'

"'Don't worry, my friend, everything around us is asleep, only the cricket in the grass and the chafer in the air can hear what I have to say to you!'

"'No, no, Sdenka, I must go!'

"'Stop, stop,' said Sdenka, 'I love you more than my soul, more than my salvation, you told me that your life and your blood are mine!'

"'But your brother, your brother, Sdenka, I have a hunch that he will come!'

"'Calm down, my soul, my brother has been lulled to sleep by the wind playing in the trees; very heavy is his rest, very long is the night and I ask you only for an hour!'

"As she said this, Sdenka was so beautiful that the vague terror that agitated me began to give way to the desire to stay with her. A mixture of fear and indescribable pleasure filled my whole being. As I weakened, Sdenka grew more tender, so much so that I made up my mind to give in, while promising myself to be on my guard. However, as I said earlier, I have never been more than half wise, and when Sdenka, noticing my reserve, offered to chase away the cold of the night with a few glasses of the generous wine that she said she got from the good hermit, I accepted her offer with an eagerness that made her smile. The wine produced its effect. From the second glass, the bad impression that the circumstance of the cross and the images had made on me was completely erased; Sdenka in the mess of her attire, with her beautiful half-braided hair, with her moonlit jewels, seemed irresistible to me. I was no longer restrained and I hugged her tight in my arms.

"Then, comrades, occurred one of those mysterious revelations which I shall never be able to explain, but the existence of which experience has forced me to believe, though hitherto I have been little inclined to admit them.

"The force with which I wrapped my arms around Sdenka made one of the points of the cross which you have just seen and which the Duchess of Gramont gave me when I left, entered my chest. The sharp pain that I felt was like a ray of light to me that went through me right through. I looked at Sdenka and saw that her features, though still beautiful, were contracted with death, that her eyes did not see and that her smile was a convulsion imprinted with agony on the face of a corpse. At the same time, I could smell in the room that nauseating odor that usually emanates from improperly closed vaults. The ugly truth stood before me in all its ugliness, and I remembered the hermit's warnings too late. I understood how precarious my position was and I felt that everything depended on my courage and my composure. I turned away from Sdenka to hide from her the horror my features must have expressed. My eyes, then, fell on the window and I saw the infamous Gorcha, leaning on a bloodied stake and fixing on me the eyes of a hyena. The other window was occupied by the pale face of Georgi, who at this moment bore a frightening resemblance to his father. They both seemed to be watching my movements and I had no doubt they would swarm at me at the slightest attempt to escape. So I did not give the impression I had seen them, and made a violent effort on myself to continue, yes, ladies, I continued to lavish on Sdenka the same caresses that I liked to give her before my terrible discovery. Meanwhile, I was thinking with anguish of how to escape. I noticed that Gorcha and Georgi were exchanging knowing looks with Sdenka and they were starting to get impatient. I also heard a woman's voice outside and the cries of children, but so dreadful they could have been taken for the howls of wild cats.

"'Now it's time to pack up,' I said to myself, 'and the sooner the better!'

"Addressing Sdenka then, I said aloud so that her hideous family could hear:

"I am very tired, my dear; I would like to go to bed and sleep for a few hours, but first I must go and see if my horse has eaten its feed. Please do not go away and wait for my return.'

"I then applied my lips to her bloodless, discolored lips and walked out. I found my horse covered in foam and free of his leash. He hadn't touched the oats, but the whinny he let out when he saw me coming gave me goosebumps, for I feared he would betray my intentions. However, the vampires, who had probably overheard my conversation with Sdenka, did not think to take alarm. I then made sure the porte-cochere was open and, springing into the saddle, I rammed my spurs into my horse's sides.

"As I rode out of the gate, I noticed that the crowd around the house had grown into a horde and that most of the newcomers pressed their eyes to the panes of the windows. It seems that my sudden flight puzzled them at first, since for some time I did not distinguish any other sounds in the stillness of the night, except for the measured tramp of my horse. I was almost congratulating myself on the success that my cunning had led to, when suddenly I heard a noise behind me—like the roar of a hurricane raging in the mountains. A thousand confused voices screamed, howled and seemed to be arguing among themselves. Then, as if by agreement, they all fell silent, and only the rapid tramp of feet was heard, as if a detachment of infantrymen were approaching at a quick pace.

"I urged on my horse, mercilessly thrusting his spurs into his sides. A fiery fever made my arteries pound, and as I exhausted myself in tremendous efforts to maintain my presence of mind, I heard a voice behind me shouting at me:

"'Stop, stop, my darling! You are dearer to me than my soul, than my salvation! Stop, stop, your blood is mine!'

"At the same time, a cold breath brushed my ear and I felt Sdenka jump up on me.

"'My heart, my soul!' she said to me, 'I only see you, I only feel you, I am not in control of myself, I obey a higher force, forgive me, my darling, forgive me!'

"And, wrapping her arms around me, she tried to pull me back and bite me in the throat. A terrible struggle ensued between us. For a long time I barely defended myself, but finally I managed to grab Sdenka with one hand by her belt and the other by her braids and, stiffening myself in my stirrups, I threw her to the ground!

"Immediately my strength gave up and delirium took hold of me. A thousand crazy and terrible figures chased me, grimacing. First Georgi and his brother Petar stalked alongside the road and tried to cut my path. They didn't succeed, and I was about to rejoice when, turning around, I saw old Gorcha using his stake to leap like Tyrolean mountaineers when they cross the abyss. I also outpaced him. Then his daughter-in-law, who was dragging her children behind her, threw one of her boys to him, and he caught him on the edge of his stake. Using it as a ballista, he hurled the child after me with all his might. I avoided the blow, but with true bulldog instinct the little bastard clung to my horse's neck, and I had a hard time pulling it off. The other child was sent to me in the same way, but they overshot and he was crushed beneath the hooves of the horse. I don't remember what else happened, but when I came to my senses, it was broad daylight and I found myself lying on the road, with my horse dying next to me.

"So ended, ladies, a love affair that should have cured me forever of the urge to seek new ones. A few contemporaries of your grandmothers could tell you if I was wiser in the future.

"Either way, I still shudder at the idea that, if I had succumbed to my enemies, I would have become a vampire too; but Heaven did not allow things to come to this point, and far from thirsting for your blood, good fellows, I am more than happy, even at my advanced age, to shed my blood for you!"

MANOR

Karl Heinrich Ulrichs

TRANSLATED BY C.S.R. CALLOWAY

from *Matrosengeschichten* (1885)

I.

A group of thirty-five sparsely populated islands lie isolated in the middle of the North Atlantic, equidistant from Scotland, Iceland and Norway. They're known as the Faroe Islands; desolate, rocky, scored by the melancholy screeches of fluttering seabirds, surrounded by surging waves, and nearly always shrouded in fog. The mountains peak two thousand feet above sea level in the summer, and from peak to shore are jagged rocks, gloomy ravines, primeval fir forests, and thousands of springs and waterfalls which often thunder and foam from great heights, tumbling down from ledge to ledge. The banks are deeply carved by bays and fjords; almost nothing is accessible due to the high rocks. The sea, equally constrained and barricaded here and there by rocks and reefs, is tormented by eddies of water and swept through by wild currents.

Only seventeen of the islands are inhabited. Streymoy and Vágar are only separated by a narrow sound, one that a brave, capable swimmer could cross. Some location names call back to the time when there were no churches in the Faroes and the old beliefs had not yet been expelled. As an example, the city Tórshavn, on the coast of Streymoy, has a name meaning "Thor's harbor."

It was in those days that a fisherman and his fifteen-year-old son rowed from Streymoy out to sea. A storm rose, capsizing the boat and throwing the son into the reefs of Vágar. A young skipper saw this from Vágar and jumped into the waves, swimming between the reefs. He grabbed the drifting body and dragged it ashore. Pulling the barely-conscious boy into his lap on the beach, he wrapped him in his arms. Eventually the boy's eyes fluttered open and into focus.

"What's your name?" the skipper asked.

"Har," the boy responded. "From Streymoy."

The skipper rowed Har back across the sound to his home in Streymoy, bringing him to Lara, his mother. As they said goodbye, the boy gratefully clung to his savior's neck.

The corpse of the boy's father was washed ashore later by the waves.

The skipper was four years older than Har, an orphan named Manor. He carried and intense love for Har and longed to see him again. He would occasionally row over to Streymoy or, once summer came, swim through the lukewarm waves in the evening when his day's work was done. Har would climb a cliff overlooking the shore and wave his handkerchief when he saw Manor's boat approaching. They would stay together for an hour or two, rowing out onto calm seas and singing shanties. Or they would undress, dive into the waves, and swim to the nearest opposite sandbank, sending the sunbathing seals fleeing. Or they would walk into the dark green forest of tall fir trees, whose rustling tops echoed Thor's own voice. Or they would sit on a stone beneath the branches of an old beech tree, chatting and making plans. They both wanted to go along whenever a ship would sail to go whaling, but most days they sat like that upon the stone. Manor would put his arm around Har's shoulders, calling him "Boy Mine," and Har was never more contented than when Manor held him like that. If it was late when he arrived, Manor would walk quietly to the lilac bush that shaded the boy's window and knock on the panes. Har would wake and steal out to him, happy as always to be with Manor.

II.

A Danish three-master came along and anchored in Vágar's dependable harbor, looking for sailors for a two-month whaling voyage. Manor went aboard where the captain immediately accepted the trim youth. Har wanted to be a cabin boy, but his mother wailed, "You are my only child! The sea has already claimed your father, taking him from me. You want to leave me, too?" So Har stayed. When the ship lifted its anchors, Manor was the only one of the two onboard.

The two months passed and it was winter again. Har climbed the cliff, looked into the distance and saw the ship coming one morning. He waved his handkerchief happily, but it was stormy and the waves rose like mountains. The ship, headed for the Bay of Vágar, got lost in the dangerous reefs of Streymoy instead, shipwrecking before Har's eyes. He saw the sailors struggling against the waves. Saw one who grasped a plank with a strong arm, but in the next instant was slurped down with the plank into a whirlpool. Har knew him. It was Manor.

Several bodies washed ashore. The villagers spread straw on the beach and laid body after body upon it. Har helped, examining the each corpse.

Eventually Manor's body was brought and laid on the straw. There he was, hair wet from the water, eyes closed, cold, with pale lips and pale cheeks, drained of the blood of life, slim in figure, yet still beautiful to look at in death.

"So, Manor, this is how we've been reunited!" Har exclaimed. Sobbing, he threw himself over his beloved's body and savored the embrace for one last moment.

The bodies were brought across the sound. Manor was buried that very day in the sand dunes of Vágar.

III.

In the evening Har sat at home heavy-hearted and unspeaking. His mother wanted to console him, but he could not be comforted. He cursed the gods and went to bed, yet couldn't fall asleep. Around midnight he sank into a light slumber.

A noise woke him. He looked up. The sound came from the window. The branches of the lilac bush buckled and its dry leaves rustled. The window opened; a figure entered. Ha! Har knew the shape! He recognized it immediately, despite the darkness. It came up with slow steps; lay down in bed with him; Har was trembling; but he didn't stop the figure. His cheeks were caressed, oh, with a cold hand! So cold, so cold! Feverish chills shivered through the boy. It kissed his warm, swelling mouth with its own ice-cold lips. Har felt the kisser's wet robe; the wet hair hung down on his forehead. A horror went through him, but it was mixed with a thrill. The figure sighed. It sounded to Har as if it wanted to say: "Longing drove me to you! I cannot find peace in the grave!"

He dared not speak. He hardly dared to breathe. And too soon did the figure rise, sighing as if to say, "Now I have to go back!"

It climbed out of the window, moving away as it had come.

"Manor was here," Har said softly to himself.

That same night a fisherman from Streymoy was out in the moonlit sound with his boat. Shimmering sparks fell from his oar. Then, shortly before midnight, he heard a strange noise and saw something shoot through the glinting waves in the direction of Streymoy, something whose shape he could not distinguish, with the speed of a large fish. But it wasn't a fish, he could see that much in the dark.

The next night Manor came back to Har, freezing like the night before, but more demanding. He wrapped around the boy with cold arms, kissed his cheek and mouth, laid his head on his soft chest. Har trembled, his heart pounding at this intimate embrace.

Manor laid his head straight on the beating heart. His lips searched for the gently swelling mound above the heart, which was set in motion by the heartbeat. There Manor began to suckle, longing and thirsting, like a baby on a mother's breast. But after a few moments he subsided; rose; moved away. Har felt as if a sucking animal had gorged itself on him until it was full.

That night, too, the fisherman was working in the sound. Exactly at the same hour as the night before, it came rushing up again—came close to him this time. In the pale moonlight he could see: it was a swimming person swimming on the right side in the manner of a sailor, but dressed in a funeral shroud. The swimmer did not seem to notice him at all, although his face was turned towards him.

He swam with eyes closed. The sight was so strange to the fisherman that he drew in his unstretched nets and rowed away, unsettled.

Manor came back to Har the next few nights as well. Sometimes he hugged the boy in his sleep, because every now and then he wouldn't wake until he was already in Manor's embrace. Each time Manor's lips sought the soft breast of the boy. When it was day, Har occasionally saw a faint droplet of blood still beading out of his left nipple. He would wipe it off with his shirt. Sometimes his shirt was already spotted with blood.

It was only on the night of the full moon that Manor did not come.

A dead person is often filled with a longing for one or the other of the loved ones he has left behind, so powerful that he leaves the grave at night and comes to him. The old belief is that Urda, the deity of fate and the past, gives some people back a short half-life at midnight and then gives them strange powers from beyond the grave. It occurs especially with young people who were dragged away by bitter death in the prime of their life. Those who return have a great need for blood and warmth at the same time. They long for the fresh blood of the living and, like a lover, for embrace, but this also communicates great longing and often causes severe agony.

Such was the case here: Har lamented and yearned for Manor all day, waiting impatiently for the night and longing for the blissful shivers of their midnight embrace.

IV.

Twelve days passed.

"You are so pale. What's come over you, Har?"

"Nothing, Mother."

"You are so quiet."

The boy sighed…

In the furthest little house in the village lived a wise woman who knew all kinds of secrets. Har's worried mother went to her. The wise woman threw runic staves.

"He is visited by the dead," the wise woman said.

"The dead?"

"Indeed, at night; and one who is visited by the dead will die as well if the visits aren't stopped before it's too late."

Lara returned home distraught.

"Is it true, Har? Are you being visited by the dead?"

He looked at the floor. "Manor has been here," he said softly, and sank weeping on her chest.

"May the gods have mercy on you!" she cried.

"The gods?" he repeated. "Pah! What should the gods do for me now! When he clung to the plank, alas! Oh dear! That was time to have mercy on me if they wanted to. But they let him sink mercilessly. How I loved him so!"

It was now that she noticed the traces of blood on his shirt, so she went to the village elders. They rowed over to Vágar with mother and son, and they also took the wise woman with them. To the the people of Vágar they said:

"Your graves are open. One leaves his grave every night and comes over to us to suck on this boy's blood."

The people responded, "We will anchor him to our island."

They seized a pine pole, as long as a man and thicker than an arm, which they cut square with an axe, tapering to a foot at the bottom. Two went with the visitors to the dunes; one carried the stake, another a heavy ax. Together, they opened Manor's grave. There he lay quietly in front of them in his shroud.

"Look!" the first Vágar islander said. "The body lies here the way we put it."

The wise woman spoke. "It's because every morning he returns to his original position."

The second Vágar islander conceded. "His face is almost fresher than before."

"No wonder," the wise woman said. "On the other hand, the living boy's face is now all the paler."

Har threw himself over his beloved corpse again.

"Manor!" he shouted in an agitated voice. "They want to stake you. Manor, wake up! Open your eyes! Your Har is calling you!"

But Manor didn't open his eyes. He lay motionless under Har's embrace, like twelve days before on the straw sprinkled beach.

Har didn't want to let go of him, so they tore him away before putting the tip of the stake on Manor's chest. With a cry, Har turned and fell onto his mother's neck. He buried his face in her shoulder.

"Mother!" he exclaimed, "why did you do this to me!"

He heard the flat back of the ax fall on the stake and the stake groan. A heavy blow; another blow and half a dozen more blows.

"Now he's secured!" the first Vágar islander asserted.

The second added, "He'll stay put now. He has to."

They carried Har away half-unconscious. "Now he will leave you alone, my dear child!" said Lara, when they were back in their hut.

Har went to bed despairing. "Now he's not coming!" he said to himself, tired and bleak. Restless and unable to sleep he tossed and turned on his bed. The minutes crept slowly; the hours crawled. Midnight came and still no sleep had fallen on his eyelashes.

Listen! What is that? In the lilac bush... Yes, no; it was impossible. And yet! Again, as before, there was rustling in the branches. The window opened. Manor was back. The corpse sighed deeply. He had a large wound in his chest that was square and went through to his back. He placed himself down next to Har again, embraced him and sucked at his breast more demanding than before.

Thirstier.

Lara remained awake in the next room, keeping watch that night; listening and trembling. She came in early in the morning and went to her son's bed.

"My poor child!" she sighed. "He's been here again."

"Yes, mother," Har replied. "He was with me again."

It was indisputable. The bed was stained with the blood that had trickled out of the corpse's great wound.

V.

A few hours later another boat rowed across the sound; this time without Har. They went back to the dunes; opened the grave again. The square stake was still there, but no longer in Manor's chest. The corpse instead draped around the shaft, prevented from lying straight in the grave.

"He was able to get loose," the wise woman said. "The stake is the same thickness at the top and bottom."

The first Vágar islander nodded. "He twisted himself up from the bottom of the post."

"Must have cost him inhuman effort," the second agreed.

On the advice of the wise woman, they hacked a stronger stake, which they left twice as thick at the top as it is at the bottom, so that it looked like a nail with a head. They pulled away the old stake and secured Manor's body with the new one.

"So! Now it's nailed," said the axman as he gave the stake the final blow on the head.

The second islander commented grimly, "Twist and squirm all he might, he won't wriggle loose from this."

Lara returned home to her son, telling him what had happened. "It's over now," Har said to himself as he went to bed. He lay there without sleep. Midnight came, but everything remained silent. Nothing rustled in the branches of the lilac bush outside by the window. No swimmer frightened the fisherman anymore, who at night cut through the sound with his eyes closed.

"Now you both can be at peace," Lara said. "He tormented you so."

"O mother!" Har replied. "Mother! He didn't torment me!" He was in heat with powerless longing. "Mother!" he said, "now it's over with me." He could no longer rise from the bed.

"You are so tired and so weak, my dear son!"

Har said simply, "He's pulling me down to him."

One early morning she sat by his bed while he was still asleep. A month had passed since the shipwreck. She cried, thinking of all that had transpired. Then her son opened his eyes.

"Mother," he said in a weak voice, "I must die."

"Oh no, my child! You're too young to die!"

"Yes, yes! Manor was with me again. We talked to each other. We sat on the stone under the old beech in the forest as usual; he wrapped his arm around my neck again and called me 'Boy Mine.' He'll come back tonight and get me. He promised me. I can't stand it without him."

She leaned over him and her tears flowed copiously onto his bed. "My poor child!" she said, and put her hand on his forehead.

When night fell, she lit a lamp and watched him by the bed. He lay there quietly; did not sleep; looked in front of himself in silence.

"Mother!" he exclaimed.

"What do you want, my dear son?"

"Put me with him in his grave, won't you? And pull the terrible stake out of his chest!"

She agreed, promising with a handshake and a kiss.

"Oh, it must be so sweet in his grave!"

Midnight approached and Har's features suddenly became transfigured. He lifted his head a little, as if listening. With shining eyes he looked at the window and at the branches of the lilac tree.

"Look, mother, here he comes!"

Those were his last words before his eyes rolled back. He sank back on the pillows and did not rise again.

They buried him as he requested.

THE OLD PORTRAIT

Hume Nisbet

(1890)

O ld-fashioned frames are a hobby of mine. I am always on the prowl amongst the framers and dealers in curiosities for something quaint and unique in picture frames. I don't care much for what is inside them, for being a painter it is my fancy to get the frames first and then paint a picture which I think suits their probable history and design. In this way I get some curious and I think also some original ideas.

One day in December, about a week before Christmas, I picked up a fine but dilapidated specimen of wood-carving in a shop near Soho. The gilding had been worn nearly away, and three of the corners broken off; yet as there was one of the corners still left, I hoped to be able to repair the others from it. As for the canvas inside this frame, it was so smothered with dirt and time stains that I could only distinguish it had been a very badly painted likeness of some sort, of some commonplace person, daubed in by a poor pot-boiling painter to fill the secondhand frame which his patron may have picked up cheaply as I had done after him; but as the frame was alright I took the spoiled canvas along with it, thinking it might come in handy.

For the next few days my hands were full of work of one kind and another, so that it was only on Christmas Eve that I found myself at liberty to examine my purchase which had been lying with its face to the wall since I had brought it to my studio.

Having nothing to do on this night, and not in the mood to go out, I got my picture and frame from the corner, and laying them upon the table, with a sponge, basin of water, and some soap, I began to wash so that I might see them the better. They were in a terrible mess, and I think I used the best part of a packet of soap-powder and had to change the water about a dozen times before the pattern began to show up on the frame, and the portrait within it asserted its awful crudeness, vile drawing, and intense vulgarity. It was the bloated, piggish visage of a publican clearly, with a plentiful supply of jewelry displayed, as is usual with such masterpieces, where the features are not considered of so much importance as a strict fidelity in the depicting of such articles as watch-guard and seals, finger rings, and breast pins; these were all there, as natural and hard as reality.

The frame delighted me, and the picture satisfied me that I had not cheated the dealer with my price, and I was looking at the monstrosity as the gaslight beat full upon it, and wondering how the owner could be pleased with himself as thus depicted, when something about the background attracted my attention—a slight marking underneath the thin coating as if the portrait had been painted over some other subject.

It was not much certainly, yet enough to make me rush over to my cupboard, where I kept my spirits of wine and turpentine, with which, and a plentiful supply of rags, I began to demolish the publican ruthlessly in the vague hope that I might find something worth looking at underneath.

A slow process that was, as well as a delicate one, so that it was close upon midnight before the gold cable rings and vermilion visage disappeared and another picture loomed up before me; then giving it the final wash over, I wiped it dry, and set it in a good light on my easel, while I filled and lit my pipe, and then sat down to look at it.

What had I liberated from that vile prison of crude paint? For I did not require to set it up to know that this bungler of the brush had covered and defiled a work as far beyond his comprehension as the clouds are from the caterpillar.

The bust and head of a young woman of uncertain age, merged within a gloom of rich accessories painted as only a master hand can paint who is above asserting his knowledge, and who has learnt to cover his technique. It was as perfect and natural in its sombre yet quiet dignity as if it had come from the brush of Moroni.

A face and neck perfectly colorless in their pallid whiteness, with the shadows so artfully managed that they could not be seen, and for this quality would have delighted the strong-minded Queen Bess.

At first as I looked I saw in the centre of a vague darkness a dim patch of grey gloom that drifted into the shadow. Then the grayness appeared to grow lighter as I sat from it, and leaned back in my chair until the features stole out softly, and became clear and definite, while the figure stood out from the background as if tangible, although, having washed it, I knew that it had been smoothly painted.

An intent face, with delicate nose, well-shaped, although bloodless, lips, and eyes like dark caverns without a spark of light in them. The hair loosely about the head and oval cheeks, massive, silky-textured, jet black, and lusterless, which hid the upper portion of her brow, with the ears, and fell in straight indefinite waves over the left breast, leaving the right portion of the transparent neck exposed.

The dress and background were symphonies of ebony, yet full of subtle coloring and masterly feeling; a dress of rich brocaded velvet with a background that represented vast receding space, wondrously suggestive and awe-inspiring.

I noticed that the pallid lips were parted slightly, and showed a glimpse of the upper front teeth, which added to the intent expression of the face. A short upper tip, which, curled upward, with the underlip full and sensuous, or rather, if color had been in it, would have been so.

It was an eerie looking face that I had resurrected on this midnight hour of Christmas Eve; in its passive pallidity it looked as if the blood had been drained from the body, and that I was gazing upon an open-eyed corpse.

The frame, also, I noticed for the first time, in its details appeared to have been designed with the intention of carrying out the idea of life in death; what had before looked like scroll-work of flowers and fruit were loathsome snake-like worms twined amongst charnel-house bones which they half covered in a decorative fashion; a hideous design in spite of its exquisite workmanship, that made me shudder and wish that I had left the cleaning to be done by daylight.

I am not at all of a nervous temperament, and would have laughed had anyone told me that I was afraid, and yet, as I sat here alone, with that portrait opposite to me in this solitary studio, away from all human contact; for none of the other studios were tenanted on this night, and the janitor had gone on his holiday; I wished that I had spent my evening in a more congenial manner, for in spite of a good fire in the stove and the brilliant gas, that intent face and those haunting eyes were exercising a strange influence upon me.

I heard the clocks from the different steeples chime out the last hour of the day, one after the other, like echoes taking up the refrain and dying away in the distance, and still I sat spellbound, looking at that weird picture, with my neglected pipe in my hand, and a strange lassitude creeping over me.

It was the eyes which fixed me now with the unfathomable depths and absorbing intensity. They gave out no light, but seemed to draw my soul into them, and with it my life and strength as I lay inert before them, until overpowered I lost consciousness and dreamt.

I thought that the frame was still on the easel with the canvas, but the woman had stepped from them and was approaching me with a floating motion, leaving behind her a vault filled with coffins, some of them shut down whilst others lay or stood upright and open, showing the grizzly contents in their decaying and stained cerements.

I could only see her head and shoulders with the sombre drapery of the upper portion and the inky wealth of hair hanging round.

She was with me now, that pallid face touching my face and those cold bloodless lips glued to mine with a close lingering kiss, while the soft black hair covered me like a cloud and thrilled me through and through with a delicious thrill that, whilst it made me grow faint, intoxicated me with delight.

As I breathed she seemed to absorb it quickly into herself, giving me back nothing, getting stronger as I was becoming weaker, while the warmth of my contact passed into her and made her palpitate with vitality.

And all at once the horror of approaching death seized upon me, and with a frantic effort I flung her from me and started up from my chair dazed for a moment and uncertain where I was, then consciousness returned and I looked round wildly.

The gas was still blazing brightly, while the fire burned ruddy in the stove. By the timepiece on the mantel I could see that it was half-past twelve.

The picture and frame were still on the easel, only as I looked at them the portrait had changed, a hectic flush was on the cheeks while the eyes glittered with life and the sensuous lips were red and ripe-looking with a drop of blood still upon the nether one. In a frenzy of horror I seized my scraping knife and slashed out the vampire picture, then tearing the mutilated fragments out I crammed them into my stove and watched them frizzle with savage delight.

I have that frame still, but I have not yet had courage to paint a suitable subject for it.

THE LAST OF THE VAMPIRES

Phil Robinson

first published in *Contemporary Review* (March 1893)

D o you remember the discovery of the "man-lizard" bones in a cave on the Amazon some time in the forties? Perhaps not. But it created a great stir at the time in the scientific world and, in a lazy sort of way, interested men and women of fashion. For a day or two it was quite the correct thing for Belgravia to talk of "connecting links," of "the evolution of man from the reptile," and "the reasonableness of the ancient myths" that spoke of Centaurs and Mermaids as actual existences.

The fact was that a German Jew, an India rubber merchant, working his way with the usual mob of natives through a cahucho forest along the Marañon, came upon some bones on the river-bank where he had pitched his camp. Idle curiosity made him try to put them together, when he found, to his surprise, that he had before him the skeleton of a creature with human legs and feet, a dog-like head and immense bat-like wings. Being a shrewd man, he saw the possibility of money being made out of such a curiosity; so he put all the bones he could find into a sack and, on the back of a llama, they were in due course conveyed to Chachapoyas, and thence to Germany.

Unfortunately, his name happened to be the same as that of another German Jew who had just then been trying to hoax the scientific world with some papyrus rolls of a date anterior to the Flood, and who had been found out and put to shame. So when his namesake appeared with the bones of a winged man, ho was treated with very scant ceremony.

However, he sold his India rubber very satisfactorily, and as for the bones, he left them with a young medical student of the ancient University of Bierundwurst, and went back to his cahucho trees and his natives and the banks of the Amazon. And there was. an end of him.

The young student one day put his fragments together, and, do what he would, could only make one thing of them—a winged man with a dog's head.

There were a few ribs too many, and some odds and ends of backbone which were superfluous; but what else could be expected of the anatomy of so extraordinary a creature? From one student to another the facts got about, and at last the professors came to hear of it; and, to cut a long story short, the student's skeleton was taken to pieces by the learned heads of the college, and put together again by their own learned hands.

But do what they would, they would only make one thing of it—a winged man with a dog's head.

The matter now became serious: the professors were at first puzzled, and then got quarrelsome; and the result of their squabbling was that pamphlets and counterblasts were published; and so all the world got to hear of the bitter controversy about the "man-lizard of the Amazon."

One side declared, of course, that such a creature was an impossibility, and that the bones were a remarkably clever hoax. The other side retorted by challenging the skeptics to manufacture a duplicate, and publishing the promise of such large rewards to any one who would succeed in doing so, that the museum was beset for months by competitors. But no one could manufacture another man-lizard. The man part was simple enough, provided they could get a human skeleton. But at the angles of the wings were set huge claws, black, polished, and curved, and nothing that ingenuity could suggest would imitate them. And then the "Genuinists," as those who believed in the monster called themselves, set the "Imposturists" another poser; for they publicly challenged them to say what animal either the head or the wings had belonged to, if not to the man-lizard? And the answer was never given.

So victory remained with them, but not, alas! the bones of contention. For the Imposturists, by bribery and burglary, got access to the precious skeleton, and lo! One morning the glory of the museum had disappeared. The man half of it was left, but the head and wings were gone, and from that day to this no one has ever seen them again.

And which of the two factions was right? As a matter of fact, neither; as the following fragments of narrative will go to prove.

Once upon a time, so say the Zaporo Indians, who inhabit the district between the Amazon and the Marañon, there came across to Pampas de Sacramendo a company of gold-seekers, white men, who drove the natives from their workings and took possession of them.

They were the first white men who had ever been seen there, and the Indians were afraid of their guns; but eventually treachery did the work of courage, for, pretending to be friendly, the natives sent their women among the strangers, and they taught them how to make tucupi out of the bread-root, but did not tell them how to distinguish between the ripe and the unripe. So the wretched white men made tucupi out of the unripe fruit (which brings on fits like epilepsy) and when they were lying about the camp, helpless, the Indians attacked them and killed them all.

All except three. These three they gave to the Vampire.

But what was the Vampire? The Zaporos did not know. "Very long ago," said they, "there were many vampires in Peru, but they were all swallowed up in the year of the Great Earthquake when the Andes were lifted up, and there was left behind only one 'Arinchi,' who lived where the Amazon joins the Marañon, and he would not eat dead bodies—only live ones, from which the blood would flow."

So far the legend; and that it had some foundation in fact is proved by the records of the district, which tell of more than one massacre of white gold-seekers on the Marañon by Indians whom they had attempted to oust from the washings; but of the Arinchi, the Vampire, there is no official mention. Here, however, other local superstitions help us to the reading of the riddle of the man-lizard of the University at Bierundwurst.

When sacrifice was made to "the Vampire," the victim was bound in a canoe, and taken down the river to a point where there was a kind of winding back-water, which had shelving banks of slimy mud, and at the end there was a rock with a cave in it. And here the canoe was left. A very slow current flowed through the tortuous creek, and anything thrown into the water ultimately reached the cave. Some of the Indians had watched the canoes drifting along, a few yards only in an hour, and turning round and round as they drifted, and had seen them reach the cave and disappear within. And it had been a wonder to them, generation after generation, that the cave was never filled up, for all day long the current was flowing into it, carrying with it the sluggish flotsam of the river. So they said that the cave was the entrance to Hell, and bottomless.

And one day a white man, a professor of that same University of Bierundwurst, and a mighty hunter of beetles before the Lord, who lived with the Indians in friendship, went up the backwater, right up to the entrance, and set afloat inside the cave a little raft, heaped up with touch-wood and knots of the oil-tree, which he set fire to, and he saw the raft go creeping along, all ablaze, for an hour and more, lighting up the wet walls of the cave as it went on either side; and then *it was put out*.

It did not "go" out suddenly, as if it had upset, or had floated over the edge of a waterfall, but just as if it had been beaten out.

For the burning fragments were flung to one side and the other, and the pieces, still alight, glowed for a long time on the ledges and points of rock where they fell, and the cave was filled with the sound of a sudden wind and the echoes of the noise of great wings flapping.

And at last, one day, this professor went into the cave himself.

"I took," he wrote, "a large canoe, and from the bows I built out a brazier of stout cask-hoops, and behind it set a gold-washing tin dish for a reflector, and loaded the canoe with roots of the resin-tree, and oil-wood, and yams, and dried meat; and I took spears with me, some tipped with the woorali poison, that numbs but does not kill. And so I drifted inside the cave; and I lit my fire, and with my pole I guided the canoe very cautiously through the tunnel, and before long it widened out, and creeping along one wall I suddenly became aware of a moving of something on the opposite side.

So I turned the light fair upon it, and there, upon a kind of ledge, sat a beast with a head like a large grey dog. Its eyes were as large as a cow's.

"What its shape was I could not see. But as I looked I began gradually to make out two huge bat-like wings, and these were spread out to their utmost as if the beast were on tiptoe and ready to fly. And so it was. For just as I had realized that I beheld before me some great bat-reptile of a kind unknown to science, except as prediluvian,[15] and the shock had thrilled through me at the thought that I was actually in the presence of a living specimen of the so-called extinct flying lizards of the Flood, the thing launched itself upon the air, and the next instant it was upon me.

"Clutching on to the canoe, it beat with its wings at the flame so furiously that it was all I could do to keep the canoe from capsizing, and, taken by surprise, I was nearly stunned by the strength and rapidity of its blows before I attempted to defend myself.

"By that time—scarcely half a minute had elapsed—the brazier had been nearly emptied by the powerful brute; and the vampire, mistaking me no doubt for a victim of sacrifice, had already taken hold of me. The next instant I had driven a spear clean through its body, and with a prodigious tumult of wings, the thing loosed its claws from my clothes and dropped off into the stream.

"As quickly as possible I rekindled my light, and now saw the Arinchi, with wings outstretched upon the water, drifting down on the current. I followed it.

"Hour after hour, with my reflector turned full upon that grey dog's head with cow-like eyes, I passed along down the dark and silent waterway. I ate and drank as I went along, but did not dare to sleep. A day must have passed, and two nights; and then, as of course I had all along expected, I saw right ahead a pale eye-shaped glimmer, and knew that I was coming out into daylight again.

"The opening came nearer and nearer, and it was with intense eagerness that I gazed upon my trophy, the floating Arinchi, the last of the Winged Reptiles.

"Already in imagination I saw myself the foremost of travelers in European fame—the hero of my day. What were Banks' kangaroos or Du Chaillu's gorilla to my discovery of the last survivor of the pterodactyls, of the creatures of Flood—the flying Saurian of the pre-Noachian epoch of catastrophe and mud?[16]

---

[15] The prediluvian or antediluvian period spans from the fall of man to the Genesis flood narrative as chronicled in the Bible's Book of Genesis. It's mostly used to describe any ancient or obscure period of time, used in geology and science until the late Victorian era.

[16] In European society, Joseph Banks is often credited with the discovery of kangaroos, while Paul Belloni Du Chaillu is widely recognized for his significant contributions in confirming the existence of gorillas.

Full of these thoughts, I had not noticed that the vampire was no longer moving, and suddenly the bow of the canoe bumped against it. In an instant it had climbed up on to the boat. Its great bat-like wings once more beat me and scattered the flaming brands, and the thing made a desperate effort to get past me back into the gloom. It had seen the daylight approaching and rather than face the sun, preferred to fight.

"Its ferocity was that of a maddened dog, but I kept it off with my pole, and seeing my opportunity as it clung, flapping its wings, upon the bow, gave it such a thrust as made it drop off. It began to swim (I then for the first time noticed its long neck), but with my pole I struck it on the head and stunned it, and once more saw it go drifting on the current into daylight.

"What a relief it was to be out in the open air! It was noon, and as we passed out from under the entrance of the cave, the river blazed so in the sunlight that after the two days of almost total darkness I was blinded for a time. I turned my canoe to the shore, to the shade of trees, and throwing a noose over the floating body, let it tow behind.

"Once more on firm land—and in possession of the Vampire!

"I dragged it out of the water. What a hideous beast it looked, this winged kangaroo with a python's neck! It was not dead; so I made a muzzle with a strip of skin, and then I firmly bound its wings together round its body. I lay down and slept. When I awoke, the next day was breaking; so, having breakfasted, I dragged my captive into the canoe and went on down the river. Where I was I had no idea; but I knew that I was going to the sea; going to Germany; and that was enough.

"For two months I have been drifting with the current down this never-ending river. Of my adventures, of hostile natives, of rapids, of alligators, and jaguars, I need say nothing. They are the common property of all travelers. But my vampire! It is alive. And now I am devoured by only one ambition—to keep it alive, to let Europe actually gaze upon the living, breathing, survivor of the great Reptiles known to the human race before the days of Noah—the missing link between the reptile and the bird. To this end I denied myself food; denied myself even precious medicine. In spite of itself I gave it all my quinine, and when the miasma crept up the river at night, I covered it with my rug and lay exposed myself. If the black fever should seize me!

"Three months, and still upon this hateful river! Will it never end? I have been ill—so ill, that for two days I could not feed it. I had not the strength to go ashore to find food, and I fear that it will die—die before I can get it home.

"Been ill again—the black fever! But *it* is alive. I caught a vicuna swimming in the river, and it sucked it dry—gallons of blood. It had been unfed three days. In its hungry haste it broke its muzzle. I was almost too feeble to put it on again. A horrible thought possesses me. Suppose it breaks its muzzle again when I am lying ill, delirious, and it is ravenous? Oh! the horror of it! To see it eating is terrible. It links the claws of its wings together, and cowers over the body; its head is under the wings, out of sight. But the victim never moves. As soon as the vampire touches it there seems to be a paralysis. Once those wings are linked there is absolute quiet. Only the grating of teeth upon bone. Horrible! Horrible! But in Germany I shall be famous. *In Germany with my Vampire!*

"**A**m very feeble. It broke its muzzle again. But it was in the daylight —when it is blind. Its great eyes are blind in sunlight. It was a long struggle. This black fever! And the horror of this thing! I am too weak now to kill it, if I would. I *must* get it home alive. Soon—surely soon—the river will end. Oh God! Does it never reach the sea, reach white men, reach home? But if it attacks me I will throttle it. If I am dying I will throttle it. If we cannot go back to Germany alive, we will go together dead. I will throttle it with my two hands, and fix my teeth in its horrible neck, and our bones shall lie together on the bank of this accursed river."

This is nearly all that was recovered of the professor's diary. But it is enough to tell us of the final tragedy.

The two skeletons were found together on the very edge of the river-bank. Half of each, in the lapse of years, had been washed away at successive floodtides. The rest, when put together, made up the man-reptile that, to use a Rabelaisian phrase, "metagrobolized all to nothing" the University of Bierundwurst.[17]

---

[17] To metagrobolize is to puzzle or mystify.

THE TRUE STORY OF A VAMPIRE

Eric Stenbock

from *Studies of Death: Romantic Tales* (1894)

Vampire stories are generally located in Styria; mine is also. Styria is by no means the romantic kind of place described by those who have certainly never been there. It is a flat, uninteresting country, only celebrated for its turkeys, its capons, and the stupidity of its inhabitants. Vampires generally arrive at night, in carriages drawn by two black horses.

Our Vampire arrived by the commonplace means of the railway train, and in the afternoon.

You must think I am joking, or perhaps that by the word "Vampire" I mean a financial vampire.

No, I am quite serious. The Vampire of whom I am speaking, who laid waste our hearth and home, was a real vampire.

Vampires are generally described as dark, sinister-looking, and singularly handsome. Our Vampire was, on the contrary, rather fair, and certainly was not at first sight sinister-looking, and though decidedly attractive in appearance, not what one would call singularly handsome.

Yes, he desolated our home, killed my brother—the one object of my adoration—also my dear father. Yet, at the same time, I must say that I myself came under the spell of his fascination, and, in spite of all, have no ill-will towards him now.

Doubtless you have read in the papers passim of "the Baroness and her beasts." It is to tell how I came to spend most of my useless wealth on an asylum for stray animals that I am writing this.

I am old now; what happened then was when I was a little girl of about thirteen. I will begin by describing our household. We were Poles: our name was Wronski: we lived in Styria, where we had a castle. Our household was very limited. It consisted, with the exclusion of domestics, of only my father, our governess—a worthy Belgian named Mademoiselle Vonnaert—my brother, and myself. Let me begin with my father: he was old and both my brother and I were children of his old age. Of my mother I remember nothing: she died in giving birth to my brother, who was only one year, or not as much, younger than in self. Our father was studious, continually occupied in reading books, chiefly on recondite subjects and in all kinds of unknown languages.

He had a long white beard, and wore habitually a black velvet skull-cap.

How kind he was to us! It was more than I could tell. Still it was not I who was the favorite.

His whole heart went out to Gabriel—Gabryel as we spelt it in Polish. He was always called by the Russian abbreviation Gavril—I mean, of course, my brother, who had a resemblance to the only portrait of my mother, a slight chalk sketch which hung in my father's study. But I was by no means jealous: my brother was and has been the only love of my life. It is for his sake that I am now keeping in Westbourne Park a home for stray cats and dogs.

I was at that time, as I said before, a little girl; my name was Carmela. My long tangled hair was always all over the place, and never would combed straight. I was not pretty—at least, looking at a photograph of me at that time. I do not think I could describe myself as such. Yet at the same time, when I look at the photograph, I think my expression may have been pleasing to some people: irregular features, large mouth, and large wild eyes.

I was by way of being naughty—not so naughty Gabriel in the opinion of Mlle Vonnaert. Mlle Vonnaert. I may intercalate, was a wholly excellent person, middle-aged, who really did speak good French, although she was a Belgian, and could also make herself understood in German, which, as you may or may not know, is the current language of Styria.

I find it difficult to describe my brother Gabriel; there was something about him strange and superhuman, or perhaps I should rather say praeterhuman, something between the animal and the divine. Perhaps the Greek idea of the Faun might illustrate what I mean: but that will not do either. He had large, wild, gazelle-like eyes: his hair, like mine, was in a perpetual tangle—that point he had in common with me, and indeed, as I afterwards heard, our mother having been of the Romani race, it will account for much of the innate wildness there was in our natures. I was wild enough, but Gabriel was much wilder. Nothing would induce him to put on shoes and stockings, except on Sundays—when he also allowed his hair to be combed, but only by me. How shall I describe the grace of that lovely mouth, shaped verily "en arc d'amour." I always think of the text in the Psalm, "Grace is shed forth on thy lips, therefore has God blessed thee eternally"—-lips that seemed to exhale the very breath of life. Then that beautiful, lithe, living, elastic form!

He could run faster than any deer: spring like a squirrel to the topmost branch of a tree: he might have stood for the sign and symbol of vitality itself. But seldom could he be induced by Mlle Vonnaert to learn lessons; but when he did so, he learnt with extraordinary quickness. He would play upon every conceivable instrument, holding a violin here, there, and everywhere except the right place: manufacturing instruments for himself out of reeds—even sticks. Mlle Vonnaert made futile efforts to induce him to learn to play the piano. I suppose he was what was called spoilt, though merely in the superficial sense of the word. Our father allowed him to indulge in every caprice.

One of his peculiarities, when quite a little child, was horror at the sight of meat. Nothing on earth would induce him to taste it. Another thing which was particularly remarkable about him was his extraordinary power over animals. Everything seemed to come tame to his hand. Birds would sit on his shoulder. Then sometimes Mlle Vonnaert and I would lose him in the woods —-he would suddenly dart away. Then we would find him singing softly or whistling to himself, with all manner of woodland creatures around him— hedgehogs, little foxes, wild rabbits, marmots, squirrels, and such like. He would frequently bring these things home with him and insist on keeping them. This strange menagerie was the terror of poor Mlle Vonnaert's heart. He chose to live in a little room at the top of a turret; but which, instead of going upstairs, he chose to reach by means of a very tall chestnut-tree, through the window. But in contradiction of all his, it was his custom to serve every Sunday Mass in the parish church, with hair nicely combed and with white surplice and red cassock. He looked as demure and tamed as possible. Then came the element of the divine. What an expression of ecstasy there was in those glorious eyes!

Thus far I have not been speaking about the Vampire. However, let me begin with my narrative at last. One day my father had to go to the neighboring town—as he frequently had. This time he returned accompanied by a guest. The gentleman, he said, had missed his train, through the late arrival of another at our station, which was a junction, and he would therefore, as trains were not frequent in our parts, have had to wait there all night. He had joined in conversation with my father in the too-late-arriving train from the town: and had consequently accepted my father's invitation to stay the night at our house. But of course, you know, in those out-of-the-way parts we are almost patriarchal in our hospitality.

He was announced under the name of Count Vardalek—the name being Hungarian. But he spoke German well enough: not with the monotonous accentuation of Hungarians, but rather, if anything, with a slight Slavonic intonation. His voice was peculiarly soft and insinuating. We soon afterwards found that he could talk Polish, and Mlle Vonnaert vouched for his good French.

Indeed he seemed to know all languages. But let me give my first impressions. He was rather tall with fair wavy hair, rather long, which accentuated a certain effeminacy about his smooth face.

His figure had something—I cannot say what—serpentine about it. The features were refined; and he had long, slender, subtle, magnetic-looking hands, a somewhat long sinuous nose, a graceful mouth, and an attractive smile, which belied the intense sadness of the expression of the eyes. When he arrived his eyes were half closed—indeed they were habitually so—so that

I could not decide their color. He looked worn and wearied. I could not possibly guess his age.

Suddenly Gabriel burst into the room: a yellow butterfly was clinging to his hair. He was carrying in his arms a little squirrel. Of course he was barelegged as usual. The stranger looked up at his approach; then I noticed his eyes. They were green: they seemed to dilate and grow larger. Gabriel stood stock-still, with a startled look, like that of a bird fascinated by a serpent.

But nevertheless he held out his hand to the newcomer Vardalek, taking his hand—I don't know why I noticed this trivial thing—pressed the pulse with his forefinger. Suddenly Gabriel darted from the room and rushed upstairs, going to his turret-room this time by the staircase instead of the tree. I was in terror what the Count might think of him. Great was my relief when he came down in his velvet Sunday suit, and shoes and stockings. I combed his hair, and set him generally right.

When the stranger came down to dinner his appearance had somewhat altered; he looked much younger. There was an elasticity of the skin, combined with a delicate complexion, rarely to be found in a man. Before, he had struck me as being very pale.

Well, at dinner we were all charmed with him, especially my father. He seemed to be thoroughly acquainted with all my father's particular hobbies. Once, when my father was relating some of his military experiences, he said something about a drummer-boy who was wounded in battle. His eyes opened completely again and dilated: this time with a particularly disagreeable expression, dull and dead, yet at the same time animated by some horrible excitement. But this was only momentary.

The chief subject of his conversation with my father was about certain curious mystical books which my father had just lately picked up, and which he could not make out, but Vardalek seemed completely to understand. At dessert-time my father asked him if he were in a great hurry to reach his destination: if not, would he not stay with us a little while: though our place was out of the way, he would find much that would interest him in his library.

He answered, "I am in no hurry. I have no particular reason for going to that place at all, and if I can be of service to you in deciphering these books, I shall be only too glad." He added with a smile which was bitter, very very bitter: "You see I am a cosmopolitan, a wanderer on the face of the earth."

After dinner my father asked him if he played the piano. He said, "Yes, I can a little," and he sat down at the piano. Then he played a Hungarian csárdás—wild, rhapsodic, wonderful.

That is the music which makes men mad. He went on in the same strain.

Gabriel stood stock-still by the piano, his eyes dilated and fixed, his form quivering. At last he said very slowly, at one particular motive—for want of a better word you may call it the relâche of a csárdás, by which I mean that point where the original quasi-slow movement begins again——"Yes, I think I could play that."

Then he quickly fetched his fiddle and self-made xylophone, and did, actually alternating the instruments, render the same very well indeed.

Vardalek looked at him, and said in a very sad voice, "Poor child! You have the soul of music within you."

I could not understand why he should seem to commiserate instead of congratulate Gabriel on what certainly showed an extraordinary talent.

Gabriel was shy even as the wild animals who were tame to him. Never before had he taken to a stranger. Indeed, as a rule, if any stranger came to the house by any chance, he would hide himself, and I had to bring him up his food to the turret chamber. You may imagine what was my surprise when I saw him walking about hand in hand with Vardalek the next morning, in the garden, talking lively with him, and showing his collection of pet animals, which he had gathered from the woods, and for which we had had to fit up a regular zoological gardens. He seemed utterly under the domination of Vardalek. What surprised us was (for otherwise we liked the stranger, especially for being kind to him) that he seemed, though not noticeably at first—except perhaps to me, who noticed everything with regard to him—to be gradually losing his general health and vitality. He did not become pale as yet; but there was a certain languor about his movements which certainly there was by no means before.

My father got more and more devoted to Count Vardalek. He helped him in his studies: and my father would hardly allow him to go away, which he did sometimes—to Trieste, he said: he always came back, bringing us presents of strange Oriental jewelry or textures.

I knew all kinds of people came to Trieste, Orientals included. Still, there was a strangeness and magnificence about these things which I was sure even then could not possibly have come from such a place as Trieste, memorable to me chiefly for its necktie shops.

When Vardalek was away, Gabriel was continually asking for him and talking about him. Then at the same time he seemed to regain his old vitality and spirits. Vardalek always returned looking much older, wan, and weary. Gabriel would rush to meet him, and kiss him on the mouth. Then he gave a slight shiver: and after a little while began to look quite young again.

Things continued like this for some time. My father would not hear of Vardalek's going away permanently. He came to be an inmate of our house. I indeed, and Mlle Vonnaert also, could not help noticing what a difference there was altogether about Gabriel. But my father seemed totally blind to it.

One night I had gone downstairs to fetch something which I had left in the drawing-room. As I was going up again I passed Vardalek's room. He was playing on a piano, which had been specially put there for him, one of Chopin's nocturnes, very beautifully: I stopped, leaning on the banisters to listen.

Something white appeared on the dark staircase. We believed in ghosts in our part. I was transfixed with terror, and clung to the ballisters. What was my astonishment to see Gabriel walking slowly down the staircase, his eyes fixed as though in a trance! This terrified me even more than a ghost would. Could I believe my senses? Could that be Gabriel?

I simply could not move. Gabriel, clad in his long white night-shirt, came downstairs and opened the door. He left it open. Vardalek still continued playing, but talked as he played.

He said—this time speaking in Polish—*Nie umiem wyrazic jak ciechi kocham*—"My darling, I fain would spare thee: but thy life is my life, and I must live, I who would rather die. Will God not have any mercy on me? Oh! Oh! life; oh, the torture of life!" Here he struck one agonized and strange chord, then continued playing softly, "O, Gabriel, my beloved! my life, yes life —oh, why life? I am sure this is but a little that I demand of thee. Sorely thy superabundance of life can spare little to one who is already dead. No, stay," he said now almost harshly, "what must be, must be!"

Gabriel stood there quite still, with the same fixed vacant expression, in the room. He was evidently walking in his sleep. Vardalek played on: then said, "Ah!" with a sign of terrible agony. Then very gently, "Go now, Gabriel; it is enough." And Gabriel went out of the room and ascended the staircase at the same slow pace, with the same unconscious stare. Vardalek struck the piano, and although he did not play loudly, it seemed as though the strings would break. You never heard music so strange and so heart-rending!

I only know I was found by Mlle Vonnaert in the morning, in an unconscious state, at the foot of the stairs. Was it a dream after all? I am sure now that it was not. I thought then it might be, and said nothing to anyone about it. Indeed, what could I say?

Well, to let me cut a long story short, Gabriel, who had never known a moment's sickness in his life, grew ill: and we had to send to Gratz for a doctor, who could give no explanation of Gabriel's strange illness. Gradual wasting away, he said: absolutely no organic complaint. What could this mean?

My father at last became conscious of the fact that Gabriel was ill. His anxiety was fearful. The last trace of grey faded from his hair, and it became quite white. We sent to Vienna for doctors.

But all with the same result.

Gabriel was generally unconscious, and when conscious, only seemed to recognize Vardalek, who sat continually by his bedside, nursing him with the utmost tenderness.

One day I was alone in the room: and Vardalek cried suddenly, almost fiercely, "Send for a priest at once, at once," he repeated. "It is now almost too late!"

Gabriel stretched out his arms spasmodically, and put them round Vardalek's neck. This was the only movement he had made, for some time. Vardalek bent down and kissed him on the lips.

I rushed downstairs: and the priest was sent for. When I came back Vardalek was not there. The priest administered extreme unction. I think Gabriel was already dead, although we did not think so at the time.

Vardalek had utterly disappeared; and when we looked for him he was nowhere to be found; nor have I seen or heard of him since.

My father died very soon afterwards: suddenly aged, and bent down with grief. And so the whole of the Wronski property came into my sole possession. And here I am, an old woman, generally laughed at for keeping, in memory of Gabriel, an asylum for stray animals—and——people do not, as a rule, believe in Vampires!

DRACULA'S GUEST

Bram Stoker

from *Dracula's Guest and Other Weird Stories* (1914)

originally written for *Dracula* (1897)

When we started for our drive the sun was shining brightly on Munich, and the air was full of the joyousness of early summer. Just as we were about to depart, Herr Delbruck (the maitre d'hotel of the Quatre Saisons, where I was staying) came down bareheaded to the carriage and, after wishing me a pleasant drive, said to the coachman, still holding his hand on the handle of the carriage door, "Remember you are back by nightfall. The sky looks bright but there is a shiver in the north wind that says there may be a sudden storm. But I am sure you will not be late." Here he smiled and added, "for you know what night it is."

Johann answered with an emphatic, "*Ja, mein Herr,*" and, touching his hat, drove off quickly. When we had cleared the town, I said, after signaling to him to stop:

"Tell me, Johann, what is tonight?"

He crossed himself, as he answered laconically: "*Walpurgis nacht.*" Then he took out his watch, a great, old-fashioned German silver thing as big as a turnip and looked at it, with his eyebrows gathered together and a little impatient shrug of his shoulders. I realized that this was his way of respectfully protesting against the unnecessary delay and sank back in the carriage, merely motioning him to proceed. He started off rapidly, as if to make up for lost time. Every now and then the horses seemed to throw up their heads and sniff the air suspiciously. On such occasions I often looked round in alarm. The road was pretty bleak, for we were traversing a sort of high windswept plateau. As we drove, I saw a road that looked but little used and which seemed to dip through a little winding valley. It looked so inviting that, even at the risk of offending him, I called Johann to stop—and when he had pulled up, I told him I would like to drive down that road. He made all sorts of excuses and frequently crossed himself as he spoke. This somewhat piqued my curiosity, so I asked him various questions. He answered fencingly and repeatedly looked at his watch in protest.

Finally I said, "Well, Johann, I want to go down this road. I shall not ask you to come unless you like; but tell me why you do not like to go, that is all I ask." For answer he seemed to throw himself off the box, so quickly did he reach the ground. Then he stretched out his hands appealingly to me and implored me not to go. There was just enough of English mixed with the German for me to understand the drift of his talk. He seemed always just about to tell me something—the very idea of which evidently frightened him; but each time he pulled himself up saying, "*Walpurgis nacht!*"

I tried to argue with him, but it was difficult to argue with a man when I did not know his language. The advantage certainly rested with him, for although he began to speak in English, of a very crude and broken kind, he always got excited and broke into his native tongue—and every time he did so, he looked at his watch. Then the horses became restless and sniffed the air. At this he grew very pale, and, looking around in a frightened way, he suddenly jumped forward, took them by the bridles, and led them on some twenty feet. I followed and asked why he had done this. For an answer he crossed himself, pointed to the spot we had left, and drew his carriage in the direction of the other road, indicating a cross, and said, first in German, then in English, "Buried him—him what killed themselves."

I remembered the old custom of burying suicides at cross roads: "Ah! I see, a suicide. How interesting!" But for the life of me I could not make out why the horses were frightened.

Whilst we were talking, we heard a sort of sound between a yelp and a bark. It was far away; but the horses got very restless, and it took Johann all his time to quiet them. He was pale and said, "It sounds like a wolf—but yet there are no wolves here now."

"No?" I said, questioning him. "Isn't it long since the wolves were so near the city?"

"Long, long," he answered, "in the spring and summer; but with the snow the wolves have been here not so long."

Whilst he was petting the horses and trying to quiet them, dark clouds drifted rapidly across the sky. The sunshine passed away, and a breath of cold wind seemed to drift over us. It was only a breath, however, and more of a warning than a fact, for the sun came out brightly again.

Johann looked under his lifted hand at the horizon and said, "The storm of snow, he comes before long time." Then he looked at his watch again, and, straightway holding his reins firmly—for the horses were still pawing the ground restlessly and shaking their heads—he climbed to his box as though the time had come for proceeding on our journey.

I felt a little obstinate and did not at once get into the carriage.

"Tell me," I said, "about this place where the road leads," and I pointed down.

Again he crossed himself and mumbled a prayer before he answered, "It is unholy."

"What is unholy?" I enquired.

"The village."

"Then there is a village?"

"No, no. No one lives there hundreds of years."

My curiosity was piqued, "But you said there was a village."

"There was."

"Where is it now?"

Whereupon he burst out into a long story in German and English, so mixed up that I could not quite understand exactly what he said. Roughly I gathered that long ago, hundreds of years, men had died there and been buried in their graves; but sounds were heard under the clay, and when the graves were opened, men and women were found rosy with life and their mouths red with blood. And so, in haste to save their lives (aye, and their souls!—and here he crossed himself) those who were left fled away to other places, where the living lived and the dead were dead and not—not something. He was evidently afraid to speak the last words. As he proceeded with his narration, he grew more and more excited. It seemed as if his imagination had got hold of him, and he ended in a perfect paroxysm of fear —white-faced, perspiring, trembling, and looking round him as if expecting that some dreadful presence would manifest itself there in the bright sunshine on the open plain.

Finally, in an agony of desperation, he cried, "*Walpurgis nacht!*" and pointed to the carriage for me to get in.

All my English blood rose at this, and standing back I said, "You are afraid, Johann—you are afraid. Go home, I shall return alone, the walk will do me good." The carriage door was open. I took from the seat my oak walking stick—which I always carry on my holiday excursions—and closed the door, pointing back to Munich, and said, "Go home, Johann—*Walpurgis nacht* doesn't concern Englishmen."

The horses were now more restive than ever, and Johann was trying to hold them in, while excitedly imploring me not to do anything so foolish. I pitied the poor fellow, he was so deeply in earnest; but all the same I could not help laughing. His English was quite gone now. In his anxiety he had forgotten that his only means of making me understand was to talk my language, so he jabbered away in his native German. It began to be a little tedious. After giving the direction, "Home!" I turned to go down the cross road into the valley.

With a despairing gesture, Johann turned his horses towards Munich. I leaned on my stick and looked after him. He went slowly along the road for a while, then there came over the crest of the hill a man tall and thin. I could see so much in the distance. When he drew near the horses, they began to jump and kick about, then to scream with terror. Johann could not hold them in; they bolted down the road, running away madly. I watched them out of sight, then looked for the stranger; but I found that he, too, was gone.

With a light heart I turned down the side road through the deepening valley to which Johann had objected. There was not the slightest reason, that I could see, for his objection; and I daresay I tramped for a couple of hours without thinking of time or distance and certainly without seeing a person or a house. So far as the place was concerned, it was desolation itself. But I did not notice this particularly till, on turning a bend in the road, I came upon a scattered fringe of wood; then I recognized that I had been impressed unconsciously by the desolation of the region through which I had passed.

I sat down to rest myself and began to look around. It struck me that it was considerably colder than it had been at the commencement of my walk— a sort of sighing sound seemed to be around me with, now and then, high overhead, a sort of muffled roar. Looking upwards I noticed that great thick clouds were drafting rapidly across the sky from north to south at a great height. There were signs of a coming storm in some lofty stratum of the air. I was a little chilly, and, thinking that it was the sitting still after the exercise of walking, I resumed my journey.

The ground I passed over was now much more picturesque. There were no striking objects that the eye might single out, but in all there was a charm of beauty. I took little heed of time, and it was only when the deepening twilight forced itself upon me that I began to think of how I should find my way home. The air was cold, and the drifting of clouds high overhead was more marked. They were accompanied by a sort of far away rushing sound, through which seemed to come at intervals that mysterious cry which the driver had said came from a wolf. For a while I hesitated. I had said I would see the deserted village, so on I went and presently came on a wide stretch of open country, shut in by hills all around. Their sides were covered with trees which spread down to the plain, dotting in clumps the gentler slopes and hollows which showed here and there. I followed with my eye the winding of the road and saw that it curved close to one of the densest of these clumps and was lost behind it.

As I looked there came a cold shiver in the air, and the snow began to fall. I thought of the miles and miles of bleak country I had passed, and then hurried on to seek shelter of the wood in front. Darker and darker grew the sky, and faster and heavier fell the snow, till the earth before and around me was a glistening white carpet the further edge of which was lost in misty vagueness. The road was here but crude, and when on the level its boundaries were not so marked as when it passed through the cuttings; and in a little while I found that I must have strayed from it, for I missed underfoot the hard surface, and my feet sank deeper in the grass and moss. Then the wind grew stronger and blew with ever increasing force, till I was fain to run before it. The air became icy-cold, and in spite of my exercise I began to suffer. The snow was now falling so thickly and whirling around me in such rapid eddies that I could hardly keep my eyes open. Every now and then the heavens were torn asunder by vivid lightning, and in the flashes I could see ahead of me a great mass of trees, chiefly yew and cypress all heavily coated with snow.

I was soon amongst the shelter of the trees, and there in comparative silence I could hear the rush of the wind high overhead. Presently the blackness of the storm had become merged in the darkness of the night. By-and-by the storm seemed to be passing away, it now only came in fierce puffs or blasts. At such moments the weird sound of the wolf appeared to be echoed by many similar sounds around me.

Now and again, through the black mass of drifting cloud, came a straggling ray of moonlight which lit up the expanse and showed me that I was at the edge of a dense mass of cypress and yew trees. As the snow had ceased to fall, I walked out from the shelter and began to investigate more closely. It appeared to me that, amongst so many old foundations as I had passed, there might be still standing a house in which, though in ruins, I could find some sort of shelter for a while. As I skirted the edge of the copse, I found that a low wall encircled it, and following this I presently found an opening. Here the cypresses formed an alley leading up to a square mass of some kind of building. Just as I caught sight of this, however, the drifting clouds obscured the moon, and I passed up the path in darkness. The wind must have grown colder, for I felt myself shiver as I walked; but there was hope of shelter, and I groped my way blindly on.

I stopped, for there was a sudden stillness. The storm had passed; and, perhaps in sympathy with nature's silence, my heart seemed to cease to beat. But this was only momentarily; for suddenly the moonlight broke through the clouds showing me that I was in a graveyard and that the square object before me was a great massive tomb of marble, as white as the snow that lay on and all around it. With the moonlight there came a fierce sigh of the storm which appeared to resume its course with a long, low howl, as of many dogs or wolves. I was awed and shocked, and I felt the cold perceptibly grow upon me till it seemed to grip me by the heart. Then while the flood of moonlight still fell on the marble tomb, the storm gave further evidence of renewing, as though it were returning on its track. Impelled by some sort of fascination, I approached the sepulcher to see what it was and why such a thing stood alone in such a place. I walked around it and read, over the Doric door, in German—

COUNTESS DOLINGEN OF GRATZ
IN STYRIA
SOUGHT AND FOUND DEATH
1801

On the top of the tomb, seemingly driven through the solid marble—for the structure was composed of a few vast blocks of stone—was a great iron spike or stake. On going to the back I saw, graven in great Russian letters: "The dead travel fast."

There was something so weird and uncanny about the whole thing that it gave me a turn and made me feel quite faint. I began to wish, for the first time, that I had taken Johann's advice. Here a thought struck me, which came under almost mysterious circumstances and with a terrible shock. This was Walpurgis Night!

Walpurgis Night was when, according to the belief of millions of people, the devil was abroad—when the graves were opened and the dead came forth and walked. When all evil things of earth and air and water held revel. This very place the driver had specially shunned. This was the depopulated village of centuries ago. This was where the suicide lay; and this was the place where I was alone—unmanned, shivering with cold in a shroud of snow with a wild storm gathering again upon me! It took all my philosophy, all the religion I had been taught, all my courage, not to collapse in a paroxysm of fright.

And now a perfect tornado burst upon me. The ground shook as though thousands of horses thundered across it; and this time the storm bore on its icy wings, not snow, but great hailstones which drove with such violence that they might have come from the thongs of Balearic slingers—hailstones that beat down leaf and branch and made the shelter of the cypresses of no more avail than though their stems were standing corn. At the first I had rushed to the nearest tree; but I was soon fain to leave it and seek the only spot that seemed to afford refuge, the deep Doric doorway of the marble tomb. There, crouching against the massive bronze door, I gained a certain amount of protection from the beating of the hailstones, for now they only drove against me as they ricochetted from the ground and the side of the marble.

As I leaned against the door, it moved slightly and opened inwards. The shelter of even a tomb was welcome in that pitiless tempest and I was about to enter it when there came a flash of forked lightning that lit up the whole expanse of the heavens. In the instant, as I am a living man, I saw, as my my eyes turned into the darkness of the tomb, a beautiful woman with rounded cheeks and red lips, seemingly sleeping on a bier. As the thunder broke overhead, I was grasped as by the hand of a giant and hurled out into the storm. The whole thing was so sudden that, before I could realize the shock, moral as well as physical, I found the hailstones beating me down. At the same time I had a strange, dominating feeling that I was not alone. I looked towards the tomb. Just then there came another blinding flash which seemed to strike the iron stake that surmounted the tomb and to pour through to the earth, blasting and crumbling the marble, as in a burst of flame. The dead woman rose for a moment of agony while she was lapped in the flame, and her bitter scream of pain was drowned in the thundercrash. The last thing I heard was this mingling of dreadful sound, as again I was seized in the giant grasp and dragged away, while the hailstones beat on me and the air around seemed reverberant with the howling of wolves. The last sight that I remembered was a vague, white, moving mass, as if all the graves around me had sent out the phantoms of their sheeted dead, and that they were closing in on me through the white cloudiness of the driving hail.

Gradually there came a sort of vague beginning of consciousness, then a sense of weariness that was dreadful. For a time I remembered nothing, but slowly my senses returned. My feet seemed positively racked with pain, yet I could not move them. They seemed to be numbed. There was an icy feeling at the back of my neck and all down my spine, and my ears, like my feet, were dead yet in torment; but there was in my breast a sense of warmth which was by comparison delicious. It was as a nightmare—a physical nightmare, if one may use such an expression; for some heavy weight on my chest made it difficult for me to breathe.

This period of semi-lethargy seemed to remain a long time, and as it faded away I must have slept or swooned. Then came a sort of loathing, like the first stage of seasickness, and a wild desire to be free of something—I knew not what. A vast stillness enveloped me, as though all the world were asleep or dead—only broken by the low panting as of some animal close to me. I felt a warm rasping at my throat, then came a consciousness of the awful truth which chilled me to the heart and sent the blood surging up through my brain. Some great animal was lying on me and now licking my throat. I feared to stir, for some instinct of prudence bade me lie still; but the brute seemed to realize that there was now some change in me, for it raised its head. Through my eyelashes I saw above me the two great flaming eyes of a gigantic wolf. Its sharp white teeth gleamed in the gaping red mouth, and I could feel its hot breath fierce and acrid upon me.

For another spell of time I remembered no more. Then I became conscious of a low growl, followed by a yelp, renewed again and again. Then seemingly very far away, I heard a "Holloa! holloa!" as of many voices calling in unison. Cautiously I raised my head and looked in the direction whence the sound came, but the cemetery blocked my view. The wolf still continued to yelp in a strange way, and a red glare began to move round the grove of cypresses, as though following the sound. As the voices drew closer, the wolf yelped faster and louder. I feared to make either sound or motion. Nearer came the red glow over the white pall which stretched into the darkness around me. Then all at once from beyond the trees there came at a trot a troop of horsemen bearing torches. The wolf rose from my breast and made for the cemetery. I saw one of the horsemen (soldiers by their caps and their long military cloaks) raise his carbine and take aim. A companion knocked up his arm, and I heard the ball whiz over my head. He had evidently taken my body for that of the wolf. Another sighted the animal as it slunk away, and a shot followed. Then, at a gallop, the troop rode forward—some towards me, others following the wolf as it disappeared amongst the snow-clad cypresses.

As they drew nearer I tried to move but was powerless, although I could see and hear all that went on around me. Two or three of the soldiers jumped from their horses and knelt beside me. One of them raised my head and placed his hand over my heart.

"Good news, comrades!" he cried. "His heart still beats!"

Then some brandy was poured down my throat; it put vigor into me, and I was able to open my eyes fully and look around. Lights and shadows were moving among the trees, and I heard men call to one another. They drew together, uttering frightened exclamations; and the lights flashed as the others came pouring out of the cemetery pell-mell, like men possessed. When the further ones came close to us, those who were around me asked them eagerly, "Well, have you found him?"

The reply rang out hurriedly, "No! no! Come away quick-quick! This is no place to stay, and on this of all nights!"

"What was it?" was the question, asked in all manner of keys. The answer came variously and all indefinitely as though the men were moved by some common impulse to speak yet were restrained by some common fear from giving their thoughts.

"It—it—indeed!" gibbered one, whose wits had plainly given out for the moment.

"A wolf—and yet not a wolf!" another put in shudderingly.

"No use trying for him without the sacred bullet," a third remarked in a more ordinary manner.

"Serve us right for coming out on this night! Truly we have earned our thousand marks!" were the ejaculations of a fourth.

"There was blood on the broken marble," another said after a pause, "the lightning never brought that there. And for him—is he safe? Look at his throat! See comrades, the wolf has been lying on him and keeping his blood warm."

The officer looked at my throat and replied, "He is all right, the skin is not pierced. What does it all mean? We should never have found him but for the yelping of the wolf."

"What became of it?" asked the man who was holding up my head and who seemed the least panic-stricken of the party, for his hands were steady and without tremor. On his sleeve was the chevron of a petty officer.

"It went home," answered the man, whose long face was pallid and who actually shook with terror as he glanced around him fearfully. "There are graves enough there in which it may lie. Come, comrades—come quickly! Let us leave this cursed spot."

The officer raised me to a sitting posture, as he uttered a word of command; then several men placed me upon a horse. He sprang to the saddle behind me, took me in his arms, gave the word to advance; and, turning our faces away from the cypresses, we rode away in swift military order.

As yet my tongue refused its office, and I was perforce silent. I must have fallen asleep; for the next thing I remembered was finding myself standing up, supported by a soldier on each side of me. It was almost broad daylight, and to the north a red streak of sunlight was reflected like a path of blood over the waste of snow. The officer was telling the men to say nothing of what they had seen, except that they found an English stranger, guarded by a large dog.

"Dog! that was no dog," cut in the man who had exhibited such fear. "I think I know a wolf when I see one."

The young officer answered calmly, "I said a dog."

"Dog!" reiterated the other ironically. It was evident that his courage was rising with the sun; and, pointing to me, he said, "Look at his throat. Is that the work of a dog, master?"

Instinctively I raised my hand to my throat, and as I touched it I cried out in pain. The men crowded round to look, some stooping down from their saddles; and again there came the calm voice of the young officer, "A dog, as I said. If aught else were said we should only be laughed at."

I was then mounted behind a trooper, and we rode on into the suburbs of Munich. Here we came across a stray carriage into which I was lifted, and it was driven off to the Quatre Saisons—the young officer accompanying me, whilst a trooper followed with his horse, and the others rode off to their barracks.

When we arrived, Herr Delbruck rushed so quickly down the steps to meet me, that it was apparent he had been watching within. Taking me by both hands he solicitously led me in. The officer saluted me and was turning to withdraw, when I recognized his purpose and insisted that he should come to my rooms. Over a glass of wine I warmly thanked him and his brave comrades for saving me. He replied simply that he was more than glad, and that Herr Delbruck had at the first taken steps to make all the searching party pleased; at which ambiguous utterance the maitre d'hotel smiled, while the officer plead duty and withdrew.

"But Herr Delbruck," I enquired, "how and why was it that the soldiers searched for me?"

He shrugged his shoulders, as if in depreciation of his own deed, as he replied, "I was so fortunate as to obtain leave from the commander of the regiment in which I serve, to ask for volunteers."

"But how did you know I was lost?" I asked.

"The driver came hither with the remains of his carriage, which had been upset when the horses ran away."

"But surely you would not send a search party of soldiers merely on this account?"

"Oh, no!" he answered, "but even before the coachman arrived, I had this telegram from the Boyar whose guest you are," and he took from his pocket a telegram which he handed to me, and I read:

Bistritz. Be careful of my guest—his safety is most precious to me. Should aught happen to him, or if he be missed, spare nothing to find him and ensure his safety. He is English and therefore adventurous. There are often dangers from snow and wolves and night. Lose not a moment if you suspect harm to him. I answer your zeal with my fortune.

DRACULA

As I held the telegram in my hand, the room seemed to whirl around me, and if the attentive maitre d'hotel had not caught me, I think I should have fallen. There was something so strange in all this, something so weird and impossible to imagine, that there grew on me a sense of my being in some way the sport of opposite forces—the mere vague idea of which seemed in a way to paralyze me. I was certainly under some form of mysterious protection. From a distant country had come, in the very nick of time, a message that took me out of the danger of the snow sleep and the jaws of the wolf.

THE STONE CHAMBER

H. B. Marriott Watson

first published in *The Heart of Miranda and Other Stories,*
Being Mostly Winter Tales (1898)

I t was not until early summer that Warrington took possession of
Marvyn Abbey. He had bought the property in the preceding autumn,
but the place had so fallen into decay through the disorders of time that
more than six months elapsed ere it was inhabitable. The delay, however, fell
out conveniently for Warrington; for the Bosanquets spent the winter abroad,
and nothing must suit but he must spend it with them. There was never a
man who pursued his passion with such ardor. He was ever at Miss
Bosanquet's skirts, and bade fair to make her as steadfast a husband as he was
attached a lover. Thus it was not until after his return from that prolonged
exile that he had the opportunity of inspecting the repairs discharged by his
architect. He was nothing out of the common in character, but was full of
kindly impulses and a fellow of impetuous blood. When he called upon me in
my chambers he spoke with some excitement of his Abbey, as also of his
approaching marriage; and finally, breaking into an exhibition of genuine
affection, declared that we had been so long and so continuously intimate
that I, and none other, must help him warm his house and marry his bride. It
had indeed been always understood between us that I should serve him at the
ceremony, but now it appeared that I must start my duties even earlier. The
prospect of a summer holiday in Utterbourne pleased me. It was a charming
village, set upon the slope of a wooded hill and within call of the sea. I had a
slight knowledge of the district from a riding excursion taken through that
part of Devonshire; and years before, and ere Warrington had come into his
money, had viewed the Abbey ruins from a distance with the polite curiosity
of a passing tourist.

I examined them now with new eyes as we drove up the avenue. The face
which the ancient building presented to the valley was of magnificent design,
but now much worn and battered.

Part of it, the right wing, I judged to be long past the uses of a dwelling,
for the walls had crumbled away, huge gaps opened in the foundations, and
the roof was quite dismantled.

Warrington had very wisely left this portion to its own sinister decay; it was the left wing which had been restored, and which we were to inhabit. The entrance, I will confess, was a little mean, for the large doorway had been bricked up and an ordinary modern door gave upon the spacious terrace and the winding gardens. But apart from this, the work of restoration had been undertaken with skill and piety, and the interior had retained its native dignity, while resuming an air of proper comfort. The old oak had been repaired congruous with the original designs, and the great rooms had been as little altered as was requisite to adapt them for daily use.

Warrington passed quickly from chamber to chamber in evident delight, directing my attention upon this and upon that, and eagerly requiring my congratulations and approval. My comments must have satisfied him, for the place attracted me vastly. The only criticism I ventured was to remark upon the size of the rooms and to question if they might dwarf the insignificant human figures they were to entertain.

He laughed. "Not a bit," said he. "Roaring fires in winter in those fine old fireplaces; and as for summer, the more space the better. We shall be jolly."

I followed him along the noble hall, and we stopped before a small door of very black oak.

"The bedrooms," he explained, as he turned the key, "are all upstairs, but mine is not ready yet.

"And besides, I am reserving it; I won't sleep in it till—you understand," he concluded, with a smiling suggestion of embarrassment.

I understood very well. He threw the door open.

"I am going to use this in the meantime," he continued. "Queer little room, isn't it? It used to be a sort of library. How do you think it looks?"

We had entered as he spoke, and stood, distributing our glances in that vague and general way in which a room is surveyed. It was a chamber of much smaller proportions than the rest, and was dimly lighted by two long narrow windows sunk in the great walls. The bed and the modern fittings looked strangely out of keeping with its ancient privacy. The walls were rudely distempered with barbaric frescos, dating, I conjectured, from the fourteenth century; and the floor was of stone, worn into grooves and hollows with the feet of many generations. As I was taking in these facts, there came over me a sudden curiosity as to those dead Marvyns who had held the Abbey for so long. This silent chamber seemed to suggest questions of their history; it spoke eloquently of past ages and past deeds, fallen now into oblivion. Here, within these thick walls, no echo from the outer world might carry, no sound would ring within its solitary seclusion. Even the silence seemed to confer with one upon the ancient transactions of that extinct House.

Warrington stirred, and turned suddenly to me. "I hope it's not damp," said he, with a slight shiver. "It looks rather solemn. I thought furniture would brighten it up."

"I should think it would be very comfortable," said I. "You will never be disturbed by any sounds at any rate."

"No," he answered, hesitatingly; and then, quickly, on one of his impulses: "Hang it, Heywood, there's too much silence here for me." Then he laughed. "Oh, I shall do very well for a month or two." And with that appeared to return to his former placid cheerfulness.

The train of thought started in that sombre chamber served to entertain me several times that day. I questioned Warrington at dinner, which we took in one of the smaller rooms, commanding a lovely prospect of dale and sea. He shook his head. Archaeological lore, as indeed anything else out of the borders of actual life, held very little interest for him.

"The Marvyns died out in 1714, I believe," he said, indifferently; "someone told me that—the man I bought it from, I think. They might just as well have kept the place up since; but I think it has been only occupied twice between then and now, and the last time was forty years ago. It would have rotted to pieces if I hadn't taken it. Perhaps Mrs. Batty could tell you. She's lived in these parts almost all her life."

To humor me, and affected, I doubt not, by a certain pride in his new possession, he put the query to his housekeeper upon her appearance subsequently; but it seemed that her knowledge was little fuller than his own, though she had gathered some vague traditions of the countryside.

The Marvyns had not left a reputable name, if rumor spoke truly; theirs was a family to which black deeds had been credited. They were ill-starred also in their fortunes, and had become extinct suddenly; but for the rest, the events had fallen too many generations ago to be current now between the memories of the village.

Warrington, who was more eager to discuss the future than to recall the past, was vastly excited by his anticipations. St. Pharamond, Sir William Bosanquet's house, lay across the valley, barely five miles away; and as the family had now returned, it was easy to forgive Warrington's elation.

"What do you think?" he said, late that evening; and clapping me upon the shoulder, "You have seen Marion; here is the house. Am I not lucky? Damn it, Heywood, I'm not pious, but I am disposed to thank God! I'm not a bad fellow, but I'm no saint; it's fortunate that it's not only the virtuous that are rewarded. In fact, it's usually contrariwise. I owe this to—Lord, I don't know what I owe it to. Is it my money? Of course, Marion doesn't care a rap for that; but then, you see, I mightn't have known her without it. Of course, there's the house, too. I'm thankful I have money. At any rate, here's my new life. Just look about and take it in, old fellow. If you knew how a man may be ashamed of himself! But there, I've done. You know I'm decent at heart—you must count my life from today." And with this outbreak he lifted the glass between fingers that trembled with the warmth of his emotions, and tossed off his wine.

He did himself but justice when he claimed to be a good fellow; and, in truth, I was myself somewhat moved by his obvious feeling. I remember that we shook hands very affectionately, and my sympathy was the prelude to a long and confidential talk, which lasted until quite a late hour.

At the foot of the staircase, where we parted, he detained me.

"This is the last of my wayward days," he said, with a smile. "Late hours—liquor—all go. You shall see. Goodnight. You know your room. I shall be up long before you." And with that he vanished briskly into the darkness that hung about the lower parts of the passage.

I watched him go, and it struck me quite vaguely what a slight impression his candle made upon that channel of opaque gloom. It seemed merely as a thread of light that illumined nothing.

Warrington himself was rapt into the prevalent blackness; but long afterwards, and even when his footsteps had died away upon the heavy carpet, the tiny beam was visible, advancing and flickering in the distance.

My window, which was modern, opened upon a little balcony, where, as the night was warm and I was indisposed for sleep, I spent half an hour enjoying the air. I was in a sentimental mood, and my thoughts turned upon the suggestions which Warrington's conversation had induced. It was not until I was in bed, and had blown out the light, that they settled upon the square, dark chamber in which my host was to pass the night. As I have said, I was wakeful, owing, no doubt, to the high pitch of the emotions which we had encouraged; but presently my fancies became inarticulate and incoherent, and then I was overtaken by profound sleep.

Warrington was up before me, as he had predicted, and met me in the breakfast-room.

"What a beggar you are to sleep!" he said, with a smile. "I've hammered at your door for half an hour."

I apologized for myself, alleging the rich country air in my defense, and mentioned that I had had some difficulty in getting to sleep.

"So had I," he remarked, as we sat down to the table. "We got very excited, I suppose. Just see what you have there, Heywood. Eggs? Oh, damn it, one can have too much of eggs!" He frowned, and lifted a third cover. "Why in the name of common sense can't Mrs. Batty give us more variety?" he asked, impatiently.

I deprecated his displeasure, suggesting that we should do very well; indeed, his discontent seemed to me quite unnecessary. But I supposed Warrington had been rather spoiled by many years of club life.

He settled himself without replying, and began to pick over his plate in a gingerly manner.

"There's one thing I will have here, Heywood," he observed. "I will have things well appointed."

"I'm not going to let life in the country mean an uncomfortable life. A man can't change the habits of a lifetime."

In contrast with his exhilarated professions of the previous evening, this struck me with a sense of amusement at the moment; and the incongruity may have occurred to him, for he went on:

"Marion's not over strong, you know, and must have things *comme il faut*. She shan't decline upon a lower level. The worst of these rustics is that they have no imagination." He held up a piece of bacon on his fork, and surveyed it with disgust. "Now, look at that! Why the devil don't they take tips from civilized people like the French?"

It was so unlike him to exhibit this petulance that I put it down to a bad night, and without discovering the connection of my thoughts, asked him how he liked his bedroom.

"Oh, pretty well, pretty well," he said, indifferently. "It's not so cold as I thought. But I slept badly. I always do in a strange bed;" and pushing aside his plate, he lit a cigarette. "When you've finished that garbage, Heywood, we'll have a stroll round the Abbey," he said.

His good temper returned during our walk, and he indicated to me various improvements which he contemplated, with something of his old ardor. The left wing of the house, as I have said, was entire, but a little apart were the ruins of a chapel. Surrounded by a low moss-grown wall, it was full of picturesque charm; the roofless chancel was spread with ivy, but the aisles were intact. Grass grew between the stones and the floor, and many creepers had strayed through chinks in the wall into those sacred precincts. The solemn quietude of the ruin, maintained under the spell of death, awed me a little, but upon Warrington apparently it made no impression. He was only zealous that I should properly appreciate the distinction of such a property. I stooped and drew the weeds away from one of the slabs in the aisle, and was able to trace upon it the relics of lettering, well-nigh obliterated under the corrosion of time.

"There are tombs," said I.

"Oh, yes," he answered, with a certain relish. "I understand the Marvyns used it as a mausoleum. They are all buried here. Some good brasses, I am told."

The associations of the place engaged me; the aspect of the Abbey faced the past; it seemed to refuse communion with the present; and somehow the thought of those two decent humdrum lives which should be spent within its shelter savored of the incongruous. The white-capped maids and the emblazoned butlers that should tread these halls offered a ridiculous appearance beside my fancies of the ancient building. For all that, I envied Warrington his home, and so I told him, with a humorous hint that I was fitter to appreciate its glories than himself.

He laughed. "Oh, I don't know," said he. "I like the old-world look as much as you do. I have always had a notion of something venerable. It seems to serve you for ancestors." And he was undoubtedly delighted with my enthusiasm.

But at lunch again he chopped round to his previous irritation, only now quite another matter provoked his anger. He had received a letter by the second post from Miss Bosanquet, which, if I may judge from his perplexity, must have been unusually confused. He read and re-read it, his brow lowering.

"What the deuce does she mean?" he asked, testily. "She first makes an arrangement for us to ride over today, and now I can't make out whether we are to go to St. Pharamond, or they are coming to us. Just look at it, will you, Heywood?"

I glanced through the note, but could offer no final solution, whereupon he broke out again:

"That's just like women—they never can say anything straightforwardly. Why, in the name of goodness, couldn't she leave things as they were? You see," he observed, rather in answer, as I fancied, to my silence, "we don't know what to do now; if we stay here they mayn't come, and if we go probably we shall cross them." And he snapped his fingers in annoyance.

I was cheerful enough, perhaps because the responsibility was not mine, and ventured to suggest that we might ride over, and return if we missed them. But he dismissed the subject sharply by saying:

"No, I'll stay. I'm not going on a fool's errand," and drew my attention to some point in the decoration of the room.

The Bosanquets did not arrive during the afternoon, and Warrington's ill-humor increased.

His love-sick state pleaded in excuse of him, but he was certainly not a pleasant companion. He was sour and snappish, and one could introduce no statement to which he would not find a contradiction. So unamiable did he grow that at last I discovered a pretext to leave him, and rambled to the back of the Abbey into the precincts of the old chapel. The day was falling, and the summer sun flared through the western windows upon the bare aisle. The creepers rustled upon the gaping walls, and the tall grasses waved in shadows over the bodies of the forgotten dead. As I stood contemplating the effect, and meditating greatly upon the anterior fortunes of the Abbey, my attention fell upon a huge slab of marble, upon which the yellow light struck sharply. The faded lettering rose into greater definition before my eyes and I read slowly:

"Here lyeth the body of Sir Rupert Marvyn."

Beyond a date, very difficult to decipher, there was nothing more; of eulogy, of style, of record, of pious considerations such as were usual to the period, not a word. I read the numerals variously as 1723 and 1745; but however they ran it was probable that the stone covered the resting-place of the last Marvyn. The history of this futile house interested me not a little, partly for Warrington's sake, and in part from a natural bent towards ancient records; and I made a mental note of the name and date.

When I returned Warrington's surliness had entirely vanished, and had given place to an effusion of boisterous spirits. He apologized jovially for his bad temper.

"It was the disappointment of not seeing Marion," he said. "You will understand that someday, old fellow. But, anyhow, we'll go over tomorrow," and forthwith proceeded to enliven the dinner with an ostentation of good-fellowship I had seldom witnessed in him. I began to suspect that he had heard again from St. Pharamond, though he chose to conceal the fact from me. The wine was admirable; though Warrington himself was no great judge, he had entrusted the selection to a good palate. We had a merry meal, drank a little more than was prudent, and smoked our cigars upon the terrace in the fresh air. Warrington was restless. He pushed his glass from him. "I'll tell you what, old chap," he broke out, "I'll give you a game of billiards. I've got a decent table."

I demurred. The air was too delicious, and I was in no humor for a sharp use of my wits. He laughed, though he seemed rather disappointed.

"It's almost sacrilege to play billiards in an Abbey," I said, whimsically. "What would the ghosts of the old Marvyns think?"

"Oh, hang the Marvyns!" he rejoined, crossly. "You're always talking of them."

He rose and entered the house, returning presently with a flagon of whisky and some glasses.

"Try this," he said. "We've had no liqueurs," and pouring out some spirit he swallowed it raw.

I stared, for Warrington rarely took spirits, being more of a wine drinker; moreover, he must have taken nearly the quarter of a tumbler. But he did not notice my surprise, and, seating himself, lit another cigar.

"I don't mean to have things quiet here," he observed, reflectively. "I don't believe in your stagnant rustic life. What I intend to do is to keep the place warm—plenty of house parties, things going on all the year. I shall expect you down for the shooting, Ned. The coverts promise well this year."

I assented willingly enough, and he rambled on again.

"I don't know that I shall use the Abbey so much. I think I'll live in town a good deal. It's brighter there. I don't know though. I like the place. Hang it, it's a rattling good shop, there's no mistake about it. Look here," he broke off, abruptly, "bring your glass in, and I'll show you something."

I was little inclined to move, but he was so peremptory that I followed him with a sigh. We entered one of the smaller rooms which overlooked the terrace, and had been diverted into a comfortable library. He flung back the windows.

"There's air for you," he cried. "Now, sit down," and walking to a cupboard produced a second flagon of whisky. "Irish!" he ejaculated, clumping it on the table. "Take your choice," and turning again to the cupboard, presently sat down with his hands under the table. "Now, then, Ned," he said, with a short laugh. "Fill up, and we'll have some fun," with which he suddenly threw a pack of cards upon the board.

I opened my eyes, for I do not suppose Warrington had touched cards since his college days; but, interpreting my look in his own way, he cried:

"Oh, I'm not married yet. Warrington's his own man still. Poker? Eh?"

"Anything you like," said I, with resignation.

A peculiar expression of delight gleamed in his eyes, and he shuffled the cards feverishly.

"Cut," said he, and helped himself to more whisky.

It was shameful to be playing there with that beautiful night without, but there seemed no help for it. Warrington had a run of luck, though he played with little skill; and his excitement grew as he won.

"Let us make it ten shillings," he suggested.

I shook my head. "You forget I'm not a millionaire," I replied. "Bah!" he cried. "I like a game worth the victory. Well, fire away." His eyes gloated upon the cards, and he fingered them with unctuous affection. The behavior of the man amazed me. I began to win.

Warrington's face slowly assumed a dull, lowering expression; he played eagerly, avariciously; he disputed my points, and was querulous.

"Oh, we've had enough!" I cried in distaste.

"By Jove, you don't!" he exclaimed, jumping to his feet. "You're the winner, Heywood, and I'll see you damned before I let you off my revenge!"

The words startled me no less than the fury which rang in his accents. I gazed at him in stupefaction. The whites of his eyes showed wildly, and a sullen, angry look determined his face.

Suddenly I was arrested by the suspicion of something upon his neck.

"What's that?" I asked. "You've cut yourself."

He put his hand to his face. "Nonsense," he replied, in a surly fashion.

I looked closer, and then I saw my mistake. It was a round, faint red mark, the size of a florin, upon the column of his throat, and I set it down to the accidental pressure of some button.

"Come on!" he insisted, impatiently.

"Bah! Warrington," I said, for I imagined that he had been overexcited by the whisky he had taken. "It's only a matter of a few pounds. Why make a fuss? Tomorrow will serve."

After a moment his eyes fell, and he gave an awkward laugh. "Oh, well, that'll do," said he.

"But I got so infernally excited."

"Whisky," said I, sententiously.

He glanced at the bottle. "How many glasses have I had?" and he whistled. "By Jove, Ned, this won't do! I must turn over a new leaf. Come on; let's look at the night."

I was only too glad to get away from the table, and we were soon upon the terrace again.

Warrington was silent, and his gaze went constantly across the valley, where the moon was rising, and in the direction in which, as he had indicated to me, St. Pharamond lay. When he said goodnight he was still pre-occupied.

"I hope you will sleep better," he said.

"And you, too," I added.

He smiled. "I don't suppose I shall wake the whole night through," he said; and then, as I was turning to go, he caught me quickly by the arm.

"Ned," he said, impulsively and very earnestly, "don't let me make a fool of myself again. I know it's the excitement of everything. But I want to be as good as I can for her."

I pressed his hand. "All right, old fellow," I said; and we parted.

I think I have never enjoyed sounder slumber than that night. The first thing I was aware of was the singing of thrushes outside my window. I rose and looked forth, and the sun was hanging high in the eastern sky, the grass and the young green of the trees were shining with dew. With an uncomfortable feeling that I was very late I hastily dressed and went downstairs. Warrington was waiting for me in the breakfast-room, as upon the previous morning, and when he turned from the window at my approach, the sight of his face startled me. It was drawn and haggard, and his eyes were shot with blood; it was a face broken and savage with dissipation. He made no answer to my questioning, but seated himself with a morose air.

"Now you have come," he said, sullenly, "we may as well begin. But it's not my fault if the coffee's cold."

I examined him critically, and passed some comment upon his appearance.

"You don't look up to much," I said. "Another bad night?"

"No; I slept well enough," he responded, ungraciously; and then, after a pause: "I'll tell you what, Heywood. You shall give me my revenge after breakfast."

"Nonsense," I said, after a momentary silence. "You're going over to St. Pharamond."

"Hang it!" was his retort, "one can't be always bothering about women. You seem mightily indisposed to meet me again."

"I certainly won't this morning," I answered, rather sharply, for the man's manner grated upon me. "This evening, if you like; and then the silly business shall end."

He said something in an undertone of grumble, and the rest of the meal passed in silence. But I entertained an uneasy suspicion of him, and after all he was my friend, with whom I was under obligations not to quarrel; and so when we rose, I approached him.

"Look here, Warrington," I said. "What's the matter with you? Have you been drinking? Remember what you asked me last night."

"Hold your damned row!" was all the answer he vouchsafed, as he whirled away from me, but with an embarrassed display of shame.

But I was not to be put off in that way, and I spoke somewhat more sharply.

"We're going to have this out, Warrington," I said. "If you are ill, let us understand that; but I'm not going to stay here with you in this cantankerous spirit."

"I'm not ill," he replied testily.

"Look at yourself," I cried, and turned him about to the mirror over the mantelpiece.

He started a little, and a frown of perplexity gathered on his forehead.

"Good Lord! I'm not like that, Ned," he said, in a different voice. "I must have been drunk last night." And with a sort of groan, he directed a piteous look at me.

"Come," I was constrained to answer, "pull yourself together. The ride will do you good. And no more whisky."

"No, by Heaven, no!" he cried vehemently, and seemed to shiver; but then, suddenly taking my arm, he walked out of the room.

The morning lay still and golden. Warrington's eyes went forth across the valley.

"Come round to the stables, Ned," he said, impulsively. "You shall choose you own nag."

I shook my head. "I'll choose yours," said I, "but I am not going with you." He looked surprised.

"No, ride by yourself. You don't want a companion on such an errand. I'll stay here, and pursue my investigations into the Marvyns."

A scowl crossed his face, but only for an instant, and then he answered: "All right, old chap; do as you like. Anyway, I'm off at once." And presently, when his horse was brought, he was laughing merrily.

"You'll have a dull day, Ned; but it's your own fault, you duffer. You'll have to lunch by yourself, as I shan't be back till late." And, gaily flourishing his whip, he trotted down the drive.

It was some relief to me to be rid of him, for, in truth, his moods had worn my nerves, and I had not looked for a holiday of this disquieting nature. When he returned, I had no doubt it would be with quite another face, and meanwhile I was excellent company for myself. After lunch I amused myself for half an hour with idle tricks upon the billiard-table, and, tiring of my pastime, fell upon the housekeeper as I returned along the corridor. She was a woman nearer to sixty than fifty, with a comfortable, portly figure, and an amiable expression. Her eyes invited me ever so respectfully to conversation, and stopping, I entered into talk. She inquired if I liked my room and how I slept.

"'Tis a nice look-out you have, Sir," said she. "That was where old Lady Martin slept."

It appeared that she had served as kitchen-maid to the previous tenants of the Abbey, nearly fifty years before.

"Oh, I know the old house in and out," she asserted; "and I arranged the rooms with Mr. Warrington."

We were standing opposite the low doorway which gave entrance to Warrington's bedroom, and my eyes unconsciously shot in that direction. Mrs. Batty followed my glance.

"I didn't want him to have that," she said; "but he was set upon it. It's smallish for a bedroom, and in my opinion isn't fit for more than a lumber-room. That's what Sir William used it for."

I pushed open the door and stepped over the threshold, and the housekeeper followed me.

"No," she said, glancing round; "and it's in my mind that it's damp, Sir."

Again I had a curious feeling that the silence was speaking in my ear; the atmosphere was thick and heavy, and a musty smell, as of faded draperies, penetrated my nostrils. The whole room looked indescribably dingy, despite the new hangings. I went over to the narrow window and peered through the diamond panes. Outside, but seen dimly through that ancient and discolored glass, the ruins of the chapel confronted me, bare and stark, in the yellow sunlight. I turned.

"There are no ghosts in the Abbey, I suppose, Mrs. Batty?" I asked, whimsically.

But she took my inquiry very gravely. "I have never heard tell of one, Sir," she protested; "and if there was such a thing I should have known it."

As I was rejoining her a strange low whirring was audible, and looking up I saw in a corner of the high-arched roof a horrible face watching me out of black narrow eyes. I confess that I was very much startled at the apparition, but the next moment realized what it was. The creature hung with its ugly fleshy wings extended over a grotesque stone head that leered down upon me, its evil-looking snout projecting into the room; it lay perfectly still, returning me glance for glance, until moved by the repulsion of its presence I clapped my hands, and cried loudly; then, slowly flitting in a circle round the roof, it vanished with a flapping of wings into some darker corner of the rafters. Mrs. Batty was astounded, and expressed surprise that it had managed to conceal itself for so long.

"Oh, bats live in holes," I answered. "Probably there is some small access through the masonry." But the incident had sent an uncomfortable shiver through me all the same.

Later that day I began to recognize that, short of an abrupt return to town, my time was not likely to be spent very pleasantly. But it was the personal problem so far as it concerned Warrington himself that distressed me even more. He came back from St. Pharamond in a morose and ugly temper, quite alien to his kindly nature. It seems that he had quarreled bitterly with Miss Bosanquet, but upon what I could not determine, nor did I press him for an explanation. But the fumes of his anger were still rising when we met, and our dinner was a most depressing meal.

He was in a degree of irritation which rendered it impossible to address him, and I soon withdrew into my thoughts. I saw, however, that he was drinking far too much, as, indeed, was plain subsequently when he invited me into the library. Once more he produced the hateful cards, and I was compelled to play, as he reminded me somewhat churlishly that I had promised him his revenge.

"Understand, Warrington," I said, firmly, "I play tonight, but never again, whatever the result In fact, I am in half the mind to return to town tomorrow."

He gave me a look as he sat down, but said nothing, and the game began. He lost heavily from the first, and as nothing would content him but we must constantly raise the stakes, in a shore time I had won several hundred pounds. He bore the reverses very ill, breaking out from time to time into some angry exclamation, now petulantly questioning my playing, and muttering oaths under his breath. But I was resolved that he should have no cause of complaint against me for this one night, and disregarding his insane fits of temper, I played steadily and silently. As the tally of my gains mounted he changed color slowly, his face assuming a ghastly expression, and his eyes suspiciously denoting my actions. At length he rose, and throwing himself quickly across the table, seized my hand ferociously as I dealt a couple of cards.

"Damn you! I see your tricks," he cried, in frenzied passion. "Drop that hand, do you hear?"

"Drop that hand, or by—"

But he got no further, for, rising myself, I wrenched my hand from his grasp, and turned upon him, in almost as great a passion as himself. But suddenly, and even as I opened my mouth to speak, I stopped short with a cry of horror. His face was livid to the lips, his eyes were cast with blood, and upon the dirty white of his flesh, right in the centre of his throat, the round red scar, flaming and ugly as a wound, stared upon me.

"Warrington" I cried, "what is this? What have you?—" And I pointed in alarm to the spot.

"Mind your own business," he said, with a sneer. "It is well to try and draw off attention from your knavery. But that trick won't answer with me."

Without another word I flung the IOU's upon the table, and turning on my heel, left the room. I was furious with him, and fully resolved to leave the Abbey in the morning. I made my way upstairs to my room, and then, seating myself upon the balcony, endeavored to recover my self-possession.

The more I considered, the more unaccountable was Warrington's behavior. He had always been a perfectly courteous man, with a great lump of kindness in his nature; whereas these last few days he had been nothing other than a savage. It seemed certain that he must be ill or going mad; and as I reflected upon this the conjecture struck me with a sense of pity. If it was that he was losing his senses, how horrible was the tragedy in face of the new and lovely prospects opening in his life. Stimulated by this growing conviction, I resolved to go down and see him, more particularly as I now recalled his pleading voice that I should help him, on the previous evening. Was it not possible that this pathetic appeal derived from the instinct of the insane to protect themselves?

I found him still in the library; his head had fallen upon the table, and the state of the whisky bottle by his arm showed only too clearly his condition. I shook him vigorously, and he opened his eyes.

"Warrington, you must go to bed," I said.

He smiled, and greeted me quite affectionately. Obviously he was not so drunk as I had supposed.

"What is the time, Ned?" he asked.

I told him it was one o'clock, at which he rose briskly.

"Lord, I've been asleep," he said. "Help me, Ned. I don't think I'm sober. Where have you been?"

I assisted him to his room, and he undressed slowly, and with an effort. Somehow, as I stood watching him, I yielded to an unknown impulse and said, suddenly:

"Warrington, don't sleep here. Come and share my room."

"My dear fellow," he replied, with a foolish laugh, "yours is not the only room in the house. I can use half-a-dozen if I like."

"Well, use one of them," I answered.

He shook his head. "I'm going to sleep here," he returned, obstinately.

I made no further effort to influence him, for, after all, now that the words were out, I had absolutely no reason to give him or myself for my proposition. And so I left him. When I had closed the door, and was turning to go along the passage, I heard very clearly, as it seemed to me, a plaintive cry, muffled and faint, but very disturbing, which sounded from the room.

Instantly I opened the door again. Warrington was in bed, and the heavy sound of his breathing told me that he was asleep. It was impossible that he could have uttered the cry. A night-light was burning by his bedside, shedding a strong illumination over the immediate vicinity, and throwing antic shadows on the walls. As I turned to go, there was a whirring of wings, a brief flap behind me, and the room was plunged in darkness. The obscene creature that lived in the recesses of the roof must have knocked out the tiny light with its wings. Then Warrington's breathing ceased, and there was no sound at all. And then once more the silence seemed to gather round me slowly and heavily, and whisper to me. I had a vague sense of being prevailed upon, of being enticed and lured by something in the surrounding air; a sort of horror circumscribed me, and I broke from the invisible ring and rushed from the room. The door clanged behind me, and as I hastened along the hail, once more there seemed to ring in my ears the faint and melancholy cry.

I awoke, in the sombre twilight that precedes the dawn, from a sleep troubled and encumbered with evil dreams. The birds had not yet begun their day, and a vast silence brooded over the Abbey gardens. Looking out of my window, I caught sight of a dark figure stealing cautiously round the corner of the ruined chapel. The furtive gait, as well as the appearance of a man at that early hour, struck me with surprise; and hastily throwing on some clothes, I ran downstairs, and, opening the hall-door, went out. When I reached the porch which gave entrance to the aisle I stopped suddenly, for there before me, with his head to the ground, and peering among the tall grasses, was the object of my pursuit. Then I stepped quickly forward and laid a hand upon his shoulder. It was Warrington.

"What are you doing here?" I asked.

He turned and looked at me in bewilderment. His eyes wore a dazed expression, and he blinked in perplexity before he replied.

"It's you, is it?" he said weakly. "I thought—" and then paused. "What is it?" he asked.

"I followed you here," I explained. "I only saw your figure, and thought it might be some intruder."

He avoided my eyes. "I thought I heard a cry out here," he answered.

"Warrington," I said, with some earnestness, "come back to bed."

He made no answer, and slipping my arm in his, I led him away. On the doorstep he stopped, and lifted his face to me.

"Do you think it's possible—" he began, as if to inquire of me, and then again paused. With a slight shiver he proceeded to his room, while I followed him. He sat down upon his bed, and his eyes strayed to the barred window absently. The black shadow of the chapel was visible through the panes.

"Don't say anything about this," he said, suddenly. "Don't let Marion know."

I laughed, but it was an awkward laugh.

"Why, that you were alarmed by a cry for help, and went in search like a gentleman?" I asked, jestingly.

"You heard it, then?" he said, eagerly.

I shook my head, for I was not going to encourage his fancies. "You had better go to sleep," I replied, "and get rid of these nightmares."

He sighed and lay back upon his pillow, dressed as he was. Ere I left him he had fallen into a profound slumber.

If I had expected a surly mood in him at breakfast I was much mistaken. There was not a trace of his nocturnal dissipations; he did not seem even to remember them, and he made no allusion whatever to our adventure in the dawn. He perused a letter carefully, and threw it over to me with a grin.

"Lor, what queer sheep women are!" he exclaimed, with rather a coarse laugh.

I glanced at the letter without thinking, but ere I had read half of it I put it aside. It was certainly not meant for my eyes, and I marveled at Warrington's indelicacy in making public, as it were, that very private matter. The note was from Miss Bosanquet, and was clearly designed for his own heart, couched as it was in the terms of warm and fond affection. No man should see such letters save he for whom they are written.

"You see, they're coming over to dine," he remarked, carelessly. "Trust a girl to make it up if you let her alone long enough."

I made no answer; but though Warrington's grossness irritated me, I reflected with satisfaction upon his return to good humor, which I attributed to the reconciliation.

When I moved out upon the terrace the maid had entered to remove the breakfast things. I was conscious of a slight exclamation behind me, and Warrington joined me presently, with a loud guffaw.

"That's a damned pretty girl!" he said, with unction. "I'm glad Mrs. Batty got her. I like to have good-looking servants."

I suddenly interpreted the incident, and shrugged my shoulders.

"You're a perfect boor this morning, Warrington," I exclaimed, irritably.

He only laughed. "You're a dull dog of a saint, Heywood," he retorted. "Come along," and dragged me out in no amiable spirit.

I had forgotten how perfect a host Warrington could be, but that evening he was displayed at his best. The Bosanquets arrived early. Sir William was an easy-going man, fond of books and of wine, and I now guessed at the taste which had decided Warrington's cellar. Miss Bosanquet was as charming as I remembered her to be; and if any objection might be taken to Warrington himself by my anxious eyes it was merely that he seemed a trifle excited, a fault which, in the circumstances, I was able to condone. Sir William hung about the table, sipping his wine.

Warrington, who had been very abstemious, grew restless, and, finally apologizing in his graceful way, left me to keep the baronet company. I was the less disinclined to do so as I was anxious not to intrude upon the lovers, and Sir William was discussing the history of the Abbey.

He had an old volume somewhere in his library which related to it, and, seeing that I was interested, invited me to look it up.

We sat long, and it was not until later that the horrible affair which I must narrate occurred.

The evening was close and oppressive, owing to the thunder, which already rumbled far away in the south. When we rose we found that Warrington and Miss Bosanquet were in the garden, and thither we followed. As at first we did not find them, Sir William, who had noted the approaching storm with some uneasiness, left me to make arrangements for his return; and I strolled along the paths by myself, enjoying a cigarette. I had reached the shrubbery upon the further side of the chapel, when I heard the sound of voices—a man's rough and rasping, a woman's pleading and informed with fear. A sharp cry ensued, and without hesitation I plunged through the thicket in the direction of the speakers. The sight that met me appalled me for the moment. Darkness was falling, lit with ominous flashes; and the two figures stood out distinctly in the bushes, in an attitude of struggle. I could not mistake the voices now. I heard Warrington's, brusque with anger, and almost savage in its tones, crying, "You shall!" and there followed a murmur from the girl, a little sob, and then a piercing cry. I sprang forward and seized Warrington by the arm; when, to my horror, I perceived that he had taken her wrist in both hands and was roughly twisting it, after the cruel habit of schoolboys. The malevolent cruelty of the action so astounded me that for an instant I remained motionless; I almost heard the bones in the frail wrist cracking; and then, in a second, I had seized Warrington's hands in a grip of iron, and flung him violently to the ground. The girl fell with him, and as I picked her up he rose too, and, clenching his fists, made as though to come at me, but instead turned and went sullenly, and with a ferocious look of hate upon his face, out of the thicket.

Miss Bosanquet came to very shortly, and though the agony of the pain must have been considerable to a delicate girl, I believe it was rather the incredible horror of the act under which she swooned. For my part I had nothing to say: not one word relative to the incident dared pass my lips. I inquired if she was better, and then, putting her arm in mine, led her gently towards the house. Her heart beat hard against me, and she breathed heavily, leaning on me for support. At the chapel I stopped, feeling suddenly that I dare not let her be seen in this condition, and bewildered greatly by the whole atrocious business.

"Come and rest in here," I suggested, and we entered the chapel.

I set her on a slab of marble, and stood waiting by her side. I talked fluently about anything; for lack of a subject, upon the state of the chapel and the curious tomb I had discovered. Recovering a little, she joined presently in my remarks. It was plain that she was putting a severe restraint upon herself. I moved aside the grasses, and read aloud the inscription on Sir Rupert's grave-piece, and turning to the next, which was rankly overgrown, feigned to search further. As I was bending there, suddenly, and by what thread of thought I know not, I identified the spot with that upon which I had found Warrington stooping that morning. With a sweep of my hand I brushed back the weeds, uprooting some with my fingers, and kneeling in the twilight, pored over the monument. Suddenly a wild flare of light streamed down the sky, and a great crash of thunder followed. Miss Bosanquet started to her feet and I to mine. The heaven was lit up, as it were, with sunlight, and, as I turned, my eyes fell upon the now uncovered stone. Plainly the lettering flashed in my eyes:

"Priscilla, Lady Marvyn."

Then the clouds opened, and the rain fell in spouts, shouting and dancing upon the ancient roof overhead.

We were under a very precarious shelter, and I was uneasy that Miss Bosanquet should run the risk of that flimsy, ravaged edifice; and so in a momentary lull I managed to get her to the house.

I found Sir William in a restless state of nerves. He was a timorous man, and the thunder had upset him, more particularly as he and his daughter were now storm-bound for some time. There was no possibility of venturing into those rude elements for an hour or more. Warrington was not inside, and no one had seen him. In the light Miss Bosanquet's face frightened me; her eyes were large and scared, and her color very dead white. Clearly she was very near a breakdown. I found Mrs. Batty, and told her that the young lady had been severely shaken by the storm, suggesting that she had better lie down for a little. Returning with me, the housekeeper led off the unfortunate girl, and Sir William and I were left together. He paced the room impatiently, and constantly inquired if there were any signs of improvement in the weather. He also asked for Warrington, irritably. The burden of the whole dreadful night seemed fallen upon me. Passing through the hall I met Mrs. Batty again. Her usually placid features were disturbed and aghast.

"What is the matter?" I asked. "Is Miss Bosanquet—"

"No, Sir; I think she's sleeping," she replied. "She's in—she is in Mr. Warrington's room."

I started. "Are there no other rooms?" I asked, abruptly.

"There are none ready, Sir, except yours," she answered, "and I thought—"

"You should have taken her there," I said, sharply. The woman looked at me and opened her mouth. "Good heavens!" I said, irritably, "what is the matter? Everyone is mad tonight."

"Alice is gone, Sir," she blurted forth.

Alice, I remembered, was the name of one of her maids.

"What do you mean?" I asked, for her air of panic betokened something graver than her words.

The thunder broke over the house and drowned her voice.

"She can't be out in this storm—she must have taken refuge somewhere," I said.

At that the strings of her tongue loosened, and she burst forth with her tale. It was an abominable narrative.

"Where is Mr. Warrington?" I asked; but she shook her head.

There was a moment's silence between us, and we eyed each other aghast. "She will be all right," I said at last, as if dismissing the subject.

The housekeeper wrung her hands. "I never would have thought it!" she repeated, dismally. "I never would have thought it!"

"There is some mistake," I said; but, somehow, I knew better. Indeed, I felt now that I had almost been prepared for it.

"She ran towards the village," whispered Mrs. Batty. "God knows where she was going! The river lies that way."

"Pooh!" I exclaimed. "Don't talk nonsense. It is all a mistake. Come, have you any brandy?" Brought back to the material round of her duties she bustled away with a sort of briskness, and returned with a flagon and glasses. I took a strong nip, and went back to Sir William. He was feverish, and declaimed against the weather unceasingly. I had to listen to the string of misfortunes which he recounted in the season's crops. It seemed all so futile, with his daughter involved in her horrid tragedy in a neighboring room. He was better after some brandy, and grew more cheerful, but assiduously wondered about Warrington.

"Oh, he's been caught in the storm and taken refuge somewhere," I explained, vainly. I wondered if the next day would ever dawn.

By degrees that thunder rolled slowly into the northern parts of the sky, and only fitful flashes seamed the heavens. It had lasted now more than two hours. Sir William declared his intention of starting, and asked for his daughter. I rang for Mrs. Batty, and sent her to rouse Miss Bosanquet.

Almost immediately there was a knock upon the door, and the housekeeper was in the doorway, with an agitated expression, demanding to see me. Sir William was looking out of the window, and fortunately did not see her.

"Please come to Miss Bosanquet, Sir," she cried, very scared. "Please come at once."

In alarm I hastily ran down the corridor and entered Warrington's room. The girl was lying upon the bed, her hair flowing upon the pillow; her eyes, wide open and filled with terror, stared at the ceiling, and her hands clutched and twined in the coverlet as if in an agony of pain. A gasping sound issued from her, as though she were struggling for breath under suffocation. Her whole appearance was as of one in the murderous grasp of an assailant.

I bent over. "Throw the light, quick," I called to Mrs. Batty; and as I put my hand on her shoulder to lift her, the creature that lived in the chamber rose suddenly from the shadow upon the further side of the bed, and sailed with a flapping noise up to the cornice. With an exclamation of horror I pulled the girl's head forward, and the candle-light glowed on her pallid face. Upon the soft flesh of the slender throat was a round red mark, the size of a florin.

At the sight I almost let her fall upon the pillow again; but, commanding my nerves, I put my arms round her, and, lifting her bodily from the bed, carried her from the room. Mrs. Batty followed.

"What shall we do?" she asked, in a low voice.

"Take her away from this damned chamber!" I cried. "Anywhere—the hall, the kitchen rather."

I laid my burden upon a sofa in the dining-room, and dispatching Mrs. Batty for the brandy, gave Miss Bosanquet a draught. Slowly the horror faded from her eyes; they closed, and then she looked at me.

"What have you?—where am I?" she asked.

"You have been unwell," I said. "Pray don't disturb yourself yet."

She shuddered, and closed her eyes again.

Very little more was said. Sir William pressed for his horses, and as the sky was clearing I made no attempt to detain him, more particularly as the sooner Miss Bosanquet left the Abbey the better for herself. In half an hour she recovered sufficiently to go, and I helped her into the carriage. She never referred to her seizure, but thanked me for my kindness. That was all. No one asked after Warrington—not even Sir William. He had forgotten everything, save his anxiety to get back. As the carriage turned from the steps I saw the mark upon the girl's throat, now grown fainter.

I waited up till late into the morning, but there was no sign of Warrington when I went to bed.

Nor had he made his appearance when I descended to breakfast. A letter in his handwriting, however, and with the London postmark, awaited me. It was a pitiful scrawl, in the very penmanship of which one might trace the desperate emotions by which he was torn. He implored my forgiveness. "Am I a devil?" he asked. "Am I mad? It was not I! It was not I!" he repeated, underlining the sentence with impetuous dashes. "You know," he wrote; "and you know, therefore, that everything is at an end for me. I am going abroad today. I shall never see the Abbey again."

It was well that he had gone, as I hardly think that I could have faced him; and yet I was loth myself to leave the matter in this horrible tangle. I felt that it was enjoined upon me to meet the problems, and I endeavored to do so as best I might. Mrs. Batty gave me news of the girl Alice.

It was bad enough, though not so bad as both of us had feared. I was able to make arrangements on the instant, which I hoped might bury that lamentable affair for the time. There remained Miss Bosanquet; but that difficulty seemed beyond me. I could see no avenue out of the tragedy. I heard nothing save that she was ill—an illness attributed upon all hands to the shock of exposure to the thunderstorm. Only I knew better, and a vague disinclination to fly from the responsibilities of the position kept me hanging on at Utterbourne.

It was in those days before my visit to St. Pharamond that I turned my attention more particularly to the thing which had forced itself relentlessly upon me. I was never a superstitious man; the gossip of old wives interested me merely as a curious and unsympathetic observer. And yet I was vaguely discomfited by the transaction in the Abbey, and it was with some reluctance that I decided to make a further test of Warrington's bedroom. Mrs. Batty received my determination to change my room easily enough, but with a protest as to the dampness of the Stone Chamber. It was plain that her suspicions had not marched with mine. On the second night after Warrington's departure I occupied the room for the first time.

I lay awake for a couple of hours, with a reading lamp by my bed, and a volume of travels in my hand, and then, feeling very tired, put out the light and went to sleep. Nothing distracted me that night; indeed, I slept more soundly and peaceably than before in that house. I rose, too, experiencing quite an exhilaration, and it was not until I was dressing before the glass that I remembered the circumstances of my mission; but then I was at once pulled up, startled swiftly out of my cheerful temper. Faintly visible upon my throat was the same round mark which I had already seen stamped upon Warrington and Miss Bosanquet. With that, all my former doubts returned in force, augmented and militant. My mind recurred to the bat, and tales of bloodsucking by those evil creatures revived in my memory. But when I had remembered that these were of foreign beasts, and that I was in England, I dismissed them lightly enough. Still, the impress of that mark remained, and alarmed me. It could not come by accident; to suppose so manifold a coincidence was absurd. The puzzle dwelt with me, unsolved, and the fingers of dread slowly crept over me.

Yet I slept again in the room. Having but myself for company, and being somewhat bored and dull, I fear I took more spirit than was my custom, and the result was that I again slept profoundly. I awoke about three in the morning, and was surprised to find the lamp still burning.

I had forgotten it in my stupid state of somnolence. As I turned to put it out, the bat swept by me and circled for an instant above my head. So overpowered with torpor was I that I scarcely noticed it, and my head was no sooner at rest than I was once more unconscious. The red mark was stronger next morning, though, as on the previous day, it wore off with the fall of evening.

But I merely observed the fact without any concern; indeed, now the matter of my investigation seemed to have drawn very remote. I was growing indifferent, I supposed, through familiarity.

But the solitude was palling upon me, and I spent a very restless day. A sharp ride I took in the afternoon was the one agreeable experience of the day. I reflected that if this burden were to continue I must hasten up to town. I had no desire to tie myself to Warrington's apron, in his interest. So dreary was the evening, that after I had strolled round the grounds and into the chapel by moonlight, I returned to the library and endeavored to pass the time with Warrington's cards.

But it was poor fun with no antagonist to pit myself against; and I was throwing down the pack in disgust when one of the manservants entered with the whisky.

It was not until long afterwards that I fully realized the course of my action; but even at the time I was aware of a curious sub-feeling of shamefacedness. I am sure that the thing fell naturally, and that there was no awkwardness in my approaching him. Nor, after the first surprise, did he offer any objection. Later he was hardly expected to do so, seeing that he was winning very quickly. The reason of that I guessed afterwards, but during the play I was amazed to note at intervals how strangely my irritation was aroused. Finally, I swept the cards to the floor, and rose, the man, with a smile in which triumph blended with uneasiness, rose also.

"Damn you, get away!" I said, angrily.

True to his traditions to the close, he answered me with respect, and obeyed; and I sat staring at the table. With a sudden flush, the grotesque folly of the night's business came to me, and my eyes fell on the whisky bottle. It was nearly empty. Then I went to bed.

Voices cried all night in that chamber—soft, pleading voices. There was nothing to alarm in them; they seemed in a manner to coo me to sleep. But presently a sharper cry roused me from my semi-slumber; and getting up, I flung open the window. The wind rushed round the Abbey, sweeping with noises against the corners and gables. The black chapel lay still in the moonlight, and drew my eyes. But, resisting a strange, unaccountable impulse to go further, I went back to bed.

The events of the following day are better related without comment.

At breakfast I found a letter from Sir William Bosanquet, inviting me to come over to St. Pharamond. I was at once conscious of an eager desire to do so: it seemed somehow as though I had been waiting for this. The visit assumed preposterous proportions, and I was impatient for the afternoon.

Sir William was polite, but not, as I thought, cordial. He never alluded to Warrington, from which I guessed that he had been informed of the breach, and I conjectured also that the invitation extended to me was rather an act of courtesy to a solitary stranger than due to a desire for my company.

Nevertheless, when he presently suggested that I should stay to dinner, I accepted promptly. For, to say the truth, I had not yet seen Miss Bosanquet, and I experienced a strange curiosity to do so. When at last she made her appearance, I was struck, almost for the first time, by her beauty. She was certainly a handsome girl, though she had a delicate air of ill-health.

After dinner Sir William remembered by accident the book on the Abbey which he had promised to show me, and after a brief hunt in the library we found it. Shortly afterwards he was called away, and with an apology left me. With a curious eagerness I turned the pages of the volume and settled down to read.

It was published early in the century, and purported to relate the history of the Abbey and its owners. But it was one chapter which specially drew my interest—that which recounted the fate of the last Marvyn. The family had become extinct through a bloody tragedy; that fact held me.

The bare narrative, long since passed from the memory of tradition, was here set forth in the baldest statements. The names of Sir Rupert Marvyn and Priscilla, Lady Marvyn, shook me strangely, but particularly the latter. Some links of connection with those gravestones lying in the Abbey chapel constrained me intimately. The history of that evil race was stained and discolored with blood, and the end was in fitting harmony—a lurid holocaust of crime. There had been two brothers, but it was hard to choose between the foulness of their lives. If either, the younger, William, was the worse; so at least the narrative would have it. The details of his excesses had not survived, but it was abundantly plain that they were both notorious gamblers.

The story of their deaths was wrapt in doubt, the theme of conjecture only, and probability; for none was by to observe save the three veritable actors— who were at once involved together in a bloody dissolution. Priscilla, the wife of Sir Rupert, was suspected of an intrigue with her brother-in-law. She would seem to have been tainted with the corruption of the family into which she had married. But according to a second rumor, chronicled by the author, there was some doubt if the woman were not the worst of the three. Nothing was known of her parentage; she had returned with the passionate Sir Rupert to the Abbey after one of his prolonged absences, and was accepted as his legal wife. This was the woman whose infamous beauty had brought a terrible sin between the brothers.

Upon the night which witnessed the extinction of this miserable family, the two brothers had been gambling together. It was known from the high voices that they had quarreled, and it is supposed that, heated with wine and with the lust of play, the younger had thrown some taunt at Sir Rupert in respect to his wife. Whereupon—but this is all conjecture—the elder stabbed him to death. At least, it was understood that at this point the sounds of a struggle were heard, and a bitter cry. The report of the servants ran that upon this noise Lady Marvyn rushed into the room and locked the door behind her. Fright was busy with those servants, long used to the savage manners of the house. According to witnesses, no further sound was heard subsequently to Lady Marvyn's entrance; yet when the doors were at last broken open by the authorities, the three bodies were discovered upon the floor.

How Sir Rupert and his wife met their deaths there was no record. "This tragedy," proceeded the scribe, "took place in the Stone Chamber underneath the stairway."

I had got so far when the entrance of Miss Bosanquet disturbed me. I remember rising in a dazed condition—the room swung about me. A conviction, hitherto resisted and stealthily entertained upon compulsion, now overpowered me.

"I thought my father was here," explained Miss Bosanquet, with a quick glance round the room.

I explained the circumstances, and she hesitated in my neighborhood with a slight air of embarrassment.

"I have not thanked you properly, Mr. Heywood," she said presently, in a low voice, scarcely articulate. "You have been very considerate and kind. Let me thank you now." And ended with a tiny spasmodic sob.

Somehow, an impulse overmastered my tongue. Fresh from the perusal of that chapter, queer possibilities crowded in my mind, odd considerations urged me.

"Miss Bosanquet," said I, abruptly, "let me speak of that a little. I will not touch on details."

"Please," she cried, with a shrinking notion as of one that would retreat in very alarm.

"Nay," said I, eagerly; "hear me. It is no wantonness that would press the memory upon you."

"You have been a witness to distressful acts; you have seen a man under the influence of temporary madness. Nay, even yourself, you have been a victim to the same unaccountable phenomena."

"What do you mean?" she cried, tensely.

"I will say no more," said I. "I should incur your laughter. No, you would not laugh, but my dim suspicions would leave you still incredulous. But if this were so, and if these were the phenomena of a brief madness, surely you would make your memory a grave to bury the past."

"I cannot do that," said she, in low tones.

"What!" I asked. "Would you turn from your lover, aye, even from a friend, because he was smitten with disease? Consider; if your dearest upon earth tossed in a fever upon his bed, and denied you in his ravings, using you despitefully, it would not be he that entreated you so. When he was quit of his madness and returned to his proper person, would you not forget—would you not rather recall his insanity with the pity of affection?"

"I do not understand you," she whispered.

"You read your Bible," said I. "You have wondered at the evil spirits that possessed poor victims. Why should you decide that these things have ceased? We are too dogmatic in our modern world. Who can say under what malign influence a soul may pass, and out of its own custody?"

She looked at me earnestly, searching my eyes.

"You hint at strange things," said she, very low.

But somehow, even as I met her eyes, the spirit of my mission failed me. My gaze, I felt, devoured her ruthlessly. The light shone on her pale and comely features; they burned me with an irresistible attraction. I put forth my hand and took hers gently. It was passive to my touch, as though in acknowledgment of my kindly offices. All the while I experienced a sense of fierce elation. In my blood ran, as it had been fire, a horrible incentive, and I knew that I was holding her hand very tightly. She herself seemed to grow conscious of this, for she made an effort to withdraw her fingers, at which, the passion rushing through my body, I clutched them closer, laughing aloud. I saw a wondering look dawn in her eyes, and her bosom thinly veiled, heaved with a tiny tremor. I was aware that I was drawing her steadily to me. Suddenly her bewildered eyes, dropping from my face, lit with a flare of terror, and, wrenching her hand away, she fell back with a cry, her gaze riveted upon my throat.

"That accursed mark! What is it? What is it?—" she cried, shivering from head to foot.

In an instant, the wild blood singing in my head, I sprang towards her. What would have followed I know not, but at that moment the door opened and Sir William returned. He regarded us with consternation; but Miss Bosanquet had fainted, and the next moment he was at her side. I stood near, watching her come to with a certain nameless fury, as of a beast cheated of its prey.

Sir William turned to me, and in his most courteous manner begged me to excuse the untoward scene. His daughter, he said, was not at all strong, and he ended by suggesting that I should leave them for a time.

Reluctantly I obeyed, but when I was out of the house, I took a sudden panic. The demoniac possession lifted, and in a craven state of trembling I saddled my horse, and rode for the Abbey as if my life depended upon my speed.

I arrived at about ten o'clock, and immediately gave orders to have my bed prepared in my old room. In my shaken condition the sinister influences of that stone chamber terrified me; and it was not until I had drunk deeply that I regained my composure.

But I was destined to get little sleep. I had steadily resolved to keep my thoughts off the matter until the morning, but the spell of the chamber was strong upon me. I awoke after midnight with an irresistible feeling drawing me to the room. I was conscious of the impulse, and combated it, but in the end succumbed; and throwing on my clothes, took a light and went downstairs. I flung wide the door of the room and peered in, listening, as though for some voice of welcome. It was as silent as a sepulcher; but directly I crossed the threshold voices seemed to surround and coax me. I stood wavering, with a curious fascination upon me. I knew I could not return to my own room, and I now had no desire to do so. As I stood, my candle flaring solemnly against the darkness, I noticed upon the floor in an alcove bare of carpet, a large black mark, which appeared to be a stain. Bending down, I examined it, passing my fingers over the stone. It moved to my touch. Setting the candle upon the floor, I put my fingertips to the edges, and pulled hard. As I did so the sounds that were ringing in my ears died instantaneously; the next moment the slab turned with a crash, and discovered a gaping hole of impenetrable blackness.

The patch of chasm thus opened to my eyes was near a yard square. The candle held to it shed a dim light upon a stone step a foot or two below, and it was clear to me that a stairway communicated with the depths. Whether it had been used as a cellar in times gone by I could not divine, but I was soon to determine this doubt; for, stirred by a strange eagerness, I slipped my legs through the hole, and let myself cautiously down with the light in my hand. There were a dozen steps to descend ere I reached the floor and what turned out to be a narrow passage. The vault ran forward straight as an arrow before my eyes, and slowly I moved on. Dank and chill was the air in those close confines, and the sound of my feet returned from those walls dull and sullen. But I kept on, and, with infinite care, must have penetrated quite a hundred yards along that musty corridor ere I came out upon an ampler chamber. Here the air was freer, and I could perceive with the aid of my light that the dimensions of the place were lofty. Above, a solitary ray of moonlight, sliding through a crack, informed me that I was not far from the level of the earth. It fell upon a block of stone, which rose in the middle of the vault, and which I now inspected with interest. As the candle threw its flickering beams upon this I realized where I was.

I scarcely needed the rude lettering upon the coffins to acquaint me that here was the family vault of the Marvyns. And now I began to perceive upon all sides whereon my feeble light fell the crumbling relics of the forgotten dead—coffins fallen into decay, bones and grinning skulls resting in corners, disposed by the hand of chance and time. This formidable array of the mortal remains of that poor family moved me to a shudder. I turned from those ugly memorials once more to the central altar where the two coffins rested in this sombre silence. The lid had fallen from the one, disclosing to my sight the grisly skeleton of a man, that mocked and leered at me.

It seemed in a manner to my fascinated eyes to challenge my mortality, inviting me too to the rude and grotesque sleep of death. I knew, as by an instinct, that I was standing by the bones of Sir Rupert Marvyn, the protagonist in that terrible crime which had locked three souls in eternal ruin. The consideration of this miserable spectacle held me motionless for some moments, and then I moved a step closer and cast my light upon the second coffin.

As I did so I was aware of a change within myself. The grave and melancholy thoughts which I had entertained, the sober bent of my solemn reflections, gave place instantly to a strange exultation, an unholy sense of elation. My pulse swung feverishly, and, while my eyes were riveted upon the tarnished silver of the plate, I stretched forth a tremulously eager hand and touched the lid. It rattled gently under my fingers. Disturbed by the noise, I hastily withdrew them; but whether it was the impetus offered by my touch, or through some horrible and nameless circumstance—God knows—slowly and softly a gap opened between the lid and the body of the coffin! Before my startled eyes the awful thing happened, and yet I was conscious of no terror, merely of surprise and—it seems terrible to admit—of a feeling of eager expectancy.

The lid rose slowly on the one side, and as it lifted the dark space between it and the coffin grew gently charged with light. At that moment my feeble candle, which had been gradually diminishing, guttered and flickered. I seemed to catch a glimpse of something, as it were, of white and shining raiment inside the coffin; and then came a rush of wings and a whirring sound within the vault. I gave a cry, and stepping back missed my foothold; the guttering candle was jerked from my grasp, and I fell prone to the floor in darkness. The next moment a sheet of flame flashed in the chamber and lit up the grotesque skeletons about me; and at the same time a piercing cry rang forth. Jumping to my feet, I gave a dazed glance at the conflagration. The whole vault was in flames. Dazed and horror-struck, I rushed blindly to the entrance; but as I did so the horrible cry pierced my ears again, and I saw the bat swoop round and circle swiftly into the flames. Then, finding the exit, I dashed with all the speed of terror down the passage, groping my way along the walls, and striking myself a dozen times in my terrified flight.

Arrived in my room, I pushed over the stone and listened. Not a sound was audible. With a white face and a body torn and bleeding I rushed from the room, and locking the door behind me, made my way upstairs to my bedroom. Here I poured myself out a stiff glass of brandy.

It was six months later ere Warrington returned. In the meantime he had sold the Abbey. It was inevitable that he should do so; and yet the new owner, I believe, has found no drawback in his property, and the Stone Chamber is still used for a bedroom upon occasions, being considered very old-fashioned. But there are some facts against which no appeal is possible, and so it was in his case. In my relation of the tragedy I have made no attempt at explanation, hardly even to myself; and it appears now for the first time in print, of course with suppositious names.

THE WOMAN WITH THE "OILY EYES"

J. E. Muddock

(WRITING AS DICK DONOVAN)

first published in *Tales of Terror* (1899)

The Story as Told by Dr. Peter Haslar, F.R.C.S. Lond.

Although often urged to put into print the remarkable story which follows I have always strenuously refused to do so, partly on account of personal reasons and partly out of respect for the feelings of the relatives of those concerned. But after much consideration I have come to the conclusion that my original objections can no longer be urged. The principal actors are dead. I myself am well stricken in years, and before very long must pay the debt of nature which is exacted from everything that lives.

Although so long a time has elapsed since the grim tragedy I am about to record, I cannot think of it even now without a shudder. The story of the life of every man and woman is probably more or less a tragedy, but nothing I have ever heard of can compare in ghastly, weird horror with all the peculiar circumstances of the case in point. Most certainly I would never have put pen to paper to record it had it not been from a sense of duty. Long years ago certain garbled versions crept into the public journals, and though at the time I did not consider it desirable to contradict them, I do think now that the moment has come when I, the only living being fully acquainted with the facts, should make them known, otherwise lies will become history, and posterity will accept it as truth. But there is still another reason I may venture to advance for breaking the silence of years. I think in the interest of science the case should be recorded. I have not always held this view, but when a man bends under the weight of years, and he sniffs the mould of his grave, his ideas undergo a complete change, and the opinions of his youth are not the opinions of his old age. There may be exceptions to this, but I fancy they must be very few. With these preliminary remarks I will plunge at once into my story.

It was the end of August 1857 that I acted as best man at the wedding of my friend Jack Redcar, C.E. It was a memorable year, for our hold on our magnificent Indian Empire had nearly been shaken loose by a mutiny which had threatened to spread throughout the whole of India. At the beginning of 1856 I had returned home from India after a three years' spell. I had gone out as a young medico in the service of the H.E.I.C., but my health broke down and I was compelled to resign my appointment. A year later my friend Redcar, who had also been in the Company's service as a civil engineer, came back to England, as his father had recently died and left him a modest fortune. Jack was not only my senior in years, but I had always considered him my superior in every respect. We were at a public school together, and both went up to Oxford, though not together, for he was finishing his final year when I was a freshman.

Although erratic and a bit wild he was a brilliant fellow; and while I was considered dull and plodding, and found some difficulty in mastering my subjects, there was nothing he tackled that he failed to succeed in, and come out with flying colors. In the early stage of our acquaintance he made me his fag, and patronized me, but that did not last long. A friendship sprang up. He took a great liking to me, why I know not; but it was reciprocated, and when he got his Indian appointment I resolved to follow, and by dint of hard work, and having a friend at court, I succeeded in obtaining my commission in John Company's service. Jack married Maude Vane Tremlett, as sweet a woman as ever drew God's breath of life. If I attempted to describe her in detail I am afraid it might be considered that I was exaggerating, but briefly I may say she was the perfection of physical beauty. Jack himself was an exceptionally fine fellow. A brawny giant with a singularly handsome face. At the time of his wedding he was thirty or thereabouts, while Maude was in her twenty-fifth year. There was a universal opinion that a better matched couple had never been brought together. He had a masterful nature; nevertheless was kind, gentle, and manly to a degree.

It may be thought that I speak with some bias and prejudice in Jack's favor, but I can honestly say that at the time I refer to he was as fine a fellow as ever figured as hero in song or story. He was the pink of honor, and few who really knew him but would have trusted him with their honor, their fortunes, their lives. This may be strong, but I declare it's true, and I am the more anxious to emphasize it because his after life was in such marked contrast, and he presents a study in psychology that is not only deeply interesting, but extraordinary.

The wedding was a really brilliant affair, for Jack had troops of friends, who vied with each other in marking the event in a becoming manner, while his bride was idolized by a doting household. Father and mother, sisters and brothers, worshipped her. She was exceedingly well connected. Her father held an important Government appointment, and her mother came from the somewhat celebrated Yorkshire family of the Kingscotes. Students of history will remember that a Colonel Kingscote figured prominently and honorably as a royalist during the reign of the unfortunate Charles I.

No one who was present on that brilliant August morning of 1857, when Jack Redcar was united in the bonds of wedlock to beautiful Maude Tremlett, would have believed it possible that such grim and tragic events would so speedily follow. The newly-married pair left in the course of the day for the Continent, and during their honeymoon I received several charming letters from Jack, who was not only a diligent correspondent, but he possessed a power of description and a literary style that made his letters delightful reading. Another thing that marked this particular correspondence was the unstinted—I may almost say florid—praise he bestowed upon his wife. To illustrate what I mean, here is a passage from one of his letters:—

> "I wish I had command of language sufficiently eloquent to speak of my darling Maude as she should be spoken of. She has a perfectly angelic nature; and though it may be true that never a human being was yet born without faults, for the life of me I can find none in my sweet wife. Of course you will say, old chap, that this is honeymoon gush, but, upon my soul, it isn't. I am only doing scant justice to the dear woman who has linked her fate with mine. I have sometimes wondered what I have done that the gods should have blest me in such a manner. For my own part, I don't think I was deserving of so much happiness, and I assure you I am happy—perfectly, deliciously happy. Will it last? Yes, I am sure it will. Maude will always be to me what she is now, a flawless woman; a woman with all the virtues that turn women into angels, and without one of the weaknesses or one of the vices which too often mar an otherwise perfect feminine character. I hope, old boy, that if ever you marry, the woman you choose will be only half as good as mine."

Had such language been used by anyone else I might have been disposed to add a good deal more than the proverbial pinch of salt before swallowing it. But, as a matter of fact, Jack was not a mere gusher. He had a thoroughly practical, as distinguished from a sentimental, mind, and he was endowed with exceptionally keen powers of observation. And so, making all the allowances for the honeymoon romance, I was prepared to accept my friend's statement as to the merits of his wife without a quibble. Indeed, I knew her to be a most charming lady, endowed with many of the qualities which give the feminine nature its charm. But I would even go a step farther than that, and declare that Mrs. Redcar was a woman in ten thousand. At that time I hadn't a doubt that the young couple were splendidly matched, and it seemed to me probable that the future that stretched before them was not likely to be disturbed by any of the commonplace incidents which seem inseparable from most lives. I regarded Jack as a man of such high moral worth that his wife's happiness was safe in his keeping. I pictured them leading an ideal, poetical life—a life freed from all the vulgar details which blight the careers of so many people—a life which would prove a blessing to themselves as well as a joy to all with whom they had to deal.

When they started on their tour Mr. and Mrs. Redcar anticipated being absent from England for five or six weeks only, but for several reasons they were induced to prolong their travels, and thus it chanced I was away when they returned shortly before Christmas of the year of their marriage. My own private affairs took me to America. As a matter of fact a relative had died leaving me a small property in that country, which required my personal attention; the consequence was I remained out of England for nearly three years.

For the first year or so Jack Redcar wrote to me with commendable regularity. I was duly apprised of the birth of a son and heir. This event seemed to put the crown upon their happiness; but three months later came the first note of sorrow. The baby died, and the doting parents were distracted. Jack wrote:—

"My poor little woman is absolutely prostrated, but I tell her we were getting too happy, and this blow has been dealt to remind us that human existence must be checkered in order that we may appreciate more fully the supreme joy of that after-life which we are told we may gain for the striving. This, of course, is a pretty sentiment, but the loss of the baby mite has hit me hard. Still, Maude is left to me, and she is such a splendid woman, that I ought to feel I am more than blest."

This was the last letter I ever received from Jack, but his wife wrote at odd times. Hers were merely gossipy little chronicles of passing events, and singularly enough she never alluded to her husband, although she wrote in a light, happy vein. This set me wondering, and when I answered her I never failed to inquire about her husband. I continued to receive letters from her, though at long intervals, down to the month of my departure from America, two years later.

I arrived in London in the winter, and an awful winter. London was indeed a city of dreadful night. Gloom and fog were everywhere. Everybody one met looked miserable and despondent. Into the public houses and gin palaces such of the poor as could scratch a few pence together crowded for the sake of the warmth and light. But in the streets sights were to be seen which made one doubt if civilization is the blessing we are asked to believe it. Starving men, women and children, soaked and sodden with the soot-laden fog, prowled about in the vain hope of finding food and shelter. But the well-to-do passed them with indifference, too intent on their own affairs, and too wrapped in self-interests to bestow thought upon the great city's pariahs.

Immediately after my arrival I penned a brief note to Jack Redcar, giving him my address, and saying I would take an early opportunity of calling, as I was longing to feel once more the hearty, honest grip of his handshake. A week later a note was put into my hand as I was in the very act of going out to keep an appointment in the city. Recognizing Mrs. Redcar's handwriting I tore open the envelope, and read, with what feelings may be best imagined, the following lines:—

> "For God's sake, come and see me at once. I am heartbroken and am going mad. You are the only friend in the world to whom I feel I can appeal. Come to me, in the name of pity.

> "MAUDE REDCAR."

I absolutely staggered as I read these brief lines, which were so pregnant with mystery, sorrow, and hopelessness. What did it all mean? To me it was like a burst of thunder from a cloudless summer sky. Something was wrong, that was certain; what that something was I could only vaguely guess at. But I resolved not to remain long in suspense. I put off my engagement, important as it was, and hailing a hansom directed the driver to go to Hampstead, where the Redcars had their residence.

The house was detached and stood in about two acres of ground, and I could imagine it being a little Paradise in brilliant summer weather; but it seemed now in the winter murk, as if a heavy pall of sorrow and anguish enveloped it.

I was shown into an exquisitely furnished drawing room by an old and ill-favored woman, who answered my knock at the door. She gave me the impression that she was a sullen, deceptive creature, and I was at a loss to understand how such a woman could have found service with my friends— the bright and happy friends of three years ago. When I handed her my card to convey to Mrs. Redcar she impertinently turned it over, and scrutinized it, and fixed her cold bleared grey eyes on me, so that I was induced to say peremptorily, "Will you be good enough to go to your mistress at once and announce my arrival?"

"I ain't got no mistress," she growled. "I've got a master;" and with this cryptic utterance she left the room.

I waited a quarter of an hour, then the door was abruptly opened, and there stood before me Mrs. Redcar, but not the bright, sweet, radiant little woman of old. A look of premature age was in her face. Her eyes were red with weeping, and had a frightened, hunted expression. I was so astounded that I stood for a moment like one dumbfounded; but as Mrs. Redcar seized my hand and shook it, she gasped in a nervous, spasmodic way:

"Thank God, you have come! My last hope is in you."

Then, completely overcome by emotion, she burst into hysterical sobbing, and covered her face with her handkerchief.

My astonishment was still so great, the unexpected had so completely paralyzed me for the moment, that I seemed incapable of action. But of course this spell quickly passed, and I regained my self-possession.

"How is it I find this change?" I asked. It was a natural question, and the first my brain shaped.

"It's the work of a malignant fiend," she sobbed.

This answer only deepened the mystery, and I began to think that perhaps she was literally mad. Then suddenly, as if she divined my thoughts, she drew her handkerchief from her face, motioned me to be seated, and literally flung herself on to a couch.

"It's an awful story," she said, in a hoarse, hollow voice, "and I look to you, and appeal to you, and pray to you to help me."

"You can rely upon my doing anything that lies in my power," I answered. "But tell me your trouble. How is Jack? Where is he?"

"In her arms, probably," she exclaimed between her teeth; and she twisted her handkerchief up, rope-wise and dragged it backward and forward through her hand with an excess of desperate, nervous energy. Her answer gave me a keynote. She had become a jealous and embittered woman. Jack had swerved from the path of honor, and allowed himself to be charmed by other eyes to the neglect of this woman whom he had described to me as being angelic. Although her beauty was now a little marred by tears and sorrow, she was still very beautiful and attractive, and had she been so disposed she might have taken an army of men captive. She saw by the expression on my face that her remark was not an enigma to me, and she added quickly: "Oh, yes, it's true, and I look to you, doctor, to help me. It is an awful, dreadful story, but, mind you, I don't blame Jack so much; he is not master of himself. This diabolical creature has enslaved him. She is like the creatures of old that one reads about. She is in possession of some devilish power which enables her to destroy men body and soul."

"Good God! This is awful," I involuntarily ejaculated; for I was aghast and horror-stricken at the revelation. Could it be possible that my brilliant friend, who had won golden opinions from all sorts and conditions of men, had fallen from his pedestal to wallow in the mire of sinfulness and deception?

"It is awful," answered Mrs. Redcar. "I tell you, doctor, there is something uncanny about the whole business. The woman is an unnatural woman. She is a she-devil. And from my heart I pity and sorrow for my poor boy."

"Where is he now?" I asked.

"In Paris with her."

"How long has this been going on!"

"Since a few weeks after our marriage."

"Good heavens, you don't say so!"

"You may well look surprised, but it's true. Three weeks after our marriage Jack and I were at Wiesbaden. As we were going downstairs to dinner one evening, we met this woman coming up. A shudder of horror came over me as I looked at her, for she had the most extraordinary eyes I have ever seen. I clung to my husband in sheer fright, and I noted that he turned and looked at her, and she also turned and looked at him.

"'What a remarkable woman,' he muttered strangely, so strangely that it was as if some other voice was using his lips. Then he broke into a laugh, and, passing his arm round my waist, said: 'Why, my dear little woman, I believe you are frightened.'

"'I am,' I said; 'that dreadful creature has startled me more than an Indian cobra would have done.'

"'Well, upon my word,' said Jack, 'I must confess she is a strange-looking being. Did ever you see such eyes? Why, they make one think of the fairy-books and the mythical beings who flit through their pages.'

"During the whole of the dinner-time that woman's face haunted me. It was a strong, hard-featured, almost masculine face, every line of which indicated a nature that was base, cruel, and treacherous. The thin lips, the drawn nostrils, the retreating chin, could never be associated with anything that was soft, gentle, or womanly. But it was the eyes that were the wonderful feature—they absolutely seemed to exercise some magic influence; they were oily eyes that gleamed and glistened, and they seemed to have in them that sinister light which is peculiar to the cobra, and other poisonous snakes. You may imagine the spell and influence they exerted over me when, on the following day, I urged my husband to leave Wiesbaden at once, notwithstanding that the place was glorious in its early autumn dress, and was filled with a fashionable and light-hearted crowd. But my lightest wish then was law to Jack, so that very afternoon we were on our way to Homburg, and it was only when Wiesbaden was miles behind me that I began to breathe freely again.

"We had been in Homburg a fortnight, and the incident of Wiesbaden had passed from my mind, when one morning, as Jack and I were on our way from the Springs, we came face to face with the woman with the oily eyes. I nearly fainted, but she smiled a hideous, cunning, cruel smile, inclined her head slightly in token of recognition, and passed on. I looked at my husband. It seemed to me that he was unusually pale, and I was surprised to see him turn and gaze after her, and she had also turned and was gazing at us. Not a word was uttered by either of us, but I pressed my husband's arm and we walked rapidly away to our apartments.

"'It's strange,' I remarked to Jack as we sat at breakfast, 'that we should meet that awful woman again.'

"Oh, not at all,' he laughed. 'You know at this time of the year people move about from place to place, and it's wonderful how you keep rubbing shoulders with the same set.'

"It was quite true what Jack said, nevertheless, I could not help the feeling that the woman with the oily eyes had followed us to Homburg. If I had mentioned this then it would have been considered ridiculous, for we had only met her once, and had never spoken a word to her. What earthly interest, therefore, could she possibly take in us who were utter strangers to her. But, looked at by the light of after events, my surmise was true. The creature had marked Jack for her victim from the moment we unhappily met on the stairs at Wiesbaden. I tell you, doctor, that that woman is a human ghoul, a vampire, who lives not only by sucking the blood of men, but by destroying their souls."

Mrs. Redcar broke down again at this stage of her narrative, and I endeavored to comfort her; but she quickly mastered her feelings sufficiently to continue her remarkable story.

"Some days later my husband and I moved along with the throng that drifted up and down the promenade listening to the band, when we met a lady whom I had known as a neighbor when I was at home with my parents. We stopped and chatted with her for some time, until Jack asked us to excuse him while he went to purchase some matches at a kiosk; he said he would be by the fountain in ten minutes, and I was to wait for him.

"My lady friend and I moved along and chatted as women will, and then she bade me goodnight as she had to rejoin her friends. I at once hurried to the rendezvous at the fountain, but Jack wasn't there. I waited some time, but still he came not. I walked about impatiently and half frightened, and when nearly three-quarters of an hour had passed I felt sure Jack had gone home, so with all haste I went to our apartments close by, but he was not in, and had not been in. Half distracted, I flew back to the promenade. It was nearly deserted, for the band had gone. As I hurried along, not knowing where to go to, and scarcely knowing what I was doing, I was attracted by a laugh—a laugh I knew. It was Jack's, and proceeding a few yards further I found him sitting on a seat under a linden tree with the woman with the oily eyes.

"'Why, my dear Maude,' he exclaimed, 'wherever have you been to? I've hunted everywhere for you.'

"A great lump came in my throat, for I felt that Jack was lying to me. I really don't know what I said or what I did, but I am conscious in a vague way that he introduced me to the woman, but the only name I caught was that of Annette. It burnt itself into my brain; it has haunted me ever since.

"Annette put out her white hand veiled by a silk net glove through which diamond rings sparkled. I believe I did touch the proffered fingers, and I shuddered, and I heard her say in a silvery voice that was quite out of keeping with her appearance:

"'If I were your husband I should take you to task. Beauty like yours, you know, ought not to go unattended in a place like this.'

"Perhaps she thought this was funny, for she laughed, and then patted me on the shoulder with her fan. But I hated her from that moment—hated her with a hatred I did not deem myself capable of.

"We continued to sit there, how long I don't know. It seemed to me a very long time, but perhaps it wasn't long. When we rose to go the promenade was nearly deserted, only two or three couples remained. The moon was shining brilliantly; the night wind sighed pleasantly in the trees; but the beauty of the night was lost upon me. I felt ill at ease, and, for the first time in my life, unhappy. Annette walked with us nearly to our door. When the moment for parting came she again offered me the tips of her fingers, but I merely bowed frigidly, and shrank from her as I saw her oily eyes fixed upon me.

"'Ta, ta!' she said in her fatal silvery voice; 'keep a watchful guard over your husband, my dear; and you, sir, don't let your beautiful little lady stray from you again, or there will be grief between you.'

"Those wicked words, every one of which was meant to have its effect, was like the poison of asps to me; you may imagine how they stung me when I tell you I was seized with an almost irresistible desire to hurl the full weight of my body at her, and, having thrown her down, trample upon her. She had aroused in me such a feeling of horror that very little more would have begotten in me the desperation of madness, and I might have committed some act which I should have regretted all my life. But bestowing another glance of her basilisk eyes upon me she moved off, and I felt relieved; though, when I reached my room, I burst into hysterical weeping. Jack took me in his arms, and kissed and comforted me, and all my love for him was strong again; as I lay with my head pillowed on his breast I felt once more supremely happy.

"The next day, on thinking the matter over, I came to the conclusion that my suspicions were unjust, my fears groundless, my jealousy stupid, and that my conduct had been rude in the extreme. I resolved, therefore, to be more amiable and polite to Annette when I again met her. But, strangely enough, though we remained in Homburg a fortnight longer we did not meet; but I know now my husband saw her several times.

"Of course, if it had not been for subsequent events, it would have been said that I was a victim of strong hysteria on that memorable night. Men are so ready to accuse women of hysteria because they are more sensitive, and see deeper than men do themselves. But my aversion to Annette from the instant I set eyes upon her, and the inferences I drew, were not due to hysteria, but to that eighth sense possessed by women, which has no name, and of which men know nothing. At least, I mean to say that they cannot understand it."

Again Mrs. Redcar broke off in her narrative, for emotion had got the better of her. I deemed it advisable to wait. Her remarkable story had aroused all my interest, and I was anxious not to lose any connecting link of it, for from the psychological point of view it was a study.

"Of course, as I have begun the story I must finish it to its bitter end," she went on. "As I have told you, I did not see Annette again in Homburg, and when we left all my confidence in Jack was restored, and my love for him was stronger than ever if that were possible. Happiness came back to me. Oh! I was so happy, and thinking I had done a cruel, bitter wrong to Jack in even supposing for a moment that he would be unfaithful to me, I tried by every little artifice a woman is capable of to prove my devotion to him.

"Well, to make a long story short, we continued to travel about for some time, and finally returned home, and my baby was born. It seemed to me then as if God was really too good to me. I had everything in the world that a human being can reasonably want. An angel baby, a brave, handsome husband, ample means, hosts of friends. I was supremely happy. I thanked my Maker for it all every hour of my life. But suddenly amongst the roses the hiss of the serpent sounded. One day a carriage drove up to our door. It brought a lady visitor. She was shown into our drawing-room, and when asked for her name made some excuse to the servant. Of course, I hurried down to see who my caller was, and imagine my horror when on entering the room I beheld Annette.

"'My dear Mrs. Redcar,' she gushingly exclaimed, emphasizing every word, 'I am so delighted to see you again. Being in London, I could not resist the temptation to call and renew acquaintances.'

"The voice was as silvery as ever, and her awful eyes seemed more oily. In my confusion and astonishment I did not inquire how she had got our address; but I know that I refused her proffered hand, and by my manner gave her unmistakably to understand that I did not regard her as a welcome visitor. But she seemed perfectly indifferent. She talked gaily, flippantly. She threw her fatal spell about me. She fascinated me, so that when she asked to see my baby I mechanically rang the bell, and as mechanically told the servant to send the nurse and baby in. When she came, the damnable woman took the child from the nurse and danced him, but he suddenly broke into a scream of terror, so that I rushed forward; but the silvery voice said:

"'Oh, you silly little mother. The baby is all right. Look how quiet he is now.'

"She was holding him at arm's length, and gazing at him with her basilisk eyes, and he was silent. Then she hugged him, and fondled him, and kissed him, and all the while I felt as if my brain was on fire, but I could neither speak nor move a hand to save my precious little baby.

"At last she returned him to his nurse, who at once left the room by my orders, and then Annette kept up a cackle of conversation. Although it did not strike me then as peculiar, for I was too confused to have any clear thought about anything—it did afterwards—she never once inquired about Jack. It happened that he was out. He had gone away early that morning to the city on some important business in which he was engaged.

"At last Annette took herself off, to my intense relief. She said nothing about calling again; she gave no address, and made no request for me to call on her. Even had she done so I should not have called. I was only too thankful she had gone, and I fervently hoped I should never see her again.

"As soon as she had departed I rushed upstairs, for baby was screaming violently. I found him in the nurse's arms, and she was doing her utmost to comfort him. But he refused to be comforted, and I took him and put him to my breast, but he still fought, and struggled, and screamed, and his baby eyes seemed to me to be bulging with horror. From that moment the darling little creature began to sicken. He gradually pined and wasted, and in a few weeks was lying like a beautiful waxen doll in a bed of flowers. He was stiff, and cold, and dead.

"When Jack came home in the evening of the day of Annette's call, and I told him she had been, he did not seem in the least surprised, but merely remarked:

"'I hope you were hospitable to her.'

"I did not answer him, for I had been anything but hospitable. I had not even invited her to partake of the conventional cup of tea.

"As our baby boy faded day by day, Jack seemed to change, and the child's death overwhelmed him. He was never absolutely unkind to me at that period, but he seemed to have entirely altered. He became sullen, silent, even morose, and he spent the whole of his days away from me. When I gently chided him, he replied that his work absorbed all his attention. And so things went on until another thunderbolt fell at my feet.

"One afternoon Jack returned home and brought Annette. He told me that he had invited her to spend a few days with us. When I urged an objection he was angry with me for the first time in our married life. I was at once silenced, for his influence over me was still great, and I thought I would try and overcome my prejudice for Annette. At any rate, as Jack's wife I resolved to be hospitable, and play the hostess with grace. But I soon found that I was regarded as of very little consequence. Annette ruled Jack, she ruled me, she ruled the household.

"You will perhaps ask why I did not rise up in wrath, and, asserting my position and dignity, drive the wicked creature out of my home. But I tell you, doctor, I was utterly powerless. She worked some devil's spell upon me, and I was entirely under the influence of her will.

"Her visit stretched into weeks. Our well-tried and faithful servants left. Others came, but their stay was brief; and at last the old woman who opened the door to you was installed. She is a creature of Annette's, and is a spy upon my movements.

"All this time Jack was under the spell of the charmer, as I was. Over and over again I resolved to go to my friends, appeal to them, tell them everything, and ask them to protect me; but my will failed, and I bore and suffered in silence. And my husband neglected me; he seemed to find pleasure only in Annette's company. Oh, how I fretted and gnawed my heart, and yet I could not break away from the awful life. I tell you, doctor, that that woman possessed some strange, devilish, supernatural power over me and Jack. When she looked at me I shriveled up. When she spoke, her silvery voice seemed to sting every nerve and fibre in my body, and he was like wax in her hands. To me he became positively brutal, and he told me over and over again that I was spoiling his life. But, though she was a repulsive, mysterious, crafty, cruel woman, he seemed to find his happiness in her company.

"One morning, after a restless, horrible, feverish night, I arose, feeling strangely ill, and as if I were going mad. I worked myself up almost to a pitch of frenzy, and, spurred by desperation, I rushed into the drawing-room, where my husband and Annette were together, and exclaimed to her:

"'Woman, do you not see that you are killing me? Why have you come here? Why do you persecute me with your devilish wiles? You must know you are not welcome. You must feel you are an intruder.'

"Overcome by the effort this had cost me, I sank down on the floor on my knees, and wept passionately. Then I heard the silvery voice say, in tones of surprise and injured innocence:

"'Well, upon my word, Mrs. Redcar, this is an extraordinary way to treat your husband's guest. I really thought I was a welcome visitor instead of an intruder; but, since I am mistaken, I will go at once.'

"I looked at her through a blinding mist of tears. I met the gaze of her oily eyes, but only for a moment, as I cowered before her, shrank within myself, and felt powerless again. I glanced at my husband. He was standing with his head bowed, and, as it seemed to me, in a pose of shame and humiliation. But suddenly he darted at me, and I heard him say:

"'What do you mean by creating such a scene as this? You must understand I am master here.' Then he struck me a violent blow on the head, and there was a long blank.

"When I came to my senses I was in bed, and the hideous old hag who opened the door to you was bending over me. It was some little time before I could realize what had occurred. When I did, I asked the woman where Mr. Redcar was, and she answered sullenly:

"'Gone.'

"'And the—Annette; where is she?' I asked.

"'Gone, too,' was the answer.

"Another blank ensued. I fell very ill, and when my brain was capable of coherent thought again I learnt that I had passed through a crisis, and my life had been in jeopardy. A doctor had been attending me, and there was a professional nurse in the house; but she was a hard, dry, unsympathetic woman, and I came to the conclusion—wrongly so, probably—she, too, was one of Annette's creatures.

"I was naturally puzzled to understand why none of my relatives and friends had been to see me, but I was to learn later that many had called, but had been informed I was abroad with my husband, who had been summoned away suddenly in connection with some professional matters. And I also know now that all letters coming for me were at once forwarded to him, and that any requiring answers he answered.

"As I grew stronger I made up my mind to keep my own counsel, and not let any of my friends know of what I had gone through and suffered; for I still loved my husband, and looked upon him as a victim to be pitied and rescued from the infernal wiles of the she-demon. When I heard of your arrival in England, I felt you were the one person in the wide world I could appeal to with safety, for you can understand how anxious I am to avoid a scandal. Will you help me? Will you save your old friend Jack? Restore him to sanity, doctor, and bring him back to my arms again, which will be wide open to receive him."

I listened to poor Mrs. Redcar's story patiently, and at first was disposed to look upon it as a too common tale of human weakness. Jack Redcar had fallen into the power of an adventuress, and had been unable to resist her influence. Such things had happened before, such things will happen again, I argued with myself. There are certain women who seem capable of making men mad for a brief space; but under proper treatment they come to their senses quickly, and blush with shame as they think of their foolishness. At any rate, for the sake of my old friend, and for the sake of his poor suffering little wife, I was prepared to do anything in reason to bring back the erring husband to his right senses.

I told Mrs. Redcar this. I told her I would redress her wrongs if I could, and fight her battle to the death. She almost threw herself at my feet in her gratitude. But when I suggested that I should acquaint her family with the facts, she begged of me passionately not to do so. Her one great anxiety was to screen her husband. One thing, however, I insisted upon. That was, the old woman should be sent away, the house shut up, and that Mrs. Redcar should take apartments in an hotel, so that I might be in touch with her. She demurred to this at first, but ultimately yielded to my persuasion.

Next I went to the old woman. She was a German Suisse—her name was Grebert. I told her to pack up her things and clear out at once. She laughed in my face, and impertinently told me to mind my own business. I took out my watch and said, 'I give you half an hour. If you are not off the premises then, I will call in the police and have you turned out. Any claim you have on Mrs. Redcar, who is the mistress here—shall be settled at once.'

She replied that she did not recognize my authority, that she had been placed there by Mr. Redcar, who was her master, and unless he told her to go she should remain. I made it plain to her that I was determined and would stand no nonsense. Mr. Redcar had taken himself off, I said; Mrs. Redcar was his lawful wife, and I was acting for her and on her behalf.

My arguments prevailed, and after some wrangling the hag came to the conclusion that discretion was the better part of valor, and consented to go providing we paid her twenty pounds. This we decided to do rather than have a scene, but three hours passed before we saw the last of the creature. Mrs. Redcar had already packed up such things as she required, and when I had seen the house securely fastened up I procured a cab, and conveyed the poor little lady to a quiet West End hotel, close to my own residence, so that I could keep a watchful eye upon her.

Of course, this was only the beginning of the task I had set myself, which was to woo back the erring husband, if possible, to his wife's side, and to restore him to the position of happiness, honor, and dignity from which he had fallen. I thought this might be comparatively easy, and little dreamed of the grim events that were to follow my interference.

Three weeks later I was in Paris, and proceeded to the Hotel de l'Univers, where Mrs. Redcar had ascertained through his bankers her husband was staying. But to my chagrin, I found he had departed with his companion, and the address he had given for his letters at the post-office was Potes, in Spain. As I had taken up the running I had no alternative but to face the long, dreary journey in pursuit of the fugitives, or confess defeat at the start.

It is not necessary for me to dwell upon that awful journey in the winter time. Suffice to say I reached my destination in due course.

Potes, it is necessary to explain, is a small town magnificently situated in the Liebana Valley, in the Asturian Pyrenees, under the shadow of Pico de Europa. Now, what struck me as peculiar was the fugitives coming to such a place at that time of the year. Snow lay heavily everywhere. The cold was intense. For what reason had such a spot been chosen? It was a mystery I could not hope to solve just then. There was only one small hotel in the village, and there Annette and Redcar were staying. My first impulse was not to let them know of my presence, but to keep them under observation for a time. I dismissed that thought as soon as formed, for I was not a detective, and did not like the idea of playing the spy. But even had I been so disposed, there would have been a difficulty about finding accommodation. Moreover, it was a small place, and the presence of a foreigner at that time of year must necessarily have caused a good deal of gossip. The result was I went boldly to the hotel, engaged a room, and then inquired for Redcar. I was directed to a private room, where I found him alone. My unexpected appearance startled him, and when he realized who I was, he swore at me, and demanded to know my business.

He had altered so much that in a crowd I really might have had some difficulty in recognizing him. His face wore a drawn, anxious, nervous look, and his eyes had acquired a restless, shifty motion, while his hair was already streaked with grey.

I began to reason with him. I reminded him of our old friendship, and I drew a harrowing picture of the sufferings of his dear, devoted, beautiful little wife.

At first he seemed callous; but presently he grew interested, and when I referred to his wife he burst into tears. Then suddenly he grasped my wrist with a powerful grip, and said:

"Hush! Annette mustn't know this—mustn't hear. I tell you, Peter, she is a ghoul. She sucks my blood. She has woven a mighty spell about me, and I am powerless. Take me away; take me to dear little Maude."

I looked at him for some moments with a keen professional scrutiny, for his manner and strange words were not those of sanity. I determined to take him at his word, and, if possible, remove him from the influence of the wicked siren who had so fatally lured him.

"Yes," I said, "we will go without a moment's unnecessary delay. I will see if a carriage and post-horses are to be had, so that we can drive to the nearest railway station."

He assented languidly to this, and I rose with the intention of making inquiries of the hotel people; but simultaneously with my action the door opened and Annette appeared. Up to that moment I thought that Mrs.

Redcar had exaggerated in describing her, therefore I was hardly prepared to find that so far from the description being an exaggeration, it had fallen short of the fact, Annette was slightly above the medium height, with a well-developed figure, but a face that to me was absolutely repellent. There was not a single line of beauty nor a trace of womanliness in it. It was hard, coarse, cruel, with thin lips drawn tightly over even white teeth. And the eyes were the most wonderful eyes I have ever seen in a human being. Maude was right when she spoke of them as "oily eyes." They literally shone with a strange, greasy lustre, and were capable of such a marvelous expression that I felt myself falling under their peculiar fascination. I am honest and frank enough to say that, had it been her pleasure, I believe she could have lured me to destruction as she had lured my poor friend. But I was forearmed, because forewarned. Moreover, I fancy I had a much stronger will than Redcar. Any way, I braced myself up to conquer and crush this human serpent, for such I felt her to be.

Before I could speak, her melodious voice rang out with the query, addressed to Jack:

"Who is this gentleman? Is he a friend of yours?"

"Yes, yes," gasped Jack, like one who spoke under the influence of a nightmare. She bowed and smiled, revealing all her white teeth, and she held forth her hand to me, a delicately shaped hand, with clear, transparent skin, and her long lithe fingers were bejeweled with diamonds.

I drew myself up, as one does when a desperate effort is needed, and, refusing the proffered hand, I said:

"Madame, hypocrisy and deceit are useless. I am a medical man, my name is Peter Haslar, and Mr. Redcar and I have been friends from youth. I've come here to separate him from your baneful influence and carry him back to his broken-hearted wife. That is my mission. I hope I have made it clear to you?"

She showed not the slightest sign of being disturbed, but smiled on me again, and bowed gracefully and with the most perfect self-possession. And speaking in a soft gentle manner, which was in such startling contrast to the woman's appearance, she said:

"Oh, yes; thank you. But, like the majority of your countrymen, you display a tendency to arrogate too much to yourself. I am a Spaniard myself, by birth, but cosmopolitan by inclination, and, believe me, I do not speak with any prejudice against your nationality, but I have yet to learn, sir, that you have any right to constitute yourself Mr. Redcar's keeper."

Her English was perfect, though she pronounced it with just a slight foreign accent. There was no anger in her tones, no defiance. She spoke softly, silvery, persuasively.

"I do not pretend to be his keeper, madame; I am his sincere friend," I answered. "And surely I need not remind you that he owes a duty to his lawful wife."

During this short conversation Jack had sat motionless on the edge of a couch, his chin resting on his hands, and apparently absorbed with some conflicting thoughts. But Annette turned to him, and, still smiling, said:

"I think Mr. Redcar is quite capable of answering for himself. Stand up, Jack, and speak your thoughts like a man."

Although she spoke in her oily, insidious way, her request was a peremptory command. I realized that at once, and I saw as Jack rose he gazed at her, and her lustrous eyes fixed him. Then he turned upon me with a furious gesture and exclaimed, with a violence of expression that startled me:

"Yes, Annette is right. I am my own master. What the devil do you mean by following me, like the sneak and cur that you are? Go back to Maude, and tell her that I loathe her. Go; relieve me of your presence, or I may forget myself and injure you."

Annette, still smiling and still perfectly self-possessed, said:

"You hear what your friend says, doctor. Need I say that if you are a gentleman you will respect his wishes?"

I could no longer control myself. Her calm, defiant, icy manner maddened me, and her silvery voice seemed to cut down on to my most sensitive nerves, for it was so suggestive of the devilish nature of the creature. It was so incongruous when contrasted with her harsh, horribly cruel face. I placed myself between Jack and her, and meeting her weird gaze, I said, hotly:

"Leave this room. You are an outrage on your sex; a shame and a disgrace to the very name of woman. Go, and leave me with my friend, whose reason you have stolen away."

She still smiled and was still unmoved, and suddenly I felt myself gripped in a grip of iron, and with terrific force I was hurled into a corner of the room, where, huddled up in a heap, I lay stunned for some moments. But as my senses returned I saw the awful woman smiling still, and she was waving her long white bejeweled hand before the infuriated Jack, as if she were mesmerizing him; and I saw him sink on to the sofa subdued and calmed. Then addressing me she said:

"That is a curious way for your friend to display his friendship. I may be wrong, but perhaps as a medical man you will recognize that your presence has an irritating effect on Mr. Redcar, and if I may suggest it, I think it desirable that you should depart at once and see him no more."

"Devil!" I shouted at her. "You have bewitched him, and made him forgetful of his honor and of what he owes to those who are dear to him. But I will defeat you yet."

She merely bowed and smiled, but deigned no reply; and holding her arm to Jack, he took it, and they passed out of the room. She was elegantly attired. Her raven hair was fascinatingly dressed in wavy bands. There was something regal in her carriage, and gracefulness in her every movement; and yet she filled me with a sense of indefinable horror; a dread to which I should have been ashamed to own to a little while ago.

I tried to spring up and go after them, but my body seemed a mass of pain, and my left arm hung limp and powerless. It was fractured below the elbow. There was no bell in the room, and I limped out in search of assistance. I made my way painfully along a gloomy corridor, and hearing a male voice speaking Spanish, I knocked at a door, which was opened by the landlord. I addressed him, but he shook his head and gave me to understand that he spoke no English. Unhappily I spoke no Spanish. Then he smiled as some idea flitted through his mind, and bowing me into the room he motioned me to be seated, and hurried away. He returned in about five minutes accompanied by Annette, whom he had brought to act as interpreter. I was almost tempted to fly at her and strangle her where she stood. She was undisturbed, calm, and still smiled. She spoke to the man in Spanish, then she explained to me that she had told him I had slipped on the polished floor, and falling over a chair had injured myself, and she had requested him to summon the village surgeon if need be.

Without waiting for me to reply she swept gracefully out of the room. Indeed, I could not reply, for I felt as if I were choking with suppressed rage. The landlord rendered me physical assistance and took me to my bedroom, where I lay down on the bed, feeling mortified, ill, and crushed. Half an hour later a queer-looking old man, with long hair twisted into ringlets, was ushered into my room, and I soon gathered that he was the village surgeon. He spoke no English, but I explained my injury by signs, and he went away, returning in a little while with the necessary bandages and splints, and he proceeded rather clumsily to bandage my broken arm. I passed a cruel and wretched night. My physical pain was great, but my mental pain was greater. The thought forced itself upon me that I had been defeated, and that the fiendish, cunning woman was too much for me. I felt no resentment against Jack. His act of violence was the act of a madman, and I pitied him. For hours I lay revolving all sorts of schemes to try and get him away from the diabolical influence of Annette. But though I could hit upon nothing, I firmly resolved that while my life lasted I would make every effort to save my old friend, and if possible restore him to the bosom of his distracted wife.

The case altogether was a very remarkable one, and the question naturally arose, why did a man so highly gifted and so intelligent as Jack Redcar desert his charming, devoted, and beautiful wife, to follow an adventuress who entirely lacked physical beauty. Theories without number might have been suggested to account for the phenomenon, but not one would have been correct. The true answer is, Annette was not a natural being. In the ordinary way she might be described as a woman of perverted moral character, or as a physiological freak, but that would have been rather a misleading way of putting it. She was, in short, a human monstrosity. By that I do not mean to say her body was contorted, twisted, or deformed. But into her human composition had entered a strain of the fiend; and I might go even further than this and say she was more animal than human. Though in whatever way she may be described, it is certain she was an anomaly—a human riddle.

The morning following the outrage upon me found me prostrated and ill. A night of racking pain and mental distress had told even upon my good constitution. The situation in which I found myself was a singularly unfortunate one. I was a foreigner in an out-of-the-way place, and my want of knowledge of Spanish, of course, placed me at a tremendous disadvantage.

The landlord came to me and brought his wife, and between them they attended to my wants, and did what they could for my comfort. But they were ignorant, uncultivated people, only one remove from the peasant class, and I realized that they could be of little use to me. Now the nearest important town to this Alpine village was Santander, but that was nearly a hundred miles away. As everyone knows who has been in Spain, a hundred miles, even on a railway, is a considerable journey; but there was no railway between Santander and Potes. An old ramshackle vehicle, called a diligence, ran between the two places every day in the summer and twice a week in the winter, and it took fourteen hours to do the journey. Even a well-appointed carriage and pair could not cover the distance under eight hours, as the road was infamous, and in parts was little better than a mule track. I knew that there was a British consul in Santander, and I was hopeful that if I could communicate with him he might be able to render me some assistance. In the meantime I had to devise some scheme for holding Annette in check and saving my friend. But in my crippled and prostrate condition I could not do much. While lying in my bed, and thus revolving all these things in my mind, the door gently opened and Annette glided in—"glided" best expresses her movement, for she seemed to put forth no effort. She sat down beside the bed and laid her hand on mine.

"You are ill this morning," she said softly. "This is regrettable, but you have only yourself to blame. It is dangerous to interfere in matters in which you have no
concern. My business is mine, Mr. Redcar's is his, and yours is your own, but the three won't amalgamate. Jack and I came here for the sake of the peace and quietness of these solitudes; unhappily you intrude yourself and disaster follows."

Her voice was as silvery as ever. The same calm self-possessed air characterized her; but in her oily eyes was a peculiar light, and I had to turn away, for they exerted a sort of mesmeric influence over me, and I am convinced that had I not exerted all my will power I should have thrown myself into the creature's arms. This is a fact which I have no hesitation in stating, as it serves better than any other illustration to show what a wonderful power of fascination the remarkable woman possessed. Naturally I felt disgusted and enraged, but I fully recognized that I could not fight the woman openly; I must to some extent meet her with her own weapons. She was cunning, artful, insidious, pitiless, and the basilisk-like power she possessed not only gave her a great advantage but made her a very dangerous opponent. At any rate, having regard to all the circumstances and my crippled condition, I saw that my only chance was in temporizing with her. So I tried to reason with her, and I pointed out that Redcar had been guilty of baseness in leaving his wife, who was devoted to him.

At this point of my argument Annette interrupted me, and for the first time she displayed something like passion, and her voice became hard and raucous.

"His wife," she said with a sneer of supreme contempt. "A poor fool, a fleshly doll. At the precise instant I set my eyes upon her for the first time I felt that I should like to destroy her, because she is a type of woman who make the world commonplace and reduce all men to a common level. She hated me from the first and I hated her. She would have crushed me if she could, but she was too insignificant a worm to do that, and I crushed her."

This cold, brutal callousness enraged me; I turned fiercely upon her and exclaimed:

"Leave me, you are a more infamous and heartless wretch than I believed you to be. You are absolutely unworthy the name of woman, and if you irritate me much more I may even forget that you have a woman's shape."

She spoke again. All trace of passion had disappeared. She smiled the wicked insidious smile which made her so dangerous, and her voice resumed its liquid, silvery tones:

"You are very violent," she said gently, "and it will do you harm in your condition. But you see violence can be met with violence. The gentleman you are pleased to call your friend afforded you painful evidence last night that he knows how to resent unjustifiable interference, and to take care of himself. I am under his protection, and there is no doubt he will protect me."

"For God's sake, leave me!" I cried, tortured beyond endurance by her hypocrisy and wickedness.

"Oh, certainly, if you desire it," she answered, as she rose from her seat. "But I thought I might be of use. It is useless your trying to influence Mr. Redcar—absolutely useless. His destiny is linked with mine, and the human being doesn't exist who can sunder us. With this knowledge, you will do well to retrace your steps; and, if you like, I will arrange to have you comfortably conveyed to Santander, where you can get a vessel. Anyway, you will waste your time and retard your recovery by remaining here."

"I intend to remain here, nevertheless," I said, with set teeth. "And, what is more, madame, when I go my friend Redcar will accompany me."

She laughed. She patted my head as a mother might pat the head of her child. She spoke in her most insidious, silvery tones.

"We shall see, *mon cher*—we shall see. You will be better tomorrow. Adieu!"

That was all she said, and she was gone. She glided out of the room as she had glided in.

I felt irritated almost into madness for some little time; but as I reflected, it was forced upon me that I had to deal with a monster of iniquity, who had so subdued the will of her victim, Redcar, that he was a mere wooden puppet in her hand. Force in such a case was worse than useless. What I had to do was to try and circumvent her, and I tried to think out some plan of action. All that day I was compelled to keep my bed, and, owing to the clumsy way in which my arm had been bandaged, I suffered intolerable pain, and had to send for the old surgeon again to come and help me to reset the fracture. I got some ease after that, and a dose of chloral sent me to sleep, which continued for many hours. When I awoke I managed to summon the landlord, and he brought me food, and a lantern containing a candle so that I might have light. And, in compliance with my request, he made me a large jug of lemonade, in order that I could have a drink in the night, for I was feverish, and my throat was parched. He had no sooner left the room than Annette entered to inquire if she could do anything for me. I told her that I had made the landlord understand all that I desired, and he would look after me, so she wished me goodnight and left. Knowing as I did that sleep was very essential in my case, I swallowed another, though smaller, dose of chloral, and then there was a blank.

How long I slept I really don't know; but suddenly, in a dazed sort of way, I saw a strange sight. The room I occupied was a long, somewhat meagerly furnished, one. The entrance door was at the extreme end, opposite the bed. Over the doorway hung a faded curtain of green velvet. By the feeble light of the candle lantern I saw this curtain slowly pulled on one side by a white hand; then a face peered in; next Annette entered. Her long hair was hanging down her back, and she wore a nightdress a soft, clinging substance, which outlined her figure. With never a sound she moved lightly towards the bed, and waved her hand two or three times over my face. I tried to move, to utter a sound, but couldn't; and yet what I am describing was no dream, but a reality. Slightly bending over me, she poured from a tiny phial she carried in the palm of her hand a few drops of a slightly acrid, burning liquid right into my mouth, and at that instant, as I believe, it seemed to me as if a thick, heavy pall fell over my eyes, for all was darkness.

I awoke hours later. The winter sun was shining brightly into my room. I felt strangely languid, and had a hot, stinging sensation in my throat. I felt my pulse, and found it was only beating at the rate of fifty-eight beats in the minute. Then I recalled the extraordinary incident of the previous night, which, had it not been for my sensations, I might have regarded as a bad dream, the outcome of a disturbed state of the brain. But as it was, I hadn't a doubt that Annette had administered some subtle and slow poison to me. My medical knowledge enabled me to diagnose my own case so far, that I was convinced I was suffering from the effects of a potent poisonous drug, the action of which was to lower the action of the vital forces and weaken the heart. Being probably cumulative, a few doses more or less, according to the strength of the subject, and the action of the heart would be so impeded that the organ would cease to beat. Although all this passed through my brain, I felt so weak and languid that I had neither energy nor strength to arouse myself, and when the landlord brought me in some food I took no notice of him. I knew that this symptom of languor and indifference was very characteristic of certain vegetable poisons, though what it was Annette had administered to me I could not determine.

Throughout that day I lay in a drowsy, dreamy state. At times my brain was clear enough, and I was able to think and reason; but there were blanks, marked, no doubt, by periods of sleep.

When night came I felt a little better, and I found that the heart's action had improved. It was steadier, firmer, and the pulse indicated sixty-two beats. Now I had no doubt that if it was Annette's intention to bring about my death slowly she would come again that night, and arousing myself as well as I could, and summoning all my will power, I resolved to be on the watch. During the afternoon I had drunk milk freely, regarding it as an antidote, and when the landlord visited me for the last time that evening I made him understand that I wanted a large jug of milk fresh from the cow, if he could get it. He kept cows of his own; they were confined in a chalet on the mountain side, not far from his house, so that he was able to comply with my request. I took a long draught of this hot milk, which revived my energies wonderfully, and then I waited for developments. I had allowed my watch to run down, consequently I had no means of knowing the time. It was a weary vigil, lying there lonely and ill, and struggling against the desire for sleep.

By-and-by I saw the white hand lift the curtain again, and Annette entered, clad as she was on the previous night.

When she came within reach of me I sprang up in the bed and seized her wrist.

"What do you want here?" I demanded angrily. "Do you mean to murder me?"

Her imperturbability was exasperating. She neither winced nor cried out, nor displayed the slightest sign of surprise. She merely remarked in her soft cooing voice, her white teeth showing as her thin lips parted in a smile:

"You are evidently restless and excited tonight, and it is hardly generous of you to treat my kindly interest in such a way."

"Kindly interest!" I echoed with a sneer, as, releasing her wrist, I fell back on the bed.

"Yes; you haven't treated me well, and you are an intruder here. Nevertheless, as you are a stranger amongst strangers, and cannot speak the language of the country, I would be of service to you if I could. I have come to see if you have everything you require for the night."

"And you did the same last night," I cried in hot anger, for, knowing her infamy and wickedness, I could not keep my temper.

"Certainly," she answered coolly; "and I found you calmly dozing, so left you."

"Yes—after you had poured poison down my throat," I replied.

She broke into a laugh—a rippling laugh, with the tinkle of silver in it—and she seemed hugely amused.

"Well, well," she said; "it is obvious, sir, you are not in a fit state to be left alone. Your nerves are evidently unstrung, and you are either the victim of a bad dream or some strange delusion. But there, there; I will pardon you. You are not responsible just at present for your language."

As she spoke she passed her soft white hand over my forehead. There was magic in her touch, and it seemed as if all my will had left me, and there stole over me a delightful sense of dreamy languor. I looked at her, and I saw her strange eyes change color. They became illumined, as it were, by a violet light that fascinated me so that I could not turn from her. Indeed, I was absolutely subdued to her will now. Everything in the room faded, and I saw nothing but those marvelous eyes glowing with violet light which seemed to fill me with a feeling of ecstasy. I have a vague idea that she kept passing her hand over my face and forehead; that she breathed upon my face; then that she pressed her face to mine, and I felt her hot breath in my neck.

Perhaps it will be said that I dreamed all this. I don't believe it was a dream. I firmly and honestly believe that every word I have written is true.

Hours afterwards my dulled brain began to awake to things mundane. The morning sun was flooding the room, and I was conscious that somebody stood over me, and soon I recognized the old surgeon, who had come to see that the splints and bandages had not shifted. I felt extraordinarily weak, and I found that my pulse was beating very slowly and feebly. Again I had the burning feeling in the throat and a strange and absolutely indescribable sensation at the side of the neck. The old doctor must have recognized that I was unusually feeble, for he went to the landlord, and returned presently with some cognac which he made me swallow, and it picked me up considerably.

After his departure I lay for some time, and tried to give definite shape to vague and dreadful thoughts that haunted me, and filled me with a shrinking horror. That Annette was a monster in human form I hadn't a doubt, and I felt equally certain that she had designs upon my life. That she had now administered poison to me on two occasions seemed to me beyond question, but I hesitated to believe that she was guilty of the unspeakable crime which my sensations suggested.

At last, unable longer to endure the tumult in my brain, I sprang out of bed, rushed to the looking-glass, and examined my neck. I literally staggered back, and fell prostrate on the bed, overcome by the hideous discovery I had made. It had the effect, however, of calling me back to life and energy, and I made a mental resolution that I would, at all hazards, save my friend, though I clearly recognized how powerless I was to cope with the awful creature single-handed.

I managed to dress myself, not without some difficulty; then I summoned the landlord, and made him understand that I must go immediately to Santander at any cost. My intention was to invoke the aid of the consul there. But the more I insisted, the more the old landlord shook his head. At length, in desperation, I rushed from the house, hoping to find somebody who understood French or English. As I almost ran up the village street I came face to face with a priest. I asked him in English if he spoke my language, but he shook his head. Then I tried him with French, and to my joy he answered me that he understood a little French. I told him of my desire to start for Santander that very day, but he said that it was impossible, as, owing to the unusual hot sun in the day time there had been a great melting of snow, with the result that a flooded river had destroyed a portion of the road; and though a gang of men had been set to repair it, it would be two or three days before it was passable.

"But is there no other way of going?" I asked.

"Only by a very hazardous route over the mountains," he answered. And he added that the risk was so great it was doubtful if anyone could be found who would act as guide. "Besides," he went on, "you seem very ill and weak. Even a strong man might fail, but you would be certain to perish from exhaustion and exposure."

I was bound to recognize the force of his argument. It was a maddening disappointment, but there was no help for it. Then it occurred to me to take the old priest into my confidence and invoke his aid. Though, on second thoughts, I hesitated, for was it not possible—nay, highly probable—that if I told the horrible story he and others would think I was mad? Annette was a Spanish woman, and it was feasible to suppose she would secure the ear of those ignorant villagers sooner than I should. No, I would keep the ghastly business to myself for the present at any rate, and wait with such patience as I could command until I could make the journey to Santander. The priest promised me that on the morrow he would let me know if the road was passable, and, if so, he would procure me a carriage and make all the preparations for the journey. So, thanking him for his kindly services, I turned towards the hotel again. As I neared the house I observed two persons on the mountain path that went up among the pine trees. The sun was shining brilliantly; the sky was cloudless, the air crisp and keen. The two persons were Annette and Redcar. I watched them for some minutes until they were lost to sight amongst the trees.

Suddenly an irresistible impulse to follow them seized me. Why I know not. Indeed, had I paused to reason with myself it would have seemed to me then a mad act, and that I was risking my life to no purpose. But I did not reason. I yielded to the impulse, though first of all I went to my room, put on a thicker pair of boots, and armed myself with a revolver which I had brought with me. During my extensive traveling about America a revolver was a necessity, and by force of habit I put it up with my clothes when packing my things in London for my Continental journey.

Holding the weapon between my knees, I put a cartridge in each barrel, and, providing myself with a stick in addition, I went forth again and began to climb the mountain path. I was by no means a sanguinary man; even my pugnacity could only be aroused after much irritation. Nevertheless, I knew how to defend myself, and in this instance, knowing that I had to deal with a woman who was capable of any crime, and who, I felt sure, would not hesitate to take my life if she got the chance, I deemed it advisable to be on my guard against any emergency that might arise. As regards Redcar, he had already given me forcible and painful evidence that he could be dangerous; but I did not hold him responsible for his actions. I regarded him as being temporarily insane owing to the infernal influence the awful woman exercised over him. Therefore it would only have been in the very last extremity that I should have resorted to lethal weapons as a defense against him. My one sole aim, hope, desire, prayer, was to rescue him from the spell that held him in thrall and restore him to his wife, his honor, his sanity. With respect to Annette, it was different. She was a blot on nature, a disgrace to humankind, and, rather than let her gain complete ascendency over me and my friend, I would have shot her if I had reason to believe she contemplated taking my life. It might have involved me in serious trouble with the authorities at first, for in Spain the foreigner can hope but for little justice. I was convinced, however, that ultimately I should be exonerated.

Such were the thoughts that filled my mind as I painfully made my way up the steep mountainside. My fractured arm was exceedingly painful. Every limb in my body ached, and I was so languid, so weak that it was with difficulty I dragged myself along. But worse than all this was an all but irresistible desire to sleep, the result, I was certain, of the poison that had been administered to me. But it would have been fatal to have slept. I knew that, and so I fought against the inclination with all my might and main, and allowed my thoughts to dwell on poor little Maude Redcar, waiting desolate and heartbroken in London for news. This supplied me with the necessary spur and kept me going.

The trees were nearly all entirely bare of snow. It had, I was informed, been an unusually mild season, and at that time the sun's rays were very powerful. The path I was pursuing was nothing more than a rough track worn by the peasants passing between the valley and their hay chalets dotted about the mountain. Snow lay on the path where it was screened from the sun by the trees. I heard no sound, saw no sign of those I was seeking save here and there footprints in the snow. I frequently paused and listened, but the stillness was unbroken save for the subdued murmur of falling water afar off.

In my weakened condition the exertion I had endured had greatly distressed me; my heart beat tumultuously, my pulses throbbed violently, and my breathing was stertorous. I was compelled at last to sit down and rest. I was far above the valley now, and the pine trees were straggling and sparse. The track had become very indistinct, but I still detected the footsteps of the people I was following. Above the trees I could discern the snow-capped Pico de Europa glittering in the brilliant sun. It was a perfect Alpine scene, which, under other circumstances, I might have reveled in. But I felt strangely ill, weak, and miserable, and drowsiness began to steal upon me, so that I made a sudden effort of will and sprang up again, and resumed the ascent.

In a little time the forest ended, and before me stretched a sloping plateau which, owing to its being exposed to the full glare of the sun, as well as to all the winds that blew, was bare of snow. The plateau sloped down for probably four hundred feet, then ended abruptly at the edge of a precipice. How far the precipice descended I could not tell from where I was, but far far below I could see a stream meandering through a thickly wooded gorge. I took the details of the scene in with a sudden glance of the eye, for another sight attracted and riveted my attention, and froze me with horror to the spot. Beneath a huge boulder which had fallen from the mountain above, and lodged on the slope, were Annette and Redcar. He was lying on his back, she was stretched out beside him, and her face was buried in his neck. Even from where I stood I could see that he was ghastly pale, his features drawn and pinched, his eyes closed. Incredible as it may seem, horrible as it sounds, it is nevertheless true that that hellish woman was sucking away his life blood. She was a human vampire, and my worst fears were confirmed.

I am aware that an astounding statement of this kind should not be made lightly by a man in my position. But I take all the responsibility of it, and I declare solemnly that it is true. Moreover, the sequel which I am able to give to this story more than corroborates me, and proves Annette to have been one of those human problems which, happily for the world, are very rare, but of which there are several well authenticated cases.

As soon as I fully realized what was happening I drew my revolver from the side pocket of my jacket and fired, not at Annette, but in the air; my object being to startle her so that she would release her victim. It had the desired effect. She sprang up, livid with rage. Blood—his blood—was oozing from the sides of her mouth. Her extraordinary eyes had assumed that strange violet appearance which I had seen once before. Her whole aspect was repulsive, revolting, horrible beyond words. Rooted to the spot I stood and gazed at her, fascinated by the weird, ghastly sight. In my hand I still held the smoking revolver, leveled at her now, and resolved if she rushed towards me to shoot her, for I felt that the world would be well rid of such a hideous monster. But suddenly she stooped, seized her unfortunate victim in her arms, and tore down the slope, and when the edge of the precipice was reached they both disappeared into space.

The whole of this remarkable scene was enacted in the course of a few seconds. It was to me a maddening nightmare. I fell where I stood, and remembered no more until, hours afterwards, I found myself lying in bed at the hotel, and the old surgeon and the priest sitting beside me. Gradually I learnt that the sound of the shot from the revolver, echoing and re-echoing in that Alpine region, had been heard in the village, and some peasants had set off for the mountain to ascertain the cause of the firing. They found me lying on the ground still grasping the weapon, and thinking I had shot myself they carried me down to the hotel.

Naturally I was asked for explanations when I was able to talk, and I recounted the whole of the ghastly story. At first my listeners, the priest and the doctor, seemed to think I was raving in delirium, as well they might, but I persisted in my statements, and I urged the sending out of a party to search for the bodies. If they were found my story would be corroborated.

In a short time a party of peasants started for the gorge, which was a wild, almost inaccessible, ravine through which flowed a mountain torrent amongst the debris and boulders that from time to time had fallen from the rocky heights. After some hours of searching the party discovered the crushed remains of Jack Redcar. His head had been battered to pieces against the rocks as he fell, and every bone in his body was broken. The precipice over which he had fallen was a jagged, scarred, and irregular wall of rock at least four thousand feet in height. The search for Annette's body was continued until darkness compelled the searchers to return to the village, which they did bringing with them my poor friend's remains. Next day the search was resumed, and the day after, and for many days, but with no result. The woman's corpse was never found. The theory was that somewhere on that frightful rock face she had been caught by a projecting pinnacle, or had got jammed in a crevice, where her unhallowed remains would moulder into dust. It was a fitting end for so frightful a life.

Of course an official inquiry was held—and officialism in Spain is appalling. It was weeks and weeks before the inevitable conclusion of the tribunal was arrived at, and I was exonerated from all blame. In the meantime Redcar's remains were committed to their eternal rest in the picturesque little Alpine village churchyard, and for all time Potes will be associated with that grim and awful tragedy. Why Annette took her victim to that out of the way spot can only be guessed at. She knew that the death of her victim was only a question of weeks, and in that primitive and secluded hamlet it would arouse no suspicion, she being a native of Spain. It would be easy for her to say that she had taken her invalid husband there for the benefit of his health, but unhappily the splendid and bracing air had failed to save his life. In this instance, as in many others, her fiendish cunning would have enabled her to score another triumph had not destiny made me its instrument to encompass her destruction.

For long after my return to England I was very ill. The fearful ordeal I had gone through, coupled with the poison which Annette had administered to me, shattered my health; but the unremitting care and attention bestowed upon me by my old friend's widow pulled me through. And when at last I was restored to strength and vigor, beautiful Maude Redcar became my wife.

THE TOMB OF SARAH

F. G. Loring

first published in *Pall Mall Magazine* (December 1900)

My father was the head of a celebrated firm of church restorers and decorators about sixty years ago. He took a keen interest in his work, and made an especial study of any old legends or family histories that came under his observation. He was necessarily very well read and thoroughly well posted in all questions of folklore and medieval legend. As he kept a careful record of every case he investigated, the manuscripts he left at his death have a special interest. From amongst them I have selected the following, as being a particularly weird and extraordinary experience. In presenting it to the public, I feel it is superfluous to apologize for its supernatural character.

MY FATHER'S DIARY

1841.—June 17th. Received a commission from my old friend Peter Grant to enlarge and restore the chancel of his church at Hagarstone, in the wilds of the West Country.

July 5th. Went down to Hagarstone with my head man Somers. A very long and tiring journey.

July 7th. Got the work well started. The old church is one of special interest to the antiquarian, and I shall endeavor while restoring it to alter the existing arrangements as little as possible. One large tomb, however, must be moved bodily ten feet at least to the southward. Curiously enough, there is a somewhat forbidding inscription upon it in Latin, and I am sorry that this particular tomb should have to be moved. It stands amongst the graves of the Kenyons, an old family which has been extinct in these parts for centuries. The inscription on it runs thus:—

"SARAH.

"1630.

FOR THE SAKE OF THE DEAD AND THE WELFARE OF THE
LIVING, LET THIS SEPULTURE REMAIN UNTOUCHED AND ITS
OCCUPANT UNDISTURBED TILL THE COMING OF CHRIST.

"IN THE NAME OF THE FATHER, THE SON, AND THE HOLY
GHOST."

July 8th. Took counsel with Grant concerning the "Sarah Tomb." We are both very loth to disturb it, but the ground has sunk so beneath it, that the safety of the church is in danger; thus we have no choice. However, the work shall be done as reverently as possible under our own direction.

Grant says there is a legend in the neighborhood that it is the tomb of the last of the Kenyons, the evil Countess Sarah, who was murdered in 1630. She lived quite alone in the old castle, whose ruins still stand three miles from here on the road to Bristol. Her reputation was an evil one even for those days. She was a witch or were-woman, the only companion of her solitude being a familiar in the shape of a huge Asiatic wolf. This creature was reputed to seize upon children, or failing these, sheep and other small animals, and convey them to the castle, where the Countess used to suck their blood. It was popularly supposed that she could never be killed. This, however, proved a fallacy, since she was strangled one day by a mad peasant woman who had lost two children, she declaring that they had both been seized and carried off by the Countess's familiar. This is a very interesting story, since it points to a local superstition very similar to that of the Vampire, existing in Slavonic and Hungarian Europe.

The tomb is built of black marble, surmounted by an enormous slab of the same material. On the slab is a magnificent group of figures. A young and handsome woman reclines upon a couch; round her neck is a piece of rope, the end of which she holds in her hand. At her side is a gigantic dog with bared fangs and lolling tongue. The face of the reclining figure is a cruel one: the corners of the mouth are curiously lifted, showing the sharp points of long canine or dog teeth. The whole group, though magnificently executed, leaves a most unpleasant sensation.

If we move the tomb, it will have to be done in two pieces, the covering slab first and then the tomb proper. We have decided to remove the covering slab tomorrow.

July 9th.—6 p.m. A very strange day.

By noon everything was ready for lifting off the covering stone, and after the men's dinner we started the jacks and pulleys. The slab lifted easily enough, though it fitted closely into its seat and was further secured by some sort of mortar or putty, which must have kept the interior perfectly airtight.

None of us were prepared for the horrible rush of foul, moldy air that escaped as the cover lifted clear of its seating. And the contents that gradually came into view were more startling still. There lay the fully dressed body of a woman, wizened and shrunk and ghastly pale as if from starvation. Round her neck was a loose cord, and, judging by the scars still visible, the story of death by strangulation was true enough.

The most horrible part, however, was the extraordinary freshness of the body. Except for the appearance of starvation, life might have been only just extinct. The flesh was soft and white, the eyes were wide open and seemed to stare at us with a fearful understanding in them. The body itself lay on mold, without any pretense to coffin or shell.

For several moments we gazed with horrible curiosity, and then it became too much for my workmen, who implored us to replace the covering slab. That, of course, we would not do; but I set the carpenters to work at once to make a temporary cover while we moved the tomb to its new position. This is a long job, and will take two or three days at least.

July 9th.—9 p.m. Just at sunset we were startled by the howling of, seemingly, every dog in the village. It lasted for ten minutes or a quarter of an hour, and then ceased as suddenly as it began. This, and a curious mist that has risen round the church, makes me feel rather anxious about the "Sarah Tomb." According to the best established traditions of the Vampire-haunted countries, the disturbance of dogs or wolves at sunset is supposed to indicate the presence of one of these fiends, and local fog is always considered to be a certain sign. The Vampire has the power of producing it for the purpose of concealing its movements near its hiding-place at any time.

I dare not mention or even hint my fears to the rector, for he is, not unnaturally perhaps, a rank disbeliever in many things that I know, from experience, are not only possible but even probable. I must work this out alone at first, and get his aid without his knowing in what direction he is helping me. I shall now watch till midnight at least.

10:15 p.m. As I feared and half-expected. Just before ten there was another outburst of the hideous howling. It was commenced most distinctly by a particularly horrible and blood-curdling wail from the vicinity of the churchyard. The chorus lasted only a few minutes, however, and at the end of it I saw a large dark shape, like a huge dog, emerge from the fog and lope away at a rapid canter towards the open country. Assuming this to be what I fear, I shall see it return soon after midnight.

12:30 p.m. I was right. Almost as midnight struck, I saw the beast returning. It stopped at the spot where the fog seemed to commence, and lifting up its head, gave tongue to that particularly horrible long-drawn wail that I had noticed as preceding the outburst earlier in the evening.

Tomorrow I shall tell the rector what I have seen; and if, as I expect, we hear of some neighboring sheepfold having been raided, I shall get him to watch with me for this nocturnal marauder. I shall also examine the "SarahTomb" for something which he may notice without any previous hint from me.

July 10th. I found the workmen this morning much disturbed in mind about the howling of the dogs. "We doan't like it, zur," one of them said to me—"we doan't like it; there was zummat abroad last night that was unholy." They were still more uncomfortable when the news came round that a large dog had made a raid upon a flock of sheep, scattering them far and wide, and leaving three of them dead with torn throats in the field.

When I told the rector of what I had seen and what was being said in the village, he immediately decided that we must try and catch or at least identify the beast I had seen. "Of course," said he, "it is some dog lately imported into the neighborhood, for I know of nothing about here nearly as large as the animal you describe, though its size may be due to the deceptive moonlight."

This afternoon I asked the rector, as a favor, to assist me in lifting the temporary cover that was on the tomb, giving as an excuse the reason that I wished to obtain a portion of the curious mortar with which it had been sealed. After a slight demur he consented, and we raised the lid. If the sight that met our eyes gave me a shock, at least it appalled Grant.

"Great God!" he exclaimed; "the woman is alive!"

And so it seemed for a moment. The corpse had lost much of its starved appearance, and looked hideously fresh and alive. It was still wrinkled and shrunken, but the lips were firm, and of the rich red hue of health. The eyes, if possible, were more appalling than ever, though fixed and staring. At one corner of the mouth I thought I noticed a slight dark-colored froth, but I said nothing about it then.

"Take your piece of mortar, Harry," gasped Grant, "and let us shut the tomb again. God help me! Parson though I am, such dead faces frighten me!"

Nor was I sorry to hide that terrible face again; but I got my bit of mortar, and I have advanced a step towards the solution of the mystery.

This afternoon the tomb was moved several feet towards its new position, but it will be two or three days yet before we shall be ready to replace the slab.

10:15 p.m. Again the same howling at sunset, the same fog enveloping the church, and at 10 o'clock the same great beast slipping silently out into the open country. I must get the rector's help and watch for its return. But precautions we must take, for if things are as I believe, we take our lives in our hands when we venture out into the night to waylay the—Vampire. Why not admit it at once? For that the beast I have seen is the Vampire of that evil thing in the tomb I can have no reasonable doubt.

Not yet come to its full strength, thank Heaven!after the starvation of nearly two centuries, for at present it can only maraud as wolf, apparently. But, in a day or two, when full power returns, that dreadful woman in new strength and beauty will be able to leave her refuge. Then it would not be sheep merely that would satisfy her disgusting lust for blood, but victims that would yield their life-blood without a murmur to her caressing touch —victims that, dying of her foul embrace, themselves must become Vampires in their turn to prey on others.

Mercifully my knowledge gives me a safeguard; for that little piece of mortar that I rescued today from the tomb contains a portion of the Sacred Host, and who holds it, humbly and firmly believing in its virtue, may pass safely through such an ordeal as I intend to submit myself and the rector to tonight.

12:30 p.m. Our adventure is over for the present, and we are back safe.

After writing the last entry recorded above, I went off to find Grant and tell him that the marauder was out on the prowl again. "But, Grant," I said, "before we start out tonight, I must insist that you will let me prosecute this affair in my own way; you must promise to put yourself completely under my orders, without asking any questions as to the why and wherefore."

After a little demur, and some excusable chaff on his part at the serious view I was taking of what he called a "dog hunt," he gave me his promise. I then told him that we were to watch tonight and try and track the mysterious beast, but not to interfere with it in any way. I think, in spite of his jests, that I impressed him with the fact that there might be after all good reason for my precautions.

It was just after eleven when we stepped out into the still night.

Our first move was to try and penetrate the dense fog round the church, but there was something so chilly about it, and a faint smell so disgustingly rank and loathsome, that neither our nerves nor our stomachs were proof against it. Instead, we stationed ourselves in the dark shadow of a yew tree that commanded a good view of the wicket entrance to the churchyard.

At midnight the howling of the dogs began again, and in a few minutes we saw a large grey shape, with green eyes shining like lamps, shamble swiftly down the path towards us.

The rector started forward, but I laid a firm hand upon his arm and whispered a warning, "Remember!" Then we both stood very still and watched as the great beast cantered swiftly by. It was real enough, for we could hear the clicking of its nails on the stone flags. It passed within a few yards of us, and seemed to be nothing more nor less than a great grey wolf, thin and gaunt, with bristling hair and dripping jaws. It stopped where the mist commenced, and turned round. It was truly a horrible sight, and made one's blood run cold. The eyes burnt like fires, the upper lip was snarling and raised, showing the great canine teeth, while round the mouth clung and dripped a dark-colored froth.

It raised its head and gave tongue to its long wailing howl, which was answered from afar by the village dogs. After standing for a few moments, it turned and disappeared into the thickest part of the fog.

Very shortly afterwards the atmosphere began to clear, and within ten minutes the mist was all gone, the dogs in the village were silent, and the night seemed to reassume its normal aspect. We examined the spot where the beast had been standing, and found, plainly enough upon the stone flags, dark spots of froth and saliva.

"Well, Rector," I said "will you admit now, in view of the things you have seen today, in consideration of the legend, the woman in the tomb, the fog, the howling dogs, and, last but not least, the mysterious beast you have seen so close, that there is something not quite normal in it all? Will you put yourself unreservedly in my hands and help me, *whatever I may do*, to first make assurance doubly sure, and finally take the necessary steps for putting an end to this horror of the night?" I saw that the uncanny influence of the night was strong upon him, and wished to impress it as much as possible.

"Needs must," he replied, "when the Devil drives; and in the face of what I have seen, I must believe that some unholy forces are at work. Yet, how can they work in the sacred precincts of a church? Shall we not call rather upon Heaven to assist us in our need."

"Grant," I said solemnly, "that we must do, each in his own way. "God helps those who help themselves, and by His help and the light of my knowledge we must fight this battle for Him and the poor lost soul within."

We then returned to the rectory and to our rooms, though I have sat up to write this account while the scene is fresh in my mind.

July 11th. Found the workmen again very much disturbed in their minds, and full of a strange dog that had been seen during the night by several people, who had hunted it. Farmer Stotman, who had been watching his sheep (the same flock that had been raided the night before) had surprised it over a fresh carcass and tried to drive it off, but its size and fierceness so alarmed him that he had beaten a hasty retreat for a gun. When he returned the animal was gone, though he found that three more sheep from his flock were dead and torn.

The "Sarah Tomb" was moved today to its new position; but it was a long, heavy business, and there was not time to replace the covering slab. For this I was glad, as in the prosaic light of day the rector almost disbelieves the events of the night, and is prepared to think everything to have been magnified and distorted by our imagination.

As, however, I could not possibly proceed with my war of extermination against this foul thing without assistance, and as there is nobody else I can rely upon, I appealed to him for one more night—to convince him that it was no delusion, but a ghastly, horrible truth, which must be fought and conquered for our own sakes, as well as that of all those living in the neighborhood.

"Put yourself in my hands, Rector," I said, "for tonight at least. Let us take those precautions which my study of the subject tells me are the right ones. Tonight you and I must watch in the church; and I feel assured that tomorrow you will be as convinced as I am, and be equally prepared to take those awful steps which I know to be proper, and I must warn you that we shall find a more startling change in the body lying there than you noticed yesterday."

My words came true; for on raising the wooden cover once more, the rank stench of a slaughterhouse arose, making us feel positively sick. There lay the Vampire, but how changed from the starved and shrunken corpse we saw two days ago for the first time! The wrinkles had almost disappeared, the flesh was firm and full, the crimson lips grinned horribly over the long pointed teeth, and a distinct smear of blood had trickled down one corner of the mouth. We set our teeth, however, and hardened our hearts. Then we replaced the cover, and put what we had collected into a safe place in the vestry. Yet even now Grant could not believe that there was any real or pressing danger concealed in that awful tomb, as he raised strenuous objections to any apparent desecration of the body without further proof.

This he shall have tonight. God grant that I am not taking too much on myself! If there is any truth in old legends, it would be easy enough to destroy the Vampire now; but Grant will not have it.

I hope for the best of this night's work, but the danger in waiting is very great.

6 p.m. I have prepared everything: the sharp knives, the pointed stake, fresh garlic, and the wild dog-roses. All these I have taken and concealed in the vestry, where we can get at them when our solemn vigil commences.

If either or both of us die with our fearful task undone, let those reading my record see that this is done. I lay it upon them as a solemn obligation. "That the Vampire be pierced through the heart with the stake, then let the Burial Service be read over the poor clay at last released from its doom. Thus shall the Vampire cease to be, and a lost soul rest."

July 12th. All is over. After the most terrible night of watching and horror, one Vampire at least will trouble the world no more . But how thankful should we be to a merciful Providence that that awful tomb was not disturbed by any one not having the knowledge necessary to deal with its dreadful occupant! I write this with no feelings of self-complacency, but simply with a great gratitude for the years of study I have been able to devote to this special subject.

And now to my tale.

Just before sunset last night, the rector and I locked ourselves into the church, and took up our position in the pulpit. It was one of those pulpits, to be found in some churches, which is entered from the vestry, the preacher appearing at a good height through an arched opening in the wall. This gave as a sense of security (which we felt we needed), a good view of the interior, and direct access to the implements which I had concealed in the vestry.

The sun set and the twilight gradually deepened and faded. There was, so far, no sign of the usual fog, nor any howling of the dogs. At nine o'clock the moon rose and her pale light gradually flooded the aisles, and still no sign of any kind from the "Sarah Tomb." The rector had asked me several times what he might expect, but I was determined that no words or thought of mine should influence him, and that he should be convinced by his own senses alone.

By half-past ten we were both getting very tired, and I began to think that perhaps after all we should see nothing that night. However, soon after eleven we observed a light mist rising from the "Sarah Tomb." It seemed to scintillate and sparkle as it rose, and curled in a sort of pillar or spiral.

I said nothing, but I heard the rector give a sort of gasp as he clutched my arm feverishly. "Great Heaven!" he whispered: "it is taking shape."

And true enough, in a very few moments we saw standing erect by the tomb the ghastly figure of the Countess Sarah!

She looked thin and haggard still, and her face was deadly white; but the crimson lips looked like a hideous gash in the pale cheeks, and her eyes glared like red coals in the gloom of the church.

It was a fearful thing to watch as she stepped unsteadily down the aisle, staggering a little as if from weakness and exhaustion. This was perhaps, natural, as her body must have suffered much physically from her long incarceration, in spite of the unholy forces which kept it fresh and well.

We watched her to the door, and wondered what would happen; but it appeared to present no difficulty, for she melted through it and disappeared.

"Now, Grant," I said, "do you believe?"

"Yes," he replied, "I must. Everything is in your hands, and I will obey your commands to the letter, if you can only instruct me how to rid my poor people of this unnameable terror."

"By God's help I will," said I; "but you shall be yet more convinced first, for we have a terrible work to do, and much to answer for in the future, before we leave the church again this morning. And now to work, for in its present weak state the Vampire will not wander far, but may return at any time, and must not find us unprepared."

We stepped down from the pulpit and, taking dog-roses and garlic from the vestry, proceeded to the tomb. I arrived first, and throwing off the wooden cover, cried, "Look! it is empty!" There was nothing there! Nothing except the impress of the body in the loose damp mold!

I took the flowers and laid them in a circle round the tomb, for legend teaches us that Vampires will not pass over these particular blossoms if they can avoid it.

Then, eight or ten feet away, I made a circle on the stone pavement, large enough for the rector and myself to stand in, and within the circle I placed the implements that I had brought into the church with me.

"Now," I said, "from this circle, which nothing unholy can step across, you shall see the Vampire face to face, and see her afraid to cross that other circle of garlic and dog-roses to regain her unholy refuge. But on no account step beyond the holy place you stand in, for the Vampire has a fearful strength not her own, and, like a snake, can draw her victim willingly to his own destruction."

Now, so far my work was done, and calling the rector, we stepped into the Holy Circle to await the Vampire's return.

Nor was this long delayed. Presently a damp, cold odor seemed to pervade the church, which made our hair bristle and flesh to creep. And then, down the aisle with noiseless feet came That which we watched for.

I heard the rector mutter a prayer, and I held him tightly by the arm, for he was shivering violently.

Long before we could distinguish the features, we saw the glowing eyes and the crimson sensual mouth. She went straight to her tomb, but stopped short when she encountered my flowers. She walked right round the tomb seeking a place to enter, and as she walked she saw us. A spasm of diabolical hate and fury passed over her face; but it quickly vanished, and a smile of love, more devilish still, took its place. She stretched out her arms towards us. Then we saw that round her mouth gathered a bloody froth, and from under her lips long pointed teeth gleamed and champed.

She spoke: a soft soothing voice, a voice that carried a spell with it, and affected us both strangely, particularly the rector. I wished to test as far as possible, without endangering our lives, the Vampire's power.

Her voice had a soporific effect, which I resisted easily enough, but which seemed to throw the rector into a sort of trance. More than this: it seemed to compel him to her in spite of his efforts to resist.

"Come!" she said, "come! I give sleep and peace—sleep and peace—sleep and peace."

She advanced a little towards us; but not far, for I noted that the Sacred Circle seemed to keep her back like an iron hand.

My companion seemed to become demoralized and spellbound. He tried to step forward, and finding me detain him whispered,—"Harry, let go! I must go! She is calling me! I must! I must!Oh, help me! help me!" And he began to struggle.

It was time to finish.

"Grant!" I cried, in a loud, firm voice, "in the name of all that you hold sacred, have done and play the man!" He shuddered violently, and gasped, "Where am I?" Then he remembered, and clung to me convulsively for a moment.

At this a look of damnable hate changed the smiling face before us, and with a sort of shriek she staggered back.

"Back!" I cried: "back to your unholy tomb! No longer shall you molest the suffering world! Your end is near."

It was fear that now showed itself in her beautiful face (for it was beautiful in spite of its horror), as she shrank back, back and over the circlet of flowers, shivering as she did so. At last, with a low mournful cry, she appeared to melt back again into her tomb.

As she did so the first gleams of the rising sun lit up the world, and I knew all danger was over for the day.

Taking Grant by the arm, I drew him with me out of the circle and led him to the tomb. There lay the Vampire once more, still in her living death as we had a moment before seen her in her devilish life. But in the eyes remained that awful expression of hate, and cringing, appalling fear.

Grant was pulling himself together.

"Now," I said, "will you dare the last terrible act, and rid the world forever of this horror?"

"By God!" he said solemnly, "I will.—Tell me what to do."

"Help me to lift her out of her tomb. She can harm us no more," I replied.

With averted faces we set to our terrible task, and laid her out upon the flags.

"Now," I said, "read the Burial Service over the poor body, and then let us give it its release from this living hell that holds it."

Reverently the rector read the beautiful words, and reverently I made the necessary responses. When it was over I took the stake, and, without giving myself time to think, plunged it with al my strength through the heart.

As though really alive, the body for a moment writhed and kicked convulsively, and an awful heart-rending shriek woke the silent church; then all was still.

Then we lifted the poor body back; and, thank God! the consolation that legend tells is never denied to those who have to do such awful work as ours came at last. Over the face stole a great and solemn peace; the lips lost their crimson hue, the prominent sharp teeth sank back into the mouth, and for a moment we saw before us the calm, pale face of a most beautiful woman, who smiled as she slept. A few minutes more, and she faded away to dust before our eyes as we watched. We set to work and cleaned up every trace of our work, and then departed for the rectory. Most thankful were we to step out of the church, with its horrible associations, into the rosy warmth of the summer morning.

With the above end the notes in my father's diary, though a few days later this further entry occurs:—

July 15th. Since the 12th everything has been quiet and as usual. We replaced and sealed up the "Sarah Tomb" this morning. The workmen were surprised to find the body had disappeared, but took it to be the natural result of exposing it to the air.

One odd thing came to my ears today. It appears that the child of one of the villagers strayed from home the night of the 11th inst., and was found asleep in a coppice near the church, very pale and quite exhausted. There were two small marks on her throat, which have since disappeared.

What does this mean? I have, however, kept it to myself, as, now that the Vampire is no more, no further danger either to that child or any other is to be apprehended. It is only those who die of the Vampire's embrace that become Vampires at death in their turn.

THE VAMPIRE

Hugh McCrae

(WRITING AS W. W. LAMBLE)

first published in *The Bulletin* (November 1901)

How well I remember my first love,—with her stuffed busks and her stuffed hair! We did not meet in the summer, nor in the green grass near running water, but in winter,—under the pale glare of gas, in the wet street and among people.

She was complexionless, her face so bleached that her black eyes and red lips positively glared; yet she had a silky fascination for me. And her smooth, evil hands brought not only flesh into contact, but mind.

She said she was hungry. I had just drawn my month's earnings, and we went arm-in-arm to a little green-curtained restaurant. It was sufficiently evil-looking,—the gas low, and the solitary waiter unobstreperous.

I was drunk. The fumes of the cheap Burgundy started an orchestra in my ears, and swelled the veins of my brain. The wind lifted the blind and blew my cigarettes in a whirring covey off the table. I stooped to pick them up, but the blood-strings in my throat stood out,—and the room darkened to my eyes. The waiter noiselessly came to my assistance, replacing them on a plate and retaining a few slyly up his sleeve. But I said nothing, only looking at Marguerite and her long, folded fingers.

She ordered some oysters and, when they had come, I watched her squeeze a lemon-quarter into the shells and over the firm fish.

I seemed to be in a garden with Marguerite. The garden was full of lilies tall, white lilies without a speck or mark; and everywhere amongst them were blue flies, trumpeting and buzzing with pleasure. Here and there a rich bee, with powdered legs, swayed on a flower, like a jewel in snow. The air was warm and soft as down, while the rounded sound of bubbling water poppled in the moss, between the bars of lily-stalks. A delicious sweetness of earth and honey mounted to my brain. I watched a butterfly, winged in old-gold and grey, as he flickered on a red tile under the steady shadow of a fern.

Gradually I grew aware of the subtle electrical hand upon my wrist—then of the eyes that made my mind hers, nay, my very soul. The small, piercing eyes, whose pupils diminished and enlarged, and enlarged and diminished, like the flame of a dying lamp. And every time the pupils diminished, they seemed to me two miser hands that gripped my brain and squeezed myself from me, like a water from cloth, opening only to grip again.

But the woman, in the body, was tall, and breasted like a young girl; her back was straight as an arrow, and her neck reared white as a rock wave carrying the magnificent head on its summit. She had a broad brow, but somewhat slanting; a long, slight nose, an eagerly insolent mouth, and the eyes I have spoken of. Her hair, where it was loose, shimmered and shook as though over a heat-mist.

Presently she lifted her hands from my wrists, and I felt her fingers thrill through my temples, as she drew me towards her and kissed me on the lips. A song seemed to set up in the garden, and the lilies shot up like stars, swayed in the sky, meeting in an arch, and crossed in stormy rushes over our heads. The noise of the water rose clamorously, and a flight of colored birds brushed my shoulder. A soft sensation went over the whole of my skin, like the dropping of a delicate veil.

And still she drew me closer.

I tried to resist, but, as in a nightmare, my arms remained limp and paralyzed. Neither could I cry out. All at once, in the midst of a million kisses, she drew back her head, and, with a gasping laugh, pushed her red lips at my throat and bit me deep, even to blood.

In vain I beat her about the face, and plucked at her cheeks. She hung like a dog. With horrible little laughs and gurgles she greeted my impotent rage.

I put both hands to her forehead, and made to thrust her from me; but again my muscles failed. And she bit deeper.

Then the lilies withered down from the skies and lay stained and yellow on the earth. The butterfly lost its old-gold, and its wings and whole form broadened into a bat's. The soft ripple of the water changed to the purring of a flame, and bale fires leapt from every corner.

Still the woman tore at my throat.

My breath shortened, and I felt as though my skull were contracting and injuring my brain. Spasm after spasm shot through my head. Goaded to madness, I hurled my tormenter away, and as she returned to me, bloody-mouthed, I saw that she too had changed. Her eyes had sunk, her teeth were old and wasted to an appearance of cloves; her nose seemed flattened, and her hair thin. Her face was almost simian.

My strength failed me, and I staggered on my feet. "Marguerite," I cried. "Woman! Devil! Vampire!"

And I fell clean to the ground, like a tree in a storm.

A great coldness rushed upon me, and an icy breath fanned my forehead. I could feel a pair of hands beneath my armpits. I was smothering. There was a bandage round my mouth.

I opened my eyes. There were stars—thousands of them—blinking and blinking, but below, turbid and swollen, lay the river without a light for miles.

The hands withdrew suddenly; and a man darted from me, fleeing up the steep stoned bank. It was the waiter of the restaurant. The bandage dropped off my jaw, and I could now understand the sweet scent of my garden dream.

My pockets were empty as the day when my clothes were made; that was a foregone conclusion.

Marguerite never again crossed my path. Yet I know that green-curtained restaurant, and someday I shall see her sanding in the doorway. If she beckons, I must go to her.

Because I dare not refuse.

MEDUSA

Phil Robinson

published anonymously in *Tales by Three Brothers*, and widely
credited to the eldest brother (1902)

I t was on the 17th of June that the world read in its morning paper that
James Westerby had died suddenly in his office at Whitehall on the
preceding day. The world may still, if its memory be jogged a little, be
able to remember that the cause of death was said to have been heart disease,
the crisis having been accelerated by overwork. As to the sadness of the event,
the newspapers of all political shades agreed.

James Westerby would have been a prominent man, even if he had not
been an Under Secretary and one of the pleasantest speakers in the House of
Commons. He was of the Westerbys of Oxfordshire, the last, I fear, of a fine
old line. "Hotspur" Westerby, of revolutionary fame, was one of his ancestors,
and the Under Secretary prided himself not a little on his resemblance to the
old hero, whom Cromwell hated so cordially. His father's place is secure in
the world of letters. James Westerby promised to be worthy of his blood. Still
young (he died when he was thirty-nine), he had borne himself admirably in
public position; and when he died there were not wanting some who spoke of
his loss as a national calamity.

To me his death was a personal sorrow. I was, and had been since his
appointment, fifteen months before, his private secretary; and, previous to
that again, for the twelve years since I came down from the 'Varsity we had
been intimate friends, though he was some years my senior.

On the morning of that 16th day of June I was sitting at my desk as usual,
between the ante-room and his private office. The last person who had been
admitted to his presence was a lady, who, dressed in black and closely veiled,
made at the time no distinct impression on my mind. The Under Secretary
had refused admittance to some ten or twelve people that morning, but, on
my handing him this lady's card, he told me to admit her. She was with him
for, perhaps, half an hour. It must have been about 11 o'clock when she passed
out. It was just 11:30 when I went into his office and found him dead in his
chair.

Some of these facts—with many more or less imaginative details—were presented to the world by the morning papers, as already mentioned, of the 17th. But in no paper was any mention made of the veiled lady, for the altogether sufficient reason that no representative of any paper knew of the veiled lady's existence.

At about a quarter before twelve we were standing—two or three others of the higher employees of the department and myself—in my office, waiting for the arrival of the doctor. The door of the Under Secretary's private room was closed. In the excitement the doorkeeper in the ante-room had presumably deserted his post, for, seeing those to whom I was talking glance toward the outer door, I turned and found myself again confronting the veiled lady.

"Can I see Mr. Westerby once more?" she asked.

"Mr. Westerby, madam," I answered, "is dead."

She did not reply at once, but with both hands raised her veil as if to obtain a clearer view of my face, to see if I spoke the truth. In doing so, she showed me the most beautiful face that I have ever seen, or ever expect to see. One dreams of such eyes. Perhaps Endymion looked into them. But I had never hoped to see them in a woman's face. I scarcely remember that she murmured in a low, incredulous but very musical voice, the one word —

"Dead?"

"He died, madam, suddenly, less than an hour ago."

We had been standing, as we spoke, within earshot of the others. She now drew back to where my desk stood, in the further corner of the room, whither I followed her.

"Was anyone with him after I left, can you remember?" she asked.

"No, madam, I had no occasion to go into his room for some little time after you went. When I did so, he was dead."

It was some time before she spoke again; then —

"Excuse me," she said, hesitatingly, "but I hope I shall not have to appear in connection with this. You can understand how very much I should dislike" —this with the faintest smile—"to have my name in all the newspapers. Of course, if there is an inquest, and if my evidence can be of service, I shall have to give it. But it does not seem to me that anything I can say could be of importance. He was well when I saw him—that is all."

Then, after a pause, during which I was silent: "If you can manage it so that my name will not be mentioned, I shall be very grateful to you," she said. As she spoke, she drew one of her cards from a small black card case and handed it to me, adding, "and I hope you will call and let me have the pleasure of thanking you."

I took the card and assured her that I would do what I could in her behalf. She lowered her veil again and left the room. I read the card now with more interest than I had the former one when taking it to my chief. It said:

Mrs. Walter F. Tierce,
19, Grasmere Crescent, W.

Mrs. Tierce had hardly gone when the doctor came in, followed a moment later by a police inspector.

"Heart disease," the doctor said. The inspector asked me a few questions and said that no inquest would be necessary.

I was hardly conscious at the time, I think, that I was telling the officer that no one had been with the Under Secretary for an hour before his death. Nor when it was over and I recognized what I had done, did my conscience disturb me much. It was a mere courtesy to a woman, such as any man would do if he had it in his power. Why should she be made to suffer because he chanced to die about the time that she happened to call upon him?

So the world next morning heard nothing of the veiled lady.

Within a month I was back in my old chambers in Lincoln's Inn trying to gather up the interrupted threads of my legal studies—a task which would, perhaps, have progressed more rapidly if it had received my entire attention. As it was, however, work had to be content to divide my thoughts somewhat unequally with another subject—Mrs. Walter Tierce.

Mrs. Tierce was a widow. When I called at her home immediately after the funeral, she met me with delightful cordiality.

I called frequently after my first visit, and never met any other visitor at the house. It was difficult to understand how so charming a woman could live in a fashionable quarter of London in such complete isolation. But I had no desire that it should be otherwise.

At the age of thirty-five I had settled down, more or less reconciled to the belief that I should never marry. In theory, I have always maintained that it is the duty to himself and to society of every healthy man to take to himself a wife and assume the responsibilities of a householder before he is thirty years of age. A bachelor's life is an inchoate existence; a species of half-life at best —"like the odd half of a pair of scissors," as Benjamin Franklin said. It is as the head of a family alone, with the care of others on his shoulders, that a man arrives at the possibility of his best development. This was my loudly proclaimed belief. And still I was unmarried. If one could only wake some morning and find himself married—in his own house, with a charming and domestic wife—perhaps with children! But the necessary preliminaries to arriving at that state terrified me. The difficulty of a selection (in the face of an apparently incurable incapacity of falling seriously in love with any one individual) was appalling.

But now the picture of a home rose frequently before me, altogether pleasant to contemplate—a home in which two wonderful black eyes smiled at me across the breakfast table-cloth in the morning and were waiting to meet mine as I looked up from my reading in our library at night.

In fact, I was in love—at times. But there were also times when my condition seemed, on analysis, curiously unsatisfactory to myself, curiously contradictory. Especially was this the case immediately after being in Mrs. Tierce's presence, when there was a certain reaction. On leaving her home, I never failed to ask myself wonderingly, if I really loved her as a man should love a woman before asking her to be his wife. She filled all my thoughts by day and a large share of my dreams by night. Those eyes haunted me. In her presence I was helpless—intoxicated—a blind worshipper. I longed to touch her with my hands, to stroke the fabric of her dress or any object which her hands had recently touched. My whole being ached with very tenderness to approach more nearly to her—to be in contact with her—to caress her. The physical attraction of her presence was overmastering.

Fifteen minutes after leaving her, however, I would be dimly wondering if this was really love—the love that a husband should feel for a wife. This absolute submission of my individuality to hers—would it last through days and weeks and months of constant companionship? Through all the stress of years of wedded life? And if it did not, if my individuality asserted itself, and I became critical of her, what then?

Not that her beauty was her only attraction. On the contrary, few women whom I have ever met have impressed me more distinctly with their intellectuality.

But her most charming characteristic was a certain admirable self-possession and self-control. She seemed so thoroughly to understand herself and to know what was her right relation to things around her; and this without a suspicion of masculinity or of the business air. Never for a moment was there danger of her losing either her mental or emotional equilibrium.

In fact, she was adorable. But, though there was no point of view from which she did not seem to me to be entirely the most delightful thing that I had ever seen, I never failed to experience that same misgiving immediately after quitting her presence. It was as short-lived as it was regular in its recurrence. An hour later, as I sat in my chambers alone, her eyes haunted me once more.

Though I had never spoken of my love, she must have read it in my eyes a hundred times, nor apparently was the perusal distasteful to her.

I had been back in Lincoln's Inn now five months, and was sitting in my chambers one dark mid-afternoon in December. Had I been reading, I must have lit the gas. But there was light enough to sit and dream of her; light enough to see those eyes in the shadow of my book-case. My one clerk was away and would not return for an hour. So I dreamed uninterruptedly until a shuffling outside my office door recalled me to myself. It would have looked more business-like in the eyes of a client to have light enough in the room to work by, and I made a movement toward the matchbox. But there was no time. A knock at the door sounded and the door itself was thrown wide open. There was an interval of some seconds and then a figure entered, moving heavily and painfully with the aid of a crutch—a man and crippled, that was all that I could see.

The figure moved laboriously halfway across the floor toward me. Then, standing on one foot, the visitor placed his crutch against the wall and allowed himself to drop heavily into a chair a few feet away from me, while I stood looking on, mutely anxious to render assistance but not knowing how to offer it.

After a short silence he spoke, simply pronouncing my name; not interrogatively, but as if to inform me that he knew to whom he was speaking and that his business was with me. I bowed in response, and with matter-of-fact business suavity asked what I could do for him.

He was silent for some moments, and as he sat fronting the window to which my back was turned, and through which came what small light there was in the office, I could see his face plainly enough. Not an old man, by any means, probably younger than myself, with features that must once have been handsome, and would be still but for the deep lines of sorrow or of pain. The figure, too, as he sat, looked full and healthy with nothing but a certain stiffness of pose to tell of its infirmity. At last he spoke, hurriedly, and in a hard, feverish-sounding voice.

"Nothing, thank you. You can do nothing for me. I have come to do something for you, instead."

I bowed acknowledgment.

"I have come to warn you," he went on, still hurriedly and shifting uneasily in his seat, like one who has an unpleasant thing to tell and is anxious to be over with it The strangeness of his voice and manner, and the intentness—almost the fierceness—with which he looked at me, made me uneasy in my turn. I doubted his sanity, and wished that there was more light or that my clerk was present.

"I came to warn you," he said again, and I saw his hands moving nervously as he leaned toward me and spoke harshly and quickly. "You are in love with her—with Mrs. Tierce. No; don't deny it I know, I know, and before heaven, if I can save you I will."

The heaviness of his breathing told the intensity of the excitement under which he was laboring as he went on, edging further forward on his chair and reaching out his hands toward me;

"She is not a woman; she is not human. Yes, I know how beautiful she is; how helpless a man must be before her. I have known it for six years; and had I not known it I should not now be what I am. You will think me mad," he said. "You probably think me so now. I do not wonder at it. What else should you think when a stranger comes into your chambers and tells you that in these matter-of-fact nineteenth-century days there exist beings who are not human—who have more than human attributes, and that one of these beings is the woman whom you love?"

He was quieter now, more serious, and spoke almost argumentatively, as one who seeks only to convince, while he almost despaired of doing it.

"You are laughing at me now—or pitying me; but I call the Almighty God to witness that I speak the truth—if a God can be almighty and let her live. I tell you, sir, that to know her is death. If you do not believe me you will become worse than I am—as her husband is who died at her feet here in London—as the American is who died before her in the café at Nice—as heaven only knows how many more are who have crossed her path."

Of course I had no doubt of his madness; but his earnestness—the utter strength of conviction with which he spoke—was strangely moving. That he, poor fellow, believed what he said, it was impossible to doubt.

"It is six years since I saw her first at Havre, in France. I chanced to be seated at the next table to her at Frascati's, and I knew that I loved her then. The American was with her. I followed her to Cannes, to Trouville, to Monaco, to Nice; and where she went the American went, too. There was no impropriety in their companionship, but he followed her as I did; only that he had her acquaintance and I had not. And I knew, or thought I knew, that it would be useless for me to try and win her while he was there. He evidently worshipped her, and she—for he was a handsome fellow (Reading was his name)—seemed to care for him. So I watched her from a distance, waiting and hoping; and as I have told you my turn came.

"It was in the Cafe Royal, and nobody saw it happen but herself. Suddenly she rushed out from the corner where they were sitting and called for help. Every one crowded around, and he was dead—dead in his chair, with his face upturned and his eyes fixed, staring like one suddenly terrified. They said it was heart disease. Heart disease!"

It had grown almost dark, and he drew his chair close to me. The paling light from the window just showed me the worn face and the sunken, feverish eyes.

"Then I came to know her," he continued, after a pause. "I hung upon her as he had done, and for three months I believed that I was the happiest man in Europe. In Venice, in Florence, in Paris, in London, I was constantly with her, day after day. She seemed to love me, and in the Bois or in Hyde Park how proud I was to be seen by her side! Then she went to stay for a month at Oxford, and I, with her permission, followed her there, and would call for her at the Mitre every morning. Under the shadow of the grey college walls and in the well-trimmed walks and gardens, it seemed that her face put on a new and holier beauty in keeping with the place. There it was that I told her that I loved her and asked her to be my wife, as we stood for a minute to rest in the cloisters of Christ Church."

His voice was very sad. It had lost its harshness, and as he remembered—or did he only imagine?—the sweetness of those days of love-making, there was more of a soft regretfulness than of anger in his tones.

"She did not refuse me," he said, "nor did she explicitly accept me. But I was idiotically happy—happy for three whole days—until that afternoon in the Magdalen Walks, when in ten minutes I became, from a healthy, strong man, the wreck you see me now."

The regretfulness was all gone, and the hard, fierce ring was in his voice again as he went on:

"It was on one of the benches in Addison's Walk, as they call it, and I pressed her for some more definite promise than she had yet given me. She did not seem to listen to me, to heed me, as she leaned back, her hands lying idly in her lap and her great, grave eyes looking out across the meadow. I grew more passionate; clasped her hands and begged for an answer. At last she turned her face towards me. I met her eyes—"

His voice broke and he stopped speaking. For a minute or more we sat in silence in the twilight, his face buried in his hands. Then he raised his head again, and in slow, unimpassioned accents, continued:

"As our eyes met, hers looked lusterless, hardly as if she saw me or was looking at me. But as I gazed into them they changed. Somewhere inside them, or behind them, a flame was lit. The pupils expanded, black and brilliant as eyes never shone before. What was it? Was it love? And leaning still closer, I gazed more intensely into the eyes that seemed now to blaze before me. And as I looked the spell came upon me. It was as though I swooned. Dimly I became aware that I was losing my power of motion, of speech, of thought. The eyes engulfed me. I was vaguely conscious that I must somehow disengage myself from the spell that was upon me; but I could not. I was powerless, and she—it was as if she fed upon my very life. I cannot phrase it otherwise. I was numb, and, though I tried to speak, could not move one muscle. Then consciousness began to leave me, and I was on the point of —God knows what—swoon or death—when the crunching of feet on the gravel path came sharply to my ears.

"Who it was that passed I do not know. I know not how long I sat there. I remember that she rose without a word and left me. When I moved it was evening. The sun was behind the college walls, and the walk was dark. With my brain hardly awake and my lower limbs still benumbed, slowly I made my way out of the college gates and up the High Street to the Clarendon Hotel, where I was staying. Next morning I awoke what you see me now—a cripple, a paralytic for life."

During all this narrative I had sat silent, engrossed in the madman's tale. As a piece of dramatic elocution, it was magnificent. When he finished I cast about for some commonplace remark to make, but in the state of my feelings it was not easy to find one, and it was he who again broke the silence:

"Tierce, poor fool! I warned him as I am warning you. It was two years afterward that she married him, and in two weeks more he was dead—dead in their house in Park Lane—died of heart disease! Heart disease!"

And as he said it, I could not help thinking of James Westerby.

My visitor was about to speak again when a footfall sounded on the stairs outside, the door opened, and my clerk stood in the entrance, astonished at the darkness.

"Come in, Jackson," I called, to let him know that I was there, "and light the gas, please."

My visitor rose painfully, and again took his crutch.

"I have told you all that is vital to the case," he said in the matter-of-fact voice of a client addressing his attorney, "and you will, of course, do as you think best."

Jackson, about to light the gas, with a burning match in his hand, held the door open for the stranger to pass out, and without another word the cripple moved laboriously away. It was not until he had gone that it occurred to me that I had not asked nor been told his name.

"Has that gentleman ever called before, Jackson?"

"I think not, sir."

But probably I should meet him again. And now, my thoughts reverted to her. He was mad, of course: and his story was absurd. But as I walked home from the office, those eyes were before me, blazing with the passion which he had lit in them. What eyes they were in truth! How lovely, and how I loved them! And how easy, too, it was to imagine them dilating and engulfing one's senses until he swooned!

I had not hoped to see her again that day, having spent part of the morning in "helping her to shop," and expecting to escort her to the theatre on the evening following. So after a solitary dinner at a restaurant, I climbed up to my chambers to dream away the evening alone.

The story which I had heard a few hours before certainly had not in any way altered my feelings towards Mrs. Tierce. Indeed, I hardly thought of the story, except to pity the poor fellow who told it and to speculate upon his history. Who was he? Had he loved her and gone mad for love of her? And should I tell her of his visit? It might pain her by bringing up unpleasant memories; but on the other hand I should like to know something more of the cripple's history.

But I was restless, and my rooms seemed more than ever lonely and unhomelike that evening; so about nine o'clock, I put on my hat and overcoat and went out into the street.

It was a cold night, damp and raw, with no sign of starlight or moonlight overhead, and a heavy, misty atmosphere through which the street lights shone blurred and twinkling.

Instinctively I turned westward, and, as a matter of course, set my face towards Grasmere Crescent, not with any intention of calling at the house, but with a lover's longing to see it and to be near to her. I passed the house on the opposite side of the street. No. 19 had a large bow-window in the drawing room, on the first floor, and as I approached, the blind of the narrow side-window facing me being raised some few inches gave a glimpse of the brightly lighted, daintily furnished room, with which I was so familiar, within. I had hoped to catch a glimpse of her, but in the small segment of the room that was visible through the aperture, no figure was to be seen.

After passing on to the end of the street I made a circuit round some by-streets and so back to Grasmere Crescent. As I approached now from the north the house looked dark, save for a narrowest chink of light which outlined the edge of the bow-window. When I had passed I turned to look back at the window of which the blind was raised; and doing so, I saw a curious thing.

It was only instantaneous; but just for that instant I saw two figures standing, herself and one of the servants, whom I recognized. They were facing one another, each, it seemed, leaning slightly forward. But even as I looked, the servant suddenly threw up her hands and fell—fell straight backward, rigidly, as if in a fit. Mrs. Tierce started towards the falling girl, as if to catch her. The movement took her out of my range of vision, the projecting woodwork of the window intervening.

It all happened so suddenly that I stood for a moment bewildered and irresolute. Had I really seen it? It was more like some tableau on a stage, or the flash of a slide from a magic lantern, than a reality.

Recovering my senses, my first impulse was to cross the street and offer my services. But why? The girl had but slipped suddenly upon the polished floor, and doubtless they were laughing over it now. It would be an impertinence for me to thrust myself in with a confession of having been playing spy. So, after standing and gazing at the window for a few moments, during which I once saw Mrs. Tierce pass quickly across the room and back, I moved on to my rooms.

The next morning as I sat at breakfast, a note was brought to me,

"I am very sorry," she wrote, "to interfere with your theatre party this evening, but a dreadful thing happened here last night. One of my servants —Mary, you know her—died very suddenly. I was talking to her, when she simply threw up her hands and fell down before me, dead. Regretting that I must ask you to excuse me, I am,

"Yours cordially,

"EDITH TIERCE."

I wished now that I had obeyed my first impulse on the preceding evening and had rung at the door to volunteer my services. I would certainly go and see her immediately after breakfast.

Fortunately my theatre party included only two other persons besides Mrs. Tierce and myself, and I was on sufficiently intimate terms with John Bradstreet and his wife to have no fear of offending them. So I wrote Mrs. Bradstreet a short note explaining the situation briefly, enclosing the tickets and hoping she would use the box or not, as she saw fit. Then I drove at once to Grasmere Crescent.

In her quiet, self-possessed way Mrs. Tierce had already done all that was necessary, and I found that there was little excuse for thrusting my services upon her. Still I saw her frequently during the next two days, though never for any length of time and rarely to talk of things not associated immediately with the melancholy ceremony that was impending. The dead girl seemed to have had no family connections, and the funeral was conducted under Mrs. Tierce's directions. I accompanied her to the church and cemetery, and left her at her own door afterwards, accepting an invitation to call again that evening.

I have spoken before of the curious self-possession, an imperturbable self-reliance, which Mrs. Tierce possessed and which sat very becomingly upon her delicate grave face. Never had this quality in her seemed more admirably perfect to me than during those days when the shadow of death hung over her home.

On the evening of the day of the funeral, she was even more reposeful than usual, in a dreamy mood in which I had seen her before more than once, and in which she seemed hardly conscious of—or rather inattentive to—what passed around her. This mood of hers the cripple had recalled to me when describing the scene in the Oxford walk.

It may have been that the events and scenes of the last few days, with all their appeals to the emotions, had predisposed us both to tenderness. Certainly from the time of my entry when our greeting had been only a hand-clasp, with hardly an audible word on either side, we had spoken constrainedly, in undertones and on personal topics. Though more than once I strove desperately to be matter-of-fact, my voice in spite of myself would sink, and wherever the conversation started from, it ended in herself.

At last some chance word of hers made me broach a subject which I had never approached before, and which she rarely alluded to—her late husband. Before I was conscious of what I was doing, I had said:

"It is not, by any means, I know, your first contact with death. You have told me very little of Mr. Tierce."

"No," she said dreamily, "there is little to tell. We were only married a few weeks."

And then:

"And is it not possible that you might marry again? Could you not?" and I crossed from my chair to take a seat on the sofa by her side, "could you not— is there any hope for me?"

Instead of replying, she sat silent and inattentive, her large swimming eyes looking far into either the past or the future—I wondered which.

"Tell me," I urged, laying my hand on one of hers, as it rested in her lap, "tell me, is there any hope?"

She did not move, did not answer me. Again I implored her, and at last she spoke, but with seeming irrelevance.

"Did you ever hear of the Court of Love?" she asked, "the court over which the Countess Ermengarde presided in the tenth or eleventh century?"

No, I knew nothing of the Court of Love or the Countess Ermengarde, though I have since looked them up.

"The Court decided, and the decision was affirmed by a later Court composed of half the queens and duchesses of Europe, that true love could not exist between married persons."

"But you do not believe it? That was nine centuries ago; and how should queens and duchesses know anything of love?"

"I do not know whether I believe it or not," she murmured, and turned her head as it lay on the cushions of the sofa, to look at me with eyes that still seemed strangely dreamy and far away.

"But you do know," I urged impulsively, leaning forward till my face was dangerously close to hers. "You know that you do not believe it. You know that I should always love you—that I must always love you. And if I may love you as my wife—"

She smiled faintly, charmingly, but did not answer me.

"My darling," I whispered, "say something! Am I to be utterly happy?"

And still she did not answer; but leaned back with the faint half-smile on her lips, and her great inscrutable eyes looking into and through mine. Then in the silence and suspense, the cripple's story came into my mind. No wonder that he should believe that he had been fascinated in some mysterious way—spellbound, benumbed—by those eyes! No wonder! And still I looked into them; and still they looked through mine. I forgot the nearness of her lips; forgot that I held her hand. I thought only of, saw only, those eyes. And still I thought only of the cripple and vaguely pitied him.

But somehow—when it began I knew not—I found that the expression of the eyes had changed. They were no longer dreamy and far away, but intensely earnest, with a passion in them that was almost hunger.

"Yes," I thought to myself (and I must have smiled in thinking it), "this is what he described. No wonder that they seemed to him to flame. They are not looking at my eyes now, but through, into my brain, into me. My eyes are no more than two pieces of glass in the path of her vision." And I felt a curious, half-gratified recognition of the accuracy of the other's description. And still the eyes seemed to expand until they were many times larger than my own; till I could see nothing but them.

Have you ever, in a half-darkened room, set your face close against a mirror and looked into your own eyes and seen what terrible things they are; how the view of everything else is shut out and all your sense is drawn into the pupils confronting you? So I felt my whole being concentrating itself in —merging itself into—drowning in—her eyes. A strange feeling of intoxication possessed me; of ecstasy. I could have laughed aloud, but that it seemed as if to do it I would somehow have to summon my faculties from too far away.

At what point this strange calmness gave way to conscious fear, I do not know. I saw the pupils of her eyes expanding and contracting, as if with the regular beats of a passionate pulse behind them. I saw, or rather I was aware, that the color flushed into her cheeks and died again, that her breath, which was warm on my face, came short and gasping. Her lips closed and parted, moist and glistening, suggesting to me somehow the craving of some animal in the presence of food which it could not reach. Her nostrils dilated, quivering, and her whole being strained with a passion which seemed carnivorous.

"It was as if she preyed upon my very life," he had said, and I understood him now. But the memory of the cripple was fading from me. I was conscious only of myself and of her; of the terror of her fierce hunger and my own helplessness. The power of motion was gone from me; even volition seemed slipping away. The burning of her eyes was in my brain which was as if laid open before her; as a hollow dish set open to the scorching sun. I was utterly at her mercy, without power of resistance; and as her breath grew yet more rapid and more heavy, I knew that she was in some way inhaling my very life.

Suddenly a flash of fear passed across her face—a spasm of agonized disappointment. For a moment it was as if she would, in one long, indrawn breath, draw the last of my strength from me; and then a man's voice sounded in my ear.

"I hope I am in time!"

She had fallen reclining against the cushions of the sofa. I looked up dazedly, and the cripple stood in the centre of the room, his hat in his hand.

"You had better let me take you away," he said, and I heard it half-consciously. Turning to look at her, I saw her lie panting and exhausted. I cannot tell the horror of her appearance. Her eyes still sought mine hungrily as before. Her hands, lying in her lap, fumbled each other, her fingers knotting and intertwining. Her lips moved, and all her body quivered with passion. It was a dreadful fancy, but I could liken her to nothing but some blood-sucking thing; some human leech or vampire, torn from its prey, quivering dumbly with its unsated appetite.

At the time I only half understood what passed around me. I knew that the danger was over and that escape lay before me. I saw the cripple waiting for me to rise and was conscious of the horror with which she inspired me. But I was bewildered. My brain seemed numb, and when I endeavored to stand up my limbs refused their office. Seeing my powerlessness the cripple moved forward and with his healthy arm assisted me. It was with difficulty that I stood, for there was no sensation in my feet or legs and it was only by leaning on my companion that I made my way laboriously to the door.

No word had been spoken beyond the two sentences which the cripple had uttered. Reaching the door of the room I turned to look at her once more, supporting myself against the door-post. She had not moved. Under the influence of the passion that was upon her she evidently had no other thought or emotion. There was no sign of shame or confusion on her face; nothing but the blind craving for the prey that was being taken from her. Even there, across the full width of the room, her eyes sought mine with the same despairing longing. But she only made me shudder now. The cripple still supporting me, we passed together from the house.

Of the remainder of that evening my memory is confused and faint. I know that I was helped to my chambers and that there, with the assistance of the cripple and some third person, though who, or whence or where he joined us, I know not, I was put to bed. That night was one long, half-waking swoon, and far into the next afternoon I lay motionless upon my back without speaking or wishing to speak, save only to tell the woman who took care of my rooms that I needed no help or food. As the twilight fell the same good woman came again, and yet again late at night. But I was scarcely conscious, and had no wishes. Even speech was an effort.

For seven days, all through the Christmas holidays, I lay in this state, talcing little nourishment; hardly speaking, hardly thinking clearly. At last, on the day after Christmas, I found courage and strength to attack the mail which had been accumulating on my sick-room table. I had expected to find her handwriting on one at least of the envelopes. In this I was disappointed. But some instinct led me to open first one envelope the address of which was written in a hand that was strange to me. It contained nothing but a newspaper clipping:

"A sad accident occurred last night at 19 Grasmere Crescent, W. The house was inhabited by Mrs. Walter Tierce, the widow of the late Walter Tierce, Esq. Last evening Mrs. Tierce, who was twenty-six years of age, retired to rest as usual. This morning she failed to answer the knock of the servant at the door, and on the maid entering the room she noticed a strong and peculiar odor. She was frightened and went out and fetched another servant. The two entered the room and found Mrs. Tierce dead, and an overturned bottle of chloroform by the pillow. It was evidently an accident, and no inquest will be held. A curious coincidence in connection with the sad affair is that this is the second death in the same house within a week. On Monday last, a maid in the service of Mrs. Tierce died suddenly of heart disease. Her funeral occurred yesterday afternoon, when Mrs. Tierce attended it."

Attached to this clipping with a pin was the date line of the evening newspaper from which it was taken—"Friday, December 19th." That was the day after that terrible evening, and a week ago now. The funeral must have already taken place.

Though, as I have said, the handwriting on the envelope was unfamiliar to me, I had my conjecture as-to whom the message was from, and after keeping the envelope for all these years, the clue has come which shows that the conjecture was correct. Six weeks ago I received information that I had been appointed executor of the estate of the late James Livingston, of Hereford. James Livingston? The name was unknown to me. Thinking that there might be some mistake, I called at the solicitor's office from which the intimation came. No, there was no mistake, the solicitor informed me; he had drawn up the will, and Mr. Livingston had given him special instructions how to communicate with me.

"And you say you never knew him at all?" he asked musingly, "that is certainly curious for he seemed to know you. But you could not well have forgotten him. He was disabled—almost entirely paralyzed in his right side."

LUELLA MILLER

Mary Wilkins Freeman

first published in *Everybody's Magazine* (December 1902)

C lose to the village street stood the one-story house in which Luella Miller, who had an evil name in the village, had dwelt. She had been dead for years, yet there were those in the village who, in spite of the clearer light which comes on a vantage-point from a long-past danger, half believed in the tale which they had heard from their childhood. In their hearts, although they scarcely would have owned it, was a survival of the wild horror and frenzied fear of their ancestors who had dwelt in the same age with Luella Miller. Young people even would stare with a shudder at the old house as they passed, and children never played around it as was their wont around an untenanted building. Not a window in the old Miller house was broken: the panes reflected the morning sunlight in patches of emerald and blue, and the latch of the sagging front door was never lifted, although no bolt secured it. Since Luella Miller had been carried out of it, the house had had no tenant except one friendless old soul who had no choice between that and the far-off shelter of the open sky. This old woman, who had survived her kindred and friends, lived in the house one week, then one morning no smoke came out of the chimney, and a body of neighbors, a score strong, entered and found her dead in her bed. There were dark whispers as to the cause of her death, and there were those who testified to an expression of fear so exalted that it showed forth the state of the departing soul upon the dead face. The old woman had been hale and hearty when she entered the house, and in seven days she was dead; it seemed that she had fallen a victim to some uncanny power. The minister talked in the pulpit with covert severity against the sin of superstition; still the belief prevailed. Not a soul in the village but would have chosen the almshouse rather than that dwelling. No vagrant, if he heard the tale, would seek shelter beneath that old roof, unhallowed by nearly half a century of superstitious fear.

There was only one person in the village who had actually known Luella Miller. That person was a woman well over eighty, but a marvel of vitality and unextinct youth. Straight as an arrow, with the spring of one recently let loose from the bow of life, she moved about the streets, and she always went to church, rain or shine. She had never married, and had lived alone for years in a house across the road from Luella Miller's.

This woman had none of the garrulousness of age, but never in all her life had she ever held her tongue for any will save her own, and she never spared the truth when she essayed to present it. She it was who bore testimony to the life, evil, though possibly wittingly or designedly so, of Luella Miller, and to her personal appearance. When this old woman spoke—and she had the gift of description, although her thoughts were clothed in the rude vernacular of her native village—one could seem to see Luella Miller as she had really looked. According to this woman, Lydia Anderson by name, Luella Miller had been a beauty of a type rather unusual in New England. She had been a slight, pliant sort of creature, as ready with a strong yielding to fate and as unbreakable as a willow. She had glimmering lengths of straight, fair hair, which she wore softly looped round a long, lovely face. She had blue eyes full of soft pleading, little slender, clinging hands, and a wonderful grace of motion and attitude.

"Luella Miller used to sit in a way nobody else could if they sat up and studied a week of Sundays," said Lydia Anderson, "and it was a sight to see her walk. If one of them willows over there on the edge of the brook could start up and get its roots free of the ground, and move off, it would go just the way Luella Miller used to. She had a green shot silk she used to wear, too, and a hat with green ribbon streamers, and a lace veil blowing across her face and out sideways, and a green ribbon flyin' from her waist. That was what she came out bride in when she married Erastus Miller. Her name before she was married was Hill. There was always a sight of 'l's' in her name, married or single. Erastus Miller was good lookin', too, better lookin' than Luella. Sometimes I used to think that Luella wa'n't so handsome after all. Erastus just about worshiped her. I used to know him pretty well. He lived next door to me, and we went to school together. Folks used to say he was waitin' on me, but he wa'n't. I never thought he was except once or twice when he said things that some girls might have suspected meant somethin'. That was before Luella came here to teach the district school. It was funny how she came to get it, for folks said she hadn't any education, and that one of the big girls, Lottie Henderson, used to do all the teachin' for her, while she sat back and did embroidery work on a cambric pocket-handkerchief. Lottie Henderson was a real smart girl, a splendid scholar, and she just set her eyes by Luella, as all the girls did. Lottie would have made a real smart woman, but she died when Luella had been here about a year—just faded away and died: nobody knew what ailed her. She dragged herself to that schoolhouse and helped Luella teach till the very last minute. The committee all knew how Luella didn't do much of the work herself, but they winked at it. It wa'n't long after Lottie died that Erastus married her. I always thought he hurried it up because she wa'n't fit to teach. One of the big boys used to help her after Lottie died, but he hadn't much government, and the school didn't do very well, and Luella might have had to give it up, for the committee couldn't have shut their eyes to things much longer. The boy that helped her was a real honest, innocent sort of fellow, and he was a good scholar, too. Folks said he overstudied, and that was the reason he was took crazy the year after Luella married, but I don't know. And I don't know what made Erastus Miller go into consumption of the blood the year after he was married: consumption wa'n't in his family. He just grew weaker and weaker, and went almost bent double when he tried to wait on Luella, and he spoke feeble, like an old man. He worked terrible hard till the last trying to save up a little to leave Luella. I've seen him out in the worst storms on a wood-sled—he used to cut and sell wood—and he was hunched up on top lookin' more dead than alive. Once I couldn't stand it: I went over and helped him pitch some wood on the cart—I was always strong in my arms. I wouldn't stop for all he told me to, and I guess he was glad enough for the help. That was only a week before he died. He fell on the kitchen floor while he was gettin' breakfast. He always got the breakfast and let Luella lay abed. He did all the sweepin' and the washin' and the ironin' and most of the cookin'. He couldn't bear to have Luella lift her finger, and she let him do for her. She lived like a queen for all the work she did. She didn't even do her sewin'. She said it made her shoulder ache to sew, and poor Erastus's sister Lily used to do all her sewin'. She wa'n't able to, either; she was never strong in her back, but she did it beautifully. She had to, to suit Luella, she was so dreadful particular. I never saw anythin' like the fagottin' and hemstitchin' that Lily Miller did for Luella. She made all Luella's weddin' outfit, and that green silk dress, after Maria Babbit cut it. Maria she cut it for nothin', and she did a lot more cuttin' and fittin' for nothin' for Luella, too. Lily Miller went to live with Luella after Erastus died. She gave up her home, though she was real attached to it and wa'n't a mite afraid to stay alone. She rented it and she went to live with Luella right away after the funeral."

Then this old woman, Lydia Anderson, who remembered Luella Miller, would go on to relate the story of Lily Miller. It seemed that on the removal of Lily Miller to the house of her dead brother, to live with his widow, the village people first began to talk. This Lily Miller had been hardly past her first youth, and a most robust and blooming woman, rosy-cheeked, with curls of strong, black hair overshadowing round, candid temples and bright dark eyes. It was not six months after she had taken up her residence with her sister-in-law that her rosy color faded and her pretty curves became wan hollows. White shadows began to show in the black rings of her hair, and the light died out of her eyes, her features sharpened, and there were pathetic lines at her mouth, which yet wore always an expression of utter sweetness and even happiness. She was devoted to her sister; there was no doubt that she loved her with her whole heart, and was perfectly content in her service. It was her sole anxiety lest she should die and leave her alone.

"The way Lily Miller used to talk about Luella was enough to make you mad and enough to make you cry," said Lydia Anderson. "I've been in there sometimes toward the last when she was too feeble to cook and carried her some blanc-mange or custard—somethin' I thought she might relish, and she'd thank me, and when I asked her how she was, say she felt better than she did yesterday, and asked me if I didn't think she looked better, dreadful pitiful, and say poor Luella had an awful time takin' care of her and doin' the work—she wa'n't strong enough to do anythin'—when all the time Luella wa'n't liftin' her finger and poor Lily didn't get any care except what the neighbors gave her, and Luella eat up everythin' that was carried in for Lily. I had it real straight that she did. Luella used to just sit and cry and do nothin'. She did act real fond of Lily, and she pined away considerable, too. There was those that thought she'd go into a decline herself. But after Lily died, her Aunt Abby Mixter came, and then Luella picked up and grew as fat and rosy as ever. But poor Aunt Abby begun to droop just the way Lily had, and I guess somebody wrote to her married daughter, Mrs. Sam Abbot, who lived in Barre, for she wrote her mother that she must leave right away and come and make her a visit, but Aunt Abby wouldn't go. I can see her now. She was a real good-lookin' woman, tall and large, with a big, square face and a high forehead that looked of itself kind of benevolent and good. She just tended out on Luella as if she had been a baby, and when her married daughter sent for her she wouldn't stir one inch. She'd always thought a lot of her daughter, too, but she said Luella needed her and her married daughter didn't. Her daughter kept writin' and writin', but it didn't do any good. Finally she came, and when she saw how bad her mother looked, she broke down and cried and all but went on her knees to have her come away. She spoke her mind out to Luella, too. She told her that she'd killed her husband and everybody that had anythin' to do with her, and she'd thank her to leave her mother alone. Luella went into hysterics, and Aunt Abby was so frightened that she called me after her daughter went. Mrs. Sam Abbot she went away fairly cryin' out loud in the buggy, the neighbors heard her, and well she might, for she never saw her mother again alive. I went in that night when Aunt Abby called for me, standin' in the door with her little green-checked shawl over her head. I can see her now. 'Do come over here, Miss Anderson,' she sung out, kind of gasping for breath. I didn't stop for anythin'. I put over as fast as I could, and when I got there, there was Luella laughin' and cryin' all together, and Aunt Abby trying to hush her, and all the time she herself was white as a sheet and shakin' so she could hardly stand. 'For the land sakes, Mrs. Mixter,' says I, 'you look worse than she does. You ain't fit to be up out of your bed.'

"'Oh, there ain't anythin' the matter with me,' says she. Then she went on talkin' to Luella. 'There, there, don't, don't, poor little lamb,' says she. 'Aunt Abby is here. She ain't goin' away and leave you. Don't, poor little lamb.'

"'Do leave her with me, Mrs. Mixter, and you get back to bed,' says I, for Aunt Abby had been layin' down considerable lately, though somehow she contrived to do the work.

"'I'm well enough,' says she. 'Don't you think she had better have the doctor, Miss Anderson?'

"'The doctor,' says I, 'I think you had better have the doctor. I think you need him much worse than some folks I could mention.' And I looked right straight at Luella Miller laughin' and cryin' and goin' on as if she was the centre of all creation. All the time she was actin' so—seemed as if she was too sick to sense anythin'—she was keepin' a sharp lookout as to how we took it out of the corner of one eye. I see her. You could never cheat me about Luella Miller. Finally I got real mad and I run home and I got a bottle of valerian I had, and I poured some boilin' hot water on a handful of catnip, and I mixed up that catnip tea with most half a wineglass of valerian, and I went with it over to Luella's. I marched right up to Luella, a-holdin' out of that cup, all smokin'. 'Now,' says I, 'Luella Miller, 'you swallar this!'

"'What is—what is it, oh, what is it?' she sort of screeches out. Then she goes off a-laughin' enough to kill.

"'Poor lamb, poor little lamb,' says Aunt Abby, standin' over her, all kind of tottery, and tryin' to bathe her head with camphor.

"'You swaller this right down,' says I. And I didn't waste any ceremony. I just took hold of Luella Miller's chin and I tipped her head back, and I caught her mouth open with laughin', and I clapped that cup to her lips, and I fairly hollered at her: 'Swaller, swaller, swaller!' and she gulped it right down. She had to, and I guess it did her good. Anyhow, she stopped cryin' and laughin' and let me put her to bed, and she went to sleep like a baby inside of half an hour. That was more than poor Aunt Abby did. She lay awake all that night and I stayed with her, though she tried not to have me; said she wa'n't sick enough for watchers. But I stayed, and I made some good cornmeal gruel and I fed her a teaspoon every little while all night long. It seemed to me as if she was jest dyin' from bein' all wore out. In the mornin' as soon as it was light I run over to the Bisbees and sent Johnny Bisbee for the doctor. I told him to tell the doctor to hurry, and he come pretty quick. Poor Aunt Abby didn't seem to know much of anythin' when he got there. You couldn't hardly tell she breathed, she was so used up. When the doctor had gone, Luella came into the room lookin' like a baby in her ruffled nightgown. I can see her now. Her eyes were as blue and her face all pink and white like a blossom, and she looked at Aunt Abby in the bed sort of innocent and surprised. 'Why,' says she, 'Aunt Abby ain't got up yet?'

"'No, she ain't,' says I, pretty short.

"'I thought I didn't smell the coffee,' says Luella. "'Coffee,' says I. 'I guess if you have coffee this mornin'

you'll make it yourself.'

"'I never made the coffee in all my life,' says she, dreadful

astonished. 'Erastus always made the coffee as long as he lived, and then Lily she made it, and then Aunt Abby made it. I don't believe I can make the coffee, Miss Anderson.'

"'You can make it or go without, jest as you please,' says I. "'Ain't Aunt Abby goin' to get up?' says she.

"'I guess she won't get up,' says I, 'sick as she is.' I was gettin' madder and madder. There was somethin' about that little pink-and-white thing standin' there and talkin' about coffee, when she had killed so many better folks than she was, and had jest killed another, that made me feel 'most as if I wished somebody would up and kill her before she had a chance to do any more harm.

"Is Aunt Abby sick?' says Luella, as if she was sort of aggrieved and injured.

"'Yes,' says I, 'she's sick, and she's goin' to die, and then you'll be left alone, and you'll have to do for yourself and wait on yourself, or do without things.' I don't know but I was sort of hard, but it was the truth, and if I was any harder than Luella Miller had been I'll give up. I ain't never been sorry that I said it. Well, Luella, she up and had hysterics again at that, and I jest let her have 'em. All I did was to bundle her into the room on the other side of the entry where Aunt Abby couldn't hear her, if she wa'n't past it—I don't know but she was—and set her down hard in a chair and told her not to come back into the other room, and she minded. She had her hysterics in there till she got tired. When she found out that nobody was comin' to coddle her and do for her she stopped. At least I suppose she did. I had all I could do with poor Aunt Abby tryin' to keep the breath of life in her. The doctor had told me that she was dreadful low, and give me some very strong medicine to give to her in drops real often, and told me real particular about the nourishment. Well, I did as he told me real faithful till she wa'n't able to swaller any longer. Then I had her daughter sent for. I had begun to realize that she wouldn't last any time at all. I hadn't realized it before, though I spoke to Luella the way I did. The doctor he came, and Mrs. Sam Abbot, but when she got there it was too late; her mother was dead. Aunt Abby's daughter just give one look at her mother layin' there, then she turned sort of sharp and sudden and looked at me.

"'Where is she?' says she, and I knew she meant Luella.

"'She's out in the kitchen,' says I. 'She's too nervous to see folks die. She's afraid it will make her sick.'

"The Doctor he speaks up then. He was a young man. Old Doctor Park had died the year before, and this was a young fellow just out of college. 'Mrs. Miller is not strong,' says he, kind of severe, 'and she is quite right in not agitating herself.'

"'You are another, young man; she's got her pretty claw on you,' thinks I, but I didn't say anythin' to him. I just said over to Mrs. Sam Abbot that Luella was in the kitchen, and Mrs. Sam Abbot she went out there, and I went, too, and I never heard anythin' like the way she talked to Luella Miller. I felt pretty hard to Luella myself, but this was more than I ever would have dared to say. Luella she was too scared to go into hysterics. She jest flopped. She seemed to jest shrink away to nothin' in that kitchen chair, with Mrs. Sam Abbot standin' over her and talkin' and tellin' her the truth. I guess the truth was most too much for her and no mistake, because Luella presently actually did faint away, and there wa'n't any sham about it, the way I always suspected there was about them hysterics. She fainted dead away and we had to lay her flat on the floor, and the Doctor he came runnin' out and he said somethin' about a weak heart dreadful fierce to Mrs. Sam Abbot, but she wa'n't a mite scared. She faced him jest as white as even Luella was layin' there lookin' like death and the Doctor feelin' of her pulse.

" 'Weak heart,' says she, 'weak heart; weak fiddlesticks! There ain't nothin' weak about that woman. She's got strength enough to hang onto other folks till she kills 'em. Weak? It was my poor mother that was weak: this woman killed her as sure as if she had taken a knife to her.'

"But the Doctor he didn't pay much attention. He was bendin' over Luella layin' there with her yellow hair all streamin' and her pretty pink-and-white face all pale, and her blue eyes like stars gone out, and he was holdin' onto her hand and smoothin' her forehead, and tellin' me to get the brandy in Aunt Abby's room, and I was sure as I wanted to be that Luella had got somebody else to hang onto, now Aunt Abby was gone, and I thought of poor Erastus Miller, and I sort of pitied the poor young Doctor, led away by a pretty face, and I made up my mind I'd see what I could do.

"I waited till Aunt Abby had been dead and buried about a month, and the Doctor was goin' to see Luella steady and folks were beginnin' to talk; then one evenin', when I knew the Doctor had been called out of town and wouldn't be round, I went over to Luella's. I found her all dressed up in a blue muslin with white polka dots on it, and her hair curled jest as pretty, and there wa'n't a young girl in the place could compare with her. There was somethin' about Luella Miller seemed to draw the heart right out of you, but she didn't draw it out of me. She was settin' rocking in the chair by her sittin'-room window, and Maria Brown had gone home. Maria Brown had been in to help her, or rather to do the work, for Luella wa'n't helped when she didn't do anythin'. Maria Brown was real capable and she didn't have any ties; she wa'n't married, and lived alone, so she'd offered. I couldn't see why she should do the work any more than Luella; she wa'n't any too strong; but she seemed to think she could and Luella seemed to think so, too, so she went over and did all the work—washed, and ironed, and baked, while Luella sat and rocked. Maria didn't live long afterward. She began to fade away just the same fashion the others had. Well, she was warned, but she acted real mad when folks said anythin': said Luella was a poor, abused woman, too delicate to help herself, and they'd ought to be ashamed, and if she died helpin' them that couldn't help themselves she would—and she did.

" 'I s'pose Maria has gone home,' says I to Luella, when I had gone in and sat down opposite her.

" 'Yes, Maria went half an hour ago, after she had got supper and washed the dishes,' says Luella, in her pretty way.

" 'I suppose she has got a lot of work to do in her own house tonight,' says I, kind of bitter, but that was all thrown away on Luella Miller. It seemed to her right that other folks that wa'n't any better able than she was herself should wait on her, and she couldn't get it through her head that anybody should think it wa'n't right.

"'Yes,' says Luella, real sweet and pretty, 'yes, she said she had to do her washin' tonight. She has let it go for a fortnight along of comin' over here.'

"'Why don't she stay home and do her washin' instead of comin' over here and doin' your work, when you are just as well able, and enough sight more so, than she is to do it?' says I.

"Then Luella she looked at me like a baby who has a rattle shook at it. She sort of laughed as innocent as you please. 'Oh, I can't do the work myself, Miss Anderson,' says she. 'I never did. Maria has to do it.'

"Then I spoke out: 'Has to do it!' says I. 'Has to do it!' She don't have to do it, either. Maria Brown has her own home and enough to live on. She ain't beholden to you to come over here and slave for you and kill herself.'

"Luella she jest set and stared at me for all the world like a doll-baby that was so abused that it was comin' to life.

" 'Yes,' says I, 'she's killin' herself. She's goin' to die just the way Erastus did, and Lily, and your Aunt Abby. You're killin' her jest as you did them. I don't know what there is about you, but you seem to bring a curse,' says I. 'You kill everybody that is fool enough to care anythin' about you and do for you.'

"She stared at me and she was pretty pale.

"'And Maria ain't the only one you're goin' to kill,' says I. 'You're goin' to kill Doctor Malcom before you're done with him.'

"Then a red color came flamin' all over her face. 'I ain't goin' to kill him, either,' says she, and she begun to cry.

"'Yes, you be!' says I. Then I spoke as I had never spoke before. You see, I felt it on account of Erastus. I told her that she hadn't any business to think of another man after she'd been married to one that had died for her: that she was a dreadful woman; and she was, that's true enough, but sometimes I have wondered lately if she knew it—if she wa'n't like a baby with scissors in its hand cuttin' everybody without knowin' what it was doin'.

"Luella she kept gettin' paler and paler, and she never took her eyes off my face. There was somethin' awful about the way she looked at me and never spoke one word. After awhile I quit talkin' and I went home. I watched that night, but her lamp went out before nine o'clock, and when Doctor Malcom came drivin' past and sort of slowed up he see there wa'n't any light and he drove along. I saw her sort of shy out of meetin' the next Sunday, too, so he shouldn't go home with her, and I begun to think mebbe she did have some conscience after all. It was only a week after that that Maria Brown died— sort of sudden at the last, though everybody had seen it was comin'. Well, then there was a good deal of feelin' and pretty dark whispers. Folks said the days of witchcraft had come again, and they were pretty shy of Luella. She acted sort of offish to the Doctor and he didn't go there, and there wa'n't anybody to do anythin' for her. I don't know how she did get along. I wouldn't go in there and offer to help her—not because I was afraid of dyin' like the rest, but I thought she was just as well able to do her own work as I was to do it for her, and I thought it was about time that she did it and stopped killin' other folks. But it wa'n't very long before folks began to say that Luella herself was goin' into a decline jest the way her husband, and Lily, and Aunt Abby and the others had, and I saw myself that she looked pretty bad. I used to see her goin' past from the store with a bundle as if she could hardly crawl, but I remembered how Erastus used to wait and 'tend when he couldn't hardly put one foot before the other, and I didn't go out to help her.

"But at last one afternoon I saw the Doctor come drivin' up like mad with his medicine chest, and Mrs. Babbit came in after supper and said that Luella was real sick.

"'I'd offer to go in and nurse her,' says she, 'but I've got my children to consider, and mebbe it ain't true what they say, but it's queer how many folks that have done for her have died.'

"I didn't say anythin', but I considered how she had been Erastus's wife and how he had set his eyes by her, and I made up my mind to go in the next mornin', unless she was better, and see what I could do; but the next mornin' I see her at the window, and pretty soon she came steppin' out as spry as you please, and a little while afterward Mrs. Babbit came in and told me that the Doctor had got a girl from out of town, a Sarah Jones, to come there, and she said she was pretty sure that the Doctor was goin' to marry Luella.

"I saw him kiss her in the door that night myself, and I knew it was true. The woman came that afternoon, and the way she flew around was a caution. I don't believe Luella had swept since Maria died. She swept and dusted, and washed and ironed; wet clothes and dusters and carpets were flyin' over there all day, and every time Luella set her foot out when the Doctor wa'n't there there was that Sarah Jones helpin' of her up and down the steps, as if she hadn't learned to walk.

"Well, everybody knew that Luella and the Doctor were goin' to be married, but it wa'n't long before they began to talk about his lookin' so poorly, jest as they had about the others; and they talked about Sarah Jones, too.

"Well, the Doctor did die, and he wanted to be married first, so as to leave what little he had to Luella, but he died before the minister could get there, and Sarah Jones died a week afterward.

"Well, that wound up everything for Luella Miller. Not another soul in the whole town would lift a finger for her. There got to be a sort of panic. Then she began to droop in good earnest. She used to have to go to the store herself, for Mrs. Babbit was afraid to let Tommy go for her, and I've seen her goin' past and stoppin' every two or three steps to rest. Well, I stood it as long as I could, but one day I see her comin' with her arms full and stoppin' to lean against the Babbit fence, and I run out and took her bundles and carried them to her house.

Then I went home and never spoke one word to her though she called after me dreadful kind of pitiful. Well, that night I was taken sick with a chill, and I was sick as I wanted to be for two weeks. Mrs. Babbit had seen me run out to help Luella and she came in and told me I was goin' to die on account of it. I didn't know whether I was or not, but I considered I had done right by Erastus's wife.

"That last two weeks Luella she had a dreadful hard time, I guess. She was pretty sick, and as near as I could make out nobody dared go near her. I don't know as she was really needin' anythin' very much, for there was enough to eat in her house and it was warm weather, and she made out to cook a little flour gruel every day, I know, but I guess she had a hard time, she that had been so petted and done for all her life.

"When I got so I could go out, I went over there one morning. Mrs. Babbit had just come in to say she hadn't seen any smoke and she didn't know but it was somebody's duty to go in, but she couldn't help thinkin' of her children, and I got right up, though I hadn't been out of the house for two weeks, and I went in there, and Luella she was layin' on the bed, and she was dyin'.

"She lasted all that day and into the night. But I sat there after the new doctor had gone away. Nobody else dared to go there. It was about midnight that I left her for a minute to run home and get some medicine I had been takin', for I begun to feel rather bad.

"It was a full moon that night, and just as I started out of my door to cross the street back to Luella's, I stopped short, for I saw something."

Lydia Anderson at this juncture always said with a certain defiance that she did not expect to be believed, and then proceeded in a hushed voice:

"I saw what I saw, and I know I saw it, and I will swear on my death bed that I saw it. I saw Luella Miller and Erastus Miller, and Lily, and Aunt Abby, and Maria, and the Doctor, and Sarah, all goin' out of her door, and all but Luella shone white in the moonlight, and they were all helpin' her along till she seemed to fairly fly in the midst of them. Then it all disappeared. I stood a minute with my heart poundin', then I went over there. I thought of goin' for Mrs. Babbit, but I thought she'd be afraid. So I went alone, though I knew what had happened. Luella was layin' real peaceful, dead on her bed."

This was the story that the old woman, Lydia Anderson, told, but the sequel was told by the people who survived her, and this is the tale which has become folklore in the village.

Lydia Anderson died when she was eighty-seven. She had continued wonderfully hale and hearty for one of her years until about two weeks before her death.

One bright moonlight evening she was sitting beside a window in her parlor when she made a sudden exclamation, and was out of the house and across the street before the neighbor who was taking care of her could stop her. She followed as fast as possible and found Lydia Anderson stretched on the ground before the door of Luella Miller's deserted house, and she was quite dead.

The next night there was a red gleam of fire athwart the moonlight and the old house of Luella Miller was burned to the ground. Nothing is now left of it except a few old cellar stones and a lilac bush, and in summer a helpless trail of morning glories among the weeds, which might be considered emblematic of Luella herself.

COUNT MAGNUS

M. R. James

from *Ghost Stories of an Antiquary* (1904)

By what means the papers out of which I have made a connected story came into my hands is the last point which the reader will learn from these pages. But it is necessary to prefix to my extracts from them a statement of the form in which I possess them.

They consist, then, partly of a series of collections for a book of travels, such a volume as was a common product of the forties and fifties. Horace Marryat's 'Journal of a Residence in Jutland and the Danish Isles' is a fair specimen of the class to which I allude. These books usually treated of some unknown district on the Continent. They were illustrated with woodcuts or steel plates. They gave details of hotel accommodation, and of means of communication, such as we now expect to find in any well-regulated guide-book, and they dealt largely in reported conversations with intelligent foreigners, racy innkeepers and garrulous peasants. In a word, they were chatty.

Begun with the idea of furnishing material for such a book, my papers as they progressed assumed the character of a record of one single personal experience, and this record was continued up to within a very short time from its termination.

The writer was a Mr. Wraxall. For my knowledge of him I have to depend entirely on the evidence his writings afford, and from these I deduce that he was a man past middle age, possessed of some private means, and very much alone in the world. He had, it seems, no settled abode in England, but was a denizen of hotels and boarding-houses. It is probable that he entertained the idea of settling down at some future time which never came; and I think it also likely that the Pantechnicon fire in the early seventies must have destroyed a great deal that would have thrown light on his antecedents, for he refers once or twice to property of his that was warehoused at that establishment.

It is further apparent that Mr. Wraxall had published a book, and that it treated of a holiday he had once taken in Britanny. More than this I cannot say about his work, because a diligent search in bibliographical works has convinced me that it must have appeared either anonymously or under a pseudonym.

As to his character, it is not difficult to form some superficial opinion. He must have been an intelligent and cultivated man. It seems that he was near being a Fellow of his college at Oxford—Brasenose, as I judge from the Calendar. His besetting fault was pretty clearly that of over-inquisitiveness, possibly a good fault in a traveller, certainly a fault for which our traveller paid dearly enough in the end.

On what proved to be his last expedition, he was plotting another book. Scandinavia, a region not widely known to Englishmen forty years ago, had struck him as an interesting field. He must have alighted on some old books of Swedish history or memoirs, and the idea had struck him that there was room for a book descriptive of travel in Sweden, interspersed with episodes from the history of some of the great Swedish families. He procured letters of introduction, therefore, to some persons of quality in Sweden, and set out thither in the early summer of 1863.

Of his travels in the North there is no need to speak, nor of his residence of some weeks in Stockholm. I need only mention that some savant resident there put him on the track of an important collection of family papers belonging to the proprietors of an ancient manor-house in Vestergothland, and obtained for him permission to examine them.

The manor-house, or herrgård, in question is to be called Råbäck (pronounced something like Roebeck), though that is not its name. It is one of the best buildings of its kind in all the country, and the picture of it in Dahlenberg's *Suecia Antiqua et Hodierna*, engraved in 1694, shows it very much as the tourist may see it today. It was built soon after 1600, and is, roughly speaking, very much like an English house of that period in respect of material—red-brick with stone facings—and style. The man who built it was a scion of the great house of De la Gardie, and his descendants possess it still. De la Gardie is the name by which I will designate them when mention of them becomes necessary.

They received Mr. Wraxall with great kindness and courtesy, and pressed him to stay in the house as long as his researches lasted. But, preferring to be independent, and mistrusting his powers of conversing in Swedish, he settled himself at the village inn, which turned out quite sufficiently comfortable, at any rate during the summer months. This arrangement would entail a short walk daily to and from the manor-house of something under a mile. The house itself stood in a park, and was protected—we should say grown up— with large old timber. Near it you found the walled garden, and then entered a close wood fringing one of the small lakes with which the whole country is pitted. Then came the wall of the demesne, and you climbed a steep knoll—a knob of rock lightly covered with soil—and on the top of this stood the church, fenced in with tall dark trees. It was a curious building to English eyes. The nave and aisles were low, and filled with pews and galleries. In the western gallery stood the handsome old organ, gaily painted, and with silver pipes. The ceiling was flat, and had been adorned by a seventeenth-century artist with a strange and hideous 'Last Judgment,' full of lurid flames, falling cities, burning ships, crying souls, and brown and smiling demons. Handsome brass coronae hung from the roof; the pulpit was like a doll's-house, covered with little painted wooden cherubs and saints; a stand with three hour-glasses was hinged to the preacher's desk. Such sights as these may be seen in many a church in Sweden now, but what distinguished this one was an addition to the original building. At the eastern end of the north aisle the builder of the manor-house had erected a mausoleum for himself and his family. It was a largish eight-sided building, lighted by a series of oval windows, and it had a domed roof, topped by a kind of pumpkin-shaped object rising into a spire, a form in which Swedish architects greatly delighted. The roof was of copper externally, and was painted black, while the walls, in common with those of the church, were staringly white. To this mausoleum there was no access from the church. It had a portal and steps of its own on the northern side.

Past the churchyard the path to the village goes, and not more than three or four minutes bring you to the inn door.

On the first day of his stay at Råbäck Mr. Wraxall found the church door open, and made those notes of the interior which I have epitomized. Into the mausoleum, however, he could not make his way. He could by looking through the keyhole just descry that there were fine marble effigies and sarcophagi of copper, and a wealth of armorial ornament, which made him very anxious to spend some time in investigation.

The papers he had come to examine at the manor-house proved to be of just the kind he wanted for his book. There were family correspondence, journals, and account-books of the earliest owners of the estate, very carefully kept and clearly written, full of amusing and picturesque detail. The first De la Gardie appeared in them as a strong and capable man. Shortly after the building of the mansion there had been a period of distress in the district, and the peasants had risen and attacked several châteaux and done some damage. The owner of Råbäck took a leading part in suppressing the trouble, and there was reference to executions of ringleaders and severe punishments inflicted with no sparing hand.

The portrait of this Magnus de la Gardie was one of the best in the house, and Mr. Wraxall studied it with no little interest after his day's work. He gives no detailed description of it, but I gather that the face impressed him rather by its power than by its beauty or goodness; in fact, he writes that Count Magnus was an almost phenomenally ugly man.

On this day Mr. Wraxall took his supper with the family, and walked back in the late but still bright evening.

"I must remember," he writes, "to ask the sexton if he can let me into the mausoleum at the church. He evidently has access to it himself, for I saw him tonight standing on the steps, and, as I thought, locking or unlocking the door."

I find that early on the following day Mr. Wraxall had some conversation with his landlord. His setting it down at such length as he does surprised me at first; but I soon realized that the papers I was reading were, at least in their beginning, the materials for the book he was meditating, and that it was to have been one of those quasi-journalistic productions which admit of the introduction of an admixture of conversational matter.

His object, he says, was to find out whether any traditions of Count Magnus de la Gardie lingered on in the scenes of that gentleman's activity, and whether the popular estimate of him were favorable or not. He found that the Count was decidedly not a favorite. If his tenants came late to their work on the days which they owed to him as Lord of the Manor, they were set on the wooden horse, or flogged and branded in the manor-house yard. One or two cases there were of men who had occupied lands which encroached on the lord's domain, and whose houses had been mysteriously burnt on a winter's night, with the whole family inside. But what seemed to dwell on the innkeeper's mind most—for he returned to the subject more than once—was that the Count had been on the Black Pilgrimage, and had brought something or someone back with him.

You will naturally inquire, as Mr. Wraxall did, what the Black Pilgrimage may have been. But your curiosity on the point must remain unsatisfied for the time being, just as his did. The landlord was evidently unwilling to give a full answer, or indeed any answer, on the point, and, being called out for a moment, trotted out with obvious alacrity, only putting his head in at the door a few minutes afterwards to say that he was called away to Skara, and should not be back till evening.

So Mr. Wraxall had to go unsatisfied to his day's work at the manor-house. The papers on which he was just then engaged soon put his thoughts into another channel, for he had to occupy himself with glancing over the correspondence between Sophia Albertina in Stockholm and her married cousin Ulrica Leonora at Råbäck in the years 1705-1710. The letters were of exceptional interest from the light they threw upon the culture of that period in Sweden, as anyone can testify who has read the full edition of them in the publications of the Swedish Historical Manuscripts Commission.

In the afternoon he had done with these, and after returning the boxes in which they were kept to their places on the shelf, he proceeded, very naturally, to take down some of the volumes nearest to them, in order to determine which of them had best be his principal subject of investigation next day. The shelf he had hit upon was occupied mostly by a collection of account-books in the writing of the first Count Magnus. But one among them was not an account-book, but a book of alchemical and other tracts in another sixteenth-century hand. Not being very familiar with alchemical literature, Mr. Wraxall spends a good deal of space which he might have spared in setting out the names and beginnings of the various treatises: The book of the Phoenix, book of the Thirty Words, book of the Toad, book of Miriam, Turba philosophorum, and so forth; and then he announces with a good deal of circumstance his delight at finding, on a leaf originally left blank near the middle of the book, some writing of Count Magnus himself headed "*Liber nigræ peregrinationis.*" It is true that only a few lines were written, but there was quite enough to show that the landlord had that morning been referring to a belief at least as old as the time of Count Magnus, and probably shared by him. This is the English of what was written:

"If any man desires to obtain a long life, if he would obtain a faithful messenger and see the blood of his enemies, it is necessary that he should first go into the city of Chorazin, and there salute the prince…" Here there was an erasure of one word, not very thoroughly done, so that Mr. Wraxall felt pretty sure that he was right in reading it as *aëris* ("of the air"). But there was no more of the text copied, only a line in Latin: "*Quære reliqua hujus materiei inter secretiora*" (See the rest of this matter among the more private things).

It could not be denied that this threw a rather lurid light upon the tastes and beliefs of the Count; but to Mr. Wraxall, separated from him by nearly three centuries, the thought that he might have added to his general forcefulness alchemy, and to alchemy something like magic, only made him a more picturesque figure; and when, after a rather prolonged contemplation of his picture in the hall, Mr. Wraxall set out on his homeward way, his mind was full of the thought of Count Magnus. He had no eyes for his surroundings, no perception of the evening scents of the woods or the evening light on the lake; and when all of a sudden he pulled up short, he was astonished to find himself already at the gate of the churchyard, and within a few minutes of his dinner. His eyes fell on the mausoleum.

"Ah," he said, "Count Magnus, there you are. I should dearly like to see you."

"Like many solitary men," he writes, "I have a habit of talking to myself aloud; and, unlike some of the Greek and Latin particles, I do not expect an answer. Certainly, and perhaps fortunately in this case, there was neither voice nor any that regarded: only the woman who, I suppose, was cleaning up the church, dropped some metallic object on the floor, whose clang startled me. Count Magnus, I think, sleeps sound enough."

That same evening the landlord of the inn, who had heard Mr. Wraxall say that he wished to see the clerk or deacon (as he would be called in Sweden) of the parish, introduced him to that official in the inn parlor. A visit to the De la Gardie tomb-house was soon arranged for the next day, and a little general conversation ensued.

Mr. Wraxall, remembering that one function of Scandinavian deacons is to teach candidates for Confirmation, thought he would refresh his own memory on a Biblical point.

"Can you tell me," he said, "anything about Chorazin?"

The deacon seemed startled, but readily reminded him how that village had once been denounced.

"To be sure," said Mr. Wraxall; "it is, I suppose, quite a ruin now?"

"So I expect," replied the deacon. "I have heard some of our old priests say that Antichrist is to be born there; and there are tales—"

"Ah! what tales are those?" Mr. Wraxall put in.

"Tales, I was going to say, which I have forgotten," said the deacon; and soon after that he said goodnight.

The landlord was now alone, and at Mr. Wraxall's mercy; and that inquirer was not inclined to spare him.

"Herr Nielsen," he said, "I have found out something about the Black Pilgrimage. You may as well tell me what you know. What did the Count bring back with him?"

Swedes are habitually slow, perhaps, in answering, or perhaps the landlord was an exception. I am not sure; but Mr. Wraxall notes that the landlord spent at least one minute in looking at him before he said anything at all. Then he came close up to his guest, and with a good deal of effort he spoke:

"Mr. Wraxall, I can tell you this one little tale, and no more—not any more. You must not ask anything when I have done. In my grandfather's time —that is, ninety-two years ago—there were two men who said: 'The Count is dead; we do not care for him. We will go tonight and have a free hunt in his wood'—the long wood on the hill that you have seen behind Råbäck. Well, those that heard them say this, they said: 'No, do not go; we are sure you will meet with persons walking who should not be walking. They should be resting, not walking.' These men laughed. There were no forest-men to keep the wood, because no one wished to live there. The family were not here at the house. These men could do what they wished.

"Very well, they go to the wood that night. My grandfather was sitting here in this room. It was the summer, and a light night. With the window open, he could see out to the wood, and hear.

"So he sat there, and two or three men with him, and they listened. At first they hear nothing at all; then they hear someone—you know how far away it is—they hear someone scream, just as if the most inside part of his soul was twisted out of him. All of them in the room caught hold of each other, and they sat so for three-quarters of an hour. Then they hear someone else, only about three hundred ells off. They hear him laugh out loud: it was not one of those two men that laughed, and, indeed, they have all of them said that it was not any man at all. After that they hear a great door shut.

"Then, when it was just light with the sun they all went to the priest. They said to him:

"Father, put on your gown and your ruff, and come to bury these men, Anders Bjornsen and Hans Thorbjorn.'

"You understand that they were sure these men were dead. So they went to the wood—my grandfather never forgot this. He said they were all like so many dead men themselves. The priest, too, he was in a white fear. He said when they came to him:

"'I heard one cry in the night, and I heard one laugh afterwards. If I cannot forget that, I shall not be able to sleep again.'

"So they went to the wood, and they found these men on the edge of the wood. Hans Thorbjorn was standing with his back against a tree, and all the time he was pushing with his hands—pushing something away from him which was not there. So he was not dead. And they led him away, and took him to the home at Nykjoping, and he died before the winter; but he went on pushing with his hands. Also Anders Bjornsen was there; but he was dead. And I tell you this about Anders Bjornsen, that he was once a beautiful man, but now his face was not there, because the flesh of it was sucked away off the bones. You understand that? My grandfather did not forget that. And they laid him on the bier which they brought, and they put a cloth over his head, and the priest walked before; and they began to sing the psalm for the dead as well as they could. So, as they were singing the end of the first verse, one fell down, who was carrying the head of the bier, and the others looked back, and they saw that the cloth had fallen off, and the eyes of Anders Bjornsen were looking up, because there was nothing to close over them. And this they could not bear. Therefore the priest laid the cloth upon him, and sent for a spade, and they buried him in that place."

The next day Mr. Wraxall records that the deacon called for him soon after his breakfast, and took him to the church and mausoleum. He noticed that the key of the latter was hung on a nail just by the pulpit, and it occurred to him that, as the church door seemed to be left unlocked as a rule, it would not be difficult for him to pay a second and more private visit to the monuments if there proved to be more of interest among them than could be digested at first. The building, when he entered it, he found not unimposing. The monuments, mostly large erections of the seventeenth and eighteenth centuries, were dignified if luxuriant, and the epitaphs and heraldry were copious. The central space of the domed room was occupied by three copper sarcophagi, covered with finely-engraved ornament. Two of them had, as is commonly the case in Denmark and Sweden, a large metal crucifix on the lid. The third, that of Count Magnus, as it appeared, had, instead of that, a full-length effigy engraved upon it, and round the edge were several bands of similar ornament representing various scenes. One was a battle, with cannon belching out smoke, and walled towns, and troops of pikemen. Another showed an execution. In a third, among trees, was a man running at full speed, with flying hair and outstretched hands. After him followed a strange form; it would be hard to say whether the artist had intended it for a man, and was unable to give the requisite similitude, or whether it was intentionally made as monstrous as it looked. In view of the skill with which the rest of the drawing was done, Mr. Wraxall felt inclined to adopt the latter idea. The figure was unduly short, and was for the most part muffled in a hooded garment which swept the ground. The only part of the form which projected from that shelter was not shaped like any hand or arm. Mr. Wraxall compares it to the tentacle of a devil-fish, and continues: "On seeing this, I said to myself, 'This, then, which is evidently an allegorical representation of some kind—a fiend pursuing a hunted soul—may be the origin of the story of Count Magnus and his mysterious companion. Let us see how the huntsman is pictured: doubtless it will be a demon blowing his horn.'" But, as it turned out, there was no such sensational figure, only the semblance of a cloaked man on a hillock, who stood leaning on a stick, and watching the hunt with an interest which the engraver had tried to express in his attitude.

Mr. Wraxall noted the finely-worked and massive steel padlocks—three in number—which secured the sarcophagus. One of them, he saw, was detached, and lay on the pavement. And then, unwilling to delay the deacon longer or to waste his own working-time, he made his way onward to the manor-house.

"It is curious," he notes, "how on retracing a familiar path one's thoughts engross one to the absolute exclusion of surrounding objects. Tonight, for the second time, I had entirely failed to notice where I was going (I had planned a private visit to the tomb-house to copy the epitaphs), when I suddenly, as it were, awoke to consciousness, and found myself (as before) turning in at the churchyard gate, and, I believe, singing or chanting some such words as, 'Are you awake, Count Magnus? Are you asleep, Count Magnus?' and then something more which I have failed to recollect. It seemed to me that I must have been behaving in this nonsensical way for some time."

He found the key of the manor-house where he had expected to find it, and copied the greater part of what he wanted; in fact, he stayed until the light began to fail him.

"I must have been wrong," he writes, "in saying that one of the padlocks of my Count's sarcophagus was unfastened; I see tonight that two are loose. I picked both up, and laid them carefully on the window-ledge, after trying unsuccessfully to close them. The remaining one is still firm, and, though I take it to be a spring lock, I cannot guess how it is opened. Had I succeeded in undoing it, I am almost afraid I should have taken the liberty of opening the sarcophagus. It is strange, the interest I feel in the personality of this, I fear, somewhat ferocious and grim old noble."

The day following was, as it turned out, the last of Mr. Wraxall's stay at Råbäck. He received letters connected with certain investments which made it desirable that he should return to England; his work among the papers was practically done, and traveling was slow. He decided, therefore, to make his farewells, put some finishing touches to his notes, and be off.

These finishing touches and farewells, as it turned out, took more time than he had expected. The hospitable family insisted on his staying to dine with them—they dined at three—and it was verging on half-past six before he was outside the iron gates of Råbäck. He dwelt on every step of his walk by the lake, determined to saturate himself, now that he trod it for the last time, in the sentiment of the place and hour. And when he reached the summit of the churchyard knoll, he lingered for many minutes, gazing at the limitless prospect of woods near and distant, all dark beneath a sky of liquid green. When at last he turned to go, the thought struck him that surely he must bid farewell to Count Magnus as well as the rest of the De la Gardies. The church was but twenty yards away, and he knew where the key of the mausoleum hung. It was not long before he was standing over the great copper coffin, and, as usual, talking to himself aloud. "You may have been a bit of a rascal in your time, Magnus," he was saying, "but for all that I should like to see you, or, rather—"

"Just at that instant," he says, "I felt a blow on my foot. Hastily enough I drew it back, and something fell on the pavement with a clash. It was the third, the last of the three padlocks which had fastened the sarcophagus. I stooped to pick it up, and—Heaven is my witness that I am writing only the bare truth—before I had raised myself there was a sound of metal hinges creaking, and I distinctly saw the lid shifting upwards. I may have behaved like a coward, but I could not for my life stay for one moment. I was outside that dreadful building in less time than I can write—almost as quickly as I could have said—the words; and what frightens me yet more, I could not turn the key in the lock. As I sit here in my room noting these facts, I ask myself (it was not twenty minutes ago) whether that noise of creaking metal continued, and I cannot tell whether it did or not. I only know that there was something more than I have written that alarmed me, but whether it was sound or sight I am not able to remember. What is this that I have done?"

Poor Mr. Wraxall! He set out on his journey to England on the next day, as he had planned, and he reached England in safety; and yet, as I gather from his changed hand and inconsequent jottings, a broken man. One of several small notebooks that have come to me with his papers gives, not a key to, but a kind of inkling of, his experiences. Much of his journey was made by canal-boat, and I find not less than six painful attempts to enumerate and describe his fellow-passengers. The entries are of this kind:

'24. Pastor of village in Skåne. Usual black coat and soft black hat.

'25. Commercial traveller from Stockholm going to Trollhättan. Black cloak, brown hat.

'26. Man in long black cloak, broad-leafed hat, very old-fashioned.'

This entry is lined out, and a note added: "Perhaps identical with No. 13. Have not not yet seen his face." On referring to No. 13, I find that he is a Roman priest in a cassock.

The net result of the reckoning is always the same. Twenty-eight people appear in the enumeration, one being always a man in a long black cloak and broad hat, and the other a "short figure in dark cloak and hood." On the other hand, it is always noted that only twenty-six passengers appear at meals, and that the man in the cloak is perhaps absent, and the short figure is certainly absent.

O n reaching England, it appears that Mr. Wraxall landed at Harwich, and that he resolved at once to put himself out of the reach of some person or persons whom he never specifies, but whom he had evidently come to regard as his pursuers. Accordingly he took a vehicle—it was a closed fly—not trusting the railway, and drove across country to the village of Belchamp St. Paul. It was about nine o'clock on a moonlight August night when he neared the place. He was sitting forward, and looking out of the window at the fields and thickets—there was little else to be seen—racing past him. Suddenly he came to a cross-road. At the corner two figures were standing motionless; both were in dark cloaks; the taller one wore a hat, the shorter a hood. He had no time to see their faces, nor did they make any motion that he could discern. Yet the horse shied violently and broke into a gallop, and Mr. Wraxall sank back into his seat in something like desperation. He had seen them before.

Arrived at Belchamp St. Paul, he was fortunate enough to find a decent furnished lodging, and for the next twenty-four hours he lived comparatively speaking, in peace. His last notes were written on this day. They are too disjointed and ejaculatory to be given here in full, but the substance of them is clear enough. He is expecting a visit from his pursuers—how or when he knows not—and his constant cry is "What has he done?" and "Is there no hope?" Doctors, he knows, would call him mad, policemen would laugh at him. The parson is away. What can he do but lock his door and cry to God?

P eople still remembered last year at Belchamp St. Paul how a strange gentleman came one evening in July years back; and how the next morning but one he was found dead, and there was an inquest; and the jury that viewed the body fainted, seven of 'em did, and none of 'em wouldn't speak to what they see, and the verdict was visitation of God; and how the people as kep' the 'ouse moved out that same week, and went away from that part. But they do not, I think, know that any glimmer of light has ever been thrown, or could be thrown, on the mystery. It so happened that last year the little house came into my hands as part of a legacy. It had stood empty since 1863, and there seemed no prospect of letting it; so I had it pulled down, and the papers of which I have given you an abstract were found in a forgotten cupboard under the window in the best bedroom.

/

A DEAD FINGER

Sabine Baring-Gould

first published in *A Book of Ghosts* (October 1904)

I.

Why the National Gallery should not attract so many visitors as, say, the British Museum, I cannot explain. The latter does not contain much that, one would suppose, appeals to the interest of the ordinary sightseer. What knows such of prehistoric flints and scratched bones? Of Assyrian sculpture? Of Egyptian hieroglyphics? The Greek and Roman statuary is cold and dead. The paintings in the National Gallery glow with color, and are instinct with life. Yet, somehow, a few listless wanderers saunter yawning through the National Gallery, whereas swarms pour through the halls of the British Museum, and talk and pass remarks about the objects there exposed, of the date and meaning of which they have not the faintest conception.

I was thinking of this problem, and endeavoring to unravel it, one morning whilst sitting in the room for English masters at the great collection in Trafalgar Square. At the same time another thought forced itself upon me. I had been through the rooms devoted to foreign schools, and had then come into that given over to Reynolds, Morland, Gainsborough, Constable, and Hogarth. The morning had been for a while propitious, but towards noon a dense umber-tinted fog had come on, making it all but impossible to see the pictures, and quite impossible to do them justice. I was tired, and so seated myself on one of the chairs, and fell into the consideration first of all of—why the National Gallery is not as popular as it should be; and secondly, how it was that the British School had no beginnings, like those of Italy and the Netherlands. We can see the art of the painter from its first initiation in the Italian peninsula, and among the Flemings. It starts on its progress like a child, and we can trace every stage of its growth. Not so with English art. It springs to life in full and splendid maturity. Who were there before Reynolds and Gainsborough and Hogarth? The great names of those portrait and subject painters who have left their canvases upon the walls of our country houses were those of foreigners—Holbein, Kneller, Van Dyck, and Lely for portraits, and Monnoyer for flower and fruit pieces. Landscapes, figure subjects were all importations, none home-grown. How came that about? Was there no limner that was native? Was it that fashion trampled on home-grown pictorial beginnings as it flouted and spurned native music?

Here was food for contemplation. Dreaming in the brown fog, looking through it without seeing its beauties, at Hogarth's painting of Lavinia Fenton as Polly Peachum, without wondering how so indifferent a beauty could have captivated the Duke of Bolton and held him for thirty years, I was recalled to myself and my surroundings by the strange conduct of a lady who had seated herself on a chair near me, also discouraged by the fog, and awaiting its dispersion.

I had not noticed her particularly. At the present moment I do not remember particularly what she was like. So far as I can recollect she was middle-aged, and was quietly yet well dressed. It was not her face nor her dress that attracted my attention and disturbed the current of my thoughts; the effect I speak of was produced by her strange movements and behavior.

She had been sitting listless, probably thinking of nothing at all, or nothing in particular, when, in turning her eyes round, and finding that she could see nothing of the paintings, she began to study me. This did concern me greatly. A cat may look at the king; but to be contemplated by a lady is a compliment sufficient to please any gentleman. It was not gratified vanity that troubled my thoughts, but the consciousness that my appearance produced—first of all a startled surprise, then undisguised alarm, and, finally, indescribable horror.

Now a man can sit quietly leaning on the head of his umbrella, and glow internally, warmed and illumined by the consciousness that he is being surveyed with admiration by a lovely woman, even when he is middle-aged and not fashionably dressed; but no man can maintain his composure when he discovers himself to be an object of aversion and terror.

What was it? I passed my hand over my chin and upper lip, thinking it not impossible that I might have forgotten to shave that morning, and in my confusion not considering that the fog would prevent the lady from discovering neglect in this particular, had it occurred, which it had not. I am a little careless, perhaps, about shaving when in the country; but when in town, never.

The next idea that occurred to me was—a smut. Had a London black, curdled in that dense pea-soup atmosphere, descended on my nose and blackened it? I hastily drew my silk handkerchief from my pocket, moistened it, and passed it over my nose, and then each cheek. I then turned my eyes into the corners and looked at the lady, to see whether by this means I had got rid of what was objectionable in my personal appearance.

Then I saw that her eyes, dilated with horror, were riveted, not on my face, but on my leg.

My leg! What on earth could that harmless member have in it so terrifying? The morning had been dull; there had been rain in the night, and I admit that on leaving my hotel I had turned up the bottoms of my trousers. That is a proceeding not so uncommon, not so outrageous as to account for the stony stare of this woman's eyes.

If that were all I would turn my trousers down.

Then I saw her shrink from the chair on which she sat to one further removed from me, but still with her eyes fixed on my leg—about the level of my knee. She had let fall her umbrella, and was grasping the seat of her chair with both hands, as she backed from me.

I need hardly say that I was greatly disturbed in mind and feelings, and forgot all about the origin of the English schools of painters, and the question why the British Museum is more popular than the National Gallery.

Thinking that I might have been spattered by a hansom whilst crossing Oxford Street, I passed my hand down my side hastily, with a sense of annoyance, and all at once touched something cold, clammy, that sent a thrill to my heart, and made me start and take a step forward. At the same moment, the lady, with a cry of horror, sprang to her feet, and with raised hands fled from the room, leaving her umbrella where it had fallen.

There were other visitors to the Picture Gallery besides ourselves, who had been passing through the saloon, and they turned at her cry, and looked in surprise after her.

The policeman stationed in the room came to me and asked what had happened. I was in such agitation that I hardly knew what to answer. I told him that I could explain what had occurred little better than himself. I had noticed that the lady had worn an odd expression, and had behaved in most extraordinary fashion, and that he had best take charge of her umbrella, and wait for her return to claim it.

This questioning by the official was vexing, as it prevented me from at once and on the spot investigating the cause of her alarm and mine—hers at something she must have seen on my leg, and mine at something I had distinctly felt creeping up my leg.

The numbing and sickening effect on me of the touch of the object I had not seen was not to be shaken off at once. Indeed, I felt as though my hand were contaminated, and that I could have no rest till I had thoroughly washed the hand, and, if possible, washed away the feeling that had been produced.

I looked on the floor, I examined my leg, but saw nothing. As I wore my overcoat, it was probable that in rising from my seat the skirt had fallen over my trousers and hidden the thing, whatever it was. I therefore hastily removed my overcoat and shook it, then I looked at my trousers. There was nothing whatever on my leg, and nothing fell from my overcoat when shaken.

Accordingly I reinvested myself, and hastily left the Gallery; then took my way as speedily as I could, without actually running, to Charing Cross Station and down the narrow way leading to the Metropolitan, where I went into Faulkner's bath and hairdressing establishment, and asked for hot water to thoroughly wash my hand and well soap it. I bathed my hand in water as hot as I could endure it, employed carbolic soap, and then, after having a good brush down, especially on my left side where my hand had encountered the object that had so affected me, I left. I had entertained the intention of going to the Princess's Theatre that evening, and of securing a ticket in the morning; but all thought of theatre-going was gone from me. I could not free my heart from the sense of nausea and cold that had been produced by the touch. I went into Gatti's to have lunch, and ordered something, I forget what, but, when served, I found that my appetite was gone. I could eat nothing; the food inspired me with disgust. I thrust it from me untasted, and, after drinking a couple of glasses of claret, left the restaurant, and returned to my hotel.

Feeling sick and faint, I threw my overcoat over the sofa-back, and cast myself on my bed.

I do not know that there was any particular reason for my doing so, but as I lay my eyes were on my great-coat.

The density of the fog had passed away, and there was light again, not of first quality, but sufficient for a Londoner to swear by, so that I could see everything in my room, though through a veil, darkly.

I do not think my mind was occupied in any way. About the only occasions on which, to my knowledge, my mind is actually passive or inert is when crossing the Channel in *The Foam* from Dover to Calais, when I am always, in every weather, abjectly seasick—and thoughtless. But as I now lay on my bed, uncomfortable, squeamish, without knowing why—I was in the same inactive mental condition. But not for long.

I saw something that startled me.

First, it appeared to me as if the lappet of my overcoat pocket were in movement, being raised. I did not pay much attention to this, as I supposed that the garment was sliding down on to the seat of the sofa, from the back, and that this displacement of gravity caused the movement I observed. But this I soon saw was not the case. That which moved the lappet was something in the pocket that was struggling to get out. I could see now that it was working its way up the inside, and that when it reached the opening it lost balance and fell down again. I could make this out by the projections and indentations in the cloth; these moved as the creature, or whatever it was, worked its way up the lining.

"A mouse," I said, and forgot my seediness; I was interested. "The little rascal! However did he contrive to seat himself in my pocket? and I have worn that overcoat all the morning!" But no—it was not a mouse. I saw something white poke its way out from under the lappet; and in another moment an object was revealed that, though revealed, I could not understand, nor could I distinguish what it was.

Now roused by curiosity, I raised myself on my elbow. In doing this I made some noise, the bed creaked. Instantly the something dropped on the floor, lay outstretched for a moment, to recover itself, and then began, with the motions of a maggot, to run along the floor.

There is a caterpillar called "The Measurer," because, when it advances, it draws its tail up to where its head is and then throws forward its full length, and again draws up its extremity, forming at each time a loop; and with each step measuring its total length. The object I now saw on the floor was advancing precisely like the measuring caterpillar. It had the color of a cheese-maggot, and in length was about three and a half inches. It was not, however, like a caterpillar, which is flexible throughout its entire length, but this was, as it seemed to me, jointed in two places, one joint being more conspicuous than the other. For some moments I was so completely paralyzed by astonishment that I remained motionless, looking at the thing as it crawled along the carpet—a dull green carpet with darker green, almost black, flowers in it.

It had, as it seemed to me, a glossy head, distinctly marked; but, as the light was not brilliant, I could not make out very clearly, and, moreover, the rapid movements prevented close scrutiny.

Presently, with a shock still more startling than that produced by its apparition at the opening of the pocket of my great-coat, I became convinced that what I saw was a finger, a human forefinger, and that the glossy head was no other than the nail.

The finger did not seem to have been amputated. There was no sign of blood or laceration where the knuckle should be, but the extremity of the finger, or root rather, faded away to indistinctness, and I was unable to make out the root of the finger.

I could see no hand, no body behind this finger, nothing whatever except a finger that had little token of warm life in it, no coloration as though blood circulated in it; and this finger was in active motion creeping along the carpet towards a wardrobe that stood against the wall by the fireplace.

I sprang off the bed and pursued it.

Evidently the finger was alarmed, for it redoubled its pace, reached the wardrobe, and went under it. By the time I had arrived at the article of furniture it had disappeared. I lit a vesta match and held it beneath the wardrobe, that was raised above the carpet by about two inches, on turned feet, but I could see nothing more of the finger.

I got my umbrella and thrust it beneath, and raked forwards and backwards, right and left, and raked out flue, and nothing more solid.

II.

I packed my portmanteau next day and returned to my home in the country. All desire for amusement in town was gone, and the faculty to transact business had departed as well.

A languor and qualms had come over me, and my head was in a maze. I was unable to fix my thoughts on anything. At times I was disposed to believe that my wits were deserting me, at others that I was on the verge of a severe illness. Anyhow, whether likely to go off my head or not, or take to my bed, home was the only place for me, and homeward I sped, accordingly. On reaching my country habitation, my servant, as usual, took my portmanteau to my bedroom, unstrapped it, but did not unpack it. I object to his throwing out the contents of my Gladstone bag; not that there is anything in it he may not see, but that he puts my things where I cannot find them again. My clothes—he is welcome to place them where he likes and where they belong, and this latter he knows better than I do; but, then, I carry about with me other things than a dress suit, and changes of linen and flannel. There are letters, papers, books—and the proper destinations of these are known only to myself. A servant has a singular and evil knack of putting away literary matter and odd volumes in such places that it takes the owner half a day to find them again. Although I was uncomfortable, and my head in a whirl, I opened and unpacked my own portmanteau. As I was thus engaged I saw something curled up in my collar-box, the lid of which had got broken in by a boot-heel impinging on it. I had pulled off the damaged cover to see if my collars had been spoiled, when something curled up inside suddenly rose on end and leapt, just like a cheese-jumper, out of the box, over the edge of the Gladstone bag, and scurried away across the floor in a manner already familiar to me.

I could not doubt for a moment what it was—here was the finger again. It had come with me from London to the country.

Whither it went in its run over the floor I do not know, I was too bewildered to observe.

Somewhat later, towards evening, I seated myself in my easy-chair, took up a book, and tried to read. I was tired with the journey, with the knocking about in town, and the discomfort and alarm produced by the apparition of the finger. I felt worn out. I was unable to give my attention to what I read, and before I was aware was asleep. Roused for an instant by the fall of the book from my hands, I speedily relapsed into unconsciousness. I am not sure that a doze in an armchair ever does good. It usually leaves me in a semi-stupid condition and with a headache. Five minutes in a horizontal position on my bed is worth thirty in a chair. That is my experience. In sleeping in a sedentary position the head is a difficulty; it drops forward or lolls on one side or the other, and has to be brought back into a position in which the line to the centre of gravity runs through the trunk, otherwise the head carries the body over in a sort of general capsize out of the chair on to the floor.

I slept, on the occasion of which I am speaking, pretty healthily, because deadly weary; but I was brought to waking, not by my head falling over the arm of the chair, and my trunk tumbling after it, but by a feeling of cold extending from my throat to my heart. When I awoke I was in a diagonal position, with my right ear resting on my right shoulder, and exposing the left side of my throat, and it was here—where the jugular vein throbs—that I felt the greatest intensity of cold. At once I shrugged my left shoulder, rubbing my neck with the collar of my coat in so doing. Immediately something fell off, upon the floor, and I again saw the finger.

My disgust—horror, were intensified when I perceived that it was dragging something after it, which might have been an old stocking, and which I took at first glance for something of the sort.

The evening sun shone in through my window, in a brilliant golden ray that lighted the object as it scrambled along. With this illumination I was able to distinguish what the object was. It is not easy to describe it, but I will make the attempt.

The finger I saw was solid and material; what it drew after it was neither, or was in a nebulous, protoplasmic condition. The finger was attached to a hand that was curdling into matter and in process of acquiring solidity; attached to the hand was an arm in a very filmy condition, and this arm belonged to a human body in a still more vaporous, immaterial condition. This was being dragged along the floor by the finger, just as a silkworm might pull after it the tangle of its web. I could see legs and arms, and head, and coat-tail tumbling about and interlacing and disentangling again in a promiscuous manner. There were no bone, no muscle, no substance in the figure; the members were attached to the trunk, which was spineless, but they had evidently no functions, and were wholly dependent on the finger which pulled them along in a jumble of parts as it advanced.

In such confusion did the whole vaporous matter seem, that I think—I cannot say for certain it was so, but the impression left on my mind was—that one of the eyeballs was looking out at a nostril, and the tongue lolling out of one of the ears.

It was, however, only for a moment that I saw this germ-body; I cannot call by another name that which had not more substance than smoke. I saw it only so long as it was being dragged athwart the ray of sunlight. The moment it was pulled jerkily out of the beam into the shadow beyond, I could see nothing of it, only the crawling finger.

I had not sufficient moral energy or physical force in me to rise, pursue, and stamp on the finger, and grind it with my heel into the floor. Both seemed drained out of me. What became of the finger, whither it went, how it managed to secrete itself, I do not know. I had lost the power to inquire. I sat in my chair, chilled, staring before me into space.

"Please, sir," a voice said, "there's Mr. Square below, electrical engineer."

"Eh?" I looked dreamily round.

My valet was at the door.

"Please, sir, the gentleman would be glad to be allowed to go over the house and see that all the electrical apparatus is in order."

"Oh, indeed! Yes—show him up."

III.

I had recently placed the lighting of my house in the hands of an electrical engineer, a very intelligent man, Mr. Square, for whom I had contracted a sincere friendship.

He had built a shed with a dynamo out of sight, and had entrusted the laying of the wires to subordinates, as he had been busy with other orders and could not personally watch every detail. But he was not the man to let anything pass unobserved, and he knew that electricity was not a force to be played with. Bad or careless workmen will often insufficiently protect the wires, or neglect the insertion of the lead which serves as a safety-valve in the event of the current being too strong. Houses may be set on fire, human beings fatally shocked, by the neglect of a bad or slovenly workman.

The apparatus for my mansion was but just completed, and Mr. Square had come to inspect it and make sure that all was right.

He was an enthusiast in the matter of electricity, and saw for it a vast perspective, the limits of which could not be predicted.

"All forces," said he, "are correlated. When you have force in one form, you may just turn it into this or that, as you like. In one form it is motive power, in another it is light, in another heat. Now we have electricity for illumination. We employ it, but not as freely as in the States, for propelling vehicles. Why should we have horses drawing our buses? We should use only electric trams. Why do we burn coal to warm our shins? There is electricity, which throws out no filthy smoke as does coal. Why should we let the tides waste their energies in the Thames? in other estuaries? There we have Nature supplying us—free, gratis, and for nothing—with all the force we want for propelling, for heating, for lighting. I will tell you something more, my dear sir," said Mr. Square. "I have mentioned but three modes of force, and have instanced but a limited number of uses to which electricity may be turned. How is it with photography? Is not electric light becoming an artistic agent? I bet you," said he, "before long it will become a therapeutic agent as well."

"Oh, yes; I have heard of certain impostors with their life-belts."

Mr. Square did not relish this little dig I gave him. He winced, but returned to the charge. "We don't know how to direct it aright, that is all," said he. "I haven't taken the matter up, but others will, I bet; and we shall have electricity used as freely as now we use powders and pills. I don't believe in doctors' stuffs myself. I hold that disease lays hold of a man because he lacks physical force to resist it. Now, is it not obvious that you are beginning at the wrong end when you attack the disease? What you want is to supply force, make up for the lack of physical power, and force is force wherever you find it —here motive, there illuminating, and so on. I don't see why a physician should not utilize the tide rushing out under London Bridge for restoring the feeble vigor of all who are languid and a prey to disorder in the Metropolis. It will come to that, I bet, and that is not all. Force is force, everywhere.

Political, moral force, physical force, dynamic force, heat, light, tidal waves, and so on—all are one, all is one. In time we shall know how to galvanize into aptitude and moral energy all the limp and crooked consciences and wills that need taking in hand, and such there always will be in modern civilization. I don't know how to do it. I don't know how it will be done, but in the future the priest as well as the doctor will turn electricity on as his principal, nay, his only agent. And he can get his force anywhere, out of the running stream, out of the wind, out of the tidal wave.

"I'll give you an instance," continued Mr. Square, chuckling and rubbing his hands, "to show you the great possibilities in electricity, used in a crude fashion. In a certain great city away far west in the States, a go-ahead place, too, more so than New York, they had electric trams all up and down and along the roads to everywhere. The union men working for the company demanded that the non-unionists should be turned off. But the company didn't see it. Instead, it turned off the union men. It had up its sleeve a sufficiency of the others, and filled all places at once. Union men didn't like it, and passed word that at a given hour on a certain day every wire was to be cut. The company knew this by means of its spies, and turned on, ready for them, three times the power into all the wires. At the fixed moment, up the poles went the strikers to cut the cables, and down they came a dozen times quicker than they went up, I bet. Then there came wires to the hospitals from all quarters for stretchers to carry off the disabled men, some with broken legs, arms, ribs; two or three had their necks broken. I reckon the company was wonderfully merciful—it didn't put on sufficient force to make cinders of them then and there; possibly opinion might not have liked it. Stopped the strike, did that. Great moral effect—all done by electricity."

In this manner Mr. Square was wont to rattle on. He interested me, and I came to think that there might be something in what he said—that his suggestions were not mere nonsense. I was glad to see Mr. Square enter my room, shown in by my man. I did not rise from my chair to shake his hand, for I had not sufficient energy to do so. In a languid tone I welcomed him and signed to him to take a seat. Mr. Square looked at me with some surprise.

"Why, what's the matter?" he said. "You seem unwell. Not got the 'flue, have you?"

"I beg your pardon?"

"The influenza. Every third person is crying out that he has it, and the sale of eucalyptus is enormous, not that eucalyptus is any good. Influenza microbes indeed! What care they for eucalyptus? You've gone down some steps of the ladder of life since I saw you last, squire. How do you account for that?"

I hesitated about mentioning the extraordinary circumstances that had occurred; but Square was a man who would not allow any beating about the bush. He was downright and straight, and in ten minutes had got the entire story out of me.

"Rather boisterous for your nerves that—a crawling finger," said he. "It's a queer story taken on end."

Then he was silent, considering.

After a few minutes he rose, and said: "I'll go and look at the fittings, and then I'll turn this little matter of yours over again, and see if I can't knock the bottom out of it, I'm kinder fond of these sort of things."

Mr. Square was not a Yankee, but he had lived for some time in America, and affected to speak like an American. He used expressions, terms of speech common in the States, but had none of the Transatlantic twang. He was a man absolutely without affectation in every other particular; this was his sole weakness, and it was harmless.

The man was so thorough in all he did that I did not expect his return immediately. He was certain to examine every portion of the dynamo engine, and all the connections and burners. This would necessarily engage him for some hours. As the day was nearly done, I knew he could not accomplish what he wanted that evening, and accordingly gave orders that a room should be prepared for him. Then, as my head was full of pain, and my skin was burning, I told my servant to apologize for my absence from dinner, and tell Mr. Square that I was really forced to return to my bed by sickness, and that I believed I was about to be prostrated by an attack of influenza.

The valet—a worthy fellow, who has been with me for six years—was concerned at my appearance, and urged me to allow him to send for a doctor. I had no confidence in the local practitioner, and if I sent for another from the nearest town I should offend him, and a row would perhaps ensue, so I declined. If I were really in for an influenza attack, I knew about as much as any doctor how to deal with it. Quinine, quinine—that was all. I bade my man light a small lamp, lower it, so as to give sufficient illumination to enable me to find some lime-juice at my bed head, and my pocket-handkerchief, and to be able to read my watch. When he had done this, I bade him leave me.

I lay in bed, burning, racked with pain in my head, and with my eyeballs on fire.

Whether I fell asleep or went off my head for a while I cannot tell. I may have fainted. I have no recollection of anything after having gone to bed and taken a sip of lime-juice that tasted to me like soap—till I was roused by a sense of pain in my ribs—a slow, gnawing, torturing pain, waxing momentarily more intense. In half-consciousness I was partly dreaming and partly aware of actual suffering. The pain was real; but in my fancy I thought that a great maggot was working its way into my side between my ribs. I seemed to see it. It twisted itself half round, then reverted to its former position, and again twisted itself, moving like a bradawl, not like a gimlet, which latter forms a complete revolution.

This, obviously, must have been a dream, hallucination only, as I was lying on my back and my eyes were directed towards the bottom of the bed, and the coverlet and blankets and sheet intervened between my eyes and my side.

But in fever one sees without eyes, and in every direction, and through all obstructions.

Roused thoroughly by an excruciating twinge, I tried to cry out, and succeeded in throwing myself over on my right side, that which was in pain. At once I felt the thing withdrawn that was awling—if I may use the word—in between my ribs.

And now I saw, standing beside the bed, a figure that had its arm under the bedclothes, and was slowly removing it. The hand was leisurely drawn from under the coverings and rested on the eider-down coverlet, with the forefinger extended.

The figure was that of a man, in shabby clothes, with a sallow, mean face, a retreating forehead, with hair cut after the French fashion, and a mustache, dark. The jaws and chin were covered with a bristly growth, as if shaving had been neglected for a fortnight. The figure did not appear to be thoroughly solid, but to be of the consistency of curd, and the face was of the complexion of curd. As I looked at this object it withdrew, sliding backward in an odd sort of manner, and as though overweighted by the hand, which was the most substantial, indeed the only substantial portion of it. Though the figure retreated stooping, yet it was no longer huddled along by the finger, as if it had no material existence. If the same, it had acquired a consistency and a solidity which it did not possess before.

How it vanished I do not know, nor whither it went. The door opened, and Square came in.

"What!" he exclaimed with cheery voice; "influenza is it?"

"I don't know—I think it's that finger again."

IV.

"Now, look here," said Square, "I'm not going to have that cuss at its pranks any more. Tell me all about it."

I was now so exhausted, so feeble, that I was not able to give a connected account of what had taken place, but Square put to me just a few pointed questions and elicited the main facts. He pieced them together in his own orderly mind, so as to form a connected whole. "There is a feature in the case," said he, "that strikes me as remarkable and important. At first—a finger only, then a hand, then a nebulous figure attached to the hand, without backbone, without consistency. Lastly, a complete form, with consistency and with backbone, but the latter in a gelatinous condition, and the entire figure overweighted by the hand, just as hand and figure were previously overweighted by the finger. Simultaneously with this compacting and consolidating of the figure, came your degeneration and loss of vital force and, in a word, of health. What you lose, that object acquires, and what it acquires, it gains by contact with you. That's clear enough, is it not?"

"I dare say. I don't know. I can't think."

"I suppose not; the faculty of thought is drained out of you. Very well, I must think for you, and I will. Force is force, and see if I can't deal with your visitant in such a way as will prove just as truly a moral dissuasive as that employed on the union men on strike in——never mind where it was. That's not to the point."

"Will you kindly give me some lime-juice?" I entreated.

I sipped the acid draught, but without relief. I listened to Square, but without hope. I wanted to be left alone. I was weary of my pain, weary of everything, even of life. It was a matter of indifference to me whether I recovered or slipped out of existence.

"It will be here again shortly," said the engineer. "As the French say, *l'appetit vient en mangeant*. It has been at you thrice, it won't be content without another peck. And if it does get another, I guess it will pretty well about finish you."

Mr. Square rubbed his chin, and then put his hands into his trouser pockets. That also was a trick acquired in the States, an inelegant one. His hands, when not actively occupied, went into his pockets, inevitably they gravitated thither. Ladies did not like Square; they said he was not a gentleman. But it was not that he said or did anything "off color," only he spoke to them, looked at them, walked with them, always with his hands in his pockets. I have seen a lady turn her back on him deliberately because of this trick.

Standing now with his hands in his pockets, he studied my bed, and said contemptuously: "Old-fashioned and bad, fourposter. Oughtn't to be allowed, I guess; unwholesome all the way round."

I was not in a condition to dispute this. I like a fourposter with curtains at head and feet; not that I ever draw them, but it gives a sense of privacy that is wanting in one of your half-tester beds.

If there is a window at one's feet, one can lie in bed without the glare in one's eyes, and yet without darkening the room by drawing the blinds. There is much to be said for a fourposter, but this is not the place in which to say it.

Mr. Square pulled his hands out of his pockets and began fiddling with the electric point near the head of my bed, attached a wire, swept it in a semicircle along the floor, and then thrust the knob at the end into my hand in the bed.

"Keep your eye open," said he, "and your hand shut and covered. If that finger comes again tickling your ribs, try it with the point. I'll manage the switch, from behind the curtain."

Then he disappeared.

I was too indifferent in my misery to turn my head and observe where he was. I remained inert, with the knob in my hand, and my eyes closed, suffering and thinking of nothing but the shooting pains through my head and the aches in my loins and back and legs.

Some time probably elapsed before I felt the finger again at work at my ribs; it groped, but no longer bored. I now felt the entire hand, not a single finger, and the hand was substantial, cold, and clammy. I was aware, how, I know not, that if the finger-point reached the region of my heart, on the left side, the hand would, so to speak, sit down on it, with the cold palm over it, and that then immediately my heart would cease to beat, and it would be, as Square might express it, "gone coon" with me.

In self-preservation I brought up the knob of the electric wire against the hand—against one of the ringers, I think—and at once was aware of a rapping, squealing noise. I turned my head languidly, and saw the form, now more substantial than before, capering in an ecstasy of pain, endeavoring fruitlessly to withdraw its arm from under the bedclothes, and the hand from the electric point.

At the same moment Square stepped from behind the curtain, with a dry laugh, and said: "I thought we should fix him. He has the coil about him, and can't escape. Now let us drop to particulars. But I shan't let you off till I know all about you."

The last sentence was addressed, not to me, but to the apparition.

Thereupon he bade me take the point away from the hand of the figure—being—whatever it was, but to be ready with it at a moment's notice. He then proceeded to catechize my visitor, who moved restlessly within the circle of wire, but could not escape from it. It replied in a thin, squealing voice that sounded as if it came from a distance, and had a querulous tone in it. I do not pretend to give all that was said. I cannot recollect everything that passed. My memory was affected by my illness, as well as my body. Yet I prefer giving the scraps that I recollect to what Square told me he had heard.

"Yes—I was unsuccessful, always was. Nothing answered with me. The world was against me. Society was. I hate Society. I don't like work neither, never did. But I like agitating against what is established. I hate the Royal Family, the landed interest, the parsons, everything that is, except the people —that is, the unemployed. I always did. I couldn't get work as suited me. When I died they buried me in a cheap coffin, dirt cheap, and gave me a nasty grave, cheap, and a service rattled away cheap, and no monument. Didn't want none. Oh! there are lots of us. All discontented. Discontent! That's a passion, it is—it gets into the veins, it fills the brain, it occupies the heart; it's a sort of divine cancer that takes possession of the entire man, and makes him dissatisfied with everything, and hate everybody. But we must have our share of happiness at some time. We all crave for it in one way or other. Some think there's a future state of blessedness and so have hope, and look to attain to it, for hope is a cable and anchor that attaches to what is real. But when you have no hope of that sort, don't believe in any future state, you must look for happiness in life here. We didn't get it when we were alive, so we seek to procure it after we are dead. We can do it, if we can get out of our cheap and nasty coffins. But not till the greater part of us is moldered away. If a finger or two remains, that can work its way up to the surface, those cheap deal coffins go to pieces quick enough. Then the only solid part of us left can pull the rest of us that has gone to nothing after it. Then we grope about after the living. The well-to-do if we can get at them—the honest working poor if we can't—we hate them too, because they are content and happy. If we reach any of these, and can touch them, then we can draw their vital force out of them into ourselves, and recuperate at their expense. That was about what I was going to do with you. Getting on famous. Nearly solidified into a new man; and given another chance in life. But I've missed it this time. Just like my luck. Miss everything. Always have, except misery and disappointment. Get plenty of that."

"What are you all?" asked Square. "Anarchists out of employ?"

"Some of us go by that name, some by other designations, but we are all one, and own allegiance to but one monarch—Sovereign discontent. We are bred to have a distaste for manual work; and we grow up loafers, grumbling at everything and quarreling with Society that is around us and the Providence that is above us."

"And what do you call yourselves now?"

"Call ourselves? Nothing; we are the same, in another condition, that is all. Folk called us once Anarchists, Nihilists, Socialists, Levelers, now they call us the Influenza. The learned talk of microbes, and bacilli, and bacteria. Microbes, bacilli, and bacteria be blowed! We are the Influenza; we the social failures, the generally discontented, coming up out of our cheap and nasty graves in the form of physical disease. We are the Influenza."

"There you are, I guess!" exclaimed Square triumphantly. "Did I not say that all forces were correlated? If so, then all negations, deficiencies of force are one in their several manifestations. Talk of Divine discontent as a force impelling to progress! Rubbish, it is a paralysis of energy. It turns all it absorbs to acid, to envy, spite, gall. It inspires nothing, but rots the whole moral system. Here you have it—moral, social, political discontent in another form; nay aspect—that is all. What Anarchism is in the body Politic, that Influenza is in the body Physical. Do you see that?"

"Ye-e-s-e-s," I believe I answered, and dropped away into the land of dreams.

I recovered. What Square did with the Thing I know not, but believe that he reduced it again to its former negative and self-decomposing condition.

/

FOR THE BLOOD IS THE LIFE

F. Marion Crawford

first published in *Collier's Weekly Magazine*
(December 1905)

We had dined at sunset on the broad roof of the old tower, because it was cooler there during the great heat of summer. Besides, the little kitchen was built at one corner of the great square platform, which made it more convenient than if the dishes had to be carried down the steep stone steps broken in places and everywhere worn with age. The tower was one of those built all down the west coast of Calabria by the Emperor Charles V early in the sixteenth century, to keep off the Barbary pirates, when the unbelievers were allied with Francis I against the Emperor and the Church. They have gone to ruin, a few still stand intact, and mine is one of the largest. How it came into my possession ten years ago, and why I spend a part of each year in it, are matters which do not concern this tale. The tower stands in one of the loneliest spots in Southern Italy, at the extremity of a curving, rocky promontory, which forms a small but safe natural harbor at the southern extremity of the Gulf of Policastro, and just north of Cape Scalea, the birthplace of Judas Iscariot, according to the old local legend. The tower stands alone on this hooked spur of the rock, and there is not a house to be seen within three miles of it. When I go there I take a couple of sailors, one of whom is a fair cook, and when I am away it is in charge of a gnome-like little being who was once a miner and who attached himself to me long ago.

My friend, who sometimes visits me in my summer solitude, is an artist by profession, a Scandinavian by birth, and a cosmopolitan by force of circumstances.

We had dined at sunset; the sunset glow had reddened and faded again, and the evening purple steeped the vast chain of the mountains that embrace the deep gulf to eastward and rear themselves higher and higher towards the south. It was hot, and we sat at the landward corner of the platform, waiting for the night breeze to come down from the lower hills. The color sank out of the air, there was a little interval of deep-grey twilight, and a lamp sent a yellow streak from the open door of the kitchen, where the men were getting their supper.

Then the moon rose suddenly above the crest of the promontory, flooding the platform and lighting up every little spur of rock and knoll of grass below us, down to the edge of the motionless water. My friend lighted his pipe and sat looking at a spot on the hillside. I knew that he was looking at it, and for a long time past I had wondered whether he would ever see anything there that would fix his attention. I knew that spot well. It was clear that he was interested at last, though it was a long time before he spoke. Like most painters, he trusts to his own eyesight, as a lion trusts his strength and a stag his speed, and he is always disturbed when he cannot reconcile what he sees with what he believes that he ought to see.

"It's strange," he said. "Do you see that little mound just on this side of the boulder?"

"Yes," I said, and I guessed what was coming.

"It looks like a grave," observed Holger.

"Very true. It does look like a grave."

"Yes," continued my friend, his eyes still fixed on the spot. "But the strange thing is that I see the body lying on the top of it. Of course," continued Holger, turning his head on one side as artists do, "it must be an effect of light. In the first place, it is not a grave at all. Secondly, if it were, the body would be inside and not outside. Therefor, it's an effect of the moonlight. Don't you see it?"

"Perfectly; I always see it on moonlight nights."

"It doesn't seem it interest you much," said Holger.

"On the contrary, it does interest me, though I am used to it. You're not so far wrong, either. The mound is really a grave."

"Nonsense!" cried Holger incredulously. "I suppose you'll tell me that what I see lying on it is really a corpse!"

"No," I answered, "it's not. I know, because I have taken the trouble to go down and see."

"Then what is it?" asked Holger.

"It's nothing."

"You mean that it's an effect of light, I suppose?"

"Perhaps it is. But the inexplicable part of the matter is that it makes no difference whether the moon is rising or setting, or waxing or waning. If there's any moonlight at all, from east or west or overhead, so long as it shines on the grave you can see the outline of the body on top."

Holger stirred up his pipe with the point of his knife, and then used his finger for a stopper. When the tobacco burned well, he rose from his chair.

"If you don't mind," he said, "I'll go down and take a look at it."

He left me, crossed the roof, and disappeared down the dark steps. I did not move, but sat looking down until he came out of the tower below. I heard him humming an old Danish song as he crossed the open space in the bright moonlight, going straight to the mysterious mound. When he was ten paces from it, Holger stopped short, made two steps forward, and then three or four backward, and then stopped again. I know what that meant. He had reached the spot where the Thing ceased to be visible—where, as he would have said, the effect of light changed.

Then he went on till he reached the mound and stood upon it. I could see the Thing still, but it was no longer lying down; it was on its knees now, winding its white arms round Holger's body and looking up into his face. A cool breeze stirred my hair at that moment, as the night wind began to come down from the hills, but it felt like a breath from another world.

The Thing seemed to be trying to climb to its feet helping itself up by Holger's body while he stood upright, quite unconscious of it and apparently looking toward the tower, which is very picturesque when the moonlight falls upon it on that side.

"Come along!" I shouted. "Don't stay there all night!"

It seemed to me that he moved reluctantly as he stepped from the mound, or else with difficulty. That was it. The Thing's arms were still round his waist, but its feet could not leave the grave. As he came slowly forward it was drawn and lengthened like a wreath of mist, thin and white, till I saw distinctly that Holger shook himself, as a man does who feels a chill. At the same instant a little wail of pain came to me on the breeze—it might have been the cry of the small owl that lives amongst the rocks—and the misty presence floated swiftly back from Holger's advancing figure and lay once more at its length upon the mound.

Again I felt the cool breeze in my hair, and this time an icy thrill of dread ran down my spine. I remembered very well that I had once gone down there alone in the moonlight; that presently, being near, I had seen nothing; that, like Holger, I had gone and had stood upon the mound; and I remembered how when I came back, sure that there was nothing there, I had felt the sudden conviction that there was something after all if I would only look back, a temptation I had resisted as unworthy of a man of sense, until, to get rid of it, I had shaken myself just as Holger did.

And now I knew that those white, misty arms had been round me, too; I knew it in a flash, and I shuddered as I remembered that I had heard the night owl then, too. But it had not been the night owl. It was the cry of the Thing.

I refilled my pipe and poured out a cup of strong southern wine; in less than a minute Holger was seated beside me again.

"Of course there's nothing there," he said, "but it's creepy, all the same. Do you know, when I was coming back I was so sure that there was something behind me that I wanted to turn around and look? It was an effort not to."

He laughed a little, knocked the ashes out of his pipe, and poured himself out some wine. For a while neither of us spoke, and the moon rose higher and we both looked at the Thing that lay on the mound.

"You might make a story about that," said Holger after a long time.

"There is one," I answered. "If you're not sleepy, I'll tell it to you."

"Go ahead," said Holger, who likes stories.

O ld Alario was dying up there in the village beyond the hill. You remember him, I have no doubt. They say that he made his money by selling sham jewelry in South America, and escaped with his gains when he was found out.. Like all those fellows, if they bring anything back with them, he at once set to work to enlarge his house, and as there are no masons here, he sent all the way to Paola for two workmen. They were a rough-looking pair of scoundrels—a Neapolitan who had lost one eye and a Sicilian with an old scar half an inch deep across his left cheek. I often saw them, for on Sundays they used to come down here and fish off the rocks. When Alario caught the fever that killed him the masons were still at work. As he had agreed that part of their pay should be their board and lodging, he made them sleep in the house. His wife was dead, and he had an only son called Angelo, who was a much better sort than himself. Angelo was to marry the daughter of the richest man in the village, and, strange to say, though the marriage was arranged by their parents, the young people were said to be in love with each other.

For that matter, the whole village was in love with Angelo, and among the rest a wild, good-looking creature called Cristina, who was more like a Romani than any girl I ever saw about here. She had very red lips and very black eyes, she was built like a greyhound, and had the tongue of the devil. But Angelo did not care a straw for her. He was rather a simpleminded fellow, quite different from his old scoundrel of a father, and under what I should call normal circumstances I really believe that he would never have looked at any girl except the nice plump little creature, with a fat dowry, whom his father meant him to marry. But things turned up which were neither normal nor natural.

On the other hand, a very handsome young shepherd from the hills above Maratea was in love with Cristina, who seems to have been quite indifferent to him. Cristina had no regular means of subsistence, but she was a good girl and willing to do any work or go on errands to any distance for the sake of a loaf of bread or a mess of beans, and permission to sleep under cover. She was especially glad when she could get something to do about the house of Angelo's father. There is no doctor in the village, and when the neighbors saw that old Alario was dying they sent Cristina to Scalea to fetch one. That was late in the afternoon, and if they had waited so long it was because the dying miser refused to allow any such extravagance while he was able to speak. But while Cristina was gone matters grew rapidly worse, the priest was brought to the bedside, and when he had done what he could he gave it as his opinion to the bystanders that the old man was dead, and left the house.

You know these people. They have a physical horror of death. Until the priest spoke, the room had been full of people. The words were hardly out of his mouth before it was empty. It was night now. They hurried down the dark steps and out into the street.

Angelo, as I have said, was away, Cristina had not come back—the simple woman-servant who had nursed the sick man fled with the rest, and the body was left alone in the flickering light of the earthen oil lamp.

Five minutes later two men looked in cautiously and crept forward toward the bed. They were the one-eyed Neapolitan mason and his Sicilian companion. They knew what they wanted. In a moment they had dragged from under the bed a small but heavy iron-bound box, and long before anyone thought of coming back to the dead man they had left the house and the village under cover of darkness. It was easy enough, for Alario's house is the last toward the gorge which leads down here, and the thieves merely went out by the back door, got over the stone wall, and had nothing to risk after that except that possibility of meeting some belated countryman, which was very small indeed, since few of the people use that path. They had a mattock and shovel, and they made their way without accident.

I am telling you this story as it must have happened, for, of course, there were no witnesses to this part of it. The men brought the box down by the gorge, intending to bury it on the beach in the wet sand, where it would have been much safer. But the paper would have rotted if they had been obliged to leave it there long, so they dug their hole down there, close to that boulder. Yes, just where the mound is now.

Cristina did not find the doctor in Scalea, for he had been sent for from a place up the valley, half-way to San Domenico. If she had found him we would have come on his mule by the upper road, which is smoother but much longer. But Cristina took the short cut by the rocks, which passes about fifty feet above the mound, and goes round that corner. The men were digging when she passed, and she heard them at work. It would not hav been like her to go by without finding out what the noise was, for she was never afraid of anything in her life, and, besides, the fishermen sometimes come ashore here at night to get a stone for an anchor or to gather sticks to make a little fire. The night was dark and Cristina probably came close to the two men before she could see what they were doing. She knew them, of course, and they knew her, and understood instantly that they were in her power. There was only one thing to be done for their safety, and they did it. They knocked her on the head, they dug the hole deep, and they buried her quickly with the iron-bound chest. They must have understood that their only chance of escaping suspicion lay in getting back to the village before their absence was noticed, for they returned immediately, and were found half and hour later gossiping quietly with the man who was making Alario's coffin. He was a crony of theirs, and had been working at the repairs in the old man's house. So far as I have been able to make out, the only persons who were supposed to know where Alario kept his treasure were Angelo and the one woman-servant I have mentioned. Angelo was away; it was the woman who discovered the theft.

It was easy enough to understand why no one else knew where the money was. The old man kept his door locked and the key in his pocket when he was out, and did not let the woman enter to clean the place unless he was there himself. The whole village knew that he had money somewhere, however, and the masons had probably discovered the whereabouts of the chest by climbing in at the window in his absence. If the old man had not been delirious until he lost consciousness he would have been in frightful agony of mind for his riches. The faithful woman-servant forgot their existence only for a few moments when she fled with the rest, overcome by the horror of death. Twenty minutes had not passed before she returned with the two hideous old hags who are always called in to prepare the dead for burial. Even then she had not at first the courage to go near the bed with them, but she made a pretense of dropping something, went down on her knees as if to find it, and looked under the bedstead. The walls of the room were newly whitewashed down to the floor and she saw at a glance that the chest was gone. It had been there in the afternoon, it had therefore been stolen in the short interval since she had left the room.

There are no carabineers stationed in the village; there is not so much as a municipal watchman, for there is no municipality. There never was such a place, I believe. Scalea is supposed to look after it in some mysterious way, and it takes a couple of hours to get anybody from there. As the old woman had lived in the village all her life, it did not even occur to her to apply to any civil authority for help. She simply set up a howl and ran through the village in the dark, screaming out that her dead master's house had been robbed. Many of the people looked out, but at first no one seemed inclined to help her. Most of them, judging her by themselves, whispered to each other that she had probably stolen the money herself. The first man to move was the father of the girl whom Angelo was to marry; having collected his household, all of whom felt a personal interest in the wealth which was to have come into the family, he declared it to be his opinion that the chest had been stolen by the two journeymen masons who lodged in the house. He headed a search for them, which naturally began in Alario's house and ended in the carpenter's workshop, where the thieves were found discussing a measure of wine with the carpenter over the half-finished coffin, by the light of one earthen lamp filled with oil and tallow. The search-party at once accused the delinquents of the crime, and threatened to lock them up in the cellar till the carabineers could be fetched from Scalea. The two men looked at each other for one moment, and then without the slightest hesitation they put out the single light, seized the unfinished coffin between them, and using it as a sort of battering ram, dashed upon their assailants in the dark. In a few moments they were beyond pursuit.

That is the end of the first part of the story. The treasure had disappeared, and as no trace of it could be found the people supposed that the thieves had succeeded in carrying it off. The old man was buried, and when Angelo came back at last he had to borrow money to pay for the miserable funeral, and had some difficulty in doing so. He hardly needed to be told that in losing his inheritance he had lost his bride. In this part of the world marriages are made on strictly business principles, and if the promised cash is not forthcoming on the appointed day, the bride or the bridegroom whose parents have failed to produce it may as well take themselves off, for there will be no wedding. Poor Angelo knew that well enough. His father had been possessed of hardly any land, and now that the hard cash which he had brought from South America was gone, there was nothing left but debts for the building materials that were to have been used for enlarging and improving the old house. Angelo was beggared, and the nice plump little creature who was to have been his, turned up her nose at him in the most approved fashion. As for Cristina, it was several days before she was missed, for no one remembered that she had been sent to Scalea for the doctor, who had never come. She often disappeared in the same way for days together, when she could find a little work here and there at the distant farms among the hills. But when she did not come back at all, people began to wonder, and at last made up their minds that she had connived with the masons and had escaped with them.

I paused and emptied my glass.

"That sort of thing could not happen anywhere else," observed Holger, filling his everlasting pipe again. "It is wonderful what a natural charm there is about murder and sudden death in a romantic country like this. Deeds that would be simply brutal and disgusting anywhere else become dramatic and mysterious because this is Italy, and we are living in a genuine tower of Charles V built against Barbary pirates."

"There's something in that," I admitted. Holger is the most romantic man in the world inside of himself, but he always thinks it necessary to explain why he feels anything.

"I suppose they found the poor girl's body with the box," he said presently.

"As it seems to interest you," I answered, "I'll tell you the rest of the story."

The mood had risen by this time; the outline of the Thing on the mound was clearer to our eyes than before.

The village very soon settled down to its small dull life. No one missed old Alario, who had been away so much on his voyages to South America that he had never been a familiar figure in his native place. Angelo lived in the half-finished house, and because he had no money to pay the old woman-servant, she would not stay with him, but once in a long time she would come and wash a shirt for him for old acquaintance' sake. Besides the house, he had inherited a small patch of ground at some distance from the village; he tried to cultivate it, but he had no heart in the work, for he knew he could never pay the taxes on it and on the house, which would certainly be confiscated by the government, or seized for the debt of the building material, which the man who had supplied it refused to take back.

Angelo was very unhappy. So long as his father had been alive and rich, every girl in the village had been in love with him; but that was all changed now. It had been pleasant to be admired and courted, and invited to drink wine by fathers who had girls to marry. It was hard to be stared at coldly, and sometimes laughed at because he had been robbed of his inheritance. He cooked his miserable meals for himself, and from being sad became melancholy and morose.

At twilight, when the day's work was done, instead of hanging about in the open space before the church with young fellows of his own age, he took to wandering in lonely places on the outskirts of the village till it was quite dark. Then he slunk home and went to bed to save the expense of a light. But in those lonely twilight hours he began to have strange waking dreams. He was not always alone, for often when he sat on the stump of a tree, where the narrow path turns down the gorge, he was sure that a woman came up noiselessly over the rough stones, as if her feet were bare; and she stood under a clump of chestnut trees only half a dozen yards down the path, and beckoned to him without speaking. Though she was in the shadow he knew that her lips were red, and that when they parted a little and smiled at him she showed two small sharp teeth. He knew this at first rather than saw it, and he knew that it was Cristina, and that she was dead. Yet he was not afraid; he only wondered whether it was a dream, for he thought that if he had been awake he should have been frightened.

Besides, the dead woman had red lips, and that could only happen in a dream. Whenever he went near the gorget after sunset she was already there waiting for him, or else she very soon appeared, and he began to be sure of her blood-red mouth, but now each feature grew distinct, and the pale face looked at him with deep and hungry eyes.

It was the eyes that grew dim. Little by little he came to know that someday the dream would not end when he turned away to go home, but would lead him down the gorge out of which the vision rose. She was nearer now when she beckoned to him. Her cheeks were not livid like those of the dead, but pale with starvation, with the furious and unappeased physical hunger of her eyes that devoured him. They feasted on his soul and cast a spell over him, and at last they were close to his own and held him. He could not tell whether her breath was as hot as fire, or as cold as ice; he could not tell whether her red lips burned his or froze them, or whether her five fingers on his wrists seared scorching scars or bit his flesh like frost; he could not tell whether he was awake or asleep, whether she was alive or dead, but he knew that she loved him, she alone of all creatures, earthly or unearthly, and her spell had power over him.

When the moon rose high that night the shadow of that Thing was not alone down there upon the mound.

Angelo awoke in the cool dawn, drenched with dew and chilled through flesh, and blood, and bone. He opened his eyes to the faint grey light, and saw the stars were still shining overhead. He was very weak, and his heart was beating so slowly that he was almost like a man fainting. Slowly he turned his head on the mound, as on a pillow, but the other face was not there. Fear seized him suddenly, a fear unspeakable and unknown; he sprang to his feet and fled up the gorge, and he never looked behind him until he reached the door of the house on the outskirts of the village. Drearily he went to his work that day, and wearily the hours dragged themselves after the sun, till at last it touched the sea and sank, and the great sharp hills above Maratea turned purple against the dove-colored eastern sky.

Angelo shouldered his heavy hoe and left the field. He felt less tired now than in the morning when he had begun to work, but he promised himself that he would go home without lingering by the gorge, and eat the best supper he could get himself, and sleep all night in his bed like a Christian man. Not again would he be tempted down the narrow way by a shadow with red lips and icy breath; not again would he dream that dream of terror and delight. He was near the village now; it was half an hour since the sun had set, and the cracked church bell sent little discordant echoes across the rocks and ravines to tell all good people that the day was done. Angelo stood still a moment where the path forked, where it led toward the village on the left, and down to the gorge on the right, where a clump of chestnut trees overhung the narrow way. He stood still a minute, lifting his battered hat from his head and gazing at the fast-fading sea westward, and his lips moved as he silently repeated the familiar evening prayer. His lips moved, but the words that followed them in his brain lost their meaning and turned into others, and ended in a name that he spoke aloud—Cristina! With the name, the tension of his will relaxed suddenly, reality went out and the dream took him again, and bore him on swiftly and surely like a man walking in his sleep, down, down, by the steep path in the gathering darkness. And as she glided beside him, Cristina whispered strange, sweet things in his ear, which somehow, if he had been awake, he knew that he could not quite have understood; but now they were the most wonderful words he had ever heard in his life. And she kissed him also, but not upon his mouth. He felt her sharp kisses upon his white throat, and he knew that her lips were red. So the wild dream sped on through twilight and darkness and moonrise, and all the glory of the summer's night. But in the chilly dawn he lay as one half dead upon the mound down there, recalling and not recalling, drained of his blood, yet strangely longing to give those red lips more. Then came the fear, the awful nameless panic, the mortal horror that guards the confines of the world we see not, neither know of as we know of other things, but which we feel when its icy chill freezes our bones and stirs our hair with the touch of a ghostly hand. Once more Angelo sprang from the mound and fled up the gorge in the breaking day, but his step was less sure this time, and he panted for breath as he ran; and when he came to the bright spring of water that rises half way up the hillside, he dropped upon his knees and hands and plunged his whole face in and drank as he had never drunk before—for it was the thirst of the wounded man who has lain bleeding all night upon the battle-field.

She had him fast now, and he could not escape her, but would come to her every evening at dusk until she had drained him of his last drop of blood. It was in vain that when the day was done he tried to take another turning and to go home by a path that did not lead near the gorge. It was in vain that he made promises to himself each morning at dawn when he climbed the lonely way up from the shore to the village. It was all in vain, for when the sun sank burning into the sea, and the coolness of the evening stole out as from a hiding-place to delight the weary world, his feet turned toward the old way, and she was waiting for him in the shadow under the chestnut trees; and then all happened as before, and she fell to kissing his white throat even as she flitted lightly down the way, winding one arm about him. And as his blood failed, she grew more hungry and more thirsty every day, and every day when he awoke in the early dawn it was harder to rouse himself to the effort of climbing the steep path to the village; and when he went to his work his feet dragged painfully, and there was hardly strength in his arms to wield the heavy hoe. He scarcely spoke to anyone now, but the people said he was "consuming himself" for love of the girl he was to have married when he lost his inheritance; and they laughed heartily at the thought, for this is not a very romantic country. At this time Antonio, the man who stays here to look after the tower, returned from a visit to his people, who live near Salerno. He had been away all the time since before Alario's death and knew nothing of what had happened. He has told me that he came back late in the afternoon and shut himself up in the tower to eat and sleep, for he was very tired. It was past midnight when he awoke, and when he looked out toward the mound, and he saw something, and he did not sleep again that night. When he went out again in the morning it was broad daylight, and there was nothing to be seen on the mound but loose stones and driven sand. Yet he did not go very near it; he went straight up the path to the village and directly to the house of the old priest.

"I have seen an evil thing this night," he said; "I have seen how the dead drink the blood of the living. And the blood is the life."

"Tell me what you have seen," said the priest in reply.

Antonio told him everything he had seen.

"You must bring your book and your holy water tonight," he added. "I will be here before sunset to go down with you, and if it pleases your reverence to sup with me while we wait, I will make ready."

"I will come," the priest answered, "for I have read in old books of these strange beings which are neither quick nor dead, and which lie ever fresh in their graves, stealing out in the dusk to taste life and blood."

Antonio cannot read, but he was glad to see that the priest understood the business; for, of course, the books must have been instructed him as to the best means of quieting the half-living Thing forever.

So Antonio went away to his work, which consists largely in sitting on the shady side of the tower, when he is not perched upon a rock with a fishing-line catching nothing. But on that day he went twice to look at the mound in the bright sunlight, and he searched round and round it for some hole through which the being might get in and out; but he found none. When the sun began to sink and the air was cooler in the shadows, he went up to fetch the old priest, carrying a little wicker basket with him; and in this they placed a bottle of holy water, and the basin, and sprinkler, and the stole which the priest would need; and they came down and waited in the door of the tower till it should be dark. But while the light still lingered very grey and faint, they saw something moving, just there, two figures, a man's that walked, and a woman's that flitted beside him, and while her head lay on his shoulder she kissed his throat. The priest has told me that, too, and that his teeth chattered and he grasped Antonio's arm. The vision passed and disappeared into the shadow. Then Antonio got the leathern flask of strong liquor, which he kept for great occasions, and poured such a draft as made the old man feel almost young again; and gave the priest his stole to put on and the holy water to carry, and they went out together toward the spot where the work was to be done. Antonio says that in spite of the rum his own knees shook together, and the priest stumbled over his Latin. For when they were yet a few yards from the mound the flickering light of the lantern fell upon Angelo's white face, unconscious as if in sleep, and on his upturned throat, over which a very thin red line of blood trickled down into his collar; and the flickering light of the lantern played upon another face that looked up from the feast, upon two deep, dead eyes that saw in spite of death—upon parted lips, redder than life itself—upon two gleaming teeth on which glistened a rosy drop. Then the priest, good old man, shut his eyes tight and showered holy water before him, and his cracked voice rose almost to a scream; and then Antonio, who is no coward after all, raised his pick n one hand and the lantern in the other, as he sprang forward, not knowing what the end should be; and then he swears that he heard a woman's cry, and the Thing was gone, and Angelo lay alone on the mound unconscious, with the red line on his throat and the beads of deathly sweat on his cold forehead. They lifted him, half-dead as he was, and laid him on the ground close by; then Antonio went to work, and the priest helped him, thought he was old and could not do much; and they dug deep, and at last Antonio, standing in the grave, stooped down with his lantern to see what he might see.

His hair used to be dark brown, with grizzled streaks about the temples; in less than a month from that day he was as grey as a badger. He was a miner when he was young, and most of these fellows have seen ugly sights now and then, when accidents have happened, but he had never seen what he saw that night—that Thing which is neither alive nor dead, that Thing that will abide neither above ground nor in the grave. Antonio had brought something with him which the priest had not noticed—a sharp stake shaped from a piece of tough old driftwood. He had it with him now, and he had his heavy pick, and he had taken the lantern down into the grave. I don't think any power on earth could make him speak of what happened then, and the old priest was too frightened to look in. He says he heard Antonio breathing like a wild beast, and moving as if he were fighting with something almost as strong as himself; and he heard an evil sound also, with blows, as of something violently driven through flesh and bone; and then, the most awful sound of all—a woman's shriek, the unearthly scream of a woman neither dead nor alive, but buried deep for many days. And he, the poor old priest, could only rock himself as he knelt there in the sand, crying aloud his prayers and exorcisms to drown these dreadful sounds. Then suddenly a small iron-bound chest was thrown up and rolled over against the old man's knee, and in a moment more Antonio was beside him, his face as white as tallow in the flickering light of the lantern, shoveling the sand and pebbles into the grave with furious haste, and looking over the edge till the pit was half full; and the priest said that there was much fresh blood on Antonio's hands and on his clothes.

I had come to the end of my story. Holger finished his wine and leaned back in his chair.

"So Angelo got his own again." he said. "Did he marry the prim and plump young person to whom he had been betrothed?"

"No; he had been badly frightened. He went to South America, and has not been heard of since."

"And that poor thing's body is there still, I suppose," said Holger. "Is it quite dead yet, I wonder?"

I wonder, too. But whether it be dead or alive, I should hardly care to see it, even in broad daylight. Antonio is as grey as a badger, and he has never been quite the same man since that night.

THE FEATHER PILLOW

Horacio Quiroga

TRANSLATED BY C.S.R. CALLOWAY

first published as "El almohadón de plumas" in *Caras y Caretas*
(July 1907)

Their honeymoon was a hot and cold experience for Alicia. Blond, angelic and reserved, her childhood dreams were met with a chilling reality in the rough nature of her husband. She loved him very much, however. Sometimes when returning at night together from the street, with a slight shudder she would sneak a glance at the tall build of Jordan, who wouldn't speak for an hour. He, for her part, loved her deeply, without outwardly showing it.

For three months—they had been married in April—they lived in special bliss. Without a doubt, she would have wanted less severity in that rigid sky of love, more expansive and incautious tenderness; but the impassive countenance of her husband restrained her at once.

The house they lived in had no small influence on her chilled shudders. The whiteness of the silent courtyard—friezes, columns, and marble statues —produced a wintery impression of an enchanted palace. Inside, the icy sheen of stucco, without the slightest scratch on the high walls, affirmed that feeling of unpleasant cold. As they crossed from one room to another, the footsteps echoed throughout the house, as if a long abandonment had sensitized their resonance.

In that strange love nest, Alicia passed the entire autumn. She laid a veil over her old dreams, living the life of a sleepwalker instead, unwilling to think on anything until her husband arrived.

It is no surprise that she began to lose weight. She had a slight bout of influenza that dragged on insidiously for days and days, and her health never recovered. One afternoon she was finally able to go out to the garden, leaning on her husband's arm. She looked indifferently from one side to the other. Jordan, with sudden deep tenderness, passed his hand over her head and Alicia immediately burst into tears, throwing her arms around her neck. She cried for a long time, releasing all of her silent fears, intensifying her weeping at the slightest attempt to comfort her. Then the sobs slowed, and she remained hidden in his neck for a long time, without moving or saying a word.

That was the last day Alicia was up. The next day she woke up feeling faint. Jordan's doctor examined her very carefully, ordering her absolute calm and rest.

"I don't know," he said to Jordan at the front door, his voice still low. "She has a great weakness that I can't explain, and without vomiting, nothing... If she wakes up like this tomorrow, call me right away."

The next day Alicia was even worse. There was a consultation. She was found to have a severely progressing anemia, completely inexplicable. Alicia had no more fainting spells, but was visibly moving towards death. All day her bedroom lights remained on and there was complete silence. Hours went by without the slightest noise being heard. Alicia dozed. Jordan now essentially lived in the living room, also constantly illuminated. He paced endlessly from one end of the room to the other with tireless persistence. The carpet muffled his steps. At times he would enter the bedroom and continue his silent pacing along the bed, looking at his wife every time he approached her.

Soon Alicia began to have hallucinations, obscure and floating at first, then descending to the floor. The young woman, her eyes wide open, did nothing but look at the carpet on either side of the head of the bed. One night she suddenly fixed upon one spot. After a while she opened her mouth to scream, and her nose and lips were beaded with sweat.

"Jordan! Jordan!" She cried out, rigid with shock, still staring at the carpet.

Jordan ran to the bedroom, and when Alicia saw him appear she screamed in horror.

"It's me, Alicia, it's me!"

Alicia looked at him wildly, looked at the carpet, looked at him again, and after a long time of dumbfounded internal conflict, she calmed down. She smiled and took the hand of her husband between her trembling ones, caressing it.

Among her most recurring hallucinations was an anthropoid, fingers balanced on the carpet, eyes fixed on her.

The doctors returned to no avail. Before them they saw a life that was ending, bleeding away day by day, hour by hour, without gaining any knowledge of exactly how. At the last consultation Alicia lay in a stupor while they took her pulse, passing her inert wrist from one to the other. They watched her for a long time in silence and withdrew to the dining room.

"Pfff..." his doctor shrugged his shoulders in dismay. "It's a serious case... there's little to be done...

"I need *something* to be done," Jordan snorted. And he pounded the table.

Alicia was wasting away in a sub-delirium of anemia, aggravated in the afternoon, but which always subsided in the early hours of dawn. During the day her illness did not advance, but every morning she woke up pale, close to unconsciousness. It seemed that only at night her life was drained in new waves of blood. She always had the feeling of being collapsed on the bed with a million kilograms on top of her when she woke up. From the third day on, this sensation of weight never left her. She could barely move her head. She didn't want her bed to be touched, not even to have her pillow fixed. Her twilight terrors advanced in the form of monsters that crawled onto the bed and scrambled up the quilt.

Then she lost consciousness. The final two days she raved incessantly in a low voice. The lights remained mournfully on in the bedroom and living room. In the agonizing silence of the house, nothing could be heard other than the monotonous delirium coming from the bed, and the muffled murmur of Jordan's endless footsteps.

At last, Alicia passed. The maid, who came in afterward in order to strip the now-empty bed, looked at the pillow for a while, puzzled.

"Sir," she called to Jordan in a low voice. "There are stains on the cushion that look like blood."

Jordan approached quickly and bent over the bed. Indeed, on the pillowcase, on both sides of the depression left by Alicia's head, there were visible dark spots.

"They look like bite marks," the maid murmured after a while of motionless observation.

"Hold it up to the light," Jordan told her.

The servant girl picked it up, but immediately dropped it, and stared at it, livid and trembling. Without knowing why, Jordan felt his hair stand on end.

"What is it?" he murmured hoarsely.

"It's quite heavy," the maid articulated, still trembling.

Jordan picked it up; it had an extraordinary weight. They went out of the room with it, and on the dining room table Jordan cut through case and pillow with one slash. The upper feathers flew, and the servant girl gave a cry of horror with her mouth wide open, raising her clenched hands.—On the bottom, among the feathers, slowly moving its hairy legs, there was a monstrous animal, a slimy, living ball. It was so swollen that its mouth was barely noticeable.

Night after night, since Alicia had fallen into bed, it had stealthily applied its mouth—its proboscis, rather—to her temples, sucking her blood. The bite was almost imperceptible. The daily removal of the pillow would have undoubtedly prevented its progress, but since the girl could not move, the consumption was dizzying. In five days, in five nights, the monster had emptied Alicia.

These parasites of birds, tiny in their natural habitat, reach enormous proportions under certain conditions. Human blood seems to be particularly beneficial to them, and it is not uncommon to find them in feather pillows.

THE TRANSFER

Algernon Blackwood

first published in *Country Life* (December 1911)

T he child began to cry in the early afternoon—about three o'clock, to be exact. I remember the hour, because I had been listening with secret relief to the sound of the departing carriage. Those wheels fading into the distance down the gravel drive with Mrs. Frene, and her daughter Gladys to whom I was governess, meant for me some hours' welcome rest, and the June day was oppressively hot. Moreover, there was this excitement in the little country household that had told upon us all, but especially upon myself. This excitement, running delicately behind all the events of the morning, was due to some mystery, and the mystery was of course kept concealed from the governess. I had exhausted myself with guessing and keeping on the watch. For some deep and unexplained anxiety possessed me, so that I kept thinking of my sister's dictum that I was really much too sensitive to make a good governess, and that I should have done far better as a professional clairvoyante.

Mr. Frene, senior, "Uncle Frank," was expected for an unusual visit from town about tea-time. That I knew. I also knew that his visit was concerned somehow with the future welfare of little Jamie, Gladys's seven-year-old brother. More than this, indeed, I never knew, and this missing link makes my story in a fashion incoherent—an important bit of the strange puzzle left out. I only gathered that the visit of Uncle Frank was of a condescending nature, that Jamie was told he must be upon his very best behavior to make a good impression, and that Jamie, who had never seen his uncle, dreaded him horribly already in advance. Then, trailing thinly through the dying crunch of the carriage wheels this sultry afternoon, I heard the curious little wail of the child's crying, with the effect, wholly unaccountable, that every nerve in my body shot its bolt electrically, bringing me to my feet with a tingling of unequivocal alarm. Positively, the water ran into my eyes. I recalled his white distress that morning when told that Uncle Frank was motoring down for tea and that he was to be "very nice indeed" to him. It had gone into me like a knife. All through the day, indeed, had run this nightmare quality of terror and vision.

"The man with the 'normous face?" he had asked in a little voice of awe, and then gone speechless from the room in tears that no amount of soothing management could calm. That was all I saw; and what he meant by "the 'normous face" gave me only a sense of vague presentiment. But it came as anticlimax somehow—a sudden revelation of the mystery and excitement that pulsed beneath the quiet of the stifling summer day. I feared for him. For of all that commonplace household I loved Jamie best, though professionally I had nothing to do with him. He was a high-strung, ultra-sensitive child, and it seemed to me that no one understood him, least of all his honest, tender-hearted parents; so that his little wailing voice brought me from my bed to the window in a moment like a call for help.

The haze of June lay over that big garden like a blanket; the wonderful flowers, which were Mr. Frene's delight, hung motionless; the lawns, so soft and thick, cushioned all other sounds; only the limes and huge clumps of guelder roses hummed with bees. Through this muted atmosphere of heat and haze the sound of the child's crying floated faintly to my ears—from a distance. Indeed, I wonder now that I heard it at all, for the next moment I saw him down beyond the garden, standing in his white sailor suit alone, two hundred yards away. He was down by the ugly patch where nothing grew—the Forbidden Corner. A faintness then came over me at once, a faintness as of death, when I saw him there of all places—where he never was allowed to go, and where, moreover, he was usually too terrified to go. To see him standing solitary in that singular spot, above all to hear him crying there, bereft me momentarily of the power to act. Then, before I could recover my composure sufficiently to call him in, Mr. Frene came round the corner from the Lower Farm with the dogs, and, seeing his son, performed that office for me. In his loud, good-natured, hearty voice he called him, and Jamie turned and ran as though some spell had broken just in time—ran into the open arms of his fond but uncomprehending father, who carried him indoors on his shoulder, while asking "what all this hubbub was about?" And, at their heels, the tailless sheepdogs followed, barking loudly, and performing what Jamie called their "Gravel Dance," because they ploughed up the moist, rolled gravel with their feet.

I stepped back swiftly from the window lest I should be seen. Had I witnessed the saving of the child from fire or drowning the relief could hardly have been greater. Only Mr. Frene, I felt sure, would not say and do the right thing quite. He would protect the boy from his own vain imaginings, yet not with the explanation that could really heal. They disappeared behind the rose trees, making for the house. I saw no more till later, when Mr. Frene, senior, arrived.

To describe the ugly patch as "singular" is hard to justify, perhaps, yet some such word is what the entire family sought, though never—oh, never!—used. To Jamie and myself, though equally we never mentioned it, that treeless, flowerless spot was more than singular. It stood at the far end of the magnificent rose garden, a bald, sore place, where the black earth showed uglily in winter, almost like a piece of dangerous bog, and in summer baked and cracked with fissures where green lizards shot their fire in passing. In contrast to the rich luxuriance of death amid life, a center of disease that cried for healing lest it spread. But it never did spread. Behind it stood the thick wood of silver birches and, glimmering beyond, the orchard meadow, where the lambs played.

The gardeners had a very simple explanation of its barrenness—that the water all drained off it owing to the lie of the slopes immediately about it, holding no remnant to keep the soil alive. I cannot say. It was Jamie—Jamie who felt its spell and haunted it, who spent whole hours there, even while afraid, and for whom it was finally labelled "strictly out of bounds" because it stimulated his already big imagination, not wisely but too darkly—it was Jamie who buried ogres there and heard it crying in an earthy voice, swore that it shook its surface sometimes while he watched it, and secretly gave it food in the form of birds or mice or rabbits he found dead upon his wanderings. And it was Jamie who put so extraordinarily into words the feeling that the horrid spot had given me from the moment I first saw it.

"It's bad, Miss Gould," he told me.

"But, Jamie, nothing in Nature is bad—exactly; only different from the rest sometimes."

"Miss Gould, if you please, then it's empty. It's not fed. It's dying because it can't get the food it wants." And when I stared into the little pale face where the eyes shone so dark and wonderful, seeking within myself for the right thing to say to him, he added, with an emphasis and conviction that made me suddenly turn cold: "Miss Gould"—he always used my name like this in all his sentences—"it's hungry, don't you see? But I know what would make it feel all right."

Only the conviction of an earnest child, perhaps, could have made so outrageous a suggestion worth listening to for an instant; but for me, who felt that things an imaginative child believed were important, it came with a vast disquieting shock of reality. Jamie, in this exaggerated way, had caught at the edge of a shocking fact—a hint of dark, undiscovered truth had leaped into that sensitive imagination. Why there lay horror in the words I cannot say, but I think some power of darkness trooped across the suggestion of that sentence at the end, "I know what would make it feel all right." I remember that I shrank from asking explanation. Small groups of other words, veiled fortunately by his silence, gave life to an unspeakable possibility that hitherto had lain at the back of my own consciousness. The way it sprang to life proves, I think, that my mind already contained it. The blood rushed from my heart as I listened. I remember that my knees shook. Jamie's idea was—had been all along—my own as well.

And now, as I lay down on my bed and thought about it all, I understood why the coming of his uncle involved somehow an experience that wrapped terror at its heart. With a sense of nightmare certainty that left me too weak to resist the preposterous idea, too shocked, indeed, to argue or reason it away, this certainty came with its full, black blast of conviction; and the only way I can put it into words, since nightmare horror really is not properly tellable at all, seems this: that there was something missing in that dying patch of garden; something lacking that it ever searched for; something, once found and taken, that would turn it rich and living as the rest; more—that there was some living person who could do this for it. Mr. Frene, senior, in a word, "Uncle Frank," was this person who out of his abundant life could supply the lack—unwittingly.

For this connection between the dying, empty patch and the person of this vigorous, wealthy, and successful man had already lodged itself in my subconsciousness before I was aware of it. Clearly it must have lain there all along, though hidden. Jamie's words, his sudden pallor, his vibrating emotion of fearful anticipation had developed the plate, but it was his weeping alone there in the Forbidden Corner that had printed it. The photograph shone framed before me in the air. I hid my eyes. But for the redness—the charm of my face goes to pieces unless my eyes are clear—I could have cried. Jamie's words that morning about the "'normous face" came back upon me like a battering-ram.

Mr. Frene, senior, had been so frequently the subject of conversation in the family since I came, I had so often heard him discussed, and had then read so much about him in the papers—his energy, his philanthropy, his success with everything he laid his hand to—that a picture of the man had grown complete within me. I knew him as he was—within; or, as my sister would have said—clairvoyantly. And the only time I saw him (when I took Gladys to a meeting where he was chairman, and later felt his atmosphere and presence while for a moment he patronizingly spoke with her) had justified the portrait I had drawn. The rest, you may say, was a woman's wild imagining; but I think rather it was that kind of divining intuition which women share with children. If souls could be made visible, I would stake my life upon the truth and accuracy of my portrait.

For this Mr. Frene was a man who drooped alone, but grew vital in a crowd—because he used their vitality. He was a supreme, unconscious artist in the science of taking the fruits of others' work and living—for his own advantage. He vampired, unknowingly no doubt, every one with whom he came in contact; left them exhausted, tired, listless. Others fed him, so that while in a full room he shone, alone by himself and with no life to draw upon he languished and declined. In the man's immediate neighborhood you felt his presence draining you; he took your ideas, your strength, your very words, and later used them for his own benefit and aggrandizement. Not evilly, of course; the man was good enough; but you felt that he was dangerous owing to the facile way he absorbed into himself all loose vitality that was to be had. His eyes and voice and presence devitalized you. Life, it seemed, not highly organized enough to resist, must shrink from his too near approach and hide away for fear of being appropriated, for fear, that is, of—death.

Jamie, unknowingly, put in the finishing touch to my unconscious portrait. The man carried about with him some silent, compelling trick of drawing out all your reserves—then swiftly pocketing them. At first you would be conscious of taut resistance; this would slowly shade off into weariness; the will would become flaccid; then you either moved away or yielded—agreed to all he said with a sense of weakness pressing ever closer upon the edges of collapse. With a male antagonist it might be different, but even then the effort of resistance would generate force that he absorbed and not the other. He never gave out. Some instinct taught him how to protect himself from that. To human beings, I mean, he never gave out. This time it was a very different matter. He had no more chance than a fly before the wheels of a huge—what Jamie used to call—"attraction" engine.

So this was how I saw him—a great human sponge, crammed and soaked with the life, or proceeds of life, absorbed from others—stolen. My idea of a human vampire was satisfied. He went about carrying these accumulations of the life of others. In this sense his "life" was not really his own. For the same reason, I think, it was not so fully under his control as he imagined.

And in another hour this man would be here. I went to the window. My eye wandered to the empty patch, dull black there amid the rich luxuriance of the garden flowers. It struck me as a hideous bit of emptiness yawning to be filled and nourished. The idea of Jamie playing round its bare edge was loathsome. I watched the big summer clouds above, the stillness of the afternoon, the haze. The silence of the overheated garden was oppressive. I had never felt a day so stifling, motionless. It lay there waiting. The household, too, was waiting—waiting for the coming of Mr. Frene from London in his big motor-car.

And I shall never forget the sensation of icy shrinking and distress with which I heard the rumble of the car. He had arrived. Tea was all ready on the lawn beneath the lime trees, and Mrs. Frene and Gladys, back from their drive, were sitting in wicker chairs. Mr. Frene, junior, was in the hall to meet his brother, but Jamie, as I learned afterwards, had shown such hysterical alarm, offered such bold resistance, that it had been deemed wiser to keep him in his room. Perhaps, after all, his presence might not be necessary. The visit clearly had to do with something on the uglier side of life—money, settlements, or what not; I never knew exactly; only that his parents were anxious, and that Uncle Frank had to be propitiated. It does not matter. That has nothing to do with the affair. What has to do with it—or I should not be telling the story—is that Mrs. Frene sent for me to come down "in my nice white dress, if I didn't mind," and that I was terrified, yet pleased, because it meant that a pretty face would be considered a welcome addition to the visitor's landscape. Also, most odd it was, I felt my presence was somehow inevitable, that in some way it was intended that I should witness what I did witness. And the instant I came upon the lawn—I hesitate to set it down, it sounds so foolish, disconnected—I could have sworn, as my eyes met his, that a kind of sudden darkness came, taking the summer brilliance out of everything, and that it was caused by troops of small black horses that raced about us from his person—to attack.

After a first momentary approving glance he took no further notice of me. The tea and talk went smoothly; I helped to pass the plates and cups, filling in pauses with little undertalk to Gladys. Jamie was never mentioned. Outwardly all seemed well, but inwardly everything was awful—skirting the edge of things unspeakable, and so charged with danger that I could not keep my voice from trembling when I spoke.

I watched his hard, bleak face; I noticed how thin he was, and the curious, oily brightness of his steady eyes. They did not glitter, but they drew you with a sort of soft, creamy shine like Eastern eyes. And everything he said or did announced what I may dare to call the suction of his presence. His nature achieved this result automatically. He dominated us all, yet so gently that until it was accomplished no one noticed it.

Before five minutes had passed, however, I was aware of one thing only. My mind focussed exclusively upon it, and so vividly that I marveled the others did not scream, or run, or do something violent to prevent it. And it was this; that, separated merely by some dozen yards or so, this man, vibrating with the acquired vitality of others, stood within easy reach of that spot of yawning emptiness, waiting and eager to be filled. Earth scented her prey.

These two active "centers" were within fighting distance; he so thin, so hard, so keen, yet really spreading large with the loose "surround" of others' life he had appropriated, so practiced and triumphant; that other so patient, deep, with so mighty a draw of the whole earth behind it, and—ugh!—so obviously aware that its opportunity at last had come.

I saw it all as plainly as though I watched two great animals prepare for battle, both unconsciously; yet in some inexplicable way I saw it, of course, within me, and not externally. The conflict would be hideously unequal. Each side had already sent out emissaries, how long before I could not tell, for the first evidence he gave that something was going wrong with him was when his voice grew suddenly confused, he missed his words, and his lips trembled a moment and turned flabby. The next second his face betrayed that singular and horrid change, growing somehow loose about the bones of the cheek, and larger, so that I remembered Jamie's miserable phrase. The emissaries of the two kingdoms, the human and the vegetable, had met, I make it out, in that very second. For the first time in his long career of battening on others, Mr. Frene found himself pitted against a vaster kingdom than he knew and, so finding, shook inwardly in that little part that was his definite actual self. He felt the huge disaster coming.

"Yes, John," he was saying, in his drawling, self-congratulating voice, "Sir George gave me that car—gave it to me as a present. Wasn't it char—?" and then broke off abruptly, stammered, drew breath, stood up, and looked uneasily about him. For a second there was a gaping pause. It was like the click which starts some huge machinery moving—that instant's pause before it actually starts. The whole thing, indeed, then went with the rapidity of machinery running down and beyond control. I thought of a giant dynamo working silently and invisible.

"What's that?" he cried, in a soft voice charged with alarm. "What's that horrid place? And someone's crying there—who is it?" He pointed to the empty patch. Then, before anyone could answer, he started across the lawn towards it, going every minute faster. Before anyone could move he stood upon the edge. He leaned over—peering down into it.

It seemed a few hours passed, but really they were seconds, for time is measured by the quality and not the quantity of sensations it contains. I saw it all with merciless, photographic detail, sharply etched amid the general confusion. Each side was intensely active, but only one side, the human, exerted all its force—in resistance. The other merely stretched out a feeler, as it were, from its vast, potential strength; no more was necessary. It was such a soft and easy victory. Oh, it was rather pitiful! There was no bluster or great effort, on one side at least. Close by his side I witnessed it, for I, it seemed, alone had moved and followed him. No one else stirred, though Mrs. Frene clattered noisily with the cups, making some sudden impulsive gesture with her hands, and Gladys, I remember, gave a cry—it was like a little scream— "Oh, mother, it's the heat, isn't it?" Mr. Frene, her father, was speechless, pale as ashes.

But the instant I reached his side, it became clear what had drawn me there thus instinctively. Upon the other side, among the silver birches, stood little Jamie. He was watching. I experienced—for him—one of those moments that shake the heart; a liquid fear ran all over me, the more effective because unintelligible really. Yet I felt that if I could know all, and what lay actually behind, my fear would be more than justified; that the thing was awful, full of awe.

And then it happened—a truly wicked sight—like watching a universe in action, yet all contained within a small square foot of space. I think he understood vaguely that if someone could only take his place he might be saved, and that was why, discerning instinctively the easiest substitute within reach, he saw the child and called aloud to him across the empty patch, "James, my boy, come here!" His voice was like a thin report, but somehow flat and lifeless, as when a rifle misses fire, sharp, yet weak; it had no "crack" in it. It was really supplication. And, with amazement, I heard my own ring out imperious and strong, though I was not conscious of saying it, "Jamie, don't move. Stay where you are!" But Jamie, the little child, obeyed neither of us. Moving up nearer to the edge, he stood there—laughing! I heard that laughter, but could have sworn it did not come from him. The empty, yawning patch gave out that sound.

Mr. Frene turned sideways, throwing up his arms. I saw his hard, bleak face grow somehow wider, spread through the air, and downwards. A similar thing, I saw, was happening at the same time to his entire person, for it drew out into the atmosphere in a stream of movement. The face for a second made me think of those toys of green India rubber that children pull. It grew enormous. But this was an external impression only. What actually happened, I clearly understood, was that all this vitality and life he had transferred from others to himself for years was now in turn being taken from him and transferred—elsewhere.

One moment on the edge he wobbled horribly, then with that queer sideways motion, rapid yet ungainly, he stepped forward into the middle of the patch and fell heavily upon his face. His eyes, as he dropped, faded shockingly, and across the countenance was written plainly what I can only call an expression of destruction. He looked utterly destroyed. I caught a sound—from Jamie?—but this time not of laughter. It was like a gulp; it was deep and muffled and it dipped away into the earth. Again I thought of a troop of small black horses galloping away down a subterranean passage beneath my feet—plunging into the depths—their tramping growing fainter and fainter into buried distance. In my nostrils was a pungent smell of earth.

And then—all passed. I came back into myself. Mr. Frene, junior, was lifting his brother's head from the lawn where he had fallen from the heat, close beside the tea-table. He had never really moved from there. And Jamie, I learned afterwards, had been the whole time asleep upon his bed upstairs, worn out with his crying and unreasoning alarm. Gladys came running out with cold water, sponge and towel, brandy too—all kinds of things. "Mother, it was the heat, wasn't it?" I heard her whisper, but I did not catch Mrs. Frene's reply. From her face it struck me that she was bordering on collapse herself. Then the butler followed, and they just picked him up and carried him into the house. He recovered even before the doctor came.

But the queer thing to me is that I was convinced the others all had seen what I saw, only that no one said a word about it; and to this day no one has said a word. And that was, perhaps, the most horrid part of all.

From that day to this I have scarcely heard a mention of Mr. Frene, senior. It seemed as if he dropped suddenly out of life. The papers never mentioned him. His activities ceased, as it were. His after-life, at any rate, became singularly ineffective. Certainly he achieved nothing worth public mention. But it may be only that, having left the employ of Mrs. Frene, there was no particular occasion for me to hear anything.

The after-life of that empty patch of garden, however, was quite otherwise. Nothing, so far as I know, was done to it by gardeners, or in the way of draining it or bringing in new earth, but even before I left in the following summer it had changed. It lay untouched, full of great, luscious, driving weeds and creepers, very strong, full—fed, and bursting thick with life.

THE SUMACH

Ulric Daubeny

from *The Elemental: Tales of the Supernormal and the Inexplicable*
(1919)

"**H**ow red that Sumach is!"
Irene Barton murmured something commonplace, for to her the tree brought painful recollections. Her visitor, unconscious of this fact, proceeded to elaborate.

"Do you know, Irene, that tree gives me the creeps! I can't explain, except that it is not a nice tree, not a *good* tree. For instance, why should its leaves be red in August, when they are not supposed to turn until October?"

"What queer ideas you have, May! The tree is right enough, although its significance to me is sad. Poor Spot, you know; we buried him beneath it too days ago. Come and see his grave."

The two women left the terrace, where this conversation had been taking place, and leisurely strolled across the lawn, at the end of which, in almost startling isolation, grew the Sumach. At least, Mrs. Watcombe, who evinced so great an interest in the tree, questioned whether it actually was a Sumach, for the foliage was unusual, and the branches gnarled and twisted beyond recognition. Just now, the leaves were stained with splashes of dull crimson, but rather than droop, they had a bloated appearance, as if the luxuriance of the growth were not altogether healthy.

For several moments they stood regarding the pathetic little grave, and the silence was only broken when Mrs. Watcombe darted beneath the tree and came back with something in her hand.

"Irene, look at this dead thrush. Poor little thing! Such splendid plumage, yet it hardly weighs a sugar plum!"

Mrs. Barton regarded it with wrinkled brows.

"I cannot understand what happens to the birds, May—unless someone lays poison. We continually find them dead about the garden, usually beneath, or very near this tree."

It is doubtful whether Mrs. Watcombe listened. Her attention seemed to wander that morning, and she was studying the twisted branches of the Sumach with thoughtful scrutiny.

"Curious that the leaves should turn at this time of year," she murmured. "It brings to mind poor Geraldine's illness. This tree had an extraordinary fascination for her, you know. It was quite scarlet then, yet that was only June, and it had barely finished shooting."

"My dear May! You have red leaves on the brain this morning!" Irene retorted, uncertain whether to be irritated or amused. "I can't think why you are so concerned about the color. It is only the result of two days' excessive heat, for scarcely a leaf was touched, when I buried poor Spot."

The conversation seemed absurdly trivial, yet, Mrs. Watcombe gone, Irene could not keep her mind from her cousin's fatal illness. The news had reached them with the shock of the absolutely unexpected. Poor Geraldine, who had always been so strong, to have fallen victim to acute anaemia! It was almost unbelievable, that heart failure should have put an end to her sweet young life after a few days' ailing. Of course, the sad event had wrought a wonderful change for Irene and her husband, giving them, in place of a cramped suburban villa, this beautiful country home, Cleeve Grange. Everything for her was filled with the delight of novelty, for she had ruled as mistress over the charmed abode for only one short week. Hilary, her husband, was yet a stranger to the more intimate of its attractions, being detained in London by the winding-up of business affairs.

Several days elapsed, for the most part given solely to the keen pleasure of arranging and rearranging the new home. As time went by, the crimson splashes on the Sumach faded, the leaves becoming green again, though drooping as if for want of moisture. Irene noticed this when she paid her daily visits to the pathetic little dog grave, trying to induce flowers to take root upon it, but do what she might, they invariably faded. Nothing, not even grass, would grow beneath the Sumach. Only death seemed to thrive there, she mused in a fleeting moment of depression, as she searched around for more dead birds. But none had fallen since the thrush, picked up by Mrs. Watcombe.

One evening, the heat inside the house becoming insupportable, Irene wandered into the garden her steps mechanically leading her to the little grave beneath the Sumach. In the uncertain moonlight, the twisted trunk and branches of the old tree were suggestive of a rustic seat, and feeling tired, she lifted herself into the natural bower, and lolled back, joyously inhaling the cool night air. Presently she dropped asleep, and in a curiously vivid manner, dreamt of Hilary; that he had completed his business in London, and was coming home. They met at evening, near the garden gate, and Hilary spread wide his arms, and eagerly folded them about her. Swiftly the dream began to change, assuming the characteristic of a nightmare. The sky grew strangely dark, the arms fiercely masterful, while the face which bent to kiss her neck was not that of her young husband: it was leering, wicked, gnarled like the trunk of some weather-beaten tree. Chilled with horror, Irene fought long and desperately against the vision, to be at last awakened by her own frightened whimpering. Yet returning consciousness did not immediately dissipate the nightmare. In imagination she was still held rigid by brutal arms, and it was only after a blind, half-waking struggle that she freed herself, and went speeding across the lawn, towards the lighted doorway.

Mrs. Watcombe called the next morning, and subjected her to a puzzled scrutiny.

"How pale you look, Irene. Do you feel ill?"

"Ill! No, only a little languid. I find this hot weather very trying."

Mrs. Watcombe studied her with care, for the pallor of Irene's face was very marked. In contrast, a vivid spot of red showed on the slender neck, an inch or so below the ear. Intuitively a hand went up, as Irene turned to her friend in explanation.

"It feels so sore. I think I must have grazed the skin, last night, while sitting in the Sumach."

"Sitting in the Sumach!" echoed Mrs. Watcombe in surprise. "How curious you should do that. Poor Geraldine used to do the same, just before she was taken ill, and yet at the last she was seized with a perfect horror of the tree. Goodness, but it is quite red again, this morning!"

Irene swung round in the direction of the tree, filled with a vague repugnance. Sure enough, the leaves no longer drooped, nor were they green. They had become flecked once more with crimson, and the growth had regained its former vigor.

"Eugh!" she breathed, hurriedly running towards the house. "It reminds me of a horrid nightmare. I have rather a head this morning; let's go in, and talk of something else."

As the day advanced, the heat grew more oppressive, and night brought with it a curious stillness, the stillness which so often presages a heavy thunderstorm. No bird had offered up its evening hymn, no breeze came sufficient to stir a single leaf: everything was pervaded by a silence of expectancy.

The interval between dinner and bedtime is always a dreary one for those accustomed to companionship, and left all alone, Irene's restlessness momentarily increased. First the ceiling, then the very atmosphere seemed to weigh heavy upon her head. Although windows and doors were all flung wide, the airlessness of the house grew less and less endurable, until from sheer desperation she made her escape to the garden, where a sudden illumination of the horizon gave warning of the approaching storm. Feeling somewhat at a loss, she roamed aimlessly awhile, pausing sometimes to catch the echoes of distant thunder, until at last she found herself standing over Spot's desolate little grave. The sight struck her with a sense of utter loneliness, and the tears sprang to her eyes, in poignant longing for the companionship of her faithful pet.

Moved by what she knew not, Irene swung herself into the comfortable branches of the Sumach, and soothed by the reposeful attitude, her head soon began to nod in slumber. Afterwards it was a doubtful memory whether she actually did sleep, or whether the whole experience was not a waking kind of nightmare. Something of the previous evening's dream returned to her, but this time with added horror; for it commenced with no pleasurable vision of her husband. Instead, relentless, stick-like arms immediately closed in upon her, their vice-like grip so tight that she could scarcely breathe. Down darted the awful head, rugged and lined by every sin, darting at the fair, white neck as a wild beast on its prey. The foul lips began to eat into her skin... She struggled desperately, madly, for to her swooning senses the very branches of the tree became endowed with active life, coiling unmercifully around her, tenaciously clinging to her limbs, and tearing at her dress. Pain at last spurred her to an heroic effort, the pain of something—perhaps a twig—digging deep into her unprotected neck. With a choking cry she freed herself, and nerved by a sudden burst of thunder, ran tottering towards the shelter of the house.

Having gained the cosy lounge-hall, Irene sank into an armchair, gasping hysterically for breath. Gusts of refreshing wind came through the open windows, but although the atmosphere rapidly grew less stagnant, an hour passed before she could make sufficient effort to crawl upstairs to bed. In her room, a further shock awaited her. The bloodless, drawn face reflected in the mirror was scarcely recognizable. The eyes lacked luster, the lips were white, the skin hung flabby on the shrunken flesh, giving it a look of premature old age. A tiny trickle of dry blood, the solitary smudge of color, stained the chalky pallor of her neck. Taking up a hand-glass, she examined this with momentary concern. It was the old wound reopened, and angry-looking sore, almost like the bite of some small, or very sharp-toothed animal. It smarted painfully...

Mrs. Watcombe, bursting into the breakfast room the next morning, with suggestions of an expedition to a neighboring town, was shocked at Irene's looks, and insisted on going at once to fetch the doctor. Mrs. Watcombe fussed continually throughout the interview, and insisted upon an examination of the scar upon Irene's neck. Patient and doctor had discarded this as a negligible detail, but finally the latter subjected it to a slightly puzzled scrutiny, advising that it should be kept bandaged. He suggested that Irene was suffering from anaemia, and would do well to keep as quiet as possible, building up her strength with food, open windows and a general selection of pills and tonics. Despite these comforting arrangements, no one was entirely satisfied. The doctor lacked something in assurance, Irene was certain that she could not really be anaemic, while Mrs. Watcombe was obsessed by inward misgivings, perfectly indefinable, yet nonetheless disturbing. She left the house as a woman bent under a load of care. Passing up the lane, her glance lighted on the old Sumach, more crimson now, more flourishing in its growth than she had seen it since the time of Geraldine's fatal illness.

"I loathe that horrid old tree!" she murmured, then added, struck by a nameless premonition, "Her husband ought to know. I shall wire to him at once."

Irene, womanlike, put to use her enforced illness, by instituting a rearrangement of the box-room, the only part of her new home which remained yet unexplored. Among the odds and ends of the rubbish to be thrown away, there was a little notebook, apparently unused. In idle curiosity, Irene picked it up, and was surprised to learn, from an inscription, that her cousin Geraldine had intended to use it as a diary. A date appeared—only a few day prior to the poor girl's death—but no entries had been made, thought the first two pages of the book had certainly been removed. As Irene put it down, there fluttered to the ground a torn scrap of writing. She stooped, and continued stooping, breathlessly staring at the words that had been written by her cousin's hand—*Sumach fascinates m—*

In some unaccountable manner this applied to her. It was obvious what tree was meant, the old Sumach at the end of the lawn; and it fascinated her, Irene, though not until that moment had she openly recognized the fact. Searching hurriedly through the notebook, she discovered, near the end, a heap of torn paper, evidently the first two pages of a diary. She turned the pieces in eager haste. Most of them bore no more than one short word, or portions of a longer one, but a few bigger fragments proved more enlightening, and filled with nervous apprehension, she carried the book to her escritoire, and spent the remainder of the afternoon in trying to piece together the torn-up pages.

Meanwhile, Mrs. Watcombe was worrying and fretting over Irene's unexplained illness. Her pallor, her listlessness, even the curious mark up on her neck, gave cause for positive alarm, so exactly did they correspond with symptoms exhibited by her cousin Geraldine, during the few days prior to her death. She wished that the village doctor, who had attended the earlier case, would return soon from his holiday, as his *locum tenens* seemed sadly wanting in that authoritative decision which is so consoling to patients, relatives, and friends. Feeling, as an old friend, responsible for the welfare of Irene, she wired to Hilary, telling him of the sudden illness, and advising him to return without delay.

The urgency of the telegram alarmed him, so much that he left London by the next train, arriving at Cleeve Grange shortly after dark.

"Where is your mistress?" was his first enquiry, as the maid met him in the hall.

"Upstairs, sir. She complained of feeling tired, and said she would go to bed."

He hurried to her room, only to find it empty. He called, rang for the servants; in a moment the whole house was astir, yet nowhere was Irene to be found. Deeming it possible that she might have gone to see Mrs. Watcombe, Hilary was about to follow, when that lady herself was ushered in.

"I saw the lights of your cab," she commenced, cutting short the sentence, as she met his questioning glance.

"Where is Irene?"

"Irene? My dear Hilary, is she not here?"

"No. We can't find her anywhere. I thought she might have been with you."

For the space of half a second, Mrs. Watcombe's face presented a picture of astonishment, then the expression changed to one of dismayed concern.

"She's in that tree! I'm certain of it! Hilary, we must fetch her in at once!"

Completely at a loss to understand, he followed the excited woman into the garden, stumbling blindly in her wake across the lawn. The darkness was intense, and a terrific wind beat them back as if with living hands. Irene's white dress at length became discernible, dimly thrown up against the pitchy background, and obscured in places by the twists and coils of the old Sumach. Between them they grasped the sleeping body, but the branches swung wildly in the gale, and to Hilary's confused imagination it was as if they had to literally tear it from the tree's embrace. At last they regained the shelter of the house, and laid their inanimate burden upon the sofa. She was quite unconscious, pale as death, and her face painfully contorted, as if with fear. The old wound on the neck, now bereft of bandages, had been reopened, and was wet with blood.

Hilary rushed off to fetch the doctor, while Mrs. Watcombe and the servants carried Irene to her room. Several hours passed before she regained consciousness, and during that time Hilary was gently but firmly excluded from the sickroom. Bewildered and disconsolate, he wandered restlessly about the house, until his attention was arrested by the unusual array of torn-up bits of paper on Irene's desk. He saw that she had been sorting out the pieces, and sticking them together as the sentences became complete. The work was barely half-finished, yet what there was to read struck him as exceedingly strange:

The seat in the old Sumach fascinates me. I find myself going back to it unconsciously, nay, even against my will. Oh, but the nightmare visions it always brings me! In them I seem to plumb the very depths of terror. Their memory preys upon my mind, and every day my strength grows less.

Dr. H. speaks of anaemia…

That was as far as Irene has proceeded. Hardly knowing why he did so, Hilary resolved to complete the task, but the chill of early morning was in the air before it was finished. Cramped and stiff, he was pushing back his chair when a footstep sounded in the doorway and Mrs. Watcombe entered.

"Irene is better," she volunteered immediately. "She is sleeping naturally, and Doctor Thomson says there is no longer any immediate danger. The poor child is terribly weak and bloodless."

"May—tell me—what is the meaning of all this? Why has Irene suddenly become so ill? I can't understand it!"

Mrs. Watcombe's face was preternaturally grave.

"Even the doctor admits that he is puzzled," she answered very quietly. "The symptoms all point to a sudden and excessive loss of blood, though in cases of acute anaemia—"

"God! But—not like Geraldine? I can't believe it!"

"Neither can I. Oh, Hilary, you may think me mad, but I can't help feeling that there is some unknown, some awful influence at work. Irene was perfectly well three days ago, and it was the same with Geraldine before she was taken ill. The cases are so exactly similar.

"Irene was trying to tell me something about a diary, but the poor girl was too exhausted to make herself properly understood."

"Diary? Geraldine's diary, do you think? She must mean that. I have just finished piecing it together, but frankly, I can't make heads or tails of it!"

Mrs. Watcombe rapidly scanned the writing, then studied it again with greater care. Finally, she read the second part aloud.

"Listen, Hilary! This seems to me important."

Dr. H. speaks of anaemia. Pray heaven, he may be correct, for my thoughts sometimes move in a direction which foreshadows nothing short of lunacy —or so people would tell me, if I could bring myself to confide these things. I must fight alone, clinging to the knowledge that it is usual for anaemic persons to be obsessed by healthy fancies. If only I had not read those horribly suggestive words in Barrett...

"Barrett? What can she mean, May?"

"Wait a moment. Barrett? Barrett's *Traditions of the County*, perhaps. I have noticed a copy in the library. Let us go there; it may give the clue!"

The book was quickly found, and a marker indicated the passage to which Geraldine apparently referred.

At Cleeve, I was reminded of another of those traditions, so rapidly disappearing before the spread of education. It concerned the old belief in vampires, spirits of the evil dead, who by night, could assume a human form, and scour the countryside in search of victims. Suspected vampires, if caught, were buried with the mouth stuffed full of garlic, and a stake plunged through the heart, whereby they were rendered harmless, or, at least, confined to that one particular locality.

Some thirty years ago, and old man pointed out a tree which was said to have grown from such a stake. So far as I can recollect, it was an unusual variety of Sumach, and had been enclosed during a recent extension to the garden of the old Grange...

"Come outside," said Mrs. Watcombe, breaking a long and solemn silence. "I want you to see that tree."

The sky was suffused with the blush of early dawn, and the shrubs, the flowers, and even the dew upon the grass caught and reflected something of the pink effulgence. The Sumach alone stood out, dark and menacing. During the night its leaves had become a hideous, mottled purple; its growth was oily, bloated, unnaturally vigorous, like that of some rank and poisonous weed.

Mrs. Watcombe, looking from afar, spoke in frightened, husky tones.

"See, Hilary! It was exactly like when—when Geraldine died!"

W hen evening fell, the end of the lawn was strangely bare. In place of the old tree, there lay an enormous heap of smoldering embers— enormous, because the Sumach had been too sodden with dark and sticky sap, to burn without the assistance of large quantities of other timber.

Many weeks elapsed before Irene was sufficiently recovered to walk as far as Spot's little grave. She was surprised to find it almost hidden in a bed of garlic.

Hilary explained that it was the only plant they could induce to grow there.

MRS. AMWORTH

E. F. Benson

from *Visible and Invisible* (1920)

The village of Maxley, where, last summer and autumn, these strange events took place, lies on a heathery and pine-clad upland of Sussex. In all England you could not find a sweeter and saner situation. Should the wind blow from the south, it comes laden with the spices of the sea; to the east high downs protect it from the inclemencies of March; and from the west and north the breezes which reach it travel over miles of aromatic forest and heather. The village itself is insignificant enough in point of population, but rich in amenities and beauty. Half-way down the single street, with its broad road and spacious areas of grass on each side, stands the little Norman Church and the antique graveyard long disused: for the rest there are a dozen small, sedate Georgian houses, red-bricked and long-windowed, each with a square of flower-garden in front, and an ampler strip behind; a score of shops, and a couple of score of thatched cottages belonging to laborers on neighboring estates, complete the entire cluster of its peaceful habitations. The general peace, however, is sadly broken on Saturdays and Sundays, for we lie on one of the main roads between London and Brighton and our quiet street becomes a race-course for flying motor-cars and bicycles. A notice just outside the village begging them to go slowly only seems to encourage them to accelerate their speed, for the road lies open and straight, and there is really no reason why they should do otherwise. By way of protest, therefore, the ladies of Maxley cover their noses and mouths with their handkerchiefs as they see a motor-car approaching, though, as the street is asphalted, they need not really take these precautions against dust. But late on Sunday night the horde of scorchers has passed, and we settle down again to five days of cheerful and leisurely seclusion. Railway strikes which agitate the country so much leave us undisturbed because most of the inhabitants of Maxley never leave it at all.

I am the fortunate possessor of one of these small Georgian houses, and consider myself no less fortunate in having so interesting and stimulating a neighbor as Francis Urcombe, who, the most confirmed of Maxleyites, has not slept away from his house, which stands just opposite to mine in the village street, for nearly two years, at which date, though still in middle life, he resigned his Physiological Professorship at Cambridge University and devoted himself to the study of those occult and curious phenomena which seem equally to concern the physical and the psychical sides of human nature. Indeed his retirement was not unconnected with his passion for the strange uncharted places that lie on the confines and borders of science, the existence of which is so stoutly denied by the more materialistic minds, for he advocated that all medical students should be obliged to pass some sort of examination in mesmerism, and that one of the tripos papers should be designed to test their knowledge in such subjects as appearances at time of death, haunted houses, vampirism, automatic writing, and possession.

"Of course they wouldn't listen to me," ran his account of the matter, "for there is nothing that these seats of learning are so frightened of as knowledge, and the road to knowledge lies in the study of things like these. The functions of the human frame are, broadly speaking, known. They are a country, anyhow, that has been charted and mapped out. But outside that lie huge tracts of undiscovered country, which certainly exist, and the real pioneers of knowledge are those who, at the cost of being derided as credulous and superstitious, want to push on into those misty and probably perilous places. I felt that I could be of more use by setting out without compass or knapsack into the mists than by sitting in a cage like a canary and chirping about what was known. Besides, teaching is very bad for a man who knows himself only to be a learner: you only need to be a self-conceited ass to teach."

Here, then, in Francis Urcombe, was a delightful neighbor to one who, like myself, has an uneasy and burning curiosity about what he called the "misty and perilous places"; and this last spring we had a further and most welcome addition to our pleasant little community, in the person of Mrs. Amworth, widow of an Indian civil servant. Her husband had been a judge in the North-West Provinces, and after his death at Peshawar she came back to England, and after a year in London found herself starving for the ampler air and sunshine of the country to take the place of the fogs and griminess of town. She had, too, a special reason for settling in Maxley, since her ancestors up till a hundred years ago had long been native to the place, and in the old church-yard, now disused, are many grave-stones bearing her maiden name of Chaston. Big and energetic, her vigorous and genial personality speedily woke Maxley up to a higher degree of sociality than it had ever known. Most of us were bachelors or spinsters or elderly folk not much inclined to exert ourselves in the expense and effort of hospitality, and hitherto the gaiety of a small tea-party, with bridge afterwards and galoshes (when it was wet) to trip home in again for a solitary dinner, was about the climax of our festivities. But Mrs. Amworth showed us a more gregarious way, and set an example of luncheon-parties and little dinners, which we began to follow. On other nights when no such hospitality was on foot, a lone man like myself found it pleasant to know that a call on the telephone to Mrs. Amworth's house not a hundred yards off, and an inquiry as to whether I might come over after dinner for a game of piquet before bed-time, would probably evoke a response of welcome. There she would be, with a comrade-like eagerness for companionship, and there was a glass of port and a cup of coffee and a cigarette and a game of piquet. She played the piano, too, in a free and exuberant manner, and had a charming voice and sang to her own accompaniment; and as the days grew long and the light lingered late, we played our game in her garden, which in the course of a few months she had turned from being a nursery for slugs and snails into a glowing patch of luxuriant blossoming. She was always cheery and jolly; she was interested in everything, and in music, in gardening, in games of all sorts was a competent performer. Everybody (with one exception) liked her, everybody felt her to bring with her the tonic of a sunny day. That one exception was Francis Urcombe; he, though he confessed he did not like her, acknowledged that he was vastly interested in her. This always seemed strange to me, for pleasant and jovial as she was, I could see nothing in her that could call forth conjecture or intrigued surmise, so healthy and unmysterious a figure did she present. But of the genuineness of Urcombe's interest there could be no doubt; one could see him watching and scrutinizing her. In matter of age, she frankly volunteered the information that she was forty-five; but her briskness, her activity, her unravaged skin, her coal-black hair, made it difficult to believe that she was not adopting an unusual device, and adding ten years on to her age instead of subtracting them.

Often, also, as our quite unsentimental friendship ripened, Mrs. Amworth would ring me up and propose her advent. If I was busy writing, I was to give her, so we definitely bargained, a frank negative, and in answer I could hear her jolly laugh and her wishes for a successful evening of work. Sometimes, before her proposal arrived, Urcombe would already have stepped across from his house opposite for a smoke and a chat, and he, hearing who my intending visitor was, always urged me to beg her to come. She and I should play our piquet, said he, and he would look on, if we did not object, and learn something of the game. But I doubt whether he paid much attention to it, for nothing could be clearer than that, under that penthouse of forehead and thick eyebrows, his attention was fixed not on the cards, but on one of the players. But he seemed to enjoy an hour spent thus, and often, until one particular evening in July, he would watch her with the air of a man who has some deep problem in front of him. She, enthusiastically keen about our game, seemed not to notice his scrutiny. Then came that evening, when, as I see in the light of subsequent events, began the first twitching of the veil that hid the secret horror from my eyes. I did not know it then, though I noticed that thereafter, if she rang up to propose coming round, she always asked not only if I was at leisure, but whether Mr. Urcombe was with me. If so, she said, she would not spoil the chat of two old bachelors, and laughingly wished me good night.

Urcombe, on this occasion, had been with me for some half-hour before Mrs. Amworth's appearance, and had been talking to me about the medieval beliefs concerning vampirism, one of those borderland subjects which he declared had not been sufficiently studied before it had been consigned by the medical profession to the dust-heap of exploded superstitions. There he sat, grim and eager, tracing, with that pellucid clearness which had made him in his Cambridge days so admirable a lecturer, the history of those mysterious visitations. In them all there were the same general features: one of those ghoulish spirits took up its abode in a living man or woman, conferring supernatural powers of bat-like flight and glutting itself with nocturnal blood-feasts. When its host died it continued to dwell in the corpse, which remained undecayed. By day it rested, by night it left the grave and went on its awful errands. No European country in the Middle Ages seemed to have escaped them; earlier yet, parallels were to be found, in Roman and Greek and in Jewish history.

"It's a large order to set all that evidence aside as being moonshine," he said. "Hundreds of totally independent witnesses in many ages have testified to the occurrence of these phenomena, and there's no explanation known to me which covers all the facts. And if you feel inclined to say 'Why, then, if these are facts, do we not come across them now?' there are two answers I can make you. One is that there were diseases known in the Middle Ages, such as the black death, which were certainly existent then and which have become extinct since, but for that reason we do not assert that such diseases never existed. Just as the black death visited England and decimated the population of Norfolk, so here in this very district about three hundred years ago there was certainly an outbreak of vampirism, and Maxley was the centre of it. My second answer is even more convincing, for I tell you that vampirism is by no means extinct now. An outbreak of it certainly occurred in India a year or two ago."

At that moment I heard my knocker plied in the cheerful and peremptory manner in which Mrs. Amworth is accustomed to announce her arrival, and I went to the door to open it.

"Come in at once," I said, "and save me from having my blood curdled. Mr. Urcombe has been trying to alarm me."

Instantly her vital, voluminous presence seemed to fill the room.

"Ah, but how lovely!" she said. "I delight in having my blood curdled. Go on with your ghost-story, Mr. Urcombe. I adore ghost-stories."

I saw that, as his habit was, he was intently observing her.

"It wasn't a ghost-story exactly," said he. "I was only telling our host how vampirism was not extinct yet. I was saying that there was an outbreak of it in India only a few years ago."

There was a more than perceptible pause, and I saw that, if Urcombe was observing her, she on her side was observing him with fixed eye and parted mouth. Then her jolly laugh invaded that rather tense silence.

"Oh, what a shame!" she said. "You're not going to curdle my blood at all. Where did you pick up such a tale, Mr. Urcombe? I have lived for years in India and never heard a rumor of such a thing. Some story-teller in the bazaars must have invented it: they are famous at that."

I could see that Urcombe was on the point of saying something further, but checked himself.

"Ah! very likely that was it," he said.

But something had disturbed our usual peaceful sociability that night, and something had damped Mrs. Amworth's usual high spirits. She had no gusto for her piquet, and left after a couple of games. Urcombe had been silent too, indeed he hardly spoke again till she departed.

"That was unfortunate," he said, "for the outbreak of—of a very mysterious disease, let us call it, took place at Peshawar, where she and her husband were. And—"

"Well?" I asked.

"He was one of the victims of it," said he. "Naturally I had quite forgotten that when I spoke."

The summer was unreasonably hot and rainless, and Maxley suffered much from drought, and also from a plague of big black night-flying gnats, the bite of which was very irritating and virulent. They came sailing in of an evening, settling on one's skin so quietly that one perceived nothing till the sharp stab announced that one had been bitten. They did not bite the hands or face, but chose always the neck and throat for their feeding-ground, and most of us, as the poison spread, assumed a temporary goiter. Then about the middle of August appeared the first of those mysterious cases of illness which our local doctor attributed to the long-continued heat coupled with the bite of these venomous insects. The patient was a boy of sixteen or seventeen, the son of Mrs. Amworth's gardener, and the symptoms were an anemic pallor and a languid prostration, accompanied by great drowsiness and an abnormal appetite. He had, too, on his throat two small punctures where, so Dr. Ross conjectured, one of these great gnats had bitten him. But the odd thing was that there was no swelling or inflammation round the place where he had been bitten. The heat at this time had begun to abate, but the cooler weather failed to restore him, and the boy, in spite of the quantity of good food which he so ravenously swallowed, wasted away to a skin-clad skeleton.

I met Dr. Ross in the street one afternoon about this time, and in answer to my inquiries about his patient he said that he was afraid the boy was dying. The case, he confessed, completely puzzled him: some obscure form of pernicious anemia was all he could suggest. But he wondered whether Mr. Urcombe would consent to see the boy, on the chance of his being able to throw some new light on the case, and since Urcombe was dining with me that night, I proposed to Dr. Ross to join us. He could not do this, but said he would look in later. When he came, Urcombe at once consented to put his skill at the other's disposal, and together they went off at once. Being thus shorn of my sociable evening, I telephoned to Mrs. Amworth to know if I might inflict myself on her for an hour. Her answer was a welcoming affirmative, and between piquet and music the hour lengthened itself into two. She spoke of the boy who was lying so desperately and mysteriously ill, and told me that she had often been to see him, taking him nourishing and delicate food. But today—and her kind eyes moistened as she spoke—she was afraid she had paid her last visit. Knowing the antipathy between her and Urcombe, I did not tell her that he had been called into consultation; and when I returned home she accompanied me to my door, for the sake of a breath of night air, and in order to borrow a magazine which contained an article on gardening which she wished to read.

"Ah, this delicious night air," she said, luxuriously sniffing in the coolness. "Night air and gardening are the great tonics. There is nothing so stimulating as bare contact with rich mother earth. You are never so fresh as when you have been grubbing in the soil—black hands, black nails, and boots covered with mud." She gave her great jovial laugh.

"I'm a glutton for air and earth," she said. "Positively I look forward to death, for then I shall be buried and have the kind earth all round me. No leaden caskets for me—I have given explicit directions. But what shall I do about air? Well, I suppose one can't have everything. The magazine? A thousand thanks, I will faithfully return it. Good night: garden and keep your windows open, and you won't have anemia."

"I always sleep with my windows open," said I.

I went straight up to my bedroom, of which one of the windows looks out over the street, and as I undressed I thought I heard voices talking outside not far away. But I paid no particular attention, put out my lights, and falling asleep plunged into the depths of a most horrible dream, distortedly suggested no doubt, by my last words with Mrs. Amworth. I dreamed that I woke, and found that both my bedroom windows were shut. Half-suffocating I dreamed that I sprang out of bed, and went across to open them. The blind over the first was drawn down, and pulling it up I saw, with the indescribable horror of incipient nightmare, Mrs. Amworth's face suspended close to the pane in the darkness outside, nodding and smiling at me. Pulling down the blind again to keep that terror out, I rushed to the second window on the other side of the room, and there again was Mrs. Amworth's face. Then the panic came upon me in full blast; here was I suffocating in the airless room, and whichever window I opened Mrs. Amworth's face would float in, like those noiseless black gnats that bit before one was aware. The nightmare rose to screaming point, and with strangled yells I awoke to find my room cool and quiet with both windows open and blinds up and a half-moon high in its course, casting an oblong of tranquil light on the floor. But even when I was awake the horror persisted, and I lay tossing and turning. I must have slept long before the nightmare seized me, for now it was nearly day, and soon in the east the drowsy eyelids of morning began to lift.

I was scarcely downstairs next morning—for after the dawn I slept late— when Urcombe rang up to know if he might see me immediately. He came in, grim and preoccupied, and I noticed that he was pulling on a pipe that was not even filled.

"I want your help," he said, "and so I must tell you first of all what happened last night. I went round with the little doctor to see his patient, and found him just alive, but scarcely more. I instantly diagnosed in my own mind what this anemia, unaccountable by any other explanation, meant. The boy is the prey of a vampire."

He put his empty pipe on the breakfast-table, by which I had just sat down, and folded his arms, looking at me steadily from under his overhanging brows.

"Now about last night," he said. "I insisted that he should be moved from his father's cottage into my house. As we were carrying him on a stretcher, whom should we meet but Mrs. Amworth? She expressed shocked surprise that we were moving him. Now why do you think she did that?"

With a start of horror, as I remembered my dream that night before, I felt an idea come into my mind so preposterous and unthinkable that I instantly turned it out again.

"I haven't the smallest idea," I said.

"Then listen, while I tell you about what happened later. I put out all light in the room where the boy lay, and watched. One window was a little open, for I had forgotten to close it, and about midnight I heard something outside, trying apparently to push it farther open. I guessed who it was—yes, it was full twenty feet from the ground—and I peeped round the corner of the blind. Just outside was the face of Mrs. Amworth and her hand was on the frame of the window. Very softly I crept close, and then banged the window down, and I think I just caught the tip of one of her fingers."

"But it's impossible," I cried. "How could she be floating in the air like that? And what had she come for? Don't tell me such—"

Once more, with closer grip, the remembrance of my nightmare seized me.

"I am telling you what I saw," said he. "And all night long, until it was nearly day, she was fluttering outside, like some terrible bat, trying to gain admittance. Now put together various things I have told you."

He began checking them off on his fingers.

"Number one," he said: "there was an outbreak of disease similar to that which this boy is suffering from at Peshawar, and her husband died of it. Number two: Mrs. Amworth protested against my moving the boy to my house. Number three: she, or the demon that inhabits her body, a creature powerful and deadly, tries to gain admittance. And add this, too: in medieval times there was an epidemic of vampirism here at Maxley. The vampire, so the accounts run, was found to be Elizabeth Chaston . . . I see you remember Mrs. Amworth's maiden name. Finally, the boy is stronger this morning. He would certainly not have been alive if he had been visited again. And what do you make of it?"

There was a long silence, during which I found this incredible horror assuming the hues of reality.

"I have something to add," I said, "which may or may not bear on it. You say that the—the spectre went away shortly before dawn."

"Yes."

I told him of my dream, and he smiled grimly.

"Yes, you did well to awake," he said. "That warning came from your subconscious self, which never wholly slumbers, and cried out to you of deadly danger. For two reasons, then, you must help me: one to save others, the second to save yourself."

"What do you want me to do?" I asked.

"I want you first of all to help me in watching this boy, and ensuring that she does not come near him. Eventually I want you to help me in tracking the thing down, in exposing and destroying it. It is not human: it is an incarnate fiend. What steps we shall have to take I don't yet know."

It was now eleven of the forenoon, and presently I went across to his house for a twelve-hour vigil while he slept, to come on duty again that night, so that for the next twenty-four hours either Urcombe or myself was always in the room where the boy, now getting stronger every hour, was lying. The day following was Saturday and a morning of brilliant, pellucid weather, and already when I went across to his house to resume my duty the stream of motors down to Brighton had begun. Simultaneously I saw Urcombe with a cheerful face, which boded good news of his patient, coming out of his house, and Mrs. Amworth, with a gesture of salutation to me and a basket in her hand, walking up the broad strip of grass which bordered the road. There we all three met. I noticed (and saw that Urcombe noticed it too) that one finger of her left hand was bandaged.

"Good morning to you both," said she. "And I hear your patient is doing well, Mr. Urcombe. I have come to bring him a bowl of jelly, and to sit with him for an hour. He and I are great friends. I am overjoyed at his recovery."

Urcombe paused a moment, as if making up his mind, and then shot out a pointing finger at her.

"I forbid that," he said. "You shall not sit with him or see him. And you know the reason as well as I do."

I have never seen so horrible a change pass over a human face as that which now blanched hers to the color of a grey mist. She put up her hand as if to shield herself from that pointing finger, which drew the sign of the cross in the air, and shrank back cowering on to the road. There was a wild hoot from a horn, a grinding of brakes, a shout—too late—from a passing car, and one long scream suddenly cut short. Her body rebounded from the roadway after the first wheel had gone over it, and the second followed. It lay there, quivering and twitching, and was still.

She was buried three days afterwards in the cemetery outside Maxley, in accordance with the wishes she had told me that she had devised about her interment, and the shock which her sudden and awful death had caused to the little community began by degrees to pass off. To two people only, Urcombe and myself, the horror of it was mitigated from the first by the nature of the relief that her death brought; but, naturally enough, we kept our own counsel, and no hint of what greater horror had been thus averted was ever let slip. But, oddly enough, so it seemed to me, he was still not satisfied about something in connection with her, and would give no answer to my questions on the subject. Then as the days of a tranquil mellow September and the October that followed began to drop away like the leaves of the yellowing trees, his uneasiness relaxed. But before the entry of November the seeming tranquillity broke into hurricane.

I had been dining one night at the far end of the village, and about eleven o'clock was walking home again. The moon was of an unusual brilliance, rendering all that it shone on as distinct as in some etching. I had just come opposite the house which Mrs. Amworth had occupied, where there was a board up telling that it was to let, when I heard the click of her front gate, and next moment I saw, with a sudden chill and quaking of my very spirit, that she stood there. Her profile, vividly illuminated, was turned to me, and I could not be mistaken in my identification of her. She appeared not to see me (indeed the shadow of the yew hedge in front of her garden enveloped me in its blackness) and she went swiftly across the road, and entered the gate of the house directly opposite. There I lost sight of her completely.

My breath was coming in short pants as if I had been running—and now indeed I ran, with fearful backward glances, along the hundred yards that separated me from my house and Urcombe's. It was to his that my flying steps took me, and next minute I was within.

"What have you come to tell me?" he asked. "Or shall I guess?"

"You can't guess," said I.

"No; it's no guess. She has come back and you have seen her. Tell me about it."

I gave him my story.

"That's Major Pearsall's house," he said. "Come back with me there at once."

"But what can we do?" I asked.

"I've no idea. That's what we have got to find out."

A minute later, we were opposite the house. When I had passed it before, it was all dark; now lights gleamed from a couple of windows upstairs. Even as we faced it, the front door opened, and next moment Major Pearsall emerged from the gate. He saw us and stopped.

"I'm on my way to Dr. Ross," he said quickly. "My wife has been taken suddenly ill. She had been in bed an hour when I came upstairs, and I found her white as a ghost and utterly exhausted. She had been to sleep, it seemed —but you will excuse me."

"One moment, Major," said Urcombe. "Was there any mark on her throat?"

"How did you guess that?" said he. "There was: one of those beastly gnats must have bitten her twice there. She was streaming with blood."

"And there's someone with her?" asked Urcombe.

"Yes, I roused her maid."

He went off, and Urcombe turned to me. "I know now what we have to do," he said. "Change your clothes, and I'll join you at your house."

"What is it?" I asked.

"I'll tell you on our way. We're going to the cemetery."

He carried a pick, a shovel, and a screwdriver when he rejoined me, and wore round his shoulders a long coil of rope. As we walked, he gave me the outlines of the ghastly hour that lay before us.

"What I have to tell you," he said, "will seem to you now too fantastic for credence, but before dawn we shall see whether it outstrips reality. By a most fortunate happening, you saw the spectre, the astral body, whatever you choose to call it, of Mrs. Amworth, going on its grisly business, and therefore, beyond doubt, the vampire spirit which abode in her during life animates her again in death. That is not exceptional—indeed, all these weeks since her death I have been expecting it. If I am right, we shall find her body undecayed and untouched by corruption."

"But she has been dead nearly two months," said I.

"If she had been dead two years it would still be so, if the vampire has possession of her. So remember: whatever you see done, it will be done not to her, who in the natural course would now be feeding the grasses above her grave, but to a spirit of untold evil and malignancy, which gives a phantom life to her body."

"But what shall I see done?" said I.

"I will tell you. We know that now, at this moment, the vampire clad in her mortal semblance is out; dining out. But it must get back before dawn, and it will pass into the material form that lies in her grave. We must wait for that, and then with your help I shall dig up her body. If I am right, you will look on her as she was in life, with the full vigor of the dreadful nutriment she has received pulsing in her veins. And then, when dawn has come, and the vampire cannot leave the lair of her body, I shall strike her with this"— and he pointed to his pick—"through the heart, and she, who comes to life again only with the animation the fiend gives her, she and her hellish partner will be dead indeed. Then we must bury her again, delivered at last."

We had come to the cemetery, and in the brightness of the moonshine there was no difficulty in identifying her grave. It lay some twenty yards from the small chapel, in the porch of which, obscured by shadow, we concealed ourselves. From there we had a clear and open sight of the grave, and now we must wait till its infernal visitor returned home. The night was warm and windless, yet even if a freezing wind had been raging I think I should have felt nothing of it, so intense was my preoccupation as to what the night and dawn would bring. There was a bell in the turret of the chapel, that struck the quarters of the hour, and it amazed me to find how swiftly the chimes succeeded one another.

The moon had long set, but a twilight of stars shone in a clear sky, when five o'clock of the morning sounded from the turret. A few minutes more passed, and then I felt Urcombe's hand softly nudging me; and looking out in the direction of his pointing finger, I saw that the form of a woman, tall and large in build, was approaching from the right. Noiselessly, with a motion more of gliding and floating than walking, she moved across the cemetery to the grave which was the centre of our observation. She moved round it as if to be certain of its identity, and for a moment stood directly facing us. In the grayness to which now my eyes had grown accustomed, I could easily see her face, and recognize its features.

She drew her hand across her mouth as if wiping it, and broke into a chuckle of such laughter as made my hair stir on my head. Then she leaped on to the grave, holding her hands high above her head, and inch by inch disappeared into the earth. Urcombe's hand was laid on my arm, in an injunction to keep still, but now he removed it.

"Come," he said.

With pick and shovel and rope we went to the grave. The earth was light and sandy, and soon after six struck we had delved down to the coffin lid. With his pick he loosened the earth round it, and, adjusting the rope through the handles by which it had been lowered, we tried to raise it. This was a long and laborious business, and the light had begun to herald day in the east before we had it out, and lying by the side of the grave. With his screwdriver he loosed the fastenings of the lid, and slid it aside, and standing there we looked on the face of Mrs. Amworth. The eyes, once closed in death, were open, the cheeks were flushed with color, the red, full-lipped mouth seemed to smile.

"One blow and it is all over," he said. "You need not look."

Even as he spoke he took up the pick again, and, laying the point of it on her left breast, measured his distance. And though I knew what was coming I could not look away. . . .

He grasped the pick in both hands, raised it an inch or two for the taking of his aim, and then with full force brought it down on her breast. A fountain of blood, though she had been dead so long, spouted high in the air, falling with the thud of a heavy splash over the shroud, and simultaneously from those red lips came one long, appalling cry, swelling up like some hooting siren, and dying away again. With that, instantaneous as a lightning flash, came the touch of corruption on her face, the color of it faded to ash, the plump cheeks fell in, the mouth dropped.

"Thank God, that's over," said he, and without pause slipped the coffin lid back into its place.

Day was coming fast now, and, working like men possessed, we lowered the coffin into its place again, and shoveled the earth over it... The birds were busy with their earliest pipings as we went back to Maxley.

BEWITCHED

Edith Wharton

from in *Here and Beyond* (1926)

I.

The snow was still falling thickly when Orrin Bosworth, who farmed the land south of Lonetop, drove up in his cutter to Saul Rutledge's gate. He was surprised to see two other cutters ahead of him. From them descended two muffled figures. Bosworth, with increasing surprise, recognized Deacon Hibben, from North Ashmore, and Sylvester Brand, the widower, from the old Bearcliff farm on the way to Lonetop.

It was not often that anybody in Hemlock County entered Saul Rutledge's gate; least of all in the dead of winter, and summoned (as Bosworth, at any rate, had been) by Mrs. Rutledge, who passed, even in that unsocial region, for a woman of cold manners and solitary character. The situation was enough to excite the curiosity of a less imaginative man than Orrin Bosworth.

As he drove in between the broken-down white gate-posts topped by fluted urns the two men ahead of him were leading their horses to the adjoining shed. Bosworth followed, and hitched his horse to a post. Then the three tossed off the snow from their shoulders, clapped their numb hands together, and greeted each other.

"Hallo, Deacon."

"Well, well, Orrin—." They shook hands.

"Day, Bosworth," said Sylvester Brand, with a brief nod. He seldom put any cordiality into his manner, and on this occasion he was still busy about his horse's bridle and blanket.

Orrin Bosworth, the youngest and most communicative of the three, turned back to Deacon Hibben, whose long face, queerly blotched and moldy-looking, with blinking peering eyes, was yet less forbidding than Brand's heavily-hewn countenance.

"Queer, our all meeting here this way. Mrs. Rutledge sent me a message to come," Bosworth volunteered.

The Deacon nodded. "I got a word from her too—Andy Pond come with it yesterday noon. I hope there's no trouble here—"

He glanced through the thickening fall of snow at the desolate front of the Rutledge house, the more melancholy in its present neglected state because, like the gate-posts, it kept traces of former elegance. Bosworth had often wondered how such a house had come to be built in that lonely stretch between North Ashmore and Cold Corners. People said there had once been other houses like it, forming a little township called Ashmore, a sort of mountain colony created by the caprice of an English Royalist officer, one Colonel Ashmore, who had been murdered by the Indians, with all his family, long before the Revolution. This tale was confirmed by the fact that the ruined cellars of several smaller houses were still to be discovered under the wild growth of the adjoining slopes, and that the Communion plate of the moribund Episcopal church of Cold Corners was engraved with the name of Colonel Ashmore, who had given it to the church of Ashmore in the year 1723. Of the church itself no traces remained. Doubtless it had been a modest wooden edifice, built on piles, and the conflagration which had burnt the other houses to the ground's edge had reduced it utterly to ashes. The whole place, even in summer, wore a mournful solitary air, and people wondered why Saul Rutledge's father had gone there to settle.

"I never knew a place," Deacon Hibben said, "as seemed as far away from humanity. And yet it ain't so in miles."

"Miles ain't the only distance," Orrin Bosworth answered; and the two men, followed by Sylvester Brand, walked across the drive to the front door. People in Hemlock County did not usually come and go by their front doors, but all three men seemed to feel that, on an occasion which appeared to be so exceptional, the usual and more familiar approach by the kitchen would not be suitable.

They had judged rightly; the Deacon had hardly lifted the knocker when the door opened and Mrs. Rutledge stood before them.

"Walk right in," she said in her usual dead-level tone; and Bosworth, as he followed the others, thought to himself; "Whatever's happened, she's not going to let it show in her face."

It was doubtful, indeed, if anything unwonted could be made to show in Prudence Rutledge's face, so limited was its scope, so fixed were its features. She was dressed for the occasion in a black calico with white spots, a collar of crochet-lace fastened by a gold brooch, and a gray woolen shawl crossed under her arms and tied at the back. In her small narrow head the only marked prominence was that of the brow projecting roundly over pale spectacled eyes. Her dark hair, parted above this prominence, passed tight and flat over the tips of her ears into a small braided coil at the nape; and her contracted head looked still narrower from being perched on a long hollow neck with cord-like throat-muscles. Her eyes were of a pale cold gray, her complexion was an even white. Her age might have been anywhere from thirty-five to sixty.

The room into which she led the three men had probably been the dining-room of the Ashmore house. It was now used as a front parlor, and a black stove planted on a sheet of zinc stuck out from the delicately fluted panels of an old wooden mantel. A newly-lit fire smoldered reluctantly, and the room was at once close and bitterly cold.

"Andy Pond," Mrs. Rutledge cried to someone at the back of the house, "step out and call Mr. Rutledge. You'll likely find him in the wood-shed, or round the barn somewheres." She rejoined her visitors. "Please suit yourselves to seats," she said.

The three men, with an increasing air of constraint, took the chairs she pointed out, and Mrs. Rutledge sat stiffly down upon a fourth, behind a rickety bead-work table. She glanced from one to the other of her visitors.

"I presume you folks are wondering what it is I asked you to come here for," she said in her dead-level voice. Orrin Bosworth and Deacon Hibben murmured an assent; Sylvester Brand sat silent, his eyes, under their great thicket of eyebrows, fixed on the huge boot-tip swinging before him.

"Well, I allow you didn't expect it was for a party," continued Mrs. Rutledge.

No one ventured to respond to this chill pleasantry, and she continued: "We're in trouble here, and that's the fact. And we need advice—Mr. Rutledge and myself do." She cleared her throat, and added in a lower tone, her pitilessly clear eyes looking straight before her: "There's a spell been cast over Mr. Rutledge."

The Deacon looked up sharply, an incredulous smile pinching his thin lips. "A spell?"

"That's what I said: he's bewitched."

Again the three visitors were silent; then Bosworth, more at ease or less tongue-tied than the others, asked with an attempt at humor: "Do you use the word in the strict Scripture sense, Mrs. Rutledge?"

She glanced at him before replying: "That's how *he* uses it."

The Deacon coughed and cleared his long rattling throat. "Do you care to give us more particulars before your husband joins us?"

Mrs. Rutledge looked down at her clasped hands, as if considering the question. Bosworth noticed that the inner fold of her lids was of the same uniform white as the rest of her skin, so that when she dropped them her rather prominent eyes looked like the sightless orbs of a marble statue. The impression was unpleasing, and he glanced away at the text over the mantelpiece, which read:

The Soul That Sinneth It Shall Die.

"No," she said at length, "I'll wait."

At this moment Sylvester Brand suddenly stood up and pushed back his chair. "I don't know," he said, in his rough bass voice, "as I've got any particular lights on Bible mysteries; and this happens to be the day I was to go down to Starkfield to close a deal with a man."

Mrs. Rutledge lifted one of her long thin hands. Withered and wrinkled by hard work and cold, it was nevertheless of the same leaden white as her face. "You won't be kept long," she said. "Won't you be seated?"

Farmer Brand stood irresolute, his purplish underlip twitching. "The Deacon here—such things is more in his line…"

"I want you should stay," said Mrs. Rutledge quietly; and Brand sat down again.

A silence fell, during which the four persons present seemed all to be listening for the sound of a step; but none was heard, and after a minute or two Mrs. Rutledge began to speak again.

"It's down by that old shack on Lamer's pond; that's where they meet," she said suddenly.

Bosworth, whose eyes were on Sylvester Brand's face, fancied he saw a sort of inner flush darken the farmer's heavy leathern skin. Deacon Hibben leaned forward, a glitter of curiosity in his eyes.

"They—*who*, Mrs. Rutledge?"

"My husband, Saul Rutledge…and her…"

Sylvester Brand again stirred in his seat. "Who do you mean by *her?*" he asked abruptly, as if roused out of some far-off musing.

Mrs. Rutledge's body did not move; she simply revolved her head on her long neck and looked at him.

"Your daughter, Sylvester Brand."

The man staggered to his feet with an explosion of inarticulate sounds. "My—my daughter? What the hell are you talking about? My daughter? It's a damned lie…it's…it's…"

"Your daughter *Ora*, Mr. Brand," said Mrs. Rutledge slowly.

Bosworth felt an icy chill down his spine. Instinctively he turned his eyes away from Brand, and, they rested on the mildewed countenance of Deacon Hibben. Between the blotches it had become as white as Mrs. Rutledge's, and the Deacon's eyes burned in the whiteness like live embers among ashes.

Brand gave a laugh: the rusty creaking laugh of one whose springs of mirth are never moved by gaiety. "My daughter *Ora?*" he repeated.

"Yes."

"My *dead* daughter?"

"That's what he says."

"Your husband?"

"That's what Mr. Rutledge says."

Orrin Bosworth listened with a sense of suffocation; he felt as if he were wrestling with long-armed horrors in a dream. He could no longer resist letting his eyes return to Sylvester Brand's face. To his surprise it had resumed a natural imperturbable expression. Brand rose to his feet. "Is that all?" he queried contemptuously.

"All? Ain't it enough? How long is it since you folks seen Saul Rutledge, any of you?" Mrs. Rutledge flew out at them.

Bosworth, it appeared, had not seen him for nearly a year; the Deacon had only run across him once, for a minute, at the North Ashmore post office, the previous autumn, and acknowledged that he wasn't looking any too good then. Brand said nothing, but stood irresolute.

"Well, if you wait a minute you'll see with your own eyes; and he'll tell you with his own words. That's what I've got you here for—to see for yourselves what's come over him. Then you'll talk different," she added, twisting her head abruptly toward Sylvester Brand.

The Deacon raised a lean hand of interrogation.

"Does your husband know we've been sent for on this business, Mrs. Rutledge?" Mrs. Rutledge signed assent.

"It was with his consent, then—?"

She looked coldly at her questioner. "I guess it had to be," she said. Again Bosworth felt the chill down his spine. He tried to dissipate the sensation by speaking with an affectation of energy.

"Can you tell us, Mrs. Rutledge, how this trouble you speak of shows itself...what makes you think...?"

She looked at him for a moment; then she leaned forward across the rickety bead-work table. A thin smile of disdain narrowed her colorless lips. "I don't think—I know."

"Well—but how?"

She leaned closer, both elbows on the table, her voice dropping. "I seen 'em."

In the ashen light from the veiling of snow beyond the windows the Deacon's little screwed-up eyes seemed to give out red sparks. "Him and the dead?"

"Him and the dead."

"Saul Rutledge and—and Ora Brand?"

"That's so."

Sylvester Brand's chair fell backward with a crash. He was on his feet again, crimson and cursing. "It's a God-damned fiend-begotten lie..."

"Friend Brand...friend Brand..." the Deacon protested.

"Here, let me get out of this. I want to see Saul Rutledge himself, and tell him—"

"Well, here he is," said Mrs. Rutledge.

The outer door had opened; they heard the familiar stamping and shaking of a man who rids his garments of their last snowflakes before penetrating to the sacred precincts of the best parlor. Then Saul Rutledge entered.

II.

As he came in he faced the light from the north window, and Bosworth's first thought was that he looked like a drowned man fished out from under the ice—"self-drowned," he added. But the snow-light plays cruel tricks with a man's color, and even with the shape of his features; it must have been partly that, Bosworth reflected, which transformed Saul Rutledge from the straight muscular fellow he had been a year before into the haggard wretch now before them.

The Deacon sought for a word to ease the horror. "Well, now, Saul—you look's if you'd ought to set right up to the stove. Had a touch of ague, maybe?"

The feeble attempt was unavailing. Rutledge neither moved nor answered. He stood among them silent, incommunicable, like one risen from the dead.

Brand grasped him roughly by the shoulder. "See here, Saul Rutledge, what's this dirty lie your wife tells us you've been putting about?"

Still Rutledge did not move. "It's no lie," he said.

Brand's hand dropped from his shoulder. In spite of the man's rough bullying power he seemed to be undefinably awed by Rutledge's look and tone.

"No lie? You've gone plumb crazy, then, have you?"

Mrs. Rutledge spoke. "My husband's not lying, nor he ain't gone crazy. Don't I tell you I seen 'em?"

Brand laughed again. "Him and the dead?"

"Yes."

"Down by the Lamer pond, you say?"

"Yes."

"And when was that, if I might ask?"

"Day before yesterday."

A silence fell on the strangely assembled group. The Deacon at length broke it to say to Mr. Brand: "Brand, in my opinion we've got to see this thing through."

Brand stood for a moment in speechless contemplation: there was something animal and primitive about him, Bosworth thought, as he hung thus, lowering and dumb, a little foam beading the corners of that heavy purplish underlip. He let himself slowly down into his chair. "I'll see it through."

The two other men and Mrs. Rutledge had remained seated. Saul Rutledge stood before them, like a prisoner at the bar, or rather like a sick man before the physicians who were to heal him. As Bosworth scrutinized that hollow face, so wan under the dark sunburn, so sucked inward and consumed by some hidden fever, there stole over the sound healthy man the thought that perhaps, after all, husband and wife spoke the truth, and that they were all at that moment really standing on the edge of some forbidden mystery. Things that the rational mind would reject without a thought seemed no longer so easy to dispose of as one looked at the actual Saul Rutledge and remembered the man he had been a year before. Yes; as the Deacon said, they would have to see it through...

"Sit down then, Saul; draw up to us, won't you?" the Deacon suggested, trying again for a natural tone.

Mrs. Rutledge pushed a chair forward, and her husband sat down on it. He stretched out his arms and grasped his knees in his brown bony fingers; in that attitude he remained, turning neither his head nor his eyes.

"Well, Saul," the Deacon continued, "your wife says you thought mebbe we could do something to help you through this trouble, whatever it is."

Rutledge's gray eyes widened a little. "No; I didn't think that. It was her idea to try what could be done."

"I presume, though, since you've agreed to our coming, that you don't object to our putting a few questions?"

Rutledge was silent for a moment; then he said with a visible effort: "No; I don't object."

"Well—you've heard what your wife says?"

Rutledge made a slight motion of assent. "And—what have you got to answer? How do you explain…?"

Mrs. Rutledge intervened. "How can he explain? I seen 'em."

There was a silence; then Bosworth, trying to speak in an easy reassuring tone, queried: "That so, Saul?"

"That's so."

Brand lifted up his brooding head. "You mean to say you…you sit here before us all and say…"

The Deacon's hand again checked him. "Hold on, friend Brand. We're all of us trying for the facts, ain't we?" He turned to Rutledge. "We've heard what Mrs. Rutledge says. What's your answer?"

"I don't know as there's any answer. She found us."

"And you mean to tell me the person with you was…was what you took to be…" the Deacon's thin voice grew thinner: "Ora Brand?"

Saul Rutledge nodded.

"You knew…or thought you knew…you were meeting with the dead?"

Rutledge bent his head again. The snow continued to fall in a steady unwavering sheet against the window, and Bosworth felt as if a winding-sheet were descending from the sky to envelop them all in a common grave.

"Think what you're saying! It's against our religion! Ora…poor child!… died over a year ago. I saw you at her funeral, Saul. How can you make such a statement?"

"What else can he do?" thrust in Mrs. Rutledge.

There was another pause. Bosworth's resources had failed him, and Brand once more sat plunged in dark meditation. The Deacon laid his quivering finger-tips together, and moistened his lips.

"Was the day before yesterday the first time?" he asked.

The movement of Rutledge's head was negative.

"Not the first? Then when…"

"Nigh on a year ago, I reckon."

"God! And you mean to tell us that ever since—?"

"Well…look at him," said his wife. The three men lowered their eyes.

After a moment Bosworth, trying to collect himself, glanced at the Deacon. "Why not ask Saul to make his own statement, if that's what we're here for?"

"That's so," the Deacon assented. He turned to Rutledge. "Will you try and give us your idea…of…of how it began?"

There was another silence. Then Rutledge tightened his grasp on his gaunt knees, and still looking straight ahead, with his curiously clear unseeing gaze: "Well," he said, "I guess it begun away back, afore even I was married to Mrs. Rutledge…" He spoke in a low automatic tone, as if some invisible agent were dictating his words, or even uttering them for him. "You know," he added, "Ora and me was to have been married."

Sylvester Brand lifted his, head. "Straighten that statement out first, please," he interjected.

"What I mean is, we kept company. But Ora she was very young. Mr. Brand here he sent her away. She was gone nigh to three years, I guess. When she come back I was married."

"That's right," Brand said, relapsing once more into his sunken attitude.

"And after she came back did you meet her again?" the Deacon continued.

"Alive?" Rutledge questioned.

A perceptible shudder ran through the room.

"Well—of course," said the Deacon nervously.

Rutledge seemed to consider. "Once I did—only once. There was a lot of other people round. At Cold Corners fair it was." "Did you talk with her then?"

"Only a minute."

"What did she say?"

His voice dropped. "She said she was sick and knew she was going to die, and when she was dead she'd come back to me."

"And what did you answer?"

"Nothing."

"Did you think anything of it at the time?"

"Well, no. Not till I heard she was dead I didn't. After that I thought of it —and I guess she drew me." He moistened his lips.

"Drew you down to that abandoned house by the pond?"

Rutledge made a faint motion of assent, and the Deacon added: "How did you know it was there she wanted you to come?"

"She…just drew me…"

There was a long pause. Bosworth felt, on himself and the other two men, the oppressive weight of the next question to be asked. Mrs. Rutledge opened and closed her narrow lips once or twice, like some beached shell-fish gasping for the tide. Rutledge waited.

"Well, now, Saul, won't you go on with what you was telling us?" the Deacon at length suggested.

"That's all. There's nothing else."

The Deacon lowered his voice. "She just draws you?"

"Yes."

"Often?"

"That's as it happens…"

"But if it's always there she draws you, man, haven't you the strength to keep away from the place?"

For the first time, Rutledge wearily turned his head toward his questioner. A spectral smile narrowed his colorless lips. "Ain't any use. She follers after me..."

There was another silence. What more could they ask, then and there? Mrs. Rutledge's presence checked the next question. The Deacon seemed hopelessly to revolve the matter. At length he spoke in a more authoritative tone. "These are forbidden things. You know that, Saul. Have you tried prayer?"

Rutledge shook his head.

"Will you pray with us now?"

Rutledge cast a glance of freezing indifference on his spiritual adviser. "If you folks want to pray, I'm agreeable," he said. But Mrs. Rutledge intervened.

"Prayer ain't any good. In this kind of thing it ain't no manner of use; you know it ain't. I called you here, Deacon, because you remember the last case in this parish. Thirty years ago it was, I guess; but you remember. Lefferts Nash —did praying help him? I was a little girl then, but I used to hear my folks talk of it winter nights. Lefferts Nash and Hannah Cory. They drove a stake through her breast. That's what cured him."

"Oh—" Orrin Bosworth exclaimed.

Sylvester Brand raised his head. "You're speaking of that old story as if this was the same sort of thing?"

"Ain't it? Ain't my husband pining away the same as Lefferts Nash did? The Deacon here knows—"

The Deacon stirred anxiously in his chair. "These are forbidden things," he repeated. "Supposing your husband is quite sincere in thinking himself haunted, as you might say. Well, even then, what proof have we that the...the dead woman...is the spectre of that poor girl?"

"Proof? Don't he say so? Didn't she tell him? Ain't I seen 'em?" Mrs. Rutledge almost screamed.

The three men sat silent, and suddenly the wife burst out: "A stake through the breast That's the old way; and it's the only way. The Deacon knows it!"

"It's against our religion to disturb the dead."

"Ain't it against your religion to let the living perish as my husband is perishing?" She sprang up with one of her abrupt movements and took the family Bible from the what-not in a corner of the parlor. Putting the book on the table, and moistening a livid finger-tip, she turned the pages rapidly, till she came to one on which she laid her hand like a stony paper-weight. "See here," she said, and read out in her level chanting voice:

"*Thou shalt not suffer a witch to live.*'

"That's in Exodus, that's where it is," she added, leaving the book open as if to confirm the statement.

Bosworth continued to glance anxiously from one to the other of the four people about the table. He was younger than any of them, and had had more contact with the modern world; down in Starkfield, in the bar of the Fielding House, he could hear himself laughing with the rest of the men at such old wives' tales. But it was not for nothing that he had been born under the icy shadow of Lonetop, and had shivered and hungered as a lad through the bitter Hemlock County winters. After his parents died, and he had taken hold of the farm himself, he had got more out of it by using improved methods, and by supplying the increasing throng of summer-boarders over Stotesbury way with milk and vegetables. He had been made a selectman of North Ashmore; for so young a man he had a standing in the county. But the roots of the old life were still in him. He could remember, as a little boy, going twice a year with his mother to that bleak hill-farm out beyond Sylvester Brand's, where Mrs. Bosworth's aunt, Cressidora Cheney, had been shut up for years in a cold clean room with iron bars in the windows. When little Orrin first saw Aunt Cressidora she was a small white old woman, whom her sisters used to "make decent" for visitors the day that Orrin and his mother were expected. The child wondered why there were bars to the window. "Like a canary-bird," he said to his mother. The phrase made Mrs. Bosworth reflect. "I do believe they keep Aunt Cressidora too lonesome," she said; and the next time she went up the mountain with the little boy he carried to his great-aunt a canary in a little wooden cage. It was a great excitement; he knew it would make her happy.

The old woman's motionless face lit up when she saw the bird, and her eyes began to glitter. "It belongs to me," she said instantly, stretching her soft bony hand over the cage.

"Of course it does, Aunt Cressy," said Mrs. Bosworth, her eyes filling.

But the bird, startled by the shadow of the old woman's hand, began to flutter and beat its wings distractedly. At the sight, Aunt Cressidora's calm face suddenly became a coil of twitching features. "You she-devil, you!" she cried in a high squealing voice; and thrusting her hand into the cage she dragged out the terrified bird and wrung its neck. She was plucking the hot body, and squealing "she-devil, she-devil!" as they drew little Orrin from the room. On the way down the mountain his mother wept a great deal, and said: "You must never tell anybody that poor Auntie's crazy, or the men would come and take her down to the asylum at Starkfield, and the shame of it would kill us all. Now promise." The child promised.

He remembered the scene now, with its deep fringe of mystery, secrecy and rumor. It seemed related to a great many other things below the surface of his thoughts, things which stole up anew, making him feel that all the old people he had known, and who "believed in these things," might after all be right. Hadn't a witch been burned at North Ashmore? Didn't the summer folk still drive over in jolly buckboard loads to see the meeting-house where the trial had been held, the pond where they had ducked her and she had floated?... Deacon Hibben believed; Bosworth was sure of it. If he didn't, why did people from all over the place come to him when their animals had queer sicknesses, or when there was a child in the family that had to be kept shut up because it fell down flat and foamed? Yes, in spite of his religion, Deacon Hibben *knew*...

And Brand? Well, it came to Bosworth in a flash: that North Ashmore woman who was burned had the name of Brand. The same stock, no doubt; there had been Brands in Hemlock County ever since the white men had come there. And Orrin, when he was a child, remembered hearing his parents say that Sylvester Brand hadn't ever oughter married his own cousin, because of the blood. Yet the couple had had two healthy girls, and when Mrs. Brand pined away and died nobody suggested that anything had been wrong with her mind. And Vanessa and Ora were the handsomest girls anywhere round. Brand knew it, and scrimped and saved all he could to send Ora, the eldest, down to Starkfield to learn book-keeping. "When she's married I'll send you," he used to say to little Venny, who was his favorite. But Ora never married. She was away three years, during which Venny ran wild on the slopes of Lonetop; and when Ora came back she sickened and died—poor girl! Since then Brand had grown more savage and morose. He was a hard-working farmer, but there wasn't much to be got out of those barren Bearcliff acres. He was said to have taken to drink since his wife's death; now and then men ran across him in the "dives" of Stotesbury. But not often. And between times he labored hard on his stony acres and did his best for his daughters. In the neglected grave-yard of Cold Corners there was a slanting head-stone marked with his wife's name; near it, a year since, he had laid his eldest daughter. And sometimes, at dusk, in the autumn, the village people saw him walk slowly by, turn in between the graves, and stand looking down on the two stones. But he never brought a flower there, or planted a bush; nor Venny either. She was too wild and ignorant...

Mrs. Rutledge repeated: "That's in Exodus."

The three visitors remained silent, turning about their hats in reluctant hands. Rutledge faced them, still with that empty pellucid gaze which frightened Bosworth. What was he seeing?

"Ain't any of you folks got the grit—?" his wife burst out again, half hysterically.

Deacon Hibben held up his hand. "That's no way, Mrs. Rutledge. This ain't a question of having grit. What we want first of all is...proof..."

"That's so," said Bosworth, with an explosion of relief, as if the words had lifted something black and crouching from his breast. Involuntarily the eyes of both men had turned to Brand. He stood there smiling grimly, but did not speak.

"Ain't it so, Brand?" the Deacon prompted him.

"Proof that spooks walk?" the other sneered.

"Well—I presume you want this business settled too?"

The old farmer squared his shoulders. "Yes—I do. But I ain't a sperritualist. How the hell are you going to settle it?"

Deacon Hibben hesitated; then he said, in a low incisive tone: "I don't see but one way—Mrs. Rutledge's."

There was a silence.

"What?" Brand sneered again. "Spying?"

The Deacon's voice sank lower. "If the poor girl *does* walk…her that's your child…wouldn't you be the first to want her laid quiet? We all know there've been such cases…mysterious visitations…Can any one of us here deny it?"

"I seen 'em," Mrs. Rutledge interjected.

There was another heavy pause. Suddenly Brand fixed his gaze on Rutledge. "See here, Saul Rutledge, you've got to clear up this damned calumny, or I'll know why. You say my dead girl comes to you." He labored with his breath, and then jerked out: "When? You tell me that, and I'll be there."

Rutledge's head drooped a little, and his eyes wandered to the window. "Round about sunset, mostly."

"You know beforehand?"

Rutledge made a sign of assent.

"Well, then—tomorrow, will it be?" Rutledge made the same sign.

Brand turned to the door. "I'll be there." That was all he said. He strode out between them without another glance or word. Deacon Hibben looked at Mrs. Rutledge. "We'll be there too," he said, as if she had asked him; but she had not spoken, and Bosworth saw that her thin body was trembling all over. He was glad when he and Hibben were out again in the snow.

III.

They thought that Brand wanted to be left to himself, and to give him time to unhitch his horse they made a pretense of hanging about in the doorway while Bosworth searched his pockets for a pipe he had no mind to light.

But Brand turned back to them as they lingered. "You'll meet me down by Lamer's pond tomorrow?" he suggested. "I want witnesses. Round about sunset."

They nodded their acquiescence, and he got into his sleigh, gave the horse a cut across the flanks, and drove off under the snow-smothered hemlocks. The other two men went to the shed.

"What do you make of this business, Deacon?" Bosworth asked, to break the silence.

The Deacon shook his head. "The man's a sick man—that's sure. Something's sucking the life clean out of him."

But already, in the biting outer air, Bosworth was getting himself under better control. "Looks to me like a bad case of the ague, as you said."

"Well—ague of the mind, then. It's his brain that's sick."

Bosworth shrugged. "He ain't the first in Hemlock County."

"That's so," the Deacon agreed. "It's a worm in the brain, solitude is."

"Well, we'll know this time tomorrow, maybe," said Bosworth. He scrambled into his sleigh, and was driving off in his turn when he heard his companion calling after him. The Deacon explained that his horse had cast a shoe; would Bosworth drive him down to the forge near North Ashmore, if it wasn't too much out of his way? He didn't want the mare slipping about on the freezing snow, and he could probably get the blacksmith to drive him back and shoe her in Rutledge's shed. Bosworth made room for him under the bearskin, and the two men drove off, pursued by a puzzled whinny from the Deacon's old mare.

The road they took was not the one that Bosworth would have followed to reach his own home. But he did not mind that. The shortest way to the forge passed close by Lamer's pond, and Bosworth, since he was in for the business, was not sorry to look the ground over. They drove on in silence.

The snow had ceased, and a green sunset was spreading upward into the crystal sky. A stinging wind barbed with ice-flakes caught them in the face on the open ridges, but when they dropped down into the hollow by Lamer's pond the air was as soundless and empty as an unswung bell. They jogged along slowly, each thinking his own thoughts.

"That's the house...that tumble-down shack over there, I suppose?" the Deacon said, as the road drew near the edge of the frozen pond.

"Yes: that's the house. A queer hermit-fellow built it years ago, my father used to tell me. Since then I don't believe it's ever been used but by the gipsies."

Bosworth had reined in his horse, and sat looking through pine-trunks purpled by the sunset at the crumbling structure. Twilight already lay under the trees, though day lingered in the open. Between two sharply-patterned pine-boughs he saw the evening star, like a white boat in a sea of green.

His gaze dropped from that fathomless sky and followed the blue-white undulations of the snow. It gave him a curious agitated feeling to think that here, in this icy solitude, in the tumble-down house he had so often passed without heeding it, a dark mystery, too deep for thought, was being enacted. Down that very slope, coming from the grave-yard at Cold Corners, the being they called "Ora" must pass toward the pond. His heart began to beat stiflingly. Suddenly he gave an exclamation: "Look!"

He had jumped out of the cutter and was stumbling up the bank toward the slope of snow. On it, turned in the direction of the house by the pond, he had detected a woman's foot-prints; two; then three; then more. The Deacon scrambled out after him, and they stood and stared.

"God—barefoot!" Hibben gasped. "Then it is...the dead..."

Bosworth said nothing. But he knew that no live woman would travel with naked feet across that freezing wilderness. Here, then, was the proof the Deacon had asked for—they held it. What should they do with it?

"Supposing we was to drive up nearer—round the turn of the pond, till we get close to the house," the Deacon proposed in a colorless voice. "Mebbe then…"

Postponement was a relief. They got into the sleigh and drove on. Two or three hundred yards farther the road, a mere lane under steep bushy banks, turned sharply to the right, following the bend of the pond. As they rounded the turn they saw Brand's cutter ahead of them. It was empty, the horse tied to a tree-trunk. The two men looked at each other again. This was not Brand's nearest way home.

Evidently he had been actuated by the same impulse which had made them rein in their horse by the pond-side, and then hasten on to the deserted hovel. Had he too discovered those spectral foot-prints? Perhaps it was for that very reason that he had left his cutter and vanished in the direction of the house. Bosworth found himself shivering all over under his bearskin. "I wish to God the dark wasn't coming on," he muttered. He tethered his own horse near Brand's, and without a word he and the Deacon ploughed through the snow, in the track of Brand's huge feet. They had only a few yards to walk to overtake him. He did not hear them following him, and when Bosworth spoke his name, and he stopped short and turned, his heavy face was dim and confused, like a darker blot on the dusk. He looked at them dully, but without surprise.

"I wanted to see the place," he merely said.

The Deacon cleared his throat. "Just take a look…yes…We thought so… But I guess there won't be anything to *see*…" He attempted a chuckle.

The other did not seem to hear him, but labored on ahead through the pines. The three men came out together in the cleared space before the house. As they emerged from beneath the trees they seemed to have left night behind. The evening star shed a luster on the speckless snow, and Brand, in that lucid circle, stopped with a jerk, and pointed to the same light foot-prints turned toward the house—the track of a woman in the snow. He stood still, his face working. "Bare feet…" he said.

The Deacon piped up in a quavering voice: "The feet of the dead."

Brand remained motionless. "The feet of the dead," he echoed.

Deacon Hibben laid a frightened hand on his arm. "Come away now, Brand; for the love of God come away."

The father hung there, gazing down at those light tracks on the snow—light as fox or squirrel trails they seemed, on the white immensity. Bosworth thought to himself "The living couldn't walk so light—not even Ora Brand couldn't have, when she lived…" The cold seemed to have entered into his very marrow. His teeth were chattering.

Brand swung about on them abruptly. "*Now!*" he said, moving on as if to an assault, his head bowed forward on his bull neck.

"Now—now? Not in there?" gasped the Deacon. "What's the use? It was tomorrow he said—." He shook like a leaf.

"It's now," said Brand. He went up to the door of the crazy house, pushed it inward, and meeting with an unexpected resistance, thrust his heavy shoulder against the panel. The door collapsed like a playing-card, and Brand stumbled after it into the darkness of the hut. The others, after a moment's hesitation, followed.

Bosworth was never quite sure in what order the events that succeeded took place. Coming in out of the snow-dazzle, he seemed to be plunging into total blackness. He groped his way across the threshold, caught a sharp splinter of the fallen door in his palm, seemed to see something white and wraithlike surge up out of the darkest corner of the hut, and then heard a revolver shot at his elbow, and a cry—

Brand had turned back, and was staggering past him out into the lingering daylight. The sunset, suddenly flushing through the trees, crimsoned his face like blood. He held a revolver in his hand and looked about him in his stupid way.

"They *do* walk, then," he said and began to laugh. He bent his head to examine his weapon. "Better here than in the churchyard. They shan't dig her up *now*," he shouted out. The two men caught him by the arms, and Bosworth got the revolver away from him.

<h1 style="text-align:center">IV.</h1>

The next day Bosworth's sister Loretta, who kept house for him, asked him, when he came in for his midday dinner, if he had heard the news.

Bosworth had been sawing wood all the morning, and in spite of the cold and the driving snow, which had begun again in the night, he was covered with an icy sweat, like a man getting over a fever.

"What news?"

"Venny Brand's down sick with pneumonia. The Deacon's been there. I guess she's dying."

Bosworth looked at her with listless eyes. She seemed far off from him, miles away. "Venny Brand?" he echoed.

"You never liked her, Orrin."

"She's a child. I never knew much about her."

"Well," repeated his sister, with the guileless relish of the unimaginative for bad news, "I guess she's dying." After a pause she added: "It'll kill Sylvester Brand, all alone up there."

Bosworth got up and said: "I've got to see to poulticing the gray's fetlock." He walked out into the steadily falling snow.

Venny Brand was buried three days later. The Deacon read the service; Bosworth was one of the pall-bearers. The whole countryside turned out, for the snow had stopped falling, and at any season a funeral offered an opportunity for an outing that was not to be missed. Besides, Venny Brand was young and handsome—at least some people thought her handsome, though she was so swarthy—and her dying like that, so suddenly, had the fascination of tragedy.

"They say her lungs filled right up...Seems she'd had bronchial troubles before...I always said both them girls was frail...Look at Ora, how she took and wasted away I And it's colder'n all outdoors up there to Brand's...Their mother, too, *she* pined away just the same. They don't ever make old bones on the mother's side of the family...There's that young Bedlow over there; they say Venny was engaged to him...Oh, Mrs. Rutledge, excuse *me*...Step right into the pew; there's a seat for you alongside of grandma..."

Mrs. Rutledge was advancing with deliberate step down the narrow aisle of the bleak wooden church. She had on her best bonnet, a monumental structure which no one had seen out of her trunk since old Mrs. Silsee's funeral, three years before. All the women remembered it. Under its perpendicular pile her narrow face, swaying on the long thin neck, seemed whiter than ever; but her air of fretfulness had been composed into a suitable expression of mournful immobility.

"Looks as if the stone-mason had carved her to put atop of Venny's grave," Bosworth thought as she glided past him; and then shivered at his own sepulchral fancy. When she bent over her hymn book her lowered lids reminded him again of marble eye-balls; the bony hands clasping the book were bloodless. Bosworth had never seen such hands since he had seen old Aunt Cressidora Cheney strangle the canary-bird because it fluttered.

The service was over, the coffin of Venny Brand had been lowered into her sister's grave, and the neighbors were slowly dispersing. Bosworth, as pall-bearer, felt obliged to linger and say a word to the stricken father. He waited till Brand had turned from the grave with the Deacon at his side. The three men stood together for a moment; but not one of them spoke. Brand's face was the closed door of a vault, barred with wrinkles like bands of iron.

Finally the Deacon took his hand and said: "The Lord gave—"

Brand nodded and turned away toward the shed where the horses were hitched. Bosworth followed him. "Let me drive along home with you," he suggested.

Brand did not so much as turn his head. "Home? What home?" he said; and the other fell back.

Loretta Bosworth was talking with the other women while the men unblanketed their horses and backed the cutters out into the heavy snow. As Bosworth waited for her, a few feet off, he saw Mrs. Rutledge's tall bonnet lording it above the group. Andy Pond, the Rutledge farm-hand, was backing out the sleigh.

"Saul ain't here today, Mrs. Rutledge, is he?" one of the village elders piped, turning a benevolent old tortoise-head about on a loose neck, and blinking up into Mrs. Rutledge's marble face.

Bosworth heard her measure out her answer in slow incisive words. "No. Mr. Rutledge he ain't here. He would 'a' come for certain, but his aunt Minorca Cummins is being buried down to Stotesbury this very day and he had to go down there. Don't it sometimes seem zif we was all walking right in the Shadow of Death?"

As she walked toward the cutter, in which Andy Pond was already seated, the Deacon went up to her with visible hesitation. Involuntarily Bosworth also moved nearer. He heard the Deacon say: "I'm glad to hear that Saul is able to be up and around."

She turned her small head on her rigid neck, and lifted the lids of marble.

"Yes, I guess he'll sleep quieter now.—And her too, maybe, now she don't lay there alone any longer," she added in a low voice, with a sudden twist of her chin toward the fresh black stain in the grave-yard snow. She got into the cutter, and said in a clear tone to Andy Pond: "'S long as we're down here I don't know but what I'll just call round and get a box of soap at Hiram Pringle's."

THE WOLF-WOMAN

Grace Jones Morgan

(WRITING AS BASSETT MORGAN)

first published in *Weird Tales* (September 1927)

B eaten back by fogs and wizards of the heights, the Stamwell party was camped in a sun-warmed valley at the base of Mount Logan, which lifts its ice-capped head in eternal solitude and awful silence above the most intensely glaciated region of the world.

Three years before, in an attempt to follow MacCarthy, who first ascended Logan, the intrepid mountain-climber Morsey had fallen into a crevasse; and Professor Stamwell was now attempting to recover his body from the glacier and by a process of his own experimentation restore it to life.

His assistant, Lieutenant Cressey, who had been more intrigued by the adventure of the climb than by Stamwell's sanguinary hope of resuscitating flesh entombed and even perfectly preserved in the ice, was reluctant to admit failure. Nevertheless, he enjoyed the sun-warmth of the valley after the terrific frost-fangs and ice-claws of the heights. Along the shores of a little river whose source lay in the glaciers, the dogs romped, catching fish with the dexterity of the husky breed and gorging themselves.

Baptiste, the big half-breed Canadian guide who looked after the comforts of the men, had been roving all day. At supper time he returned, tossing his cap in the air and yelling excitedly.

"*M'sieus*," he shouted, "I have find wan funny mans what makes t'ings of ivory. You come an' see. You lak heem ver' much."

Nothing loth to leave the discussion of their defeat, Stamwell and Cressey followed the exuberant Baptiste for a mile or two along the river to a stoutly timbered cabin beside which an old man watched his supper cooking over a fire outside. At sight of him, Cressey laughed, while Baptiste explained his new acquaintance.

"Hees name ees Jo. He ees half Indian, half Eskimo. An' I savvy hees talk ver' fine."

While Baptiste talked in tribal jargon, Cressey's amusement mounted. The old man was toothless and wrinkled. A beaded band kept the lank hair from obscuring his sight, and as his jaw wagged constantly on a quid of chewing tobacco, two knobbed knucklebones of seals thrust through slits in his cheeks gave the appearance of tusks. Ragged wolf-skin trousers and elk-hide moccasins completed his attire, but he smiled grotesquely as he led the way inside the cabin. There he lighted a wick floating on a dish of oil, threw wide a window-shutter and let in sunlight, which revealed a collection of carved ivory objects on shelves about the walls.

Baptiste was even more eager than the carver to display his skill. He handed Stamwell a figure copied from comic supplements of newspapers and familiar in homes from the arctic circle to the Florida Keys. A moment later he brought forth its mate. Stamwell held in his hands cleverly chiseled likenesses of Mutt and Jeff. Flattered by the interest of these white men, Jo showed them the source of his inspiration, a sheaf of old newspapers from the pages of which he took his ivory models. Baptiste, convulsed with mirth, laid in Cressey's hand a figure which brought a responsive laugh.

"She got bellyache!" he shouted.

Even Professor Stamwell chuckled at his description of a lovely little "September Morn."

They spent a good deal of time with the contents of the shelf before Jo took up the oil dish and threw a flickering light on a recumbent figure in the cabin corner. Stamwell went on his knees, and Cressey gasped at the beauty of a woman, carved in ivory, lying as if asleep with one arm under her head and her long hair draped over her shoulder. The figure was almost life-size, and the ivory block showed no seam or joint. Stamwell touched the slender leg with gentle fingers, then looked at Cressey.

"Cressey, this ivory is of different texture from the small figurines. I should say it was fossilized, but where on earth would the old fellow obtain such a huge block of material?"

"And the woman-model!" exclaimed Cressey. "A white woman, undoubtedly. Look at the sensitive nostrils and straight nose, and the rounded cheeks. No Kogmollyc or Indian squaw posed for this. The old fellow didn't create her, either. He couldn't. You can see he has only a great skill in imitating and copying. Baptiste, ask Jo where he saw such a woman, asleep."

Baptiste's conversation with the old man occupied some time, and before it ended the big guide was fingering his scapular.

"Jo, he say dees woman froze een ice. He git dees big chunk'ivory from ver' beeg land-whale, also froze een ice."

"A land-whale! Cressey, he means a mammoth. We've come across real treasure. Baptiste, tell Jo we would like to see this land-whale."

Baptiste interpreted. The ivory-carver nodded good-naturedly and started at once to lead them to the source of his art-material.

"Jo, he say," offered Baptiste when the dogs were harnessed and food on the sled in case of an overnight trip, "he say dees womans ees froze een ice long tarn. Maybe dis summer fetch her out. She come down ver' fast. Long tarn ago, Jo see her ver' high up. Jo say more as hunderd snows when he first see her."

"Frozen in the glacier more than a hundred years ago! Preposterous! The old fellow exaggerates." Starnwell waved aside Jo's veracity. "We've evidently stumbled on a tragedy. Snow madness makes its victims strip naked, usually, which would account for her nudity, and Jo looks aged, but I don't credit his hundred-year memory."

"Her hair must have touched the ground, Professor. That dates her pretty far back."

For some hours the ice-trail, steep though not perilous, claimed their attention. The sun swung down to the horizon for the brief moments of northern midnight, then began its upward arc. They found that Jo had cut steps on the glacial river which wound down from the grim sides of Mount Logan. Mounting steadily, they reached a terrace which led to lofty pinnacles of ice so clearly blue it was like a fairy palace, where steps led to an outstanding archway and natural grotto of rock that had been broken from its base and carried down.

Inside the grotto the light was weirdly blue, the ice underfoot clear as glass. Jo pointed and Cressey knelt, and a moment later his cry echoed from the grotto walls. Under the crystal shell lay the carver's model, more beautiful than the carved ivory, a woman, young, lovely, golden hair half robing her form, tawny eyelashes on her rounded cheeks. Near by, as if they had lain down to sleep and been caught by instant and painless death, were seven large hounds or wolves, with snow-white pelts.

Baptiste, plagued by superstitions fear, gazed long and earnestly, then leaped from the cave with a wild cry and ran down the steps which led to the broken end of the lower terrace. Cressey and Stamwell, engrossed by the sight beneath their feet, did not miss Baptiste until he returned, holding his nose and grimacing.

"Name of a Name! She smell ver' dead, dat land-whale!"

They followed him to the terrace, below which lay the enormous carcass of a hairy mammoth in advanced stages of putrefaction, smelling, as Baptiste had said, "very dead."

One great tusk lay on the tundra, the other had been sawn off, proving Jo's assertion about the source of his ivory. Cressey was staring at the mass below in absorbed silence, when Stamwell clutched his arm and exclaimed: "Cressey, we did not find Morsey. But we've found this woman. By heaven, we'll take her and the dogs from their ice-tomb!"

"But—but what a pity!" cried Cressey.. "The air will finish them in no time, like that mammoth. And she is beautiful in death!"

"Another summer would bring her down to that finish anyway," argued Stamwell. "And what if it isn't death? What about its being merely suspended animation? Here is our chance to test my discovery. I meant to try it on Morsey. We can't do that for him, but what a triumph to bring this woman back to life after God alone knows how many years of sleep; a Diana of eld and her hunting pack!"

"But aren't you interested in this mammoth at all, Stamwell?"

"What is a mammoth, decayed at that?" Stamwell's eyes burned with the passion of a zealot. "Mammoths have been found everywhere, their skeletons mounted and their existence traced. We shouldn't have even the satisfaction of originality. But to carry out a living woman who has been buried in the ice, no one can say how long—Cressey, look at those hounds!" Stamwell was hurrying to the cave and growing more excited every moment. "Do you know of a living breed of dogs like them? They are true wolf, even larger than the timber wolves. And albinos. It is stupendous, staggering, the antiquity revealed under this shell of ice. And to think, if we had been a year later this superb discovery would have moved down with the glacier and broken off at the terrace, the prey of wild animals, the bones scattered. That will happen next year unless we rescue her!"

Cressey did not answer. The idea of taking this frozen beauty from the ice and restoring her to life sounded like the talk of a man demented. Yet, as he heard the calculating plan of Stamwell unfold, Cressey admitted to himself that it was a new and alluring adventure. At Stamwell's succinct commands, he accompanied Baptiste to the valley camp to bring back their packs and establish a camp in the grotto which penetrated the floe for a hundred feet or more and would serve admirably as a shelter.

By the time Baptiste had made beds of pine boughs and started a fire with wood hauled from below, Cressey found that Stamwell had made remarkable progress in chipping the ice from the entombed woman and her dogs. The guide cooked breakfast. The cave had assumed an appearance of comfort exceeding their valley tents, and after a meal of flapjacks they slept.

Cresset was wakened by the noise of Stamwell's pick on the ice. "What if that hammering should start an avalanche?" he asked.

"There isn't much danger. The sun warmth melting the ice also welds it, and the floe is less crisp here than in higher altitudes. Don't think up discouragements, Cressey. Get busy and help me."

They worked all day, cutting a rectangular space which included the entire group. Baptiste and the half-breeds had slept huddled in parkas, in the tents erected outside the grotto, which they refused to enter except to carry out the broken ice., It was apparent to both Stamwell and Cressey that their men regarded this disturbance of the ice-entombed woman as a sacrilege that would brew trouble, and Baptiste solemnly voiced prophetic warning.

"Dogs!" he snorted. "Who ever see dogs lak dem? Dey look more lak ghost-wolf, the loup-garou. Me, I don' lak dees bisniss. I come for to climb mountain, not dig up dead womans." Nor would be gaze into the deepening hole where Stamwell and Cressey labored until only a thin shell of ice covered the bodies of the woman and hounds, when Stamwell called a halt.

"We must prepare things for her resuscitation, Cressey. Help me with these packs."

They toiled until Cressey reeled with weariness, preparing ice slabs covered with furs, arranging apparatus, pulmonary respirators, hypodermics, bottles of precious distillations known only to Professor Stamwell, blankets and kettles of hot water.

"If you should be tempted to give an account of this to the world, Cressey, I trust you will guard the secret of my process," said Stamwell that night.

"Obviously," answered Cressey, "since I haven't the faintest idea of success in such a preposterous attempt to cheat death."

Buoyed up by excitement, Stamwell seemed unwearied, but Cressey was glad to lie down, and it seemed only a few moments of sleep when again he was awakened by Stamwell's chipping ice in the task of extricating one of the white hounds. By noontime, they were lifting it from the hole and placing it on a fur-covered slab of ice to roll in blankets and be gradually warmed with hot water cans until the nine-inch length of fur fell wet and limp as it thawed.

It was some time before the flesh grew pliable, for the beast measured eleven feet from snout to tail-tip and was all the two men could manage. With sweat pouring down his face, Cressey obeyed the crisp commands of Stamwell with trained military precision while the professor applied one after another of his processes and both took turns in expanding and contracting the great fur-clad chest by sheer strength, and manipulating the hypodermic of fluid which started heart action. Then Cressey felt a twitching of the body muscles and saw the legs jerk. He could scarcely credit his sight as Stamwell poured small doses of prepared broth down the dog's throat, and it swallowed them with a faint, gurgling whimper. Stamwell's cry held triumph.

In vain Baptiste announced mealtime.. The sun had dipped and begun another day before the great hound was swathed in blankets and furs and the two white men took the hot coffee they sorely needed.

"Eureka!" shouted Stamwell, beside himself with joy.

"And now that the beast is alive, what will we do with him?" was Cressey's rejoinder.

"Take excellent care of him. Take him down to the valley as soon as possible, where Baptiste can feed and look after him."

After a brief three hours of sleep, Stamwell roused Cressey and they exhumed another hound, going through the same laborious work as before, to be rewarded eventually by a whimpering whine and the signs of recurring animation. By that time the first hound was able to take boiled meat and showed ravenous greed, and after the meal it attempted to struggle to its feet but was still weak. In three days it left the blankets and took a few staggering steps, then lifted its magnificent head and howled mournfully again and again, a sound at which Baptiste made the sign of the cross and muttered Chippewan incantations against evil.

When ten days were gone, Baptiste was delegated to escort a pack of seven white hounds, for which stout leather collars and light chains were provided, to the valley. With him went all the half-breeds except one who remained to cook for the white men in the grotto. Baptiste had orders to hunt game and feed the hounds and keep the sled dogs on leash at the cabin of the ivory-carver for greater safety.

With the grotto cleared of the dogs, Stamwell turned his attention to the central block of ice. The hypodermic needles were carefully sterilized, and the greatest care and precautions taken as they lifted the crystal casket from the hole and carefully thawed the ice embedding the woman. Sweat poured off both men while they worked, and their breaths came in sharp hisses long before the first sign of life was evinced in a whispered sigh from the pale lips.

Stamwell's eyes were shadowed to the cheekbones and he seemed to have aged years when the muscular twitching of her slender legs began and a sigh of agony quivered into the silence.

"If you've had your flesh frozen and thawed, you will understand the pain she feels," said Stamwell. "I almost regret inflicting this suffering upon her, but when she pulls through and realizes that she is alive, then, Cressey, I shall be repaid."

Cressey's thoughts denied that potential gratitude. Suppose this woman had been dead any great length of time and found none of her own generation alive in the world, would she thank them? Cressey doubted it, but she was so lovely that he lost all sense of dread and felt only a vast pity in his heart for the beautiful creature lying in the red blankets, her golden hair spread like a silken veil on the colored wool.

It was almost midnight when her eyelids fluttered open and the two men saw eyes of purple softness which moved slowly as she seemed aware of the two men and firelight illuminating the dark ice of the cave. The blueness left her fingernails and color returned to her lips as she was fed hot milk and broth; then her eyelids closed and her body relaxed in sleep. Stamwell was like a man insane with fear until he applied a stethoscope to her breast.

"Thank God, it is sleep!" he cried. "But there will be no peace for me until she is out of danger. While I watch her, you had better rest. Cressey, do you realize that I have brought the dead to life?"

To Cressey his cry was a challenge, a sacrilege. He felt something of the same uncanny fear which Baptiste had displayed at Stamwell's assumption of supernatural power, and wondered if it were beneficence or crime to restore that lovely creature to life after her long sleep.

His sleep was troubled because in the valley the great hounds howled all night. Dozing, waking to curse them, he saw Stamwell beside the woman's couch, and rising he bade the professor sleep while he watched. He made coffee and carried a steaming cup to his seat beside the sleeping beauty, sipping it as he gazed at the sun-gold creeping down the glacier to the grotto door. A sigh roused him. A white hand touched his wrist. Turning, Cressey was aware that the violet eyes of the woman gazed at him and she smiled, then her fingers touched the tin cup he held as if she was thirsty.

"I can't give you that," he found himself telling her as if she understood his talk. He reached for a bowl of broth simmering on the alcohol stove, heavy with meat juices and nourishing tonic medicines, and fed her. Color tinted her throat and cheeks. She seemed momentarily to gain strength. Cressey was thrilled and awed by the miracle happening before his eyes, and shocked at the languorous coquetry of her glance and the white fingers clinging to his hand.

Again he fed her, aware that she was ravenously hungry, until the broth was finished. He thought she was again asleep until her hand lifted her golden hair and trailed it across his face and a low-toned, throaty laugh startled him. Feeling helpless in face of a crisis, he replaced the golden tress on the couch and felt his fingers tingling as from a light galvanic shock at its touch. He leaned forward and instantly his neck was circled by her arms and she pressed her face against his throat. Cressey was so astonished that he did not try to draw back, and an instant later he felt her teeth on the flesh of his neck.

Alarm and swift revulsion seized him. He was afraid to tear her arms away for fear of bruising the tender skin. He knew her heart beat under the forced stimulation of Stamwell's drugs and feared a sudden shock might halt its action, then while he hesitated a strange drowsiness clouded his senses and stole over his body. He felt ho pain where her teeth pierced the skin of his throat; her arms were satin-smooth, the warmth of her lips tempted him to rest in the alluring embrace.

Then a cry from Stamwell roused Cressey from drowsiness that nearly swung into blissful unconsciousness. He was wrenched from her arms and felt the sting of flesh her teeth released. Glancing at her, he saw her lips moist and crimson-stained, and she was struggling in the clutch of Stamwell.

"Fill that hypo with the medicine in the third bottle, quickly, Cressey. She is so strong I can scarcely control her."

Cressey obeyed, even to inserting the needle into the skin of her arm. Her scream was piercing as she fought Stamwell, who held her until the drug took effect and she sank back, relaxed. Then Stamwell turned to Cressey.

"Good God, man, I trusted you to stay awake and watch."

Cressey did not reply. Stamwell was disinfecting the wound on his neck, to which he applied a pad of cotton gauze and adhesive tape. Cressey could not even smile, nor would he tell Stamwell how she had coquetted with him before catching him in her arms.

A few minutes later they saw Baptiste toiling up the glacial drift, and from outside the grotto door he called to them.

"*M'sieus*, I can not hold dose dog, dey grow so beeg, so strong, an' my men ees scare' dey break dem chain. I am ver' scare' of dose dog my own self.. Me, I am good dogman, but not dat kind of dog. I feed heem nineteen rabbit, seven coyote, wan elk and much fish in wan week. All my men do ees hunt for feed dose dog., Me, I am 'bout ready quit my job. I tak sled dogs an' tie heem across rivaire cause eef dose white dog git loose…well, we walk back outside."

"Cressey, the white hounds must not kill our sled dogs and Baptiste must be pacified, for if he deserted we should never get our menagerie out alive. I think we can take the woman down to the valley by tomorrow. Suppose you go down Mow and look after the camp."

Following Baptiste down the ice-trail, Cressey saw the ivory-carver industriously sawing off the remaining tusk of the mammoth, and watching him a moment, he slipped and fell headlong. He w r as only slightly stunned, hut a worse calamity had befallen, for in extricating his foot from a small fissure, he felt the snapping of bone and a dull pain. Cressey cursed.

"Baptiste, I've snapped a bone!"

The warm-hearted Baptiste lifted him to his shoulder and made his way down to the valley, where their arrival started a terrific din of howling dogs and answering yelps of the sled huskies leashed across the river. Baptiste muttered oaths.

"Eef dose white dog git loose, dey swallow my dog lak I swallow loche-liver without chew heem," he commented and grumbled his distaste of the whole business of the grotto miracle. Baptiste was about ready to desert, and it occurred to Cressey that he had better summon Stamwell at once. The great white hounds leaped the length of their chains and the sturdy pine trees were swaying and jerking from the lunge of their powerful bodies.

"Baptiste, you had better fetch Professor Stamwell and his packs down at once, and we'll make a start outside," he said. Again Baptiste took the trail to the grotto, while Cressey soaked his foot in hot water, then bound it with wet moss and cotton. The cook was preparing supper, the other men had gone to assist old Jo to fetch his big mammoth tusk to his cabin, then they all came to where Cressey sat and one of the breeds translated Jo's talk.

"*M'sieu*, he say eet ees not good to stay where devils come to life. Dees white wolf ees devil-wolf. Dis woman ees devil-woman. Jo, he say we better froze de dogs and womans again and go out, queeck."

"He's a timid, superstitious old man," said Cressey. "The dogs are savage but the woman can not harm anyone."

Yet as he spoke Cressey felt uneasy. The gauze pad on his neck was a reminder of his personal experience with the woman. He ate supper and waited impatiently for the coming of Stamwell, but it was nearly midnight when he saw Baptiste coming down swiftly, alone. The big guide broke into excited cries as he ran toward Cressey.

"*M'sieu! Le professeur* ees dead, an' *la femme*, she ees gone!"

"Gone! Stamwell dead!" echoed Cressey. Baptiste crossed himself and muttered broken snatches of Chippewan mingled with Roman Catholic prayers, looking apprehensively at the hounds. The dogs stood silent but alert, ears stiffly pointed, and sniffing the wind.

"*M'sieu*, een de cave ev'ting toss dees way an' dat. Le professeur he ees lay on floor and hees t'roat ees got bite. Hees hands dey look laic dey soak in water long tam."

Like a blow from a bludgeon the explanation crashed on Cressey. When Stamwell dozed, the woman had caught him as she seized Cressey, possibly drained his blood like vampire bats of southern caves, and with renewed strength had left the grotto. He remembered that she was unclad and the air of the ice-fields bitterly cold. With his injured foot he was hampered in reaching the glacier, and nothing he could say or do would persuade Baptiste and his men to search and bring the woman to the valley.

Stamwell's death had come so suddenly he could not yet realize the tragedy. Then he noticed that the dogs were rousing to uncanny excitement, whining and growling, tugging strenuously at their chains. Cressey began to regret bitterly what had been done and longed to break camp and escape from the weird influences loosed by Stamwell and himself.

Baptiste saw him look toward the ivory-carver's cabin. "Good, *M'sieu*. We camp tonight een Jo's house. Eet ees not good to be here. *Non!*"

U nder Baptiste's commands the men toiled to carry everything to the cabin, then they set about strengthening it with a barricade of young firs quickly cut down and heaped about the log walls.

"The good priest, he say all trees ees made by *le bon Dieu*," explained Baptiste, "an', Name of a Name! we need Heem dis night to keep us safe." Cressey could only nod assent, for as he dropped on a couch of freshly cut pine branches, he was aware that stealing over him was that same blissful unrest he had felt in the arms of the death-delivered woman of the glacier. He felt possessed of a wild desire to find her and thrill again to the touch of her satin arms and her mouth warm on his flesh. He knew it for an evil thing, a worse craving than whisky or dope, and found himself battling the weakness of flesh with arguments prompted by reason which his lips betrayed to Baptiste.

"It is cruel to let the woman wander alone on the ice. If you do not go and find her, Baptiste, I will."

The breed's dark face was grim with dogged determination.

"*M'sieu*, you do not leave dis cabin, not eef we must chain you lak wan dog. Me, I t'ink you have evil curse on you!"

And Baptiste barred both door and window of the cabin which held eight men, until within an hour of midnight the air had grown hot and foul and Cressey demanded fresh air. Reluctantly, Baptiste threw open the window-shutter and admitted a bar of diminishing sunlight. The white hounds were giving tongue in unearthly howlings, mournful as dog wailings which to the superstitious folk announce death, and the blood of Cressey was leaping as at the cry of a hunting pack. He hobbled to the window and looked toward the glacier where Stamwell lay. Even now he could scarcely realize that his friend was dead, and again he urged Baptiste to open the door.

"No, for my life, *M'sieu*. Look!"

There in the river of slow-moving ice stood the huntress, poised daintily on her toes as if in a dance, her arms uplifted to cup her hands at her lips, her long golden hair blowing about a body as softly rounded as a young girl. And on the midnight silence came a clear, ringing cry.

Instantly pandemonium broke loose among the white hounds. Their howls were deafening and the clank of chains made wild, metallic music, and they leaped, and fell back, and leaped again. With their heads thrust through the window opening, Baptiste and Cressey watched, leaning back against men crowded behind them, as one of the hounds snapped his chain and raced like a white cloud in great, swift bounds toward the glacier.

Within a few moments they were all free and flying to the heights, where they leaped about the woman with joyous yelps until she was hidden by a frenzied tumult of gigantic hounds. Then, seemingly at her command, their yelps ceased and they were squatted on their haunches at her feet, pink eyes shining like rubies in the soft twilight, red tongues lolling and quivering from white-fanged jaws. Again she cupped hands to her lips and sent out her hunting cry. At the sound, Cressey shivered. In every nerve he felt the piercing lure of that wail. She was calling him forth, and some hell-born desire to answer and go to her was fighting every prompting of reason. Again came her call, and Cressey plunged from the window toward the door.

Baptiste was too quick for him and thrust his own great bulk against the timbers, flinging Cressey aside.

"*Non! M'sieu*, are you crazee? Look!" Baptiste had snatched a small silver crucifix from inside his shirt and clamped it against Cressey's forehead. He felt it searing his skin, like white-hot metal, and he sank to the pine couch, shuddering, sweat breaking out on his face. At Baptiste's command the men held Cressey down, and again Baptiste flattened the crucifix over his breast and repeated bits of prayers strangely mixed with the incantations of his Chippewan mother's teachings. The sweat grew clammy on his body before Baptiste released him and gave him whisky from an emergency flask.

A somber group of men waited in the cabin until the sun was sailing high and the last faint howling of the white hounds had dwindled to silence. Cressey slept and wakened to see the door open and feel the warm wind blowing through the cabin, then Baptiste brought him coffee and flapjacks hot from the pan.

"*M'sieu*, I say to Jo that we use wan sled to carry out hees beeg tusk. We have sled to spare now we don' carry out medicine packs. Today we break camp."

Cressey considered in silence, his mind quite clear, the horror of the night-frenzy vanished with the sunlight. He could not, would not go outside and leave Stamwell's body without decent burial and said so.

"*M'sieu*, what happen hees body makes no nev' mind. Me, Baptiste, say you do not go to dat cave no more. Eet ees *la Chasse du Diable!*"

"Call it what you will, Baptiste. I do not leave here without placing the body of my friend out of reach of wolves. Perhaps already the white hounds have found it. If so, I shall be haunted for life."

"Me, I t'ink dat ees happen already, *M'sieu*," commented Baptiste, "but now dey are gone, maybe we go fetch down *le professeur*." Baptiste had clashed wills with Cressey before, and met defeat, yet when they dragged Cressey up the ice-trail on a sled the breed wore crucifix and scapular in full view on his breast and every man did likewise.

They found no trace of the hounds, not even pad-marks on the snow. The grotto showed signs of a struggle, but fortunately Stamwell had packed his medicines and instruments. His body lay on the couch, relaxed before rigor mortis set in, and his face had even the semblance of a smile, but on his throat was an ominous white mark of strong, even teeth, and the visible skin was puckered as if his veins were empty. Otherwise the corpse was unmolested, at which Cressey marveled until he remembered that the white hounds had been supplied with meat by the men. The gaping ice-hole presented a solution of a temporary tomb, and Professor Stamwell, blanket-wrapped, was laid deep, the broken ice shoveled in, and heated water poured until the grave was filled and already freezing, safe against depredation.

It was while that task engrossed him that Cressey felt the force of the tragedy and a growing desire to avenge the murder of Stamwell, and he forgot the weird spell of the night in which the untombed woman had tempted him to follow her by the memory of her beauty and blissful languor of her caress. It was cowardly to run away now, nor had he any proof of the tale he must tell of Stamwell's death when he was again outside.. Then he remembered that since the conquest of Mount Logan by MacCarthy, other parties had set out, and he knew approximately the location of three groups headed for that ascent, all hard-headed mountain-climbers and scientists. Giving orders to Baptiste to dispatch men in search of these expedition-groups, he started up the glacier in spite of the vehement protests of the guide, who, just before leaving on the valley trail, tossed over Cressey's head the deerskin thong holding the crucifix.

"Wan ver' good priest bless it, M'sieu. You take care of heem for Baptiste."

Irreligious himself, Cressey respected the faiths of other men and humored Baptiste. Then, drawn on a sled by two breeds, he adventured the heights, watching for a glimpse of the woman.

They had traversed a considerable distance, had seen ptarmigan tame as chickens, and edelweiss growing through the snow. Halting to pluck one of these brave little blooms, Cressey saw something glittering over a flower that seemed withered in first unfolding, and he picked from it a long, glistening thread of golden hair that curled, by some attraction of warm blood, about his fingers.

The snow-glare was blinding, the wind whistled keen as whip-lashes, and to eat their meal sheltered from its cutting blast, Cressey ordered a detour toward a group of ice-spires which on closer inspection proved a labyrinthine entrance of shining columns leading to a second grotto. Leaning on a stout fir branch used as a cane, he limped down the passage, then "halted in alarm. Low, menacing growls and clanking metal told of the hounds within, and a moment later they had leaped forth, a cloud of white death!

Cressey turned to run, knowing how meager was his chance for life. His revolver was in his hand, but as shots rang out, the hounds circled past him, apparently untouched, while he reeled in shocked amazement that he had missed a hit at such close range. Screams from the ice entrance brought his heart to his throat, cries of the two breeds that were drowned in the bay of wolves on the kill.

Cressey stood paralyzed, unable to prevent the dreadful carnage, unable to save his men even while he pumped lead into that swirling, milling cloud of destruction now fighting fiercely over the mangled remains of their victims.

Weakly, he leaned against the ice wall, his senses reeling as he reloaded his revolver with trembling fingers, knowing lead was impotent against those ghost-wolves. For he knew them, now, to be more than flesh and blood. They were some infernal incarnation invulnerable to man-dealt destruction.

A high-pitched, ringing call, clear as a bugle, brought his gaze to the grotto and he saw the woman standing against the blue gloom, golden hair wind-blown, poised on her toes. She glided, dazzlingly lovely, toward him with arms outstretched, and in his last moment of reason Cressey threw one wrist up to shield his eyes from that dread allure. Then again he felt the fierce desire of her and flung out his arms. She came within five feet of him and halted, a puzzled expression on her features, her hands sweeping and weaving as if she tried to tear from between them some barrier invisible to Cressey. When he tried to seize her, she retreated, still fighting at the space separating them until man and woman reached the entrance to the ice passage, where the dogs leaped back from too close a contact, and with a gesture of despair she turned and ran, calling in her ringing voice and leading her pack to the heights. Cressey fell on his knees beside the gnawed bones of his men and heard his own cries imploring her to return.

Sweat rained from his face, his body quivered; he was a man corroded by the poison of an evil desire. After a long time his head lifted and he clutched at the crucifix on his breast, then reason gradually conquered and as he pressed it to his head and lips he felt the sun-warmth and cool wind and knew he was himself. Slowly, painfully, he retraced his trail down the glacier and found Baptiste had reached the lower grotto and was searching for him, frantic with fear.

"The two men are dead, eaten by the white hounds," he told Baptiste, and shuddered at the breed's cry of horror. "Take me down and bind me in the cabin, Baptiste. I am a man accursed."

"Help will come wit' dose men I send out, M'sieu," comforted Baptiste. But they waited for three days, seeing nothing of the white hounds and woman, until one man returned, a trapper old on the trails, and with chattering teeth told a tale of horror.

"White wolves broke into the first camp I git to, M'sieu, an' I find only wan man alive. He tell me of La Chasse du Diable, then he die. M'sieu, I am ver' old man.. But I hear when I was babee, of this Chasse du Diable, from my gran'-gran'-pere, an' hees gran'-pere tell heem."

For a week they waited the return of the second man sent out, then one morning Baptiste reported men coming up the valley, and Cressey hobbled to meet them.

"Thank God you've come!" he cried. "My name is Cressey. My companion, Professor Stamwell, is dead, and I have a tale to tell almost beyond belief."

"I'm Johnson," said the leader of the newcomers, "and I think I know something of your story. Your man told us a little and we found the Stillwell camp ravaged—a terrible sight. I'm worried about another party toward the west, for we had a friendly wager as to who would first climb Logan. But I am amazed at the hunger of wolves in summer, that they attack men."

"These are more than wolves, Johnson, as Baptiste will tell you." Cressey began to relate his adventures, omitting nothing, not even his own accursed desire which had recurred each night and which Baptiste fought with incantation and holy symbol.

"Laugh if you will. To me it is horrible," he ended.

"I'm not even smiling. Your face shows the strain, Cressey. But have you nerve enough to accompany me and the men to the grotto again?"

"Of course. Waiting here is hell."

Johnson and Baptiste held weighty consultations while Cressey lay on the grass, too pain-racked to take part. His lips twisted in a sneer when the men made rude crosses of wood and gathered a blanket full of windflowers, those pale blooms which Indian converts say "spring up where angels' tears have fallen," and loaded sleds. Cressey was oblivious to everything but the fact that he was returning to the grotto where he had seen the Huntress, and with a low cunning that shamed him he was plotting a meeting with her that should cradle him in her arms.

They threaded the passageway of ice turrets, carrying pine torches which gave smoky light to the blueness of the grotto as Johnson examined it, then flung himself on the ice floor with a cry.

"Cressey, for God's sake, look! Here's a mammoth, as I'm alive! And other beasts. Lord, man, some mighty convulsion of nature must have herded your huntress, her wolves, and other denizens of her long-departed era into close quarters and caught them. Good heavens, if your secret process will restore the woman and wolves, why not try it on bigger game?"

Cressey laughed. The evil spell of the place had caught Johnson, and if he could be persuaded to carry out this wild scheme of digging up this frozen mammoth, there would be time...time to seek again his Huntress and find the Lethe of her embrace.

Through ensuing talk, Cressey was enthusiastic. The men were sent to bring the packs from the first grotto, and the digging began. About the cave entrance, the wooden crosses were arranged with arms touching and draped with windflowers that were also scattered on the ice trail.

Cressey's own men and Baptiste refused to assist the ice-digging. Jo, the ivory-carver, was still below in his cabin. Nothing would persuade him to take part.

"Old Jo declares this woman and her dogs are evil, yet he seems unafraid," Cressey remarked one day.

"Jo," interrupted Baptiste, "he say he too old, an' have not much blood. He say he make charm een hees ivory womans. When dis hunter-womans come, he pick up ax and smash ivory womans, an' the ghost-womans go 'way an' nev' come back."

"Oddly enough, the natives of the south seas and Africa have the same belief," said Johnson. "They make an image of .some enemy and either burn it or put it in water to rot, and the object of their venom sickens and dies. The world, Cressey, is small."

That night, as the sun sank lower, came the howling of wolves, and Cressey felt the prickling of his scalp and leap of blood. Although toil-weary, the men were awake, and guns in hand they watched the great white hounds streaking down the glacier, led by the flying huntress. Cressey started for the ice-passage, but Baptiste leaped and bore him down, his great weight pressing the breath from the smaller man as he struggled and fought in sudden rage. Subsiding, he laughed, but the sound of his laughter was unpleasant even to his own hearing.

It seemed as if the party had small chance of defense against those ghastly, ravening death-wolves, but to the amazement of every man, the pack halted abruptly beyond the wooden crosses, and the huntress stood there twisting her white hands as if baffled. The crosses and blessed windflowers had turned the hunt, but there began hours of fearful waiting until the pack circled the pinnacles, even leaping over the grotto arch and howling from behind the fence of crosses over the cave entrance. The sun was well above the horizon when they drifted away.

Night after night the diabolic chase returned only to retreat, baffled by barriers they could not break down. By day the men slaved to unearth the frozen beasts belonging to an era when the norths was tropic swale. Baptiste, who hunted in the valley for fresh meat, reported that Jo was carving a second figure of the huntress, standing upright, extremely lifelike, and that he scarcely left his work to eat or sleep.

A t last the great hairy mammoth lay clear of ice, and because they had no means of lifting its immense weight from the hole, Cressey and Johnson built fires about it, shielded from the carcass by screens of flattened oil-cans until it was thawed and restoratives from Stamwell's stores applied. Blankets and fur robes were shoved under it by leverage of cut pine sticks, and all hands rubbed the gigantic limbs and trunk with rough pads of twigs bound together by coarse grass. It was a Herculean task and the men were exhausted before the monster shuddered, stirred his mighty body, strained ponderously, while everyone scrambled out of the ice-hole; then heaving himself to his knees, the mammoth staggered slowly to his feet. As the puny humans fled from his path, he crushed the ice under his forefeet, burst the ropes with which he had been bound, and lumbered out of his tomb, his tusks crashing down the ice-pinnacles of the passage and scattering the protecting crosses, then he lunged to the glacial river and went tottering to the valley.

Cressey, white-faced and shaking as he realized the titanic grimness of the thing he and Johnson had loosed, ordered the trek to begin immediately down the ice-floe to the valley. At the same time he realized that, working with pick and shovel, concentrating on the healthful task of manual labor, he had liberated his mind and body from the huntress' evil sway. He no longer paid attention to the midnight *Chanse du Diable*, and he slept soundly through the baying of ghost-wolves. He breathed deep drafts of the balsam-laden valley warmth as they approached Jo's cabin, reverently thankful for his release.

"Baptiste," he said gently, "you have looked after me and I am grateful. I have been caught in the power of hell, but it is gone."

Baptiste caught him by the arms and looked deep into his eyes.

"*Oui, M'sieu.* No more I can see dat woman-shape in your eyeball. All dees time, eet was dere an' I know you are een her power. Now, eet ees gone!"

Cressey felt a tremor of apprehension. He had not known that, the image of the huntress was photographed on the retinas of his eyes until Baptiste spoke of it. He held out his hand and the breed gripped it in solemnity of silence that was like prayer, then he pointed to the almost finished figure at which Jo worked assiduously, never lifting his hands from the task. The delicacy of his skill was never so apparent as now. From the ivory base still shrouding her feet, the huntress seemed to dance, wind-blown hair, curving limbs, round young breasts so perfect that it seemed a pity he could not, like Pygmalion of old, breathe life into this Galatea. Cressey put out a hand to touch it but Jo waved him aside and yelped a warning.

"He say you mus' not touch her, or you have devil in your liver some more," translated Baptiste.

"Tell him I shall buy her and pay well," said Cressey, but Baptiste returned a disconcerting negative.

"Jo say, he keep her for to lay curse you have loos' een dees world. Now, *M'sieu*, we go outside."

But this time it was Jo who demurred at departure. His harangue, interpreted by Baptiste, told Cressey that he was responsible for releasing the powers of darkness in the valley and it was no longer safe to be caught on the trail at night until the evil was overcome. This simple acceptance by the old ivory-carver of the presence of terrifying supernatural powers did more to persuade Johnson than all Cressey's talk.

"They're merely flesh and blood animals," he argued. "We may have to take precautions as we would with any wild beasts, but I mean to follow that mammoth and herd him into some museum."

In the sun-warmed valley, where fires and cooking spread the comfort of commonplace occurrences, it was easier to lay aside superstitious fears, but when Baptiste's convictions were strengthened by Jo's calm acceptance of peril, Cressey realized he would better bow to their opinion that they take the river instead of land trails on their way out, and for this purpose Baptiste was already cutting timber to make rafts, which were the quickest and most serviceable solution of their need.

The long day passed and night closed in again. The crosses, carried down by the careful Baptiste, stood like a fence about the cabin, draped with fresh windflowers, with one gap left by which the men went to and fro on the way to logs they rolled to the river for the raft.

Johnson fell into heavy sleep and Cressey lay near him, smoking a last pipe. The old ivory-carver worked by the light of his oil lamp in the corner, although sunlight still shone in at the open window. The sled dogs had been brought and leashed inside the encircling crosses, but Cressey had scarcely dozed off when he heard their whimperings. Rising, he went outside.

From far off came the baying of the chase, and he saw the huntress flying down the ice, followed by her hounds. Johnson came from the cabin and both men stood in that twilight which had grown longer in the waning of summer which would soon give way to winter. A pale crescent moon danced on one silver toe, a fit companion for that lovely Diana dancing on the ice.

"Even now," said Johnson. "I can't believe but that she is a flesh and blood woman. Cressey, I'd like to clasp her hand and know for myself."

Cressey did not reply. The huntress was coming nearer, the baying of the hounds grew louder. He looked to see that the crosses were in place and did not observe that Johnson had stepped past them until he heard the cry of Baptiste. Then he saw the dark figure of the man, the radiant white fire of the huntress' beauty, and they melted into each other's arms. With a yell, Cressey leaped the barrier of crosses and raced to where the two stood swaying in close embrace.

As if the hounds sensed the symbol on Cressey's breast, they fell back as he approached. He had a swift wonder at their timidity until his hands seized Johnson, who screamed and writhed at his touch and fought being rescued as the huntress' head lifted from his shoulder and she slowly retreated, step by step, her moistened red lips parted, showing her strong white teeth in almost a snarl of hatred.

Cressey fought to draw Johnson to safety, and as he came nearer the cabin, the huntress advanced, hands reaching, weaving, tearing at the space separating her from her victim, unable to brush aside or combat the force for good protecting him.. Slowly the hounds advanced with her, and the cries of the sled dogs made the night hideous, when suddenly the huntress threw back her head and shrilled her wild call.

Once inside the barrier of crosses, Cressey dropped the half-crazed Johnson into Baptiste's arms, then he stared into the brightening light of dawn on the mountains. There were sounds from far off, of crashing brush and thunderingly ominous tread, and into their view loomed the giant of the ancient world, lumbering forward with incredible speed until it reached the woman's side, a dreadful menace which only for the frail barrier could have crushed the cabin and scattered the last vestige of men and dogs.

The howling of sled dogs and cries of men were terror-muted for a few moments. Then they were alert. Guns cracked in sharp fusillade, but the ghost-beasts neither quivered nor showed signs of a wound. The huntress was screaming at her beasts and waving white arms to urge them on, but they slunk aside until she howled at the mammoth, who caught her in his trunk and swung her to his broad head. There she stood, ethereally lovely and evil, her lips stained by the interrupted draft of human life, while the night waned and the blessed sun shot from the curving breasts of snow on Mount Logan. A cry as of frenzied despair came from her. The mammoth turned, the hounds leaped ahead, and the whole cavalcade vanished in the direction of the ice-fields.

Cressey turned to find Johnson as mad as he himself had been.

"You cur," he howled, "to come between me and my woman! You've had your day and now you begrudge me my hour of happiness."

"Johnson, she killed Stamwell, drained his body of life. She almost killed me. Left me like a maniac, as she will leave you. Here, this trinket of Baptiste's protected me; you shall wear it."

He dropped the thong of the crucifix over Johnson's head and heard his cry of pain. Cressey knew the white-hot searing of that symbol on flesh accursed and felt only pity for the man. All that day Johnson moaned, watched over by Cressey, while Baptiste directed the men in their task of making the raft.

"No ghost can pass running water," he said, and that night the logs were lashed together and the rafts moored to shore trees, and the barrier of crosses was strengthened.

Meanwhile, working ceaselessly, Jo had cut the ivory from the feet of the huntress he was carving, and was chiseling her pretty toes with their filbert-shaped nails. He had truly caught the grace of her dancing poise in the slender ankles, and she stood like a fairy molded of mellow gold when the sun touched the far horizon and brief night began in violet-tinted twilight.

Cressey was fascinated by the figure. "Tell Jo that I must have it. I will pay well, five hundred dollars, even a thousand. I will take her out with me."

Reluctantly Baptiste interpreted his demand and for the first time the old ivory-carver showed emotion. Fire leaped in his eyes as he wrathfully waved Cressey aside and refused to consider even so great a sum of money for his statue of the woman.

Cressey did not argue, but in his heart he determined to obtain the ivory figure, and fell asleep planning a means to that end. He slept lightly, dreaming of the huntress, and muttering in his sleep. His broken talk wakened Johnson, who looked toward Cressey with hatred in his eyes, which changed to cunning.

Johnson cautiously slipped the thong of the crucifix from his neck and it dropped on the floor. Then for a time he lay still except for the convulsive twitching of his body and the rolling of his tortured eyes.

A t midnight came the whimpering of the sled-dogs and baying of white hounds from afar. Immediately every man in the cabin was alert. They grabbed guns and plunged outside, waiting that dread visitation. The moon was fuller and gave silver light pricked out by velvet dark blotches of the trees. The glacial river gleamed like pearl. Another day and the party would have escaped, afloat on rafts carried by the swift-running stream, but this one night must be endured.

The huntress was not alone with her dogs, for she stood on the head of the mammoth which thundered into the plain cleared by his voracious feeding, and about them raced the white hounds. The hearts of the men were seized by icy fingers of fear even while they poured volley after volley of shots at the advancing horror and realized as they pulled the triggers that no man-invented mode of death could halt them.

The old ivory-carver, Jo, alone seemed fearless or careless of those terrific ghouls of eld, for he came leisurely from the cabin, toddling toward the barrier fence of wooden crosses and peering as if to feast his sight, on the vision he had foregone during those nights he toiled at the ivory figure of the woman.

Cressey stepped to Jo's side. He had forgotten Johnson in the cabin. There was none to see Johnson spring from the couch and with the desperation of a madman seize the ivory huntress in his arms and rush from the door on shoeless feet that made no sound.

Cressey's first glimpse of him came when Johnson leaped the barrier of crosses and headed for the river raft. But the huntress had also seen that plunging human and her cry rang like the long-drawn note of a silver horn. The mammoth lunged forward, the hounds leaped in white arcs of flying fur, and Johnson's scream stabbed through the din of animal howls.

They saw the huntress leap from her titanic steed to catch Johnson in her arms; saw the ivory figure knocked from his grasp. The golden hair of the huntress enveloped him like a ruddy silk mantle and her mouth was pressed to his throat.

But a greater tragedy was imminent. As if the scent of human blood maddened it, the mammoth plunged forward, his great tusks lunging between the leaping hounds to stab his human enemy; and the hounds closed in with unearthly yelpings.

Transfixed by the sight, the men at the cabin stared at the calamity they were powerless to avert, until there came a loud crunch as the mammoth's foot trod on the ivory figure of the huntress which Johnson had dropped.

Then, as if at a signal, the ghost-beasts seemed frozen in their tracks, and from them came a glistening white mist which swayed to and fro as it rose and drifted across the face of the young moon, and the watchers saw, like a frail cloud, the shining form of that lovely, hell-born huntress, as it blew away on the wind of dawn.

Light grew swiftly. The sun came up and shone on a mountainous mass of hairy mammoth flesh and long-furred hounds lying on the tundra.

As they stood, chained to the spot by paralysis of horror, every nerve taut, the men at the cabin saw that mound of flesh subside to pulp, and a dreadful stench arose in a smoky steam. By noon there was a gelatinous mass, which by nightfall had soaked into the earth, leaving only the skeletons. A clean, cold wind from the snows sweetened the air where Jo prodded the bones with a stick to recover all that was left of his ivory huntress, a head on which the features faithfully depicted her inscrutable smile, with lips and teeth slightly parted.

Cressey did not offer to buy it, and the head still hangs above Jo's cabin door. One glance at that lovely face had power to recall all too vividly the fate of Stamwell and Johnson, for whom crosses were erected in the valley and lop-sticks near by carved with their names. Cressey did not smile nor dispute the assertion of Baptiste that he should never return to that valley.

"M'sieu," said Baptiste, "dat devil-womans have dreenk your blood wan time, an' eef someday she come back, she catch you again, because all womans ees jealous, an' eef a womans git jealous eet open doors of ver' bad hells. You do what Baptiste say, you wear a li'l crucifix all time." And though not a religious man, Cressey has never since been without that symbol.

/

THE CANAL

Everil Worrell

first published in *Weird Tales* (December 1927)

Past the sleeping city the river sweeps; along its left bank the old canal creeps.

I did not intend that to be poetry, although the scene is poetic—somberly, gruesomely poetic, like the poems of Poe. Too well I know it—too often have I walked over the grass-grown path beside the reflections of black trees and tumble-down shacks and distant factory chimneys in the sluggish waters that moved so slowly, and ceased to move at all.

I shall be called mad, and I shall be a suicide. I shall take no pains to cover up my trail, or to hide the thing that I shall do. What will it matter, afterward, what they say of me? If they knew the truth—if they could vision, even dimly, the beings with whom I have consorted—if the faintest realization might be theirs of the thing I am becoming, and of the fate from which I am saving their city—then they would call me a great hero. But it does not matter what they call me, as I have said before. Let me write down the things I am about to write down, and let them be taken, as they will be taken, for the last ravings of a madman. The city will be in mourning for the thing I shall have done—but its mourning will be of no consequence beside that other fate from which I shall have saved it.

I have always had a taste for nocturnal prowling. We as a race have grown too intelligent to take seriously any of the old, instinctive fears that preserved us through preceding generations. Our sole remaining salvation, then, has come to be our tendency to travel in herds. We wander at night—but our objective is somewhere on the brightly lighted streets, or still somewhere where men do not go alone. When we travel far afield, it is in company. Few of my acquaintance, few in the whole city here, would care to ramble at midnight over the grass-grown path I have spoken of; not because they would fear to do so, but because such things are not being done.

Well, it is dangerous to differ individually from one's fellows. It is dangerous to wander from the beaten road. And the fears that guarded the race in the dawn of time and through the centuries were real fears, founded on reality.

A month ago, I was a stranger here. I had just taken my first position—I was graduated from college only three months before, in the spring. I was lonely, and likely to remain so for some time, for I have always been of a solitary nature, making friends slowly.

I had received one invitation out—to visit the camp of a fellow employee in the firm for which I worked, a camp which was located on the farther side of the wide river—the side across from the city and the canal, where the bank was high and steep and heavily wooded, and little tents blossomed all along the water's edge. At night these camps were a string of sparkling lights and tiny, leaping campfires, and the tinkle of music carried faintly far across the calmly flowing water. That far bank of the river was no place for an eccentric, solitary man to love. But the near bank, which would have been an eyesore to the campers had not the river been so wide,—the near bank attracted me from my first glimpse of it.

We embarked in a motor-boat at some distance downstream, and swept up along the near bank, and then out and across the current. I turned my eyes backward. The murk of stagnant water that was the canal, the jumble of low buildings beyond it; the lonely, low-lying waste of the narrow strip of land between canal and river, the dark, scattered trees growing there—I intended to see more of these things.

That week-end bored me, but I repaid myself no later than Monday evening, the first evening when I was back in the city, alone and free. I ate a solitary dinner immediately after leaving the office. I went to my room and slept from seven until nearly midnight. I wakened naturally, then, for my whole heart was set on exploring the alluring solitude I had discovered. I dressed, slipped out of the house and into the street, started the motor in my roadster which I had left parked at the curb, and drove through the lighted streets.

I left behind that part of town which was thick with vehicles carrying people home from their evening engagements, and began to thread my way through darker and narrower streets. Once I had to back out of a cul-de-sac, and once I had to detour around a closed block. This part of town was not alluring, even to me. It was dismal without being solitary.

But when I had parked my car on a rough, cobbled street that ran directly down into the inky waters of the canal, and crossed a narrow bridge, I was repaid. A few minutes set my feet on the old tow-path where mules had drawn river-boats up and down only a year or so ago. Across the canal now, as I walked upstream at a swinging pace, the miserable shacks where miserable people lived seemed to march with me, and then fell behind. They looked like places in which murders might be committed, every one of them.

The bridge I had crossed was near the end of the city going north, as the canal marked its western extremity. Ten minutes of walking, and the dismal shacks were quite a distance behind, the river was farther away and the strip of waste land much wider and more wooded, and tall trees across the canal marched with me as the evil-looking houses had done before. Far and faint, the sound of a bell in the city reached my ears. It was midnight.

I stopped, enjoyed the desolation around me. It had the savor I had expected and hoped for. I stood for some time looking up at the sky, watching the low drift of heavy clouds, which were visible in the dull reflected glow from distant lights in the heart of the city, so that they appeared to have a lurid phosphorescence of their own. The ground under my feet, on the contrary, was utterly devoid of light. I had felt my way carefully, knowing the edge of the canal partly by instinct, partly by the even more perfect blackness of the water in it, and even holding pretty well to the path, because it was perceptibly sunken below the ground beside it.

Now as I stood motionless in this spot, my eyes upcast, my mind adrift with strange fancies, suddenly my feelings of satisfaction and well-being gave way to something different. Fear was an emotion unknown to me—for those things which make men fear, I had always loved. A graveyard at night was to me a charming place for a stroll and meditation.

But now, the roots of my hair seemed to move upright on my head, and along all the length of my spine I was conscious of a prickling, tingling sensation—such as my forefathers may have felt in the jungle when the hair on their backs stood up as the hair of my head was doing now. Also, I was afraid to move; and I knew that there were eyes upon me, and that that was why I was afraid to move. I was afraid of those eyes—afraid to see them, to look into them.

All this while, I stood perfectly still, my face uptilted toward the sky. But after a terrible mental effort, I mastered myself.

Slowly—slowly, with an attempt to propitiate the owner of the unseen eyes by my casual manner, I lowered my own. I looked straight ahead—at the softly swaying silhouette of the tree-tops across the canal as they moved gently in the cool night wind; at the mass of blackness that was those trees, and the opposite shore; at the shiny blackness where the reflections of the clouds glinted vaguely and disappeared, that was the canal. And again I raised my eyes a little, for just across the canal where the shadows massed most heavily, there was that at which I must look more closely. And now, as I grew accustomed to the greater blackness and my pupils expanded, I dimly discerned the contours of an old boat or barge, half sunken in the water.

An old, abandoned canal-boat.

But was I dreaming, or was there a white-clad figure seated on the roof of the low cabin aft; a pale, heart-shaped face gleaming strangely at me from the darkness, the glow of two eyes seeming to light up the face, and to detach it from the darkness?

Surely, there could be no doubt as to the eyes. They shone as the eyes of animals shine in the dark—with a phosphorescent gleam, and a glimmer of red! Well, I had heard that some human eyes have that quality at night.

But what a place for a human being to be—a girl, too, I was sure. That daintily heart-shaped face was the face of a girl, surely—I was seeing it clearer and clearer, either because my eyes were growing more accustomed to peering into the deeper shadows, or because of that phosphorescence in the eyes that stared back at me.

I raised my voice softly, not to break too much the stillness of the night.

"Hello! Who's there? Are you lost, or marooned, and can I help?"

There was a little pause. I was conscious of a soft lapping at my feet. A stronger night wind had sprung up, was ruffling the dark waters. I had been over-warm, and where it struck me the perspiration turned cold on my body, so that I shivered uncontrollably.

"You can stay—and talk awhile, if you will. I am lonely, but not lost—I—I live here."

I could hardly believe my ears. The voice was little more than a whisper, but it had carried clearly—a girl's voice, sure enough. And she lived there—in an old, abandoned canal-boat, half submerged in the stagnant water.

"You are not alone there?"

"No, not alone. My father lives here with me, but he is deaf—and he sleeps soundly."

Did the night wind blow still colder, as though it came to us from some unseen, frozen sea—or was there something in her tone that chilled me, even as a strange attraction drew me toward her? I wanted to draw near to her, to see closely the pale, heart-shaped face, to lose myself in the bright eyes that I had seen shining in the darkness. I wanted—I wanted to hold her in my arms, to find her mouth with mine, to kiss it-

With a start, I realized the nature of my thoughts, and for an instant lost all thought in surprise. Never in my twenty-two years had I felt love before. My fancies had been otherwise directed—a moss-grown, fallen gravestone was a dearer thing to me to contemplate than the fairest face in all the world. Yet, surely, what I felt now was love!

I took a reckless step nearer the edge of the bank.

"Could I come over to you?" I begged. "It's warm, and I don't mind a wetting. It's late, I know—but I would give a great deal to sit beside you and talk, if only for a few minutes before I go back to town. It's a lonely place here for a girl like you to live—your father should not mind if you exchange a few words with someone occasionally."

Was it the unconventionality of my request that made her next words sound like a long-drawn shudder of protest? There was a strangeness in the tones of her voice that held me wondering, every time she spoke.

"No—no. Oh, no! You must not swim across."

"Then—could I come tomorrow, or someday soon, in the daytime; and would you let me come on board then—or would you come on shore and talk to me, perhaps?"

"Not in the daytime—never in the daytime!"

Again the intensity of her low-toned negation held me spellbound.

It was not her sense of the impropriety of the hour, then, that had dictated her manner. For surely, any girl with the slightest sense of the fitness of things would rather have a tryst by daytime than after midnight—yet there was an inference in her last words that if I came again it should be again at night.

Still feeling the spell that had enthralled me, as one does not forget the presence of a drug in the air that is stealing one's senses, even when those senses begin to wander and to busy themselves with other things, I yet spoke shortly.

"Why do you say, 'Never in the daytime'? Do you mean that I may come more than this once at night, though now you won't let me cross the canal to you at the expense of my own clothes, and you won't put down your plank or drawbridge, or whatever you come on shore with, and talk to me here for only a moment? I'll come again, if you'll let me talk to you instead of calling across the water. I'll come again, any time you will let me—day or night, I don't care. I want to come to you. But I only ask you to explain. If I came in the daytime and met your father, wouldn't that be the best thing to do? Then we could be really acquainted—we could be friends."

"In the night time, my father sleeps. In the daytime, I sleep. How could I talk to you, or introduce you to my father then? If you came on board this boat in the daytime, you would find my father—and you would be sorry. As for me, I would be sleeping. I could never introduce you to my father, do you see?"

"You sleep soundly, you and your father." Again there was pique in my voice.

"Yes, we sleep soundly."

"And always at different times?"

"Always at different times. We are on guard—one of us is always on guard. We have been hardly used, down there in your city. And we have taken refuge here. And we are always—always—on guard."

The resentment vanished from my breast, and I felt my heart go out to her anew. She was so pale, so pitiful in the night. My eyes were learning better and better how to pierce the darkness, they were giving me a more definite picture of my companion—if I could think of her as a companion, between myself and whom stretched the black water.

The sadness of the lonely scene, the perfection of the solitude itself, these things contributed to her pitifulness. Then there was that strangeness of atmosphere of which, even yet, I had only partly taken note. There was the strange, shivering chill, which yet did not seem like the healthful chill of a cool evening. In fact, it did not prevent me from feeling the oppression of the night, which was unusually sultry. It was like a little breath of deadly cold that came and went, and yet did not alter the temperature of the air itself, as the small ripples on the surface of water do not concern the water even a foot down.

And even that was not all. There was an unwholesome smell about the night—a dank, moldy smell that might have been the very breath of death and decay. Even I, the connoisseur in all things dismal and unwholesome, tried to keep my mind from dwelling overmuch upon that smell. What it must be to live breathing it constantly in, I could not think. But no doubt the girl and her father were used to it; and no doubt it came from the stagnant water of the canal and from the rotting wood of the old, half-sunken boat that was their refuge.

My heart throbbed with pity again. Their refuge—what a place! And my clearer vision of the girl showed me that she was pitifully thin, even though possessed of the strange face that drew me to her. Her clothes hung around her like old rags, but hers' was no scarecrow aspect. Although little flesh clothed her bones, her very bones were beautiful. I was sure the little, pale, heart-shaped face would be more beautiful still, if I could only see it closely. I must see it closely—I must establish some claim to consideration as a friend of the strange, lonely crew of the half-sunken wreck.

"This is a poor place to call a refuge," I said finally. "One might have very little money, and yet do somewhat better. Perhaps I might help you—I am sure I could. If your ill-treatment in the city was because of poverty—I am not rich, but I could help that. I could help you a little with money—if you would let me—or, in any case, I could find a position for you. I'm sure I could do that."

The eyes that shone fitfully toward me like two small pools of water intermittently lit by a cloud-swept sky seemed to glow more brightly. She had been half crouching, half sitting on top of the cabin; now she leaped to her feet with one quick, sinuous, abrupt motion, and took a few rapid, restless steps to and fro before she answered.

When she spoke, her voice was little more than a whisper; yet surely rage was in its shrill sibilance.

"Fool! Do you think you would be helping me, to tie me to a desk, to shut me behind doors, away from freedom, away from the delight of doing my own will, of seeking my own way? Never, never would I let you do that. Rather this old boat, rather a deserted grave under the stars, for my home!"

A boundless surprise swept over me, and a positive feeling of kinship with this strange being, whose face I had hardly seen, possessed me. So I myself might have spoken—so I had often felt, though I had never dreamed of putting my thoughts so definitely, so forcibly. My regularized daytime life was a thing I thought little of; I really lived only in my nocturnal prowlings. Why, this girl was right! All of life should be free—and spent in places that interested and attracted.

How little, how little I knew, that night, that dread forces were tugging at my soul, were finding entrance to it and easy access through the morbid weakness of my nature! How little I knew at what a cost I deviated so radically from my kind, who herd in cities and love well-lit ways and the sight of man, and sweet and wholesome places to be solitary in, when the desire for solitude comes over them!

That night it seemed to me that there was but one important thing in life —to allay the angry passion my unfortunate words had aroused in the breast of my beloved, and to win from her some answering feeling.

"I understand—much better than you think," I whispered tremulously.

"What I want is to see you again, to come to know you. And to serve you in any way that I may. Surely, there must be something in which I can be of use to you. All you have to do from tonight on forever, is to command me. I swear it!"

"You swear that—you do swear it?"

Delighted at the eagerness of her words, I lifted my hand toward the dark heavens.

"I swear it. From this night on, forever—I swear it."

"Then listen. Tonight you may not come to me, nor I to you. I do not want you to board this boat, not tonight, not any night. And most of all, not any day. But do not look so sad. I will come to you. No, not tonight. Perhaps not for many nights—yet before very long. I will come to you there, on the bank of the canal, when the water in the canal ceases to flow."

I must have made a gesture of impatience, or of despair. It sounded like a way of saying "never"—for why should the water in the canal cease to flow? She read my thoughts in some way, for she answered them.

"You do not understand. I am speaking seriously—I am promising to meet you there on the bank, and soon. For the water within these banks is moving slower, always slower. Higher up, I have heard that the canal has been drained. Between these lower locks, the water still seeps in and. drops slowly, slowly downstream. But there will come a night when it will be quite, quite stagnant—and on that night I will come to you. And when I come, I will ask of you a favor. And you will keep your oath."

I t was all the assurance I could get that night. She had come back to the side of the cabin where she had sat crouched before, and she resumed again that posture and sat still and silent, watching me. Sometimes I could see her eyes upon me, and sometimes not. But I felt that their gaze was unwavering. The little cold breeze, which I had finally forgotten while I was talking with her, was blowing again, and the unwholesome smell of decay grew heavier before the dawn.

She would not speak again, nor answer me when I spoke to her, and I grew nervous, and strangely ill at ease.

At last I went away. And in the first faint light of dawn I slipped up the stairs of my rooming-house, and into my own room.

I was deadly tired at the office next day. And day after day slipped away and I grew more and more weary. For a man cannot wake day and night without suffering, especially in hot weather, and that was what I was doing. I haunted the old tow-path and waited, night after night, on the bank opposite the sunken boat. Sometimes I saw my lady of the darkness, and sometimes not. When I saw her, she spoke little; but sometimes she sat there on the top of the cabin and let me watch her till the dawn, or until the strange uneasiness that was like fright drove me from her and back to my room, where I tossed restlessly in the heat and dreamed strange dreams, half waking, till the sun shone in on my forehead and I tumbled into my clothes and down to the office again.

Once I asked her why she had made the fanciful condition that she would not come ashore to meet me until the waters of the canal had ceased to run. (How eagerly I studied those waters; how I stole away at noontime more than once, not to approach the old boat, but to watch the almost imperceptible downward drift of bubbles, bits of straw, twigs, rubbish!)

My questioning displeased her, and I asked her that no more. It was enough that she chose to be whimsical. My part was to wait.

It was more than a week later that I questioned her again, this time on a different subject. And after that, I curbed my curiosity relentlessly.

"Never speak to me of things you do not understand about me. Never again, or I will not show myself to you again. And when I walk on the path yonder, it will not be with you."

I had asked her what form of persecution she and her father had suffered in the city, that had driven them out to this lonely place, and where in the city they had lived.

Frightened seriously lest I lose the ground I was sure I had gained with her, I was about to speak of something else. But before I could find the words, her low voice came to me again.

"It was horrible—horrible! Those little houses below the bridge, those houses along the canal—tell me, are they not worse than my boat? Life there was shut in, and furtive. I was not free as I am now—and the freedom I will soon have will make me forget the things I have not yet forgotten. The screaming, the reviling and cursing! Fear and flight! As you pass back by those houses, think how you would like to be shut in one of them, and in fear of your life. And then think of them no more—for I would forget them, and I will never speak of them again!"

I dared not answer her. I was surprised that she had vouchsafed me so much. But surely her words meant this—that before she had come to live on the decaying, water-rotted old boat, she had lived in one of those horrible houses I passed by on my way to her. Those houses, each of which looked like the predestined scene of a murder!

As I left her that night, I felt that I was very daring.

"One or two nights more and you will walk beside me," I called to her. "I have watched the water at noon, and it hardly moves at all. I threw a scrap of paper into the canal, and it whirled and swung a little where a thin skim of oil lay on the water down there—oil from the big, dirty city you are well out of. But though I watched and watched, I could not see it move downward at all. Perhaps tomorrow night, or the night after, you will walk on the bank with me. I hope it will be clear and moonlight; and I will be near enough to see you clearly—as well as you seem always to see me in darkness or moonlight, equally well. And perhaps I will kiss you—but not unless you let me."

And yet, the next day, for the first time my thoughts were definitely troubled. I had been living in a dream—I began to speculate concerning the end of the path on which my feet were set.

I had conceived, from the first, such a horror of those old houses by the canal! They were well enough to walk past, nursing gruesome thoughts for a midnight treat. But, much as I loved all that was weird and eery about the girl I was wooing so strangely, it was a little too much for my fancy that she had come from them.

By this time, I had become decidedly unpopular in my place of business. Not that I had made enemies, but that my peculiar ways had caused too much adverse comment. It would have taken very little, I think, to have made the entire office force decide that I was mad. After the events of the next twenty-four hours, and after this letter is found and read, they will be sure that they knew it all along! At this time, however, they were punctiliously polite to me, and merely let me alone as much as possible—which suited me perfectly. I dragged wearily through day after day, exhausted for lack of sleep, conscious of their speculative glances, living only for the night to come.

But on this day, I approached the man who had invited me to the camp across the river, who had unknowingly shown me the way that led to my love.

"Have you ever noticed the row of tumble-down houses along the canal on the city side?" I asked him.

He gave me an odd look. I suppose he sensed the significance of my breaking silence after so long to speak of them—sensed that in some way I had a deep interest in them.

"You have odd tastes, Morton," he said after a moment. "I suppose you wander into strange places sometimes—I've heard you speak of an enthusiasm for graveyards at night. But my advice to you is to keep away from those houses. They're unsavory, and their reputation is unsavory. Positively, I think you'd be in danger of your life, if you go poking around there. They have been the scene of several murders, and a dope den or two has been cleaned out of them. Why in the world you should want to investigate them—"

"I don't expect to investigate them," I said testily. "I was merely interested in them—from the outside. To tell you the truth, I'd heard a story, a rumor—never mind where. But you say there have been murders there—I suppose this rumor I heard may have had to do with an attempted one. There was a girl who lived there with her father once—and they were set upon there, or something of the sort, and had to run away. Did you ever hear that story?"

Barrett gave me an odd look such as one gives in speaking of a past horror so dreadful that the mere speaking of it makes it live terribly again.

"What you say reminds me of a horrible thing that was said to have happened down there once," he said. "It was in all the papers. A little child disappeared in one of those houses—and a couple of poor lodgers who lived there, a girl and her father, were accused of having made away with it. They were accused—they were accused—oh, well, I don't like to talk about such things. It was too dreadful. The child's body was found—part of it was found. It was mutilated, and the people in the house seemed to believe it had been mutilated in order to conceal the manner of its death—there was an ugly wound in the throat, it finally came out, and it seemed as if the child might have been bled to death. It was found in the girl's room, hidden away. The old man and his daughter escaped, before the police were called. The countryside was scoured for them—the whole country was scoured, but they were never found. Why, you must have read it in the papers, several years ago."

I nodded, with a heavy heart. I had read it in the papers, I remembered now. And again, a terrible questioning came over me. Who was this girl, what was this girl, who seemed to have my heart in her keeping?

Why did not a merciful God let me die then?

Befogged with exhaustion, bemused in a dire enchantment, my mind was incapable of thought. And yet, some soul-process akin to that which saves the sleepwalker poised at perilous heights sounded its warning now.

My mind was filled with doleful images. There were women—I had heard and read—who slew to satisfy a blood-lust. There were ghosts, specters—call them what you will, their names have been legion in the dark pages of that lore which dates back to the infancy of the races of the earth—who retained even in death this blood-lust. Vampires—they had been called that. I had read of them. Corpses by day, spirits of evil by night, roaming abroad in their own forms or in the forms of bats or unclean beasts, killing body and soul of their victims—for whoever dies of the repeated "kiss" of the vampire, which leaves its mark on the throat and draws the blood from the body, becomes a vampire also—of such beings I had read.

And, horror of horrors! In that last cursed day at the office, I remembered reading of these vampires—these undead—that in their nocturnal flights they had one limitation—they could not cross running water.

That night I went my usual nightly way with tears of weakness on my face—for my weakness was supreme, and I recognized fully at last the misery of being the victim of an enchantment stronger than my feeble will. But I went.

I approached the neighborhood of the canal-boat as the distant city clock chimed the first stroke of 12. It was the dark of the moon and the sky was overcast. Heat-lightning flickered low in the sky, seeming to come from every point of the compass and circumscribe the horizon, as if unseen fires burned behind the rim of the world. By its fitful glimmer, I saw a new thing— between the old boat and the canal bank stretched a long, slim; solid-looking shadow—a plank had been let down! In that moment, I realized that I had been playing with powers of evil which had no intent now to let me go, which were indeed about to lay hold upon me with an inexorable grasp. Why had I come tonight? Why, but that the spell of the enchantment laid upon me was a thing more potent, and far more unbreakable, than any wholesome spell of love? The creature I sought out—oh, I remembered now, with the cold perspiration beading my brow, the lore hidden away between the covers of the dark old book which I had read so many years ago and half forgotten! —until dim memories of it stirred within me, this last day and night.

My lady of the night! No woman of wholesome flesh and blood and odd perverted tastes that matched my own, but one of the undead. In that moment, I knew it, and knew that the vampires of old legends polluted still, in these latter days, the fair surface of the earth.

And on the instant, behind me in the darkness there was the crackle of a twig, and something brushed against my arm!

This, then, was the fulfillment of my dream. I knew, without turning my head, that the pale, dainty face with its glowing eyes was near my own—that I had only to stretch out my arm to touch the slender grace of the girl I had so longed to draw near. I knew, and should have felt the rapture I had anticipated. Instead, the roots of my hair prickled coldly, unendurably, as they had on the night when I had first sighted the old boat. The miasmic odors of the night, heavy and oppressive with heat and unrelieved by a breath of air, all but overcame me, and I fought with myself to prevent my teeth clicking in my head. The little waves of coldness I had felt often in this spot were chasing over my body; yet they were not from any breeze; the leaves on the trees hung down motionless, as though they were actually wilting on their branches.

With an effort, I turned my head.

Two hands caught me around my neck. The pale face was so near, that I felt the warm breath from its nostrils fanning my cheek.

And, suddenly, all that was wholesome in my perverted nature rose uppermost. I longed for the touch of the red mouth, like a dark flower opening before me in the night. I longed for it—and yet more I dreaded it. I shrank back, catching in a powerful grip the fragile wrists of the hands that strove to hold me. I must not—I must not yield to the faintness that I felt stealing languorously over me.

I was facing down the path toward the city. A low rumble of thunder—the first—broke the torrid hush of the summer night. A glare of lightning seemed to tear the night asunder, to light up the whole universe. Overhead, the clouds were careening madly in fantastic shapes, driven by a wind that swept the upper heavens without as yet causing even a trembling in the air lower down. And far down the canal, that baleful glare seemed to play around and hover over the little row of shanties—murder-cursed, and haunted by the ghost of a dead child.

My gaze was fixed on them, while I held away from me the pallid face and fought off the embrace that sought to overcome my resisting will. And so a long moment passed. The glare faded out of the sky, and a greater darkness took the world. But there was a near, more menacing glare fastened upon my face—the glare of two eyes that watched mine, that had watched me as I, unthinking, stared down at the dark houses.

This girl—this woman who had come to me at my own importunate requests, did not love me, since I had shrunk from her. She did not love me; but it was not only that. She had watched me as I gazed down at the houses that held her dark past—and I was sure that she divined my thoughts. She knew my horror of those houses—she knew my new-born horror of her. And she hated me for it, hated me more malignantly than I had believed a human being could hate.

And at that point in my thoughts, I felt my skin prickle and my scalp rise again: could a human being cherish such hatred as I read, trembling more and more, in those glowing fires lit with what seemed to me more like the fires of hell than any light that ought to shine in a woman's eyes?

And through all this, not a word had passed between us!

So far I have written calmly. I wish that I could write on so, to the end. If I could do that there might be one or two of those who will regard this as the document of a maniac, who would believe the horrors of which I am about to write.

But I am only flesh and blood. At this point in the happenings of the awful night, my calmness deserted me—at this point I felt that I had been drawn into the midst of a horrible nightmare from which there was no escape, no waking! As I write, this feeling again overwhelms me, until I can hardly write at all—until, were it not for the thing which I must do, I would rush out into the street and run, screaming, until I was caught and dragged away, to be put behind strong iron bars. Perhaps I would feel safe there—perhaps!

I know that, terrified at the hate I saw confronting me in those redly gleaming eyes, I would have slunk away. The two thin hands that caught my arm again were strong enough to prevent that, however. I had been spared her kiss—I was not to escape from the oath I had taken to serve her.

"You promised—you swore," she hissed in my ear. "And tonight you are to keep your oath."

I felt my senses reel. My oath—yes, I had an oath to keep. I had lifted my hand toward the dark heavens, and sworn to serve her in any way she chose—freely, and of my own volition, I had sworn.

I sought to evade her.

"Let me help you back to your boat," I begged. "You have no kindly feeling for me—and—you have seen it—I love you no longer. I will go back to the city—you can go back to your father, and forget that I broke your peace."

The laughter that greeted my speech I shall never forget—not in the depths under the scummy surface of the canal—not in the empty places between the worlds, where my tortured soul may wander.

"So you do not love me, and I hate you! Fool! Have I waited these weary months for the water to stop, only to go back now? After my father and I returned here and found the old boat rotting in the drained canal, and took refuge in it; when the water was turned into the canal while I slept, so that I could never escape until its flow should cease, because of the thing that: I am —even then I dreamed of tonight.

"When the imprisonment we still shared ceased to matter to my father— come on board the deserted boat tomorrow, and see why, if you dare!—still I dreamed on, of tonight!

"I have been lonely, desolate, starving—now the whole world shall be mine! And by your help!"

I asked her, somehow, what she wanted of me, and a madness overcame me so that I hardly heard her reply. Yet somehow, I knew that there was that on the opposite shore of the great river where the pleasure camps were, that she wanted to find. In the madness of my terror, she made me understand and obey her.

I must carry her in my arms across the long bridge over the river, deserted in the small hours of the night!

The way back to the city was long tonight—long. She walked behind me, and I turned my eyes neither to right nor left. Only as I passed the tumble-down houses, I saw their reflection in the canal and trembled so that I could have fallen to the ground, at the thoughts of the little child this woman had been accused of slaying there, and at the certainty I felt that she was reading my thoughts.

And now the horror that engulfed me darkened my brain.

I know that we set our feet upon the long, wide bridge that spanned the river. I know the storm broke there, so that I battled for my footing, almost for my life, it seemed, against the pelting deluge. And the horror I had invoked was in my arms, clinging to me, burying its head upon my shoulder. So increasingly dreadful had my pale-faced companion become to me, that I hardly thought of her now as a woman at all—only as a demon of the night.

The tempest raged still as she leaped down out of my arms on the other shore. And again I walked with her against my will, while the trees lashed their branches madly around me, showing the pale undersides of their leaves in the vivid frequent flashes that rent the heavens.

On and on we went, branches flying through the air and missing us by a miracle of ill fortune. Such as she and I are not slain by falling branches. The river was a welter of whitecaps, flattened down into strange shapes by the pounding rain. The clouds as we glimpsed them were like devils flying through the sky.

Past dark tent after dark tent we stole, and past a few where lights burned dimly behind their canvas walls. And at last we came to an old quarry. Into its artificial ravine she led me, and up to a crevice in the rock wall.

"Reach in your hand and pull out the loose stone you will feel," she whispered. "It closes an opening that leads into deep caverns. A human hand must remove that stone—your hand must move it!"

Why did I struggle so to disobey her? Why did I fail? It was as though I knew—but my failure was foreordained—I had taken oath!

If you who read have believed that I have set down the truth thus far, the little that is left you will call the ravings of a madman overtaken by his madness. Yet these things happened.

I stretched out my arm, driven by a compulsion I could not resist. At arm's length in the niche in the rock, I felt something move—the loose rock, a long, narrow fragment, much larger than I had expected. Yet it moved easily, seeming to swing on a natural pivot. Outward it swung, toppling toward me —a moment more and there was a swift rush of the ponderous weight I had loosened. I leaped aside and went down, my forehead grazed by the rock.

For a brief moment I must have been unconscious. But only for a moment. My head a stabbing agony of pain, unreal lights flashing before my eyes, I yet knew the reality of the storm that beat me down as I struggled to my feet. I knew the reality of the dark, loathsome shapes that passed me in the dark, crawling out of the orifice in the rock and flapping through the wild night, along the way that led to the pleasure camps.

So the caverns I had laid open to the outer world were infested with bats. I had been inside unlit caverns, and had heard there the squeaking of the things, felt and heard the flapping of their wings—but never in all my life before had I seen bats as large as men and women!

Sick and dizzy from the blow on my head, and from disgust, I crept along the way they were going. If I touched one of them, I felt that I should die of horror.

Now, at last, the storm abated, and a heavy darkness made the whole world seem like the inside of a tomb.

Where the tents stood in a long row, the number of the monster bats seemed to diminish. It was as though—horrible thought!—they were creeping into the tents, with their slumbering occupants.

At last I came to a lighted tent, and paused, crouching so that the dim radiance that shone through the canvas did not touch me in the shadows. And there I waited, but not for long. There was a dark form silhouetted against the tent—a movement of the flap oft-the tent—a rustle and confusion, and the dark thing was again in silhouette—but with a difference in the quality of the shadow. The dark thing was inside the tent now, its bat wings extending across the entrance through which it had crept.

Fear held me spellbound. And as I looked the shadow changed again— imperceptibly, so that I could not have told how it changed.

But now it was not the shadow of a bat, but of a woman.

"The storm—the storm! I am lost, exhausted—I crept in here, to beg for refuge until the dawn!"

That low, thrilling, sibilant voice—too well I knew it!

Within the tent I heard a murmur of acquiescent voices. At last I began to understand.

I knew the nature of the woman I had carried over the river in my arms, the woman who would not even cross the canal until the water should have ceased utterly to flow. I remembered books I had read—Dracula—other books, and stories. I knew they were true books and stories, now—I knew those horrors existed for me.

I had indeed kept my oath to the creature of darkness—I had brought her to her kind, under her guidance. I had let them loose in hordes upon the pleasure camps. The campers were doomed—and through them, others-

I forgot my fear. I rushed from my hiding-place up to the tent door, and there I screamed and called aloud.

"Don't take her in—don't let her stay—nor the others, that have crept into the other tents! Wake all the campers—they will sleep on to their destruction! Drive out the interlopers—drive them out quickly! They are not human—no, and they are not bats. Do you hear me?—do you understand?"

I was fairly howling, in a voice that was strange to me.

"She is a vampire—they are all vampires. Vampires!"

Inside the tent I heard a new voice. "What can be the matter with that poor man?" the voice said. It was a woman's, and gentle.

"Crazy—somebody out of his senses, dear," a man's voice answered. "Don't be frightened."

And then the voice I knew so well—so well: "I saw a falling rock strike a man on the head in the storm. He staggered away, but I suppose it crazed him."

I waited for no more. I ran away, madly, through the night and back across the bridge to the city.

Next day—today—I boarded the sunken canal-boat. It is the abode of death—no woman could have lived there—only such a one as she. The old man's corpse was there—he must have died long, long ago. The smell of death and of decay on the boat was dreadful.

Again, I felt that I understood. Back in those awful houses, she had committed the crime when first she became the thing she is. And he—her father—less sin-steeped, and less accursed, attempted to destroy the evidence of her crime, and fled with her, but died without becoming like her. She had said that one of those two was always on watch—did he indeed divide her vigil on the boat? What more fitting—the dead standing watch with the undead! And no wonder that she would not let me board the craft of death, even to carry her away.

And still I feel the old compulsion. I have been spared her kiss—but for a little while. Yet I will not let the power of my oath to her draw me back, till I enter the caverns with her and creep forth in the form of a bat to prey upon mankind. Before that can happen, I too will die.

Today in the city I heard that a horde of strange insects or small animals infested the pleasure camps last night. Some said, with horror-bated breath, that they perhaps were rats. None of them was seen; but in the morning nearly every camper had a strange, deep wound in his throat. I almost laughed aloud. They were so horrified at the idea of an army of rats, creeping into the tents and biting the sleeping occupants on their throats! If they had seen what I saw—if they knew that they are doomed to spread corruption-

So my own death will not be enough. Today I bought supplies for blasting. Tonight I will set my train of dynamite, from the hole I made in the cliff where the vampires creep in and out, along the row of tents, as far as the last one—then I shall light my fuse. It will be done before the dawn. Tomorrow, the city will mourn its dead and execrate my name.

And then, at last, in the slime beneath the unmoving waters of the canal, I shall find peace! But perhaps it will not be peace—for I shall seek it midway between the old boat with its cargo of death and the row of dismal houses where a little child was done to death when first she became the thing she is. That is my expiation.

RED THIRST

Henry Kuttner

first published as "I, the Vampire" in *Weird Tales* (February 1937)

I. CHEVALIER FUTAINE

The party was dull. I had come too early. There was a preview that night at Grauman's Chinese, and few of the important guests would arrive until it was over. Jack Hardy, ace director at Summit Pictures, where I worked as assistant director, hadn't arrived—yet—and he was the host. But Hardy had never been noted for punctuality.

I went out on the porch and leaned against a cocktail and looking down at the lights of Hollywood. Hardy's place was on the summit of a hill overlooking the film capital, near Falcon Lair, Valentino's famous turreted castle. I shivered a little. Fog was sweeping in from Santa Monica, blotting out the lights to the west.

Jean Hubbard, who was an ingenue at Summit, came up beside me and took the glass out of my hand.

"Hello, Mart," she said, sipping the liquor. "Where've you been?"

"Down with the Murder Desert troupe, on location in the Mojave," I said. "Miss me, honey?" I drew her close.

She smiled up at me, her tilted eyebrows lending a touch of diablerie to the tanned, lovely face. I was going to marry Jean, but I wasn't sure just when.

"Missed you lots," she said, and held up her lips. I responded.

After a moment I said, "What's this about the vampire man?"

She chuckled. "Oh, the Chevalier Futaine. Didn't you read Lolly Parsons', write-up in *Script*? Jack Hardy picked him up last month in Europe. Silly rot. Bill it's good publicity."

"Three cheers for publicity," I said. "Look what it did for *Birth of a Nation*. But where does the vampire angle come in?"

"Mystery man. Nobody can take a picture of him, scarcely anybody can meet him. Weird tales are told about his former life in Paris. Going to play in Jack's *Red Thirst*. The kind of build-up Universal gave Karloff for *Frankenstein*. Our Chevalier Futaine"—she rolled out the words with amused relish—"is probably a singing waiter from a Paris cafe. I haven't seen him—but the deuce with him, anyway. Mart, I want you to do something for me. For Deming."

"Hess Deming?" I raised my eyebrows in astonishment. Hess Deming, Summit's biggest box-office star, whose wife, Sandra Colter, had died two day before. She, too, had been an actress, although never the great star her husband was. Hess loved her, I knew—and now I guessed what the trouble was. I said, "I noticed he was a bit wobbly."

"He'll kill himself," Jean said, looking worried. "I—I feel responsible for him somehow, Mart. After all, he gave me my start at Summit. And he's due for the DTs any time now."

"Well, I'll do what I can," I told her. "But that isn't a great deal. After all, getting tight is probably the best thing he could do. I know if I lost you, Jean —"

I stopped. I didn't like to think of it.

Jean nodded. "Sec what you can do for him, anyway. Losing Sandra that way was—pretty terrible."

"What way?" I asked. "I've been away, remember. I read something about it, but—"

"She just died," Jean said. "Pernicious anemia, they said. But Hess told me the doctor really didn't know what it was. She just seemed to grow weaker and weaker until—she passed away."

I nodded, gave Jean a hasty kiss, and went back into the house. I had just seen Hess Deming walk past, a glass in his hand. He turned as I tapped his shoulder.

"Oh, Mart," he said, his voice just a bit fuzzy. He could hold his liquor, but I could tell by his bloodshot eyes that he was almost at the end of his rope. He was a handsome devil, all right, well-built, strong-featured, with level gray eyes and a broad mouth that was usually smiling. It wasn't smiling now. It was slack, and his face was bedewed with perspiration.

"You know about Sandra?" he asked.

"Yeah," I said. "I'm sorry, Hess."

He drank deeply from the glass, wiped his mouth with a grimace of distaste. "I'm drunk, Mart," he confided. "I had to get drunk. It was awful— those last few days. I've got to burn her up."

I didn't say anything.

"Burn her up. Oh, my God, Mart—that beautiful body of hers, crumbling to • In i -and I've got to watch it! She made me promise I'd watch to make sure they burned her."

I said, "Cremation's a clean ending, Hess. And Sandra was a clean girl, and a damned good actress."

He put his flushed face close to mine. "Yeah—but I've got to burn her up. It'll kill me, Mart. Oh, God!" He put the empty glass down on a table and looked around dazedly.

I was wondering why Sandra had insisted on cremation. She'd given an interview once in which she stressed her dread of fire. Most write-ups of stars are applesauce, but I happened to know that Sandra did dread fire. Once, on the set, I'd seen her go into hysterics when her leading man lit his pipe too near her face.

"Excuse me, Mart," Hess said. "I've got to get another drink."

"Wait a minute," I said, holding him. "You want to watch yourself, Hess, you've had too much already."

"It still hurts," he said. "Just a little more and maybe it won't hurt so much." But he didn't pull away. Instead he stared at me with the dullness of intoxication in his eyes. "Clean," he said presently.

"She said that too. Mart. She said burning was a clean death. But, God, that beautiful white body of hers—I can't stand it, Mart! I'm going crazy, I think. Get me a drink, like a good fellow."

I said, "Wait here, Hess. I'll get you one." I didn't add that it would be watered—considerably.

He sank down in a chair, mumbling thanks. As I went off I felt sick. I'd seen too many actors going on the rocks to mistake Hess's symptoms. I knew that his box office days were over. There would be longer and longer waits between features, and then personal appearances, and finally Poverty Row and serials. And in the end maybe a man found dead in a cheap hall bedroom on Main Street, with the gas on.

There was a crowd around the bar. Somebody said, "Here's Mart. Hey, come on and meet the vampire."

Then I got a shock. I saw Jack Hardy, my host, the director with whom I'd on many a hit. He looked like a corpse. And I'd seen him looking plenty bad before. A man with a hangover or a marijuana jag isn't a pretty sight, but I'd never seen Hardy like this. He looked as though he was keeping going on his nerve alone. There was no blood in the man.

I'd last seen him as a stocky, ruddy blond, who looked like nothing so much as a wrestler, with his huge biceps, his ugly, good-natured face, and his bristling crop of yellow hair. Now he looked like a skeleton, with skin hanging loosely on the big frame. His face was a network of sagging wrinkles. Pouches bagged beneath his eyes, and those eyes were dull and glazed. About his neck a black silk scarf was knotted tightly.

"Good God, Jack!" I exclaimed. "What have you done to yourself?"

He looked away quickly. "Nothing," he said brusquely. "I'm all right. I want you to meet the Chevalier Futaine—this is Mart Prescott."

"Pierre," a voice said. "Hollywood is no place for titles. Mart Prescott—the pleasure is mine."

I faced the Chevalier Pierre Futaine.

We shook hands. My first impression was of icy cold, and a slick kind of dryness—and I let go of his hand too quickly to be polite. He smiled at me.

A charming man, the chevalier. Or so he seemed. Slender, below medium height, his bland, round face seemed incongruously youthful. Blond hair was plastered close to his scalp. I saw that his cheeks were rouged—very deftly, but I know something about makeup. And under the rouge I read a curious, deathly pallor that would have made him a marked man had he not disguised it. Some disease, perhaps, had blanched his skin—but his lips were not artificially reddened. And they were as crimson as blood.

He was clean-shaved, wore impeccable evening clothes, and his eyes were black pools of ink.

"Glad to know you," I said. "You're the vampire, eh?"

He smiled. "So they tell me. But we all serve the dark god of publicity, eh Mr. Prescott? Or—is it Mart?"

"It's Mart," I said, still staring at him. I saw his eyes go past me, and an extraordinary expression appeared on his face—an expression of amazement, disbelief. Swiftly it was gone.

I turned. Jean was approaching, was at my side as I moved. She said, "Is this the chevalier?"

Pierre Futaine was staring at her, his lips parted a little. Almost inaudibly he murmured, "Sonya." And then, on a note of interrogation, "Sonya?"

I introduced the two. Jean said, "You see, my name isn't Sonya."

The chevalier shook his head, an odd look in his black eyes.

"I once knew a girl like you," he said softly. "Very much like you. It's strange."

"Will you excuse me?" I broke in. Jack Hardy was leaving the bar. Quickly I followed him.

I touched his shoulder as he went out the French windows. He jerked out a snarled oath, turned a white death mask of a face to me.

"Damn you, Mart," he snarled. "Keep your hands to yourself."

I put my hands on his shoulders and swung him around.

"What the devil has happened to you?" I asked. "Listen, Jack, you can't bluff me or lie to me. You know that. I've straightened you out enough times in the past, and I can do it again. Let me in on it."

His ruined face softened. He reached up and took away my hands. His own were ice-cold, like the hands of the Chevalier Futaine.

"No," he said. "No use, Mart. There's nothing you can do. I'm all right, really. Just—overstrain. I had too good a time in Paris."

I was up against a blank wall. Suddenly, without volition, a thought popped into my mind and out of my mouth before I knew it.

"What's the matter with your neck?" I asked abruptly.

He didn't answer. He just frowned and shook his head.

"I've a throat infection," he told me. "Caught it on the steamer."

His hand went up and touched the black scarf.

There was a croaking, harsh sound from behind us—a sound that didn't seem quite human. I turned. It was Hess Deming. He was swaying in the portal, his eyes glaring and bloodshot, a little trickle of saliva running down his chin.

He said in a dead, expressionless voice that was somehow dreadful, "Sandra died of a throat infection, Hardy."

Jack didn't answer. He stumbled back a step. Hess went on dully.

"She got all white and died. And the doctor didn't know what it was, although the death certificate said anemia. Did you bring back some filthy disease with you, Hardy? Because if you did I'm going to kill you."

"Wait a minute," I said. "A throat infection? I didn't know—"

"There was a wound on her throat—two little marks, close together. That wouldn't have killed her, unless some loathsome disease—"

"You're crazy, Hess," I said. "You know you're drunk. Listen to me: Jack couldn't have had anything to do with—that."

Hess didn't look at me. He watched Jack Hardy out of his bloodshot eyes. He went on in that low, deadly monotone:

"Will you swear Mart's right, Hardy? Will you?"

Jack's lips were twisted by some inner agony. I said, "Go on, Jack. Tell him he's wrong."

Hardy burst out, "I haven't been near your wife! I haven't seen her since I got back. There's—"

"That's not the answer I want," Hess whispered. And he sprang for the other man—reeled forward, rather.

Hess was too drunk, and Jack too weak, for them to do each other any harm, but there was a nasty scuffle for a moment before I separated them. As I pulled them apart, Hess's hand clutched the scarf about Jack's neck, ripped it away.

And I saw the marks on Jack Hardy's throat. Two red, angry little pits, white rimmed, just over the left jugular.

II. THE CREMATION OF SANDRA

It was the next day that Jean telephoned me.

"Mart," she said, "we're going to run over a scene for *Red Thirst* tonight at the studio—Stage 6. You've been assigned as assistant director for the pic, so you should be there. And—I had an idea Jack might not tell you. He's been—so odd lately."

"Thanks, honey," I said. "I'll be there. But I didn't know you were in the flicker."

"Neither did I, but there's been some wire-pulling. Somebody wanted me in it—the chevalier, I think—and the big boss phoned me this morning and let me in on the secret. I don't feel up to it, though. Had a bad night."

"Sorry," I sympathized. "You were okay when I left you."

"I had a—nightmare," she said slowly. "It was rather frightful, Mart. It's funny, though, I can't remember what it was about. Well—you'll be there tonight?"

I said I would, but as it happened I was unable to keep my promise. Hess Deming telephoned me, asking if I'd come out to his Malibu place and drive him into town. He was too shaky to handle a car himself, he said, and Sandra's cremation was to take place that afternoon. I got out my roadster and sent it spinning west on Sunset. In twenty minutes I was at Deming's beach house The houseboy let me in, shaking his head gravely as he recognized me. "Mist' Doming pretty bad," he told me. "All morning drinking gin straight—"

From upstairs Hess shouted, "That you, Mart? Okay—I'll be down right away. Come up here, Jim!"

The Japanese, with a meaningful glance at me, pattered upstairs.

I wandered over to a table, examining the magazines upon it. A little breeze of wind came through the half-open window, fluttering a scrap of paper. A word on it caught my eye, and I picked up the note. For that's what it was. It was addressed to Hess, and after one glance I had no compunction about scanning it. "Hess dear," the message read. "I feel I'm going to die very soon. And I want you to do something for me. I've been out of my head, I know, saying things I didn't mean. Don't cremate me, Hess. Even though I were dead I'd feel the fire—I know it. Bury me in a vault in Forest Lawn—and don't embalm me. I shall be dead when you find this, but I know you'll do as I wish, dear. And alive or dead, I'll always love you."

The note was signed by Sandra Colter, Hess's wife. This was odd. I wondered whether Hess had seen it yet.

There was a little hiss of indrawn breath from behind me. It was Jim, the houseboy. He said, "Mist' Prescott, I find that note last night. Mist' Hess not seen it. It Mis' Colter's writing."

He hesitated, and I read fear in his eyes—sheer, unashamed fear. He put a brown forefinger on the note.

"See that, Mist' Prescott?"

He was pointing to a smudge of ink that half obscured the signature. I said, "Well?"

"I do that, Mist' Prescott. When I pick up the note. The ink—not dry."

I stared at him. He turned hastily at the sound of footsteps on the stairs. Hess Deming was coming down, rather shakily.

I think it was then that I first realized the horrible truth. I didn't believe it, though—not then. It was too fantastic, too incredible; yet something of the truth must have crept into my mind, for there was no other explanation for what I did then.

Hess said, "What have you got there, Mart?"

"Nothing," I said quietly. I crumpled the note and thrust it into my pocket. "Nothing important, anyway. Ready to go?"

He nodded, and we went to the door. I caught a glimpse of Jim staring after us, an expression of—was it relief?—in his dark, wizened face.

The crematory was in Pasadena, and I left Hess there. I would have stayed with him, but he wouldn't have it. I knew he didn't want anyone to be watching him when Sandra's body was being incinerated. And I knew it would be easier for him that way. I took a short cut through the Hollywood hills, and that's where the trouble started.

I broke an axle. Recent rains had gullied the road, and I barely saved the car from turning over. After that I had to hike miles to the nearest telephone, and then I wasted more time waiting for a taxi to pick me up. It was nearly eight o'clock when I arrived at the studio.

The gateman let me in, and I hurried to Stage 6. It was dark. Cursing under my breath, I turned away, and almost collided with a small figure. It was Forrest, one of the cameramen. He let out a curious squeal, and clutched my arm.

"That you, Mart? Listen, will you do me a favor? I want you to watch a I uint—"

"Haven't time," I said. "Seen Jean around here? I was to—"

"It's about that," Forrest said. He was a shriveled, monkey-faced little chap, but a mighty good cameraman. "They've gone—Jean and Hardy and the chevalier. There's something funny about that guy."

"Think so? Well, I'll phone Jean. I'll look at your rushes tomorrow."

"She won't be home," he told me. "The chevalier took her over to the Grove Listen, Mart, you've got to watch this. Either I don't know how to handle a grinder any more, or that Frenchman is the damnedest thing I've ever shot, come over to the theater. Mart I've got the reel ready to run. Just developed the rough print myself."

"Oh, all right," I assented, and followed Forrest to the theater.

I found a seat in the dark little auditorium, and listened to Forrest moving about in the projection booth. He clicked on the amplifier and said: "Hardy didn't warn any pictures taken—insisted on it, you know. But the boss told me to leave one of the automatic cameras going—not to bother with the sound—just to get an idea how the French guy would screen. Lucky it wasn't one of the old rattler cameras, or Hardy would have caught on. Here it comes, Mart!"

I heard a click as the amplifier was switched off. White light flared on the screen. It faded, gave place to a picture—the interior of Stage 6. The set was incongruous—a mid-Victorian parlor, with overstuffed plush chairs, gilt-edged paintings, even a particularly hideous what-not. Jack Hardy moved into the range of the camera. On the screen his face seemed to leap out at me like a death's-head, covered with sagging, wrinkled skin. Following him came Jean, wearing a tailored suit—no one dresses for rehearsals—and behind her —

I blinked, thinking that my eyes were tricking me. Something like a glowing fog—oval, tall as a man—was moving across the screen. You've seen the nimbus of light on the screen when a flashlight is turned directly on the camera? Well—it was like that, except that its source was not traceable. And, horribly, it moved forward at about the pace a man would walk.

The amplifier clicked again. Forrest said, "When I saw it on the negative I thought I was screwy, Mart. I saw the take—there wasn't any funny light there—"

The oval, glowing haze was motionless beside Jean, and she was looking directly at it, a smile on her lips. "Mart, when that was taken, Jean was looking right at the French guy!"

I said, somewhat hoarsely, "Hold it, Forrest. Right there."

The images slowed down, became motionless. Jean's profile was toward the camera. I leaned forward, staring at something I had glimpsed on the girl's neck. It was scarcely visible save as a tiny, discolored mark on Jean's throat, above the jugular—but unmistakably the same wound I had seen on the throat of Jack Hardy the night before!

I heard the amplifier click off. Suddenly the screen showed blindingly white, and then went black.

I waited a moment, but there was no sound from the booth.

"Forrest," I called. "You okay?"

There was no sound. The faint whirring of the projector had died. I got up quickly and went to the back of the theater. There were two entrances to the booth, a door which opened on stairs leading down to the alley outside, and a hole in the floor reached by means of a metal ladder. I went up this swiftly, an ominous apprehension mounting within me.

Forrest was still there. But he was no longer alive. He lay sprawled on his back, his wizened face staring up blindly, his head twisted at an impossible angle. It was quite apparent that his neck had been broken almost instantly.

I sent a hasty glance at the projector. The can of film was gone! And the door opening on the stairway was ajar a few inches.

I stepped out on the stairs, although I knew I would see no one. The white-lit broad alley between Stages 6 and 4 was silent and empty.

The sound of running feet came to me, steadily growing louder. A man came racing into view. I recognized him as one of the publicity gang. I hailed him.

"Can't wait," he gasped, but slowed down nevertheless.

I said, "Have you seen anyone around here just now? The—Chevalier Futaine?"

He shook his head. "No, but—" His face was white as he looked up at me. "Hess Deming's gone crazy. I've got to contact the papers."

Ice gripped me. I raced down the stairs, clutched his arm.

"What do you mean?" I snapped. "Hess was all right when I left him. A bit tight, that's all."

His face was glistening with sweat. "It's awful—I'm not sure yet what happened. His wife—Sandra Colter—came to life while they were cremating her. They saw her through the window, you know—screaming and pounding at the glass while she was being burned alive. Hess got her out too late. He went stark, raving mad. Suspended animation, they say—I've got to get to a phone, Mr. Prescott!"

He tore himself away, sprinted in the direction of the administration buildings.

I put my hand in my pocket and pulled out a scrap of paper. It was the note I had found in Hess Deming's house. The words danced and wavered before my eyes. Over and over I was telling myself, "It can't be true! Such things can't happen!"

I didn't mean Sandra Colter's terrible resurrection during the cremation. That, alone, might be plausibly explained—catalepsy, perhaps. But taken in conjunction with certain other occurrences, it led to one definite conclusion —and it was a conclusion I dared not face.

What had poor Forrest said? That the chevalier was taking Jean to the Cocoanut Grove? Well—

The taxi was still waiting. I got in.

"The Ambassador," I told the driver grimly. "Twenty bucks if you hit the green lights all the way."

III. THE BLACK COFFIN

All night I had been combing Hollywood—without success. Neither the Chevalier Futaine nor Jean had been to the Grove, I discovered. And no one knew the Chevalier's address. A telephone call to the studio, now ablaze with the excitement over the Hess Deming disaster and the Forrest killing, netted me exactly nothing. I went the rounds of Hollywood night life vainly. The Trocadero, Sardi's, all three of the Brown Derbies, the smart, notorious clubs of the Sunset eighties—nowhere could I find my quarry. I telephoned Jack Hardy a dozen times, but got no answer. Finally, in a "private club" in Culver City, I met with my first stroke of good luck.

"Mr. Hardy's upstairs," the proprietor told me, looking anxious. "Nothin' wrong, I hope, Mr. Prescott? I heard about Deming."

"Nothing," I said. "Take me up to him."

"He's sleeping it off," the man admitted. "Tried to drink the place dry, and I put him upstairs where he'd be safe."

"Not the first time, eh?" I said, with an assumption of lightness. "Well, bring up some coffee, will you? Black. I've got to—talk to him."

But it was half an hour before Hardy was in any shape to understand what I was saying. At last he sat up on the couch, blinking, and a gleam of realization came into his sunken eyes.

"Prescott," he said, "can't you leave me alone?"

I leaned close to him, articulating carefully so he would be sure to understand me. "I know what the Chevalier Futaine is," I said.

And I waited for the dreadful, impossible confirmation, or for the words which would convince me that I was an insane fool.

Hardy looked at me dully. "How did you find out?" he whispered.

An icy shock went through me. Up to that moment I had not really believed, in spite of all the evidence. But now Hardy was confirming the suspicions which I had not let myself believe.

I didn't answer his question. Instead, I said, "Do you know about Hess?" He nodded, and at sight of the agony in his face I almost pitied him. Then the thought of Jean steadied me.

"Do you know where he is now?" I asked.

"No. What are you talking about?" he flared suddenly. "Are you mad, Mart? Do you—"

"I'm not mad. But Hess Deming is."

He looked at me like a cowering, whipped dog.

I went on grimly: "Are you going to tell me the truth? How you got those marks on your throat? How you met this—creature? And where he's taken Jean?"

"Jean!" He looked genuinely startled. "Has he got—I didn't know that, Mart—I swear I didn't. You—you've been a good friend to me, and—and I'll tell you the truth—for your sake and Jean's—although now it may be too late." My involuntary movement made him glance at me quickly. Then he went on. "I met him in Paris. I was out after new sensations—but I didn't expect anything like that. A Satanist club—devil-worshippers, they were. The ordinary stuff—cheap, furtive blasphemy. But it was there that I met—him.

"He can be a fascinating chap when he tries. He drew me out, made me tell him about Hollywood—about the women we have here. I bragged a little. He asked me about the stars, whether they were really as beautiful as they seemed. His eyes were hungry as he listened to me, Mart.

"Then one night I had a fearful nightmare. A monstrous, black horror crept in through the window and attacked me—bit me in the throat, I dreamed, or thought I did. After that—

"I was in his power. He told me the truth. He made me his slave, and I could do nothing. His powers—are not human."

I licked dry lips.

Hardy continued: "He made me bring him here, introducing him as a new discovery to be starred in *Red Thirst*—I'd mentioned the picture to him, before I—knew. How he must have laughed at me! He made me serve him, keeping away photographers, making sure that there were no cameras, no mirrors near him. And for a reward—he let me live."

I knew I should feel contempt for Hardy, panderer to such a loathsome evil. But somehow I couldn't.

I said quietly, "What about Jean? Where does the chevalier live?"

He told me. "But you can't do anything, Mart. There's a vault under the house, where he stays during the day. It can't be opened, except with a key he always keeps with him—a silver key. He had a door specially made, and then did something to it so that nothing can open it but that key. Even dynamite wouldn't do it, he told me."

I said, "Such things—can be killed."

"Not easily. Sandra Colter was a victim of his. After death she, too, became a vampire, sleeping by day and living only at night. The fire destroyed her, but there's no way to get into the vault under Futaine's house."

"I wasn't thinking of fire," I said. "A knife—"

"Through the heart," Hardy interrupted almost eagerly. "Yes—and decapitation. I've thought of it myself, but I can do nothing. I—am his slave, Mart."

I said nothing, but pressed the bell. Presently the proprietor appeared.

"Can you get me a butcher knife?" I measured with my hands. "About so long? A sharp one?"

Accustomed to strange requests, he nodded. "Right away, Mr. Prescott." As I followed him out, Hardy said weakly, "Mart."

I turned.

"Good luck," he said. The look on his wrecked face robbed the words of their pathos.

"Thanks," I forced myself to say. "I don't blame you, Jack, for what's happened. I—I'd have done the same."

I left him there, slumped on the couch, staring after me with eyes that had looked into hell.

It was past daylight when I drove out of Culver City, a long, razor-edged knife hidden securely inside my coat. And the day went past all too quickly. A telephone call told me that Jean had not yet returned home. It took me more than an hour to locate a certain man I wanted—a man who had worked for the studio before on certain delicate jobs. There was little about locks he did not know, as the Police had sometimes ruefully admitted.

His name was Axel Ferguson, a bulky, good-natured Swede, whose thick fingers seemed more adapted to handling a shovel than the mechanisms of locks. Yet he was as expert as Houdini—indeed, he had at one time been a professional magician.

The front door of Futaine's isolated canyon home proved no bar to Ferguson's fingers and the tiny sliver of steel he used. The house, a modern two-story place, seemed deserted. But Hardy had said below the house.

We went down the cellar stairs and found ourselves in a concrete-lined passage that ran down at a slight angle for perhaps thirty feet. There the corridor ended in what seemed to be a blank wall of bluish steel. The glossy surface of the door was unbroken, save for a single keyhole.

Ferguson set to work. At first he hummed under his breath, but after a time he worked in silence. Sweat began to glisten on his face. Trepidation assailed me as I watched.

The flashlight he had placed beside him grew dim. He inserted another battery, got out unfamiliar-looking apparatus. He buckled on dark goggles, and handed me a pair. A blue, intensely brilliant flame began to play on the door. It was useless. The torch was discarded after a time, and Ferguson returned to his tools. He was using a stethoscope, taking infinite pains in the delicate movements of his hands.

It was fascinating to watch him. But all the time I realized that the night was coming, that presently the sun would go down, and that the life of the vampire lasts from sunset to sunrise.

At last Ferguson gave up. "I can't do it," he told me, panting as though from a hard race. "And if I can't, nobody can. Even Houdini couldn't have broken this lock. The only thing that'll open it is the key."

"All right, Axel," I said dully. "Here's your money."

He hesitated, watching me. "You going to stay here. Mr. Prescott?"

"Yeah," I said. "You can find your way out. I'll—wait awhile."

"Well, I'll leave the light with you," he said. "You can let me have it sometime, eh?"

He waited, and, as I made no answer, he departed, shaking his head.

Then utter silence closed around me. I took the knife out of my coat, tested its edge against my thumb, and settled back to wait.

Less than half an hour later the steel door began to swing open. I stood up. Through the widening crack I saw a bare, steel-lined chamber, empty save for a long, black object that rested on the floor. It was a coffin.

The door was wide. Into view moved a white, slender figure—Jean, clad in a diaphanous, silken robe. Her eyes were wide, fixed and staring. She looked like a sleepwalker.

A man followed her—a man wearing impeccable evening clothes. Not a hair was out of place on his sleek blond head, and he was touching his lips delicately with a handkerchief as he came out of the vault.

There was a little crimson stain on the white linen where his lips had brushed.

IV. I, THE VAMPIRE

Jean walked past me as though I didn't exist. But the Chevalier Futaine paused, his eyebrows lifted. His black eyes pierced through me.

The handle of the knife was hot in my hand. I moved aside to block Futaine's way. Behind me came a rustle of silk, and from the corner of my eye I saw Jean pause hesitatingly.

The chevalier eyed me, toying negligently with his handkerchief. "Mart," he said slowly. "Mart Prescott." His eyes flickered toward the knife, and a little smile touched his lips.

I said, "You know why I'm here, don't you?"

"Yes," he said. "I—heard you. I was not disturbed. Only one thing can open this door."

From his pocket he drew a key, shining with a dull silver sheen.

"Only this," he finished, replacing it. "Your knife is useless, Mart Prescott."

"Maybe," I said, edging forward very slightly. "What have you done to Jean?"

A curious expression, almost of pain, flashed into his eyes. "She is mine," he shot out half angrily. "You can do nothing, for—"

I sprang then, or, at least, I tried to. The blade of the knife sheared down straight for Futaine's white shirtfront. It was arrested in midair. Yet he had not moved. His eyes had bored into mine, suddenly, terribly, and it seemed as though a wave of fearful energy had blasted out at me—paralyzing me, rendering me helpless. I stood rigid. Veins throbbed in my temples as I tried to move—to bring down the knife. It was useless. I stood as immovable as a statue.

The chevalier brushed past me.

"Follow," he said almost casually, and like an automaton I swung about, began to move along the passage. What hellish hypnotic power was this that held me helpless?

Futaine led the way upstairs. It was not yet dark, although the sun had gone down. I followed him into a room, and at his gesture dropped into a chair. At my side was a small table. The chevalier touched my arm gently, and something like a mild electric shock went through me. The knife dropped from my fingers, clattering to the table.

Jean was standing rigidly nearby, her eyes dull and expressionless. Futaine moved to her side, put an arm about her waist. My mouth felt as though it were filled with mud, but somehow I managed to croak out articulate words.

"Damn you, Futaine! Leave her alone!"

He released her, and came toward me, his face dark with anger.

"You fool, I could kill you now, very easily. I could make you go down to the busiest corner of Hollywood and slit your throat with that knife. I have the power. You have found out much, apparently. Then you know my—my power."

"Yes," I muttered thickly. "I know that. You devil—Jean is mine!"

The face of a beast looked into mine. He snarled. "She is not yours. Nor is she—*Jean*. She is Sonya!"

I remembered what Futaine had murmured when he had first seen Jean. He read the question in my eyes.

"I knew a girl like that once, very long ago. That was Sonya. They killed her—put a stake through her heart, long ago in Thurn. Now that I've found this girl, who might be a reincarnation of Sonya—they are so alike—I shall not give her up. Nor can anyone force me."

"You've made her a devil like yourself," I said through half-paralyzed lips. "I'd rather kill her—"

Futaine turned to watch Jean. "Not yet," he said softly. "She is mine—yes. She bears the stigmata. But she is still—alive. She will not become—*wampyr* until she has died, or until she has tasted the red milk. She shall do that tonight." I cursed him bitterly, foully. He touched my lips, and I could utter no sound. Then they left me—Jean and her master. I heard a door close quietly.

The night dragged on. Futile struggles had convinced me that it was useless to attempt escape—I could not even force a whisper through my lips. More than once I felt myself on the verge of madness—thinking of Jean, and remembering Futaine's ominous words. Eventually agony brought its own surcease, and I fell into a kind of coma, lasting for how long I could not guess. Many hours had passed, I knew, before I heard footsteps coming toward my prison.

Jean moved into my range of vision. I searched her face with my eyes, seeking for some mark of a dreadful metamorphosis. I could find none. Her beauty was unmarred, save for the terrible little wounds on her throat. She went to a couch and quietly lay down. Her eyes closed.

The chevalier came past me and went to Jean's side. He stood looking down at her. I have mentioned before the incongruous youthfulness of his face. That was gone now. He looked old—old beyond imagination.

At last he shrugged and turned to me. His fingers brushed my lips again, and I found that I could speak. Life flooded back into my veins, benign lancing twinges of pain. I moved an arm experimentally. The paralysis was leaving me. The chevalier said, "She is still—clean. I could not do it."

Amazement flooded me. My eyes widened in disbelief.

Futaine smiled wryly. "It is quite true. I could have made her as myself—undead. But at the last moment I forbade her." He looked toward the windows. "It will be dawn soon."

I glanced at the knife on the table beside me. The chevalier put out a hand and drew it away.

"Wait," he said. "There is something I must tell you, Mart Prescott. You say that you know who and what I am."

I nodded.

"Through the ages I have come, since first I fell victim to another vampire —for thus is the evil spread. Deathless and not alive, bringing fear and sorrow always, knowing the bitter agony of Tantalus, I have gone down through the weary centuries. I have known Richard and Henry and Elizabeth of England, and ever have I brought terror and destruction in the night, for I am an alien thing, I am the undead."

The quiet voice went on, holding me motionless in its weird spell.

"I, the vampire. I, the accursed, the shining evil, *negotium perambulans in tenebris*...but I was not always thus.[18] Long ago in Thurn, before the shadow

---

[18] Roughly translated from the Latin as "trouble roaming the darkness." Notably, a 1922 short story by E. F. Benson about a leech-like monster includes this exact phrase—deriving its title from it, in fact—and, with poetic license, translates it as "the pestilence that walketh in darkness."

leapt upon me, I loved a girl—Sonya. But the vampire visited me, and I sickened and died—and awoke. Then I arose.

"It is the curse of the undead to prey upon those they love. I visited Sonya.

"I made her my own. She, too, died, and for a brief while we walked the earth together, neither alive nor dead. But that was not Sonya. It was her body, yes, but I had not loved her body alone. I realized too late that I had destroyed her utterly."

"One day they opened her grave, and the priest drove a stake through her heart, and gave her rest. Me they could not find, for my coffin was hidden too well. I put love behind me then, knowing that there was none for such as I.

"Hope came to me when I found—Jean. Hundreds of years have passed since Sonya crumbled to dust, but I thought I had found her again. And—I took her. Nothing human could prevent me."

The chevalier's eyelids sagged. He looked infinitely old.

"Nothing human. Yet in the end I found that I could not condemn her to the hell that is mine. I thought I had forgotten love. But, long and long ago, I loved Sonya. And, because of her, and because I know that I would only destroy, as I did once before, I shall not work my will on this girl."

I turned to watch the still figure on the couch. The chevalier followed my gaze and nodded slowly.

"Yes, she bears the stigmata. She will die, unless"—he met my gaze unblinkingly—"unless I die. If you had broken into the vault yesterday, if you had sunk that knife into my heart, she would be free now." He glanced at the windows again. "The sun will rise soon."

Then he went quickly to Jean's side. He looked down at her for a moment. "She is very beautiful," he murmured. "Too beautiful for hell."

The chevalier swung about, went toward the door. As he passed me he threw something carelessly on the table, something that tinkled as it fell. In the portal he paused, and a little smile twisted the scarlet lips. I remembered him thus, framed against the black background of the doorway, his sleek blond head erect and unafraid. He lifted his arm in a gesture that should have been theatrical, but, somehow, wasn't.

"And so farewell. I who am about to die—"

He did not finish. In the faint grayness of dawn I saw him striding away, heard his footsteps on the stairs, receding and faint—heard a muffled clang as of a great door closing. The paralysis had left me. I was trembling a little, for I realized what I must do soon. But I knew I would not fail.

I glanced down at the table. Even before I saw what lay beside the knife, I knew what would be there. A silver key...

ABOUT THE EDITOR

C. S.R. CALLOWAY is a prolific writer across a multitude of mediums and genres. His horror novels include *Desiderio*, *The Ungodly Hours*, and *The Veil and the Shade*. In addition to creating, curating, and editing the entire HORROR HISTORIA anthology, he is best known as creator and showrunner of the award-winning series *Pretty Dudes*. Calloway currently lives in Los Angeles with his Venus flytraps Betsy, Bootsie, and Itsy Bitsy.

CHANCECALLOWAY.COM